From the
EDITOR-IN-CHIEF

Dear Reader,

I hear the line "They don't write 'em like they used to" all the time. And it's true—the 2008 reading audience is very different from audiences of twenty or thirty years ago, so the books and authors are very different, too. Favorite genres have fallen out of favor or are transformed. For instance, hospital medical dramas have morphed into futuristic biotech thrillers. Boy-meets-girl romances are now more often boy-stalks-girl romantic suspense. And sweeping historical sagas such as the ones James Michener once wrote are thin on the ground— although Ken Follett has recently published a sequel to his wonderful 1989 historical *Pillars of the Earth.*

There seems to be a special hankering for the whimsical, pastoral stories of the type that James Herriot, who died in 1995, used to write. Well, for all those sighing nostalgists, I'm happy to report that Patrick Taylor is here to fill the void with his wonderful novel *An Irish Country Doctor.* Taylor's doctor ministers to Irish country folk, not British livestock, but you'll delight in the same type of wry observations and quirky characters as those of that beloved veterinarian from Yorkshire.

Die-hard nostalgists ourselves, we Select Editions editors are now on the lookout for the twenty-first-century version of Erma Bombeck—people still want to laugh, don't they? Wish us luck!

Very truly yours,

Laura E. Kelly

Turn the page for a fun trivia quiz based on the SELECT EDITIONS online blog.

selecteditions.blogspot.com

What is a blog? And other trivia....

The editors at SELECT EDITIONS have put together this quiz as a way of introducing you to our online blog, **selecteditions.blogspot.com**. All the answers can be found in postings on the blog. Visit us online today!

1. What is a blog?
a) a small spiny mammal
b) a stain on the kitchen counter
c) an Internet diary
d) a spongy marsh

2. Who on the staff calls himself the Word Nerd?

a) Tom   b) Joe   c) Jim

3. Fannie Flagg and Stephen King share which biographical fact?

a) They both live in Chicago
b) They have the same birthday
c) They have both written novels about killer dogs

4. Which of the following is NOT an acceptable profession for a romance book hero?

a) carpenter
b) musician
c) accountant
d) chef

5. Who on the staff is related (by marriage) to someone who was in Sing Sing prison?

a) Laura   b) Barbara   c) Amy

6. Which George Gershwin song does NOT feature the line "Who could ask for anything more?"

a) "I Got Rhythm"
b) "Nice Work If You Can Get It"
c) " 'S Wonderful"

7. Which recent SE author once logged timber in the Rockies?

a) Lee Child
b) Peter Pezzelli
c) Jeffery Deaver
d) William Kent Krueger

8. Who said "I cannot live without books"?

a) Thomas Jefferson
b) Mark Twain
c) Oscar Wilde
d) Benjamin Franklin

Answers: 1-c; 2-a; 3-b; 4-c; 5-b; 6-c; 7-d; 8-a

SELECT EDITIONS

Selected and Edited by Reader's Digest

THE READER'S DIGEST ASSOCIATION, INC.

PLEASANTVILLE, NEW YORK • MONTREAL

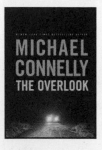
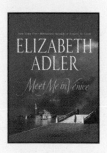

STEP ON A CRACK
James Patterson and Michael Ledwidge

A mysterious group of thugs pulls off what may be the crime of the century. Nonstop excitement introduces a new Patterson hero.

AFTER WORDS: *Sharing the spotlight with James Patterson, and a "Statue of Faith."*

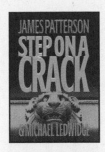

page 306

EXCITING NEW AUTHOR!

AN IRISH COUNTRY DOCTOR
Patrick Taylor

Wisdom, trust, and love are the rewards that await a young doctor in this magical tale of a small-town medical practice in the 1960s.

AFTER WORDS: *A conversation with Patrick Taylor, plus a look at the ancestral isle.*

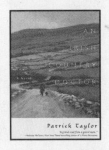

page 432

page 158   *page 303*   *page 429*   *page 574*

MICHAEL CONNELLY

THE OVERLOOK

ONE

THE call came at midnight. Harry Bosch was awake and sitting in the living room in the dark. He liked to think that he was doing this because it allowed him to hear the saxophone better. By masking one of the senses, he accentuated another. But deep down, he knew the truth. He was waiting.

The call was from Larry Gandle, his supervisor

in Homicide Special. It was Bosch's first call out in the new job. And it was what he had been waiting for.

"Harry, you up?"

"I'm up."

"Who's that you got playing?"

"Frank Morgan, live at the Jazz Standard in New York. That's George Cables you're hearing now on piano."

"Good stuff. I hate to take you away from it."

Bosch used the remote to turn the music off.

"What's the call, Lieutenant?"

"Hollywood wants you and Iggy to come out and take over a case. They've already caught three today and can't handle a fourth. This one also looks like it might become a hobby. It looks like an execution."

The Los Angeles Police Department had seventeen geographic divisions, each with its own station and detective bureau, including a homicide squad. But the divisional squads were the first line and couldn't get bogged down on long-running cases. When a murder came with any sort of political, celebrity, or media attachment, it was usually shuttled down to Homicide Special, which operated out of RHD—the Robbery-Homicide Division—in Parker Center. Any case that appeared to be particularly difficult and time-consuming—that would invariably stay active, like a hobby—would also be an immediate candidate for Homicide Special. This was one of those.

"Where is it?" Bosch asked.

"Up on that overlook above the Mulholland Dam."

Bosch got up and walked to the dining-room table. He opened a drawer designed for silverware and took out a pen and a small note-book. On the first page of the notebook, he wrote down the date and the location of the murder scene.

"Any other details I should know?" Bosch asked.

"Not a lot," Gandle said. "Like I said, it was described to me as an execution. Two in the back of the head. Somebody took this guy up there and blew his brains out all over that pretty view."

Bosch let this register a moment before asking the next question. "Do they know who the dead guy is?"

"The divisionals are working on it. Maybe they'll have something by the time you get over there. It's practically in your neighborhood, right?"

"Not too far."

Gandle gave Bosch more specifics on the location of the crime scene and asked if Harry would make the next call out to his partner. Bosch said he would take care of it.

"Okay, Harry, get up there and see what's what, then call me and let me know. Just wake me up. Everybody else does."

Bosch thought it was just like a supervisor to complain about getting woken up to a person he would routinely wake up over the course of their relationship.

"You got it," Bosch said.

Bosch hung up and immediately called Ignacio Ferras, his new partner. They were still feeling their way. Ferras was more than twenty years younger and from another culture. The bonding would happen, Bosch was sure, but it would come slowly. It always did.

Ferras was awakened by Bosch's call but became alert quickly and seemed eager to respond, which was good. The only problem was that he lived all the way out in Diamond Bar, which would put his ETA at the crime scene at least an hour off. Bosch had talked to him about it the first day they had been assigned as partners, but Ferras wasn't interested in moving. He had a family support system in Diamond Bar and wanted to keep it.

Bosch knew that he would get there well ahead of Ferras, and that would mean handling any divisional friction on his own. Taking a case away from the divisional squad was always a delicate thing. It was a decision usually made by supervisors, not by the homicide detectives on the scene. No homicide detective worth the gold trim on his badge would ever want to give away a case.

"See you there, Ignacio," Bosch said.

"Harry, I told you. Call me Iggy. Everybody does."

Bosch said nothing. He didn't want to call him Iggy. He didn't think it was a name that matched the weight of the assignment and mission. He wished that his partner would come to that realization and then stop asking him.

Bosch thought of something and added an instruction, telling Ferras to swing by Parker Center on his way in and pick up the city car they were assigned. It would add minutes to his arrival time, but Bosch planned to drive his own car to the scene, and he knew he was low on gas.

"Okay, see you there," Bosch said, leaving names out.

He hung up and grabbed his coat out of the closet by the front door. As he put his arms into it, he glanced at himself in the mirror on the inside of the door. At fifty-six years old, he was trim and fit and could even stand to add a few pounds, while other detectives his age were getting round in the middle. In Homicide Special, there was a pair of detectives known as Crate and Barrel because of their widening dimensions. Bosch didn't have to worry about that.

The gray had not yet chased all of the brown out of his hair, but it was getting close to victory. His dark eyes were clear and bright and ready for the challenge awaiting him at the overlook.

He reached across his body with his left hand to pull the gun out of the holster on his right hip. It was a Kimber Ultra Carry. He quickly checked the magazine and the action and then returned the weapon to its holster.

He was ready. He opened the door.

The lieutenant had not known a lot about the case, but he had been right about one thing: The crime scene was not far from Bosch's home. He dropped down to Cahuenga and then took Barham across the 101 Freeway, then up Lake Hollywood Drive to a neighborhood of homes clustered on the hills surrounding the reservoir and the Mulholland Dam. They were expensive homes.

He worked his way around the fenced reservoir, stopping only for a moment when he came upon a coyote in the road. The animal's eyes caught the headlights and glowed brightly. It then turned and sauntered slowly across the road, disappearing into the brush.

It was in no hurry to get out of the way, almost daring Bosch to do something. It reminded him of his days on patrol, when he saw the same challenge in the eyes of most of the young men he encountered on the street.

After passing the reservoir, he took Tahoe Drive farther up into the hills and then connected with the eastern terminus of Mulholland Drive. There was an unofficial overlook of the city here. It was posted with NO PARKING and OVERLOOK CLOSED AT DARK signs. But these were routinely ignored at all hours of the day and night.

Bosch pulled in behind the grouping of official vehicles—the forensics van and the coroner's wagon, as well as several marked and unmarked police cars. There was an outer perimeter of yellow police tape surrounding the crime scene, and inside this boundary was a silver Porsche Carrera with its hood open. It had been sectioned off by more yellow tape.

Bosch parked and got out. A patrol officer assigned to the outer perimeter took down his name and badge number and allowed him under the yellow tape. He approached the crime scene. Portable lights had been erected on either side of the body, which was in the center of a clearing that looked down upon the city. Forensics techs and coroner's people were working on and around the body. A tech with a video camera was documenting the scene as well.

"Harry, over here."

Bosch turned and saw Detective Jerry Edgar leaning against the hood of an unmarked detective cruiser. He had a cup of coffee in his hand and appeared to be just waiting. He pushed himself off the car as Bosch came over.

Edgar had been Bosch's partner once, back when he had worked in Hollywood Division. Back then Bosch was a team leader on the homicide squad. Now Edgar was in that position.

"Been waiting on somebody from RHD," Edgar said. "Didn't know it would be you, man. You working this solo?"

"No. My partner's on the way."

"Your new partner, right? I haven't heard from you since that mess over in Echo Park last year."

"Yeah. So what do you have here?"

Bosch didn't want to talk about Echo Park with Edgar or with anyone, as a matter of fact. He wanted to stay focused on the case at hand. It was his first call out since his transfer to Homicide Special. He knew there would be a lot of people watching his moves. Some of them would be people hoping he would fail.

Edgar turned so that Bosch could see what was spread out on the trunk of the car. Bosch took out glasses and put them on as he leaned in close to look. An array of evidence bags contained items taken from the body. These included a wallet, a key ring, and a clip-on name tag. There was also a money clip with a thick fold of currency and a BlackBerry that was still on, its green light flashing and ready to transmit calls its owner would never make or receive.

"The coroner's guy just gave me all of this," Edgar said. "They should be done with the body in about ten minutes."

Bosch picked up the bag containing the ID tag and angled it toward the light. It said SAINT AGATHA'S CLINIC FOR WOMEN. On it was a photograph of a man with dark hair and dark eyes. It identified him as Dr. Stanley Kent. Bosch noticed that the ID tag was also a swipe key that could open locked doors.

"Why don't you run down what you've got, Jerry?" Bosch said.

"Happy to," Edgar said. "The stiff was found about an hour ago. Hollywood always has a patrol swing by here a few times a night to chase lookyloos away. Keeps the rich locals up here happy. I am told that house over there is Madonna's. Or it was."

He pointed to a sprawling mansion about a hundred yards from the clearing. The mansion was on a promontory that afforded a magnificent, sweeping view of the city below. Bosch imagined the pop star looking down on the city that lay at her command.

"The patrol car swings around about eleven and sees the Porsche with the hood open. Engine's in the back of those Porsches. It means the trunk was open."

"Got it."

"The patrol car pulls up; they don't see anybody in or around the Porsche, so the two officers get out. One of them walks out into the clearing and finds our guy. He's facedown and has two in the back of the head. An execution, clean and simple."

Bosch nodded at the ID tag in the evidence bag.

"And this is the guy, Stanley Kent?"

"Looks that way. The tag and the wallet both say he's Stanley Kent, forty-two years old, from around the corner on Arrowhead Drive. We ran the plate on the Porsche, and it comes back to a business called K and K Medical Physicists. I ran Kent through the box, and he came up pretty clean. He's got a few speeding tickets on the Porsche, but that's it. A straight shooter."

Bosch nodded as he registered all the information.

"You are going to get no grief from me, taking over this case, Harry," Edgar said. "I got one partner in court this month, and I left my other one at the first scene we caught today—a three-bagger, with a fourth victim on life support at Queen of Angels."

Bosch remembered that Hollywood ran its homicide squad in three-man teams instead of the traditional partnerships.

"Any chance the three-bagger is connected to this?"

"No. That's a straight gang shoot-'em-up," Edgar said. "I think this thing is a whole different ball game, and I'm happy for you to take it."

"Good," Bosch said. "I'll cut you loose as soon as I can. Anybody look in the car yet?"

"Not really. Waiting on you."

"Okay. Anybody go to the victim's house on Arrowhead?"

"No on that, too."

"Anybody knock on any doors?"

"Not yet. We were working the scene first."

Edgar obviously had decided early that the case would be passed to RHD. It bothered Bosch that nothing had been done, but at the same time, he knew it would be his and Ferras's to work fresh from the start, and that wasn't a bad thing. There was a long history in the department of cases getting damaged or bungled while in transition from divisional to downtown detective teams.

He looked at the lighted clearing and counted a total of five men working on or near the body for the forensics and coroner's teams.

"Well," he said, "since you're working the crime scene first, did anybody look for foot impressions around the body before you let the techs approach?"

Bosch couldn't keep the tone of annoyance out of his voice.

"Harry," Edgar said, his tone now showing annoyance with Bosch's annoyance, "a couple hundred people stand around on this overlook every day. We coulda been looking at footprints till Christmas if we'd wanted to take the time. I didn't think we did. We had a body lying out here in a public place and needed to get to it. Besides that, it looks like a professional hit. That means the shoes, the gun, the car—everything's already long gone by now."

Bosch nodded. He wanted to dismiss this and move on.

"Okay," he said evenly, "then I guess you're clear."

After Edgar left, Bosch went to his car and got the Maglite out of the trunk. He walked to the Porsche, put on gloves, and opened the driver-side door. He leaned in and looked around. On the passenger seat was a briefcase. It was unlocked, and when he popped the snaps, it opened to reveal several files, a calculator, and various pads, pens, and papers. He closed it and left it in its place. Its position on the seat told him that the victim had likely arrived at the overlook by himself. He had met his killer here. He had not brought his killer with him. This, Bosch thought, might be significant.

He opened the glove box next, and several more clip-on IDs fell to the floorboard. He picked them up one by one and saw that each access badge had been issued by a different local hospital. But the swipe cards all bore the same name and photo: Stanley Kent.

He noticed that on the back of several of the tags there were handwritten notations. He looked at these for a long moment. Most were numbers with the letters *L* or *R* at the end and he concluded that they were lock combinations.

Bosch looked farther into the glove box and found even more IDs and access key cards. As far as he could tell, the dead man—if he was Stanley Kent—had clearance access to just about every hospital in Los Angeles County. He also had the combinations to security locks at almost every one of the hospitals. Bosch briefly considered that the IDs and key cards might be counterfeits used in some sort of hospital scam.

Bosch returned everything to the glove box and closed it. He looked under and between the seats and found nothing of interest. He backed out of the car and went to the open trunk.

The trunk was small and empty. But in the beam of his flashlight, he noted that there were four indentations in the carpet lining the bottom. It was clear that something square and heavy with four legs or wheels had been carried in the trunk. Because the trunk was found in the open position, it was likely that the object—whatever it was—had been taken during the killing.

"Detective?"

Bosch turned and put the beam of his light into the face of a patrolman. It was the officer who had taken his name and badge number at the perimeter. He lowered the light. "What is it?"

"There's an FBI agent here. She's asking permission to enter the crime scene."

"Where is she?"

The officer led the way back to the yellow tape. As Bosch got close, he saw a woman standing next to the open door of a car. She was alone, and she wasn't smiling. Bosch felt the thud of uneasy recognition hit his chest.

"Hello, Harry," she said when she saw him.

"Hello, Rachel," he said.

TWO

IT HAD been almost six months since he had seen Special Agent Rachel Walling of the FBI. As he approached her at the tape, Bosch was sure that not a day had gone by in that time when he hadn't thought about her. She was dressed in jeans, an oxford shirt, and a dark blue blazer. Her dark hair was unkempt, but she still looked beautiful. She obviously had been called in from home, just as Bosch had. She wasn't smiling, and Bosch was reminded of how badly things had ended the last time.

"Look," he said, "I know I've been ignoring you, but you didn't have to go to all the trouble of tracking me down at a crime scene just to—"

"It's not really a time for humor," she said, cutting him off. "If this is what I think it might be."

They'd last had contact on the Echo Park case. He had found her at the time working for a shadowy FBI unit called Tactical Intelligence. She had never explained what exactly the unit did, and Bosch had never pushed it, since it wasn't important to the Echo Park investigation. He had reached out to her because of her past tenure as a profiler—and their past personal history. The Echo Park case had gone sideways, and so had any chance for another romance. As Bosch looked at her now, he knew she was all business, and he had a feeling he was about to find out what the Tactical Intelligence Unit was all about.

"What is it you think it might be?" he asked.

"I'll tell you when I can tell you. Can I please see the scene?"

Reluctantly, Bosch lifted the crime-scene tape and returned her perfunctory attitude with his standard sarcasm.

"Come on in, then, Agent Walling," he said. "Why don't you just make yourself at home?"

She stepped under and stopped, at least respecting his right to lead her to his crime scene.

"I actually might be able to help you here," she said. "If I can see the body, I might be able to make a formal identification for you."

She held up a file that she had been carrying at her side.

"This way, then," Bosch said.

He led her to the clearing, where the victim was cast in the sterilizing fluorescent light from the mobile units. The dead man was lying on the orange dirt about five feet from the drop-off at the edge of the overlook. Beyond the body and over the edge, the moonlight reflected off the reservoir below. Past the dam the city spread out in a blanket of a million lights.

The victim had been rolled over by the medical examiner and was now faceup. There were abrasions on the dead man's face and forehead, but Bosch thought he could recognize the man in the photos on the hospital tags in the glove box. Stanley Kent. His shirt was open, exposing a hairless chest of pale white skin. There was an incision mark on one side of the torso where the medical examiner had pushed a temperature probe into the liver.

"Evening, Harry," said Joe Felton, the medical examiner. "Or I guess I should say, Good morning. Who's your friend there? I thought they teamed you with Iggy Ferras."

"I am with Ferras," Bosch responded. "This is Special Agent Walling from the FBI's Tactical Intelligence Unit."

"Tactical Intelligence? What will they think of next?"

"I think it's one of those Homeland Security–type operations. You know, don't ask, don't tell, that sort of thing. She says she might be able to confirm an ID for us."

Walling gave Bosch a look that told him he was being juvenile.

"All right if we come in, Doc?" Bosch asked.

"Sure, Harry, we're pretty much squared away here."

Bosch started to step forward, but Walling moved quickly in front of him and walked into the harsh light. Without hesitation, she took a position over the body. She opened the file and took out an 8 x 10 face shot. She bent down and held it next to the dead man's face.

"It's him," she said. "Stanley Kent."

Bosch nodded his agreement and then offered his hand to her so that she could step back over the body. She ignored it and did it without help. Bosch looked down at Felton, who was squatting next to the body.

"So, Doc, you want to tell us what we've got here?"

"We've got a man who was brought here or came here for whatever reason and was made to get down on his knees."

Felton pointed to the victim's pants. There were smudges of orange dirt on both knees.

"Then somebody shot him twice in the back of the head, and he went down face-first. The facial injuries you see came when he hit the ground. He was already dead by then."

Bosch nodded.

"No exit wounds," Felton added. "Probably something small, like a twenty-two, with the ricochet effect inside the skull."

Bosch realized now that Lieutenant Gandle had been speaking figuratively when he mentioned that the victim's brains had been blown across the view from the overlook. He would have to remember Gandle's tendency toward hyperbole in the future.

"Time of death?" he asked Felton.

"Going by the liver temp, I would say four or five hours," the medical examiner replied. "Eight o'clock, give or take."

That last part troubled Bosch. By eight, it would have been dark and all the sunset worshippers would have been long gone. But the two shots would have echoed from the overlook and into the nearby houses. Yet no one had called the police, and the body wasn't found until a patrol car happened by three hours later.

"I know what you are thinking," Felton said. "What about the sound? There is a possible explanation. Guys, roll him over."

Bosch stepped out of the way while Felton's assistants turned the body over, exposing the bullet entry wounds in the back of the head. The victim's black hair was matted with blood. The back of his white shirt was spattered with a fine spray of a brown substance that immediately drew Bosch's attention.

"That's not blood, is it?"

"No, it's not," Felton said. "I think we'll find out from the lab that it's good old Coca-Cola syrup. The residue you might find in the bottom of an empty bottle or can."

Before Bosch could respond, Walling did.

"An improvised silencer," she said. "You tape an empty plastic liter Coke bottle to the muzzle of the weapon, and the sound of the shot is significantly reduced as sound waves are projected into the bottle rather than the open air. If the bottle had a residue of Coke in it, the liquid would be spattered onto the target."

Felton looked at Bosch and nodded approvingly.

"Where'd you get her, Harry? She's a keeper."

Bosch looked at Walling. He, too, was impressed.

"Internet," she said.

Bosch nodded, though he didn't believe her.

"And there is one other thing you should note," Felton said. He reached across the body to point at the hand on Bosch's side. "We have one of these on each hand."

He was pointing to a red plastic ring on the middle finger. Bosch looked at it and then checked the other hand. There was a matching red ring. On the inside of each hand, the ring had a white facing that looked like some sort of tape.

"What are they?" Bosch asked.

"I don't know yet," Felton said. "But I think—"

"I do," Walling said.

Bosch looked up at her. He nodded. Of course she knew.

"They're called TLD rings," Walling said. "Stands for thermal luminescent dosimetry. It's an early-warning device. It's a ring that reads radiation exposure."

The news brought an eerie silence to the gathering.

"And I'll give you a tip," Walling continued. "When they are turned inward like that, with the TLD screen on the inside of the hand, that usually means the wearer handles radioactive materials."

Bosch stood up. "Okay, everybody," he ordered. "Back away from the body. Everybody just back away."

The crime-scene techs, the coroner's people, and Bosch all started moving away. But Walling didn't move. She raised her hands like she was calling for a congregation's attention in church.

"Hold on," she said. "Nobody has to back away. It's safe."

Everybody paused, but nobody moved to their original positions.

"If there was an exposure threat here, then the TLD screens on the rings would be black," she said. "That's the early warning. But they haven't turned black, so we're safe. Additionally, I have this."

She pulled back her jacket to reveal a small black box clipped to her belt like a pager.

"Radiation monitor," she explained. "If we had a problem, believe me, this thing would be screaming bloody murder and I'd be running at the front of the pack. But we don't. Everything is cool here, okay?"

The people at the crime scene started to return to their positions. Harry Bosch moved in close to Walling and took her by an elbow.

"Can we talk over here for a minute?"

They moved out of the clearing toward the curb at Mulholland. Bosch was agitated. He didn't want to lose control of the crime scene, and this sort of information threatened to do just that.

"What are you doing here, Rachel?" he asked. "What's going on?"

"Just like you, I got a call in the middle of the night. I was told to roll out. I assure you that I am here to help."

"Then start by telling me exactly what you are doing here and who sent you out. That would help me a lot."

Walling looked around and then back at Bosch. She pointed out beyond the yellow tape. "Can we?"

Bosch held out his hand, telling her to lead the way. They went under the tape and out into the street to where they were out of earshot of everyone else at the crime scene.

"Okay, this is far enough," he said. "What is going on here?"

She locked eyes with him again.

"Listen, what I tell you here has to remain confidential," she said. "For now."

"Look, Rachel, I don't have time for—"

"Stanley Kent is on a list. When you or one of your colleagues ran his name on the National Crime Index Computer tonight, a flag went up in Washington, D.C., and a call went out to me at Tactical."

"What, was he a terrorist?"

"No. He was a medical physicist. And as far as I know, a law-abiding citizen."

"Then what's with the radiation rings and the FBI showing up in the middle of the night? What list was Stanley Kent on?"

Walling ignored the question. "Let me ask you something, Harry. Has anyone checked on this man's home or wife yet?"

"Not yet. We were working the crime scene first. I plan to—"

"Then I think we need to do that right now," she said in an urgent tone. "You can ask your questions along the way. Get the guy's keys in case we need to go in. And I'll go get my car."

Walling started to move away, but Bosch caught her by the arm. "I'm driving," he said.

He pointed toward his Mustang and left her there. He headed to the patrol car, where the evidence bags were still spread on the trunk. As he made his way, he signaled the watch sergeant over.

"Listen, I have to leave the scene to check on the victim's house. I shouldn't be gone long, and Detective Ferras should be here any minute. Just maintain the scene until one of us gets here."

"You got it."

Bosch pulled out his cell phone and called his partner.

"Where are you?"

"I just cleared Parker Center. I'm twenty minutes away."

Bosch explained that he was leaving the scene and that Ferras needed to hurry. He disconnected, grabbed the evidence bag containing the key ring, and shoved it into his coat pocket.

As he got to his car, he saw Walling already in the passenger seat. She was finishing a call and closing her cell phone.

"Who was that?" Bosch asked after getting in. "The president?"

"My partner," she replied. "I told him to meet me at the house. Where's your partner?"

"He's coming." Bosch started the car and pulled out. "If Stanley Kent wasn't a terrorist, what list was he on?"

"As a medical physicist, he had direct access to radioactive materials. That put him on a list."

Bosch thought of all the hospital name tags he had found in the dead man's Porsche. "Access where? In the hospitals?"

"Exactly. That's where it's kept. These are materials primarily used in the treatment of cancer."

Bosch nodded. "So what am I missing here? Lay it out for me."

"Stanley Kent had direct access to materials that some people in the world would like to get their hands on. Materials that could be very valuable to these people, but not in the treatment of cancer."

"Terrorists."

"Exactly."

"Are you saying that this guy could just waltz into a hospital and get this stuff? Aren't there regulations?"

"There are always regulations, Harry. But just having them is not always enough. Repetition, routine—these are the cracks in any security system. We used to leave the cockpit doors on commercial airlines unlocked. Now we don't. It takes an event of life-altering consequences to change procedures and strengthen precautions."

He thought of the notations on the back of some of the ID cards in the victim's Porsche. Could Stanley Kent have been so lax about the security of these materials that he wrote access combinations on the back of his ID cards? The answer was probably yes.

"I understand," he told Walling.

"So if you were going to circumvent an existing security system, who would you go to?" she asked. "Somebody with intimate knowledge of that security system."

Bosch nodded. He turned onto Arrowhead Drive and started looking at address numbers on the curb.

"So you're saying this could be an event of life-altering consequences?"

"No, I'm not saying that. Not yet."

"Did you know Kent?" Bosch looked at Walling as he asked, and she looked surprised by the question. It had been a long shot, but he threw it out there for the reaction. Walling turned from him and looked out her window before answering. Bosch knew the move. A classic tell. He knew she would now lie to him.

"No, I never met the man."

Bosch pulled into the next driveway and stopped the car.

"What are you doing?" she asked.

"This is it. It's Kent's house."

They were in front of a house that had no lights on inside or out. It looked like no one lived there.

"No, it isn't," Walling said. "His house is down another block—"

She stopped when she realized Bosch had smoked her out. Bosch stared at her for a moment in the dark car before speaking.

"You want to level with me now?"

"Look, Harry, I told you. There are things I can't—"

"Get out of the car, Agent Walling. I'll handle this myself."

"Look, you have to under—"

"This is a homicide. *My* homicide. Get out of the car."

She didn't move. "I can make one phone call and you'd be removed from this investigation before you got back to the scene."

"Then do it. I'd rather be kicked to the curb right now than be a mushroom for the feds. Isn't that one of the Bureau's slogans? Keep the locals in the dark and bury them in cow manure? Well, not me, not tonight, and not on my own case."

He started to reach across her lap to open her door. Walling pushed him back and raised her hands in surrender.

"All right, all right," she said. "What is it you want to know?"

"I want the truth this time. All of it."

THREE

BOSCH turned in his seat to look directly at Walling. He was not going to move the car until she started talking.

"You obviously knew who Stanley Kent was and where he lived," he said. "You lied to me. Now, was he a terrorist or not?"

"I told you no, and that is the truth. He was a citizen. He was a physicist. He was on a watch list because he handled radioactive sources that could be used—in the wrong hands—to harm members of the public."

"What are you talking about? How would this happen?"

"Through exposure. And that could take many different forms. Individual assault—you remember last Thanksgiving the Russian who was dosed with polonium in London? The material Kent had access to could also be used on a larger scale—a mall, a subway, whatever. It all depends on the quantity and the delivery device."

"Delivery device? Are you talking about a bomb? Somebody could make a dirty bomb with the stuff he handled?"

"In some applications, yes."

"I thought that was an urban legend, that there's never actually been a dirty bomb."

"The official designation is IED—improvised explosive device. And put it this way, it's only an urban legend until precisely the moment that the first one is detonated."

Bosch nodded. He gestured to the house in front of them. "How did you know this isn't the Kent house?"

Walling rubbed her forehead as though she were tired of his annoying questions and had a headache.

"Because I have been to his house before. Okay? Early last year my partner and I came to Kent's house and briefed him and his wife on the potential dangers of his profession. We did a security check on their home and told them to take precautions. We had been asked to do it by the Department of Homeland Security. Okay?"

"Yeah, okay. And was that routine for Tactical Intelligence, or was that because there had been a threat to him?"

"Not a threat specifically aimed at him, no. We were simply taking precautions. Sixteen months ago someone entered a cancer clinic in Greensboro, North Carolina, circumvented security measures, and removed twenty-two small tubes of a radioisotope called cesium one thirty-seven. The legitimate medical use of this material in that setting was in the treatment of gynecological cancer. We don't know who got in there or why, but the material was taken. When news of the theft went out on the wire, somebody in the Joint Terrorism Task Force here in L.A. thought it would be a good idea to assess the security of these materials in local hospitals and to warn those who have access to and handle the stuff to take precautions and to be alert. Can we *please* go now?"

"And that was you."

"*Yes.* You got it. It was the federal trickle-down theory at work.

It fell to me and my partner to go out and talk to people like Stanley Kent. We met him and his wife at their house so we could do a security check of the place at the same time we told him that he should start watching his back. That is the same reason I was the one who got the call when his name came up on the flag."

Bosch dropped the transmission into reverse and quickly pulled out of the driveway.

"Why didn't you just tell me this up front?"

In the street, the car jerked forward as Bosch threw it into drive.

"Because nobody got killed in Greensboro," Walling said. "This whole thing could be something different. I was told to approach with caution and discretion. I'm sorry I lied to you."

"A little late for that, Rachel. Did your people get the cesium back in Greensboro?"

"No, not yet. The word is that it was sold on the black market. The material itself is quite valuable on a monetary basis, even if used in the proper medical context. That's why we are not sure what we've got here. That's why I was sent."

In ten more seconds, they were at the correct block of Arrowhead Drive, and Bosch started looking at address numbers again. But Walling directed him.

"That one up on the left, I think. With the black shutters. It's hard to tell in the dark."

Bosch pulled in and chunked the transmission into park. He jumped out and headed to the front door. The house was dark, but as Bosch approached the front door, he saw that it had been left ajar.

"It's open," he said.

Bosch and Walling drew their weapons. Bosch placed his hand on the door and slowly pushed it open. With guns up, they entered the dark and quiet house. Bosch found a light switch, and the lights came on, revealing a living room that was neat but empty, with no sign of trouble.

"Mrs. Kent?" Walling called out loudly. Then to Bosch in a lower voice, she said, "There's just his wife, no children."

Walling called out once more, but the house remained silent.

There was a hallway to the right. Bosch found another light switch and illuminated a passageway with four closed doors and an alcove.

The alcove was a home office that was empty. He saw a blue reflection on the window that was cast by a computer screen. They passed the alcove and went door by door, clearing what looked like a guest bedroom and then a home gym, with cardio machines and with workout mats hanging on the wall. The third door was to a guest bathroom. The fourth led to the master bedroom.

They entered the master, and Bosch once more flicked up a wall switch. They found Mrs. Kent.

She was on the bed naked, gagged, and hog-tied, with her hands behind her back. Her eyes were closed. Walling rushed to see if she was alive, while Bosch moved through the bedroom to clear the bathroom and a walk-in closet. There was no one.

When he got back to the bed, he saw that Walling had removed the gag and used a pocketknife to slice through the black plastic snap ties that had been used to bind the woman's wrists and ankles together behind her back. Rachel was pulling the bedspread over the woman's naked body. There was a distinct odor of urine.

"Is she alive?" Bosch asked.

"She's alive. I think she's just passed out."

Walling started rubbing the woman's wrists and hands. They had turned dark and almost purple from lack of blood circulation.

"Get help," she told him.

Annoyed with himself for not reacting until ordered, Bosch pulled out his phone and walked out into the hallway while he called the central communications center to get paramedics rolling.

"Ten minutes," he said, coming back into the bedroom.

Bosch felt a wave of excitement go through him. They now had a live witness. He knew that it would be vitally important to get the woman talking as soon as possible.

There was a loud groan as she regained consciousness.

"Mrs. Kent, it's okay," Walling said. "You're safe now."

The woman tensed, and her eyes widened when she saw the two strangers in front of her. Walling held up her credentials.

"FBI, Mrs. Kent. Do you remember me?"

"What? What is— Where's my husband?"

She started to get up but then realized she was naked beneath the bedcovers and tried to pull them tightly around herself. Her fingers were apparently still numb and couldn't find purchase. Walling helped pull the spread around her.

"Where is Stanley?"

"Mrs. Kent, your husband is not here," Bosch said. "I am Detective Bosch with the LAPD, and this is Agent Walling with the FBI. We're trying to find out what happened to your husband."

The woman looked up at Bosch and then at Walling, and her eyes held on the federal agent. "I remember you," she said. "You came to the house to warn us. Is that what is happening? Do the men who were here have Stanley?"

Rachel leaned in close and spoke in a calming voice.

"Mrs. Kent, we— It's Alicia, right? Alicia, we need for you to calm down a little bit so that we can talk and possibly help you. Would you like to get dressed?"

Alicia Kent nodded.

"Okay. We'll give you some space here," Walling said. "You get dressed, and we'll wait for you in the living room. First, let me ask, Have you been injured in any way?"

The woman shook her head.

"Are you sure . . ."

Walling didn't finish, as though she were intimidated by her own question. Bosch wasn't. He knew they needed to know precisely what had happened here.

"Mrs. Kent, were you sexually assaulted here tonight?"

The woman shook her head again.

"They made me take off my clothes. That was all they did."

Bosch studied her eyes, hoping to read them and be able to tell if she was telling a lie.

"Okay," Walling said, interrupting the moment. "We'll leave you to get dressed. When the paramedics arrive, we will still want them to check you for injuries."

"I'll be fine. What happened to my husband?"

"We're not sure," Bosch said. "You get dressed and come out to the living room; then we'll tell you what we know."

Clutching the bedspread around herself, she tentatively stood up from the bed. Bosch saw the stain on the mattress and knew that Alicia Kent had either been so scared during her ordeal that she had urinated or the wait for rescue had been too long.

She took one step toward the closet and appeared to be falling over. Bosch moved in and grabbed her before she fell.

"Are you all right?"

"I'm fine. I think I'm just a little dizzy. What time is it?"

Bosch looked at the digital clock on the right-side bed table, but its screen was blank. It was turned off or unplugged. He turned his right wrist without letting go of her and looked at his watch.

"It's almost one in the morning."

Her body seemed to tighten in his grasp. "Oh, my God!" she cried. "It's been hours. Where is Stanley?"

Bosch helped her stand up straight. "You get dressed and we'll talk about it," he said.

She walked unsteadily to the closet and opened the door. A full-length mirror was attached to the outside of the door. Her opening it swung Bosch's reflection back at him. In the moment, he thought that maybe he saw something new in his eyes. A look of discomfort, perhaps even a fear of the unknown. It was understandable, he decided. He had worked a thousand murder cases in his time, but never one that had taken him in the direction he was now traveling. Maybe fear was appropriate.

Alicia Kent took a white terry-cloth robe off a hook inside the closet and carried it with her to the bathroom. She left the closet door open, and Bosch had to look away from his own reflection.

Walling headed out of the bedroom, and Bosch followed.

He decided to make another survey of the house while waiting for Alicia Kent to get dressed. This time he checked the backyard and the garage, as well as every room again. He found nothing amiss, though he did note that the two-car garage was empty. If the

Kents had another car in addition to the Porsche, then it wasn't on the premises.

Following the walk-through, he stood in the backyard looking up at the Hollywood sign and calling central communications again to ask that a second forensics team be dispatched to process the Kent house. Next, he called Lieutenant Gandle, waking him at his home. His supervisor listened quietly as Bosch updated him. The federal involvement and the rising possibility of a terrorism angle to the investigation gave Gandle pause.

"Well," he said when Bosch was finished, "it looks like I will have to wake some people up."

He meant he was going to have to send word up the department ladder of the case and its larger dimensions. The last thing an RHD lieutenant would want would be to get called into the OCP in the morning and asked why he hadn't alerted command staff earlier. Bosch knew that Gandle would now act to protect himself as well as to seek direction from above. This was fine with Bosch, and expected. But it gave him pause as well. The LAPD had its own Office of Homeland Security. It was commanded by a man most people in the department viewed as a loose cannon and unqualified for the job.

"Is one of those wake-ups going to Captain Hadley?" Bosch asked.

Captain Don Hadley was the twin brother of James Hadley, who happened to be a member of the Police Commission, the politically appointed panel with LAPD oversight and the authority to appoint and retain the chief of police. Less than a year after James Hadley was placed on the commission, his twin brother jumped from being second in command of the Valley Traffic Division to being commander of the newly formed Office of Homeland Security. This was seen at the time as a political move by the then–chief of police, who was desperately trying to keep his job. It didn't work. He was fired and a new chief appointed. But in the transition, Hadley kept his job commanding the OHS.

The mission of the OHS was to maintain a flow of intelligence data with federal agencies. In the last six years, Los Angeles had been targeted by terrorists at least two times. In each incident, the LAPD found out about the threat after it had been foiled by the feds. This was embarrassing to the department, and the OHS had been formed so that the LAPD could make intelligence inroads and know what the feds knew about its own backyard.

The problem was that in practice, it was largely suspected that the LAPD remained shut out by the feds. And in order to hide this failing and to justify his position and unit, Captain Hadley had taken to holding grandstanding press conferences and showing up with his black-clad OHS unit at any crime scene where there was a remote possibility of terrorist involvement. An overturned tanker truck on the Hollywood Freeway brought the OHS out in force until it was determined that the tanker was carrying milk. A shooting of a rabbi at a temple in Westwood brought the same response, until the incident was determined to have been the product of a love triangle.

And so it went. After about the fourth misfire, the commander of the OHS was baptized with a new name among the rank and file. Captain Don Hadley became known as Captain Done Badly. But he remained in his position, thanks to the thin veil of politics that hung over his appointment. The last Bosch had heard about Hadley through the department grapevine was that he had put his entire squad back into the academy for training in urban assault tactics.

"I don't know about Hadley," Gandle said in response to Bosch. "I'll start with my captain, and he'll make the call on who gets the word from there. But that's not your concern, Harry. You do your job and don't worry about Hadley. The people you have to watch your back with are the feds. With them it's always time to worry when they start telling you just what you want to hear."

"Got it," Bosch said. The advice followed a time-honored LAPD tradition of distrusting the FBI. And, of course, it was a tradition honored for just as long by the FBI in terms of distrusting the LAPD right back. It was the reason the OHS was born.

When Bosch came back into the house, he found Walling on her cell phone and a man he had never seen before standing in the living room. He was tall, mid-forties, and he exuded that undeniable FBI confidence. The man put out his hand.

"You must be Detective Bosch," he said. "Jack Brenner. Rachel's my partner."

Bosch shook his hand. The way he said Rachel was his partner was a small thing, but it told Bosch a lot. There was something proprietary about it. Brenner was telling him that the senior partner was now on the job.

"So you two have met."

Bosch turned. Walling was off the phone now.

"Sorry," she said. "I was filling in the special agent in charge. He's decided to devote all of Tactical to this. He's running out three teams to start hitting the hospitals to see if Kent has been in any of the hot labs today."

"The hot lab is where they keep the radioactive stuff?" Bosch asked.

"Yes. Kent had access to just about all of them in the county. We have to figure out if he was inside any of them today."

Bosch knew that he could probably narrow the search down to one medical facility. Saint Agatha's Clinic for Women. Kent was wearing an ID tag from the hospital when he was murdered. Walling and Brenner didn't know that, and Bosch decided not to tell them yet. He wanted to hold on to what might be the one piece of inside information he still had.

"What about the LAPD?" he asked instead.

"The LAPD?" Brenner said, jumping on the question ahead of Walling. "You mean, what about you, Bosch?"

"Yeah, that's right. Where do I stand in this?"

Brenner spread his hands in a gesture of openness.

"Don't worry, you're in. You're with us all the way."

"Good," Bosch said. "That's just what I wanted to hear."

He looked at Walling for confirmation of her partner's statement, but she looked away.

FOUR

WHEN Alicia Kent finally came out of the master bedroom, she had brushed her hair and washed her face but had put on only the white robe. Bosch now saw how attractive she was. Small and dark and exotic-looking in some way. He guessed that taking her husband's name had hidden a bloodline from somewhere far away. Her black hair had a luminescent quality to it. It framed an olive face that was beautiful and sorrowful at the same time.

She noticed Brenner, and he nodded and introduced himself. Alicia Kent seemed so dazed by what was happening that she showed no recognition of Brenner in the way that she had remembered Walling. Brenner directed her to the couch and told her to sit down.

"Where is my husband?" she demanded, this time with a voice that was stronger and calmer than before. "I want to know what is going on."

Rachel sat down next to her, ready to console if necessary. Brenner took a chair near the fireplace. Bosch remained standing. He never liked to be sitting down all cozy when he delivered this sort of news.

"Mrs. Kent," Bosch said, taking the lead in a proprietary effort to keep his hold of the case. "I am a homicide detective. I am here because earlier tonight we found the body of a man we believe to be your husband. I am very sorry to tell you this."

Her head dropped forward as she received the news; then her hands came up and covered her face. A shudder went through her body, and the sound of a helpless moan came from behind her hands. Then she started to cry, deep sobs that shook her shoulders. Walling reached over and put a hand on the back of her neck.

Brenner offered to get her a glass of water, and she nodded.

While he was gone, Bosch studied the woman. It was dirty work, telling someone that their loved one was dead. He had done it hundreds of times, but it wasn't something you ever got used to or even good at. It had also been done to him. When his own mother was murdered more than forty years before, he got the news from a cop just after Bosch had climbed out of a swimming pool at a youth hall. His response was to jump back in and try to never come back up.

Brenner delivered the water, and the brand-new widow drank half of it down. Before anyone could ask a question, there was a knock on the door, and Bosch stepped over and let in two paramedics carrying big equipment boxes. While they came forward to assess the woman's physical condition, Bosch signaled Walling and Brenner into the kitchen, where they could confer in whispers.

"So how do you want to handle her?" Bosch asked.

Brenner spread his hands wide again, as though he was open to suggestions. "I think you keep the lead. We'll step in when needed. If you don't like that, we could—"

"No, that's good. I'll keep the lead."

He looked at Walling, waiting for an objection, but she was fine with it, too. He turned to leave the kitchen, but Brenner stopped him.

"Bosch, I want to be up front with you," Brenner said. "I had you checked out. The word is, you—"

"What do you mean you checked me out?"

"I needed to know who we're working with. I wanted—"

"If you have any questions, you can ask me."

Brenner raised his hands, palms out. "Fair enough."

Bosch left the kitchen and stood in the living room, waiting for the paramedics to finish with Alicia Kent. One of the medical men was taking a blood-pressure reading. Bandages had been placed on her neck and one wrist, apparently covering wounds that he hadn't noticed before.

His phone buzzed, and Bosch went back into the kitchen to take the call. He noticed that Walling and Brenner were gone, apparently having slipped into another part of the house. It made Bosch anxious. He didn't know what they were up to.

The call was from his partner. Ferras had finally made it to the crime scene.

"Is the body still there?" Bosch asked.

"No. The ME just cleared the scene," Ferras said.

Bosch updated him on the direction the case appeared to be going, telling him about the federal involvement and the potentially dangerous materials Stanley Kent had had access to. He then directed him to start knocking on doors and looking for witnesses who might have seen or heard something. He knew it was a long shot, because no one had called 911 after the shooting.

"Should I do that now, Harry? It's the middle of the night and people are sleep—"

"Yes, Ignacio, you should do it now."

Bosch wasn't worried about waking people up. It was always better to find witnesses sooner rather than later.

When Bosch came out of the kitchen, the paramedics had packed up and were leaving. They told Bosch that Alicia Kent was physically fine, with minor wounds and abrasions. They said they had given her a pill to help calm her and a tube of cream to apply to the chafe marks on her wrists and ankles.

Walling was sitting on the couch next to her again, and Brenner sat by the fireplace. Bosch sat down on the chair directly across the glass coffee table from Alicia Kent.

"Mrs. Kent," he began, "we are very sorry for your loss and the trauma you have been through. But it is very urgent that we move quickly with the investigation. In a perfect world, we would wait until you were ready to talk to us. But it's not a perfect world. You know that better than we do now. We need to ask you questions about what happened here tonight."

She folded her arms across her chest and nodded.

"Then let's get started," Bosch said. "Can you tell us what happened?"

"Two men," she responded tearfully. "There was a knock at the door, and I answered. There was no one there. Then, when I started to close the door, they jumped out. They had on masks and hoods—like a sweatshirt with a hood. They pushed their way in and grabbed me. They had a knife, and one of them grabbed me and held it against my throat. He told me he would cut my throat if I didn't do exactly what he told me to do."

She lightly touched the bandage on her neck.

"Do you remember what time this was?" Bosch asked.

"It was almost six o'clock," she said. "It had been dark for a while, and I was about to start dinner. Stanley comes home most nights at seven."

The reminder of her husband's habits brought a new rush of tears. Bosch tried to keep her on point by moving to the next question. He thought he already detected a slowing down of her speech. The pill the paramedics gave her was taking effect.

"What did the men do, Mrs. Kent?" he asked.

"They took me to the bedroom. They made me sit down on the bed and take off all my clothes. Then one of them started to ask me questions. I was scared. I guess I got hysterical, and he slapped me. He told me to calm down and answer his questions."

"What did he ask you?"

"I can't remember everything. I was so scared."

"Try, Mrs. Kent. It's important."

"He asked me if we had a gun and where the—"

"Wait a minute, Mrs. Kent," Bosch said. "Let's go one at a time. He asked you if you had a gun. What did you tell him?"

"I was scared. I said yes, we had a gun. He asked where it was, and I told him it was in the drawer by the bed on my husband's side. It was the gun we got after you warned us about the dangers Stan faced with his job."

She said this last part while looking directly at Walling.

"Weren't you afraid that they would kill you with it?" Bosch asked. "Why did you tell them where the gun was?"

Alicia Kent looked down at her hands. "I was sitting there naked. I was already sure they were going to rape me and kill me. I guess I thought it didn't matter anymore."

Bosch nodded as if he understood.

"What else did they ask you, Mrs. Kent?"

"They wanted to know where the keys to the car were. I told them. I told them everything they wanted to know."

"Is that your car they were talking about?"

"Yes, my car. In the garage. I keep the keys on the kitchen counter."

"I checked the garage. It's empty."

"I heard the garage door—after they were here. They must've taken the car."

Brenner abruptly stood up.

"We need to get this out," he interjected. "Can you tell us what kind of car it is and the license plate number?"

"It's a Chrysler Three hundred. I can't remember the number. I could look it up in our insurance file."

Brenner held up his hands to stop her from getting up.

"Not necessary. I'll be able to get it. I'll call it in right away."

He got up to go to the kitchen to make the call without disturbing the interview. Bosch went back to his questions.

"What else did they ask you, Mrs. Kent?"

"They wanted our camera. The camera that worked with my husband's computer. I told them Stanley had a camera in his desk. Whenever I answered a question, one man—the one who asked them—would translate to the other, and then that man left the room. I guess he went to get the camera."

Now Walling stood up and headed toward the hallway leading to the bedrooms.

"Rachel, don't touch anything," Bosch said. "I have a crime-scene team coming."

Walling waved him off as she disappeared down the hall. Brenner then came back into the room and nodded to Bosch.

"The BOLO's out," he said.

Alicia Kent asked what a BOLO was.

"It means 'Be on the lookout,'" Bosch explained. "They'll be looking for your car. What happened next, Mrs. Kent?"

She grew tearful again as she answered.

"They . . . They tied me in that awful way and gagged me with one of my husband's neckties. Then after the one came back with the camera, the other took a picture of me like that."

Bosch noted the look of burning humiliation on her face.

"He took a photograph?"

"Yes, that's all. Then they both left the room. The one who spoke English bent down and whispered that my husband would come to rescue me. Then he left."

That brought a long space of silence before Bosch continued. "After they left the bedroom, did they leave the house right away?"

The woman shook her head.

"I heard them talking for a little while; then I heard the garage door. It opened and closed. After that, I thought they were gone."

Brenner cut in. "When I was in the kitchen, I think I heard you say that one of the men translated for the other. Do you know what language they were speaking?"

Bosch was annoyed with Brenner for jumping in. He intended to ask about the language the intruders used but was carefully covering one aspect of the interview at a time. He had found in previous cases that it worked best with traumatized victims.

"I'm not sure. The one who spoke in English had an accent, but I don't know where it was from. I think Middle Eastern. I think when they spoke to each other, it was Arabic or something. It was foreign, very guttural."

Brenner nodded. "You said they wore masks. What kind of masks?"

She thought for a moment before answering.

"The pullover kind. Like you see robbers put on in movies."

"A wool ski mask."

She nodded. "Yes, exactly."

"Okay. Were they the kind with one hole for both eyes, or was there a separate hole for each eye?"

"Um, separate, I think. Yes, separate."

"Was there an opening for the mouth?"

"Uh . . . yes, there was. I remember watching the man's mouth when he spoke in the other language."

"That's good, Mrs. Kent. You're being very helpful. What detail do you remember that I haven't asked you for?"

She thought about it and then shook her head. "I don't know. I think I've told you everything I can remember."

Bosch wasn't convinced. He began to go through the story with her again, coming at the same information from new angles. It was a tried-and-true interview technique for eliciting new details, and it did not fail him. The most interesting bit of new information to emerge in the second telling was that the man who spoke English also asked her what the password was to her e-mail account.

"Why would he want that?" Bosch asked.

"I don't know," she said. "I just gave them what they wanted."

When the forensics team arrived, Bosch called for a break in the questioning. He walked the tech team back to the master bedroom so they could start there. He then stepped into a corner of the room and called his partner. Ferras reported that he had found nobody so far who had seen or heard anything on the overlook. Bosch told him that when he wanted a break from knocking on doors, he should check into Stanley Kent's ownership of a gun. It was looking like he was killed with his own gun.

As Bosch closed the phone, Walling called to him from the home office. Harry found her and Brenner standing behind the desk and looking at a computer screen.

"Look at this," Walling said.

"I told you," he said, " you shouldn't be touching anything yet."

"We don't have the luxury of time," Brenner said. "Look at this."

Bosch came around the desk to look at the computer.

"Her e-mail account was left open," Walling said. "I went into the Sent Mail folder. And this was sent to her husband's e-mail at six-twenty-one p.m. last night."

The e-mail subject line said HOME EMERGENCY: READ IMMEDIATELY!

Embedded in the body of the e-mail was a photograph of Alicia

Kent naked and hog-tied on the bed. The impact of the photo would be obvious to anyone, not just a husband.

Below the photograph was a message:

> We have your wife. Retrieve for us all cesium sources available to you. Bring them in safe containment to the Mulholland overlook near your home by eight o'clock. We will be watching you. If you tell anyone or make a call, we will know. The consequence will be your wife being raped, tortured, and left in to many pieces to count. Use all precautions while handling sources. Do not be late or we will kill her.

Bosch read the message twice and believed he felt the same terror Stanley Kent must have felt.

" 'We will be watching . . . we will know . . . we will kill her,' " Walling said. "No contractions. The 'too' in 'too many pieces' is spelled wrong. I don't think this was written by someone whose original language is English."

As she said it, Bosch saw it and knew that she was right.

"They send the message right from here," Brenner said. "The husband gets it at the office or on his PDA. Did he have a PDA?"

Bosch had no expertise in this area. He hesitated.

"A personal digital assistant," Walling prompted. "You know, like a Palm Pilot or a phone with all the gadgets."

Bosch nodded.

"I think so," he said. "There was a BlackBerry cell phone recovered. It looks like it has a mini keyboard."

"That works," Brenner said. "So no matter where he is, he gets this message and can probably view the photo, too."

All three of them were quiet while the impact registered. Finally Bosch spoke, feeling guilty now about holding back earlier.

"I just remembered something. There was an ID tag on the body. From Saint Aggy's up in the Valley."

Brenner's eyes took on a sharpness.

"You just remembered a key piece of information like that?"

"That's right. I for—"

"It doesn't matter now," Walling interjected. "Saint Aggy's is a women's cancer clinic. Cesium is used almost exclusively for treating cervical and uterine cancer."

Bosch nodded. "Then we better get going," he said.

FIVE

SAINT Agatha's Clinic for Women was in Sylmar at the north end of the San Fernando Valley. Because it was the dead of night, they were making good time on the 170 Freeway. Bosch was behind the wheel of his Mustang, one eye on the fuel needle. He knew he was going to need gas before coming back down into the city. It was him and Brenner in the car. Brenner had decided that Walling should stay behind with Alicia Kent to continue questioning her. Walling didn't seem happy about the assignment, but Brenner, asserting his seniority, didn't give her room to debate it.

Brenner spent most of the drive taking and making a series of cell calls to and from superiors and fellow agents. It was clear to Bosch from the side of things that he was able to hear that the big federal machine was gearing up for battle. A greater alarm had now been sounded. The e-mail sent to Stanley Kent had brought things into better focus, and what was once a federal curiosity had now gone completely off the scale.

When Brenner finally closed the phone, he turned slightly in his seat and looked over at Bosch.

"I've got a RAT team heading to Saint Aggy's," he said. "They'll go into the materials safe to check it out."

"A rat team?"

"Radiological-attack team."

"What's their ETA?"

"Didn't ask, but they might beat us. They've got a chopper."

Bosch was impressed. It meant that there had been a rapid-response team on duty somewhere in the middle of the night. He thought about how he had been awake and waiting for the call out that night. The members of the radiological-attack team must wait for the call they hope never comes. He remembered what he had heard about the LAPD's own OHS unit taking training in urban assault tactics. He wondered if Captain Hadley had a RAT team, too.

"They're going full field on this," Brenner said. "The Department of Homeland Security is overseeing from D.C. This morning at nine, there will be meetings on both coasts to bring everybody together on it."

"Who is everybody?"

"There's a protocol. We'll bring in Homeland, the JTTF, everybody. It'll be alphabet soup. The NRC, the DOE, RAP. It's going to be federal pandemonium."

Bosch didn't know what all the acronyms stood for, but he didn't need to. They all spelled out *feds* to him.

"Who will be running the show?"

"Everybody and nobody. If we open up that safe at Saint Aggy's and the cesium is gone, then our best shot at tracking it and getting it back will be to do it before all hell breaks loose at nine and we get micromanaged to death from Washington."

Bosch nodded. He thought maybe he had misjudged Brenner. The agent seemed to want to get things done, not wallow in the bureaucratic mire.

"And what's the LAPD status going to be?"

"I already told you, the LAPD remains in. Nothing changes on that. You remain in, Harry. My guess is that bridges are already being built between our people and your people. I know the LAPD has its own Homeland Security office. I'm sure they will be brought in. We're obviously going to need all hands on deck with this."

Bosch glanced over at him. Brenner looked serious.

"Have you worked with our OHS before?" Bosch asked.

"On occasion. We shared some intelligence on a few things."

Bosch nodded but felt that Brenner was being disingenuous or was completely naïve about the gulf between the locals and the feds.

But he noted that he had been called by his first name and wondered if that was one of the bridges being built.

"You said you checked me out. Who did you check with?"

"Harry, we're working well here. Why stir it up?"

"Who'd you check me out with?"

"Look, all I'm going to tell you is that I asked Agent Walling who the LAPD point man was, and she gave me your name. I made a few calls. I was told you were a very capable detective. That you had more than thirty years, that a few years back you retired, didn't like it much, and came back to the job to work cold cases. Things went sideways in Echo Park—a little thing you dragged Agent Walling into. You were off the job a few months while that was, uh, cleared up, and now you're back and assigned to Homicide Special."

"What else?"

"Harr—"

"What else?"

"Okay. The word I got is that you can be difficult to get along with, especially when it comes to working with the federal government. But I have to say, so far I don't see any of that at all."

Bosch figured that most of this information had come from Rachel. He was disappointed if she had said such things about him. And he knew that Brenner was probably holding back most of it. The truth was that he'd had so many run-ins with the feds that they probably had a file on him as thick as a murder book.

After a minute or so of silence, Bosch decided to change direction and spoke again.

"Tell me about cesium," he said.

"It's a by-product. The fission of uranium and plutonium creates cesium. When Chernobyl hit meltdown, cesium was the stuff that was dispersed into the air. It comes in powder or a silver-gray metal. When they conducted nuke tests in the South Pacific—"

"I don't mean the science. I don't care about the science. Tell me about what we are dealing with here."

Brenner thought for a moment.

"Okay," he said. "The stuff we're talking about comes in pieces about the size of a pencil eraser. It is contained in a sealed stainless-steel tube about the size of a forty-five-caliber bullet cartridge. When used in the treatment of a gynecological cancer, it's placed inside the woman's uterus for a calculated amount of time and irradiates the targeted area. It is supposed to be very effective in quick doses. It's the job of a guy like Stanley Kent to make that calculus—to run the physics down and determine how long a dose is called for. He would then go and get the cesium out of the hospital's hot safe and deliver it to the oncologist in the operating room. The doctor administering the treatment handles the stuff as little as possible. Because the surgeon can't wear any protection while performing a procedure, he's got to limit his exposure."

Bosch nodded. "Do these tubes protect whoever handles them?"

"No. The only thing that knocks down the gamma rays from cesium is lead. The safe they keep the tubes in is lined with lead. The device they transport them in is made of lead."

"So how bad is this stuff going to be if it gets out in the world?"

Brenner gave it some thought before answering. "Out in the world, it is all about quantity, delivery, and location. If you set off a good amount of this stuff in an enclosed environment—like maybe a subway station or an office building—then that place could be shut down for three hundred years."

Bosch was stunned. "What about people?" he asked.

"Also depends on dispersal and containment. A high-intensity exposure could kill you within a few hours. But if it's dispersed by an IED in a subway station, then my guess is that the immediate casualties would be very low. But a body count is not what this would be about. It's the fear factor that would be important to these people. You set something off like this domestically, and what's important is the wave of fear it sends through the country. A place like Los Angeles? It would never be the same again."

AT SAINT Aggy's, they entered through the main lobby and asked the receptionist for the chief of security. They were told that he worked days but that she would locate the night-shift security supervisor. While they waited, they heard the helicopter land on the front lawn of the medical center, and soon the four-member radiological team came in, each man wearing a radiation suit and carrying a face guard. The leader of the group—it said KYLE REID on his nameplate—carried a handheld radiation monitor.

Finally a man who looked like he had been roused from a bed in a spare patient room greeted them in the lobby. He said his name was Ed Romo, and he couldn't seem to take his eyes off the hazmat suits worn by the lab team. Brenner badged Romo and took charge. Bosch didn't object. He knew that they were now on turf where the federal agent would be best suited to walk point.

"We need to go to the hot lab and check the materials inventory," Brenner said. "We also need to see any records or key-card data that will show us who has been in and out of there in the last twenty-four hours."

Romo didn't move. He paused as if groping for understanding. "What's this about?" he finally asked.

"I just told you what it's about," Brenner said. "We need to get into the hot lab in oncology. If you can't get us in there, then find somebody who can. Now."

"I gotta make a call first," Romo said.

"Good. Make it. I'll give you two minutes, and then we're going to run you over."

The whole time he was making the threat, Brenner was smiling and nodding.

Romo took out a cell phone and stepped away from the group to make the call.

Brenner looked at Bosch with a sardonic smile. "Last year I did a security survey here. They had a key lock on the lab and the safe and that was it. They upgraded after that. But you build a better mousetrap and the mice just get smarter."

Ten minutes later Bosch, Brenner, Romo, and the rest of the lab team stepped out of the elevator into the medical clinic's basement. Romo's boss was on his way in, but Brenner was not waiting. Romo used a key card to gain entrance to the oncology lab.

The lab was deserted. Brenner found an inventory sheet and a lab log on an entrance desk and started reading. There was a small video monitor on the desk that showed a camera view of a safe.

"He was here," Brenner said. "Seven o'clock, according to this."

Reid pointed to the monitor. "Does that record?" he asked Romo. "Can we see what Kent did when he was in there?"

Romo looked at the monitor as though it were the first time he had ever seen it. "Um, no, it's just a monitor. Whoever's on the desk is supposed to watch what's taken out of the safe."

Romo pointed to the far end of the lab, where there was a large steel door. The trefoil warning symbol for radioactive materials was posted on it at eye level, along with a sign:

CAUTION! RADIATION HAZARD.
PROTECTIVE EQUIPMENT MUST BE WORN.

Bosch noticed that the door had a push-button combination lock as well as a magnetic key-card swipe slot.

"It says here that he took one source of cesium," Brenner said. "One tube. He was taking the source over to Burbank Medical Center for a procedure there. It says that there were thirty-one pieces of cesium left in inventory."

"Is that all you need, then?" Romo asked.

"No," Brenner said. "We have to physically inspect the inventory. We'll need to enter the safe room and then open the safe. What's the combination?"

"I don't have it," Romo said.

"Who does?"

"The physicists. The head of the lab. The chief of security."

"Get the chief on the speaker."

Brenner pointed to the phone on the desk. Romo sat down and tapped in a number. It was answered immediately.

"This is Richard Romo."

Ed Romo leaned forward to the phone and looked as though he was embarrassed by the revelation of the obvious nepotism at play.

"Uh, yeah, Dad, this is Ed. The man from the FB—"

"Mr. Romo?" Brenner cut in. "This is Special Agent John Brenner of the FBI. I believe we met and spoke about security issues a year ago. We need to open the hot-lab safe right now to determine its contents."

"You can't open that without hospital approval."

"Mr. Romo, we have reason to believe the contents of the safe were turned over to people without the interests or safety of the American people in mind. We need to open the safe so that we know exactly what is here and what is missing. And we can't wait. We have to *move,* sir. Now, how do we open the safe?"

There was silence from the speakerphone for a few moments. Then Richard Romo relented.

"Ed, I take it you are calling from the desk in the lab?"

"Yeah."

"Okay, unlock it and open the bottom-left drawer."

Ed Romo rolled his chair back and studied the desk. There was a key lock on the upper-left drawer that apparently unlocked all three drawers. He pulled a key ring off his belt, inserted it into the lock, and turned it. He pulled open the bottom drawer.

"Got it."

"Okay, there's a binder in the drawer. Open it up and look for the page with the combination lists for the safe room. It's changed week to week."

Holding the binder in his hands, Romo started to open it. Brenner roughly took it from him. He opened it on the desk and started leafing through pages of safety protocols.

"Where is it?" he said impatiently to the speakerphone.

"It should be in the final section. It will be clearly marked as hot-lab combinations. There is one catch, though. We use the previous week. The combination for the current week is wrong. Use last week's combo."

Brenner found the page and drew his finger down the listing until he found the combination for the previous week.

"Okay, got it. What about the safe inside?"

"You will use the key card again and another combination. That one I know. It doesn't change. It is six six six."

"Original."

Brenner held his hand out to Ed Romo. "Give me your key card."

Romo complied, and Brenner then handed the card to Reid. "The door combo is five six one eight four, and you heard the rest."

Reid turned and pointed to one of the others in hazmat suits.

"It'll be tight in there. Just Miller and I go in."

The leader and his chosen second snapped on their face guards and used the key card and combination to open the safe-room door. Miller carried the radiation monitor, and they entered the safe room, pulling the door closed behind them.

"You know, people go in there all the time, and they don't wear space suits," Ed Romo said.

"I'm happy for them," Brenner said. "This situation is a little different, don't you think? We don't know what may or may not have been let loose in that environment."

"I was just saying," Romo said defensively.

"Then do me a favor and don't say anything. Let us do our job."

Bosch watched on the monitor and soon saw a glitch in the security system. The camera was mounted overhead, but as soon as Reid bent down to type the combination into the safe, he blocked the camera's view of what he was doing. Bosch knew that even if someone had watched Kent when he went into the safe at seven p.m. the evening before, he could easily have hidden what he was taking.

Less than a minute after going into the safe room, the two men in hazmat suits stepped out. Brenner stood up. The men unsnapped their face guards, and Reid looked at Brenner. He shook his head.

"The safe's empty," he said.

Brenner pulled his phone from his pocket. But before he could punch in a number, Reid stepped forward, holding out a piece of paper torn from a spiral notebook.

"This was all that was left," he said.

Bosch looked over Brenner's shoulder at the note. It was scribbled in ink and difficult to decipher. Brenner read it out loud.

" 'I am being watched. If I don't do this, they'll kill my wife. Thirty-two sources, cesium. God forgive me. No choice.' "

SIX

BOSCH and the federal agents stood silently. There was an almost palpable sense of dread hanging in the air. They had just confirmed that Stanley Kent took thirty-two capsules of cesium from the safe and then most likely turned them over to persons unknown. Those persons had then executed him up on the Mulholland overlook.

"Thirty-two capsules of cesium," Bosch said. "How much damage could that do?"

"It could get the job done," Brenner said. "If somebody out there wants to send a message, it would be heard loud and clear."

Bosch suddenly thought of something that didn't fit.

"Wait a minute," he said. "Stanley Kent's radiation rings showed no exposure. How could he have taken all the cesium out of here and not lit up those warning devices like a Christmas tree?"

Brenner shook his head dismissively.

"He obviously used a pig."

"A what?"

"The pig is what they call the transfer device. It basically looks like a lead mop bucket on wheels. With a secured top, of course. It's heavy and built low to the ground—like a pig."

"And he could just waltz right in and out of here with something like that?"

Brenner pointed at the clipboard on the desk.

"Interhospital transfers of radioactive sources for cancer treatment are not unusual," he said. "He signed out one source but then took them all. That's what was unusual, but who was going to open up the pig and check?"

Bosch thought about the indentations he had seen in the floor of the Porsche's trunk. Something heavy had been carried in the car and was then removed. Now Bosch knew what it was, and it was one more indication of the worst-case scenario.

"I have to make a call," Brenner said.

He moved away from the others and pulled out his cell phone. Bosch decided to make his own call. He pulled out his phone, found a corner for privacy, and called his partner.

"Ignacio, it's me. I'm just checking in."

"Call me Iggy, Harry. What's happening with you?"

"Nothing good. Kent emptied the safe. All the cesium is gone."

"Are you kidding me? That's the stuff you said could be used to make a dirty bomb?"

"That's the stuff. Are you still at the scene?"

"Yeah, and listen, I've got a kid here who might be a witness."

"What do you mean, *might* be? Who is it, a neighbor?"

"No. It's sort of a screwy story. You know that house that was supposedly Madonna's?"

"Yeah."

"Yeah, well, she used to own it but doesn't anymore. I go up there to knock on the door, and the guy who lives there now says he didn't see or hear anything. So I'm leaving, when I spot this guy hiding behind these big potted trees in the courtyard. I draw down on him and call backup, you know, thinking maybe he's our shooter from the overlook. But turns out it's a kid—twenty years old and just off the bus from Canada—and he thinks Madonna's still living in the house. He's got a star map that still lists her as living there, and he's trying to see her or something—like a stalker. He climbed over a wall to get into the courtyard."

"Did he see the shooting?"

"He claims he didn't see or hear anything, but I don't know,

Harry. I'm thinking he might've been stalking Madonna's place when the thing went down on the overlook. He then hides and tries to wait it out. Only I find him first."

Bosch was missing something in the story.

"Why would he hide? Why wouldn't he just get the hell out of there? We didn't find the body till three hours after the shooting."

"Yeah, I know. That part doesn't make sense. Maybe he was just scared or thought that if he was seen in the vicinity of the body, he might get tagged as a suspect or something."

Bosch nodded. It was a possibility.

"You holding him on the trespass?" he asked.

"Yeah. I talked to the guy who bought the place from Madonna, and he'll work with us. He'll press charges if we need him to. So don't worry. We can hold him and work him with it."

"Good. Take him downtown, put him in a room, and warm him up. And Ignacio, don't tell anybody about the cesium."

"You got it, Harry."

Bosch closed the phone before Ferras could tell him to call him Iggy again. He listened to the end of Brenner's conversation. Brenner's manner was deferential. He was talking to a boss.

"According to the log here, seven o'clock," he said. "That puts the transfer at the overlook at around eight, so we're talking about a six-and-a-half-hour lead at this point."

Brenner listened some and then started to speak several times but was repeatedly cut off by the person on the other end of the line.

"Yes, sir," he finally said. "We're on our way back in now."

He closed the phone and looked at Bosch.

"I'm going back in on the chopper. I have to lead a teleconference debriefing with Washington. I'd take you with me, but I think you'd be better off on the ground, chasing the case. I'll have someone pick up my car later."

"No problem."

"Did your partner find a witness? Is that what I heard?"

Bosch had to wonder how Brenner had picked that up while conducting his own phone conversation.

"Maybe, but it sounds like a long shot. I'm going downtown to see about that right now."

Brenner nodded solemnly, then handed Bosch a business card.

"If you get anything, give me a call. Anything at all, call."

Bosch took the card and put it in his pocket. He and the agents then left the lab, and a few minutes later he watched the federal chopper take off into the black sky. He got into his car and pulled out of the clinic's parking lot to head south. Before hitting the freeway, he gassed up at a station on San Fernando Road.

Traffic coming down into the center of the city was light, and he cruised at a steady eighty. The driving helped Bosch smooth out his thoughts. He realized the case was shifting. The feds, at least, were chasing the missing cesium instead of the killers. There was a subtle difference there that Bosch thought was important. He knew that he needed to keep his focus on the overlook and not lose sight of the fact that this was a murder investigation.

"Find the killers, you find the cesium," he said out loud.

When he got downtown, he took the Los Angeles Street exit and parked in the front lot at police headquarters. At this hour, nobody would care that he wasn't a VIP or a member of command staff.

Parker Center was on its last legs. A new building was under way, but it was an estimated four years from completion. Many who worked in Parker Center wondered if the current headquarters could last that long.

The RHD squad room on the third floor was deserted when Bosch got there. He opened his cell phone and called his partner.

"Where are you?"

"Hey, Harry. I'm at SID. I'm getting what I can so I can start putting the murder book together. Are you in the office?"

"I just got here. Where'd you put the wit?"

"I've got him cooking in room two. You want to start with him?"

"Might be good to hit him with somebody he hasn't seen before. Somebody older."

It was a delicate suggestion. The potential witness was Ferras's find. Bosch wouldn't move in on him without his partner's at least tacit approval. But the situation dictated that someone with Bosch's experience would be better conducting such an important interview.

"Have at him, Harry. When I get back, I'll watch in the media room. If you need me to come in, just give me the signal."

"Right."

"I made fresh coffee in the captain's office if you want it."

"Good. I need it. But first tell me about the witness."

"His name is Jesse Mitford. From Halifax. He's kind of a drifter. He told me he hitchhiked down here and has been staying in shelters and sometimes up in the hills. That's about it."

"Maybe he was going to sleep up there in Madonna's courtyard. That's why he didn't split."

"I didn't think about that, Harry. You might be right."

Bosch ended the call, got his coffee mug out of his desk drawer, and headed to the RHD captain's office. There was an anteroom where the secretary's desk was located, as well as a table with a coffeemaker. The smell of fresh-brewed coffee hit Bosch as he entered, and that alone almost gave him the caffeine charge he needed. He poured a cup, dropped a buck in the basket, and then headed back to his desk.

The squad room was designed with long rows of facing desks so that partners sat across from each other. The design afforded no personal or professional privacy. Since Bosch and Ferras were the newest additions to the squad, their desk tandem was located at the end of a line in a windowless corner, where the air circulation was bad and they would be furthest from the exit in the case of an emergency, like an earthquake.

Bosch's work space was neat and clean, just as he had left it. He noticed a backpack and a plastic evidence bag on his partner's desk, across from him. He grabbed the backpack first. It contained mostly clothing and other personal items belonging to the potential witness. There was a book called *The Stand* by Stephen King and a bag with toothpaste and a toothbrush in it. It all amounted to the meager belongings of a meager existence.

He reached across for the evidence bag. It contained a small amount of U.S. currency, a set of keys, a thin wallet, and a Canadian passport. It also contained a folded "Homes of the Stars" map, the kind sold on street corners all around Hollywood. Bosch unfolded it and located the overlook above Lake Hollywood. Just to the left of the location there was a black star with the number 23 in it. It had been circled with an ink pen. He checked the map's index, and star number 23 said, "Madonna's Hollywood Home."

The map had obviously not been updated, and Bosch suspected that few of the star locations were accurate. This explained why Mitford had been stalking a house where Madonna no longer lived.

Bosch refolded the map, put all the property back into the evidence bag, and returned it to his partner's desk. He then got a legal pad and a rights waiver out of a drawer and stood up to go to interview room 2.

Jesse Mitford looked younger than his years. He had curly dark hair and ivory white skin. He had silver rings piercing one nostril and one eyebrow. He looked alert and scared. He was seated at a small table. Mitford was sweating, which of course was the objective. Bosch had checked the thermostat in the hallway before coming in. Ferras had set the temperature in the room to eighty-two.

"Jesse, how are you doing?" Bosch asked as he took the empty seat across from him.

"Uh, not so good. It's hot in here."

"Really?"

"Are you my lawyer?"

"No, Jesse, I'm your detective. My name's Harry Bosch. I'm a homicide detective, and I am working the overlook case."

Bosch put both his legal pad and his coffee mug down on the table. He noticed that Mitford still had handcuffs on. It was a nice touch by Ferras to keep the kid confused, scared, and worried.

"I told the Mexican detective I didn't want to talk anymore. I want a lawyer."

Bosch nodded. "He's Cuban American, Jesse," he said. "And you don't get a lawyer. Lawyers are for U.S. citizens only."

This was a lie, but Bosch was banking on the twenty-year-old's not knowing this.

"You're in trouble, kid," he continued. "It's one thing to be stalking an old girlfriend or boyfriend. It's something else with a celebrity. This is a celebrity town, Jesse, and we take care of our own. I don't know what you've got up there in Canada, but the penalties here for what you were doing tonight are pretty stiff."

Mitford shook his head. "But I was told that she doesn't even live there anymore. Madonna, I mean. So I wasn't really stalking her. It would just be trespassing."

Now Bosch shook his head. "It's about intent, Jesse. You thought she might be there. You had a map that said she *was* there. You even circled the spot. That constitutes stalking a celebrity."

"Then why do they sell maps to stars' homes?"

"And why do bars have parking lots when drunk driving is illegal? We're not going to play that game, Jesse. The point is, there's nothing on the map that says anything about it being okay to jump over a wall and trespass, you know what I mean?"

Mitford dropped his eyes and sadly nodded.

"Tell you what, though," Bosch said. "You can cheer up, because things aren't as bad as they seem. You've got stalking and trespassing charges here, but I think we can probably get this all fixed up and taken care of if you agree to cooperate with me."

Mitford leaned forward. "But like I told that Mexi—that Cuban detective, I didn't see anything."

"I don't care what you told him. You're dealing with me now, son. And I think you're holding back on me."

"No, I'm not. I swear to God."

He held his hands open and as wide as the cuffs allowed in a pleading gesture. But Bosch wasn't buying it. He decided to go right at him.

"Let me tell you something, Jesse. My partner is good, and he's going places in the department. But right now he's a baby. He's been a detective for about as long as you've been growing that peach fuzz on your chin. Me, I've been around, and that means I've been around a lot of liars. And Jesse, I can tell. You're lying to me, and nobody lies to me."

"No! I—"

"And so what you've got here is about thirty seconds to start talking to me or I'm just going to take you down and book you into county lockup. I'm sure there's going to be somebody waiting in there who will have a guy like you singing *O Canada!* into the mike before sunup."

Mitford stared down at his hands on the table. Bosch waited, and twenty seconds slowly went by. Finally Bosch stood up.

"Okay, Jesse, stand up. We're going."

"Wait, wait, wait!"

"For what? I said, stand up! Let's go. This is a murder investigation, and I'm not wasting time on—"

"All right, all right, I'll tell you. I saw the whole thing, okay?"

Bosch studied him for a moment. "You're talking about the overlook? You saw the shooting on the overlook?"

"I saw everything, man."

Bosch pulled his chair out and sat back down.

SEVEN

BOSCH stopped Jesse Mitford from speaking until he signed a rights waiver. It didn't matter that he was now considered a witness. Whatever it was that he witnessed, he saw because he was in the act of committing his own crime—trespassing and stalking. Bosch had to make sure there were no mistakes on the case. No fruit-of-the-poison-tree appeal. No blowback. The stakes were high, the feds were classic second-guessers, and he knew he had to do this right.

"Okay, Jesse," he said when the waiver form was signed. "You are going to tell me what you saw and heard up on the overlook. If you are truthful and helpful, I am going to drop all charges and let you walk out of here a free man."

Technically, Bosch was overstating his hand. He had no authority to drop charges or make deals with criminal suspects. But he didn't need it in this case, because Mitford had not yet been formally charged with anything. Therein lay Bosch's leverage. It came down to semantics. What Bosch was really offering was to not proceed with charging Mitford in exchange for the Canadian's cooperation.

"I understand," Mitford said.

"Just remember, only the truth. Only what you saw and heard. Nothing else."

"I understand."

"Hold up your hands."

Mitford raised his wrists, and Bosch used his own key to remove his partner's handcuffs. Mitford immediately began to rub them to get circulation going again. It reminded Bosch of seeing Rachel rub Alicia Kent's wrists earlier.

"Okay, let's start from the top. Tell me where you came from, where you were going, and what you saw up on the overlook."

Mitford nodded and then took Bosch through a twenty-minute story that began on Hollywood Boulevard with the purchase of the star map from a curbside vendor and his long trek on foot up into the hills. His journey took nearly three hours, and he told Bosch that by the time he got up to Mulholland Drive, it was getting dark and he was tired. The house where the map said Madonna lived was dark inside. No one appeared to be home. Disappointed, he decided to wait and see if the pop singer would arrive home later. He found a spot behind some bushes where he could rest against the exterior of the wall that surrounded the home. Mitford said he fell asleep there until something woke him up.

"What woke you up?" Bosch asked.

"Voices. I heard voices."

"What was said?"

"I don't know. It was just what woke me up."

"How far were you from the overlook?"

"I don't know. Like fifty meters. I was pretty far away."

"What was said after you were awake and could hear?"

"Nothing. They stopped."

"All right, then what did you see when you woke up?"

"I saw three cars parked by the clearing. One was a Porsche, and the other two were bigger. I don't know the kind."

"Did you see the men on the overlook?"

"No, I didn't see anybody. It was too dark out there. But then I heard a voice again, and it was coming from over there. In the dark. It was like a yell. Right at the moment I looked, there were two quick flashes and shots. Like muffled shots. I could see somebody in the clearing on his knees. You know, in the flash of light. But it was so quick that was all I saw."

Bosch nodded. "This is good, Jesse. You're doing good. Let's just go over this part again so we have it right. You were asleep, and then voices woke you up and you saw the three cars, right?"

"Yes."

"Okay, good. Then you heard a voice again and you looked toward the overlook. Just then the shots were fired. Is that right?"

"Right."

Bosch nodded. But he knew that Mitford might simply be telling him what he wanted to hear. He had to test the kid to make sure that wasn't happening.

"Now, you said that in the flash from the gun, you saw the victim drop to his knees. Is that right?"

"No. I think he was on his knees already. It was so fast I wouldn't have seen him drop to his knees, like you said."

Bosch nodded. Mitford had passed the first test.

"Okay, good point. Now let's talk about what you heard. You said you heard somebody yell right before the shots. What did that person yell?"

The young man thought for a moment and then shook his head. "I'm not sure."

"Okay, that's all right. We don't want to say anything we're not sure about. Let's try an exercise. Close your eyes."

"What?"

"Just close your eyes," Bosch said. "Think about what you saw. Try to bring up the visual memory and the audio will follow. You are looking at the three cars, and then a voice pulls your attention toward the overlook. What did the voice say?"

Mitford closed his eyes. Bosch waited.

"I'm not sure," the young man finally said. "I think he was saying something about Allah, and then he shot the guy."

Bosch held perfectly still for a moment before responding.

"Allah? You mean the Arabic word *Allah?*"

"I'm not sure. I think so."

"What else did you hear?"

"Nothing else. The shots cut it off, you know?"

"You mean like 'Allah Akbar.' Is that what he yelled?"

"I don't know. I just heard the *Allah* part."

Bosch thought about this for a few moments. He remembered what he had read about the cockpit recordings from the 9/11 attacks. The terrorists called out "Allah Akbar"—God is greatest—at the last moment. Did one of Stanley Kent's killers do the same?

Again, he knew he had to be careful. Much of the investigation could hinge on the one word Mitford thought he had heard.

"Jesse, what did Detective Ferras tell you about this case before he put you in this room?"

The witness shrugged. "He didn't tell me anything, really."

"He didn't tell you what we think we're looking at here or what direction the case may be going?"

"No, none of that."

Bosch looked at him for a few moments.

"Okay, Jesse," he finally said. "What happened next?"

"After the shots, somebody ran from the clearing to the cars. There was a streetlight out there, and I saw him. He got into one of the cars, and he backed it up close to the Porsche. Then he popped the trunk and got out. The Porsche's trunk was already open."

"Where was the other man while he did this?"

Mitford looked confused. "I guess he was dead."

"No. I mean the second bad guy. There were two bad guys and one victim, Jesse. Three cars, remember?"

"I only saw one bad guy," Mitford said. "The shooter. Somebody else stayed in the car that was behind the Porsche. Right after the shooting, that car made a U-turn and drove away."

Bosch thought about this for a moment. What Mitford had described indicated a real division of labor between the two suspects. This mirrored the description of events that Alicia Kent had given earlier; one man questioning her and then translating and giving orders to the second. Bosch assumed it was the English speaker who had remained in the car.

"Okay," he finally said, "go back to the story, Jesse. Right after the shooting, one guy drives away while the other backs up closer to the Porsche and pops the trunk. Then what happened?"

"He got out and took something from the Porsche and put it in the other car's trunk. It was really heavy, and he had a hard time with it. It looked like it had handles on the sides because of the way he was holding it."

Bosch knew that he was describing the pig used to transport radioactive materials. "Then what?"

"He just got back in the car and drove off."

"And you saw nobody else?"

"Nobody else. I swear."

"Describe the man you did see."

"I can't really describe him. He was wearing a sweatshirt with the hood up. I never really saw his face or anything. I think that under the hood, he was wearing a ski mask, too."

"Was he big? Was he small?"

"I think he was average. Maybe a little short."

"What did he look like?" Bosch had to try again. It was important. He didn't give up. "White, black, Middle Eastern?"

"I couldn't tell. He had the hood and the mask, and I was so far away."

"Think about the hands, Jesse. You said there were handles on the thing he transferred from one car to the other. Could you see his hands? What color were his hands?"

Mitford thought for a moment, and his eyes brightened. "No. He wore gloves. I remember the gloves because they were those real big kind, like the guys wear who work on the trains back in Halifax. Heavy-duty with the big cuffs so they don't get burned."

Bosch nodded. He had been fishing for one thing but got something else. Protective gloves. He wondered if they were gloves specifically designed for handling radioactive material.

Bosch paused. Sometimes the silences are the most uneasy moments for a witness. They start to fill in the blanks.

But Mitford said nothing. After a long moment, Bosch continued.

"Okay, we had two cars up there besides the Porsche. Describe the car that backed up to the Porsche."

"I can't, really. I know what Porsches look like, but I couldn't tell about the other cars. Both were a lot bigger, with four doors."

"The one in front of the Porsche, was it a sedan? Four doors, trunk—like a police car?"

"Yes, like that."

Bosch thought about Alicia Kent's description of her missing car. "Do you know what a Chrysler Three hundred looks like?"

"No."

"What color was the car you saw?"

"I don't know for sure, but it was dark. Black or dark blue."

"What about the other car? The one behind the Porsche."

"Same thing. A dark sedan. It was different from the one in front—maybe a little bit smaller."

Bosch nodded. He considered things for a moment. Mitford's story matched up with information provided by Alicia Kent. The two intruders to the Kent house had to have had transportation to get there. One would have taken the original vehicle, while the other took Alicia Kent's Chrysler to transport the cesium. It seemed like the obvious thing.

His thoughts prompted a new question for Mitford.

"Which way did the second car go when he drove off?"

"He also made a U-turn and drove down the hill."

"What did you do then?"

"Me? Nothing. I just stayed where I was."

"Why?"

"I was scared. I had just seen some guy get murdered."

"You didn't go check on him to see if he was alive and needed help?"

Mitford looked away from Bosch and shook his head.

"No. I was afraid. I'm sorry."

"It's okay, Jesse. You don't have to worry about that. He was already dead. He was dead before he hit the ground. But what I'm curious about is why you stayed in hiding for so long. Why didn't you go down the hill? Why didn't you call nine one one?"

Mitford raised his hands and dropped them on the table.

"I don't know. I was afraid, I guess. I followed the map up the hill, so that was the only way I knew back. I would have had to walk right by there, and I thought, What if the cops come while I'm walking right there? I could get blamed. And I thought, if it was like the mafia or something that did it and they found out I had seen everything, then I'd be killed or something."

Bosch nodded. "I think you watch too much American TV up there in Canada. You don't have to worry. We'll take care of you. How old are you, Jesse?"

"Twenty."

"So what were you doing at Madonna's house? Isn't she a little old for you?"

"No. It wasn't like that. It was for my mother."

"You were stalking her for your mother?"

"I'm not a stalker. I just wanted to get my mother her autograph or see if she had a picture or something I could have. I wanted to send something back to my mom. You know, just to show her I'm okay. I thought if I told her I had met Madonna, then I wouldn't feel like such a . . . you know. I grew up listening to Madonna because my mom listens to her stuff. I just thought it would be kind of cool to send her something."

"Why'd you come to L.A., Jesse?"

"I don't know. It just seemed like the place to go. I was hoping I could get in a band or something."

Bosch thought Mitford had adopted the pose of the wandering troubadour, but there had been no guitar or other mobile instrument with his backpack in the squad room.

"Are you a musician or a singer?"

"I play the guitar, but I had to pawn it a few days ago."

"Where are you staying?"

"I don't really have a place right now. I was going to sleep up in the hills last night. I guess it's the real answer to why I didn't leave after I saw what happened to that guy up there. I really didn't have anyplace to go."

Bosch understood. Jesse Mitford was no different from a thousand others who got off the bus every month or thumbed it into town. More dreams than plans or currency. More hope than cunning, skill, or intelligence. Not all of those who fail to make it stalk those who do. But the one thing they all share is that desperate edge. And some never lose it, even after their names are put up in lights and they buy houses on top of the hills.

"Let's take a break here, Jesse," Bosch said. "I need to make a few phone calls, and then we'll probably need to go over it all again. You cool with that? I'll also see about maybe getting you a hotel room or something."

Mitford nodded, and Bosch left him there.

In the hallway, Bosch switched on the air-conditioning in the interview room and set it at sixty-four. It would soon cool off in the room, and instead of sweating, Mitford would start to get cold—though coming from Canada, maybe not. After he chilled for a while, Bosch would take another run at him and see if anything new came out. He checked his watch. It was almost five a.m., and the case meeting the feds were organizing was not for another four hours.

Out in the squad room, Bosch found Ignacio Ferras working at his desk, typing on his laptop. Bosch noticed that Mitford's property had been replaced on the desk by other evidence bags and file folders. It was everything from SID that the case had spawned so far on the two crime scenes.

"Harry, sorry I didn't get back in there to watch," Ferras said. "Anything new from the kid?"

"We're getting there. I'm just taking a break."

Ferras was thirty years old and had an athlete's body. He was also handsome, with mocha skin and short-cropped hair. He had piercing green eyes.

Bosch stepped over to his own desk to use the phone. He was going to wake up Lieutenant Gandle one more time to give him another update.

"You track the vic's gun yet?" he asked Ferras.

"Yeah. I got it off the ATF computer. He bought a twenty-two-caliber belly gun six months ago. Smith and Wesson."

Bosch nodded. "A twenty-two fits. No exit wounds."

"Bullets check in, but they don't check out."

Ferras delivered the line like a television commercial huckster and laughed at his own joke. Bosch thought about what was lying beneath the humor. Stanley Kent had been warned that his profession made him vulnerable. His response was to purchase a gun for protection.

And now Bosch was betting that the gun he'd bought had been used to kill him by a terrorist who called out the name of Allah as he pulled the trigger. What a world it was, Bosch thought, when someone could draw the courage to pull the trigger on another man by calling out to his God.

"Not a good way to go," Ferras said.

Bosch looked across the two desks at him.

"Let me tell you something," he said. "You know what you find out on this job?"

"No, what?"

"That there are no good ways to go."

EIGHT

BOSCH went to the captain's office to refill his coffee mug. When he reached into his pocket for another buck for the basket, he came out with Brenner's card, and it reminded him of Brenner's request to be updated on the possibility of a witness. But Bosch had just finished updating Lieutenant Gandle on what the Canadian said he had seen and heard, and together they had decided to keep Mitford under wraps for the time being. Until at least the nine a.m. meeting, when it would be time to put up or shut up. If the feds were going to keep the LAPD involved, it would become clear at that meeting. Then it would be quid pro quo time. Bosch would share the witness's story in exchange for a share of the investigation.

Meantime, Gandle said he would send another update through the department's chain of command. With the word *Allah* cropping up in the investigation, it was incumbent upon him to make sure the growing gravity of the case was communicated upward.

With his mug full, Bosch went back to his desk and started going through the evidence collected from the murder scene and the house where Alicia Kent had been held.

He started removing Stanley Kent's personal belongings from the evidence bags and examining them. At this stage, they had been processed by Forensics and it was okay to handle them.

The first item was the physicist's BlackBerry. Bosch was not adept in a digital world. He had mastered his own cell phone, but it was a basic model that made and received calls, stored numbers in a directory, and did nothing else. This meant that he was quite lost as he tried to manipulate the higher-evolution device.

"Harry, you need help with that?"

Bosch looked up and saw Ferras smiling at him. Bosch was embarrassed by his lack of technological skill, but not to the point where he wouldn't accept help. "You know how to work this?"

"Sure."

"It has e-mail, right?"

"It should."

Bosch handed the phone across both of their desks.

"About six o'clock yesterday, Kent was sent an e-mail that was marked urgent from his wife. It had the photo in it of her tied up on their bed. I want you to find it and see if there is a way you can somehow print it out with the photo. I want to look at the photo again, but bigger than on that little screen."

"No problem," Ferras said. "What I can do is forward the e-mail to my own e-mail account. Then I'll open it up and print it out."

Ferras started using his thumbs to type on the phone's tiny keyboard. It looked like some sort of child's toy to Bosch. Like the ones he had seen kids use on planes. He didn't understand why people were always typing feverishly on their phones. He was sure it was some sort of warning, a sign of the decline of civilization or humanity, but he couldn't put his finger on the right explanation for what he felt. The digital world was always billed as a great advancement, but he remained skeptical.

"Okay, I found it and sent it," Ferras finally said. "It'll probably come through in a couple minutes. What else?"

"Does that show what calls he made and what calls came in?"

Ferras manipulated the controls on the phone. "How far back do you want to go?" he asked.

"For now, how about going back till about noon yesterday."

"Okay, I'm on the screen. You want me to show you how to use this thing, or do you want me to just give you the numbers?"

Bosch got up and came around the row of desks so he could look over his partner's shoulder at the phone's small screen.

"Just give me an overview for now. "If you tried to teach me, we'd be here forever."

Ferras nodded. "Well," he said, "it shows a lot of calls to and from the office and various hospitals all through the afternoon. Three calls are marked 'Barry.' I'm assuming that was his partner. I looked up the state corporate records online, and K and K Medical Physicists is owned by Kent and someone named Barry Kelber."

"Yeah," Bosch said, "that reminds me that we have to talk to the partner first thing this morning."

He leaned across Ferras's desk to reach the notepad on his own desk. He wrote the name Barry Kelber down while Ferras continued to scroll through the cell phone's call log.

"Now, here we are after six, and he starts alternately calling his home and his wife's cell phone. I get the feeling that these weren't answered, because he's got ten calls logged in three minutes. He was calling and calling. And these were all made after he received that urgent e-mail from his wife's account."

Bosch saw the picture beginning to fill in a little bit. Kent had a routine day on the job, then got the e-mail from his wife's account. He saw the photo attached and started calling home. She didn't answer, which only alarmed him further. Finally, he went out and did what the e-mail instructed him to do.

"So what went wrong?" he asked out loud.

"What do you mean, Harry?"

"Up at the overlook. I still don't understand why they killed him. He did what they wanted. What went wrong?"

"I don't know. Maybe he saw one of their faces."

"The witness says the shooter was wearing a mask."

"Well, then maybe nothing went wrong. Maybe the plan was to kill him all along. They made that silencer, remember? And the way the guy yells out 'Allah' doesn't make it sound like something went wrong. Makes it sound like part of a plan."

Bosch nodded. "Then if that was the plan, why kill him and not her? Why leave a witness?"

"I don't know, Harry. But don't those hard-core Muslims have a rule about hurting women? Like it keeps them out of nirvana or heaven or whatever they call it?"

Bosch didn't answer the question, because he didn't know about the cultural practices his partner had crudely referred to. But the question underlined for him how out of his element he was on the case. He was used to chasing killers motivated by greed or lust or any one of the big seven sins. Religious extremism wasn't often on the list.

Ferras put the BlackBerry down and turned back to his computer. Like many detectives, he preferred to use his own laptop because the computers provided by the department were old and slow and most of them carried more viruses than a Hollywood Boulevard hooker.

He saved what he had been working on and opened up his e-mail screen. The e-mail forwarded from Kent's account was there. Ferras opened it and whistled when he saw the embedded photograph of Alicia Kent naked and tied up on the bed.

"Yeah, that would do it," he said.

Meaning that he understood why Kent had turned over the cesium. Ferras had been married for less than a year and had a baby on the way. Bosch was just starting to get to know his young partner but knew already that he was deeply in love with his wife. Under the glass top of his desk, Ferras had a collage of photos of his bride. Under the glass on his side of the workstation, Bosch had photos of murder victims whose killers he was still looking for.

"Make me a printout of that," Bosch said. "Blow it up if you can. And keep playing with that phone. See what else you can find."

Bosch went back to his side of the workstation and sat down. Ferras enlarged and printed out the e-mail and photo on a color printer located at the back of the squad room. He went over and retrieved it and then brought it to Bosch.

Bosch already had his reading glasses on, but from a desk drawer he pulled a rectangular magnifying glass he'd bought when he noticed that his prescription was no longer strong enough for close-up work. He never used the magnifying glass when the squad room was crowded with detectives. He didn't want to give the others something to ridicule him with—either in jest or not.

He put the printout on his desk and leaned over it with the magnifier. He studied the bindings that held the woman's limbs behind her torso. The intruders had used six snap ties, placing one loop around each wrist and ankle, then one to link the ankles, and the last one to link the wrist loops to the loop connecting the ankles.

It seemed like an overly complicated way to bind the woman's extremities. It was not the way Bosch would have done it if he were trying to quickly hog-tie a perhaps struggling woman. He would have used fewer bindings and made the work easier and quicker.

He wasn't sure what this meant, or if it meant anything at all. Perhaps Alicia Kent hadn't struggled, and in return for her cooperation, her captors used the extra links in order to make the time she was left bound on the bed less difficult. It seemed to Bosch that the way she had been bound meant that her arms and legs were not pulled behind her as far as they could have been.

Still, remembering the bruising on Alicia Kent's wrists, he realized that no matter what, the time she had spent hog-tied naked on the bed had not been easy. He decided that he needed to talk with Alicia Kent again and go over what had happened in more detail.

Nothing else came to mind during his study of the photograph. When he was finished, he put the magnifier aside and started skimming through the forensics reports from the murder scene. Nothing grabbed his attention there either, and he quickly moved on to the reports and evidence from the Kent house. Because he and Brenner had quickly left the house for Saint Agatha's, Bosch had not been there when the SID techs searched for evidence left behind by the intruders. He was anxious to see what, if anything, had been found.

But there was only one evidence bag, and it contained the black plastic snap ties that had been used to bind Alicia Kent's wrists and ankles and that Rachel Walling had cut in order to free her.

"Wait a minute," Bosch said, holding up the clear plastic bag. "Is this the only evidence they bagged at the Kent house?"

Ferras looked up. "It's the only bag they gave me. Did you check the evidence log? It should be in there."

Bosch looked through the documents Ferras had obtained until he found the forensic evidence log. Every item removed from a crime scene by the technicians was always entered on the log. It helped track the chain of evidence.

He found the log and noticed that it included several items removed by technicians from the Kent house, most of them tiny hair and fiber specimens. There was no telling if any of the specimens was related to the suspects, but in all his years working cases, Bosch had yet to come across the immaculate crime scene. A crime always leaves its mark—no matter how small—on the environment. There is always a transfer. It is just a matter of finding it.

On the list, each snap tie had been individually entered, and these were followed by numerous hair and fiber specimens extracted from locations ranging from the master bedroom carpet to the sink trap in the guest bathroom. The mouse pad from the office computer was on the list, as well as a Nikon camera lens cap, which had been found beneath the bed in the master bedroom. The last entry on the list was the most interesting to Bosch. The evidence was simply described as a cigarette ash.

Bosch could not think what value as evidence a cigarette ash could be. "Is anybody still up there in SID from the Kent house search?" he asked Ferras.

"There was a half hour ago," Ferras answered. "Buzz Yates and the latents woman whose name I always forget."

Bosch picked up the phone and called the SID office.

"Scientific Investigation Division, Yates."

"Buzz, Harry Bosch. On the search of the Kent house, tell me about this cigarette ash you collected."

"Oh, yeah. The FBI agent who was there asked me to collect it. She found it on top of the toilet tank in the guest bedroom. Like somebody had put their smoke down while they took a leak and then forgot about it."

"It was just ashes when she found it?"

"Right. A gray caterpillar. But she wanted us to collect it for her. She said their lab might be able to do something with—"

"Wait a minute, Buzz. You gave her the evidence from my crime scene?"

"Yes," Yates conceded. "But not without a lot of discussion and assurances, Harry. She said the Bureau's science lab could analyze the ashes and determine the type of tobacco, which would then allow them to determine country of origin. We can't do anything like that, Harry. We can't even touch that. She said it would be important to the investigation because they might be dealing with terrorists from outside the country. So I went along with it. She told me that she worked an arson case once where they found a single ash from the cigarette that lit the fire. They were able to tell what brand, and that tied it to a specific suspect."

"And you believed her?"

"Well . . . yeah, I believed her."

"So you gave her my evidence," Bosch said in a resigned tone.

"Harry, it's not *your* evidence. We all work and play on the same team, don't we?"

"Yeah, Buzz, we do."

Bosch hung up the phone and cursed. Ferras asked him what was wrong, but Bosch waved the question away.

"Just typical Bureau bull."

"Harry, did you get any sleep at all before the call out?"

Bosch looked across the desks at his partner. He knew exactly where Ferras was headed with that question.

"No," Bosch answered. "But lack of sleep has nothing to do with my frustration with the FBI. I've been doing this for more years than you've been alive. I know how to handle sleep deprivation."

He held up his mug of coffee. "Cheers," he said.

Bosch went back to thoughts about the cigarette ash.

"What about photos?" he asked Ferras. "Did you pick up photos from the Kent house?"

"Yeah. They're here somewhere."

Ferras looked through the files on his desk and came up with the folder containing the photos and passed it across. Bosch found three shots from the guest bathroom. A full shot, an angled shot of the toilet that showed the line of ash on the tank lid, and a close-up of the gray caterpillar, as Buzz Yates had called it.

He spread the three shots out and used his magnifier once again to study them. In the close-up shot of the ash, the photographer had put a six-inch ruler down on the tank lid to give the shot scale. The ash was almost two inches long, almost a full cigarette.

"See anything yet, Sherlock?" Ferras asked.

Bosch looked up at him. His partner was smiling. Bosch didn't smile back. "Not yet, Watson," he said.

He thought that might keep Ferras quiet. Nobody wanted to be Watson.

He studied the shot of the toilet and noted the seat had been left up. The indication was that a male had used the bathroom to urinate. The cigarette ash would further indicate that it had been one of the two intruders'. Bosch looked at the wall above the toilet. There was a small framed photograph of a winter scene of New York or somewhere else in the East.

The photo prompted Bosch to remember a case he had closed a year ago while he was in the Open-Unsolved Unit. He picked up the phone and called SID again. When Yates answered, Bosch asked for the person who checked the Kent house for latent fingerprints.

"Hold on," Yates said.

Apparently still annoyed with Bosch from the earlier phone call, Yates took his time getting the latents tech to the phone. Bosch ended up holding for about four minutes, using his glass to go over the photos from the Kent house the whole time.

"This is Wittig," a voice finally said.

Bosch knew her from prior cases.

"Andrea, it's Harry Bosch. I want to ask you about the Kent house. Did you laser the guest bathroom?"

"Where they found the ash and the seat was up? Yes, I did that."

"Anything?"

"No, nothing. It was wiped."

"How about the wall up above the toilet?"

"Yes, I checked there, too. There was nothing."

"That's all I wanted to know. Thanks, Andrea."

Bosch hung up and looked at the photo of the ash. Something about it bugged him, but he wasn't sure what.

"Harry, what were you asking about the wall over the toilet?"

Bosch looked at Ferras. Part of the reason the young detective was partnered with Bosch was so that the experienced detective could mentor the inexperienced detective. Bosch decided to put the Sherlock Holmes crack aside and tell him the story.

"About thirty years ago there was a case in Wilshire. This woman and her dog found drowned in her bathtub. The whole place had been wiped clean, but the lid was left up on the toilet. That told them they were looking for a man. The toilet had been wiped, but on the wall up behind it, they found a palm print. The guy had taken a leak and leaned on the wall while doing it. By measuring the height of the palm, they were able to figure out the guy's height. They also knew he was left-handed."

"How?"

"Because the print on the wall was a right palm. They figured a guy holds his tool with his preferred hand while taking a leak."

Ferras nodded in agreement.

"So they matched the palm to a suspect?"

"Yeah, but only after thirty years. We cleared it last year in Open-Unsolved. Not a lot of palms in the data banks back then. My partner and I came across the case and sent the palm through the box. We got a hit. We traced the guy to Ten Thousand Palms in the desert and went out there to get him. He pulled a gun and killed himself before we could make the arrest."

"Wow."

"Yeah. I always thought it was weird, you know?"

"What? Him killing himself?"

"No. That we traced his palm to Ten Thousand Palms."

"Oh, yeah. Ironic. So you didn't get a chance to talk to him?"

"Not really. But we were sure it was him. And I sort of took his killing himself in front of us as an admission of guilt."

Ferras went back to his work, and Bosch leaned back in his chair and considered things about the case at hand. At the moment, it was a jumble of thoughts and questions. And once again most prominent in his mind was the basic question of why Stanley Kent was killed. Alicia Kent said the two men who held her captive had worn ski masks. Jesse Mitford said he thought the man he saw kill Kent on the overlook was wearing a ski mask. To Bosch this begged the questions: Why shoot Stanley Kent if he couldn't even identify you, and why wear the mask if the plan all along was to kill him? He supposed that wearing the mask could have been a ploy to falsely reassure Kent and to make him cooperative. But that conclusion didn't feel right to him either.

Once more he put the questions aside, deciding that he didn't have enough information yet to properly go at them. He drank some coffee and got ready to take another shot at Jesse Mitford in the interview room. But first he pulled out his phone. He still had Rachel Walling's number from the Echo Park case. He pushed the button, but when he heard her voice, it was a recording.

"It's Harry Bosch," he said. "I need to talk to you about things, and I want my cigarette ashes back. That crime scene was mine."

He hung up. He knew the message would annoy her. He knew that he was inextricably heading toward a confrontation with Rachel and the Bureau. But Bosch couldn't bring himself to roll over. Not even for Rachel and the memory of what they once had. Not even for the hope of a future with her that he still carried like a number in a cell phone's heart.

NINE

BOSCH and Ferras stepped out the front door of the Mark Twain Hotel and surveyed the morning. The light was just beginning to enter the sky. The marine layer was coming in gray and thick and was deepening the shadows in the streets. It made it look like a city of ghosts, and that was fine with Bosch. It matched his outlook.

"You think he'll stay put?" Ferras asked.

Bosch shrugged. "He's got no place else to go."

They had just checked their witness into the hotel under the alias

Stephen King. Jesse Mitford had turned into a valuable asset. Though he had not been able to provide a description of the man who shot Stanley Kent and took the cesium, Mitford had been able to give them a clear understanding of what had transpired at the overlook. He would also be useful if the investigation ever led to an arrest and trial. A prosecutor could use his story as the narrative of the crime, a way to connect the dots for the jury.

After Bosch had consulted with Lieutenant Gandle, it was decided that they shouldn't lose track of the young drifter. Gandle approved a hotel voucher that would keep Mitford in the Mark Twain for four days. By then things would be clearer in regard to which way the case was going to go.

Bosch and Ferras got into the Crown Victoria that Ferras had earlier checked out of the car shed and headed down Wilcox to Sunset. Bosch was behind the wheel. At the light, he got out his cell phone. He hadn't heard back from Rachel Walling, so he called her partner. Brenner answered right away.

Bosch proceeded cautiously. "Just checking in," he said. "We still on for the meeting at nine?" Bosch wanted to make sure he was still part of the investigation before updating Brenner on anything.

"Uh, yes, we're still on, but it's been pushed back. I think it's ten now. We'll let you know."

The answer didn't make it sound like the meeting with the locals was a done deal. He decided to press Brenner. "Where will it be? At Tactical?"

Bosch knew from working with Walling before that the Tactical Unit was off campus in a secret location. He wanted to see if Brenner would slip.

"No, in the federal building downtown. Fourteenth floor. Just ask for the TIU meeting. How helpful was the witness?"

Bosch decided to hold his cards close until he had a better idea of his standing. "He saw the shooting from a distance. Then he saw the transfer. He said one man did it all, killed Stanley Kent and then moved the pig from the Porsche to the back of another vehicle. The other guy waited in another car and just watched."

"You get any plates from him?"

"No. Mrs. Kent's car was probably the one used to make the transfer. That way there would be no cesium trace in their own car."

"What about the suspect he did see?"

"Like I said, he couldn't ID him. He was still wearing a ski mask. Other than that, nada."

"Too bad," Brenner said. "What did you do with him?"

"The kid? We just dropped him off."

"Where's he live?"

"Halifax, Canada."

"Bosch, you know what I mean."

Bosch noticed the change in tone. That and the use of his last name. "He's got no local address," he replied. "He's a drifter. We just dropped him off at the Denny's on Sunset. That's where he wanted to go. We gave him a twenty to cover breakfast."

Bosch felt Ferras staring at him as he lied.

"Can you hold a second, Harry?" Brenner said. "I've got another call coming in here. It might be Washington."

Back to first names, Bosch noted. "Sure, Jack."

Bosch heard the line go to music, and he looked over at Ferras. His partner started to speak.

"Why'd you tell him we—"

Bosch held a finger to his lips, and Ferras stopped.

Half a minute went by. The light changed, and Bosch turned onto Sunset. Then Brenner came back on the line.

"Harry? Sorry about that. That was Washington. As you can imagine, they're all over this thing. Homeland is sending a fleet of choppers with equipment that can track a radiation trail. They'll start up at the overlook and try to pick up a signature specific to cesium. But the reality is, it's got to come out of the pig before they'll pick up a signal. Meantime, we're organizing the status meeting so that we can make sure everybody's on the same page."

"That's all the big G has accomplished?"

"Well, we're just getting organized. There's always a learning curve. I think after the meeting we'll be hitting this thing on all cylinders."

Bosch now knew for sure that things had changed. Brenner's defensive response told him the conversation was either being taped or overheard by others.

"It's still a few hours till the meeting," Brenner said. "What's your next move, Harry?"

Bosch hesitated, but not for long. "My next move is to go back up to the house and talk to Mrs. Kent again. I have some follow-up. Then we'll go over to the south tower at Cedars. Kent's office is there, and we need to see it and to talk to his partner."

There was no response. Bosch was coming up on the Denny's on Sunset. He pulled into the lot and parked. Through the windows, he could see that the twenty-four-hour restaurant was largely deserted.

"You still there, Jack?"

"Uh, yeah, Harry. I should tell you that it probably won't be necessary, you going back to the house and then by Kent's office."

Bosch shook his head. I knew it, he thought.

"You've already scooped everybody up, haven't you?"

"Wasn't my call. Anyway, from what I hear, the office was clean, and we have Kent's partner in here being questioned right now. We brought Mrs. Kent in as kind of a precautionary thing. We're still talking to her, too."

Bosch killed the car's engine and thought about how to respond. "Then maybe my partner and I should head downtown. This is still a homicide investigation. And last I heard, I was still working it."

There was a long thread of silence before Brenner responded.

"Look, Detective, the case is taking on larger dimensions. You have been invited to the status meeting. You and your partner. And at that time, you will be updated on what Mr. Kelber has had to say and a few other things. If Mr. Kelber is still here with us, I will do my best to get you in to speak with him. And with Mrs. Kent, too. But to be clear, the priority here is not the homicide. The priority is finding the cesium, and we're now almost ten hours behind."

"I have a feeling that if you find the killer, you find the cesium," Bosch said.

"That may be so," Brenner responded. "But the experience is

that this material is moved very quickly. Hand to hand. It takes an investigation with a lot of velocity. That's what we're engaged in now. Building velocity. We don't want to be slowed down."

"By the local yokels."

"You know what I mean."

"Sure. I'll see you at ten, Agent Brenner."

Bosch closed his phone and got out. As he and his partner crossed the lot, Ferras barraged him with questions.

"Why did you lie to him about the wit, Harry? What's going on? What are we doing here?"

Bosch held his hands up in a calming motion.

"Hold on, Ignacio. Let's sit down and have some coffee and maybe something to eat and I'll tell you what is going on."

They almost had their pick of the place. Bosch went to a booth in a corner that would allow them a clear view of the front door. The waitress came over quickly. She was an old battle-ax, with her steel-gray hair in a tight bun. Working graveyard at a Denny's in Hollywood had leached the life out of her eyes.

"Harry, it's been a long time," she said.

"Hey, Peggy. I guess it's been a while since I've had to chase a case through the night."

"Well, welcome back. What can I get you and your much younger partner?"

Bosch ignored the dig. He ordered coffee, toast, and eggs. Ferras ordered an egg-white omelet and a latte. When the waitress smirked and told him that neither could be accomplished, he settled for scrambled eggs and regular coffee. As soon as the waitress left them alone, Bosch answered Ferras's questions.

"We're being cut out," he said. "That's what's going on here."

"Are you sure? How do you know?"

"Because they've already scooped up our victim's wife and partner, and I can guarantee they are not going to let us talk to them."

"Harry, did they say that? Did they tell you that we couldn't talk to them? There's a lot at stake here, and I think you're being a little paranoid. You're jumping to—"

"Am I? Well, wait and see, partner. Watch and learn."

"We're still going to the meeting at nine, aren't we?"

"Supposedly. Except now it's at ten. And it will probably be a dog and pony show just for us. They're not going to tell us anything. They're going to sweet-talk us and brush us aside. 'Thanks a lot, fellas, we'll take it from here.' "

"Have a little faith, Harry."

"I have faith in myself. That's it. I've been on this road before. I know where it goes. On the one hand, who cares? Let them run with the case. But on the other hand, I care. I can't trust them to do it right. They want the cesium; I want the bastards who terrorized Stanley Kent for two hours and then forced him down on his knees and put two slugs in the back of his head."

"This is national security, Harry. This is different. There's a greater good here. You know, the good of the order."

It sounded to Bosch like Ferras was quoting from an academy textbook or the code of some sort of secret society. He didn't care. He had his own code.

"The good of the order starts with that guy lying dead on the overlook. If we forget about him, then we can forget about everything else."

Ferras nodded as though he was taking the advice to heart. But then he spoke from somewhere else.

"I still don't think we should have lied to them about the witness. He might be very valuable to them. Something he told us might fit with something they know about already. What's the harm in telling them where he is?"

Bosch emphatically shook his head. "No way. Not yet. The wit is ours, and we don't give him up. We trade him for access and information, or we keep him for ourselves."

The waitress brought their plates, and Bosch immediately dug into his food, holding a fork in one hand and a piece of toast in the other. He was starved and had a feeling they'd be on the move soon. When they would next have time for a meal was anybody's guess.

He was halfway through his eggs when he saw four men in dark suits walk in with unmistakable federal purpose in their strides. Wordlessly, they split into twos and started walking through the restaurant.

There were less than a dozen diners in the place, most of them strippers and their boyfriend pimps heading home from four-o'clock clubs. Bosch calmly continued to eat and watched the men in suits stop at each table, show credentials, and ask for IDs. Ferras was too busy splashing hot sauce on his eggs to notice what was happening. Bosch got his attention and nodded toward the agents.

Most of the people scattered among the tables were too tired or buzzed to do anything but comply with the demands to show identification. One young woman with a Z shaved into the side of her head started giving one pair of agents some lip, but she was a woman and they were looking for a man, so they ignored her and waited patiently for her boyfriend with the matching Z to show some ID.

Finally, a pair of agents came to the table in the corner. Their creds identified them as FBI agents Ronald Lundy and John Parkyn. They ignored Bosch because he was too old and asked Ferras for his ID.

"Who are you looking for?" Bosch asked.

"That's government business, sir. We just need to check IDs."

Ferras opened his badge wallet. On one side it had his photo and police ID, and on the other side his detective's badge. It seemed to freeze the two agents.

"It's funny," Bosch said. "If you're looking at IDs, that means you have a name. But I never gave Agent Brenner the witness's name. Makes me wonder. You guys over there in Tactical Intelligence don't happen to have a bug in our computer or maybe our squad room, do you?"

Lundy, the one obviously in charge of the pickup detail, looked squarely at Bosch. "And you are?" he asked.

"You want to see my ID, too? I haven't passed for a twenty-year-old in a long time, but I'll take it as a compliment."

He pulled out his badge wallet and handed it to Lundy. The agent opened it and examined the contents very closely. He took his time.

"Hieronymus Bosch," he said, reading the name on the ID. "Wasn't there some sick creep of a painter named that?"

Bosch smiled back at him. "Some people consider the painter a master of the Renaissance period," he said.

Lundy dropped the badge wallet on Bosch's plate. Bosch hadn't finished his eggs yet, but luckily the yolks were overcooked.

"I don't know what the game is here, Bosch. Where's Mitford?"

Bosch picked up his badge wallet and used his napkin to clean egg off it. He looked back up at Lundy. "Who's Mitford?"

Lundy leaned down and put both hands on the table.

"You know damn well who he is, and we need to take him in."

Bosch nodded as though he understood the situation perfectly.

"We can talk about Mitford and everything else at the meeting at ten. Right after I interview Kent's partner and his wife."

Lundy smiled in a way that carried no friendliness or humor.

"You know something, pal? You're going to need a Renaissance period yourself when this is all over."

Bosch smiled again. "See you at the meeting, Agent Lundy."

TEN

THE sun was still below the ridgeline, but dawn had a full grip on the sky. In daylight, the Mulholland overlook showed no sign of the violence of the night before. Even the debris usually left behind at a crime scene—rubber gloves, coffee cups, and yellow tape—had somehow been cleaned up or maybe had blown away. It was as if Stanley Kent had not been shot to death, his body never left on the promontory with the jetliner view of the city below.

Bosch kicked at the soft orange ground. He made a decision and headed back toward the car. Ferras watched him go.

"What are you going to do?" Ferras asked.

"I'm going in. If you're coming, get in the car."

Ferras hesitated and then trotted after Bosch. They got back in the Crown Vic and drove over to Arrowhead Drive. Bosch knew that the feds had Alicia Kent, but he still had the key ring from her husband's Porsche.

The fed car they had spotted when they had driven by ten minutes earlier was still parked in front of the Kent house. Bosch pulled into the driveway, got out, and headed with purpose to the front door. He ignored the car in the street, even when he heard its door open. He managed to find the right key and get it into the lock before they were hit with a voice from behind.

"FBI. Hold it right there."

Bosch put his hand on the knob, turned, and looked at the man approaching on the front walkway. He knew that whoever was assigned to watch the house would be the lowest man on the Tactical Intelligence totem pole, a screwup or an agent with baggage. He knew he could use this to his advantage.

"LAPD Homicide Special," he said. "We're just going to finish up in here."

"No, you're not," the agent said. "The Bureau has taken over jurisdiction and will be handling everything from here on."

"Sorry, man, I didn't get the memo," Bosch said.

He turned back to the door.

"Do not open that door," the agent said. "This is a national security investigation. You can check with your superiors."

Bosch shook his head.

"You may have superiors. I have supervisors."

"Harry," Ferras said. "Maybe we—"

Bosch waved a hand and cut him off. He turned back to the agent. "Let me see some ID," he said.

The agent put an exasperated look on his face and dug out his creds. He flipped them open and held them out. Bosch was ready. He grabbed the agent by the wrist and pivoted. The agent's body came forward and past him, and Bosch used a forearm to press him face-first against the door. He pulled his hand—still clutching his credentials—behind his back.

The agent started struggling and protesting, but it was too late. Bosch leaned his shoulder into him to keep him against the door and slipped his free hand under the man's jacket. He jerked the handcuffs off the agent's belt and started cuffing him up.

"Harry, what are you doing?" Ferras yelled.

"I told you. Nobody's pushing us aside."

Once he had the agent's hands cuffed behind him, he grabbed the credentials out of his hand. He opened them and checked the name. Clifford Maxwell. Bosch turned him around and shoved the creds into the side pocket of his jacket.

"Your career is over," Maxwell said calmly.

"Tell me about it," Bosch said.

Maxwell looked at Ferras.

"You go along with this and you're in the toilet, too," he said.

"Shut up, Cliff," Bosch said. "The only one who is going to be in the toilet is you when you go back to Tactical and tell them how you let two of the local yokels get the drop on you."

That shut him up. Bosch opened the door and walked the agent in. He pushed him down into a chair in the living room.

"Have a seat," he said. "And shut up."

He reached down and opened Maxwell's jacket so he could see where he carried his weapon. His gun was in a pancake holster under his left arm. He would not be able to reach it with his wrists cuffed behind his back. Bosch frisked the agent's legs to make sure he wasn't carrying a throw-down. Satisfied, he stepped back.

"Relax now," he said. "We won't be long."

Bosch started down the hallway, signaling his partner to follow him. "You start in the office, and I'll start in the bedroom," he instructed. "We're looking for anything and everything. We'll know it when we see it. Check the computer. Anything unusual, I want to know about it."

"Harry."

Bosch stopped in the hallway and looked at Ferras. He could tell that his young partner was running scared.

"We shouldn't be doing it this way," Ferras said.

"How should we be doing it, Ignacio? Do you mean we should be going through channels? Have our boss talk to his boss, grab a latte, and wait for permission to do our job?"

"I understand the need for speed," Ferras said. "But do you think he's going to let this go? He's going to have our badges, Harry, and I don't mind going down in the line of duty, but not for what we just did."

Bosch admired Ferras for saying *we,* and that gave him the patience to calmly step back and put a hand on his partner's shoulder. He lowered his voice so Maxwell would not hear him.

"Listen to me, Ignacio. Not one thing is going to happen to you because of this. I've been around a little longer than you, and I know how the Bureau works. Hell, my ex-wife is ex-Bureau, okay? And the one thing I know better than anything is that the number one FBI priority is not to be embarrassed. So when we are done here and we cut that guy loose, he's not going to tell a single soul what we did or that we were even here. Why do you think they had him sitting on the house? Because he's working off an embarrassment—either to himself or the Bureau. And he's not going to do or say a thing that brings him any more heat."

Bosch paused to allow Ferras to respond. He didn't.

"So let's just move quickly here and check out the house," Bosch continued. "When I was here this morning, it was all about the widow and dealing with her, and then we had to run out the door to Saint Aggy's. I want to take my time but be quick, you know what I mean? I want to see the place in daylight and grind the case down for a while. This is how I like to work. You'd be surprised what you come up with sometimes. The thing to remember is that there's always a transfer. Those two killers left their mark somewhere in this house, and I think everybody else missed it. Let's go find it."

Ferras nodded. "Okay, Harry."

"Good. I'll start in the bedroom. You check the office."

Bosch moved down the hallway and was almost to the bedroom when Ferras called his name again. Bosch turned and went back to the office alcove. His partner was behind the desk.

"Where's the computer?" Ferras asked.

Bosch shook his head in frustration. "They took it."

"The FBI?"

"Who else? It wasn't on the SID log, only the mouse pad. Just look around, go through the desk. See what else you can find."

Bosch went down the hall to the master bedroom. It appeared to be undisturbed since he had last seen it. There was still a slight odor of urine due to the soiled mattress.

He walked over to the night table on the left side of the bed. He saw black fingerprint powder dusted across the knobs on the two drawers. On top of the table was a framed photograph of Stanley and Alicia Kent. The couple was standing next to a rosebush in full bloom. Alicia was smiling, as if she were standing proudly next to her own child. Bosch could tell that the rosebush was hers, and in the background, he could see others just like it. Farther up the hillside were the first three letters of the Hollywood sign, and he realized the photo was taken in the backyard of the house.

Bosch slid open the table's drawers one by one. They were full of personal items belonging to Stanley. Various reading glasses and prescription bottles. The lower drawer was empty, and Bosch remembered that it was where Stanley had kept his gun.

Bosch closed the drawers and stepped into the corner of the room. He was looking for a new angle, some sort of fresh take on the crime scene. He realized that he needed the crime-scene photos, and he had left them in a file in the car.

He walked down the hallway toward the front door. When he got to the living room, he saw Maxwell lying on the floor. He had managed to move his handcuffed wrists down over his hips. His knees were bent up with his wrists cuffed behind them. He looked up at Bosch with a red and sweating face.

"I'm stuck," Maxwell said. "Help me out."

Bosch almost laughed. "In a minute."

He walked out to the car, where he retrieved the crime-scene photos. He had put the copy of the e-mailed photo of Alicia Kent in there as well.

As he walked back into the house, Maxwell called to him.

"Come on, help me out, man."

Bosch ignored him. He walked down the hallway and glanced into the home office as he passed. Ferras was going through the drawers of the desk.

In the bedroom, Bosch got the e-mail photo out and put the files down on the bed. He held the photo up so he could compare it to the room. He then went to the mirrored closet door and opened it at an angle that matched the photograph. He noticed in the photo the white terry-cloth robe draped over a lounge chair in the corner of the room. He stepped into the closet and looked for the robe, found it, and put it in the same position on the lounge chair.

Bosch moved to the place in the room from which he believed the e-mail photo had been taken. He scanned the room, hoping something would poke through and speak to him. He noticed the dead clock on the bed table and then checked it against the e-mail photo. The clock was dead in the photo, too.

Bosch walked over to the table, crouched, and looked behind it. The clock was unplugged. He reached behind the table and plugged it back in. The digital screen started flashing 12:00 in red numerals. The clock worked. It just needed to be set.

Bosch thought about this and knew it would be something to ask Alicia Kent about. He assumed the men who were in the house had unplugged the clock. The question was why. Perhaps they didn't want Alicia Kent to know how much or how little time had gone by while she waited tied up on the bed.

Bosch moved to the bed, where he opened one of the files and took out the crime-scene photographs. He studied these and noticed that the closet door was open at a slightly different angle from the one in the e-mail photo and that the robe was gone, obviously because Alicia Kent had put it on after her rescue. He stepped over to the closet, matched the door's angle to the one in the crime scene photograph, and then stepped back and scanned the room.

Nothing broke through. The transfer still eluded him. He felt discomfort in his gut. He felt as though he was missing something. Something that was right there in the room with him.

He left the bedroom and made his way down the hall toward the kitchen, stopping in each room and checking closets and drawers and finding nothing suspicious. In the workout room, he noticed a rectangular discoloration on the wall next to the hooks, where rubber workout mats hung. There were slight tape marks indicating that a poster or maybe a large calendar had been taped to the wall.

When he got to the living room, Maxwell was still on the floor, red-faced and sweating from struggling. He now had one leg through the loop created by his cuffed wrists, but he apparently couldn't get the other through in order to bring his hands to the front of his body. He was lying on the tiled floor with his wrists bound between his legs.

"We're almost out of here, Agent Maxwell," Bosch said.

Maxwell didn't respond.

In the kitchen, Bosch went to the back door and stepped out onto a rear patio and garden. Seeing the yard in daylight changed his perspective. It was on an incline, with rosebushes going up the embankment. Some were in bloom, and some weren't. Some relied on support sticks that carried markers identifying the different kinds of roses. He studied a few of these, then returned to the house.

After locking the door behind him, he walked across the kitchen and opened another door, which he knew led to the adjoining two-car garage. A bank of cabinets stretched along the back wall of the garage. One by one he opened them and surveyed the contents. There were mostly tools for gardening and household chores, and several bags of fertilizer and soil nutrients for growing roses.

There was a wheeled trash can in the garage. Bosch opened it and saw one plastic trash bag in it. He pulled it out, loosened the pull strap, and discovered it contained what appeared to be only basic kitchen trash. On top was a cluster of paper towels that were stained purple. It looked like someone had cleaned up a spill. He held one of the towels up and smelled grape juice on it.

After returning the trash to the container, Bosch left the garage.

In the kitchen, he checked the cabinets and the walk-in pantry and studied all the groceries and supplies. After that he went to the guest bathroom in the hall and looked at the spot where the cigarette ash had been collected. On the white porcelain tank top, there was a brown discoloration about half the length of a cigarette.

Bosch stared at the mark, curious. It had been seven years since he had smoked, but he didn't remember ever leaving a cigarette to burn like that. If he had finished it, he would have thrown it into the toilet and flushed it away. It was clear that this cigarette had been forgotten.

With his search complete, he stepped back into the living room and called to his partner. "Ignacio, you ready?"

Maxwell was still on the floor but looked tired from his struggle and resigned to his predicament.

"Come on, damn it!" he finally cried out. "Uncuff me!"

Bosch stepped close to him. "Where's your key?"

"Coat pocket. Left side."

Bosch pulled a set of keys out of the agent's pocket. He found the cuff key, grabbed the chain between the two cuffs, and pulled up so he could work the key in. He wasn't gentle about it.

"Now be nice if I do this," he said.

"Nice? I'm going to kick your ass."

Bosch let go of the chain. Maxwell's wrists fell to the floor.

"What are you doing?" Maxwell yelled. "Undo me!"

"Here's a tip, Cliff. Next time you threaten to kick my ass, you might want to wait until after I've cut you loose."

Bosch straightened up and tossed the keys onto the floor on the other side of the room. "Uncuff yourself."

Bosch headed to the front door. When he got to the car, he looked over the roof at his partner. Ferras looked as mortified as some of the suspects who had ridden in the backseat.

"Cheer up," Bosch said.

As he got in, he had a vision of the FBI agent crawling in his nice suit across the living-room floor to the keys.

Bosch smiled.

ELEVEN

ON THE way back down the hill to the freeway, Ferras was silent, and Bosch knew he had to be thinking about the jeopardy his young and promising career had been placed in because of his old and reckless partner's actions. Bosch tried to draw him out of it.

"Well, that was a bust," he said. "I got nada. You find anything in the office?"

"Nothing much. I showed you, the computer was gone."

There was a sullen tone in his voice.

"What about the desk?" Bosch asked.

"The desk was mostly empty. One drawer had tax returns. Another had a copy of a trust. Their house, an investment property in Laguna, insurance policies, everything like that is held in a trust."

"Got it. How much the guy make last year?"

"A quarter million take-home. He also owns fifty-one percent of the company."

"The wife make anything?"

"No income. Doesn't work."

Bosch grew quiet as he contemplated things. When they got down off the mountain, he decided not to get on the freeway. Instead, he turned east. Ferras quickly noticed the detour.

"What's going on? I thought we were going downtown."

"We're going to Los Feliz first."

"What's in Los Feliz?"

"The Donut Hole on Vermont."

"We just ate an hour ago."

Bosch checked his watch. It was almost eight, and he hoped he wasn't too late. "I'm not going for the doughnuts."

Ferras cursed and shook his head. "You're going to talk to the Man? Are you kidding?"

"Unless I missed him already. If you're worried about it, you can stay in the car."

"You're jumping about five links in the chain, you know. Lieutenant Gandle is going to have our asses for this."

"He'll have *my* ass. You stay in the car. It will be like you weren't even there."

"Except what one partner does, the other always gets equal blame for. You know that. That's how it works. That's why they call them *partners,* Harry."

"Look, I'll take care of it. There's no time to go through proper channels. The chief should know what is what, and I'm going to tell him. He'll probably end up thanking us for the heads-up."

The partners drove the rest of the way in silence.

The LAPD was one of the most insular bureaucracies in the world. It had survived for more than a century by rarely looking outward for ideas, answers, or leaders. A few years earlier the city council decided that after years of scandal and community upset, it required leadership from outside the department. The outsider who was brought in to run the show was viewed with tremendous curiosity, not to mention skepticism. His movements and habits were documented, and the data was all dumped into an informal police pipeline that connected the department's ten thousand officers like the blood vessels in a closed fist. The intelligence was passed around in roll calls and locker rooms, text messages, e-mails and phone calls, at cop bars and backyard barbecues. It meant that street officers in South L.A. knew what Hollywood premiere the new chief had attended the night before. Vice officers in the Valley knew where he took his dress uniforms to be pressed, and the gang detail in Venice knew what supermarket his wife liked to shop at.

It also meant that Detective Harry Bosch and his partner Ignacio Ferras knew what doughnut shop the chief stopped at for coffee every morning on his way into Parker Center.

At eight a.m. Bosch pulled into the parking lot of the Donut Hole but saw no sign of the chief's unmarked car. Bosch killed the engine and looked over at his partner.

"You staying?"

Ferras nodded without looking at Bosch.

"Suit yourself," Bosch said.

"Listen, Harry, no offense, but this isn't working. You don't want a partner. You want a gofer and somebody who doesn't question anything you do. I think I'm going to talk to the lieutenant about hooking me up with someone else."

Bosch looked at him and composed his thoughts.

"Ignacio, it's our first case together. Don't you think you should give it some time? That's all Gandle's going to tell you. He's going to tell you that you don't want to start out in RHD with a reputation as a guy who cuts and runs on his partner."

"I'm not cutting and running. It's just not working right."

Bosch stared at him for a long moment before turning to the door. "Like I said, suit yourself."

Bosch got out and headed toward the doughnut shop. He was disappointed in Ferras's reaction but knew he should cut him some slack. The guy had a kid on the way and needed to play it safe. Bosch was not one to ever play it safe, and it had lost him more than a partner in the past. He would take another shot at changing the young man's mind once the case settled down.

Inside the shop, Bosch waited in line behind two people and then ordered a black coffee from the Asian man behind the counter. The man turned to a brewer on the back wall and filled a cup. When he turned back around, Bosch had his badge out.

"Has the chief been in yet?"

The man hesitated. He had no idea about the intelligence pipeline and was unsure about responding. He knew he could lose a high-profile customer if he spoke out of turn.

"It's all right," Bosch said. "I'm supposed to meet him here. I'm late." Bosch tried to smile as though he were in trouble.

"He not here yet," the counterman said.

Relieved he hadn't missed him, Bosch paid for the coffee and went to an empty table in the corner. It was mostly a takeout operation at this time of morning. For ten minutes, Bosch watched a cross section of the city's culture step up to the counter, all united by the addiction to caffeine and sugar.

Finally, he saw the black Town Car pull in. The chief was in the front passenger seat. Both he and the driver got out. Both scanned their surroundings and headed toward the doughnut shop. Bosch knew the driver was an officer and served as a bodyguard as well.

There was no line at the counter when they came in.

"Hiyou, Chief," the counterman said.

"Good morning, Mr. Ming. I'll have the usual."

Bosch stood up and approached. The bodyguard turned and squared himself in Bosch's direction. Bosch stopped.

"Chief, can I buy you a cup of coffee?" Bosch asked.

The chief turned and did a double take when he recognized Bosch. For a moment, Bosch saw a frown move across the man's face—he was still dealing with some of the fallout from the Echo Park case—but then it quickly disappeared into impassivity.

"Detective Bosch," he said. "You're not here to give me bad news, are you?"

"More like a heads-up, sir."

The chief turned away to accept a cup of coffee and a small bag from Ming. "Have a seat," he said. "I have about five minutes, and I'll pay for my own coffee."

Bosch went back to the same table and sat down and waited while the chief paid for his coffee and doughnuts, took his purchase to another counter, and put cream and sweetener into his coffee. Bosch believed that the chief had been good for the department. He had made a few missteps politically and some questionable choices in command staff assignments but had largely been responsible for raising the morale of the rank and file. Crime stats were even down, which to Bosch meant there was a good possibility that actual crime was down as well—he viewed crime statistics with suspicion.

But all of that aside, Bosch liked the chief for one overarching reason. Two years earlier he had given Bosch his job back. Bosch had retired and gone private. It didn't take him long to realize it was a mistake, and when he did, the new chief welcomed him back.

It made Bosch loyal, and that was one reason he was forcing the meeting at the doughnut shop.

The chief sat down across from him. "You're lucky, Detective. Most days I would have been here and gone an hour ago. But I worked late last night hitting crime-watch meetings in three parts of the city."

Rather than open his doughnut bag and reach in, the chief tore it down the middle so he could spread it and eat his two doughnuts off it. He had a powdered sugar and a chocolate glazed.

"Here's the most dangerous killer in the city," he said as he raised the chocolate-glazed doughnut and took a bite.

Bosch nodded. "You're probably right." He smiled uneasily and tried an icebreaker. His old partner, Kiz Rider, had just come back to work after recovering from gunshot wounds. She transferred out of Robbery-Homicide to the chief's office, where she had worked once before.

"How's my old partner doing, Chief?"

"Kiz? Kiz is good. She does fine work for me. I think she's in the right spot. Are you in the right spot, Detective?"

Bosch looked at the chief and wondered if he might already be questioning his jumping the chain of command. Before he could work up an answer, the chief asked another question.

"Are you here about the Mulholland overlook case?"

Bosch nodded. He assumed that the word had gone up the pipe from Lieutenant Gandle and that the chief had been briefed in some detail about the case.

"I know it's got federal interest. Captain Hadley called me this morning. He said there is a terrorism angle."

Bosch was surprised to learn that Captain Done Badly and the OHS were already in the picture.

"What's Captain Hadley doing?" he asked. "He hasn't called me."

"The usual. Checking our own intelligence, trying to open lines with the feds."

Bosch nodded.

"So what can you tell me, Detective? Why did you come here?"

Bosch gave him a fuller rundown on the case, accenting the federal involvement and what was looking like an effort to shut the LAPD out of its own investigation. Bosch acknowledged that the missing cesium was a priority and true cause for the feds to throw their weight around. But he said the case was a homicide, and that cut the LAPD in. He went over the evidence he had collected and laid out some of his theories.

The chief had consumed both doughnuts by the time Bosch was finished. He wiped his mouth with a napkin before responding. "What aren't you telling me?" he asked.

Bosch shrugged. "Not much. I had a little dustup at the victim's house with an agent, but I don't think anything will come of it."

"Why isn't your partner in here? Why is he waiting in the car?"

Bosch understood. The chief had seen Ferras when he scanned the lot upon his arrival.

"We're having a little disagreement on how to proceed. He's a good kid, but he wants to roll over for the feds a little too easy."

"Did your partner think it was appropriate to ignore the department's chain of command by coming directly to me with this?"

Bosch dropped his eyes to the table. The chief's voice had taken on a stern tone.

"He wasn't happy about it, Chief," Bosch said. "It wasn't his idea. It was mine. I just didn't think there was enough time to—"

"Doesn't matter what you thought. It's what you did. So if I were you, I would keep this meeting to yourself, and I will as well. Don't ever do it this way again, Detective. Are we clear on that?"

"Yes, clear."

The chief glanced toward the glass display case where the doughnuts were lined up on trays. "And by the way, how did you know that I would be here?" he asked.

Bosch shrugged. "I don't remember. I just sort of knew. It's just something that gets around the department."

"It's too bad," the chief said. "I liked this place. Convenient, good doughnuts, and Mr. Ming takes care of me. What a shame."

Bosch realized that the chief would now have to change his routine. It did not serve him well if it was known where he could be found and when.

"Sorry, sir," Bosch said. "But if I might make a recommendation. There's a place in the Farmer's Market called Bob's Coffee and Doughnuts. It's a bit out of the way for you, but the coffee and doughnuts would be worth it."

The chief nodded thoughtfully. "I'll keep it in mind. Now, what is it you want from me, Detective Bosch?"

Bosch decided that the chief obviously wanted to get down to business. "I need access to Alicia Kent and her husband's partner, a guy named Kelber. The feds have them both, and I think my window of access closed about five hours ago. That's why I'm here, Chief. I need access. I figure you can get it for me."

The chief nodded. "I can make some calls, raise some hell, and probably open the window. As I said before, we have Captain Hadley's unit on this already, and perhaps he can open up the channels of communication."

To Bosch it sounded like the chief was going to go to bat for him.

"You know what reflux is, Detective?"

"Reflux?"

"It's a condition where all the bile backs up into your throat. It burns, Detective. If I make these moves and I get that window open for you, I don't want any reflux. You understand me?"

"I understand."

The chief wiped his mouth again and put the napkin down on his torn bag. He then crumpled it all into a ball, careful not to spill any powdered sugar on his black suit.

"I'll make the calls, but it's going to be tough. You don't see the political angle here, do you, Bosch?"

Bosch looked at him. "Sir?"

"The bigger picture, Detective. You see this as a homicide investigation. It is actually much more than that. You have to understand that it serves the federal government extremely well with this thing on the overlook being part of a terrorism plot. A bona fide domestic threat would go a long way toward deflecting public attention and easing the pressure in other areas. The war's gone to hell; the election was a disaster. You've got the Middle East, the price of a gallon of gasoline, and a lame-duck president's approval ratings. The list goes on and on, and there would be an opportunity here for redemption. A chance to shift public attention and opinion."

Bosch nodded. "Are you saying that they might try to keep this thing going, maybe even exaggerate the threat?"

"I'm not saying anything, Detective. I am just trying to broaden your perspective. A case like this, you have to be aware of the political landscape. You can't be running around like a bull in a china shop—which in the past has been your specialty."

The chief stood up, ready to go. "Think about it and be careful," he said. "Remember, no reflux. No blowback."

"Yes, sir."

TWELVE

BOSCH didn't speak until they were out of the parking lot. He decided that the Hollywood Freeway would be overrun by the morning commute and Sunset was the fastest way downtown.

Ferras made it only two blocks before asking what had happened in the doughnut shop.

"Don't worry, Ignacio. We both still have our jobs."

"Then, what happened?"

"He said you were right. I shouldn't have jumped command. But he said he would make some calls and try to open things up with the feds."

They drove in silence for a while until Bosch brought up his partner's plan to ask for a new assignment.

"You still going to talk to the lieutenant?"

Ferras paused before answering. He was uncomfortable with the question.

"I don't know, Harry. I still think it would be best. Best for both of us. Maybe you work best with female partners."

Bosch almost laughed. Ferras didn't know Kiz Rider, his last partner. She never went along to get along with Harry. Like Ferras, she objected every time Bosch went alpha dog on her. He was about to set Ferras straight, when his cell phone started buzzing and he pulled it out of his pocket. It was Lieutenant Gandle.

"Harry, where are you?"

His voice was louder than usual and more urgent. He was excited about something, and Bosch wondered if he had already heard about the Donut Hole meeting. Had the chief betrayed him?

"I'm on Sunset. We're heading in."

"Did you pass Silver Lake yet?"

"Not yet."

"Good. Head up to Silver Lake. Go to the rec center at the bottom of the reservoir. The Kent car's been located. Hadley and his people are already out there setting up the Command Post. They've requested the investigators on scene."

"Hadley? Why's he there? Why is there a CP?"

"Hadley's office got the tip and checked it out before deciding to clue us in. The car is parked in front of a house belonging to a person of interest. They want you on the scene."

"Person of interest? What's that mean?"

"The house is the residence of a suspected terrorist sympathizer. I don't have all the details. Just get there, Harry. Call me and let me know what's happening."

"All right. We're on the way."

Bosch closed the phone and tried to pick up speed, but the traffic was too thick for him to get anywhere. He filled Ferras in on what little he knew from the phone call.

"What about the FBI?" Ferras asked. "Do they know?"

"I didn't ask."

"What about the meeting at ten?"

"I guess we'll worry about that at ten."

In ten minutes, they finally got to Silver Lake Boulevard, and

Bosch turned north. This part of the city took its name from the Silver Lake Reservoir, which sat in the middle of a middle-class neighborhood of bungalows and post–World War Two homes.

As they approached the recreation center, Bosch saw two shiny black SUVs that he recognized as the signature vehicles of the OHS. Apparently, he thought, there was never much trouble getting funding for a unit that supposedly hunted terrorists. There were two patrol cars and a city sanitation truck as well. Bosch parked behind one of the patrol cars, and he and Ferras got out.

There was a group of ten men in black fatigues—also distinctive to the OHS—gathered around the fold-down rear gate of one of the SUVs. Bosch approached them, and Ferras trailed a couple of steps behind. Their presence was immediately noticed, and the crowd parted, and there was Captain Don Hadley sitting on the gate. Bosch had never met him but had seen him often enough on television. He was a large red-faced man with sandy hair. He was about forty years old and looked like he had been in the gym working out for half of them.

"Bosch?" Hadley asked. "Ferras?"

"I'm Bosch. This is Ferras."

"Fellas, good to have you here. I think we're going to tie your case up for you in a bow in short order. We're just waiting on one of my guys to bring the warrant, and then we go in."

He stood up and signaled to one of his men. Hadley had a definite air of confidence about him.

"Perez, check on that warrant, will you? I'm tired of waiting. Then check the OP and see what's happening up there."

He then turned back to Bosch and Ferras.

"Walk with me, men."

Hadley headed away from the group, and Bosch and Ferras followed. He led them to the back of the sanitation truck, where he adopted a command pose, putting his foot up on the back end of the truck. Bosch noticed that he carried his sidearm in a leg holster that was strapped around his thick right thigh. Like an Old West gunslinger. He was chewing gum and not trying to hide it.

Bosch had heard many stories about Hadley. He now had the feeling that he was about to become part of one.

"I wanted you men to be here for this," Hadley said. "We've located your Chrysler Three hundred two and a half blocks from here. The plate matches the BOLO, and I eyeballed the vehicle myself. It's the car we've been looking for."

That part was good, Bosch, thought. What's the rest?

"The vehicle is parked in front of a home owned by a man named Ramin Samir," Hadley continued. "He's a guy we've been keeping our eye on for a few years. A real person of interest to us."

The name was familiar to Bosch, but he couldn't place it at first.

"Why is he of interest, Captain?" he asked.

"Mr. Samir is a known supporter of religious organizations that want to hurt Americans and damage our interests. What's worse is, he teaches our young people to hate their own country."

That last part jogged Bosch's memory, and he put things together. He could not recall which Middle Eastern country Ramin Samir was from, but Bosch remembered that he was a former visiting professor of international politics at USC who had gained widespread notice for espousing anti-American sentiment in the classroom and in the media.

He was making media ripples before the 9/11 domestic terrorist attacks. Afterward, the ripples became a wave. He openly postulated that the attacks were warranted because of U.S. intrusion and aggression all around the globe. He was able to parlay the attention this brought him into a position as the media go-to guy for the ever ready anti-American quote or sound bite.

Samir's role as agent provocateur was good for a few years of guest shots on the cable-news debate programs, where everybody tends to yell at one another. Meantime, he used his soapbox and celebrity status to help start and fund a number of organizations that were quickly accused of being connected to terrorist organizations and anti-American jihads. But while Samir was often investigated, he was never charged with any crime. He was, however, fired by USC on a technicality—he had not stated that his opinions were his own and not those of the school when he wrote an op-ed piece for the *Los Angeles Times* that suggested the Iraq war was an American-planned genocide of Muslims.

Samir was eventually discounted in the media as a narcissistic provocateur who made outlandish statements in order to draw attention to himself rather than to thoughtfully comment on the issues of the day. His star waned, and he dropped from public sight. But all the rhetoric aside, the fact that Samir was never charged with a crime during a period when the climate in the United States was hot with fear of the unknown and the desire for vengeance always indicated to Bosch that there was nothing there. If there had been fire behind the smoke, then Ramin Samir would be in a prison cell or behind a fence at Guantánamo Bay. But here he was, living in Silver Lake, and Bosch was skeptical of Captain Hadley's claims.

"I remember this guy," he said. "He was just a talker, Captain. There was never any solid link between Samir and—"

Hadley held up a finger like a teacher demanding silence.

"Never a solid link *established*," he corrected. "But that doesn't mean anything. This guy raises money for the Palestinian Jihad and other Muslim causes."

"The Palestinian Jihad?" Bosch asked. "What is that? And what Muslim causes? Are you saying Muslim causes can't be legit?"

"Look, all I'm saying is that this is a bad dude, and he's got a car that was used in a murder and zesium heist sitting right in front of his house."

"Cesium," Ferras said. "It was cesium that was stolen."

Not used to being corrected, Hadley narrowed his eyes and stared at Ferras for a moment before speaking.

"Whatever. It's not going to make much difference what you call it, son, if he dumps it into the reservoir across the street or is in that house putting it in a bomb while we're sitting here waiting on a warrant."

"The FBI didn't say anything about it being a water-borne threat," Bosch said.

Hadley shook his head. "Doesn't matter. Bottom line is that it's a threat. I'm sure the FBI said that. Well, the Bureau can talk about it. We're going to *do* something about it."

Bosch stepped back, trying to draw some fresh air into the discussion. This was moving too quickly.

"So you're going to go in?" he asked.

Hadley was working his jaw in quick, powerful bites of the gum. He seemed not to notice the strong odor of garbage emanating from the back of the truck.

"You're damn right we're going to go in," he said. "Just as soon as that warrant gets here."

"You got a judge to sign a warrant that's based on a stolen car being parked in front of the house?" Bosch asked.

Hadley signaled to one of his men.

"Bring the bags, Perez," he called. Then to Bosch he said, "No, that's not all we got. Today's trash day, Detective. I sent the garbage truck up the street, and a couple of my men emptied the two cans that were in front of Samir's house. Perfectly legal, as you know. And lookee at what we got."

Perez hustled over with the plastic evidence bags.

"Captain, I checked the OP," Perez said. "Still quiet up there."

"Thank you, Perez." Hadley took the bags and turned back to Bosch and Ferras. Perez went back to the SUV.

"Our observation post is a guy in a tree," Hadley said with a smile. "He'll let us know if anybody makes a move up there."

He handed Bosch the bags. Two of them contained black woolen ski masks. The third contained a slip of paper with a hand-drawn map on it. Bosch looked closely at it. It was a series of crisscrossing lines with two of them marked as Arrowhead and Mulholland. The map was a fairly accurate rendering of the neighborhood where Stanley Kent had lived and died.

Bosch handed the bags back and shook his head.

"Captain, I think you should hold up."

"Hold up? We're not holding up. If this guy and his pals contaminate the reservoir with that poison, do you think the people of this city are going to accept that we held up to make sure we dotted every *i* and crossed every *t?* As far as I'm concerned, we've got the leader of a terrorist cell operating out of that house, and we're going to go in and shut it down. What's your problem with that?"

"It's too easy, that's my problem. It's not about us dotting every *i,* because that's what the killers already did. This was a carefully planned crime, Captain. They wouldn't have just left the car in front of the house or put this stuff in the trash cans. Think about it."

Bosch held there and watched Hadley work it over for a few moments. He then shook his head.

"Maybe the car wasn't left there," he said. "Maybe they still plan to use it as part of the delivery. There are a lot of variables, Bosch. We're still going in. We laid it all out to the judge, and he said we have probable cause. That's good enough for me."

Bosch refused to give up. "Where did the tip come from, Captain? How did you find the car?"

"One of my sources," Hadley said. "We've been building an intelligence network for four years. Today it's paying off."

"Are you telling me you know who the source is, or did it come in anonymously?"

Hadley waved his hands in a dismissive manner. "Doesn't matter. The info was good. That's the car up there. There's no doubt about that."

Bosch knew by Hadley's sidestepping that the tip was anonymous, the hallmark of a setup.

"Captain, I urge you to stand down," he said. "There is something not right about this. It's too simple, and this wasn't a simple plan. It's some sort of misdirection, and we need to figure—"

"We're not standing down. Lives could hang in the balance."

Bosch shook his head. He wasn't going to get through to Hadley. The man believed he was poised at the edge of some sort of victory that would redeem every mistake he had ever made.

"Where's the FBI?" Bosch asked. "Shouldn't they be—"

"We don't need the FBI," Hadley said, getting in Bosch's face. "We have the training, the equipment, and the skills. We're going to take care of what's in our own backyard ourselves."

He gestured to the ground as if the place where he stood was the last battlefield between the Bureau and the LAPD.

"What about the chief? Does he know? I was just—" Bosch stopped, remembering the chief's admonishment about keeping their meeting at the Donut Hole to themselves.

"You were just what?" Hadley asked.

"I just want to know if he knows and approves."

"The chief has given me full authority to run my unit. Do you call the chief every time you go out and make an arrest?"

He turned and marched imperiously back to his men, leaving Bosch and Ferras to watch him go.

"Uh-oh," Ferras said.

"Yeah," Bosch said.

Bosch stepped away from the back of the foul-smelling sanitation truck and pulled out his phone. He scrolled through his directory to Rachel Walling's name. He had just pressed the CALL button when Hadley was there in his face again. Bosch hadn't heard him coming.

"Detective! Who are you calling?"

Bosch didn't hesitate.

"My lieutenant. He told me to update him after we got here."

"No cellular or radio transmissions. They could be monitoring."

"They who?"

"Give me the phone."

"Captain?"

"Give me the phone, or I will have it taken from you. We're not going to compromise this operation."

Bosch closed the phone without ending the call. If he was lucky, Walling would answer the call and be listening. She might be able to put it together and get the warning. The Bureau might even be able to triangulate the cell transmission and get to Silver Lake before things went completely wrong.

He handed the phone to Hadley, who turned to Ferras.

"Your phone, Detective."

"Sir, my wife is eight months pregnant and I need—"

"Detective, you are either with us or against us."

Hadley held his hand out, and Ferras reluctantly took his phone from his belt and gave it to him.

Hadley marched over to one of the SUVs, opened the passenger door, and put the two phones into the glove box. He slammed the compartment shut with authority and looked back at Bosch and Ferras as if challenging them to try to retrieve their phones.

The captain's attention was distracted when a third SUV pulled into the lot. The driver gave the captain a thumbs-up. Hadley then pointed a finger into the air and started a twirling motion.

"All right, warriors," he called out. "We have the warrant, and you know the plan. Perez, call air support and get us the eye in the sky. The rest of you, mount up! We're going in."

Bosch watched with growing dread as the members of the OHS chambered rounds in their weapons and put on helmets with face shields. Two of the men began putting on space suits, as they had been designated the radiation-containment team.

"This is crazy," Ferras said in a whisper.

"Charlie don't surf," Bosch replied.

"What?"

"Nothing. Before your time."

THIRTEEN

THE slick banked over a thirty-acre rubber plantation and put down in the LZ with the usual spine-compressing final drop. Hari Kari Bosch, Bunk Simmons, Ted Furness, and Gabe Finley rolled out into the mud, and Captain Gillette was there waiting for them, holding his helmet on top of his head so he wouldn't lose it in the rotor wash. The chopper labored as it pulled its skids out of the mud—it was the first dry day after six days of rain—and took off back in the direction of III Corps HQ.

"Walk with me, men," Gillette said.

Bosch and Simmons had been in the country long enough to have nicknames, but Furness and Finley were fresh and strictly OJT—on-the-job training—and Bosch knew they were scared. This was going to be their first drop, and nothing they taught you back at tunnel school in San Diego could prepare you for the sights, sounds, and smells of the real thing.

The captain led them to a card table set up under the command tent and outlined his plan. The tunnel system under Ben Cat was extensive and needed to be taken out as part of a first-wave attempt to take control of the village above. Already the casualties from sappers and sneak attacks inside the camp perimeter were mounting. The captain explained that he was getting chewed out on a daily basis by III Corps command. He didn't mention anything about being bothered by the dead and wounded he was losing. They were replaceable, but his favor with the colonel at III Corps was not.

The plan was a simple crimp operation. The captain unrolled a map drawn with the aid of villagers who had been in the tunnels. He pointed to four separate spider holes and said the four tunnel rats would go down simultaneously and force the VC in the tunnels toward a fifth hole, where the warriors of Tropic Lightning would be on top waiting to massacre them. Along the way, Bosch and his fellow rats would set charges, and the operation would finish with the implosion of the entire tunnel system.

The plan was simple enough until they got down there in the darkness and the labyrinth didn't match the map they had studied. Four went down, but only one came back up alive. Tropic Lightning got zero kills that day. And that was the day that Bosch knew the war was lost—for him, at least. That was when he knew that men of rank often fought battles with enemies that were inside.

Bosch and Ferras rode in the backseat of Captain Hadley's SUV. Perez drove, and Hadley rode shotgun, wearing a radio headset so he could command the operation. The vehicle's radio speaker was set to the operation's back-channel frequency—one not listed in any public directories.

They were third in line in the entourage of black SUVs. Half a block from the target house, Perez braked to let the other two vehicles move in as planned.

Bosch leaned forward between the front seats so he could see better through the windshield. Each of the other SUVs had four men riding on runners on either side. The vehicles picked up speed and then turned sharply toward the Samir house. One went down the driveway of the small Craftsman-style bungalow toward the rear yard, while the other jumped the curb and crossed the front lawn. One of the OHS men lost his grip when the heavy vehicle impacted the curb, and he went tumbling across the lawn.

The others leaped from the runners and moved toward the front door. Bosch assumed the same thing was happening at the back door. He didn't agree with the plan but admired its precision. There was a loud popping sound when the front door was breached with an explosive device. Almost immediately there was another, from the rear.

"All right, move up," Hadley commanded Perez.

As they drove up, the radio came alive with reports from inside the house.

"We're inside!"

"We're in the back!"

"Front room clear! We—"

The voice was cut off by the sound of automatic gunfire.

"Shots fired!"

Bosch heard more gunfire, but not over the radio. They were now close enough for him to hear it live. Perez jammed the SUV into park at an angle crossing the street in front of the house. All four doors opened at once as they jumped out.

"All clear! All clear!"

"One suspect down. We need medical for one suspect down. We need medical!"

It was all over in less than twenty seconds.

Bosch ran across the lawn behind Hadley and Perez. Ferras was to his left side. They entered through the front door with weapons out and up. Immediately they were met by one of Hadley's men. Above the right pocket of his fatigue shirt was the name Peck.

"We're clear! We're clear!"

Bosch dropped his weapon to his side. He looked around. It was a sparsely furnished living room. He smelled gunpowder.

"What have we got?" Hadley demanded.

"One down, one in custody," Peck said. "Back here."

They followed Peck down a short hallway to a room with woven-grass mats on the floor. A man Bosch recognized as Ramin Samir was on his back on the floor, blood from two chest wounds flowing over a cream-colored robe onto the floor and one of the mats. A young woman in a matching robe was lying facedown and whimpering, her hands cuffed behind her back.

Bosch saw a revolver on the floor by the open drawer of a small cabinet with lit votive candles on top of it. The gun was about eighteen inches from where Samir was lying.

"He went for the gun, and we took him down," Peck said.

Bosch looked down at Samir. He wasn't conscious, and his chest was rising and falling in a broken rhythm.

"He's circling the drain," Hadley said. "What've we found?"

"So far, no materials," Peck said. "We're bringing in the equipment now."

"All right. Let's get the car checked," Hadley ordered. "And get her out of here."

While two OHS men raised the crying woman up and carried her out of the room like a battering ram, Hadley headed back out of the house to the curb, where the Chrysler 300 awaited. Bosch and Ferras followed.

They looked into the car but didn't touch it. Bosch noticed that it was unlocked and the keys were in it. He pulled a pair of latex gloves from his coat pocket, stretched them, and put them on.

"Let's get a reading on it first, Bosch," Hadley said.

The captain signaled one of his men who was carrying over a radiation monitor. The man swept the device over the car and picked up only a few low pops by the trunk.

"We could have something right here," Hadley said.

"I doubt it," Bosch said. "It's not here."

He opened the driver-side door, leaned in, and popped the trunk. He backed out of the car and walked to the rear. The trunk was empty, but Bosch saw the same four indentations he had seen earlier, in the trunk of Stanley Kent's Porsche.

"It's gone," Hadley said, looking into the trunk. "They must've already made the transfer."

"Yeah. Long before the car was brought here." Bosch looked Hadley squarely in the eyes. "This was a misdirection, Captain. I told you that."

Hadley moved toward Bosch so he could speak without his whole crew hearing him. But he was intercepted by Peck.

"Captain?"

"What?" Hadley barked.

"The suspect went code seven."

"Then call off the paramedics and call the coroner."

"Yes, sir. The house is clear. No materials, and the monitors are picking up no signature."

Hadley glanced at Bosch, then looked back at Peck. "Tell them to check the place again," he ordered. "He went for a gun. He had to have been hiding something. Tear the place apart if you have to. Especially that room—it looks like a meeting place for terrorists."

"It's a prayer room," Bosch said. "And maybe the guy went for the gun because he was scared when people came busting through the doors."

Peck hadn't moved. He was listening to Bosch.

"Go!" Hadley ordered. "The material was in a lead container. Just because you got no reading doesn't mean it's not in there!"

Peck hustled back to the house, and Hadley turned his stare to Bosch.

"We need Forensics to process the car," Bosch said. "And I don't have a phone to make the call."

"Go get your phone and make the call."

Bosch went back to the SUV. He watched as the woman who had been in the house was placed in the back of the SUV parked on the lawn. She was still crying, and Bosch assumed the tears wouldn't stop anytime soon. For Samir now, herself later.

As he leaned through the door of Hadley's SUV, he realized that the vehicle was still running. He turned off the engine, then opened the glove compartment and took out the two phones. When he turned from the door, Hadley was standing there. They were away from the others, and no one would hear them.

"Bosch, if you try to make trouble for this unit, I will make trouble for you. You understand?"

Bosch studied him for a moment before responding.

"Sure, Captain. I'm glad you're thinking about the unit."

"I have connections that go all the way up. I can hurt you."

"Thanks for the advice."

Bosch started to walk away from him but then stopped. He wanted to say something but hesitated.

"What?" Hadley said. "Say it."

"I was just thinking about a captain I once worked for. This was a long time ago and in another place. He kept making all the wrong moves, and his screwups kept costing people their lives. Good people. So eventually it had to stop. That captain ended up getting fragged in the latrine by some of his own men."

Bosch walked away, but Hadley stopped him.

"What's that supposed to mean? Is that a threat?"

"No, it's a story."

"And you're calling that guy in there *good* people? Let me tell you, a guy like that stood up and cheered when the planes hit the buildings."

Bosch kept walking as he answered.

"I don't know what kind of people he was, Captain. I just know he wasn't part of this and he was set up just like you. If you figure out who it was who tipped you to the car, let me know. It might help us."

Bosch walked over to Ferras and gave him back his phone. He

told his partner to remain on the scene to supervise the forensic analysis of the Chrysler.

"Where are you going, Harry?"

"Downtown."

"What about the meeting with the Bureau?"

Bosch didn't check his watch.

"We missed it. Call me if SID comes up with anything."

Bosch left him there and started walking down the street toward the recreation center, where the car was parked. When he was halfway back to the rec center, the first TV truck passed him on its way to Samir's house.

FOURTEEN

BOSCH was hoping to get to the federal building downtown before news of the raid on Ramin Samir's house did. He had tried to call Rachel Walling but got no answer. He knew that she might be at the Tactical Intelligence location, but he didn't know where that was. He was banking on the idea that the growing size and importance of the investigation would dictate that it be directed from the main federal building and not a secret satellite office.

He entered the building through the law-enforcement door and told the U.S. marshal who checked his ID that he was going up to the FBI. He took the elevator to the fourteenth floor and was greeted by Brenner as soon as the doors came open. The word that Bosch was in the building had obviously been sent up from below.

"I thought you got the message," Brenner said.

"What message?"

"That the status conference was canceled."

"I think I should've gotten the message as soon as you people showed up. There never was going to be a conference, was there?"

Brenner ignored the question. "Bosch, what do you want?"

"I want to see Agent Walling."

"I'm her partner. Anything you want to tell her, you can tell me."

"Only her. I want to talk to her."

Brenner studied him. "Come with me," he finally said.

He used a clip-on ID card to open a door, and Bosch followed him through. They went down a long hallway, and Brenner threw questions over his shoulder as he walked.

"Where's your partner?" he asked.

"He's back at the crime scene," Bosch said. It wasn't a lie. Bosch just neglected to say which crime scene Ferras was at.

"Besides," he added, "I thought it would be safer for him there. I don't want you people leaning on him to get to me."

Brenner suddenly stopped, pivoted sharply, and was in Bosch's face. "Do you know what you are doing, Bosch? You're compromising an investigation that could have far-reaching implications. Where is the witness?"

Bosch shrugged as if to say his response was obvious.

"Where's Alicia Kent?"

Brenner shook his head but didn't answer.

"Wait in here," he said. "I'll go get Agent Walling."

Brenner opened a door and stepped back for Bosch to enter. As he stepped through, Bosch saw that it was a small interview room. He was suddenly shoved into the room, and he turned just in time to see Brenner out in the hallway pulling the door closed.

"Hey!"

Bosch grabbed for the doorknob, but it was too late. The door was locked from the outside. He pounded twice on it but knew that Brenner was not about to open it. He turned away and looked at the small space he was confined in. The room contained only three items of furniture. A small square table and two chairs. Assuming there was a camera somewhere, he raised his hand and shot his middle finger into the air.

Bosch pulled one of the chairs out and sat down, ready to wait them out. He took his cell phone out and opened it. He knew that if they were watching him, they wouldn't want him calling out and reporting his situation—it could be embarrassing for the Bureau. But when he looked at the screen, there was no signal. It was a safe room. Radio signals could not get out or in. Leave it to the feds, Bosch thought. They think of everything.

A long twenty minutes went by, and then the door finally opened. Rachel Walling stepped in. She closed the door, took the chair opposite Bosch, and quietly sat down.

"Sorry, Harry, I was over at Tactical."

"What, Rachel, you people hold cops against their will now?"

She looked surprised. "What are you talking about?"

"Your partner locked me in here."

"It wasn't locked when I came in. Try it now."

Bosch waved it away. "Forget it. I don't have time to play games. What's going on with the investigation?"

"What's going on is that you and your department have been running around like thieves in a jewelry store, smashing every case in sight. You can't tell the glass from the diamonds."

Bosch nodded. "So you know about Ramin Samir."

"Who doesn't? It's already on I-Missed-It News. What happened up there?"

"A class-A screwup is what happened. We were set up. OHS was set up."

"Sounds like somebody was."

Bosch leaned across the table. "But it means something, Rachel. The people who put the OHS onto Samir knew who he was and that he'd make an easy target. They left the Kents' car right in front of his house because they knew we'd end up spinning our wheels."

"It also could have worked as a payback to Samir."

"What do you mean?"

"All those years he was on CNN fanning the flames. He could've been seen as hurting their cause because he was giving the enemy a face and heightening American anger and resolve."

Bosch didn't get it. "I thought agitation was one of their tools. I thought they loved this guy."

"Maybe. It's hard to say."

Bosch wasn't sure what she was trying to say. But he suddenly could see how angry she was.

"Now let's talk about you and how you have been screwing things up since before the car was even found."

"What are you talking about? I'm trying to solve a homicide. That's my—"

"Yes, trying to solve a homicide at the possible cost of endangering the entire city with this petty self-righteous insistence on—"

"Come on, Rachel. Don't you think I have an idea about what could be at stake here?"

She shook her head. "Not if you are holding back a key witness from us. Don't you see what you are doing? You have no idea where this investigation is headed, because you've been busy hiding witnesses and sucker punching agents."

Bosch leaned back, clearly surprised.

"Is that what Maxwell said? That I sucker punched him?"

"It doesn't matter what he said. We are trying to control a potentially devastating situation here, and I don't understand why you are making the moves you are making."

Bosch nodded. "That makes sense," he said. "You shut somebody out of his own investigation, and it stands to reason you won't know what he is up to."

She held her hands up as if to stop an oncoming train.

"Okay, let's just stop right here. Talk to me, Harry."

Bosch looked at her and then up at the ceiling. He studied the upper corners of the room and dropped his eyes back to hers.

"You want to talk? Let's take a walk outside."

She didn't hesitate. "Okay, fine," she said. "Let's walk and talk. And then you'll give me Mitford."

Walling got up and opened the unlocked door. Brenner and another agent were waiting in the hallway.

"We're going to take a little walk," Walling said. "Alone."

"Have a great time," Brenner said. "We'll be in here trying to track the cesium, maybe save a few lives."

Walling led Bosch down the hall. Just as they were at the door to the elevator hall, Bosch heard a voice from behind him.

"Hey, buddy!"

He turned just in time to take Agent Maxwell's shoulder in the chest. He was driven into the wall and held up against it.

"You're a little outnumbered this time, aren't you, Bosch!"

"Stop!" Walling shouted. "Cliff, stop it!"

Bosch brought his arm up around Maxwell's head and was going to pull him down into a headlock, but Walling pulled Maxwell away and then pushed him back up the hallway.

"Cliff, get back! Get away!"

Maxwell started moving backward up the hall. He pointed a finger over Walling's shoulder at Bosch.

"Get out of my building! Get out and stay out!"

Walling shoved him into the first open office and then closed the door on him. By then, several other agents had come into the hallway to see what the commotion was about.

"It's over," Walling announced. "Everybody go back to work."

She came back to Bosch and pushed him through the door to the elevator. "You okay?"

"Only hurts when I breathe."

"Son of a bitch! That guy is getting out of control."

They took the elevator down and walked up an incline and out onto Los Angeles Street, heading away from the noise of the freeway. She checked her watch and then pointed toward a modern office building.

"There's decent coffee in there," she said. It was the new Social Security Administration building.

"Another federal building." Bosch sighed. "Agent Maxwell might think that's his, too."

"Can you drop that, please?"

He shrugged. "I'm just surprised Maxwell even admitted we came back to the house."

"Why wouldn't he?"

"Because I figured he was posted on the house because he was already in the doghouse for being a screwup. Why admit that we got the drop on him and have to stay in there longer?"

"You don't understand." Walling shook her head. "First of all, Maxwell has been wound a little tight lately, but no one in Tactical Intelligence is in the doghouse. The work is too important to have any screwups on the team. Secondly, he didn't care what anyone would think. What he did think was that it was important for everyone to know about the way *you're* messing things up."

He tried another direction. "Let me ask you something. Do they know about you and me over there? Our history, I mean."

"It would be hard for them not to know after Echo Park. But that is not important today. What is wrong with you? We've got enough cesium out there to shut down an airport, and you don't seem all that concerned. You are looking at this like it's a murder. Yes, a man is dead, but this is a heist, Harry. Get it? They wanted the cesium, and now they've got it. And it would help us if maybe we could talk to the only known witness. So where is he?"

"He's safe. Where's Alicia Kent? And where's her husband's partner?"

"They're safe. The partner is being questioned here, and we're keeping the wife at Tactical until we are sure we have everything there is to get from her."

"She's not going to be very helpful. She couldn't—"

"You're wrong. She's already been quite helpful."

Bosch couldn't hold back the look of surprise in his eyes.

"How? She said she didn't even see their faces."

"She didn't. But she heard a name. When they were speaking to each other, she heard a name."

"What name? She didn't say this before."

Walling nodded. "That's why you should turn over your witness. We have people who have one expertise: getting information from witnesses. We can get things from her that you are unable to get. We got them from her; we can get them from him."

Bosch felt his face turning red.

"What was the name this master interrogator got from her?"

She shook her head. "We're not trading. This involves national security. You're on the outside. And by the way, that's not going to change no matter who you get your police chief to call."

Bosch knew then that his meeting at the Donut Hole had been for nothing. Even the chief was on the outside looking in. Whatever name Alicia Kent gave up, it must have lit up the federal scoreboard like Times Square.

"All I've got is my witness," he said. "I'll trade you straight up for the name."

"Why do you want the name? You're not going to get anywhere near this guy."

"Because I want to know."

She folded her arms across her chest and thought about things for a moment. Finally, she said, "You first."

Bosch hesitated while he studied her eyes. Six months earlier he would have trusted her with his life. Now things had changed. Bosch wasn't so sure. "I stashed him at my place," he said. "I think you remember where that is."

She pulled a phone from her blazer pocket and opened it.

"Wait a second there, Agent Walling," he said. "What was the name Alicia Kent gave you?"

"Sorry, Harry."

"We had a deal."

"National security, sorry." She started punching in a number on her cell. Bosch nodded. He had called it right.

"I lied," he said. "He's not at my place."

She slapped the phone closed. "What is with you?" she asked angrily, her voice getting shrill. "We're running more than fourteen hours behind the cesium. Do you realize it may already be in a device? It may already be—"

"Give me the name, and I'll give you the witness."

"All *right!*" He knew she was angry with herself for being caught in the lie. It was the second time in less than twelve hours.

"She said she heard the name Moby, okay? She didn't think anything about it at the time, because she didn't realize that what she had heard was actually a name."

"Okay, who is Moby?"

"There is a Syrian terrorist named Momar Azim Nassar. He is believed to be in this country. He is known by friends and associates as Moby. We don't know why, but he does happen to resemble the performer named Moby."

"Who?"

"Never mind. Not your generation."

"But you are sure she heard this name?"

"Yes. Now, where is the witness?"

"Just hold on. You already lied to me once."

Bosch pulled out his phone, opened the directory, found the number for Kiz Rider, and pushed the CALL button.

Rider answered immediately. Bosch's number had showed up on caller ID. "Hello, Harry. You've been busy today."

"The chief tell you that?"

"I've got a few sources. What's up?"

Bosch spoke while staring at Walling and watching the anger darken her eyes. "I need a favor from my old partner. You still carry that laptop with you to work?"

"Of course. What favor?"

"I have a name. I want you to check to see if it's been in any stories in the *New York Times* archives."

"Hold on. I have to go online."

Several seconds went by. Bosch's phone started to beep because he was getting another call, but he stayed with Rider, and soon she was ready.

"What's the name?"

Bosch asked Walling the full name of the Syrian terrorist again. He then repeated it to Rider and waited.

"Yeah, multiple hits," she said. "Going back eight years."

"Give me a rundown."

"Uh, a bunch of stuff from the Middle East. He's suspected of involvement in a number of abductions and bombings and so on. He's connected to al Qaeda, according to federal sources."

"What's the most recent story say?"

"Uh, let's see. It's about a bus bombing in Beirut. Sixteen people killed. This is January third, 2004. Nothing after that."

"Does it give any nicknames or aliases?"

"Um . . . no. I don't see anything."

"Okay, thanks. I'll call you later."

"Wait a minute. Harry? I just want to tell you, be careful, okay? This is a whole different league you're playing in."

"Okay, I got it," Bosch said. "I gotta go."

Bosch ended the call and looked at Rachel. "There's nothing in the *New York Times* about this guy being in this country."

"Because it's not known. That is why Alicia Kent's information was so genuine."

"What do you mean? You take her word for it that the guy's in this country just because she heard a word that might not even be a name?"

She folded her arms. She was losing her patience.

"No, Harry, we *know* he's in this country. We have video of him checking out the Port of Los Angeles last August. We just didn't get there in time to grab him. We believe he was with another al Qaeda operative, named Muhammad el-Fayed. They've somehow slipped into this country—hell, the border's a sieve—and who knows what they've got planned."

"And you think they have the cesium?"

"We don't know that. But the intelligence on el-Fayed is that he smokes unfiltered Turkish cigarettes and—"

"The ashes on the toilet."

She nodded. "That's right. They're still being analyzed, but the betting in the office is that it was a Turkish cigarette."

Bosch nodded and suddenly felt foolish about the moves he had been making, the information he had held back.

"We put the witness in the Mark Twain Hotel on Wilcox," he said. "Room three-oh-three, under the name Stephen King."

"Cute."

"And Rachel? He told us he heard the shooter call out to Allah before he pulled the trigger."

She looked at him with the eyes of judgment as she opened her phone again. She pushed a single button. When her call was picked up, she delivered the information without identifying herself.

"He's at the Mark Twain on Wilcox. Room three-oh-three. Go pick him up."

She closed her phone and looked at Bosch. Worse than judgment, he saw disappointment and dismissal in her eyes now.

"I have to go," she said. "I'd stay away from airports, subways, and the malls until we find that cesium."

She turned and left him there. Bosch was watching her walk away when his phone started to buzz again, and he answered without taking his eyes off her. It was Joe Felton, the deputy coroner.

"Harry, I've been trying to reach you."

"What's up, Joe?"

"We just swung by Queen of Angels to make a pickup—some gangbanger in Hollywood."

"Yeah?" Bosch knew that the medical examiner wouldn't have called to waste his time. There was a reason.

"So we're here now and I go into the break room to grab some caffeine, and I overhear two paramedics talking about a pickup they just made. They said the ER evaluation was ARS, and it made me wonder if it could be connected with the guy up on the overlook. You know, since he was wearing the radiation alert rings."

Bosch calmed his voice. "Joe, what is ARS?"

"Acute radiation syndrome. The medics said they didn't know what the guy had. He was burned, and he was puking all over the place. They transported him, and the ER doc said it was a pretty bad exposure, Harry. Now the medics are waiting to see if they're exposed."

Bosch started walking toward Rachel Walling.

"Where'd they find this guy?"

"I didn't ask, but I assume it was somewhere in Hollywood if they brought him in here."

Bosch started picking up speed.

"Joe, I want you to hang up and get somebody from hospital security to watch this guy. I'm on my way."

Bosch clapped the phone closed and began running toward Rachel as fast as he could.

FIFTEEN

THE traffic on the Hollywood Freeway was all flowing into downtown at a slow crawl. Under the laws of traffic physics—that for every action, there is an equal and opposite reaction—Harry Bosch had clear sailing on the northbound lanes out. Of course, this was aided by the siren and flashing lights on his car, making what little traffic there was in front of him move quickly out of the way. Applied force was another law Bosch knew well. He had the old Crown Vic up to ninety.

"Where are we going?" Rachel Walling yelled over the sound of the siren.

"I told you. I'm taking you to the cesium."

"What does that mean?"

"It means paramedics just brought a man with acute radiation syndrome into the emergency room at Queen of Angels. We'll be there in four minutes."

"Damn it! Why didn't you tell me?"

The answer was that he wanted a head start, but he didn't tell her this. He remained silent while she opened her cell phone and punched in a number. She then reached up to the car's roof and flicked off the siren toggle.

"What are you doing?" Bosch exclaimed. "I need that to—"

"I need to be able to talk!"

Bosch took his foot off the accelerator and dropped it down to seventy to be safe. A moment later her call was connected, and Bosch listened to her bark commands. He hoped it was at Brenner and not Maxwell.

"Divert the team from the Mark Twain to Queen of Angels. Scramble a contamination team and get them there, too. Send backup units and a DOE assessment team. We have an exposure case that may lead us to the missing materials. Do it and call me back. I'll be on site in three minutes."

She closed the phone, and Bosch hit the siren toggle.

"I said four minutes!" he yelled.

"Impress me!" she yelled back.

He pinned the accelerator again, even though he didn't need to. He was confident they would be first to the hospital.

"Who is the victim?" Rachel shouted.

"No idea."

They were silent for a long period. Bosch concentrated on the driving. And his thoughts. There were so many things that bothered him about the case. Soon he had to share them.

"How do you think they targeted him?" he said.

"What?" Walling replied, coming out of her own thoughts.

"Moby and el-Fayed. How'd they zero in on Stanley Kent?"

"I don't know. Maybe if this is one of them at the hospital, we'll get to ask."

Bosch let some time go by. He was tired of yelling. But then he called over another question. "Doesn't it bother you that everything came out of that house?"

"What are you talking about?"

"The gun, the camera, the computer they used. Everything. There's Coke in liter bottles in the pantry, and they tied Alicia Kent up with the same snap ties she uses to hold her roses up in the backyard. Doesn't that bother you? They had nothing but a knife and ski masks when they went through that door."

"You have to remember, these people are resourceful. They teach them that in the camps. El-Fayed was trained in an al Qaeda camp in Afghanistan. He in turn taught Nassar. They make do with what's available. You could say that they took down the World Trade Center with a couple of airliners or a couple of box cutters. It's all in how you look at it."

Bosch came up on the exit, and in two minutes he killed the siren and pulled into the ambulance run at Queen of Angels.

Felton met them in the crowded emergency room and led the way to the treatment area, where there were six bays. A private security cop stood outside one of the curtained spaces, and Bosch showed his badge. He split the curtain and moved into the treatment bay.

The patient, a small dark-haired man with brown skin, was lying beneath a spiderweb of tubes and wires extending from overhead medical machinery to his limbs, chest, mouth, and nose. The hospital bed was encased in a clear plastic tent. The man's eyes were half-lidded and unmoving. Most of his body was exposed. A modesty towel had been taped over his genitals, but his legs and torso were visible. The right side of his stomach and right hip were covered with blooms of thermal burns. His right hand exhibited the same burns—painful-looking red rings surrounding purplish wet eruptions in the skin. A clear gel had been spread over the burns.

"Where is everybody?" Bosch asked.

"Harry, don't get close," Walling warned. "He's not conscious, so let's just back out and talk to the doctor before we do anything."

Bosch pointed to the patient's burns. "Could this be from the cesium? It can happen that fast?"

"From direct exposure in a concentrated amount, yeah. It depends on how long the exposure was. It looks like this guy was carrying the stuff in his pocket."

"Does he look like Moby or el-Fayed?"

"No, he doesn't look like either one of them. Come on."

She stepped back through the curtain, and Bosch followed. She ordered the security man to get the ER doctor who was treating the man. She flipped open her phone and pushed a single button. Her call was answered quickly.

"This is legit," she said. "We have a direct exposure. We need to set up a command post and a containment protocol here."

She listened and then answered a question.

"No, neither one. I don't have an ID yet. I'll call as soon as I do."

She closed the phone. "The radiation team will be here inside of ten minutes," she told Bosch. "I'll be directing the command post."

A woman in hospital blues walked up to them carrying a clipboard. "I'm Dr. Garner. You need to stay away from that patient until we know more about what happened to him."

Walling and Bosch showed her their credentials.

"What can you tell us?" Walling asked.

"Not much. He's in full prodromal syndrome—the first symptoms of exposure. The trouble is, we don't know what he was exposed to or for how long. That gives us no gray count, and without that we don't have a specific treatment protocol. We're winging it."

"What are the symptoms?" Walling asked.

"Well, you see the burns. Those are the least of our problems. The most serious damage is internal. His immune system is shutting down, and he's aspirated most of the lining of his stomach. His GI tract is shot. The stress on the body pushed him into cardiac arrest. We just had the blue team in here fifteen minutes ago."

"How long is it between exposure and the start of this produro-whatever syndrome?" Bosch asked.

"Prodromal. It can happen within an hour of first exposure."

Bosch looked at the man beneath the plastic canopy enclosing the bed. He remembered the phrase Captain Hadley had used when Samir was dying on the floor of his prayer room. *He's circling the drain.* He knew the man on the hospital bed was circling it as well.

"What can you tell us about who he is and where he was found?" Bosch asked the doctor.

"You'll have to talk to the paramedics about that. All I heard was that he was found in the street. He had collapsed. And as far as who he is . . ." She raised the clipboard and read from the top sheet.

"He's listed as Digoberto Gonzalves, age forty-one. There's no address here. That's all I know right now."

Walling stepped away, pulling her phone out again. Bosch knew she was going to call in the name, have it run through the terrorism databases.

"Where are his clothes and his wallet?" he asked the doctor.

"His clothing and all his possessions were removed from the ER because of exposure concerns."

"Where was it all taken?"

"You'll have to get that information from the nursing staff."

She pointed to a nursing station in the center of the treatment area. Bosch headed that way. The nurse at the desk told Bosch that everything from the patient was placed in a medical-waste container that was then taken to the hospital's incinerator.

"Where's the incinerator?"

Rather than give him directions, the nurse called over the security guard and told him to take Bosch to the incinerator room. Before Bosch could go, Walling called to him.

"Take this," she said, holding out the radiation-alert monitor she had taken off her belt. "And remember, we have a radiation team coming. Don't risk yourself. If that goes off, you back away."

"Got it."

Bosch put the alert monitor in his pocket. He and the guard took a stairway to the basement, then took a hallway that seemed to run at least a block to the far side of the building.

When they got to the incinerator room, the space was empty. There appeared to be no active burning of medical waste occurring. There was a three-foot canister on the floor. It was sealed with tape that said CAUTION: HAZARDOUS WASTE.

Bosch took out his key chain, which had a small penknife on it. He squatted down next to the canister and cut the security tape. In his peripheral vision, he noticed the security guard step back.

"Maybe you should wait outside," Bosch said. "There's no need for both of us to—" He heard the door close behind him before he finished the sentence.

He looked down at the canister, took a breath, and removed the top. Digoberto Gonzalves's clothes had been haphazardly dropped into the container.

Bosch took the monitor Walling had given him and waved it over the open canister like a magic wand. The monitor remained silent. He let his breath out. Then he turned the canister upside down and dumped its contents onto the concrete floor. He rolled the canister aside and once again moved the monitor in a circular pattern over the clothes. There was no alarm.

Gonzalves's clothes had been cut off his body with scissors. There were a pair of dirty jeans, a work shirt, T-shirt, underwear, socks, a pair of work boots with the laces cut. Lying loose on the floor in the middle of the clothing was a small black leather wallet.

Bosch started with the clothing. In the pocket of the work shirt were a pen and a tire pressure gauge. He found work gloves sticking out of one of the rear pockets of the jeans and then removed a set of keys and a cell phone from the left front pocket. He thought about the burns he had seen on Gonzalves's right hip and hand. But when he opened the right front pocket of the jeans, there was no cesium. The pocket was empty.

Bosch put the cell phone and keys down next to the wallet and studied what he had. On one of the keys, Bosch saw a Toyota insignia. Now he knew that a vehicle was part of the equation. He opened the phone and tried to find the call directory but couldn't figure it out. He put it aside and opened the wallet.

There wasn't much. The wallet contained a Mexican driver's license with the name and photo of Digoberto Gonzalves. In one of the slots, he found photos of a woman and three young children. There was no green card or citizenship document. There were no credit cards, and in the billfold section, there were only six dollar bills along with several tickets from pawnshops in the Valley.

Bosch put the wallet down next to the phone, stood up, and got out his own phone. He scrolled the directory until he found Walling's cell number. She answered immediately.

"I checked his clothes. No cesium."

There was no response.

"Rachel, did you—"

"Yes, I heard. I just wish you had found it, Harry. I just wish this could be over."

"Me, too. Did anything come through on the name?"

"Gonzalves? No, nothing. Not even a driver's license."

"I've got a Mexican driver's license here. I think the guy's an illegal."

She gave that some thought before responding.

"Well, it's believed that Nassar and el-Fayed came in across the Mexican border. Maybe this guy was working with them."

"I don't know, Rachel. I've got work clothes here. Work boots. I think this guy—"

"Harry, I've gotta go. My team is here."

"All right. I'm heading back up."

Bosch pocketed his phone, then gathered the clothing and boots and put them all back in the canister. He put the wallet, keys, and cell phone on top and took the canister with him. On the long walk back to the stairs, he pulled out his phone again and called the city's communications center. He asked the dispatcher to dig out the details on the paramedic call that had brought Gonzalves to Queen of Angels and was put on hold. He got all the way up the steps and back to the ER before the dispatcher came back on the line.

"The call you asked about came in at ten-oh-five from a phone registered to Easy Print at nine-thirty Cahuenga Boulevard. Man down in the parking lot. Fire department paramedics responded from station fifty-four. Anything else?"

"What's the nearest cross at that location?"

After a moment, the dispatcher told him the cross street was Lankershim Boulevard. Bosch thanked her and disconnected.

The address where Gonzalves collapsed was not far from the Mulholland overlook. Bosch realized that almost every location associated with the case so far—from the murder site to the victim's house to Ramin Samir's house and now to the spot where Gonzalves collapsed—could fit on one page of a Thomas Brothers map book.

Murder cases in L.A. usually dragged him all over the map book. But this one wasn't roaming. It was staying close.

Bosch looked around the ER. He noticed that all the people who had been crowding the waiting room before were now gone. There had been an evacuation, and agents in protective gear were moving about the area with radiation monitors. He spotted Rachel Walling by the nursing station and walked over to her.

He held out the canister. "Here's the guy's stuff."

She called over to one of the men in protection gear. She told him to take charge of the canister. She then looked back at Bosch.

"There's a cell phone in there," he told her. "They might be able to get something out of that."

"I'll tell them."

"How's the victim doing?" Bosch asked.

"Victim?"

"Whether he's involved in this or not, he is still a victim."

"If you say so. He's still out of it. I don't know if we'll ever get the chance to talk to him."

"Then I'm leaving."

"What? Where? I'm going with you," Walling said.

"I thought you had to run the CP."

"I passed it off. If there's no cesium here, I'm not staying. I'll stick with you. Let me just tell some people I'm leaving to follow a lead."

Bosch hesitated. But deep down he knew he wanted her with him. "I'll be out front in the car."

"Where are we going?"

"I don't know if Digoberto Gonzalves is a terrorist or just a victim, but I do know one thing. He drives a Toyota. And I think I know where we'll find it."

SIXTEEN

THE Hollywood Freeway always moved slowly in both directions through the bottleneck created by the cut in the mountain chain. Bosch decided to stay on surface streets and take Highland Avenue up into the pass. He filled Rachel Walling in along the way.

"The call for paramedics came from a print shop on Cahuenga near Lankershim. Gonzalves must have been in the area when he collapsed. The initial call said a man was down in the parking lot. I'm hoping the Toyota he was driving is right there. I'm betting that if we find it, we find the cesium. The mystery is why he had it."

"And why he was foolish enough to put it in his pocket unprotected," Walling added.

"You're basing that on him knowing what he had. Maybe he didn't. Maybe this isn't what we think it is."

"There's got to be a connection, Bosch, between Gonzalves and Nassar and el-Fayed. He probably brought them across the border."

Bosch almost smiled. He knew she had used his last name as a term of endearment. He remembered how she used to do that.

"And don't forget about Ramin Samir," he said.

Walling shook her head. "I'm still thinking he was a red herring," she said. "A misdirection."

"A good one," Bosch responded. "It took the mighty Captain Done Badly out of the picture."

She laughed. "Is that what they call him?"

Bosch nodded. "Not to his face, of course."

"And what do they call you? Something tough and hardheaded, I'm sure."

He glanced over at her and shrugged. He thought about telling her that his Vietnam nickname was Hari Kari, but that would require further explanation and this wasn't the time.

"You know, I still had your number in my cell's directory," he said. "I guess I never wanted to delete it."

"I was wondering about that when you left me that mean message today about the cigarette ash."

"I don't suppose you kept mine, Rachel."

She paused a long moment before answering. "I think you're still on my phone, too, Harry."

This time he had to smile, even though he was back to being Harry with her. There's hope after all, he thought.

They were approaching Lankershim Boulevard. To the right, it dropped down into a tunnel that went beneath the freeway. To the left, it ended at a strip shopping center that included the Easy Print franchise from which the call to paramedics had originated. Bosch's eyes searched the vehicles in the parking lot, looking for a Toyota.

He glided into the left-turn lane and waited to pull into the lot. He swiveled in his seat and checked the parking along both sides of Cahuenga. A quick glance showed no Toyotas, but he knew that the make had many different car models and pickup trucks.

"Do you have a plate or any description?" Walling asked. "How about a color?"

"No, no, and no."

Bosch remembered then that she had the habit of asking multiple questions at once.

He made the turn on yellow and pulled into the lot. There were no parking spaces available, but he wasn't interested in parking. He cruised slowly, checking each car. There were no Toyotas.

"It's got to be in this area somewhere," he said.

"Maybe we should check the street," Walling suggested.

He nodded and nosed his car into the alley at the end of the parking lot. He was going to turn left to turn around and go back to the street. But when he checked to see if he was clear on the right, he saw an old white pickup truck with a camper shell parked half a block down the alley next to a green trash Dumpster. The truck was facing them, and he couldn't tell what the make of it was.

"Is that a Toyota?" he asked.

Walling turned and looked. "Bosch, you're a genius."

Bosch drove toward the truck, and as he got closer, he could see that it was indeed a Toyota. So could Walling. She pulled out her phone, but Bosch reached across and put his hand on it.

"Let's just check it out first. I could be wrong about this."

"No, Bosch, you're on a roll." But she put the phone away.

Bosch pulled slowly past the pickup, giving it a once-over. He then turned around at the end of the block and came back. He stopped ten feet behind it. There was no plate on the back. A cardboard LOST TAG sign had been put in its place.

Bosch wished he had brought the keys he had found in Digoberto Gonzalves's pocket. They got out and approached the truck, coming up on either side of it. Bosch noticed that the rear window hatch of the camper shell had been left open a couple of inches. He pulled it up all the way. An air-pressure hinge had held it open. Bosch leaned in close to look into the interior. It was dark because the truck was parked in shadow and the windows were darkly tinted.

"Harry, you have that monitor?"

He pulled her radiation monitor out of his pocket and held it up as he leaned into the darkness of the truck's cargo hold. No alarm sounded. He leaned back out and put the monitor on his belt. He then reached in and lowered the truck's rear gate.

The back of the truck was piled with junk. There were empty bottles and cans strewn everywhere, a leather desk chair with a broken leg, scrap pieces of aluminum, an old watercooler, and other debris. And there, by the raised wheel well on the right side, was a lead gray container that looked like a small mop bucket on wheels.

"There," he said. "Is that the pig?"

"I think it is," Walling said excitedly. "I think it is!"

There was no warning sticker on it or radiation-alert symbol. They had been peeled off. Bosch leaned in and grabbed one of the handles. He pulled it clear of the debris around it and rolled it to the tailgate. The top was latched in four places.

"Do we open it and make sure the stuff is in there?" he asked.

"No," Walling said. "We back off and call in the team. They have protection."

She pulled her phone out again. While she called for the radiation team and backup units, Bosch moved to the front of the truck. He looked through the window and saw a half-eaten breakfast burrito sitting on a flattened brown bag on the center console. And he saw more junk on the passenger side. His eyes held on a camera that was sitting on an old briefcase with a broken handle on the passenger seat. The camera looked brand new.

Bosch checked the door and found it unlocked. He realized that Gonzalves had forgotten about his truck and his possessions when the cesium started burning through his body. He had gotten out and stumbled toward the parking lot, seeking help, leaving everything else behind and unlocked.

Bosch opened the driver's door and reached in with the radiation monitor. Nothing happened. No alert. He replaced it on his belt. From his pocket, he got out a pair of latex gloves and put them on while listening to Walling talking to someone about finding the pig.

"No, we didn't open it," she said. "Just get here as fast as you can and maybe this will all be over."

Bosch leaned into the truck and picked up the camera. It was a Nikon digital, and he remembered that the lens cover found beneath the master bed at the Kent house had said Nikon on it. He believed he was holding the camera that had taken the photograph of Alicia Kent. He turned it on, and for once, he knew what he was doing as he examined a piece of electronic equipment. He had a digital camera of his own. His wasn't a Nikon, but he was able to quickly determine that the camera he had just found had no photos in its memory because the chip had been removed.

Bosch put the camera down and began looking through the things piled on the passenger seat. In addition to the broken briefcase, there was a child's lunch box, as well as a manual for operating an Apple computer and a poker from a fireplace tool set. Nothing connected. He noticed a golf putter and a rolled-up poster on the floor.

He moved the brown bag and the burrito out of the way and shifted his weight to one elbow on the armrest between the seats so he could reach over and open the glove compartment. And there, sitting in the otherwise empty space, was a handgun. Bosch lifted it out. It was a Smith & Wesson .22-caliber revolver.

"I think we've got the murder weapon here," he called out.

There was no response from Walling. She was still at the back of the truck talking on her phone, issuing orders in an animated voice.

Bosch returned the weapon to the glove box and closed it, deciding to leave the weapon in place for the forensics team. He noticed the rolled-up poster again and decided for no reason other than curiosity to take a look at it. Using his elbow on the center armrest for support, he unrolled it across all of the junk on the passenger seat. It was a chart depicting twelve yoga positions.

Bosch immediately thought about the discolored space he had seen on the wall in the workout room at the Kent house. He wasn't sure, but he thought the dimensions of the poster would be a close match to that space on the wall. He quickly rerolled the poster and started to back out of the cab so he could show Walling.

But as he was pulling out, he noticed that the armrest between the seats was also a storage compartment. He opened it.

He froze. There was a cup holder, and in it were several steel capsules resembling bullet cartridges closed flat on both ends. The steel was so polished it almost looked like silver. It might even have been mistaken for silver.

Bosch moved the radiation monitor over the capsules in a circular pattern. There was no alarm. He turned the device over and looked at it. He saw a small switch on its side. With his thumb, he pushed it up. A blaring alarm suddenly went off, the frequency of tones so fast that they sounded like one long eardrum-piercing siren.

Bosch jumped back out of the truck and slammed the door shut. The poster fell to the ground.

"Harry!" Walling yelled. She rushed toward him.

Bosch pushed the switch again and turned the monitor off.

"What is it?" she yelled.

Bosch pointed toward the truck's door.

"The gun's in the glove box, and the cesium's in the center compartment."

"What?"

"The cesium is in the compartment under the armrest. He took the capsules out of the pig. That's why they weren't in his pocket. They were in the center armrest."

He touched his right hip, the place where Gonzalves was burned by radiation. The same spot would have been next to the armrest compartment when he was sitting in the truck.

Rachel didn't say anything for a long moment. She just stared at his face. "Are you okay?"

Bosch almost laughed. "I don't know. Ask me in ten years."

"You should be checked out."

"What are they going to be able to do? Look, I wasn't in the truck that long. It's not like Gonzalves, who was sitting in there with it. He was practically eating off of it."

She didn't answer. Bosch handed her the monitor. "It was never on. I thought it was on when you gave it to me."

She took it and looked at it. "I thought it was, too."

Bosch thought about how he had carried the monitor in his pocket rather than clipped to his belt. He had probably switched it off unknowingly when he had twice put it in and removed it. He looked back at the truck and wondered if he had possibly just hurt or killed himself.

"I need a drink of water," he said. "I've got a bottle in the trunk."

Bosch walked back to the rear of his car. Using the open trunk lid to shield Walling's view of him, he leaned his hands down on the bumper for support and tried to decipher the messages his body was sending to his brain. He felt something happening but didn't know if it was something physiological or if the shakes he felt were just an emotional response to what had just happened. He remembered what the ER doctor had said about Gonzalves and how the most serious damage was internal. Was his own immune system shutting down? Was he circling the drain? He cursed out loud.

"Harry?"

Bosch looked around the trunk lid. Rachel was walking toward him.

"The teams are headed this way. How do you feel?"

"I think I'm okay."

"Good. I talked to the head of the team. He thinks the exposure was too short to be anything serious. But you still should go to the ER and get checked out."

"We'll see."

He reached into the trunk and got a liter bottle of water out of his kit. It was an emergency bottle he kept for long surveillances. He opened it and took two strong pulls.

Bosch recapped the bottle and put it back in the kit. He stepped around the car. As he walked toward Walling, he looked past her to the south. He realized that the alley extended several blocks past the back of the Easy Print. Every twenty yards or so was a green Dumpster positioned perpendicular to the rear of the structures. Bosch realized they had been pushed out of spaces between the buildings and fenced corrals. Just like in Silver Lake, it was pickup day, and the Dumpsters were waiting for the city trucks to come.

Suddenly it all came to him. Like fusion. Two elements coming together and creating something new. The thing that bothered him about the crime-scene photos, the yoga poster, everything. The gamma rays had shot right through him, but they had left him enlightened. He knew. He understood.

"He's a scavenger."

"Who is?"

"Digoberto Gonzalves," Bosch said, his eyes looking down the alley. "It's collection day. The Dumpsters are all pushed out for the city trucks. Gonzalves is a scavenger, a Dumpster diver, and he knew this would be a good time to come here."

He looked at Walling before completing the thought.

"And so did somebody else," he said.

"You mean he found the cesium in a Dumpster?"

Bosch nodded and pointed down the alley.

"All the way at the end, that's Barham. Barham takes you up to Lake Hollywood. Lake Hollywood takes you to the overlook. This case never leaves the map page."

Walling came over and stood in front of him, blocking his view. Bosch could now hear sirens in the distance.

"What are you saying? That Nassar and el-Fayed took the cesium and stashed it in a Dumpster at the bottom of the hill? Then this scavenger comes along and finds it?"

"I'm saying you've got the cesium back, so now we're looking at this as a homicide again. You come down from the overlook and you can be in this alley in five minutes."

"So what? They stole the cesium and killed Kent just so they could come down here and stash it? Is that what you're saying? Or are you saying they just threw it all away? Why would they do that? I mean, does that make any sense at all? I mean, I don't see how that would scare people in the way we know they want to scare us."

Bosch noted that she had asked six questions at once this time, possibly a new record. "Nassar and el-Fayed were never near the cesium," he said. "That's what I'm saying."

He walked over to the truck and picked the rolled poster up off the ground. He handed it to Rachel. The sirens were getting louder.

She unrolled the poster. "What is this? What does it mean?"

Bosch took it back from her and started rolling it up.

"Gonzalves found that in the same Dumpster where he found the gun and the camera and the lead pig."

"So? What does it *mean,* Harry?"

Two fed cars pulled into the alley a block away and started making their way toward them, weaving around the Dumpsters. As they got close, Bosch could see that the driver of the lead car was Jack Brenner.

"Do you hear me, Harry? What does it—"

Bosch's knees suddenly seemed to give out, and he fell into her, throwing his arms around her to stop himself from hitting the ground.

"Bosch!" She grabbed on and held him.

"Uh . . . I'm not feeling so good," he mumbled. "I think I better . . . Can you take me to my car?"

She helped him straighten up and then started walking him toward his car. He put his arm over her shoulders. Car doors were slamming behind them as the agents got out.

"Where are the keys?" Walling asked.

He held the key ring out to her just as Brenner ran up to them.

"What is it? What's wrong?"

"He was exposed. The cesium is in the center console in the truck cab. Be careful. I'm going to take him to the hospital."

Brenner stepped back, as if whatever Bosch had were contagious. "Okay," he said. "Call me when you can."

Bosch and Walling kept moving toward the car.

"Come on, Bosch," Walling said. "Stay with me. Hang in there and we'll get you taken care of."

She had called him by his last name again.

SEVENTEEN

THE car jerked forward as Walling pulled out of the alley and into southbound traffic on Cahuenga.

"I'm taking you back to Queen of Angels so Dr. Garner can take a look at you," she said. " Just hang in there for me, Bosch."

He knew it was likely that the last-name endearments were about to come to an end. He pointed toward the left-turn lane that led onto Barham Boulevard.

"Never mind the hospital," he said. "Take me to the Kent house."

"What?"

"I'll get checked out later. The Kent house. Here's the turn. Go!"

She slipped into the left-turn lane. "What's going on?"

"I'm fine. I'm okay."

"What are you telling me, that that little fainting spell was—"

"I had to get you away from the crime scene and away from Brenner so I could check this out and talk to you. Alone."

"Check what out? Talk about what? Do you realize what you just did? I thought I was saving your life. Now Brenner or one of those other guys will take the credit for the recovery of the cesium. Thanks a lot. That was my crime scene."

He opened his jacket and pulled out the yoga poster.

"Don't worry about it," he said. "You can get the credit for the arrests. You just might not want it."

He opened the poster, letting the top half flop over his knees. He was only interested in the bottom half.

"Dhanurasana," he said.

Walling glanced over at him and then down at the poster.

"Would you start telling me what's going on?"

"Alicia Kent practices yoga. I saw the mats in the workout room at the house."

"I saw them, too. So what?"

"Did you see the sun discoloration on the wall where a picture or a calendar or maybe a poster had been taken down?"

"Yes, I saw it."

Bosch held up the poster. "I'm betting that this will be a perfect fit. This is a poster Gonzalves found with the cesium."

"And what will that mean—if it's a perfect fit?"

"It will mean that it was almost a perfect crime. Alicia Kent conspired to kill her husband, and if it hadn't been for Digoberto Gonzalves just happening to find the tossed-out evidence, she would have gotten away with it."

Walling shook her head dismissively. "Come on, Harry. Are you saying she conspired with international terrorists to kill her husband in exchange for the cesium?"

"Alicia Kent conspired with someone, but it wasn't a terrorist. The cesium being dumped in the trash proves that. You said it yourself—there is no way that Moby and el-Fayed would steal this stuff to just dump it. So what does that tell you? This *wasn't* a heist. It actually *was* a murder. The cesium was just a red herring. Just like

Ramin Samir. And Moby and el-Fayed? They were part of the misdirection as well. This poster will help prove it."

"How?"

"Dhanurasana, the rocking bow."

He held the poster up so she could glance at the yoga pose depicted in the bottom corner. It showed a woman with her arms behind her back, holding her ankles and creating a bow with the front of her body. She looked like she was hog-tied.

Walling glanced at the poster and the pose.

"We go into the house and see if this fits that space on the wall," Bosch said. "If it fits, that means she and the killer took it off the wall because they didn't want to risk that we might see it and connect it with what happened to her."

"It's a stretch, Harry. A huge one."

"Not when you put it in context."

"Which you, of course, can do."

"As soon as we get to the house."

"Hope you still have a key."

"You bet I do."

Walling turned onto Arrowhead Drive and punched the accelerator. But after a block, she slowed down.

"This is ridiculous. She gave us the name Moby. There is no way she could have known he was in this country. And then up on the overlook, your own witness said that the shooter called out to Allah as he pulled the trigger. How can—"

"Let's just try the poster on the wall. If it fits, I'll lay the whole thing out for you. I promise. If it doesn't fit, then I will quit bothering you with it."

She relented and drove the remaining block to the Kent house without another word. There was no longer a Bureau car sitting out front. Bosch guessed that it was all hands on deck at the cesium recovery scene.

"Thank God I don't have to deal with Maxwell again," he said.

Walling didn't even smile.

Bosch got out with the poster and his file containing the crime-scene photos. He used Stanley Kent's keys to open the front door, and they proceeded to the workout room. They took positions on either side of the rectangular sun-discoloration mark, and Bosch unrolled the poster. They each took a side and held the top corner of the poster to the top corner of the mark. Bosch put his other hand on the center of the poster and flattened it against the wall. The poster was a perfect fit. What was more, the tape marks on the wall matched up with tape marks on the poster. To Bosch, there was no doubt. The poster had come from Alicia Kent's home yoga studio.

Rachel let go of her side of the poster and headed out of the room. "I'll be in the living room. I can't wait to hear you put this together."

Bosch rolled the poster up and followed. Walling took a seat in the same chair Bosch had put Maxwell in a few hours earlier. He remained standing in front of her.

"The fear was that the poster could be a tip-off," he said. "Some smart agent or detective would see the rocking-bow pose and start thinking, This woman does yoga; maybe she could handle being hog-tied like that; maybe it was her idea; maybe she did it to help sell the misdirection. So the poster had to go. It went into the Dumpster with the cesium, the gun, and everything else they used. Except for the ski masks and the phony map they planted with the car at Ramin Samir's house."

"She's a master criminal," Walling said sarcastically.

Bosch was undeterred. He knew he'd convince her.

"If you get your people out there to check that line of Dumpsters, you'll find the rest—the Coke-bottle silencer, the gloves, the first set of snap ties, every—"

"The first set of snap ties?"

"That's right. I'll get to that. Just hold on. I need some water. My throat is raw from all of this talking."

He went into the kitchen, remembering that he saw bottles of water in the refrigerator while searching earlier in the day.

"You want anything?" he called out.

"No," she called back. "It's not our house, remember?"

He opened the refrigerator, took out a bottle of water, and drank half of it while standing in front of the open door. The cool air felt good, too. He closed the door but then immediately reopened it. He had seen something. On the top shelf was a plastic bottle of grape juice. He remembered that when he went through the trash bag in the garage, he had found paper towels with grape juice on them.

Another piece of the puzzle fell into place.

He returned to the living room, where Rachel was waiting.

"Okay. When was it that you captured the terrorist known as Moby on video at the port?"

"August twelfth last year."

"Okay, August twelfth. Then what? Some sort of alert went out through the Bureau and all of Homeland Security?"

She nodded. "Not for a while, though. It took almost two months of video analysis to confirm it was Nassar and el-Fayed. I wrote the bulletin. It went out October ninth as a confirmed sighting."

"Fine. So the bulletin went out October ninth. That was the day the plan to kill Stanley Kent began."

Walling folded her arms across her chest and just stared at him. Bosch thought that maybe she was beginning to see where he was going with the story and she didn't like it.

"It works best if you start from the end and go backward," Bosch said. "Alicia Kent gave you the name Moby. How could she have gotten that name?"

"She overheard one of them calling the other one that."

Bosch shook his head. "No. She told you she overheard it. But if she was lying, how would she know the name to lie about it? Just coincidence that she gives the nickname of a guy who less than six months ago was confirmed as being in the country—in L.A. County, no less? I don't think so, Rachel, and neither do you."

"Okay, so you're saying that somebody in the Bureau or another agency that received the FBI bulletin gave her the name."

"Right. He gave her the name so she could come out with it while being questioned by the FBI's master interrogator. That name, along with the plan to dump the car in front of Ramin Samir's house, would act in concert to send this whole thing down the wrong road with the FBI and everybody else chasing after terrorists."

"He?"

"I'm getting to that now. You are right. Anybody who got a look at that bulletin would have been able to give her that name. So how would we narrow it down to one?"

"You tell me."

Bosch opened the bottle and drank the rest of the water.

"You narrow it down by continuing to go backward. Where would Alicia Kent's life have intersected with one of those people in the agencies who knew about Moby?"

Walling frowned and shook her head. "That could have been anywhere. In line at the supermarket or when she was buying fertilizer for her roses. Anywhere."

Bosch now had her right where he wanted her to be.

"Then narrow the parameters," he said. "Where would she have intersected with someone who knew about Moby but also knew that her husband had access to the sort of radioactive materials Moby might be interested in?"

"Nowhere. It would take a monumental coincidence to—" She stopped when it came to her. Enlightenment. And shock as she fully understood where Bosch was going. "My partner and I visited the Kents to warn them early last year. I guess what you're saying is that that makes me a suspect."

Bosch shook his head.

"I said *he,* remember? You didn't come here alone."

Her eyes fired when she registered the implication.

"That's ridiculous. There's no way. I can't believe . . ."

She didn't finish as her mind snagged on something, some memory that undermined her trust and loyalty to her partner.

Bosch picked up on the tell and moved in closer. "What?" he asked.

"Look," she insisted, "take my advice and tell no one this theory of yours. You're lucky you told me first. Because this makes you sound like some kind of crackpot with a vendetta. You have no evidence, no motive, no incriminating statements, nothing. You just have this thing you've spun out of . . . out of a yoga poster."

"There is no other explanation that fits with the facts. And I'm talking about the facts of the case. Not the fact that the Bureau and Homeland Security and the rest of the federal government would love this to be a terrorism event so they can justify their existence and deflect criticism from other failings. Contrary to what you want to think, there *is* evidence, and there *are* incriminating statements. If we put Alicia Kent on a lie detector, you'll find out that everything she told me, you, and the master interrogator downtown is a lie. The real master was Alicia Kent. As in master manipulator."

Walling leaned forward and looked down at the floor.

"Thank you, Harry. That master interrogator you love deriding happens to have been me."

Bosch's mouth dropped open for a moment before he spoke.

"Oh . . . well . . . then, sorry . . . but it doesn't matter. The point is, she is a master liar. She lied about everything, and now that we know the story, it will be easy to smoke her out."

Walling got up from her seat and walked over to the front picture window. The vertical blinds were closed, but she split them with a finger and stared out into the street. Bosch could see her working the story over, grinding it down.

"What about the witness?" she asked. "He heard the shooter yell 'Allah.' Are you saying he's part of this? Or they just happened to know he was there and yelled 'Allah' as part of this master manipulation?"

Bosch gently tried to clear his throat. It was burning and making it difficult for him to talk.

"No. On that I think it's just a lesson in hearing what you want to hear. I plead guilty to not being much of a master interrogator myself. The kid told me that he heard the shooter yell it as he pulled the trigger. He said he wasn't sure but that it sounded like 'Allah,' and that, of course, worked with what I was thinking at the time. I heard what I wanted to hear."

Walling came away from the window and sat back down.

Bosch continued. "But how would the witness know it was the shooter and not the victim who yelled?" he asked. "It was dark. How would he know that it wasn't Stanley Kent yelling out his last word before execution? The name of the woman he loved, because he was about to die not even knowing that she'd betrayed him."

"Alicia."

"Exactly. 'Alicia' interrupted by a gunshot becomes 'Allah.' "

Walling relaxed her arms and leaned forward. As body language went, it was a good sign. It told Bosch he was pushing through.

"You said the *first* set of snap ties before," she said. "What were you talking about?"

Bosch nodded and handed across the file containing the crime-scene photos. "Look at the photos. What do you see?"

She opened the file and started looking at the photos. They depicted the master bedroom in the Kent house from all angles.

"It's the master bedroom," she said. "What am I missing?"

"Exactly. It's what you don't see. There are no clothes in the shot. She told us they told her to sit on the bed and take off her clothes. What are we supposed to believe, that they let her put the clothes away before they hog-tied her? Look at the last shot. It's the e-mail photo Stanley Kent got."

Walling looked through the file, found the printout of the e-mail photo, and stared at it. He saw recognition break in her eyes.

"Now what do you see?"

"The robe," she said excitedly. "When we let her get dressed, she went to the *closet* to get her robe. There was no robe on that lounge chair!"

Bosch nodded. "What does that tell us?" he asked. "That these considerate terrorists hung the robe up in the closet for her after taking the photo?"

"Or that maybe Mrs. Kent was tied up twice and the robe was moved in between?"

"And look again. The clock on the bed table is unplugged."

"Why?"

"Maybe they didn't want to worry about having a time stamp on the photo. Maybe the first photo wasn't even taken yesterday. Maybe it came from a dry run two days ago or even two weeks."

Rachel nodded. "She was tied up once for the photo and then once again for the rescue."

"Exactly. And that left her free to help carry out the plan on the overlook. She didn't kill her husband, but she was up there in the other car. And once Stanley was dead and the cesium was dumped and the car was ditched at Samir's, she and her partner came back home and she was tied up all over again."

"She wasn't passed out when we got there. That was an act and part of the plan. And her wetting the bed was a nice little touch to help sell it to us."

"The urine smell also covered up the smell of grape juice."

"What do you mean?"

"The purple bruises on her wrists and ankles. Now we know she wasn't tied up for hours. But she still had those bruises. There's an opened bottle of grape juice in the fridge and paper towels soaked with it in the trash can. She used grape juice to create the bruises."

"Oh, my gosh, I can't believe this."

"What?"

"When I was in the room with her at TIU. That small space. I thought I smelled grape in the room. I thought somebody had been in there before us and had been drinking grape juice. I smelled it!"

"There you go."

There was no doubt now. Bosch had her. But then a shadow of concern and doubt moved across Walling's face.

"What about motive?" she asked. "This is a federal agent we're talking about. To move on this, we need everything, even motive. There can be nothing left open to chance."

Bosch had been ready for the question.

"You saw the motive. Alicia Kent is a beautiful woman. Jack Brenner wanted her, and Stanley Kent was in the way of that."

Walling's eyes widened in shock. Bosch pressed on.

"That's the motive, Rachel. You—"

"But he—"

"Let me just finish. It goes like this. You and your partner show up here that day last year to give the Kents the warning about his occupation. Some kind of vibe is exchanged between Alicia and Jack. He gets interested; she gets interested. They meet on the sly for coffee or for drinks or whatever. One thing leads to another. An affair begins, and it lasts to the point that it's time to start thinking about doing something. Leaving the husband. Or getting rid of him because there's insurance and half a company at stake. That's enough motive right there, Rachel, and that's what this case is about. It's not about cesium or terrorism. It's the basic equation: Sex plus money equals murder."

She frowned and shook her head. "You don't know what you are talking about. Jack Brenner is married and has three children. He's stable, boring, and not interested. He wasn't—"

"Every man is interested. It doesn't matter if they're married or how many kids they have."

She spoke quietly.

"Would you listen and let me finish now? You are wrong about Brenner. He never met Alicia Kent before today. He wasn't my partner when I came here last year, and I never told you he was."

Bosch was jolted by the news. "Who was your partner last year, Rachel?"

She held his eyes for a long moment. "It was Cliff Maxwell."

EIGHTEEN

HARRY Bosch almost laughed but was too shocked to do anything but shake his head. "I can't believe this," he finally said. "About five hours ago I had the killer handcuffed on the floor right here!"

Rachel looked mortified by the realization that the murder of Stanley Kent was an inside job and the theft of the cesium was nothing more than a well-played misdirection.

"You see the rest now?" Bosch asked. "You see how he would work it? Her husband's dead, and he starts coming around out of sympathy and because he's on the case. They start dating, fall in love, and nobody ever raises an eyebrow about it. They're still out there looking for Moby and el-Fayed."

"And what if we ever catch those guys?" Walling said, taking up the story. "They could deny being a part of this thing until Osama bin Laden dies in a cave of old age, but who would believe them or care? There's nothing more ingenious than framing terrorists with a crime they didn't commit. They can never defend themselves."

Bosch nodded. "A perfect crime," he said. "The only reason it blew up was because Digoberto Gonzalves checked that Dumpster. Without him, we'd still be chasing Moby and el-Fayed, probably thinking that they had used Samir's place as a safe house."

"So what do we do now, Bosch?"

"I say we set up a classic rattrap. Put them both in rooms, ring the bell, and say the first one who talks gets the deal. I'd bet on Alicia. She'll break and give him up, probably blame him for everything, say she was acting under his influence and control."

"Something tells me you're right. And the truth is, I don't think Maxwell was smart enough to pull this off. I worked with—"

Her cell phone started buzzing. She took it out of her pocket and looked at the screen. "It's Jack."

"Find out where Maxwell is."

She answered the call and first replied to a few questions about Bosch's status, telling Brenner that he was okay but was losing his voice because his throat hurt. Bosch got up for another bottle of water but listened from the kitchen. Walling casually steered the call toward Maxwell.

"Hey, where's Cliff, by the way? I wanted to talk to him about that thing with Bosch in the hallway. I didn't like what he—"

She stopped and listened to the answer, and Bosch saw her eyes immediately become alert. Something was wrong.

"When was that?" she asked.

She listened again and stood up. "Jack, I've got to go. Bosch is about to be discharged. I'll check in as soon as I'm clear here."

She closed the phone and looked at Bosch.

"I can't stand lying to him. He won't forget it."

"What did he say?"

"He said there were too many agents at the recovery scene. Just about everybody came out from downtown, and they were standing around waiting on the radiation team. So Maxwell volunteered to go pick up the witness at the Mark Twain. Nobody had gotten around to it because I'd pulled off the original pickup team."

"How long ago?"

"A half hour."

"He's going to kill him."

Bosch started moving quickly toward the door.

BOSCH drove this time. On the way toward Hollywood, he told Walling that Jesse Mitford had no phone in his room. The Mark Twain wasn't much when it came to full service. Instead, Bosch called the watch commander at Hollywood Division and asked him to send a patrol car to the hotel to check on the witness. He then called the front desk at the Mark Twain.

"Alvin, this is Detective Bosch. From this morning? Has anyone come in asking for Stephen King?"

"Mmm, nope."

"In the last twenty minutes, have you buzzed in anybody who looked like a cop or who wasn't a tenant there?"

"No, Detective. What's going on?"

"Listen, I need you to go up to that room and tell Stephen King to get out of there and then to call me on my cell."

"I got nobody to watch the desk, Detective."

"It's an emergency, Alvin. I need to get him out of there. It will take you less than five minutes. Here, write this down." Bosch gave him his number. "And if anybody but me comes in there looking for him, say he checked out and left. Go, Alvin, and thanks."

Bosch closed the phone and looked over at Rachel. His face showed his lack of confidence in the deskman.

"I think the guy's a tweaker."

Bosch increased his speed. They had just turned south on Cahuenga off Barham. He was thinking that, depending on traffic in Hollywood, they could get to the Mark Twain in another five minutes. This conclusion made him shake his head. With a half-hour lead, Maxwell should already be at the Mark Twain. He wondered if he had slipped in the back way and already gotten to Mitford.

"Maxwell may have already gone in through the back," he told Walling. "I'm going to come in from the alley."

"You know," Walling said, "maybe he's not going to hurt him. He'll pick him up and talk to him, judge for himself if he saw enough at the overlook that he'd be a threat."

Bosch shook his head. "No way. Maxwell's got to know that once the cesium was found, his plan was going down the toilet. He's got to take action against all threats. First the witness, then Alicia Kent."

"Alicia Kent? You think he'd make a move against her? This whole thing is because of her."

"Doesn't matter now. Survival instincts take over now, and she's a threat. It goes with the territory. You cross the big line to be with her. You cross it again to save your—"

Bosch stopped talking as a sudden realization thudded in his chest. He cursed out loud and pinned the accelerator as they came out of the Cahuenga Pass. He cut across three lanes of Highland Avenue in front of the Hollywood Bowl and made a screeching U-turn in front of oncoming traffic. He punched it, and the car fishtailed wildly as he headed toward the southbound entrance to the Hollywood Freeway. Rachel grabbed the dashboard and a door handle to hold on.

"Harry, what are you doing? This is the wrong way!"

He flicked on the siren and the blue lights and yelled his response to Walling. "Mitford is a misdirection. This is the right way. Who is the greater threat to Maxwell?"

"Alicia?"

"You bet, and now's the best shot he has of getting her out of Tactical. Everybody's up in that alley with the cesium."

The freeway was moving pretty well, and the siren helped open it up further. Bosch figured Maxwell could have already gotten to downtown, depending on what kind of traffic he encountered.

Rachel opened her phone and started punching in numbers. She tried number after number, but no one was answering.

"I can't get anybody," she yelled.

"Where's TIU?"

"On Broadway. You know where the Million Dollar Theater is? Same building. Entrance on Third."

Bosch flicked off the siren and opened his phone. He called his partner, and Ferras answered right away.

"Ignacio, where are you?"

"Just got back to the office. Forensics worked the car for—"

"Listen to me. Drop what you're doing and meet me at the Third Street entrance to the Million Dollar Theater building. You know where that is?"

"Yeah, I know where it is. What's going on?"

"I'll explain when I get there."

He closed the phone and hit the siren again.

THE next ten minutes took ten hours. Bosch moved in and out of traffic and finally reached the Broadway exit downtown. He killed the siren as he made the turn, and headed down the hill toward their destination. They were three blocks away.

The Million Dollar Theater was built in a time when the movie business showed itself off in magnificent theater palaces that lined Broadway downtown. But it had been decades since a first-run film had been projected there. Now the theater waited unused for renovation and redemption while above it a once grand office building was twelve stories of office space and residential lofts.

"Good place for a secret unit to have a secret office," Bosch said as the building came into sight. "Nobody would've guessed."

Walling didn't respond. She was trying to make another call. She then slapped the phone closed in frustration.

"I can't even get our secretary. She takes lunch after one so there will be somebody in the office when the agents go to lunch earlier."

"Where exactly is the squad, and where would Alicia Kent be?"

"We have the whole seventh floor. There's a lounge room with a couch and a TV. They put her in there so she could watch TV."

"How many in the squad?"

"Eight agents, the secretary, and an office manager. The office manager just went out on maternity leave, and the secretary must be at lunch. I hope. But they wouldn't have left Alicia Kent alone. It's against policy. Somebody had to have stayed there with her."

Bosch turned right on Third and immediately pulled to the curb. Ignacio Ferras was already there, leaning casually against his Volvo station wagon. In front of it was another parked car. A federal cruiser. Bosch and Walling got out. Bosch approached Ferras, and Walling went to look inside the fed car.

"Have you seen Agent Maxwell?" Bosch asked.

"Who?"

"The guy we put on the floor at the Kent house this morning."

"No, I haven't seen anybody. What—"

"It's his car," Walling said as she joined them.

"Ignacio, this is Agent Walling."

"Call me Iggy."

"Rachel."

They shook hands.

"Okay, then he's gotta be up there," Bosch said. "How many stairwells?"

"Three," Walling said. "But he'll use the one that comes out by his car."

She pointed to a pair of double steel doors near the corner of the building. Bosch headed over that way to see if they were locked. Ferras and Walling followed.

"What is going on?" Ferras asked.

"Maxwell is our shooter," Bosch said. "He is up—"

"What?"

Bosch checked the exit doors. There was no outside handle or knob. He turned to Ferras.

"Look, there's not a lot of time. Trust me. Maxwell is our guy, and he's in this building to take out Alicia Kent. We're—"

"What is she doing here?"

"The FBI has a location here. She's here. No more questions, okay? Just listen. Agent Walling and I are going up in the elevator. I want you out here by this door. If Maxwell comes out, you take him down. You understand? You take him down."

"Got it."

"Good. Call for backup. We're going up."

Bosch reached over and tapped Ferras on the cheek.

"And stay frosty."

They left Ferras there and headed through the building's main entrance. There was no lobby to speak of, just an elevator. It opened at the push of the button, and Walling used a key card to engage the seven button. They started going up.

"Something tells me you're never going to call him Iggy," Walling said.

Bosch ignored the comment. "Does this thing have a bell or a tone that sounds when it reaches the floor?"

"I can't remem— I think it does. . . . Yes, definitely."

"Great. We'll be sitting ducks."

Bosch pulled his Kimber out of its holster and chambered a round. Walling did the same with her weapon. Bosch pushed Walling to one side of the elevator while he took the other. He raised his gun. The elevator reached seven, and there was a soft bell tone from outside. The door began to slide open, exposing Bosch first.

No one was there.

Rachel pointed to the left, signaling that the offices were to the left. Bosch crouched and stepped out, his gun up and ready.

Again, no one was there.

He started moving to his left. Rachel came out and moved with him on his right flank. They came to a loft-style office with two rows of cubicles—the squad room—and three private rooms that had been built freestanding in the open floor plan. There were large racks of electronic equipment between the cubicles, and every desk had two computer screens on it.

Bosch stepped farther in, and through the window in one of the private offices, he saw a man sitting in a chair, his head back and eyes open. He looked like he was wearing a red bib. But Bosch knew it was blood. The man had been shot in the chest.

He pointed, and Rachel saw the dead man. She reacted with a quick intake of breath and a low-volume sigh.

The door to the office was ajar. They moved toward it, and Bosch pushed it open while Walling covered them from behind. Alicia Kent was sitting on the floor, her back to the wall.

Bosch crouched beside her. Her eyes were open but dead. A gun was on the floor between her feet, and the wall behind her was spattered with blood and brain matter.

Bosch turned and surveyed the room. He understood the play. It was set up to look like Alicia Kent had grabbed the agent's gun from his holster, shot him, and then sat down on the floor and took her own life. No note or explanation, but it was the best Maxwell could come up with in the short amount of time that he had.

Bosch turned to Walling. She had let her guard down and was just standing there looking at the dead agent.

"Rachel," he said. "He's gotta still be here."

He stood and moved toward the door so he could search the squad room. As he glanced through the window, he saw movement behind the electronics racks. He stopped, raised his weapon, and tracked someone moving behind one of the racks toward a door with an exit sign on it.

In a moment, he saw Maxwell break free of the cover and dash toward the door.

"Maxwell!" Bosch yelled. "Stop!"

Maxwell spun and raised a weapon. At the same moment that his back hit the exit door, he started firing. The window shattered, and glass sprayed across Bosch. He returned fire and put six shots into the opening of the exit door, but Maxwell was gone.

"Rachel?" he called without taking his eyes off the door. "Okay?"

"I'm fine." Her voice came from below him. He knew she had hit the floor when the shooting had started.

"Which exit is that door?"

Rachel stood up. Bosch moved toward the door, glancing at her, and saw glass all over her clothes. She had been cut on the cheek.

"Those stairs go down to his car."

Bosch ran from the room toward the exit door. He opened his phone as he went and pushed the speed dial for his partner. The call was answered on half a ring. Bosch was already in the stairwell.

"He's coming down!"

Bosch dropped the phone and started down the stairs. He could hear Maxwell running on the steel steps below and instinctively knew that he was too far ahead.

NINETEEN

BOSCH covered three more landings, taking three steps at a time. He could now hear Walling coming down behind him. He then heard the booming sound from below as Maxwell hit the exit door at the bottom. There were immediate shouts, and then there were shots. They came so close together it was impossible to determine which had come first or how many shots had been fired.

Ten seconds later Bosch hit the exit door. He came out onto the sidewalk and saw Ferras leaning against the back bumper of Maxwell's fed car. He was holding his weapon with one hand and his elbow with the other. A red rose of blood was blooming on his shoulder. Traffic had stopped in both directions on Third, and pedestrians were running down the sidewalks to safety.

"I hit him twice," Ferras yelled. "He went that way."

He nodded in the direction of the Third Street tunnel under Bunker Hill. Bosch stepped closer to his partner and saw the wound in the ball of his shoulder. It didn't look too bad.

"Did you call for backup?" Bosch asked.

"On the way." Ferras grimaced as he adjusted his hold on his injured arm.

"You did good, Iggy. Hang in there while I go get this guy."

Ferras nodded. Bosch turned and saw Rachel come through the door, a smear of blood on her face.

"This way," he said. "He's hit."

They started down Third in a spread formation. After a few steps, Bosch picked up the trail. Maxwell was obviously hurt badly and was losing a lot of blood. It would make him easy to track.

But when they got to the corner of Third and Hill, they lost the trail. There was no blood on the pavement. Bosch looked into the long Third Street tunnel and saw no one moving in the traffic on foot. He looked up and down Hill Street and saw nothing, until his attention was drawn to a commotion of people running out of the Grand Central Market.

"This way," he said.

They moved quickly toward the huge market. Bosch picked up the blood trail again just outside and started in. The market was a two-story-high conglomeration of food booths and retail and produce concessions. The place was crowded and noisy, and that made it difficult for Bosch to follow the blood and track Maxwell.

Then suddenly there were shouts from directly ahead, and two quick shots were fired into the air. It caused an immediate human stampede. Dozens of screaming shoppers and workers flooded into the aisle where Bosch and Walling stood and started running toward them. Bosch realized they were going to be trampled. In one motion, he moved to his right, grabbed Walling around the waist, and pulled her behind one of the wide concrete support pillars.

The crowd moved by, and then Bosch looked around the pillar. The market was now empty. There was no sign of Maxwell, but then Bosch picked up movement in one of the cold cases that fronted a butcher shop at the end of the aisle. He looked again closely and realized that the movement came from behind the case. Looking through the glass panels and over the display of beef and pork, Bosch could see Maxwell's face. He was on the ground, leaning his back against a refrigerator in the rear of the butcher shop.

"He's up ahead in the butcher shop," he whispered to Walling. "You go to the right and down that aisle. You'll be able to come up on his right. I'll go straight on and get his attention."

"Or we could wait for backup."

"I'm not waiting."

"I didn't think so."

"Ready?"

"No. Switch. I go head-on and get his attention, and you come around the side."

Bosch knew it was the better plan, because she knew Maxwell and he knew her. But it also meant she would face the most danger.

"You sure?" Bosch asked.

"Yes. It's right."

Bosch looked around the pillar one more time and saw that Maxwell had not moved. His face looked red and sweaty. Bosch looked back at Walling. "He's still there."

"Good. Let's do it."

They separated and started moving. Bosch quickly moved down an aisle of concessions one over from the aisle that ended at the butcher shop. When he came to the end, he was at a Mexican coffee shop with high walls. He was able to protect himself and look around the corner at the butcher shop. This gave him a side view behind the counter. He saw Maxwell twenty feet away. He was slouched against the refrigerator door, still holding his weapon in two hands. His shirt was completely soaked in blood.

Bosch leaned back into cover, gathered himself, and got ready to step out and approach Maxwell. But then he heard Walling's voice.

"Cliff? It's me, Rachel. Let me get you some help."

Bosch looked around the corner. Walling was standing out in the open, five feet in front of the deli counter, her gun down at her side.

"There is no help," Maxwell said. "It's too late for me."

Bosch recognized that if Maxwell wanted to take a shot at her, the bullet would have to go through both the front and back glass panels of the deli case. With the front plate set at an angle, it would take a miracle bullet to get to her. But miracles did happen. Bosch raised his weapon, braced it against the wall, and was ready to shoot if he needed to.

"Come on, Cliff," Walling said. "Don't end it like this."

"No other way."

Maxwell's body was suddenly racked by a deep, wet coughing. Blood came to his lips. "That guy really got me," he said before coughing again.

"Cliff?" Walling said. "Let me come in there. I want to help."

"No, you come in and I'm going to—"

His words were lost when he opened fire on the deli case, sweeping his gun and shooting out the glass doors all the way down. Rachel ducked, and Bosch stepped out and straightened his arms in a two-handed grip. He held himself from shooting but keyed on the barrel of Maxwell's weapon. If the muzzle zeroed in on Walling, he was going to shoot Maxwell in the head.

Maxwell lowered his weapon and started to laugh, blood rolling down from his mouth and creating a freak clown look.

"I think . . . I think I just killed a porterhouse."

He laughed again, but it made him start to cough once more, and that looked painful. When it subsided, he spoke.

"I just want to say . . . that it was her. She wanted him dead. I just . . . I just wanted her. That's all. But she wouldn't have it any other way . . . and I did what she wanted. For that . . . I am damned."

Bosch took a step closer. He didn't think that Maxwell had noticed him yet.

"I'm sorry," Maxwell said. "Rachel? Tell them I'm sorry."

"Cliff," Walling said. "You can tell them that yourself."

As Bosch watched, Maxwell brought his gun up and put the muzzle under his chin. Without hesitation, he pulled the trigger. The impact snapped his head back and sent a spatter of blood up the refrigerator door. The gun dropped onto the concrete floor between his outstretched legs. In his suicide, Maxwell had adopted the same position as his lover, the woman he had just killed.

Walling came around the case and stood next to Bosch, and together they looked down at the dead agent. She said nothing. Bosch checked his watch. It was almost one. He had ridden the case from beginning to end in little more than twelve hours. The tally was five dead, one wounded, and one dying of radiation exposure.

And then there was himself. Bosch wondered if he was going to be part of the tally by the time all was said and done. His throat was now blazing, and there was a feeling of heaviness in his chest.

He looked at Rachel and saw blood running down her cheek again. She would need stitches to close the wound.

"You know what?" he said. "I'll take you to the hospital if you take me."

She looked at him and smiled sort of sadly.

"Throw in Iggy and you've got yourself a deal."

Bosch left her there with Maxwell and walked back to the Million Dollar Theater building to check on his partner. While he was on his way, backup units were pulling in everywhere and crowds were forming. Bosch decided he would leave it to the patrol officers to take charge of the crime scenes.

Ferras was sitting in the open door of his car, waiting for the paramedics. He was holding his arm at an awkward angle and was clearly in pain. The blood had spread on his shirt.

"You want water?" Bosch asked. "I've got a bottle in my trunk."

"No, I'll just wait. I wish they'd get here."

The signature siren of a fire-rescue paramedic truck could be heard in the distance, getting closer.

"What happened, Harry?"

Bosch leaned against the side of the car and told him that Maxwell had just killed himself as they had closed in on him.

"Hell of a way to go, I guess," Ferras said. "Cornered like that."

Bosch nodded but kept silent. As they waited, his thoughts carried him down the streets and up the hills to the overlook, where the last thing Stanley Kent ever saw was the city spread before him in beautiful shimmering lights. Maybe to Stanley it looked like heaven was waiting for him at the end.

But Bosch thought that it didn't really matter if you died cornered in a butcher shop or on an overlook glimpsing the lights of heaven. You were gone, and the finale wasn't the part that mattered. We are all circling the drain, he thought. Some are closer to the black hole than others. Some will see it coming, and some will have no clue when the undertow of the whirlpool grabs them and pulls them down into darkness forever.

The important thing is to fight it, Bosch told himself. Always keep kicking. Always keep fighting the undertow.

The rescue unit turned the corner at Broadway, working its way around several stopped cars before braking at the mouth of the alley and killing the siren. Bosch helped his partner out of the car, and they walked to the paramedics.

The Serialized
Michael Connelly

Vital Stats

BORN: Philadelphia, PA, 1956
RESIDENCE: Tampa, FL
FAMILY: Wife, one daughter
EDUCATION: University of Florida, Gainesville
FAVORITE THRILLER NOVEL: *Red Dragon* by Thomas Harris
PREFERRED WRITING HOURS: 7 a.m. to noon
WEBSITE: www.MichaelConnelly.com

FOR Michael Connelly, a key goal when writing his best-selling Harry Bosch series is to keep things fresh and interesting. So for *The Overlook,* the thirteenth Bosch entry, Connelly wrote the original story as a sixteen-part series that premiered in *The New York Times Magazine.*

Years ago, serialized tales were more commonplace in magazines than they are today. Famous authors such as Charles Dickens and Sir Arthur Conan Doyle frequently published their stories first as serials. Recently, *The New York Times Magazine* revived this tradition with authors such as Scott Turow and Patricia Cornwell.

The *Times* initially approached Connelly to write a serialized story a couple of years ago, but the busy author's schedule did not allow it at the time. When they asked again a year later, Connelly was happy to grant the request.

Connelly soon learned that writing a serialized book held unexpected challenges. "I had to write each installment to fit a three-thousand-word hole," he explains. "That is not how I normally write. When I am writing a novel, I don't care about the length of a chapter. I concentrate on its content only."

As he realized the limitations on his writing style, Connelly knew he'd eventually want to expand and rework the story in order to publish it in book form. The rewrite was a pleasure, he says. "I got to look at it again with a totally fresh mind and take it apart and rebuild it and write it the way I prefer, with the pacing that I wanted, and also throw in some more current events to make it topical."

Connelly made some significant changes, including adding a whole new character who was not in the serialization. He'd wanted to add this character for the magazine but simply didn't have the space. He also added material to the novel to ensure that it met his perfectionist expectations. The result is another top-notch Harry Bosch story.

Along with writing—and rewriting—*The Overlook,* Connelly has been busy working on a new legal thriller featuring Mickey Haller, whom he introduced in *The Lincoln Lawyer*

Prussian Blue

In *The Overlook,* Harry Bosch confronts the terrifying possibility that terrorists might possess radioactive cesium, with the intent of poisoning the unsuspecting citizens of Los Angeles. In the event of such a threat in real life, does an antidote exist?

Fortunately, yes. A mineral compound known as Prussian blue can limit the body's exposure to radioactive materials. It works by trapping these materials in the intestines and keeping them from being reabsorbed by the body. Then they move through the colon and are excreted. Hopefully Bosch, who has a brush with radiation in the line of duty, knows enough to get himself to the doctor before his next novel!

(2005). (Bosch makes a cameo appearance.) In addition, he's writing a screenplay for a film version of the 1980s television show *The Equalizer,* about a shadowy former secret agent who helps others to make up for sins from his past.

But Harry Bosch fans need not panic. Connelly also plans another Bosch mystery, this one a follow-up to *Echo Park* (2006), set partially in Hong Kong. ∎

ELIZABETH ADLER

Meet Me in Venice

A Novel

Prologue

ANA Yuan, a plain young woman in a summery blue dress and sandals, never felt even a hint of danger when she boarded the double-decker train from Shanghai to Suzhou on the borders of the Taihu Lake.

The landscape was dreamlike, more than sixty percent water with low hills bordering cultivated fields. Canals intersected the ancient city, framed by graceful arched bridges. There were leafy lanes and centuries-old pavilions and famous gardens dating back through four dynasties. It was no wonder Suzhou was described by Marco Polo as "the Venice of the East."

The journey took only ninety minutes, but when the train stopped, Ana was dismayed to find it was raining. Still, always uncertain of the temperamental weather, she had carried an umbrella. Regretting the summery blue dress and the sandals, she hurried into a taxi.

Arriving at her destination, Ana paid off the driver. She put up her umbrella and began to walk down the cobblestone pathway by the edge of the canal. It was late, and the area was deserted. The rain was coming down hard now, and what with the clouds and the dusk and the pathway covered by dense leafy trees, it was darker and more lonely than she would have liked.

Ana's sandals clattered noisily on the slick wet stones as she hurried toward her rendezvous. Head tucked under the umbrella, shivering in the damp, she did not notice the observer behind her, keeping carefully to the shadows under the trees.

She paused at the arched bridge that resembled the ones in Venice, looking around her, half-smiling. She did not hear the observer approaching on soft feet.

He struck her a vicious blow behind the knees, sending her sprawling. Her skull smacked on the stone path, and her eyes rolled up in her head. He dragged her to the canal and pushed her into the water. The heavy rain conveniently washed her blood from the path. It was the perfect murder.

The next morning Ana's body in her summery blue dress was found where it had drifted, caught in the reeds further down the canal. Her death was judged an accident: a fall on the slippery stones when she must have hit her head; a tumble unconscious into the canal; a drowning.

She was buried with great ceremony in the wealthy Yuan family's plot in Shanghai. Her handsome young American husband, Bennett Yuan, sobbed, heartbroken, but despite their sorrow her Chinese family remained impassive and dignified.

Tragic, the mourners said. A sweet girl, with everything to live for. And what on earth was she doing in Suzhou anyway?

One

Shanghai, Six Months Later

LILY Song was eating breakfast at the Happybird Tea House, an open-fronted place in an alley off the Renmin Road, named for the tiny birds, the pets of the customers that accompanied them in their little bamboo cages, singing their morning songs. She ate there every morning at eight o'clock, and she always had shrimp dim sum with vegetables and green tea with semolina. Her fellow breakfasters, all men, were all too immersed in their newspapers and noodles to notice her.

She was small and very slender, with a shoulder-length swing of glossy black hair and dark brown eyes. She had the fair skin of her European mother and the delicate nose of her Chinese father, and she wore either conservative Western clothes bought at the better boutiques or the traditional brocade dress, tailored specifically to her directions in a tiny shop near the Bubbling Well Road. Either way, she gave the impression of an attractive, successful woman. Which, in a sense, she was.

This morning, however, she was wearing narrow black pants with a black linen top. Her hair was pulled back, and large sunglasses hid her eyes. She could have passed unnoticed in any Shanghai crowd. She glanced up as a man entered, a foreigner, older, smart in a lightweight beige business suit. Lily lifted her hand, beckoning him over.

He came and sat in the chair opposite. With a gruff "good morning" he placed a leather document case on the table. A soft-footed server hovered nearby, and Lily ordered plain green tea for her guest. She asked if he would like to eat, but he said he would not. He was Swiss and conservative, and he did not like Chinese food. The teahouse was not a place he would have chosen to do business.

"My client is interested in anything you can show him," he said. "Provided it can be authenticated, that is."

Lily had done business with him before. His client's identity was preserved under a cloak of strict anonymity, which suited her just fine. Antiques and, in particular, stolen antiques were what she had dealt in since she was sixteen.

"I have some things your client might be interested in," she said in a low voice. "I expect delivery soon of a batch of antiquities. Cloisonné, famille verte, statues . . ."

"When will you have them?" His eyes bored into her.

"Within a few weeks. Meanwhile, here is something very special. The most important piece I have ever come across." She reached in her purse and handed a photograph to him.

The man studied it carefully. "My client doesn't care for jewelry," he said curtly.

"I think he will care for this when he hears its provenance." Lily took another sip of green tea, meeting his eyes across the table. "Your client will no doubt have heard of the great Dragon Lady, Cixi, the Dowager Empress of China?" She pronounced the name *chee shee* and spelled it so that he could make his notes correctly. "Cixi was once a concubine, but eventually she ruled China and was said to have been even more powerful than her contemporary, Queen Victoria. The Empress lived in great splendor in the Forbidden City. In preparation for her death she built herself a magnificent tomb, a lavish complex of temples and pavilions glittering in gold and precious stones.

"Eventually, she was buried there, wearing her elaborate crown and magnificent robes, along with her wonderful jewels and precious ornaments. In accordance with Imperial custom, a large and very rare pearl, the size of a robin's egg, was placed in her mouth to preserve the royal corpse from decay."

Lily paused. The man was looking at the photograph, and she could tell from his body language he was interested, even though he pretended otherwise. It was all about money, she thought cynically.

"Twenty years later," she said, "the revolutionary troops dynamited the entrance to Cixi's burial chamber, looted all the treasures and opened Cixi's coffin. They ripped off her Imperial robes and crown, then threw her naked corpse to the ground."

The man's stunned eyes met hers.

"And from her mouth," Lily said softly, "they stole that single, massive, rare pearl. A moonbeam of light and cool as death itself."

The man lowered his eyes to the photograph.

"Yes," she said softly, "it's the very same one. All the jewels disappeared into obscurity and into hidden collections, until suddenly, sixty or so years ago, a necklace surfaced, embedded with emeralds and rubies, diamonds and jade, all said to be from Cixi's tomb. And at its center was the famous pearl."

She saw him take a deep breath. Then he said, "And you are telling me you have this necklace in your possession?"

She lowered her eyes. "Let us just say I know where to lay my hands on it. Obviously, it will not be cheap. There is always a premium on a history and provenance as sinister as this one. Many men would enjoy handling the pearl from the mouth of the dead Empress, once a famous concubine. It would give them a special thrill, I think." She smiled. "I'm sure we can do business together," she said, offering him her hand.

The little birds trilled joyously as she left.

Paris

Six thousand miles away, Lily's cousin, Precious Rafferty, was sitting in a crowded café near the rue de Buci on Paris's Left Bank. It was ten o'clock on a rainy Saturday morning. She was sipping her café crème and nibbling on a slab of toasted baguette, watching the shoppers at the bustling street market putting up their umbrellas and walking a little faster past the piled displays of fruits and vegetables and the fragrant herbs and cheeses. A rainy Saturday was not good for business.

She finished her coffee and waved good-bye to the waiter who knew her well because she had been breakfasting there for years, then pushed her way out through the crowded tables. Under the awning a young couple, probably tourists, sat braving the elements, holding hands, and she thought wistfully how happy they looked.

How, she wondered, did you go about finding that kind of happiness? Was there some invisible element in the air you caught hold of, unknowing, and suddenly there you were, in love, a couple instead of one? Whatever it was, she certainly hadn't found it.

Stopping at the patisserie for a raspberry napoleon to get her through the morning, she hurried back through the rain to the rue Jacob, where she lived over her antiques store.

Preshy had run the business for fifteen years, ever since her grandfather Hennessy died, but it still gave her a thrill to see RAFFERTY ANTIQUES written in flowing gilt script across the window. She stopped to peer inside, imagining herself a customer, admiring the soft fuchsia walls and the alabaster sconces that added a muted glow to the narrow room crammed with antique pieces. There was a lovely marble head of a boy with the tight curls of youth, a small Etruscan bowl, a life-sized marble of Aphrodite emerging from the sea, her delicate hand outstretched.

Next to the store, tall wooden gates led into one of those charming secretive Parisian courtyards, centered with an old paulownia tree. Preshy's grandfather Arthur Hennessy, who'd fought with the U.S. Army in France and fallen in love with Paris, had discovered the apartment in the secret courtyard. He'd bought it for a song and opened his antiques store specializing in artifacts from Italy and the Balkans that were easy to come by after the conflict.

When she was six, Preshy's parents were killed in a plane crash. Her grandmother had also died young, so it was Aunt Grizelda—the Countess von Hoffenberg, a woman of the world, eccentric, glamorous, with absolutely no clue as to proper child-rearing etiquette—who'd brought Preshy up. Grizelda hired a French governess and simply hauled Preshy everywhere with her, upping stakes every few months from the von Hoffenberg castle near Salzburg, to her suite at the Carlyle in New York, or the one at Paris's Ritz Hotel. Preshy adored Aunt Grizelda, and she also loved her grandfather, who became interested in her when she was old enough to attend college in Boston and visit him in Paris, where she learned about the antiques trade.

Confident that she would do well, her grandfather willed her the store and the apartment over it. But within a few weeks of his death, Preshy discovered that the business was in chaos. He had let things slip in his old age, and there was not much stock and very little money. Gradually, with hard work and dedication, she had revamped it. She wasn't making a fortune yet, but she was making a living, and she was optimistic for better things to come.

Meanwhile, she suddenly seemed to have reached the age of thirty-eight without committing to a serious relationship. Oh sure, there had been love affairs and men she'd thought exciting or romantic for a while, but somehow none of them had worked out.

"You're too picky," Aunt Grizelda complained as yet another suitor bit the dust, but Preshy just laughed. Inside though, she was beginning to wonder if she would ever meet someone she really *liked*. Someone she enjoyed, someone who would sweep her off her feet. She thought it very unlikely.

There was nothing wrong with her. She was a tall, lanky, attractive woman with a cloud of curly copper-blond hair that frizzed horribly in the rain, her mother's jutting cheekbones and the wide Hennessy mouth. She didn't care much about clothes but dressed reasonably well when she had to, relying on that old standby, the little black dress. But day to day it was jeans and white T-shirts.

She was educated and charming, enjoyed good food and wine; she went to the latest movies, to gallery openings, concerts, theater. In fact she enjoyed life, but she thought sadly, she might enjoy it more if she ever found a soul mate.

She let herself into the courtyard and climbed the steps to the sixteenth-century stone apartment "over the shop." Her home was a cozy refuge in winter, and in summer, with the tall windows flung open to the breeze, it was a cool city space filled with sunlight and the sound of birds in the paulownia tree.

The phone was ringing, and she grabbed it. "Hello?"

"Hi, sweets, it's me."

Her best friend Daria's loud Boston twang bounced in her ear. "Isn't it a bit early for you to be calling?" she asked, trying to calculate the time difference.

"Yeah, well, Super-Kid's been up all night. Presh, what are you supposed to do when your three-year-old has bad dreams? Take her to a shrink?"

Preshy laughed. "Stop feeding her soft drinks and candy, I'd think. She hasn't enough vocabulary to talk to a shrink."

Daria's three-year-old's name was Lauren, but she'd always been known as Super-Kid, and she was Preshy's goddaughter. Daria was married to a physics professor, Tom, and she was always on to Preshy about finding "the right one." Today was no exception.

"So, it's Saturday," Daria began. "What are you going to do tonight?"

"Oh, you know, Daria, it's been a long week. There's a gallery opening I could go to, right down the street, but I don't like his work. And I'm too tired for a movie."

"You've got to get a life, Presh," Daria said sternly. "Remember, we only get to go around once. Why not come on over here and let me introduce you to some nice tenured professor?"

"Sure. And he'd live in Boston, and I'd live in Paris."

"Then have Sylvie set you up with someone."

Sylvie was their other "best friend." She was French, a chef who'd opened her own successful Paris bistro, Verlaine.

"Sylvie only knows other chefs, and with their hours who needs that?" Preshy replied. "Anyhow, did you ever stop to think I might be quite happy as I am? I don't want any changes. I have my life, I go out when I want. . . ."

"With whom?" Daria said. "I mean it, sweets. Just come on over here. I promise we'll show you a good time."

Preshy said she'd think about it, and they chatted for a while longer. When she rang off, she went to the shelf and looked at the silver-framed photo of the three friends, aged eighteen.

Daria was in the middle, her long straight blond hair floating on the sea breeze, steady blue eyes smiling as usual, preppie personified in shorts and a polo shirt. Sylvie was on the left, with a glossy black gamine haircut and solemn dark eyes, plump even then from working in a local restaurant. Preshy was on the right, taller than the others and skinny, her gold hair frizzing into a halo in the humid sea air, green-blue eyes sparkling with fun.

The three of them had spent weeks at Daria's family's tumbledown gray-shingled cottage on Cape Cod, idling away summer hours that seemed to stretch pleasantly into infinity. Preshy had met Sylvie at one of the schools she occasionally attended whenever she was in Paris and later met Daria at school in Boston, and she loved them like sisters.

She put the photo back on the shelf next to the one of Grandfather Hennessy and his pretty blond Austrian bride. It was taken on their wedding day, and she was wearing a necklace of what looked to be diamonds and emeralds with a robin's egg–sized pearl in the center. It seemed a bizarre piece of jewelry to wear with her traditional dress. Preshy had never seen the real thing, as it had not turned up amongst Grandfather's possessions.

Of course there was a photo of Preshy's parents, whose faces for her were just a blur from the past. And there were several pictures of Aunt Grizelda: one of her sipping a gin fizz with Prince Rainier on a terrace on the Côte d'Azur; another in a cloud of scarlet tulle at a table of international celebrities at the Red Cross Gala in Monte Carlo, her long sweep of hair even redder than the dress. And with her was her longtime best friend, blond, rangy, ex–Follies showgirl Mimi Moskowitz, widow of a rich investment banker.

Grizelda adored the warm South of France climate, the fashions, the parties, the entertaining company. Now the two widows shared a lavish penthouse apartment in Monte Carlo. Neither of them had children, and they considered Preshy their daughter, so of course, over the years they'd done their best to spoil her.

"But let's face it, darling," Grizelda had said, finally defeated. "The girl's unspoilable. She cares nothing for jewels and clothes. All she likes are those boring antiques. She's never even seriously cared about a man."

And she was, Preshy thought, smiling, probably right.

Nevertheless, thinking of what Daria had said, she decided that tonight she would put on the little black dress and the heels, and the thin little rope of diamonds Aunt Grizelda had given her for her sixteenth birthday. Preshy always felt elegant when she wore it, and Daria said it added a little class to her act.

Preshy heaved a sigh. She would go to that gallery opening after all, then have a late after-hours dinner with Sylvie at Verlaine. It was just another Saturday night in Paris.

Two

Shanghai

LILY lived in an old Colonial-style house in the historic part of Shanghai known as the French Concession. In the late nineteenth and early twentieth century the area had been home to French diplomats, businessmen and entrepreneurs, as well as hard-partying socialites, but after the Revolution it had fallen on hard times. Now it was being brought back to life with a mix of the old small traditional businesses and open-fronted shops set alongside smart restaurants and bars, with chic boutiques scattered amongst its alleys and broad tree-lined avenues.

Tucked back on a narrow lane with a nightclub on one side and a noodle shop on the other, Lily's house was a gem from the past, set in its private courtyard with a red-tiled roof, tall green-painted shutters and a large verandah. It had been owned by the Song family for generations and was the only possession Lily's father had not been able to gamble away. It had been the single anchor in their chaotic lives, and the only thing Lily had felt no one could ever take from her.

Lily's father had gambled himself into financial oblivion playing baccarat and *pai gow* in the gambling capitals of the world. While Henry Song played the tables, Lily's mother attempted to make a living selling cheap copies of antiques. When she was sixteen, her father died, and Lily left school and took over the business. Her mother died five years later. Lily was alone in the world with no one to rely on but herself.

She ran her antiques business from the house and did most of her buying searching out old family pieces from simple country people who had no idea of their true value. She did not consider this stealing, merely good business. More recently, though, when the Yangtze, the Great Yellow River, had been gouged out to create a dam, gangs of robbers had discovered tombs hidden near the old villages and were secretly stealing the treasures of the ancestors.

Superstitious, this had made Lily nervous, but she soon shrugged it off and found herself a lucrative new source of income, buying from the gangs, then selling on to private customers acting on behalf of rich collectors. As a front for her illegal activities, she kept up her regular business of manufacturing replicas of antiquities: the traditional Buddhas and Mao souvenirs and the famous terra-cotta warriors of Xi'an that she sold to tourist shops.

She parked her black SUV in the courtyard and pressed the electronic buzzer that closed the gates behind her. Though the house was French Colonial in style, the garden was strictly Chinese, with a pond of fat goldfish, symbols of prosperity and money, and a simple wall fountain trickling serenely onto pink lotus blossoms. It was where she enjoyed sitting in the evening, when she had a free moment that is, with a glass of wine and only her thoughts and her little canary songbird for company.

Mary-Lou Chen came out onto the terrace. "Oh, there you are, Lily," she called. "Someone telephoned a few minutes ago. He wouldn't leave his name." She grinned at Lily. "A new boyfriend?"

"Hah!" Lily tossed her head disdainfully. "Fat chance. I think I know who it might be, though."

"He said he'd call back in half an hour."

"Good." Lily knew for sure now she had the Swiss hooked.

Mary-Lou Chen was her best friend and coworker. They had known each other forever. At school they had been the only biracial outsiders, with their Chinese fathers and Caucasian mothers. And both their families were poor, Lily's from the downward spiral familiar to gamblers, and Mary-Lou's from her father's bad business methods. They both grew up harboring the same burning ambition, to be rich any way they could.

Mary-Lou was a beauty, with the smooth porcelain skin of her mother and enormous slightly tilted eyes the color of speckled amber orchids. She wore her thick black hair in the traditional short Chinese bob. With her high cheekbones and delicate features, she had tried to become a movie star but had no talent for acting. She'd had plenty of offers to star in other kinds of movies, and with poverty beckoning, to tell the truth she'd been tempted. Lily had saved her from that and brought her into the business.

Mary-Lou had a modern apartment on the Bund, the smartest street in Shanghai overlooking the Huangpu River and lined with palatial office buildings, smart high-rise restaurants, chic bars and deluxe condos. The small apartment was on the third floor, the least expensive, but she had furnished it extravagantly with modern pieces imported from Italy. She shopped at the smartest boutiques for the latest European fashions and, unknown to Lily, secretly dealt in stolen jewelry.

Mary-Lou didn't believe in morals or scruples. She owed loyalty to no one. Not even Lily.

She followed Lily into the house. It was sparsely furnished with a hard-looking sofa, a couple of good elm-wood chairs and an antique altar table topped with a golden Buddha, with scented joss sticks burning in a cloisonné holder, and a sheaf of bronze chrysanthemums. There was also a framed picture of Lily's mother over the altar table, but no picture of her father.

Apart from the chairs and the altar table, there were few antiques in Lily's home. Her bedroom contained the only true classic—a

Chinese marriage bed lacquered a deep red, the color of success and of happiness. It was built into the wall with a wooden canopy and shutters, like a small room all to itself. And that's where, Mary-Lou knew, Lily slept alone. No man, she was sure, had ever penetrated past that bedroom door.

Mary-Lou helped Lily stack cartons of replica terra-cotta warriors in the cellar; then Lily sent her out on an errand. Mary-Lou guessed Lily wanted to be alone for the phone call. She got the feeling something was going on, and it did not include her. And she resented that.

WHEN the call came, Lily picked up the phone on the first ring.

"My client is very interested." The businessman's voice was firm and crisp. "He will need to see authentication."

"Age and authenticity can be proven, though obviously we need to use a discreet expert. One guaranteed to keep his mouth shut."

"That could be arranged. The next thing to discuss is price."

"Come to me with an offer," Lily said, hanging up. She wasn't about to dicker over money. It would take time, maybe months, but the businessman would come up with the right sum eventually. And it would be many millions of Swiss francs. Enough to set her free.

She walked to the very back of the cellar. It was dark, but she knew her way. She pressed the button hidden behind a beam, and a panel slid back exposing an old iron safe, the kind you had to spin-dial a special combination. She knew the numbers by heart, and the heavy door swung open. Amongst the sheafs of banknotes was a flat dark red jewel case. Lily walked into the light and opened it.

The necklace glowed back at her from its black velvet nest, the old jewels, emeralds, rubies and diamonds in their heavy gold setting. And the great pearl, shining like a living thing in the gloom. She put out a tentative finger and felt the shock of its coldness against her flesh. Quickly, she snatched back her hand.

Lily had had this necklace for only a few weeks. On her fortieth birthday, she had been paid a visit by a stranger, an elderly man, gray-bearded and dressed like a scholar in the old days, in a long gray gown over narrow trousers, a picture from another era.

"My name is Tai Lam," he told her. "I come as a friend of your mother."

Surprised, she invited him in; she served him tea, treating him as an honored guest. She told him she had not known her mother had any friends. He inclined his head gravely and said indeed that was the case.

"For most of her life your mother was a good woman," he said. "Only one time did she stoop to thievery, out of resentment because she could not obtain her parents' permission to marry." He offered the parcel he was clutching to Lily. "She asked me to give this to you when you turned forty years, to do with it whatever you wished. And then she told me how it came into her possession.

"The necklace belonged to her own mother, a Mrs. Arthur Hennessy of Paris. It was said her husband had bought it with a batch of antiques slipped into France via the melting pot of a postwar market, and though it came with a history attached, he had no real concept of its worth. He knew only that the stones were extraordinary, a fitting wedding gift for his wife.

"When their daughter—your mother—ran off with Henry Song, she stole the necklace. She never forgave herself for that, but she was too proud to give it back. And for all those years she hid it from her gambler husband. Finally, when she was ill and knew she might die, she came to me. 'Take this; keep it for my daughter, Lily,' she said. 'It's all I have to leave her, with a letter that tells its true history. But do not give it to her until she reaches forty years because only then will she be smart enough to not allow a man to steal it from her just because she thinks she is in love.' Your mother also left the letter for you. In it she tells the story that came with the necklace. It is the true history."

Listening to him, Lily had clasped the long red case to her chest. Tears had stung her eyes. Her mother had given her the only thing of value she possessed in the world.

Lily knew about her French family, the Hennessys, and that she had a cousin who, her mother had said, was called Precious Rafferty. But that was all.

Later, when she was alone, she had read the story of the necklace, painstakingly pieced together from the information her grandfather had discounted as some sort of fairy tale about the Dragon Lady Empress. She'd investigated further and found photographs and evidence. And now the notorious pearl was Lily's to do with as she wished. But it must be kept a secret. If the authorities found out about it, she would end up in jail.

MARY-LOU had several "little secrets," only one of which was dealing in stolen jewelry. Another was that she spied on Lily. And that morning when Lily sent her off on the errand, instead she followed her and hid in the cellar's shadows. She saw Lily press the button that revealed the iron safe.

Mary-Lou already knew all about that safe. She'd found out about it several months ago. Lurking in the cellar, she'd held her cell-phone camera as Lily dialed the numbers. Later, when Lily was out, she'd walked back down, past all the crates of plaster Qin Dynasty warriors and Maos and Buddhas. She dialed the combination, the safe opened, and its contents were hers.

Up until now it had contained only money. She'd realized she had found Lily's stolen stash, her profits from plundered antiquities. Mary-Lou was almost certain Lily never counted the neat bundles. Why should she, when she believed no one else knew about the hidden safe and its combination? Mary-Lou had helped herself plentifully over the months.

This morning, however, sensing something was going on, she again lifted her cell-phone camera. She took a photograph as Lily opened the case she removed from the safe, and was scarcely able to hold back a gasp when she saw what it contained.

She had never seen jewels like that: the massive emeralds, diamonds and rubies, and the pearl the size of a robin's egg. Where, she wondered, astonished, had Lily gotten her hands on it?

She stole silently back upstairs, her pulse throbbing with excitement, adrenaline flowing. The necklace must be worth a fortune. All you needed was the right buyer. Hah! Of course, that was the call Lily had been waiting for. She had a buyer in mind!

Mary-Lou hurried out onto the street, got in her little car and drove quickly away, her mind ticking over. It would be easy to steal the necklace, but first she needed to find a buyer.

The next day when Lily was out, Mary-Lou went down to the basement and opened up the safe. She took out the necklace, marveling at the weight and clarity of the jewels, and the size of the glowing white pearl. Her eyes opened even wider when she read Lily's note about the provenance.

The fact was that the necklace would give her the millions she needed for the good life she believed she deserved. It was worth any risk. And if Lily gave her any trouble, she would deal "appropriately" with her. Her only problem now was to find that buyer.

A FEW days later, Mary-Lou was coming out of the diamond cutter's office, on the second floor of a mean little building in a bad quarter, sandwiched between a cheap "massage parlor" and one of those half-hidden stores where gamblers came to buy lottery tickets, hoping for the big win.

The building was shuttered behind double steel gates, and the narrow street flickered with neon signs hung over tacky bars and teahouses that smelled of fried eels and sheeps' brains. Ragged men squatted on the sidewalks, smoking and staring into space.

Mary-Lou's perfect nose curled in disgust. She hated coming here. She knew she attracted attention with her exotic looks; that was why she always dressed down in jeans and a T-shirt, no jewelry, not even a watch. Even so, she feared for her car, small and cheap though it was. Nothing was safe on these streets, and it made her nervous, especially with what she had hidden in her pocket: two stolen diamonds each about four carats, now recut and untraceable. Using Lily's money, she had made a deal with the thieves, and now the diamonds were hers to sell.

Putting on her dark glasses, she stepped into the street. She had parked her car right outside the building, but now an old truck was parked in its place. She let out a howl of rage and swung round, glaring accusingly at the street bums. They glared back, laughing, and one spat at her.

She stepped back, disgusted, and felt her heel strike a foot. A man's arms snaked around her, and she screamed. Furious, she swung round and let the man holding her have it with a right to the face. The man caught her arm before the punch connected.

"Careful," he said. "You could hurt somebody like that."

Mary-Lou stared up at the best-looking man she had ever seen. Tall, broad-shouldered, rangy in that American way, dark-haired and with intense unsmiling blue eyes that linked sexily with her own. She knew who he was. Not long ago, the stories about the accidental death of his wealthy wife had dominated the media.

"I know you," she said, still scowling.

"And I would like to know you," he said. "That is if you promise not to keep on punching."

She looked in his eyes a long time. "Okay," she said finally.

He let go of her arm. "So what happened?"

"Someone stole my car."

He nodded. "I'm not surprised. They'd steal the teeth from your mouth around here. You should always bring a guard, let him stay with the car while you take care of business."

He did not ask her what that business might be, nor did she ask why he was there. Direct questions about why you were in this shady area were off-limits.

"My car's just down the street," he said. "How about I give you a lift; then you can contact the police, tell them the details."

"Much good it'll do," she said bitterly, making him laugh.

"Hey," he said. "It's only a car. I assume it was insured."

"Yes," she said gloomily, "but it'll be ages and mountains of paperwork before they settle. I know how they are, too."

"For such a beautiful woman, you're a true cynic," he said, motioning his guard to open the car door for her.

Mary-Lou got into the camouflage green Hummer. He got in the other side. "Where to?" he asked.

She turned to look at him, a long deep look. "To the nearest good bar," she said in her throaty whisper.

BENNETT Yuan took her to the Bar Rouge on the Bund, not far from where Mary-Lou lived. It was a chic modernist place with huge blowup photos of pouting red-lipsticked Asian beauties in red-lacquered frames screening the booths. Ruby red Venetian chandeliers spilled pink light, and the windows and terrace offered views of the Shanghai skyline.

He sat opposite, not next to her as she had expected, and she pouted prettily. "I can see you better this way," he explained. He looked her in the eyes, a long deep look that made Mary-Lou shiver right down to the pit of her belly. "You haven't yet told me your name," he said. "Or do you prefer to be anonymous?"

"It's Mary-Lou Chen. I've seen your name in the newspapers."

He shrugged, dismissively. "And what would you like to drink, Mary-Lou Chen?"

He summoned the waiter. "I'd like a glass of champagne," Mary-Lou decided, but Bennett ordered a bottle.

They sat in silence, still looking deep into each other's eyes, recognizing the possibility of what might happen between them, until the waiter reappeared with the champagne. He uncorked it expertly, filled two flutes and left them a dish of tiny biscuits.

Bennett Yuan picked up his glass. He lifted it to hers and said, "Here's to us, Mary-Lou Chen."

"Yes," she said, suddenly nervous. There was an intensity about him she had never encountered before. He was, she thought, a man who would always get what he wanted.

"So, tell me about yourself." Bennett leaned back, one arm spread along the top of the booth.

Suddenly disconnected from her eyes, he seemed to take on a different persona. More casual, comfortable. And so handsome Mary-Lou could see no flaw. His dark hair brushed smoothly back; those intense deep blue eyes under straight dark brows; a nose almost too perfect for a man; the square jaw and a wide firm mouth that made her wonder what it would feel like to kiss him.

She shook her short swinging bob of black hair, took a sip of champagne and began to talk about her work and about Lily.

"So, who is this Lily Song?" he asked, refilling her glass.

"An old school friend. She's always dealt in antiques, but mostly she makes and sells the tourist stuff. You know, the Mao memorabilia, the warriors, Buddhas."

"And is that profitable?"

"Some of it is," she said, peering at him from under her bangs. "Why are we talking so much about me anyway? I want to know all about you."

"There's not much to tell that I suspect you don't already know. I'm involved in the furniture components business." He shrugged impatiently, as though he disliked what he did for a living. "I'm based here in Shanghai, but I travel a lot."

"Maybe that's a good thing," she said, thinking about his dead wife, Ana Yuan. "Considering what happened . . ." He gave her a cold look, and she stopped. She drank down the champagne.

"And what are we going to do about your car?" Bennett said. She'd forgotten all about the car being stolen. He handed her his cell phone. "Here, better report it," he said.

Reporting it took longer than she'd thought, and by the time she was finished, so was a second bottle of champagne, and Mary-Lou was feeling deliciously woozy.

"I live just down the road," she said, inviting him with her eyes.

He nodded, understanding. He paid the waiter and took her arm. The guard was waiting with the Hummer, and they drove a few short blocks to Mary-Lou's building, not talking, thinking of what was to come.

Bennett eyed the modern skyscraper appreciatively. "Tell me, Mary-Lou Chen," he said, "how can a woman who sells copies of Mao and Buddha afford to live in a place like this?"

She smiled at him as the elevator took them up. "That's because

I'm a clever woman. Or hadn't you noticed?" She opened the door, and they went in.

"I was too busy noticing how beautiful you are," he said, shutting the door behind him and grabbing her close. "You feel like soft Chinese silk," he murmured, kissing her left ear. "And you smell spicy, of ginger flowers and sandalwood." He was kissing her throat, then moving up to her lips. "And your mouth tastes of champagne," he said, drinking her in until she could hardly breathe.

Pushing him away, she took his hand and led him to a bedroom with poppy red walls, sweeping red silk curtains and a king-sized bed with a black silk spread.

IN THE next few weeks, when she wasn't thinking about Bennett Yuan, Mary-Lou was thinking about the necklace. It was the answer to all her prayers—if she ever prayed that is. The problem was to find a buyer rich enough to pay what she wanted. She didn't know the international superrich; they moved in a different world from hers.

She stood at the window of her apartment, smoking a cigarette and staring at the busy barge traffic on the river, thinking she was okay as a "girlfriend" to a rich man, but no one had ever mentioned marriage. Rich men simply didn't marry girls like her. They forged alliances. Money married money, especially in China.

Bennett Yuan was different, though. She'd heard that when the Yuans' daughter had married Bennett, the wealthy family had insisted he change his name to theirs, so that their "dynasty" would continue through their children. She'd seen the pictures of Bennett's wife on TV. Ana Yuan was a plain young woman, and of course rumors abounded that the handsome young American had married her for her money.

Nothing wrong with that, Mary-Lou thought. But again, so rumor had it, the Yuans had Ana's money tied up in a family trust, and after Ana's death, all the money and property, including the lavish marital apartment in one of Shanghai's most exclusive towers, reverted back to the family.

Bennett had not inherited a penny. He had told Mary-Lou that he'd loved his wife and was devastated by her tragic death. But Bennett was on his own now, and he was definitely not a rich man. In fact Bennett was like her: a "soldier of fortune," a good-looking man who believed he was entitled to the good life, whichever way he could get it. He would marry another heiress, she was sure of that. And she was just as sure he would not marry her.

She scowled with frustration as she stubbed out her cigarette. She wanted two things from life. She wanted Bennett. And she wanted to sell the necklace and get rich. Somehow the two were tied together . . . the necklace and Bennett.

The answer came to her suddenly. *Of course!* Bennett knew wealthy businesspeople, not only in China, but also abroad. He was the perfect candidate to help her find a buyer. It would mean she would have to part with fifty percent of the profit. . . . Another idea struck her, and this time she smiled. She knew how to get exactly the two things she wanted. Bennett *and* the money.

She laughed at how clever—how *simple*—her plan was. Bennett would find a buyer, and she would steal the necklace from the safe. *But* she would not hand it over unless he married her first. Then he'd sell it, and they'd both be rich.

Pleased with her plan, she called Bennett and arranged to meet at seven at the Cloud 9 bar atop the Grand Hyatt hotel, across the river in the business section called Pudong.

MARY-LOU drove through the tunnel that connected the two districts in her new red Mini Cooper. She handed over the car to the valet and entered the imposing Jin Mao Tower, the world's third tallest building. Taking the high-speed elevator to the very top, she emerged into the glittering art deco bar with its stunning view over all Shanghai, so high in the sky that the clouds hovered outside the very windows. Hence the bar's name, Cloud 9.

Looking around, she didn't see Bennett, so she took a seat at a booth and ordered a vodka martini. She sipped the drink and was thinking about her tactics when she saw Bennett enter the bar and speak to the pretty hostess, who smiled engagingly as she escorted him to the table. Bennett gave the girl that deep, very personal smile back, and it irritated the hell out of Mary-Lou.

"Sorry I'm late," Bennett slid into the booth opposite. He didn't kiss her or reach for her hand, merely gave her a tired smile.

Mary-Lou waited until he'd ordered a Jack Daniel's on the rocks. "I have a secret," she said, looking him in the eye.

"I'll bet you do. I just hope it doesn't concern me." He lit a cigarette without offering her one, and she frowned. Something was wrong.

"I just might not tell you," she said.

"So okay, don't," he said. "It's a safe way to keep a secret."

"Ah, but it's something you would be very pleased to know." Unable to contain herself any longer, she laid her cell phone on the table between them. "Check out the photograph," she said.

Sighing, Bennett picked up the phone and pressed the button. A picture of the necklace appeared on the screen. He looked at it for a few moments, then clicked off the phone and handed it back to her. "So?" he asked, sitting back and sipping his bourbon.

Mary-Lou put her elbows on the table and leaned closer. "That necklace is the real thing," she said softly. "Not only does it have jewels worth a fortune, it has a provenance discriminating international buyers will be prepared to pay a premium for." She recounted the history of the Dragon Lady Empress's famous pearl. "I can get my hands on it right now, but first I need a buyer. And that, my darling Bennett, is where you come in." A triumphant smile lit her lovely face as she sat back, looking at him.

He looked coldly back at her. "I'm guessing the necklace is stolen. Are you asking me to become a fence, Mary-Lou?"

"Not a fence. A partner. I have the goods; you get the buyer." She would not tell him the third part of the equation—marriage— until the buyer was ready and eager to hand over his money.

Bennett lifted his shoulder in a casual shrug. "I don't need this kind of deal. I have my own business to run."

She had made it her own business to find out about Bennett's "business." The Yuans had set him up exporting furniture components, but with the end of his marriage that too was drying up.

"Bennett, this necklace could make both of us very rich. You would never have to think of furniture again."

He finished his drink in one gulp and signaled the waiter for another. Bennett thought Mary-Lou was beautiful. She was sexy and amusing, but for him she had been an exciting temporary diversion. But it was time to move on, and tonight he'd planned on telling her that. Now she had come up with this scheme that appealed to him, though he doubted its veracity. "Exactly *who* has this necklace?"

"I can't tell you that."

He glanced up, brows raised. "You mean you expect me to sell jewels for you without knowing where they come from? How do I know you're not going to kill someone to get your hands on that necklace?"

Her amber-speckled eyes turned cold. "I will," she said. "If I have to."

Bennett sat back, looking at her. "I wouldn't work with you without knowing the whereabouts of the necklace."

"I can't tell you that." She was stubborn, but he knew she was softening.

He reached across the table for her hand. "Look, sweetheart," he said in the patronizing tone she knew well from other "rich" men who'd dumped her for the next pretty girl, "you're asking me to put myself in possible legal jeopardy without knowing the facts. Get real. Tell me what's what, or let's just say, 'Good-bye, it was fun while it lasted.' Right now."

Tears swam in those beautiful eyes, just as he'd known they would. "Don't say that," she whispered. "Please don't say that, Bennett."

He sat back with an indifferent shrug. "You ask too much," he said, summoning the waiter for the check.

He heard her take a deep quavering breath. Then, "It's my partner, Lily," she admitted. "She has the necklace. It's been in her family for generations. I don't know how, or why she has it now. She didn't before; otherwise she would have sold it. I know she's looking for a buyer though."

Bennett thought about Lily, the woman Mary-Lou had implied she was prepared to kill if she had to. He wondered whether he might not be better off with Lily than with Mary-Lou. After all, Lily had the necklace legitimately. It was worth exploring.

"I'd like to meet Lily," he said, paying the check and adding a generous tip. "I need to know exactly who we're dealing with, if we are to be in business together." He got up from the table and held out his hand. "Come on, partner," he said, "let's call Lily and take her out to dinner."

LILY was in her peaceful courtyard garden, feeding the goldfish. The gentle slide of water over the smooth copper surface of the wall fountain was the only sound, until the phone rang. Resentful, she thought for a moment of not answering it, but then she checked and saw it was Mary-Lou. Sighing, she pressed the talk button.

"I don't want to discuss business," she said abruptly. "Can't it wait until tomorrow?"

"Oh, Lily, I don't want to talk business. It's just that I'm with someone special, someone I want you to meet. . . ."

Mary-Lou's voice was sugary-sweet, and Lily guessed whoever this special "someone" was, he was standing right next to her. "Can't it wait?" she asked, thinking of a cool glass of wine and the trickle of the fountain and the little canary who always sang so charmingly when she came to sit near him in his bamboo cage. Then all thoughts of desecrated tombs, and of the wrath of her ancestors, would slide temporarily to the back of her mind.

"We want to take you to dinner. Come on, Lily, it's important."

To you it is, Lily thought, but Mary-Lou sounded excited, as though she needed her approval. And after all, she was her friend. "Oh, all right," she sighed, "just tell me where and when."

"The Italian restaurant at the Grand Hyatt, in half an hour."

"Forty-five minutes," Lily said, thinking of the traffic.

In fact it was an hour, and they were already seated at a discreet table, half-hidden behind a screen, waiting for her. Lily had chosen to wear a jade green knee-length cheongsam that showed off her pretty legs, and she carried a vintage embroidered satin bag. She looked cool and self-assured, neither of which she was feeling. She was wishing she had not bothered to dress up and battle the traffic all the way to Pudong just to meet Mary-Lou's latest beau.

Bennett got to his feet as she approached. He had no doubt Lily Song was a tough cookie, but he'd never yet met a woman who didn't fall for his special brand of charm.

"Lily," he said, smiling into her eyes. "Mary-Lou has talked about you so much I feel I already know you, but I must confess I didn't expect you to be so beautiful."

She raised a skeptical dark eyebrow, studying him as he held her hand slightly longer than necessary. A professional charmer, she thought, and just the sort of guy Mary-Lou would fall for.

Mary-Lou was watching them anxiously, thinking Lily was probably the only woman in Shanghai who did not recognize Bennett Yuan. But then Lily rarely watched TV or bothered with the news.

"This is Bennett Yuan," she said, and saw the flutter of response that crossed Lily's face. It seemed she was wrong, and even Lily had heard of the tragic death of Ana Yuan.

"Good evening, Mr. Yuan." Removing her hand from his, Lily glanced sideways and caught Mary-Lou's eye, wondering what she was doing with the newly widowed Bennett.

"Bennett's the man who helped me when my car was stolen," Mary-Lou said. "Remember, I told you?"

"Ah, yes, I remember."

The waiter arrived with the menus and began to tell them the night's specials, and the talk turned to food. After that, though, Bennett put himself out to be amusing: He asked Lily about the French Concession, saying he enjoyed its Colonial history.

"So do I," Lily said. "Especially since my mother was French. That is, her parents were American and Austrian, but she was born and brought up in Paris and considered herself a Frenchwoman."

Bennett had ordered a bottle of Chianti. The waiter filled their glasses, and Lily took a sip. She noticed that for some reason Mary-Lou was watching Bennett like a hunting dog, while he was Mr. Cool, talking about Shanghai and Paris and New York.

"Since your mother lived in Paris, you must know the city well," he said, but Lily said she had never been there, and then she found herself telling him about how her mother had run away from her family to marry Henry Song.

"*Not* great thinking," she added with a grim smile. "She should have stuck with the Hennessys. She told me they were very rich. There was Grandmother's castle in Austria and fabulous old furniture and paintings, and of course the antiques store. Too bad she gave it all up."

"And is it all still there?" Bennett toyed with his grilled branzino. "The antiques store? And the castle?"

"I believe so. Hennessy Antiques, it was called. My mother had a sister, with a daughter younger than I, Mother said. All the aunts and uncles were rich, too, and I imagine they left my cousin the family money, and probably Grandmother's Austrian castle." She gave Bennett a knowing glance. "Her name's Precious Rafferty. Maybe you should go visit her next time you're in Paris. I've heard you're keen to know women with money."

Mary-Lou gave her a furious kick under the table, but Bennett laughed and said what was the point of knowing people "without"? "I can tell you and I are alike, Lily," he said admiringly. "On our own and determined to get on in life."

"To get rich," Lily said, lifting her glass in a toast to Mary-Lou and their old mantra. Bennett lifted his glass, too, thinking that the only words she should have added were "at any cost." Desperate though he was to make money, the idea of dealing in stolen jewels did not appeal. His thoughts turned instead to Paris and the rich Hennessy granddaughter, the one who had inherited all the money, as well as the castle. An heiress was more his style.

Claiming she was tired, Lily left before dessert. She thanked Bennett, who again held her hand too long. He said he hoped they could get together again, and then Mary-Lou insisted on walking her to the door.

"Well?" she asked, eyes glowing. "What do you think?"

"He's Ana Yuan's widower, and I think he's dating awfully early after her tragic death, if you want the truth. Which," she added, looking at her friend's furious face, "I suspect you do not."

"He can't be expected to just sit home. A man like that, he needs a woman—"

"I'm sure he does. But, do you need a man like Bennett?" And with that Lily stepped into the elevator and was gone.

Mary-Lou flounced back to the table, where Bennett had paid the check and was ready to leave. She'd expected them to linger over drinks and coffee, but he seemed in a hurry.

He dropped her off in front of her apartment with only the briefest kiss and said he was tired and needed sleep.

"But we need to talk," she said desperately.

"Not tonight. I'll call you," he said, and he got in the car and, with a wave, drove off.

She watched his Hummer weave into the busy traffic along the Bund, feeling suddenly very much alone.

The next day, he didn't call. Nor the day after that. And when she called him, there was no answer. A week went by, and Mary-Lou did not know what to think. He was her only hope. And besides, she was in love with him.

Three

Paris

PRESHY was happy. Daria was visiting Paris with her professor husband, on business, and though Tom couldn't make it, she was looking forward to seeing her friend for dinner. Sylvie could not make it either, because of course she had her restaurant to run.

So it was on with the little black dress again, and the diamonds. Late, as always, Preshy ran down the steps to her shop, checked the blue alarm light, then dashed off.

They were meeting at La Coupole, the most Parisian of brasseries. Opened in the twenties, it was large and lofty with massive pillars wonderfully painted by Montparnasse artists. With its colorful murals, art deco lights, red banquettes, a famous bar and crammed rows of tables with white cloths, it was usually jammed with a hodgepodge of actors, politicians, publishing types, models and tourists.

It was eight o'clock, still early for Parisians, and the place was half-empty. Daria and Preshy were shown to one of the tables lined up against the wall and so close to each other you could eavesdrop on every word spoken by your neighbors. Daria ordered fish, and Preshy the *steak frites*. They were sitting contentedly sipping red wine, enjoying a catch-up conversation about life and family and friends in Boston, when Daria nudged her.

"Just look what's coming our way," she said under her breath.

Preshy followed her gaze, and then she saw him. Tall and dark and handsome as an Armani model, the man of every woman's dreams. And at that instant he turned his head and looked at her, and his eyes seemed to collide with hers. It was as though he was absorbing her deep into their blueness, drinking her in. A shiver ran down Preshy's spine as she finally dragged her eyes away.

The maître d' was showing him to a table across from them, but then she heard him say, "No, this one will do." And he came and sat at the table next to her.

She sipped her wine, not looking at him, but little electric signals seemed to pass between them. He was so close she could have reached out and touched him.

"*Bonsoir, mesdames,*" he said, acknowledging them, the way the polite French did when they were at close quarters in a restaurant, but she could tell from his accent he was American.

"*Bonsoir, m'sieur,*" they replied, just as their food arrived.

"Pardon me," the stranger said, "I don't mean to intrude, but I don't know what to order here, and what you're eating looks awfully good. Can you tell me what it is?"

Since it was quite obviously steak and fries, Preshy slid him an amused sideways look. She swept her long coppery-blond curls flirtatiously back over her shoulder, thinking what a stroke of luck she was wearing her good little black dress.

"Hi, I'm Bennett James," the handsome stranger said. "I'm in Paris on business."

"Where are you from?" Preshy asked.

"Shanghai." He frowned. "It's a long way."

"Shanghai?" she said, surprised. "I have a cousin there. I've never met her, but her name is Lily Song."

Bennett James shrugged. "Shanghai's a big city," he said. "And your name is?"

"Precious Rafferty." She blushed as she said it, and she added quickly, "But when I was nine, I cut it down to Preshy."

"I don't blame you," he said, and they all laughed. Then Preshy introduced Daria, who definitely recommended the *steak frites*, so he ordered that and a bottle of red wine, and they got to talking about Boston and Paris. They only talked a little bit about Shanghai, though. Bennett did say that he ran a big export business and was in Paris to recruit new management to help him out.

He sipped his wine, and his eyes locked with Preshy's again, and again there was that electric jolt of attraction.

She felt Daria's elbow in her ribs, and there was a grin on Daria's face as she said, "Sorry, my darling, but I'm running late. I promised Tom I'd be back at the hotel by nine." She gathered up her bag and her pale-blue blazer and slid out from the banquette.

"You're leaving me alone with him," Preshy whispered, as Daria bent to kiss her good-bye.

"You betcha," Daria whispered back.

Bennett James got to his feet. "So nice to have met you, Daria," he said, holding her hand in both of his.

She nodded. "Enjoy the rest of your stay in Paris." With a wave she strode away through the now-crowded tables.

Preshy felt the hot flush of panic up her spine; she was alone with a man she had only just met and whom she fancied strongly. She felt his eyes on her and turned to meet them. In the silence it was as though he had touched her. Finally he said, "Have you ever taken the sightseeing boat on the Seine?"

She shook her head. "Only tourists do that."

He grinned. "Then be a tourist with me. We could see Paris by night from the river. Could anything be more beautiful?" He reached out, took her hand.

"I'll do it," she breathed.

"Good!" He signaled the waiter for the check and insisted on paying hers and Daria's, too. "I'm just glad I met you," he said, giving her that all-enveloping look again.

IN THE taxi on the way to the Pont de l'Alma, Bennett kept a discreet distance between them, filling in the silence that had fallen by asking Preshy questions about her life in Paris. The taxi finally squealed to a halt at the *quai,* and he hurried her to the sleek, brightly lit *Bateau Mouche.*

As the glass-topped boat slid smoothly down the river, Bennett led the way to a seat in the bow. The boat's floodlights lit up the magical scene as they glided under Paris's loveliest bridges, illuminating in turn magnificent public buildings and gilded monuments; the white dome of the Sacré-Coeur; the massive buttresses and towering gargoyle-topped finials of Notre-Dame.

Preshy had never seen Paris from this angle before, and she was dazzled. "It's breathtaking," she murmured, instinctively reaching for his hand. Then as the boat slid silently into the darkness under a bridge, he leaned in and kissed her. Preshy's lips trembled under his. The kiss was not passionate, rather filled with a questioning tenderness. Bennett James seemed to know not to rush things; he seemed to be holding back, taking his time with her, letting her get used to the newness of it.

Still enchanted by the magic of Paris and by their kiss, they took a taxi to the Café Deux Magots, just around the corner from

Preshy's shop on the boulevard St. Germain, and sat over a glass of champagne, talking and watching the street performers on the cobbled square, the acrobats and the jugglers, while a solitary guitarist played out-of-tune flamenco music, making them laugh. And then later Bennett walked her back to the rue Jacob.

They stood in the courtyard, facing each other. He took both her hands, and again Preshy felt that electric connection between them. She studied his lean finely sculpted face; he was without doubt the most beautiful man she had ever seen.

"I don't know when I've enjoyed Paris so much," Bennett said. "Thank you for a wonderful evening." He hesitated. "Would you give me your phone number?"

Preshy scrambled in her purse for a business card. Of course she couldn't find one, so she wrote her name and number with a lip pencil on a tissue and handed it to him.

He shook his head, smiling. "What kind of businesswoman doesn't have her card handy?"

"I'm not such a hotshot businesswoman; I just happen to love antiques."

He nodded, then put a finger gently to her lips. "I'll call," he said; then he turned and strode out onto the street.

AT TEN the next morning, the phone rang. Preshy pounced on it, hoping it was him, yet surprised when it was.

"Preshy, it's Bennett."

"Ohhh . . . Bennett, hi . . . how are you?" Pulling her wits together, she said, "I hope you slept well," then wished she hadn't because it sounded as though she'd been thinking about him—which she had, but she didn't want him to know that.

"Not very," he said. "I was too busy thinking about you."

This time words escaped her completely.

"Listen, Preshy, I'm returning to Shanghai tomorrow. Will you have dinner with me tonight?"

"Tonight? Why, yes, I'd love to."

"Tell me where, and I'll make a reservation," he said.

Preshy thought quickly. "No, I'll make the reservation," she said.

She would take him to Verlaine. Sylvie would keep an eye on her. She wouldn't let her get into any trouble.

Verlaine was one of those small storefront bistros in a narrow tree-lined street near the church of St. Sulpice. Its walls were lined with faded silvery mirrors that reflected the rosy lamplight as though through a fog, and dark green taffeta curtains swept across the windows. Everything else was very simple: pale green linens, sturdy gilt chairs with green cushions. A great bouquet of field flowers that looked fresh-picked from some sunny meadow greeted you as you walked in. And the fact that Sylvie used only what was seasonal and fresh in the market, combined with her true talent as a chef, kept her customers coming back.

Sylvie was small and round and gamine-cute, with merry brown eyes, short black hair and a temper when she was crossed. Which, in her job as chef and owner of the Bistro Verlaine, meant a good deal of the time. Sous-chefs were the bane of her life. Every dish turned out at Verlaine had to be perfect: perfect ingredients perfectly prepared and perfectly presented.

They arrived at eight-thirty, windblown and a little wet from a sudden rainsquall. "Welcome, welcome," Sylvie said, greeting them in her chef's whites. A flushed, smiling Preshy introduced Bennett.

Sylvie put them at a corner table, told them there was no choice and that she was in charge of dinner, sent over a chilled bottle of Heidsieck Rosé Sauvage Champagne and an *amuse-bouche* of curried crab, then went back to her kitchen.

As she sent out the first course of lobster ravioli, she peeked round the door. They were sitting close together on the banquette, holding hands. Humph! This looked serious.

"She's a fabulous chef," Bennett said later, taking Preshy's hand and lifting it to his lips. Their glance smoldered.

"You're taking my breath away," she murmured, releasing her hand. "I think I need more wine."

"Will it bring back your breath?" he asked as he filled her glass with the chilled Brouilly Sylvie had recommended.

"I confess, I don't want it back." She smiled at him. "I kind of like being breathless," she said, then tucked into the moist, tender Bresse chicken that tasted the way no other chicken in the entire world did.

"Everything all right?" Sylvie asked, passing by.

"Sylvie, this food is . . ." Bennett seemed stumped for words. "I've never eaten anything so good in all my life."

Sylvie beamed. "I'll welcome you anytime," she assured him, and then, while they ate a small but perfect salad, followed by a selection of impeccable cheeses, she went back to her kitchen and prepared a light egg custard topped with meltingly soft egg whites whipped with sugar, then shaped with a tablespoon into "islands" that she "floated" on the custard, finished with a dusting of crushed pralines.

"Floating islands," Bennett exclaimed when she presented it. "It almost sounds Chinese. I might have to abduct you, Sylvie."

They laughed, and glancing at Preshy who was gazing admiringly at Bennett, Sylvie was glad to see her so happy. And the man couldn't take his eyes off her.

Later Sylvie sat with them as they lingered over coffee. Finally Bennett glanced regretfully at his watch. He said they had to go, and they left in a flurry of good-night kisses and promises to return. As soon as they'd gone, Sylvie was on the phone to Daria.

"Well?" Daria said.

"It's too late; she's sunk."

"Is it that bad?"

"He seems too good to be true. The only flaw is the Shanghai bit. Six thousand miles is a long way."

"They could always find a way around that," Daria said, then laughed. "Listen to us, talking like a pair of old matchmakers, and Preshy's only known him twenty-four hours."

"Maybe it's enough," Sylvie said, remembering how they had looked at each other.

"DID you really enjoy it?" Preshy asked as they strolled hand in hand through little side streets back to the rue Jacob.

"I thought it was wonderful." Bennett was looking at her. Raindrops misted her hair, and her eyes had an underwater aquamarine quality. "But I was happy just to be with you," he added.

She squeezed his hand, smiling. "Me, too," she said shyly.

Ignoring the rain, they stopped to look in the illuminated shopwindows, criticizing the paintings in the many galleries and admiring the antiques and clothing boutiques. When they finally found themselves back in the courtyard, Preshy asked if he would like to come up for a nightcap, which of course sounded like a ploy, because it was. She wasn't about to let him get away tonight.

Bennett followed her in, looking around at the pleasant place she had made home. He helped her off with her wet jacket, removed his own, then took her in his arms.

"No nightcaps," he murmured, pushing her wet curls behind her ears. "It's just us, Preshy . . . you and me." She twined her arms around his neck. "But I don't want to hurry you."

"You're not hurrying me." Her lips were a mere breath away from his.

As they kissed, she was melting into him, into the scent of him, the feel of his mouth on hers, his body against hers. She had never felt this wondrous emotion before, never known that wanting someone could be like this, where all you wanted to do was give yourself.

Bennett picked her up and carried her into the bedroom for what Preshy knew was to be the defining moment of her life.

As DAWN broke, she fell into an exhausted slumber. She did not hear Bennett get up, shower, put on his clothes and walk into the living room. He stood for a few minutes looking out the window, a frown on his face as he thought how to play this game out.

He turned and scanned the array of photographs on the shelves by the fireplace. He picked up one he guessed was Preshy's rich aunt, resplendent in scarlet chiffon in Monte Carlo. He studied her face for a few minutes; then his eye was taken by the wedding picture of Grandfather Hennessy and his bride in her traditional

Austrian dirndl. And a jeweled necklace with a single giant pearl. He looked at it for a long time. So Mary-Lou was right. He put the photo in his pocket and went back into the bedroom.

Preshy heard Bennett speak her name. He was sitting on the edge of the bed, fully dressed, looking at her. "I have a flight to catch," he said. He took her chin in his hand, tilting her face up to him. "You know I'll be back," he said gently.

She nodded, suddenly numb with fear that he might not be.

"Preshy, I mean it. I'll be back for you." He leaned in and kissed her gently; then he got up and walked to the door. He turned to look at her one last time, her eyes round and sad. "Soon," he said.

And then he was gone. Thousands of miles away, to Shanghai.

TEN days later, true to his promise, he walked unannounced into Preshy's store, laughing at her stunned expression when she swung round and saw him there. And within minutes it was as though he had never been away.

He gave her his cell-phone number and his e-mail address, and he returned every ten days or so after that. In two months they saw each other six times. But, Preshy thought, it was as if they had known each other forever.

They talked endlessly, and there was nothing Bennett didn't know about her and, she was sure, nothing she didn't know about him. She knew about his past lovers—not as many as she had expected. She knew how he felt about food, exercise and travel, world events and movies and books. She also knew about his childhood.

Bennett told her he had been abandoned by his single mother when he was five and spent his childhood years in New Hampshire, in a home for boys. "I never saw her again. As for my father, I don't even know who he was," he said, a coldness in his eyes. "You don't make friends in an environment like that. All you want to do is get out. I won a scholarship to Dartmouth, and now I'm so busy making money, trying to eliminate those years of poverty, I'm always on the move, so there's no time for real friendships or for any close relationships." He smiled ruefully. "Until you, Preshy."

She was in love with the romance of it all: in love with their partings when he went away and called her to say, Good night, sleep well, regardless of the time difference; in love with their reunions when he came back to Paris, back to rue Jacob, to her waiting arms. She shared everything with him, the stories of her life, of her family; of Grandfather Hennessy and rich Aunt Grizelda; of her parents and the little she knew about Grandfather's other granddaughter, Lily, who lived in Shanghai and whom she had never met.

She bought him gifts: a rare edition of John Donne's poems that seemed to say all there was to say about passion and love; a silly key ring with the Eiffel Tower on it—"to remind you of Paris and me." And he arrived with champagne and flowers and took her to stay at a vast château made over into a hotel, where they dined like royalty surrounded by servants.

How could romance not bloom, Preshy asked herself, lying in a silk-draped seventeenth-century bed in a vast gilded room with the moon outside the window bathing the gardens and parkland. And the beautiful sleeping man next to her.

As though he felt her gaze, Bennett's eyes flew open. "Preshy," he said sleepily, "I don't think I can live without you. Will you please marry me?"

In love with the moment, the romance, the place, Preshy didn't hesitate. "Yes," she said, and covered his face with kisses.

"When?" he demanded.

"Right now," she said, laughing. Then, "Oh, but I can't. First I have to tell Aunt Grizelda."

"Don't worry about Aunt Grizelda," Bennett said. "I'll go to Monte Carlo and ask her for your hand in marriage."

THE next day, he took her to the restaurant Jules Verne high atop the Eiffel Tower, where over champagne and oysters he solemnly presented her with a ring, an antique cushion-cut diamond surrounded by smaller diamonds. He put it on her finger while the other diners applauded with encouraging cries of "Bravo."

What, Preshy wondered, as she looked at her diamond engagement ring sparkling like the lights of Paris spread out before them, could be more romantic than this?

"We'll live here," he decided. "I'll commute from Shanghai, but I'll get home as often as I can." His eyes devoured her, sending tingles through places she hadn't known could tingle. "And tomorrow I'll ask your aunt Grizelda if she will hand you over to me. I hope she'll approve." He looked suddenly doubtful.

She laughed. "Of course she will; you can't fail," she said.

THE penthouse in Monte Carlo that the two widows and old friends, Grizelda von Hoffenberg, the aristocrat, and Mimi Moskowitz, the ex-showgirl, called home was like a movie set from the 1930s, white on white with chrome and silver accents. A wall of windows overlooking the bay was lined with voile curtains. Shaggy white rugs were flung across pale limestone floors, and oversized sofas were covered in white brocade. There were glass consoles and chrome-legged glass coffee tables, mirrored tables and cabinets.

There were flowers everywhere because Grizelda said she couldn't live without them. There were always roses—white or palest pink—and swags of blossoming cherry or lilies. And of course there was Mimi's teacup-sized Yorkie, called Lalah, and Grizelda's miniature poodle, Schnuppi.

Today, because Preshy was bringing her new boyfriend, Grizelda had gone all out, with enough flowers, Mimi said, to stock a florist shop. Jeanne and Maurice, the couple who had worked for them for twenty-five years and who Grizelda and Mimi considered "family," had prepared a special dinner, setting the smaller round dining table with the Vietri china and Christofle silverware.

"We have to make a good impression," Grizelda said to Mimi, tweaking the centerpiece of white gardenias floating in a crystal bowl. "It's not the first time Preshy's brought a boyfriend home, but it's the first time I've heard her sound like this."

"High on love," Mimi said with a grin.

"What do you think? Do we look intimidating enough?"

Grizelda was wearing a white Saint-Laurent pantsuit with a gold necklace and an armload of gold bracelets. Her red hair waved over one eye, exactly like the fifties movie actress Rita Hayworth.

"We look as good as the Lord and expensive plastic surgeons can make us," Mimi said crisply. She was wearing silver gray, a simple dress that skimmed her knees and fluttered over her ample bosom. Diamonds dangled from her ears.

"I really got the feeling from Preshy this is important," Grizelda said. "What if he's The One?"

"Then we just have to hope he passes the von Hoffenberg–Moskowitz test."

"And if he doesn't?"

"She'll probably end up with him anyway. And you'll cut her out of your will."

"She's not in my will, you know that. And so does Preshy. Of course I'll leave her my jewelry, but apart from that she can make her own way in the world."

Jeanne came in to light the dozens of gardenia-scented votive candles. "Everything's ready, madame," she said, in French. They always spoke French in this household.

"Bien, merci, Jeanne." Grizelda smiled.

Right then the concierge called to say they were on their way up. Followed by the bouncing dogs, the women hurried into the foyer, staring expectantly as the elevator door opened. And there they were; Preshy, casual as always in jeans and a white linen shirt, her big eyes smiling, wild gold hair tumbled from the wind. And Bennett James, knockout handsome in a blue shirt, a dark blue blazer, immaculately pressed pants and soft suede loafers.

Grizelda thought if first impressions were anything to go by, this was a winner. And Mimi thought he was too good to be true.

Bennett smiled warmly as Preshy introduced him. He said how pleased he was to meet them. He patted the excited Lalah, who was jumping up at him, and said how beautiful Schnuppi was, and that she was obviously shyer because she was keeping a wary distance.

They took him to the silvery white living room, wafted in on the scent of flowers and votives, and he exclaimed at its beauty and at the way the voile curtains softened the light. "Like a Matisse painting," he said, accepting a glass of champagne.

Maurice had poured the champagne, and now Jeanne came in with a tray of hors d'oeuvres. Preshy went to hug them, then introduced them to Bennett, who said he was happy to meet anybody who'd known Preshy for twenty years and maybe they had some true-life stories to tell him. They all laughed, and Grizelda took a seat on the white brocade sofa with Schnuppi, and Lalah snuggled on Mimi's knee on the sofa opposite.

Grizelda patted the sofa and said, "Come sit here, Bennett, why don't you, and tell us all about yourself."

"There's not that much to tell." He glanced at Preshy on the tufted white ottoman. "Not really much more than, no doubt, you've heard from Preshy already."

"In fact we heard nothing, only that you live in Shanghai."

"I do. And unfortunately, it's a long way from Paris."

"And what exactly do you do there, Bennett?"

Jeanne offered him the tray of hors d'oeuvres, and he took a small square of *socca,* the chickpea pancake with goat cheese and black olive that was a specialty of the Nice area.

"I own James Exports. Actually, I manufacture parts for the furniture business in the U.S. We make components that are assembled in North Carolina by the major companies."

"And is that profitable?" Mimi asked, looking as innocent as she could while obviously trying to find out his worth.

"Profitable enough," he replied, smiling.

"You needn't worry; I think I know everything there is to know about him," Preshy said, taking a sip of her champagne.

"Well, we certainly don't," Mimi said. "I'd like to know what you think of our girl, Bennett."

He gave her that long intimate look that endeared him to women. "I think your girl is wonderful, Mimi. In fact the reason I'm here is that I very much want to make her my girl. I've come to ask your permission, Aunt Grizelda, Mimi, to marry Precious."

"Oh my Lord." Grizelda hadn't really expected things to move this fast. She glanced at her niece. "And what does Preshy say?"

"I've said yes, of course." Preshy could contain herself no longer. She stuck out her left hand with the sparkling diamond. "But Bennett insisted on asking your permission."

Grizelda and Mimi leapt up to examine the ring, sending the dogs yapping. Grizelda's eyes met Mimi's: The ring was just small enough for good taste and just big enough to be expensive. They were thinking the same thing. That they loved the old-fashioned touch of a man asking permission to marry their beloved girl; that he was the right age, good-looking, charming, cultured and apparently well enough off.

"As long as you love each other, I couldn't wish for anyone better," Grizelda said, and Bennett got up and kissed her on both cheeks. Then he kissed Mimi. And then he kissed Preshy.

Later, over dinner, Grizelda said thoughtfully, "Would you prefer, I wonder, to have the wedding here or in Paris?"

"Neither." Preshy stroked Lalah, who was on her lap, hiding under the tablecloth, hoping for handouts. "I want to be married in Venice, at the Santa Maria della Salute. You know it has special memories for me. And we want to be married as soon as possible."

Grizelda looked doubtful. "Arrangements have to be made—the dress, the flowers, the invitations . . ."

"Next month," Preshy said firmly. "And we're leaving it all to you, darling Aunt G. Just tell us when, and we'll show up."

"Where will you live? Not in Shanghai, I hope?" Mimi said.

"We'll live in Paris, and Bennett will commute to Shanghai."

"That's a hefty commute," Grizelda commented.

"Don't worry," Bennett said. "I won't leave Preshy alone long enough to get lonely."

"It couldn't be more perfect, could it?" Preshy said contentedly, lifting up Lalah and kissing her sweet black nose.

THERE was no time to be lost, and Grizelda plunged headfirst into the wedding arrangements. First she had to use all her influence, rounding up people she knew in Venice to get permission for the wedding to take place at the Basilica. Then she had to call the Hotel Cipriani, where she had stayed many times over the years, to arrange for the celebration dinner and for the wedding cake.

She also called in a few favors and managed to rent the fourteenth-century Palazzo Rendino on the Grand Canal, where the bridal party would stay. She had a fight with Preshy on the phone about the wedding dress because Preshy refused to wear white. But she was flying to Paris to sort that out.

Meanwhile, there were the flowers to be taken care of, and right now she was driving along the precipitous Grande Corniche road, heading for the flower market in Nice. She'd been using the same man there for years and trusted him completely. She'd ask him to order those marvelous huge cabbage roses imported all the way from Colombia and to come personally to Venice to decorate the church and the reception, as well as do the bouquets.

With everything down to three weeks, she was as tight with nerves as if she were getting married herself.

Today the morning was blue and clear, the way it so often was in the South of France at the end of October. And without the heavy summer traffic it was a pleasure to drive high above the coast with the sea stretching to the sky. Grizelda knew the Corniche road like the back of her hand. It was carved from the side of the mountain, and she'd been driving it for years. It held no terrors for her, even though a second's lack of attention was all it would take to end up in the rocky gorge to her left.

She idled along in the big silver Bentley, taking her time, thinking over the arrangements. The road began to descend, winding around curves. It was quiet. Only a couple of cars had passed on the other side. Glancing in her rearview mirror, she noticed a white truck behind her, traveling too fast, and frowning, she honked her horn. The driver took no notice. She flashed her lights and put her foot to the metal, taking the curves faster than she liked, in an attempt to get out of his way. But still he did not slow down.

She slammed her hand on the horn and left it there. He was almost upon her, close enough that, had the truck's windows not been so dark, she would have been able to see his face. Fear hit her. *He was trying to run her off the road. . . .*

She felt the thud as the truck grazed her bumper. . . . He was crazy. . . . Oh Lord, what was happening? . . . She couldn't drive at this speed. . . . She would die . . . but she couldn't die yet. . . . She couldn't miss Preshy's wedding. . . . Think, she told herself, think! There was an emergency lay-by carved from the rock just around the bend. . . .

Praying there was nothing coming the other way, she swung the Bentley across the road and slammed on the brakes. The car slid sideways, hitting the rock face. The air bags exploded, and she was slammed back in her seat, screaming her head off. But she was alive. And the madman in the white truck had flown past.

Shaking, she sat with the air bag in her face, telling herself not to panic. The car ticked and groaned; steam surged from the hood. It might burst into flames any minute. To her surprise the door opened easily, and she was out on the road, cursing the mad bastard who had done this to her—and to her beautiful Bentley.

Later Mimi said, in tears, "*Chérie,* somebody wanted to kill you. They wanted you dead."

Grizelda glared at her. "Don't be ridiculous, Mimi. Why would anyone want me dead? No, it was just the act of a madman, and I don't want you to bother Preshy with it. She'd only worry about nothing."

Four

Shanghai

WHEN Bennett arrived at Pudong Airport, he called Mary-Lou.

"I'm back," he said, when she answered.

There was a long silence; then, "I didn't even know you'd gone," she retorted, though in truth she'd been unable to concentrate for weeks with no word from him.

"You mean you didn't miss me?"

"Not one bit."

"Then you don't want to see me tonight?"

"Only if you beg me."

Bennett laughed. "I'm begging. Your place, at eight?"

And at exactly eight, when he rang her bell, she was at the door to greet him. No words passed between them. She was in his arms, kissing him. Holding the bottle of champagne in one hand, he hooked a foot behind him and slammed the door shut.

"That's quite a welcome," he said, smiling down at her.

She led him to the small bar, where she waited for him to open the champagne. He filled two flutes, picked them up and gave her one.

"To us," he said, smiling right into her eyes, the way he always used to, sending nervous little tremors down her spine. Still, she was careful not to mention the thing uppermost on her mind, and she asked how his trip was instead.

"Paris was okay," he said, walking to the window and staring out at the sludge-colored river and the surging traffic below.

Mary-Lou paced nervously behind him. Because she was concerned about good *feng shui,* she had hung a large crystal in front of the window, to repel the bad *chi* from the evil Dragon River Gods. She never questioned whether she really believed this; she just went along with it on the basis that her ancestors had believed in it for centuries. But watching Bennett staring out of her window, she surely hoped it was working now. She had told her single contact in the jewelry world about the necklace, hoping he'd find her a buyer. She still hadn't heard back, and she needed all the luck she could get.

"Shall we eat now?" she said. "Or shall we go to bed?"

Bennett turned to look at her. "Guess," he said.

MUCH later, while Bennett showered, Mary-Lou opened the take-out cartons she'd had the forethought to buy from the local restaurant. She put them on the coffee table with a bottle of Tsingtao beer and a chilled glass. Bennett liked his beer cold.

His clothes were flung across the sofa, and she gathered them up, stooping to pick up the wallet that had fallen from his pants pocket. Something bulky was stuffed inside. It was a tissue. Smoothing it out, she read the phone number written in lipstick. And the name. "Preshy Rafferty."

"Oh my God," she whispered. *"Oh my God, you bastard. . . ."*

When Bennett came out of the bathroom, she said nothing about the tissue, now carefully tucked away in her own purse. She poured his beer and served his food, and they knelt on cushions at the low table to eat.

Bennett wanted to talk business, but he was aware of Mary-Lou's silence. The truth was he had never intended to see her again. But now he wanted to have his cake and eat it, too. He needed her.

"Do you love me, Bennett?" she asked after a while.

His eyes flicked coldly toward her. Love was not an issue between them. He picked up a spear of asparagus with his chopsticks. "We are alike, you and I, Mary-Lou," he said. "We both have hearts of steel. I doubt you've ever loved anyone in your entire life."

"And did you love Ana?"

His glance turned even colder. "You and I have a business deal," he said. "I came here to tell you I've found a buyer in Paris who's willing to pay a deposit, but he wants a guarantee he'll get what he's promised. I need to see that necklace."

"I can't do that." She stared angrily at him, eating his dinner calmly while she was in a turmoil. "Who is Preshy Rafferty?"

He put down the chopsticks. "Why do you ask?"

"Her number was in your wallet. Written in lipstick."

He got to his feet and shrugged on his jacket. "Thanks for dinner, Mary-Lou," he said, walking to the door.

"Wait," she called.

But Bennett did not wait. He knew he didn't have to. He knew he would get the necklace. She'd be back to him, and soon.

THE CONTACT MARY-LOU HAD asked to find a buyer for the necklace was a diamond cutter, a shabby, soft-bellied Dutchman named Voortmann. But Voortmann was having trouble. No matter how he tried, he could not get his contacts in Amsterdam to understand the special circumstances of the Empress's jewels, and especially the giant pearl. He'd need to look elsewhere for a buyer, and where better than right here in Shanghai?

At seven that evening Voortmann was in the Surging Hot Waters Bar, a massive low-end dive patronized by three groups: men out for a night's social drinking enhanced by the hot "bar girls"; men escaping from their families and marital woes; and alcoholics like himself. The first two groups were a shifting population, different every night, but he knew everyone in the third group. Like him, they were always there. And at least two of them came from rich families. He'd done business with them before, in a small way, fencing jewels stolen from their wives.

Spotting them at a table in a dark corner, he pushed his way through the crowd. "Good evening," he said.

They nodded good evening, and not waiting for their invitation, he pulled up a chair and signaled the barkeep for another drink.

Mary-Lou had given him a photograph, and he laid it between them. "Feast your eyes on this, gentlemen," he said, smiling. "I guarantee it will put money in all our pockets."

The two men peered through the gloom at the photo. One picked it up, studying it. "Did you steal this?" he asked.

Voortmann shook his head. "I know where it is," he said. "I could have it to you tomorrow. At a price."

"Such as?"

"First I have a story to tell you, my friends," he said softly.

When he had finished, the two Shanghainese glanced at each other. "We could go to jail for this," one said.

"How much?" said the other.

"Thirty million." Voortmann came up with a number. "But for you, I'll make it ten, so you can sell it on and make a good profit."

The Shanghainese didn't need to risk being imprisoned. "Tell us," one said, "who has this priceless object?"

Voortmann shook his head. "Just let me know if you want it or not, my friends."

But the Shanghainese were no friends of his.

MARY-LOU couldn't resist. She called Preshy Rafferty's number and got an answering machine.

"Bonjour, Rafferty Antiques, Preshy Rafferty speaking," the voice said in French. *"If you wish, please leave a message at the tone."*

Anger churned like molten lead in Mary-Lou's stomach. She felt sick. She'd lost Bennett, she knew it. And she hadn't heard from Voortmann. Bennett said he had a buyer willing to pay a deposit. She had no choice but to work with him. She *had* to get the necklace. There was no time to be lost.

She remembered that Lily went for breakfast at eight every morning to the Happybird Tea House. And the next morning Mary-Lou arrived at work early, waiting until she saw Lily's car emerge from the courtyard and disappear down the alley. She opened the gate with her own electronic key and drove in.

The little canary bird in its cage gave her a hopeful chirrup as she crossed the verandah, but she ignored it and unlocked the door. She walked down to the cellar and past the piled boxes and pressed the button. The panel slid away, and the iron safe was revealed. It took only a minute to open it. And there was the red leather jewel case.

She ran her palm across the smooth expensive leather and clicked the case open. Her eyes widened as she touched the pearl, thinking of it in the dead Empress Cixi's mouth. What a waste, she thought contemptuously, clicking the box shut.

She was about to close the safe when she heard a noise. Lifting her head, she listened.

"Mary-Lou? Is that you down there?" Lily's voice echoed down the cellar steps.

Heart throbbing, Mary-Lou flung the case back into the safe, slammed the door and locked it. She leapt backward and pressed the panel shut just as Lily appeared at the top of the steps. She stood, hands behind her back, facing her.

"Mary-Lou, what on earth are you doing here?" Lily said.

"I came early to take care of packing the rest of the Buddha replicas. We have to deliver them today."

Lily came down the steps. She looked disturbed. "That's very unusual for you. What's wrong? Couldn't you sleep?"

Mary-Lou allowed a few tears to trickle down her cheeks. "No, I couldn't. And it's all Bennett's fault. He came back last night, just showed up as though nothing had happened. And do you know where he'd been? To Paris. With your cousin, Precious Rafferty."

"What!" Lily was shocked.

"That's right. Remember, you told him she was a rich girl? Well, that's exactly what Bennett's looking for. Maybe the rumors were right and he really did marry Ana Yuan for her money. Maybe he killed her for it. Maybe he's thinking of doing the same to your cousin. Who knows? With Bennett anything's possible."

"Come on, you can't be serious," Lily said. "You're just upset, that's all."

Mary-Lou looked at her blankly. "He came over to my place. We made love. Then I found the phone number in his wallet. I have it upstairs; I'll show you." She didn't want Lily to notice she hadn't packed a single one of the Buddhas.

Lily led the way upstairs. Mary-Lou had left her purse on a chair, and she took out the tissue and handed it to Lily.

"Keep it," she said disdainfully. "Maybe you'll want to call your cousin someday. And I certainly don't want it."

Lily put the tissue in her pocket. She looked worriedly at her friend. "Are you sure you're all right? Listen, I was just going for breakfast, but I forgot my purse. Why don't we go and get a bite, and you can pour out your heart to me."

The heart that's made of steel, Mary-Lou thought bitterly, as she closed the cellar door and followed Lily out to her car.

LATER THAT EVENING, MARY-LOU called Bennett. "I tried to get the necklace today," she said.

"And you failed. You are letting me down, Mary-Lou. 'Tried' simply isn't good enough. I want it by tomorrow evening. Or . . ."

"Or . . . what?"

"Or you and I have lost a multimillion-dollar deal."

He rang off, and she slumped in her chair. Real tears coursed down her cheeks this time. Voortmann had given her his cell-phone number, and she punched it in.

He answered after a dozen rings. "Voortmann." His voice was gruff, and there was a lot of background noise and the clink of glasses. It didn't take a genius to figure out he was in a bar and drunk.

"What news do you have for me, Voortmann?" she said.

"Hah, Mary-Lou. You'll be pleased to know I have a couple of customers interested, wealthy Shanghainese—"

"Shanghainese?" she repeated, horrified. This was much too close to home. Rich or not, it was too dangerous a game for them.

"I showed them the photo," Voortmann boasted. "Don't worry; they'll get back to me soon."

Mary-Lou cut him off. The man had shown the picture to his co-horts in the bar. It didn't take long for rumors to start in this town, and she knew she was in trouble.

Tomorrow, she had to get the necklace out of the safe.

LILY was in her office. The necklace was still uppermost in her mind, and she got on the phone and called her Swiss contact. He told her his client feared the price might be exorbitant, even for a rich collector.

Lily backed down. "We can come to some arrangement."

But he demurred. "I'll get back to you" was all he said.

As if to reassure herself that the necklace was worth the fortune she believed it was, she walked down the cellar stairs and dialed the combination to the safe. When the door swung back, she stared, stunned, at its contents.

The jewel case was flung to the very back, and the packets of banknotes were tumbled untidily to one side. She was a neat woman, everything had its place—and this was not it. She took out the case and, fearful, opened it. Relief made her hands shake. The necklace was there.

She sank onto a packing crate, clutching it to her heart. Someone had been there. But who? She got to her feet again and went and counted the money. A substantial amount was missing. She remembered Mary-Lou down here alone so early in the morning when she had known Lily would be taking breakfast a couple of miles away. But how did Mary-Lou know about the safe and the combination?

Taking the jewel case, she locked the safe. She had to find another hiding place for the necklace. She thought about hiding it under her mattress, but that was the obvious place anyone might look. She heard her little canary chirping out on the verandah. Of course—she would hide it under the sandpaper base in the bottom of his cage. No one would ever think of looking there.

The bird came and sat on her hand while she accomplished her task, singing with delight at her attention. He was a sweet little creature, she thought smiling. Little did he know he was sitting on top of a fortune.

She decided to set a trap for Mary-Lou, try to catch her in the act. She called her, said she had a meeting with a dealer and expected to be away for several hours. Would Mary-Lou please come hold the fort while she was gone? As she had expected, Mary-Lou said yes.

THE first thing Mary-Lou did after Lily called was telephone Bennett. To her surprise he answered on the first ring.

"Well?" he said coldly, and she sighed.

"I'll have it for you tonight," she said.

"Where and what time?"

Mary-Lou hesitated. There was something icy about Bennett that had her scared. She didn't want to risk being alone with him while she handed over the necklace. She didn't trust him.

"At the Cloud 9 bar, eight o'clock," she said.

She drove over to Lily's house, and once inside, she went directly to the cellar. She opened the safe, then stepped back in horror. The jewel case was not there!

Oh—My—God. Lily had sold it. Or else she'd hidden it someplace new. She ran back upstairs, found the key to Lily's little "home safe" hidden under a pile of sweaters, then opened it. The necklace wasn't there. She rummaged through every drawer and cupboard. She even looked under the mattress. Nothing.

She stared with empty eyes at her pale reflection in Lily's bedroom mirror. She would have to stall Bennett again until she found out the whereabouts of the necklace. It was her only chance.

Shaking with nerves, she walked out onto the verandah. The canary fluttered on its perch, then burst into shrill warbling that darted like needles into her head, and she wanted to kill it. She stood looking at it in its pretty little cage. Her hands shook with fury, but of course it wasn't the bird's fault.

She needed a drink, and praying it might get her through the day, she drove to a crowded bar in the Old City patronized mostly by antiques dealers. She found a free stool and, still shaky, ordered a vodka martini.

"Mary-Lou, how are you?" A dealer she knew slightly slipped smiling onto the next barstool. "So how's business?"

Everyone knew everyone else's business and just how well they were doing, except for the secret trading of course. "Much as usual." She took a gulp of the martini.

"There's a rumor about a special piece going around. Have you heard it? Some necklace said to have belonged to the Dowager Empress. Now wouldn't I like to get my hands on that!" He laughed loudly. "And so no doubt would the cops."

Mary-Lou's blood ran as cold as the martini. "I hadn't heard," she said. "Where does this rumor come from anyway?"

The man shrugged. "Ohh, you know how rumors are here; it's all just hearsay. Still, you never know."

Mary-Lou drank down the rest of her martini. She slid off the barstool. "I'm supposed to be working," she said, heading for the door.

"See you around," he called after her.

Trembling with anger, Mary-Lou headed for her car. "Voortmann," she muttered. "The crazy drunken fool."

LILY heard the rumor that morning, at a café on the Wuzhong Road, near the Dongtai Antiques Market, whispered over cups of hot green tea and *xiao long bao,* her favorite steamed pork dumplings. Her face flamed with anger, and she left abruptly.

Bennett heard it on the treadmill at the splendidly equipped gym at the J.W. Marriott Hotel on the Nanjing Road, where he worked out every morning. He overheard the conversation behind him, turned to look and saw that he knew one of the speakers. He was the son of an electronics exporter, a notorious lowlife.

Realizing what must have happened, he cursed Mary-Lou. He was so angry he could have killed her, but before he did, he needed to see if she'd gotten the necklace.

MARY-LOU was back at the house when Lily returned, busily sorting orders for the replica figurines. She had decided to put a good face on things and pretend nothing was wrong.

"Business looks good this month," she said, smiling as Lily walked in.

"Stand up," Lily said. "I have something to say to you."

Mary-Lou stood, looking uncertainly at her. "What's wrong?"

"You are a liar and a cheat. You've stolen from me with no regard for our friendship, nor for the helping hand I offered when you were down on your luck. I trusted you, and you have betrayed that trust. And now half of Shanghai knows about the necklace."

"What necklace?" Mary-Lou tried to maintain her innocence.

"The one you saw in my secret safe. The one you attempted to sell on the low end of the market to the most dangerous of buyers. A Chinese." She put up a hand as Mary-Lou began to protest.

"Don't try to find excuses; I know they are all lies. I just want you out of my house."

Mary-Lou saw there was no point in arguing. She picked up her jacket and her bag and walked to the door. "I won't wish you luck with your sale, Lily," she said bitterly. "In fact I'll do everything I can to sabotage you. Including going to the authorities."

"Do that," Lily retorted. "They'll find nothing. Only a safe with my meager savings, earned from selling replicas to the tourist trade. Don't think I'm a fool, Mary-Lou. Neither you nor the authorities can ever touch me."

Maybe not, but Bennett Yuan can, Mary-Lou thought as she stormed out of the house for the last time.

BENNETT was already waiting for her at the Cloud 9 bar at eight that evening. She had taken particular care with her appearance and was wearing a new short cream silk dress and pale suede mules with very high heels. Her eyes were emphasized with bronze shadow, and her full lips were glazed their usual shiny red. She looked beautiful, and she knew it.

"Sit down, Mary-Lou," Bennett said without preamble. "I assume you have the necklace in that purse you're holding?"

"Not exactly," she admitted. "But tomorrow . . ."

He threw her a disgusted look, and she turned away. She called the waiter to bring her a martini.

"You may not have the necklace," Bennett continued, "but half of Shanghai knows about it. How do you explain that?"

Oh God, he'd heard the rumors. "You didn't seem interested, and I needed to find a buyer quick, so I went to Voortmann."

"That cheap diamond cutter? Were you out of your mind?"

She hung her head, while the waiter placed the martini in front of her. She grabbed it and took a long drink.

Bennett leaned across the table. "To tell the truth," he said softly, "I wouldn't have believed the story of the necklace if I hadn't found evidence of it myself. Of course Lily Song has it, doesn't she? And now I'm asking myself, why go to the salesman when I can go to the source? Lily owns it, my dear, and you do not."

She watched, dumbstruck, as he got to his feet. He didn't even say good-bye as he left.

She had lost her job and lost the necklace. And now she had lost Bennett. The world as she knew it had come to an end.

BENNETT knew that the rumor was rampant throughout the city, fueled by speculation as to how much the necklace might be worth and who had it. He also knew that stolen jewels of that kind of museum quality would be impossible to sell at any of the world auction houses. Only a private collector obsessed with the idea of the fabulous sinister jewel would be prepared to pay millions and then keep it hidden, to take out when he was alone, to handle it, remembering where it had come from. No one knew better than Bennett that men were strange, and this special kind of collector was a rare breed. Still, he had a few ideas.

But for now the bottom had dropped out of the market. No buyer would even bite. Lily would have to play it safe and hold on to her secret. It was too dangerous to try to sell.

Meanwhile, he was pursuing the easier of the two options that would eventually make him a rich man. He was off to Venice to get married.

MARY-LOU tried interminably to contact Bennett in an attempt to salvage their relationship. Finally, in desperation she went to find him at the Marriott gym but was told that Mr. Yuan was away. He'd gone to Europe, the hostess there told her. "To get married," she added smiling.

Mary-Lou thought she would faint. Her heart fluttered and jumped, and the girl brought her a glass of water and made her sit down for a while. In fact she had no memory of leaving the hotel, nor of driving home, but she went up to her apartment and stood by the big window with the crystal for good *chi,* screaming silently.

She had no one. Nothing. And nothing left to lose.

Five

Venice

GRIZELDA had everything perfectly organized: the Basilica; the flowers; the wedding reception. A compromise had been reached on the dress: Preshy was to wear long mist-colored chiffon and, because it was cold in Venice in November, a sweeping gold brocade hooded cape lined with bronze velvet and trimmed with fur.

Daria and her family and Sylvie would stay with them at the fourteenth-century Palazzo Rendino, but in keeping with tradition, Bennett was not sleeping under the same roof. He'd chosen instead to stay on the Lido, at the luxurious fin-de-siècle Hotel des Bains, because, he said, he wanted to be able to speed across the lagoon to his wedding like a buccaneer of old.

The night before the ceremony, Grizelda and Mimi threw a party for all fifty guests, in the faded gilt luxury of the Palazzo. Grizelda was glamorous in red lace Valentino, and Mimi in apple green chiffon Versace, bustling around, making sure everyone was having a good time. Daria, in a tailored cream suit, held hands with her bearded professor husband, Tom, who held Lauren the Super-Kid and future flower girl, who was overexcited and a bit cranky. Sylvie wore black. "It makes me look thinner," she said with a regretful sigh. The others, mostly friends of Aunt Grizelda's and Mimi's, wore everything that was elegant and in fashion and very probably too young for them. And of course, the bride-to-be was as chic as her aunt could make her, in a dark blue wrap dress that, with her long curly hair flowing free, Bennett said, made her look like a Pre-Raphaelite angel.

Fires burned in the great hearths at either end of the gilded salon, and the old Murano chandeliers, illuminating the faded ceiling frescoes, softened the lofty room into an intimate space. A string quartet played Vivaldi, Venice's own composer, and white-jacketed waiters circulated bearing large silver trays of champagne and hors d'oeuvres, while Lalah and Schnuppi yapped and snapped and ran excitedly through everybody's legs.

Outside the tall windows the canal glimmered in the deepening dusk. "How beautiful it is," Bennett said, standing by the window, looking out at it. "So dark and still."

Preshy squeezed his hand. "Now you understand why I love Venice so much."

He nodded. "Yes," he said thoughtfully. "Now I know."

Soon Grizelda was marshaling the guests to the entrance where gondolas waited to ferry them to the restaurant chosen for the prewedding dinner. Their little flotilla glided down the canal to a trattoria on the Fondamenta Nuevo, with a view over the misty lagoon to the Isola di San Michele. Dinner turned out to be a merry raucous event of silly toasts and singing and too much wine and a terrific seafood risotto Sylvie said was the best she had ever tasted.

Preshy was enjoying it all, laughing with her friends, when she noticed Bennett involved in a serious conversation with Aunt Grizelda. "Aunt G's reminding him of his responsibilities as her 'son-in-law,' " she said, nudging Daria and laughing.

Much later, full of good food and wine, she and Bennett decided to walk back alone to the Palazzo Rendino. Arms around each other's waists, they strolled through the narrow cobblestoned *calli* and over the many little bridges. At the street door of the Palazzo, her future husband held her close, and she smiled up into his handsome face. "Tomorrow, my love," she whispered.

"Tomorrow," Bennett promised, with a final lingering kiss. "I can't wait."

Preshy watched him walk away, a tall, elegant, handsome man in a dark suit. He turned at the corner and lifted his hand in farewell. He was every woman's dream, and for her, that dream was about to become a reality.

HER wedding day dawned clear and blue. The tranquil lagoon shimmered under a pale sun, ruffled here and there by the froth of a *motoscafo*'s wake. Preshy stood for a moment, alone in her wedding finery, on the Palazzo's embarcadero. She thought she had never seen Venice look more beautiful. Her gondola awaited, moored to a striped pole, its canopy swagged with garlands of greenery, intertwined with tiny white blossoms.

The gondolier helped her on board, and she smiled her thanks, arranging her long mist-colored dress on the cushions and adjusting the cape's fur-trimmed hood over her upswept hair. She clutched the small trail of honey-colored orchids, nervous but happy.

People turned to stare as the gondolier poled along the Grand Canal. At the *vaporetto* stop, the crowd waiting for the water bus waved good luck, and Preshy waved back, smiling. She felt like Cleopatra entering Rome.

Since there was no male relative to give her away, she had chosen, despite Aunt Grizelda's protests, to ride to her wedding and walk down the aisle alone. And there were no personal guests for Bennett James because he had no family and no close friends. That was why Daria's Tom had agreed to be his best man.

As the gondola slid alongside the Basilica, Preshy stared up at its great glimmering dome. It was her favorite church in all of Venice. She had been brought here by her parents when she was four years old, and she remembered its soaring height, rich colors, the glitter of gold and mosaics. And she remembered her mother holding one hand and her father the other as they walked down that aisle to inspect the great altar. It was the only true memory she had of them, and it was because of that memory that she was here today, for her wedding.

Her gold brocade cape billowed behind her as she stepped from the gondola, her face half-hidden behind her soft fur-trimmed hood. A mystery bride, she thought, smiling and feeling like a heroine in a romance novel.

The church was cold, and the scent of two thousand roses filled the air. Aunt Grizelda hurried to meet her, a flamboyant ageless redhead in a pearly white suit and a vermilion hat, wearing a diamond brooch Queen Elizabeth might have envied. But there was a frown on her face instead of a smile.

"Come here, darling." Grizelda pulled her to one side.

Preshy glanced at her, astonished. The organist was playing Vivaldi, and she knew he was simply marking time until he could segue into Haydn for her walk down the aisle.

"He's not here," Aunt Grizelda said.

"Who's not here?" she asked, bewildered.

"Bennett. My dear, he's not here."

"Oh . . . well, it must be the traffic, that's all."

Grizelda gripped her hand tighter. "I called the hotel, Preshy. They said he checked out last night."

Preshy stared, bug-eyed, at her aunt. She clutched her honey-colored orchids in a death grip. Grizelda unhooked her fingers and threw the orchids to the floor. She took both Preshy's hands in her own. They were cold.

Tears stood in Aunt Grizelda's eyes. "There will be no wedding," she said. "Bennett's gone."

Preshy felt as though she were floating somewhere in space. She was aware of Mimi, pale as a lily, and of the flutter of old friends, glamorous in their big hats, quiet now, watching. Her bridesmaids, Sylvie and Daria, lovely in pale apricot with big anxious eyes.

She looked at them and then at her aunt, still clinging to her icy hands. "There must be some mistake," she whispered. "Surely he'll call, tell us what's happened. . . . We can wait. . . ."

No one said anything.

"We can check the hotel again," she said desperately. "They've made a mistake."

"Oh, my dear . . ." Tears spilled down her aunt's cheeks.

Preshy had never seen her cry before. "Don't," she said, suddenly calm. "Don't cry, Aunt Grizelda. Your mascara will run."

Suddenly furious, her aunt yelled, "How *dare* he do this to you? I'll kill him; I'll wring his neck with my bare hands!"

Daria and Sylvie came and put their arms around Preshy, murmuring that they loved her, that it would be all right soon.

Preshy was the eye in the center of a storm of anger and sorrow, the shamed bride left at the altar. She looked around, thinking of what to do. "It's all right, everyone," she said. "Remember the old saying, 'The show must go on'? The water taxis are waiting to take us to the reception, so let's go."

And followed by Daria and Sylvie, she led the way out of the great church and to what, when she thought about it afterward, felt more like a wake than a wedding.

Six

Paris

IT WAS the thought of winter, with its long dark days closing in on her, all alone in her now empty-feeling apartment, that got Preshy on a plane to Boston and to Daria.

She had been home for a couple of weeks, fending off smiling inquiries by neighbors and friends as to how married life was with the curt answer that she wouldn't know, since she was not married and didn't plan to be, and people were either too polite or perhaps just too kind to ask why and what went wrong.

At Logan Airport, Daria took one look at her, a sorrowful, stringy-haired waif with only one small carry-on bag, and they both burst into tears.

In the car on their way to Cambridge, Daria handed Preshy a box of Kleenex, glancing at her out of the corner of her eye. "You can't go on like this, you know."

Preshy gave a little sob and stared blankly out at the rain. "He's never contacted me, you know. Not even a phone call, or an e-mail, to explain. And I'm too proud to try to contact him. Aunt G, though, she's had detectives searching, and there is no Bennett James in Shanghai, no grand apartment, no James Export Company. And nobody ever heard of him at Dartmouth. Bennett James really doesn't exist. Exactly who he is and why he did what he did is a mystery, though Aunt G says he was after my money."

"What money?" Daria said.

"That's exactly what I said to Aunt G. What money? All I have is my shop from which I make a fair living but nothing extravagant. But Aunt G said, well, I looked rich with my diamonds and my Paris apartment. She said Bennett thought I was rich, especially when he found out she was my aunt and only living relative. 'Add it up, girl,' she said. But then she had a confession to make."

"A confession? What on earth had she done?" Daria parked in front of her small Federal-style house.

"Remember the night before the wedding, at the lovely little trattoria on the Fondamenta Nuevo? We were all having such a good time, making silly toasts and laughing at each other's jokes. . . ." Daria nodded. "All except Bennett. I noticed him deep in conversation with Aunt G. She told me what that conversation was about. She said she was telling Bennett how some madman almost sideswiped her off the Grande Corniche a few weeks previously, and her first thought was she was damned if she was going to die and miss my wedding. Bennett laughed and said, 'Maybe it was Preshy, trying to get you out of the way to get her hands on your money.'

"Aunt G was a bit surprised, but she put him straight right away. 'Oh, no,' she told him. 'Preshy knows she won't inherit. She's a strong girl, and she's clever. I want her to make her own way in the world. Everything I have will go to the Princess Grace Foundation, and children's cancer care, and to take care of retired racehorses. Mimi's doing the same thing,' she said she told him. Bennett became very quiet after that, and I remember now, he did fall kind of silent on the walk back to the Palazzo."

"The bastard." Daria reached out so they could hug across the center console; then Preshy mopped her eyes prior to going inside and meeting her goddaughter.

Lauren the Super-Kid hurled herself at Preshy as soon as she stepped through the door. Preshy grabbed her, swinging her up high, groaning at how heavy she was getting. "You're growing up on me, Super-Kid," she complained, "and you promised you wouldn't."

"I'll try, Aunt Presh, really I will," Super-Kid said between giggles.

Tom was waiting for them, shabby as ever in his professorial style, in an old sweater and cords. Not only was Tom an esteemed physics professor, he was also a good cook, and he had dinner ready and the table set with a mishmash of old dishes and paper napkins.

The great room that was the entire ground floor of the house, with a combined kitchen, dining and living area, was in its usual chaotic state, with coats, kid's wellies and toys scattered all around. Neil Young played on the stereo while Anderson Cooper mouthed silently on the turned-down TV.

Tom opened a bottle of inexpensive Côtes du Rhône. "Welcome to the lovelorn," he said, pouring Preshy a glass. "Here, baby, drown your sorrows in this."

"Oh, Tom . . ." She gazed at him, all wide teary eyes, and he shook his head.

"Gotta get over it, baby. Bennett's not coming back, and if he tried, it would be over my dead body." He poured wine for his wife and handed Super-Kid her orange juice.

"Here's the deal," Daria said, as Preshy plumped down on the sagging slipcovered sofa. "We've decided to allow you exactly thirty 'Pity Days.' That means thirty days when you can cry and moan and complain and feel sorry for yourself. After that—it's all over." She sat down next to her friend. "Get it, Presh? Thirty days to wallow in self-pity, then you've got to get on with things."

Preshy glanced doubtfully at her. "Okay. I'll try."

"Trying is not enough. You *will* do this, Presh. You'll survive. No one's died; no one got hurt—only your pride and your feelings. You have a life; you *will* move on. Promise me that, and we promise to listen for exactly thirty Pity Days. Okay?"

Preshy took a deep breath. She wasn't sure she could live up to it, but she promised anyway.

Tom raised his glass. "Bravo," he said. Then he took the pot of boeuf bourguignon off the stove, plonked it down on the trivet in the center of the table, sliced up a crusty loaf and took out the salad. "Come and get it, kids."

Preshy thought it was the most comforting food she had ever eaten, right there with her true friends, surrounded by their love and free to weep into her wine on the first of her Pity Days.

DARIA and Super-Kid certainly kept her busy, taking her to the Montessori school and for walks by the Charles River, shopping in the Harvard Coop, browsing in the book and CD stores. But when even that and the Pity Days got on top of her, she escaped to the tumbledown family cottage on Cape Cod with its youthful happy memories.

She walked the winter beach alone, staring at the crashing waves. And later, huddled on the deck, swathed in blankets to stave off the cold, she asked herself over and over how the man she believed loved her could do such a terrible thing.

But then she began to ask herself a few other questions. Like, did she really still love Bennett? Had she ever loved him? Or had she simply been "swept off her feet" by his looks, his charm and sheer romance? Swept away by the telephoned "good night, sleep wells" from wherever he was in the world; by the flowers; the champagne; the country weekends; the engagement ring? Thinking back, she did not really know that much about Bennett, only the things he'd told her—all of which she had believed. She didn't even know his home address.

She knew she had been a fool. Much as she didn't want to believe it, he'd never loved her, and he'd only been marrying her for her supposed money. And he'd simply disappeared into thin air.

Feeling a little better, she returned to Boston and told Daria she had come to terms with everything. She was back on her feet, and the hell with Bennett James.

"You've still got some Pity Days left," Daria reminded her, and as if on cue, she burst into tears and sat weeping on the sofa.

"You've got to get a life, Presh," Daria said, sadly. "It's time to move on."

A WEEK later, Preshy was back home. It was a bright December morning, but the shutters were closed, and she was lying on the sofa. There was no sound in the room. No phones ringing, no music playing. Normally, she would have been taking her coffee and baguette at the café, but she couldn't even face that. She was deep into Pity Day twenty, and deep into the same old questions. Was Bennett really that wicked? Had he really intended to marry her for her supposed inheritance? How could he do that? He was so nice, so loving, so charming.

Last night Aunt Grizelda had called, begging her to come and stay. "We could go skiing," she promised, making Preshy laugh because the idea of Aunt G skiing at her age was scary, and anyhow she knew it was an excuse and that her aunt simply wanted to keep an eye on her. "I want to make sure you don't do anything foolish," Aunt G said.

"No man is worth doing anything 'foolish' for," Preshy had promised her, but it still didn't change the facts. It was stalemate with nowhere to go. Except, as Daria and Sylvie both told her, *Forward*.

Sighing, she slid off the sofa and went and looked at herself in the ornate gilt-framed Louis XVI mirror over the mantelpiece. She did not like what she saw. Her unmade-up face was pale and splotchy, her eyes red-rimmed, her untrimmed hair a tangled mess. She dragged her fingers through it, skewering it away from her face as a tear stole down her cheek.

"You idiot," she told her image sternly. "*Wallowing* in self-pity. Do you think Bennett is doing this? Oh no." She let her hair fall back around her face. "Well, I can't do anything about Bennett," she said out loud. "But I can do something about my hair."

An hour later she was sitting in the chair at a salon on the boulevard St. Germain. "Cut it all off," she told the stylist.

He picked up a curly lock, running it admiringly through his fingers. "Are you sure?" he asked. "Short is a drastic change."

"That's exactly what I want," Preshy said firmly. "A drastic change. I want to look like Audrey Hepburn."

Two hours later she didn't look exactly like Audrey Hepburn, but it was certainly a drastic change. Her mane of curls was gone, and in its place was a sleek copper-blond cap, short in the nape with deep bangs dangling in her eyes. She shook her head, fluffed it with her fingers. Somehow she felt freed from the weak romantic woman she had been. *This* was the new Preshy Rafferty.

As if to emphasize the point, she took the Métro to the boulevard Haussmann and Galeries Lafayette, where she headed for the lingerie department. An hour there netted a treasure trove of pretty underthings that, even though she was the only one who was ever going to see them, somehow made her feel better. Next, sitting in a chair at the Chanel counter, she had her face made over by a dazzlingly chic young woman who insisted she buy a pink lipstick and a pink blusher. Then she took a taxi over to Verlaine, where she found Sylvie busy assembling her menu for the evening.

Sylvie looked up as Preshy pushed through the door and gave her a little twirl.

"Well?" Preshy asked.

"You look completely different. I don't know whether it's the hair or the pink lipstick, but I think I like it."

"*Think?*" Preshy's face fell. "This is the new me, and you're not knocked out by it?"

Sylvie laughed. "Of course I am. It's just I hardly recognized you without that great cloud of hair. I can see your face now, though, and it looks good. Come on, let's go get a cup of coffee and a sandwich. I'll leave the boys in charge. They can't do too much damage in half an hour."

It was good, the time spent with Sylvie, but later that night, alone in her apartment, Preshy was back thinking about Bennett. Remembering the *Bateau Mouche,* the intimate dinners at little neighborhood restaurants, the welcome when he came "home" to the rue Jacob. *Oh God,* she thought, *what am I going to do?*

She was browsing the Internet when she came across a picture of a bunch of big-eyed, big-eared, skinny little kittens. She melted just a little, looking at their innocence. On an impulse she called the breeder, who said there were no kittens left but that a slightly older cat, nine months, had been returned because the buyer was allergic.

"I'll take her," Preshy said immediately.

"Maybe you want to meet her first, see if you're compatible," the breeder said doubtfully.

"Oh, we are. I know we are," Preshy replied. After all, hadn't they both been rejected? Both been "returned to sender" so to speak. And so the seal point Siamese with the fancy kennel name of Mirande de la Reine d'Or became hers.

Preshy drove to pick her up the next day, a cream and chocolate beauty with eyes more glitteringly blue than any sapphires. She brought her home, safe, or so she thought, in a cardboard traveling box, but she hadn't reckoned with the ingenuity of a determined Siamese. Soon the cat was on her lap. "Maow," she said, gazing earnestly into Preshy's face at the red light.

"And maow to you, too," she retorted, grinning. And so Maow the cat became.

And of course, Preshy immediately confessed all her troubles into Maow's delicate chocolate ear, and the cat gazed knowingly back, rumbling with faint purrs of sympathy.

The next day she bought a rather chic travel carrier and took the cat to visit the aunts in Monte Carlo.

Lalah and Schnuppi galloped toward her, barking as she stood in the foyer clutching the carrier to her chest, while from behind the safety of the mesh door, Maow yowled and stared them down.

The aunts watched, bemused, as their dogs tucked tail and ran.

"Of course, the cat's obviously a substitute for a man," Aunt Grizelda said suspiciously.

"And what's so wrong about that?" Preshy demanded. "At least I know where I am with her."

The dogs sat quietly. Maow emerged and curled triumphantly on the sofa, in pride of place between the aunts.

It was, Preshy thought, patting her new short hair that Grizelda said made her look like a shorn duck and smiling at the people she loved, a good new start.

Seven

Shanghai

IF LILY had thought to make a list of people she never expected to hear from again, Bennett would have headed it, with Mary-Lou in second place. So she was surprised when she heard from each of them in turn.

Bennett did not call; he came round to see her, ringing her doorbell at seven o'clock one evening about a month after she had fired Mary-Lou. When Lily checked the security camera at the gates, she was astonished to see him standing there. Pressing the intercom, she said curtly, "What is it you want?"

He said, "I'd like to speak to you, if you can take the time."

She was curious to see what he wanted, so she opened the gate to let him in, then stood on the verandah as he walked toward her holding a large bouquet of Casablanca lilies.

He said, "I meant to be in touch, but I've been in Europe. When we met, I thought we had so much to talk about. Won't you please invite me in?" He gave her that gentle heart-melting smile that, despite herself, she reacted to.

He walked up the steps, stopping to admire the canary. Her heart beat so loudly as he stared into the cage with the hidden necklace, she was surprised he didn't hear it. The scent of the lilies wafted toward her as they went into the house.

"Lilies for a Lily," he said. "But I'm sure I'm not the first man to say that to you."

She took the flowers and, with a brief unsmiling thank-you, dropped them onto a side table, then waved him to a chair.

"I suppose you've come to plead for Mary-Lou," she said, sitting on the sofa, watching him carefully.

His brows rose in surprise. "Why should I do that? What happened to her?"

She thought he was a good actor. "You mean you don't know?"

"I told you, I've been away, and anyway, things are finished between us." He shrugged. "It was fun while it lasted, but it was time to move on."

"Then that makes us equals. Mary-Lou no longer works for me. So, may I ask exactly why you are paying this visit?"

"I was impressed when I met you. This is a woman of substance, I thought. A woman I could do business with."

"And what business would that be?"

"I have a proposition to put to you," he said. "You have an exceptional piece of property. Rumors are rife in this city, but so far only you and I and Mary-Lou know where the truth lies."

"The rumors have nothing to do with me."

"That's not what Mary-Lou said. And I have good reason to believe her."

Lily's cheeks flared with heat. Mary-Lou had betrayed her one more time. She said, "I think you should know that I fired Mary-Lou because she was stealing from me. A disgruntled ex-employee will say anything to exact revenge."

He shook his head, looking regretful. "I know she tried to sell the necklace, and a rich Shanghainese no-good blabbed the story to the world. If he had not, I'm sure you would have already sold it. Too bad your deal with the Swiss agent fell through." He put up a hand to stop her protests. "Don't ask me how I know, but now that leaves the way open for a new deal. And this time, Lily, the deal is foolproof."

Lily's stomach was churning. She went to the kitchen and came back with a bottle of San Pellegrino and two glasses. Filling them, she took one and sat back in the elm-wood chair.

"Shall we drink to our collaboration?" He lifted his glass.

"Tell me exactly what you are talking about," she said, sipping the water.

"It's very simple. You have the corpse necklace. I have a buyer. My buyer is prepared to pay a substantial deposit pending delivery, but he needs to know exactly what he's getting. Therefore I need to see the necklace. I also need written documentation of its authenticity. And of course, we need a price. My guess would be about thirty million."

Did he really think she would hand over the necklace and say, "Okay, let's take it"?

"Fifty-fifty." Bennett leaned forward eagerly. "You'll never sell fake antiques again. What do you say, Lily? Are we partners?"

"You'll have to look elsewhere for your partner, Bennett. I don't have this corpse necklace, and I don't know who does. Rumor is all it is." She got to her feet, dismissing him. "Just a rumor."

Bennett also got up. He went and stood close to her. Fear shot up her spine as his suddenly cold eyes bored into her.

"Oh, but you do have it, Lily," he said softly. "And I intend to get it. Any way I can. Why don't we just do this the nice way? Because no matter what it takes, I intend to have that necklace." He stepped back, and the charming smile flashed again. "I'll give you time to think it over. Let's say until this time tomorrow?"

His threat dangled in the air, and Lily remembered Mary-Lou saying maybe Bennett had killed his rich wife for her money. Shivering, she now believed he was capable of it.

"Until tomorrow night at seven," Bennett said.

MARY-LOU had purposely befriended the young woman receptionist at the health club Bennett frequented. They met for drinks, had the occasional lunch together, did a little shopping.

That same evening Bennett called on Lily, they were in a smoky, crowded bar called Sasha's, just off the Hengshan Road. Over martinis the girl told Mary-Lou that Bennett was back in town and that the "wedding" had fallen through.

"He changed his mind." She smiled over the rim of her glass at Mary-Lou, whom she greatly admired for her beauty and her chic style. "I'll bet he just couldn't forget about you," she added.

Shock, then relief, left Mary-Lou limp. But she knew Bennett was finished with her. And she wanted revenge, no matter how, where or when.

Leaving her new friend at the bar, she drove over to Lily's. Outside the gates, she telephoned her. When Lily answered, she said, "I need to speak to you. Please let me in. It's about Bennett."

Lily hesitated, but then she thought about Bennett's threat, and she pressed the buzzer. She stood on the verandah, arms folded, as Mary-Lou walked past the fountain and the serene goldfish pond. Lily thought how beautiful she was. And how treacherous.

Mary-Lou stood at the bottom of the steps. Recognizing her, the canary bird gave a little trill, and Lily quickly covered his cage with a cloth. "I need to speak to you," Mary-Lou said.

"So speak."

"Bennett's back in town. He went to Europe to marry your cousin, but something went wrong. Maybe she didn't inherit enough, and to Bennett a woman without a lot of money isn't a woman worth marrying. Or killing. Not after what happened with the Yuans."

Bennett marrying Precious? Lily smelled danger, not only for herself but for her cousin. She suddenly knew, without a shadow of a doubt, that Bennett would kill her to get the necklace. She had to get out before tomorrow night when he came back for her.

She said, "I don't want to hear any more. Please go away."

Mary-Lou stared numbly. She'd thought Lily would be shocked, that she would join her in seeking vengeance. "He knows about the necklace," she said quickly. "He wanted me to get it from you; that's why I broke into your safe. . . ."

"I know," Lily said wearily. "And I don't care anymore."

Mary-Lou's shoulders sagged. She walked back through the courtyard, then turned to look at Lily.

"He'll kill you for it," she said as the gates clanged shut behind her.

LILY paced the bamboo floorboards, filled with fear. She had to leave Shanghai, and she had to warn her cousin. Then something occurred to her. Precious was in the antiques trade. *She* might know collectors who'd be interested in the necklace. She was the only one who could help her now.

She looked up Rafferty Antiques in Paris, found the e-mail address and sent her cousin an urgent message.

"I need your help. It is imperative I speak to you." She calculated the time difference and the flying time and how to prevent Bennett from finding her. *"Please book me into the Ritz Hotel for one week under your name. I will arrive Saturday on Cathay Pacific. This is urgent. Please do not let me down. Your cousin, Lily Song."*

Next she called Cathay Pacific and booked the earliest flight to Paris, via Hong Kong, leaving the following morning. She walked back out onto the verandah and looked at her little canary bird, sleeping in his ornate bamboo cage. She removed the red leather case from under the sandpaper base and put it in a zip-lock bag in the crisper section of the refrigerator. Then she carried the canary to her next-door neighbor at the nightclub and asked if he would take care of the bird while she was gone.

That done, she went to the cellar, selected one of the fake warrior statues and packed it. She called a courier to pick it up immediately and ship it on to Cousin Precious.

She hastily packed her bags, then arranged for a limo to pick her up the next morning. Knowing she wouldn't sleep, she sat bolt upright and frightened, staring at the TV until dawn came. Very early that morning, she would be gone.

BACK at her apartment, Mary-Lou was forced to face the fact that soon she would no longer be able to afford it. She had money in the bank but certainly not enough to maintain her extravagant lifestyle. Yet she loved her Italian sofas and modernist paintings and the red and black bedroom in which she had spent so many happy hours. She stared at the Huangpu River outside the floor-to-ceiling windows, and for the first time in many years she felt like crying.

She *knew* Lily had the necklace, and now she regretted she hadn't stolen it while she had the chance.

When Mary-Lou worked with Lily, she'd had an expert hack into Lily's computer, so she would always know what was going on. Now, sitting at her chic little desk, Mary-Lou typed in the password on her laptop, and suddenly she was looking at Lily's e-mail to Precious Rafferty in Paris.

Stunned, she realized that Lily was taking the necklace out of the country and that she must be going to ask her cousin to find a buyer. She wondered for a moment what to do, but then she knew she had only one chance.

She called Cathay Pacific and got a seat on the same flight as Lily. She knew Lily would be flying business and booked coach for herself. She also knew that first- and business-class passengers were always boarded before the others, and that their section was separate. She would be sure Lily would never know she was there.

A while later she sat back on the black silk bedspread in her poppy-red bedroom. The steam had gone out of her, and now her plan seemed ridiculous. Even if she managed to somehow get the necklace, how would she sell it? She shook her head, despairing as all her wild plans seemed to disappear out the window, no doubt flying across the river into the arms of the Dragon River Gods, who she was sure now were against her. She could not do this alone. She would have to go crawling back to Bennett and, even though she didn't trust him, take a fifty-fifty deal.

She dialed Bennett's number. "It's Mary-Lou," she said in a low scared voice. "I have something to tell you."

"I don't want to hear it," he said abruptly.

"Lily's running away to Paris. She's going to see Precious; she's taking the necklace. . . ." The story poured out of her. She told him she would get the necklace somehow, that they still needed each other, that they would go fifty-fifty as he had suggested. . . .

"When does she leave?" he asked.

"Tomorrow morning. I'm booked on the same flight."

"I'll get the flight out via Singapore," he said. "I'll call you when I get to Paris."

"Bennett?" He hadn't said what he planned to do, nor had he agreed to her fifty-fifty deal.

"I'll call you when I get there," he said again, and rang off.

Mary-Lou didn't trust him. She was afraid. She needed a gun.

She was a very small cog in the wheel of Shanghai's crime machine, but she knew a man who was "connected." She called and told him what she wanted delivered to her in Paris. It would cost, but the deed was done.

Next she called the Paris Ritz. Then she packed a bag and, like Lily, waited for morning to come.

Paris

UNUSUALLY for the time of year, Preshy had had a busy day, with a dozen customers, at least two of whom had expressed strong interest in her Etruscan bowl, even after she had told them that she believed it might be a fake. At four o'clock, with the cat under her arm, she ran up the stairs to her apartment, slamming the door quickly behind her to keep out the cold.

Maow sat on the kitchen counter, watching as Preshy fixed herself a cup of hot chocolate. Throwing all thoughts of calorie counting to the wind, she piled on the whipped cream and, with the cat at her heels, put on a CD of Joni Mitchell singing about her failures at the game of love. She sank into the cushy sofa with her feet on the coffee table, sipping the hot creamy, silky smooth chocolate, with her eyes closed, dreaming of a new life. One where she would be strong and glamorous and in charge of her own destiny. Hah! She drained the mug. Unfortunately, real life never worked out quite like that. It was much, much harder.

She went to her desk, did the day's necessary paperwork and turned on the TV. Bad weather was approaching. Snowstorms, the forecaster said. She sighed. There went her business. She checked her e-mails. The usual stuff—but then something strange. An e-mail from Cousin Lily Song.

She read Lily's message. Then read it again, still not sure she understood. *Lily* was coming to Paris? Book her into the Ritz—but under Preshy's own name? Why would she want her to do that? It was *"imperative"* she speak to her. . . . Of course, it was exciting to think she would finally get to meet Lily, but why so mysterious?

Feeling foolish, and a little like a fraud, she dialed the Ritz and booked the room as requested.

THE next morning, a freezing January Saturday, Preshy was in the crowded café near the rue de Buci breakfasting on her usual double café crème, when outside the steamed-up windows the first flakes of snow began to fall. Dragging her fingers exasperatedly through her new hair—frizzing in the steam when she'd imagined being short it wouldn't—Preshy made a quick call to Cathay Pacific to make sure Lily's flight was still on time, which it was.

She drained the last dregs of coffee and stood up to leave, wrapping her winter coat closely around her. Actually, it was Grandfather Hennessy's old sheepskin, a shapeless olive green garment that reached to her ankles, but it kept her warm. She pulled a Russian-looking fur hat with droopy earflaps over her shorn hair; then, with a good-bye wave to her waiter, she prepared to brave the elements.

Head down against the now heavily falling snow, she bought cheese from her favorite market stall, and with a crusty loaf fresh from the baker's oven under her arm, she headed for home, tearing off bits of bread to eat on the way.

The pretty apartment seemed to welcome her. Its tall narrow windows let in streams of snowy gray light. The cat unfurled herself from the cushioned window seat and ran toward her.

"Okay, Maowsie," she murmured. "Time for work, though I don't think we'll be getting many customers today."

She was right. Traffic down the usually busy street was light, and the snow was already settling on the narrow sidewalks. In the shop, the cat parked herself on a cushion in the window, while Preshy dusted her stock, then took care of some paperwork. At five, without a single customer, she closed up and carried Maow back upstairs.

She put a match to the fireplace, waiting until the small logs caught. She and the cat established themselves on the slouchy linen sofa watching the flames dance and the snow falling even more heavily outside. Sighing, Preshy picked up the phone and dialed the airline. But this time she was told that the airport was closed and that the Cathay Pacific flight had been diverted to Frankfurt.

She twirled a short strand of hair in her fingers. Even with Lily's surprise visit, a long gray winter seemed to stretch interminably in front of her. Maow shoved her nose against her face, and she stroked the cat absently. Today was the last of her Pity Days, but she was lonely in the quiet apartment with the clock ticking and the falling snow. A log slipped in the grate; the radiators hissed in the silence. Preshy thought forlornly about the bread and cheese and glass of wine awaiting her in the kitchen. The hell with it, she wasn't that French. She needed comfort food. She needed steak and fries.

She grabbed her bag, slashed on the new pink lipstick, slung on Grandfather Hennessy's ancient coat, thrust her feet into her old furry après-ski boots and headed out in search of food and . . . well, other people, she supposed.

LILY was waiting at carousel 5 in the baggage claim at Frankfurt-Main, half-expecting to see Bennett materialize.

She had the uneasy feeling of being followed, that someone's eyes were on her. Her black Tumi bag slid down the ramp, and she grabbed it. Then, tight as a drum with nerves, she hurried through the green customs light and into the terminal to look at listed departure destinations. Many flights had been canceled. There was a flight to Venice in an hour. It was the last place Bennett would ever think of looking for her.

She ran to departures. She was lucky, they had not yet closed the gate, and she was able to buy a ticket. Tension flowed out of her as the plane took off. But she still didn't feel safe.

At Venice's Marco Polo Airport she called the Bauer Hotel. It was out of season, and she was able to get a room. She took a water taxi there, hardly noticing the beauty all around her because she was too busy watching a second water taxi she suspected was following her. But when she got out at the hotel, it went right on past, and again she breathed a sigh of relief.

Exhausted, she fell into bed and slept like a dead woman.

WITH the unexpected diversion and then Lily's quick decision to take a flight to Venice, it hadn't been easy for Mary-Lou. Still, by always keeping to the back of the line and many rows away on the aircraft, somehow she managed it.

She had followed Lily's *motoscafo,* instructing the driver to go on past when Lily got out at the Bauer. A half hour later, Mary-Lou checked in and got a room on the same floor.

She called Bennett, who had been diverted to Lyon, and told him where they were. Next, without taking into consideration the time difference, she called her contact in Shanghai, who said to wire him extra money and she would have the gun in Venice instead of Paris the next day. Mary-Lou made the arrangements, then went to bed. She was worn out, and she knew she would need all her strength and all her wits to pull off what she was about to do.

LA COUPOLE was one of the few places in Paris to remain open in the storm, and despite the bad memories it held for Preshy, it was a good place for a woman alone.

Snow blistered her windshield as she crawled down the boulevard du Montparnasse in her little Smart car, which looked like a regular small car but with the back chopped off making it even smaller. For once parking was easy. The place was almost empty, and she took a seat well away from where she had sat with Bennett. She ordered a half carafe of red and the *steak frites* and was sipping the wine, wondering where Lily was, when the waiter showed a man to the table next to her. Her eyes met the stranger's briefly; then, indifferent, he looked away.

Preshy sighed with relief. This man was no beautiful Bennett James. He was very tall and thin and wiry, brown-haired and brown-eyed behind gold-rimmed glasses. He had a narrow face, a stubbled jaw and a bitter expression. He wore jeans and a black turtleneck sweater under a leather jacket, and a wedding ring, and he ordered a double vodka on the rocks that he downed fast, immediately signaling for a second. He then proceeded to order a fish called Saint-Pierre, one of her favorites, and a bottle of good Bordeaux far too heavy for the fish, which established him in her mind as a philistine.

Looking around the nearly deserted restaurant, she wondered uneasily why he had chosen to sit next to her. But then she told herself it was a public place and anyone could sit anywhere. It was her newfound paranoia clicking in, that was all.

She sipped her wine, thinking gloomily of the icy drive back to the rue Jacob in her tiny Smart car, and her lonely apartment. She wondered again where Lily was. Taking out her cell phone, she checked her messages. Zero. She tasted her steak and poured the last of the wine into her glass.

"Do you mind?" The stranger spoke. He was holding up a pack of Marlboros, a question in his eyes. She didn't like it, but this was France and smoking was permitted, and she shrugged it was okay. Behind the glasses his eyes were dark, intense. And weary. And he was American. She asked where he was from.

"Charleston, South Carolina," he said. She told him she was American and had gone to college in Boston.

He glanced indifferently at her. "I'm stuck here in Paris thanks to the weather," he said. "No flights out—no flights in."

"If you have to be stuck somewhere, Paris isn't so bad." She resented him for casting even an implied slur on her beautiful city.

"I should never have come here in the first place." He stared into space, sipping Bordeaux and smoking his cigarette, looking like a man who couldn't wait to get out of there.

"Why are you so pissed off?" she asked, wishing immediately she hadn't because it was none of her business.

"Why am I pissed off? Hah!" He laughed. "I just spent three hours sitting on a plane, on the runway, waiting for the wings to be de-iced, and by the time our turn came, a full-blown blizzard was blowing. I was disembarked along with thousands of other travelers in search of a hotel room. Of course, there were none."

Preshy's "oh" was sympathetic.

"Someone gave me the name of a third-rate joint on the rue de Rennes, where I finally got a room with a plastic shower and the smallest washbasin known to man." He took a gulp of his wine. "Since I'm six three, this only added to my torture, so—here I am." He looked at her. "So much for lousy Paris."

"Ohh," she said again, a little nervously. "Well, at least you found La Coupole."

"I've been here before," he said curtly. "I knew it was a place where you could get a solid drink, a decent bite and a bottle of good wine. I guessed it was open. If not, I was about to slit my wrists."

She stopped in midbite, alarmed, but to her relief he smiled.

"Sorry," he said, "it's been a long day. A long week."

She busied herself with her steak, which was blood-rare, thin as a washboard and tough, but that was the way the French liked it.

"So, what d'you do, here in Paris?" he asked, as though it was a mystery what anyone did in Paris.

"I work," she told him brusquely. "Antiques."

His eyes swiveled her way. He seemed to take her in properly for the first time. As though she were actually a real person, she thought resentfully.

"I own Rafferty Antiques on the rue Jacob," she said. "I deal mostly in early artifacts, Etruscan, Roman, Greek."

"Then you must be quite knowledgeable."

"I like to think so. I learned at my grandfather's knee, you might say." Then, while he ate his fish and loneliness and the wine got to her, she went on to tell him the story of Grandfather Hennessy and about the aunts. Draining her glass, she also told him the story of the Songs and the mysterious message out of the blue from Lily.

"So what d'you think she wants?" he asked, lighting up another cigarette.

Preshy said she had no idea, frowning as she wafted away the smoke. He apologized and put the cigarette out, then picked up the half-full bottle of Bordeaux, took a clean glass, poured the wine and set it before her.

Preshy thanked him. "And what do you do?" she asked.

"I'm a writer."

"So what do you write?"

"Novels."

"Really?" She eyed him respectfully. "Should I know you?"

He threw her a withering glance. "Why?"

"I mean, well, know your name?"

"It depends on whether your taste runs to mysteries."

"So what is your name?"

"Sam Knight."

Of course. "My best friend Daria's your biggest fan."

"And what about you?"

"Oh, I never have time to read." Of course it wasn't true, but mysteries were simply not her style.

"Just what every author wants to hear." He refilled his glass, lifting it in a toast. "To the solving of the Lily mystery," he said with a smile that lifted his face from the lines of bitterness into a sudden boyishness. "And anyhow, what's your name?" When she told him, he laughed. "I could never call any woman 'Precious,' " he said. "And besides, you don't look like one. You're definitely a Rafferty."

"Okay," she agreed, pleased. She wondered how old he was. In his forties obviously. "And here's to your stay in Paris," she said with a smile. "You have to admit we have good wine."

He laughed again, a deep throaty laugh that made her join in. "I should never have come in the first place," he said again.

"Then why did you?"

His eyes behind the glasses searched hers for a moment. He was not laughing now. "I was looking for the past," he said quietly.

Then he got up abruptly, said he was off to the bar to have a cigarette in peace, and left her sitting there, as alone as when she came in and wondering what on earth he could have meant.

She finished the glass of wine, which was as good as it gets, and when he came back, she offered him a lift to his hotel. "It's on my way," she said, knowing there would be no taxis.

She noticed him grin when she put on the ancient sheepskin coat, and she felt sure he was still grinning behind her as she clomped her way out in her gigantic furry boots. Embarrassed, she thought he might at least have done it to her face.

Outside, Sam Knight stared at her little Smart car. "This is it?" he said. And it was her turn to snigger as he attempted to fold his lanky frame into it. He didn't grumble though, *and* he waited patiently while she checked her messages again.

"No luck?" he asked as she crawled and slid in low gear down the empty boulevard and onto the rue de Rennes.

"No Lily. And therefore no solution to the mystery," she added with a grin.

She felt sorry for Sam when she stopped outside his seedy hotel. He got out of the car, then leaned back in, looking into her eyes, almost as weary as his own by now.

"Thanks a lot, Rafferty," he said. "I appreciate the lift. Without you, I'd have had to walk all the way back."

"You're welcome. And thanks for the company."

"Good luck with the mysterious Lily Song." He straightened up to close the door. Then he bent back in again. "Why don't you give me your phone number?" he said, coolly. "Just in case I ever get back to Paris. Then you'll be able to fill me in on the Lily story."

"Everybody's got a story," she said, and he smiled.

Eight

SHE was awakened by the sullen gray light filtering through the curtains. Struggling from sleep, she remembered Lily and immediately called the airline. She was told the flight had landed in Frankfurt the previous evening and that all the passengers had disembarked there.

She showered, dressed and went out for her coffee, slushing through piled snow, smiling and feeling like a little kid on a no-school day. She expected Lily would contact her sometime soon. Lily did not, but Sam Knight did.

She answered on the first ring. "Lily?" she demanded breathlessly.

"Rafferty, you're not still waiting for the mystery woman, are you?" he said.

"Yeah." She recognized his voice. "I'm getting sick of it. Anyhow, why are you still here?"

"I can't get a flight out. How about I take you for lunch?"

Preshy didn't hesitate. "Pick me up in half an hour," she said. "I know just the spot for a day like this."

He found her place easily enough, and when he pressed Preshy's bell, she buzzed him into the courtyard and was waiting at the top of the stone stairs that led to her apartment.

"Look," she called joyously, pointing to the paulownia tree. Every branch was rimed with a line of snow, and thin icicles dripped from the tips. "Did you ever see anything so beautiful?" she asked reverently. "I wish I could preserve it like that forever."

He stood looking at it for a long moment. "It is," he said finally, "the loveliest thing I've seen in Paris."

"Hmm." She surveyed him, arms folded over her pale-blue sweater. He was a bit of a downer, but he had possibilities, and that beat charm anytime. "Come meet Maow while I get my coat."

The cat was sleeping in the window seat. She opened an indifferent eye, and she and Sam surveyed each other for a brief moment before she closed it again. He was equally indifferent. He was a dog man himself. He helped Preshy on with the sheepskin coat that weighed, he said, about a ton.

She explained that it was her grandfather's, and that it was still the best coat for weather like this. She smoothed it doubtfully with her fingers. "I hope you don't think I look too scruffy."

Sam laughed out loud. He couldn't remember a woman ever saying anything like that. "Not *too,* but we'd better not go anywhere smart just in case they throw you out."

She laughed, too, wrapping a long blue woolen muffler around her neck, the ends dangling to her knees. She noticed he was still wearing the turtleneck and jeans and leather jacket. "Anyway, you don't look so hot yourself," she said, inspecting his stubbled jaw.

"It's obvious you've never read any of my novels; otherwise you'd have noticed the author photograph. With the beard."

"Ohh, well . . ." She beamed at him. "There you go. That's why I didn't recognize you in La Coupole."

He took her arm protectively as they walked down the icy steps and across the courtyard. "I get the feeling," he said, "that you have an excuse for everything."

"You're probably right. Daria says I lack a sense of reality. That's why I ended up—" She stopped, about to say, "dumped at the altar," but she suddenly remembered she was talking to a stranger.

"Ended up . . . what?"

"Oh, ended up with an antiques store. I guess it's easier dealing with the past."

"Not always," he said curtly.

It was her turn to stare. She wondered what he meant. "I thought we'd go to a little place on the Île St. Louis," she said. "It's a bit of a walk, but it's a treat to see a traffic-free Paris."

"As long as they have good wine."

"They do, as long as you promise not to drink a good Bordeaux with your fish."

"But I like red wine with my fish," he protested. "Whenever I'd go fishing off the Outer Banks, I'd grill my catch on the beach and we'd share a bottle of good Carolina red. They make decent wines in Carolina, you know. Maybe not like Bordeaux, but good."

The restaurant was a dark cave of a place. Old blackened beams crisscrossed the low ceiling, fake red roses topped tables covered with white butcher's paper, and a fire blazed in a big rough-stone chimney. It smelled of roasting lamb and wine-rich gravy and was as welcome on a freezing Sunday as Santa at Christmas.

It was the kind of place where a bottle of the house red already waited on the table, and to Preshy's surprise, Sam did not send it back. Instead he poured it into their glasses without even tasting it first. "Remember, I'm trusting you," he said with a smile as they clinked glasses. She watched him anxiously as he took the first sip.

"Almost as good as the Carolina red," he said.

The proprietor bustled forward with the daily menu. "You must have the soup, *madame, m'sieur,*" he said. "It's lentil with ham, very good for a cold day like this. And then I recommend the lamb, the whole leg roasted *à point.* Of course it comes with the *flageolets,* the little flat green beans, and a *tian* of potatoes *forestière,* cooked with garlic, onions and mushrooms."

Sam's eyes met Preshy's. "Let's do it," he said, and she nodded enthusiastically.

The soup was as good as promised and sent little squiggles of heat from her mouth all the way down to her toes. She looked at Sam with a question in her mind. "So, you know all about me. Now, how about you?"

"What do you want to know?"

"Hmmmm . . . Well, I know what you do. But I don't know *who* you are."

He gave her a withering look. "And you're telling me I really know who you are, Precious Rafferty, antiques dealer with a Paris apartment and Grandfather's coat?"

"Maybe I was getting too personal," she admitted. "But you

know where I live. Can't you at least tell me about that house on the beach where you drank Carolina red?"

He sat back as the proprietor removed their empty soup dishes. "I've owned the house for ten years," he said. "It was love at first sight, and I bought it with my first royalties. It's outside a small town, kind of isolated, set back on stilts above the dunes in a patch of saw grass, sheltered by tamarisk trees I planted myself, and that are now ten feet tall. It's just a gray-shingled cube, fronted with glass to catch every nuance of that ever-changing sea, and with a wraparound covered porch for long lazy summer evenings."

He fell quiet, and Preshy thought he must be feeling homesick. "You speak like a writer," she said. "The house is coming to life as you tell me about it."

But his eyes were sad. "The house is as simple inside as out," he said. "Bleached wood-plank floors, pale rugs, a comfortable sofa or two, a fireplace. In winter the fire seduces you into sitting before it, watching the flames instead of the ocean pounding savagely on the sand while the wind whistles through the tops of the trees. The house is like an island," he added softly, "my own personal island, where everything is perfect and nothing can ever go wrong."

"And did it?" The question was out before she thought about it. "Sorry. I felt as though I was in the middle of a story."

"You were, though it's not a story that will ever be written." He refilled their glasses as the proprietor bustled back with their lamb.

Looking at Sam's wedding ring, Preshy was dying to ask about his wife, but if he was such a devoted husband, he would have mentioned her by now.

Sam tasted the lamb and smiled. "This is wonderful."

"Didn't I promise you?"

"I can see you're a trustworthy person. But you know what? I forgot to ask about Lily."

Lily's name came at her out of the blue, and Preshy was surprised to find she had also forgotten about her. "Haven't heard a word," she said, tasting the potatoes under their thin golden crust and smiling with delight. "She might at least have called. But she was so mysterious anyway. I wouldn't be in the least bit surprised if she never showed up. Except . . ." She thought for a moment. "No, she said it was urgent. That she *had* to speak to me." Preshy shrugged.

"It'll be some family thing. She's probably heard you inherited Grandfather Hennessy's coat and wants to get her hands on it."

They laughed together, clinking wineglasses again. Sam glanced approvingly at the now-crowded little room. "I'm enjoying this. It's real, not at all like that big Paris out there."

"But that big Paris is made up of hundreds of little places like this. It's like your Outer Banks; you have to know it to appreciate it, other than just its beauty, of course. And you can't deny that my city is beautiful."

He stared at her across the table, taking in her flushed cheeks, the light eyes under the tangled golden fringe curling slightly in the heat. "I admit, Paris is beautiful," he agreed.

"And when you finally get a flight to New York, will you go directly to the beach house?"

To her surprise he said, "I haven't been there in years." Then he signaled for a second bottle of wine, changing the subject abruptly to what they should order for dessert.

"The apple tart," she exclaimed. "With vanilla ice cream. They get their ice cream from Berthillon, right here on the Île St. Louis. It's simply the best."

They enjoyed another glass of wine and their apple tart with the best ice cream in the world, though Sam said, personally, he was a Häagen-Dazs fan; then they lingered over rich dark coffee into which he poured enough sugar, she said, to stand a spoon in.

A WHILE later, they wandered back through the maze of small streets to Preshy's apartment.

She stopped at the courtyard door and turned to look at him. "Thank you for a lovely lunch," she said. "It was fun."

"Surprisingly, it was. Thanks for coming, Rafferty. You were good company."

"Good company for a lonely man," she said, recognizing that, in fact, that was exactly what he was. He gave her a long bleak look; then he turned and walked away.

Again, she had said the wrong thing, and feeling bad, she called after him. "Look, you can't just spend the evening in that awful hole of a hotel. Why not come on up? We'll have more coffee, play some music, maybe watch a little TV." He stood, looking at her, obviously undecided. "No obligation," she added, hoping he would come because she was lonely, too.

He walked back to her. "Thanks," he said.

As they crossed the courtyard, the concierge emerged from her ground-floor lair. "A package came for you, Mademoiselle," she said. "Special courier delivery. And on a Sunday. I told them to leave it outside your door."

Surprised, Preshy thanked her. She wasn't expecting anything, but there was the parcel, actually a crate, about three feet by two. There was a lot of Chinese writing on the labels, and she saw it came from Song Antiquities in Shanghai. "It must be from Lily," she said, opening the door as Sam hoisted it inside.

He deposited the crate on the kitchen floor, and Maow came running to sniff it suspiciously. Preshy rummaged in a drawer and came up with a screwdriver.

"I'm dying to know what's in it," she said.

Sam got busy with the screwdriver while she fixed the coffee, setting out cups on a black lacquer tray, remembering he liked sugar, pouring milk into a little jug. The crate crackled open, and Sam removed a brown wrapped parcel. He peeled back the paper, uncovering yet another layer, this time a padded blanket.

"Must be something special," Sam said.

It was a terra-cotta figurine, and Preshy saw instantly that it was a copy of the famous ones in Xi'an, China. She ran a hand over the telltale marks of the commercial mold it had been cast from. "Why would Lily bother to send me something like this?" she asked, puzzled. "They sell them in tourist shops around the world. The shipping expense was more than it's worth. Oh well." She shrugged and carried it into the living room, where she cleared a space on the shelf for it. Then, glancing along the shelf of photographs, she frowned.

"That's odd," she said. "Where's Grandfather's wedding picture? It's always right next to Aunt Grizelda."

"Did it have any value?" Sam asked.

"Only to me. I've no idea how long it's been missing. I daresay it'll turn up. Anyway, let's have our coffee, shall we?"

She carried in the tray. When Sam sat on the sofa, the cat jumped onto the arm, fixing him with an unblinking blue stare.

He eyed it warily. "Is it always like this?"

"You mean *her*. And her name is Maow. Remember?"

Preshy set the tray with the coffee things on the tufted leather ottoman in front of him. It was already getting dark, and she drew the curtains, shutting out the frigid gray sky, then poured the coffee.

"I take it you don't like cats?" She offered him a dish of pastel-colored macaroons. "Try them; they're good. And try to be nice to Maow. She's just not used to men."

Sam noticed her blush when she realized she had left herself wide open to questioning as to exactly *why* there were never any men in her apartment, but she was saved by the phone.

It was Lily.

Preshy didn't know whether to be glad or just relieved. "Lily!" she said. "At last. I was beginning to think you didn't exist." There was silence. "Lily? Are you still there?"

"Why did you say that?" Lily demanded, sounding upset. "That I didn't exist."

"Well, first you didn't show up, then you didn't call, and I've never even met you." Preshy laughed.

"Precious, you don't understand. Soon I might not *exist*. I'm being followed. Somebody wants to kill me."

"*What?* To *kill* you? Why would anybody want to *kill* you?"

"I can't talk on the phone," Lily said.

"But where *are* you? And *who* is following you?"

"I'm in Venice," Lily said, and the mention of that fateful city sent a shiver down Preshy's spine.

"But I thought you were coming to Paris."

"I was. I thought he wouldn't be able to trace me. I thought he'd never look for me in Venice. . . ."

"Just stop for a minute," Preshy said, bewildered. "Tell me exactly what you're talking about."

"I'm talking about murder, Precious. I have something he wants, and he'll kill me to get it. You must come here immediately. Please, *please,* I'm begging you to meet me in Venice. Only you can help me. I'm at the Bauer Hotel." There was a long pause, and then, "It has to do with the man you know, called Bennett."

Lily rang off. Shocked, Preshy turned to look at Sam.

"What kind of long-lost-cousinly talk was that?" he said.

She sank into a chair, hands tightly clasped between her knees. "I could hear the fear in Lily's voice," she said, stunned.

"What exactly did she say?"

"That somebody is following her. That he wants to kill her because she has something he wants." She shook her head, still disbelieving. "She wants me to meet her in Venice."

"Did she say who *he* was?" Sam asked.

"His name is Bennett. We were getting married, and he left me at the altar. In Venice. Just a couple of months ago."

MAOW stretched out along the back of the sofa. "That's probably more information than you needed to know," Preshy said.

"It was very brave of you to tell me. You needn't have."

"It's the simple truth. I was ditched at the altar by a man I believed loved me. He disappeared without a trace. Aunt Grizelda tried to find him, but the detectives said he must have been using an assumed name. He told me he lived in Shanghai, claimed to have an export business, James Export Company, but it turned out not to exist." Preshy shrugged. "The real mystery is Lily. I don't know how she knows Bennett's name."

"He probably has several. Men like that usually do."

"Men like what?"

"Con men, criminals. Do you really think Lily believes it's this Bennett who's going to kill her?"

"Oh no, it couldn't be him. Bennett was a gentle man; he was never violent." Preshy slumped in the chair and took a gulp of her coffee, thinking. It all sounded crazy, but there was no doubt Lily was terrified. And if it had something to do with Bennett, she needed to find out.

"Lily's in trouble," she said to Sam. "She's my cousin, and she needs my help. I'm going to Venice to meet her."

"And exactly how do you propose to get there? Have you forgotten the airport's closed?"

"Then I'll drive."

"In *that* little car? In this weather?"

She gazed defiantly at him. "I'm a good driver; I'll stop off at Aunt Grizelda's. I can get a flight out from Nice."

"I'm not driving all that way in that Smart car," he said coolly. "We'll have to rent one."

Preshy gawped at him. "You mean you're coming with me? Why would you do that?"

"Hey, I'm stuck here in Paris anyway, so why not Venice? At least I'll get a better hotel room." He grinned disarmingly at her. "Besides, I can't let you go alone, not after an intriguing story like Lily's. So . . . Venice, here we come."

SAM took Preshy's car and went to pick up a rental while she called her aunts. She knew the two women always raced to be first to the phone, and this time they picked up simultaneously.

"Hi, aunts," she said, smiling. "I've decided to come visit."

"When?" they asked, in unison; then Mimi got off the phone and let Grizelda do the talking.

"I'm leaving right now, driving through the night. I'll be with you by lunchtime tomorrow."

"But Presh, you can't drive all that way alone."

"I'm not alone. I'm bringing a man with me."

"What *man?*" Aunt G sounded pleased.

"Oh, just some guy, an American writer I met in La Coupole last night."

She heard Aunt G yell to Mimi, "She picked up a man in La Coupole again last night." And then Mimi yelled back, "It's becoming a habit. I hope he's better than the other one."

"Anyhow, how long can you stay?" Aunt G said.

"I don't know if I can; we might go straight on to Venice. But I'll definitely get to see you." She winced, wishing she hadn't told her about going to Venice. Now some kind of explanation was needed.

"She's off to Venice," she heard Aunt G say in a shocked aside to Mimi. Then, to her, "*Why* are you going back there?"

"It's Cousin Lily Song. Her flight to Paris got diverted. She ended up in Venice and said she needed me." Preshy hesitated. "She said it was something to do with Bennett."

"You mean Lily *knows* Bennett?"

"All I know is what she said. That's why I have to go to Venice, to find out."

"Okay, we'll discuss this tomorrow. Call when you get close, and we'll meet you in Nice. Le Chantecler at the Hôtel Negresco does a good lunch. You can introduce the new pickup and tell us all about it."

PRESHY shoved the reluctant Maow into the travel carrier. Grumbling, the cat twirled a few times before settling down.

"What's that?" Sam asked. "The *cat's* coming with us?"

"Maow comes everywhere with me. Anyhow, what else would I do with her at this time on a Sunday?" He gave her an exasperated stare, and she said, "Let's get this straight, Sam Knight. Where I go, Maow goes. You don't like it, you know what to do."

He rolled his eyes but said nothing, so she led the way downstairs to the street where the rental car was parked. She put the carrier on the backseat, wedged next to her own packed duffel and Sam's bag that he'd picked up from the hotel.

Preshy made to get in the driver's seat, but he grabbed her arm. "Nope," he said, guiding her back to the passenger side and opening the door for her. "I'm driving."

"But I know the road well," she protested.

"But I don't know how you drive." He got behind the wheel; then he glanced sideways at her and gave her a grin. "Okay, Rafferty, so we'll take turns," he said generously.

She was fastening her seat belt when she had a sudden flash of the crusty bread and the good cheese still in her kitchen.

"Hang on," she said, sliding out again. She ran back through the courtyard and up the stairs, grabbed them and a couple of glasses, plates, knives and a bottle of wine, then ran back again. "Just in case frostbite sets in and the Saint Bernards can't reach us," she said, stuffing them into the already crowded backseat.

Sam was silent as he followed her directions, negotiating his way out of snowy Paris's complicated one-way system onto the *périphérique,* then onto the autoroute. On the motorway, driving through the dark frosty night, Preshy's eyes soon closed, and she fell asleep.

When she awoke a couple of hours later, it took a few seconds to remember where she was. She glanced quickly at Sam's stern profile as he drove, concentrating on the road, and she realized she knew virtually nothing about him except that he was a writer with a house on the Outer Banks. She wondered what his story really was. "Tell me about your wife," she said into the silence.

He turned his head fractionally. "I thought you were sleeping."

"I was."

He said nothing.

"Sorry," she said. "I don't mean to pry; I'm just curious about you."

"Her name is Leilani. I met her on one of those author's jaunts organized by the publisher. I was in Santa Fe, signing books. Leilani came in, she stayed around, and we got to chatting." He shrugged. "Three months later we were married."

"How romantic. What does she look like?"

He was silent for a long while; then finally he said, "She's kind of low-key beautiful. Half Hawaiian; long black hair; golden skin; slender; graceful. She's an artist. There's a big artists' colony in Santa Fe. We bought a house out in the desert a little bit. Just the two of us with my German shepherd, Cent. Leilani painted, and I wrote. It was ideal for her, but I'm a Low-Country boy, and I pined for the smell of the ocean. I missed the way the rivers flow through the marshlands, the call of the seabirds and the scudding low clouds. I needed them for my peace of mind, for the energy of my writing. So Leilani agreed to move, and we bought my dream house on the beach."

"And that's where you've lived ever since."

"I have an apartment in New York, on Gramercy Park."

"The best of both worlds," Preshy said, wondering why he was in Paris without his beautiful wife. "Any children?"

"No kids."

She thought of him returning to New York, and of Leilani waiting to greet him. "I guess you'll be awfully glad to see her again."

He pulled off the road into an autoroute café. "Time for coffee," he said.

THEY arrived a few minutes early and took the opportunity to freshen up in the Negresco's posh restrooms. Leaving Maow in the care of the concierge, Preshy and Sam made their way into Le Chantecler restaurant, where they ordered glasses of champagne.

She had warned Sam not to be surprised when he saw two old Las Vegas showgirls coming their way. Nevertheless, Sam's eyebrows rose when Mimi strutted across the ornate dining room, Riviera-smart in a pale pink wool suit and platform shoes that made her still-fabulous legs look even longer. Her blond hair was sleeked back into a chignon, and her rows of diamond bracelets glittered as she shook Sam's hand.

"*Enchantée*, M'sieur Knight," she said, sinking into a chair.

"There you are." Grizelda slinked toward them in a clinging red dress with a little sable jacket. She was carrying a beautiful white Valentino coat, which she handed to Preshy. "I knew you'd be wearing that green 'horror,' " she said. She held out her hand to Sam. "I hear you picked up my girl in La Coupole."

Sam smiled. "Should I apologize?"

She considered him. "I don't think so," she decided. "Come, sit down. Oh, you've already got champagne, good." She signaled the waiter and ordered two gin fizzes. "They know us here," she confided to Sam. "They understand exactly how Mimi and I like them." Then she turned to Mimi. "What d'you think, darling? Is he good enough for our girl?"

"Oh God!" Preshy shrank back in her chair. "Would you please stop it, Aunt Grizelda!" she said, but Sam just laughed.

They all ordered the filet of beef with capers and potato ravioli, then a quince tart with Granny Smith ice cream. With it they would drink a Provençal rosé.

"Now," Mimi said when that was taken care of, "let's get down to business. What's all this about Lily Song?"

So Preshy told them the whole story, and that Bennett was involved. "And that's the reason I have to go back to Venice," she finished. She looked warily at them. "Grandfather would have expected me to help her."

Grizelda had to admit she was right. "But you're going to have to be very careful," she said. "I don't like the sound of this." She glanced sharply at Sam. "Can I trust you to take care of her?"

Sam's eyes met hers. "I'll do my best," he said calmly.

She heaved a grateful sigh. "It's a pity you don't have the time to visit. I would have thrown a *petite soirée* for you, introduced you to some of my friends, though I must remind you, Preshy, never to drive the Corniche road to Monaco. I haven't driven it myself, since I was almost forced off the edge of the cliff by that madman after you and Bennett visited us."

Sam asked if Grizelda had reported the incident to the police, and she said she had, but of course by then it was too late to try to trace the white van.

"And so as far as you knew Bennett wasn't in the country?"

Puzzled, Grizelda said she didn't think so, and the subject was dropped.

Sam had managed to get them seats on the four o'clock Venice flight, and they walked outside to say their good-byes, leaving Maow with the aunts.

"Well?" Grizelda asked, her green eyes alight with curiosity as she hugged Preshy good-bye, while Sam went to get the car.

"Well *what?*"

"Ohh—*you know,*" Mimi said, exasperated.

"If you mean am I interested in him, the answer is no. We are two strangers passing in the night, that's all."

"If 'that's all,' what's he doing here with you?" Mimi said.

Preshy groaned. "Will you two stop with the matchmaking. He's just a guy I know. And anyhow, he's married."

"What!" Two pairs of stunned eyes stared at her.

"You mean you didn't notice the ring?"

"So where's the wife?"

"I don't know. In fact, I don't know much about him at all. He simply offered to come to Venice to help me with the Lily situation. And to tell you the truth, I was kind of glad he did."

"Hmmm . . . me, too," Aunt G said, thoughtfully, "though I do wonder why he did. Be careful this time, Preshy."

Nine

Venice

IT WAS dark when they landed in Venice, and Marco Polo Airport brought back a slew of memories of the last time Preshy had arrived there with Sylvie and Daria, carrying her beautiful wedding dress and cape, and of how elated she had been.

"I guess this brings back some difficult memories," Sam said out of the blue.

"It does," she admitted. "But I'm not going to think about it." Still, she closed her eyes so as not to catch a glimpse of the illuminated dome of the Santa Maria della Salute as they passed.

"This place is a real live Canaletto," Sam said.

She smiled. "Sometimes I wonder if he painted it first and they built it after; it's just so perfect," she said.

The *motoscafo* idled to a stop at the Bauer Hotel's private landing stage, where their luggage was whisked away and they were escorted inside. The luxurious hotel overlooked the Grand Canal, and its salons and rooms were redolent of the romance of another era. They checked in; then Preshy asked the desk clerk if there were any messages from a Miss Song, who was also staying at the hotel. The clerk checked, but there were none.

Sam said he wanted to see something of the city and was going out for a walk, but to her surprise he did not ask her to go with him.

In her room she drew back the curtains, and there across the canal was the Salute, its dome moonlike in the night sky. It seemed there was no escaping the past, and saddened, she went off to drown her sorrows in the shower, where her tears mingled with the water. She wondered if the heartache would ever really end.

IT WAS already evening when Lily awoke from a deep sleep that left her unrefreshed. She glanced at her phone, then remembered she had turned it off and of course there were no messages. Sitting up, she glanced nervously around the darkened hotel room. She still didn't feel safe, even though, logically, no one could know where she was. Except for Cousin Preshy, who, she fervently hoped, was on her way to meet her.

A short while later, showered and dressed, she contemplated room service but told herself she was being ridiculous. She was in Venice, one of the wonders of the world, a city she had never seen. At least she should see its glory and taste its food.

She walked through the narrow busy streets until she came to the Piazza San Marco with its magical views across the Grand Canal to the lagoon. Hearing music, she went inside its magnificent Basilica. A mass was about to begin, and she stood awed by the mosaics and the glitter of gold; by the Madonnas and the saints in their arched niches; by the great altar; and by the soaring singing of the choir. At that moment she felt a sense of peace and serenity that she prayed would stay with her forever.

After a while she left the Basilica and walked alongside the canal, thinking about her future once she had sold the necklace. A whole new world would open up to her. She hoped Cousin Precious would get here soon because she wanted so badly to talk to her, not only about the necklace, but now about so many more things.

Turning down a narrow side street, she came across a small restaurant. Liking the look of its simple dark-wood interior, she took a seat, ordering pasta with clams and a glass of white wine. Afterward she lingered over an espresso.

It was dark when she left, and there was no one about. Quickening her pace, she made for the bigger street alongside the canal, smiling when it came in view, gleaming under an almost full moon. She stopped to look, taking a deep wondering breath, admiring the silhouetted skyline with its domes and pinnacles. This was something she would never forget.

The blow to the head took her completely by surprise. She cried out once, then lifted her hands. The warm blood trickled through her fingers. Suddenly all around her it was growing dark; it was as though the lights of Venice were being extinguished, one by one. The push sent her staggering. Another push, and she was in the canal. And then everything was black. The dark water closed over her head with barely a ripple.

A perfect murder.

RESTLESS, Preshy decided to go for a walk. She flung on some clothes—jeans, a sweater, boots. It was cold out, and she put on the winter white wool coat Aunt G had given her, wrapped her long blue woolen muffler round her neck, then went downstairs and out the Bauer's street entrance.

She wandered idly through the narrow *calli,* shivering in the icy night wind. Every corner brought back a memory. The very stones under her feet and the peeling stucco walls seemed to breathe romance. There was the scent of coffee and of wood fires, aromas of pizza and bread and wine. The lit shopwindows offered a million temptations, and everywhere there was the sound of water lapping eternally at the edges of the sinking city.

Turning a corner, she found herself in front of the Palazzo Rendino. Her feet had simply taken her there without her even thinking. It wasn't lit up, though, the way it had been for her wedding festivities, and the little square was in darkness. She closed her eyes, feeling the stab of pain in the place where her heart used to be before it was broken. She walked to the spot by the entry where she and Bennett had stood with their arms wrapped around each other the night before he walked out of her life.

She wanted to believe there was still, somewhere, a flicker of hope, a logical explanation. She wanted so badly for Bennett to apologize to her, to tell her again that he loved her. But that could never be. Lonely, she wandered on, emerging into the glorious open vista of St. Mark's Square. It was filled with light and the flutter of pigeons, and busy people. Music wafted from the rival *caffès*, Quadri and Florian. The illuminated Basilica dominated her left, and on her right, the ancient stone arcades gleamed in the lamplight. And in front was the most magnificent view in all of Venice: the Grand Canal, with, beyond, in the mist, the islands and the lagoon.

Deciding that the Venetian specialty, a double espresso fortified with grappa, was exactly what she needed on this cold night, Preshy pushed through the etched glass doors into Quadri's rosy velvet rooms. And into a fog of cigarette smoke and laughter and string-quartet music. Hearing her name called, she looked up and saw Sam at a table with what looked like a double vodka on the rocks.

"Hi." She beamed, taking a seat next to him.

"It seemed to me it was about time for a drink," he said. "What d'you say?"

"Espresso with grappa. When in Italy . . ."

He called over the waiter, who quickly produced her coffee, and they clinked glasses and said *"cin cin,"* Italian style. Then he sipped his vodka, something she noticed he drank quite a lot of, while she called the hotel and asked if there was a message. Which there wasn't. "Still no Lily," she said. "She really is the most mysterious woman."

"A combination of Greta Garbo and Mata Hari," he agreed. "Since Lily's not around, let's have dinner."

So she took him to a small place she knew, an old monastery where, under an arched stone ceiling lit by sconces, they dined on tiny spider crabs and the Venetian classic, calves' liver with onions. And she was so busy talking about Venice that she forgot all about Lily.

MARY-LOU was on her third espresso, sitting opposite Bennett in the hotel bar.

Signaling the waiter, Bennett ordered a second grappa. He ordered one for her, too. "You look as though you need it," he said with a contemptuous lift of his lips that, she assumed, was his real smile.

Nevertheless, she downed the liquor, shuddering as it hit her stomach. Her black suede purse was on the table in front of her, with the new Beretta nestled in its shocking pink satin lining. She placed the purse on her lap. It gave her a feeling of security.

Bennett said, "Our only hope is that Lily's hidden the necklace in her suitcase or in the room safe." He fixed her with that hard implacable gaze. "We have her room key. If the maid sees you, she'll assume you are Lily."

Mary-Lou knew he wasn't about to allow her to go alone. Shivering, she ran the tips of her fingers over the bump that was the Beretta. She hated Bennett. She would shoot him rather than hand over the necklace.

They walked together to the elevator, then down the corridor to Lily's room. The maid on duty gave them a passing glance and a *"buona sera."* A lamp was lit, and the bed had been turned down. Lily's suitcase was on the luggage stand. She had not bothered to unpack, and Mary-Lou went quickly through its contents.

She glanced up at Bennett, standing, arms folded, watching her. "Not here," she said.

"Try the safe."

She did. It was empty. Mary-Lou sat on the bed and began to cry. She had gone to the limit—and for nothing.

Despising her, Bennett walked out of the room and out of the hotel. Mary-Lou was of no more use to him, and she was too involved now to go to the police. She had served her purpose and would go home like a good girl, and he would never hear from her again.

He walked the darkened backstreets of Venice for hours, trying to figure out what Lily might have done with the necklace. Suddenly the answer came to him. Of course. Preshy Rafferty must have it.

BACK at the hotel, Sam and Preshy went up to her room to check the phone for messages. The red light was not blinking. Preshy called Lily's room. No answer.

She looked at Sam. "What shall we do now?" she asked.

He threw up his hands wearily. "Check again in the morning."

They said good night, but worried and unable to sleep, Preshy called Daria in Boston and filled her in on what was going on. Of course Daria was alarmed.

"Presh, why did you go to Venice?" she said. "It sounds dangerous to me. And the Bennett part, that's all over for you."

"But I'm the only one who can help Lily. She truly has no one else," Preshy said. "Anyway, I'm not alone. I have a new friend with me. His name is Sam Knight. You might have heard of him," she added with a little smile in her voice.

"*What?* You're with *Sam Knight?* Presh, how'd you meet him?"

"You're not going to believe this. I picked him up in La Coupole Saturday night, in a snowstorm."

"You picked up *Sam Knight?*"

"Sure. Why not? He was stranded in Paris—no flights, airport closed. . . . Why? What's wrong with that?"

Daria sighed ominously. "I have to give you credit," she said. "You surely know how to pick 'em. I don't think you're going to like this, but about three years ago Sam Knight's wife disappeared."

"Disappeared?" Preshy's heart did a little jump. "What do you mean disappeared?"

"Here's the story. Sam told the police that the last time he saw his wife was at their beach house. He'd gone out fishing. He had a small boat, and he said he often fished at night. She didn't like the sea and never went with him. He said he'd left her in the house, with just their dog for company."

"What happened to her?"

"There was no sign of violence; nothing was disturbed, no robbery. The dog was still there. The bed was unslept in; the TV still on. She had simply disappeared. It was exactly like one of his mystery novels. Forensics took that house apart and came up with nothing. And to this day, Leilani Knight has not been found. I believe Sam is still 'a person of interest' to the police. They suspected he'd killed her. Everyone did."

"I don't believe it," Preshy said, shakily. "Of course he didn't kill her. Perhaps she ran off with another man."

"Do you seriously think she wouldn't have been found by now if she'd run off with somebody? It's been *three years,* Presh."

Preshy gripped the phone tight. That was why Sam was reluctant to talk about Leilani . . . because maybe he had killed her. "Life used to be so uncomplicated, Daria. I'm here with Sam, looking for Lily—and now I'm wondering exactly *why* he came with me."

"Be careful," Daria warned. "And get the next flight home. Without Sam Knight. I'm begging you, Preshy, get out of there."

Promising she would, Preshy said good-bye. She turned out the lamp and lay, rigid with shock, staring into the darkness.

Sam's lean face came into her mind; the brown eyes behind the glasses, his stern aloof profile as he drove the autoroute that dark night. She thought about how he had come to sit next to her in La Coupole, even though the place had been half-empty. *Exactly the way Bennett had.* And how he had said, so quickly, that he was coming with her to Venice. Was there something Sam knew that she didn't? Could he possibly be involved in this Lily saga, too? As well as in his wife's disappearance?

Oh my God. She was in Venice with a man suspected of murder, searching for another man who might also be involved in murder. *What had she done?*

FOR Sam, sleep was a lost art. He had been drinking all night, and it was still dark when, a little after six a.m., he left the hotel and retraced his steps along the canal-side walkway. There was no one around. After a while it began to rain, icy needle-sharp slivers that chilled him to the bone. He turned up his collar, zipped the jacket and walked on, uncaring, waiting for the dawn.

There was some activity on the canal. The fruit and vegetable delivery boats were heading for the Rialto market. And a police boat's blue lights flashed, just ahead of him.

A small crowd had gathered. He watched a police recovery team grapple with something in the water, then haul it in.

"Probably some tourist," he heard an Englishman in the crowd say. "The fish delivery boat spotted her. An Asian woman. Probably got drunk, fell in. It happens."

Sam turned and walked quickly down the maze of little lanes until he came to an open *caffè*-bar. He stood at the counter alongside men in suits and overcoats, newspapers tucked under their arms, grabbing coffee and *cornetti* on their way to the office. He ordered a double espresso, piled in the sugar, drank it down and ordered a second. He lit a cigarette, wincing at the acrid taste. It was almost eight before the caffeine cleared his liquor-overloaded head.

Back at the hotel, he stopped at the concierge's desk and asked him to get a seat on the flight to New York. He returned to his room and phoned Preshy.

"Isn't it a bit early to be calling?" she said coldly.

"There have been some developments. Get your clothes on, Rafferty. I'll give you five minutes."

He put down the phone, glancing at the empty bottle of vodka, then at the minibar. No, he wasn't going in that direction again. He had things to take care of.

SHE ANSWERED THE DOOR IN jeans and a T-shirt. Her pale eyes were ringed with shadows, and she looked exhausted.

Without speaking, she led the way into her room, then sat looking at him. "Well?" she said distantly.

Sam thought *frigid* was the word that might best describe her attitude. He wondered what had happened. He pulled up a chair and sat opposite her. "The police found the body of an Asian woman in the canal this morning. I'm guessing it's Lily."

"Oh my God," she whispered. "I *knew* it. I knew something was wrong." Her eyes narrowed. "How do you know about this?"

"I happened to be there when they fished the body from the canal, very early this morning."

"Oh. Right. You *just happened* to be out walking, before dawn, when the police found a body? That just might be Lily's? Isn't that a bit of a coincidence? I mean, you still can't find your wife, but you find Lily right away. What exactly *happened* to Leilani, Sam? Was it something similar to what's happened to Lily?"

Sam shrugged. Now he knew the reason for her iciness. "You've obviously heard the story, so why bother to ask?"

"Because I need to hear it from you."

"The truth and nothing but the truth," he said bitterly. "It's going to haunt me for the rest of my life."

He got up and walked to the door, hesitated, then turned to face her, staring silently down at the floor.

Finally he said, "My wife, Leilani, was a depressive. She was a fragile soul, shy and insubstantial; serene one minute, in the depths of despair the next. She left me that night, just as she had threatened to do so many times before. She didn't want to 'trouble' me any longer. What 'trouble,' I'd ask, angry she didn't understand I loved her and that was all that mattered. But Leilani hated the ocean. She was afraid of it. It was the reason she had left Hawaii. Santa Fe was a landlocked island of peace for her, and selfishly, I took her away from that.

"I don't know what happened to Leilani, but I guessed she had done what she'd always threatened to do. Left me so she wouldn't be any 'trouble.' " He lifted his eyes to look at Preshy. "She was such a very private woman; I couldn't share her personal torment with the world. The media would have had a field day. So instead I said nothing. After all, I was the guilty party. I'd taken her from the place she felt secure, to live in the place that finally drove her mad."

Despite Preshy's misgivings, he sounded so—defeated. "You think she . . . ?" She couldn't bring herself to say "killed herself."

"I don't think about it," he said abruptly. "At least I try not to. In my waking moments, that is."

She knew what he meant. At night, alone in the dark, all the whys and why nots, and if onlys. "I understand," she said, wanting to believe him, but still unsure.

His eyes behind the glasses were steely. "Do you?" he asked indifferently. He came back and sat opposite her again. "We have to talk about Lily. You'll have to tell the police you were supposed to meet your cousin here, and you think the body might be hers." His eyes met hers. "They'll want you to identify it."

Preshy gasped, horrified. "But I've never met her. I can't identify her. I don't even know what she looks like."

"Her passport will be at the desk or in her room."

Preshy's hand shook as she poured a glass of water from a half-empty bottle of San Pellegrino. It was warm and flat.

"There'll be an autopsy immediately, of course; then the body will be released to you." Sam glanced at his watch. "Better get going," he said. "Get it over with."

Getting a grip on her nerves, Preshy threw on Aunt G's coat and the muffler. "You're coming with me, aren't you?"

"I can't," he said quietly.

She stared at him, stunned. He was involved in this. . . . He couldn't just walk away, leave her to pick up the dreadful pieces.

"You're looking at a man who's been there before. I can't go through it again. Knowing what you know now, you have to understand. I'm flying back to New York. I'm sorry, Rafferty."

They stood, silently, looking at each other for a long moment. Then he shook his head and walked out of her room.

Somehow Preshy pulled herself together. She called Aunt Grizelda on her cell phone and told her the terrible news.

"Do nothing" was Aunt G's horrified response. "Mimi and I will be there with a lawyer in a few hours."

Pacing her room, Preshy went over and over again what Sam had said. Of course she knew that a man suspected of one murder could not afford to become a suspect in another. Again, she wondered why he had gotten involved with her. Could he know something about Bennett? And what was it Lily had possessed that someone wanted badly enough to kill for?

She wished she had never heard from Lily, or met Sam Knight, whose past was anyhow as murky as Lily's. *How could he leave me? He was there when they found the body. He was a part of this. He had no right to skip town.*

Aunt G arrived a couple of hours later on a private plane with a lawyer in tow. "You look terrible, *chérie,*" were her first encouraging words. "And where's the Knight in shining armor?"

"I *feel* terrible." Preshy burrowed her face in Aunt G's scented shoulder. "And the Knight left me to face the music alone. I can't blame him," she added, as the tears finally flowed. "He's been through all this when his wife disappeared and never came back."

"*What?*" Mimi let out a shriek and Aunt G gasped, and now Preshy was forced to tell them Sam's story.

"So you see," she concluded, "he's a suspect in his own wife's disappearance or possibly murder."

"Imagine, a nice man like that," Mimi marveled, thinking of the pleasant lunch at Chantecler. But Grizelda snorted and said as far as she was concerned all men were alike and none were to be trusted.

"Of course Maître Deschamps is an exception," she said with a sugary smile at the lawyer: a tall, imposing, silver-haired Frenchman with forty years of criminal law under his belt.

"Thank you for that, Countess," he said with a courtly bow. "But now I must accompany Precious to the *polizia*. And you, my dear," he said looking sternly at Preshy, "will not say one word. You will leave it all to me."

Preshy promised to keep her mouth shut, and Maître Deschamps informed the aunts they could not come along because he knew from experience he had no control over Grizelda.

The interview was not as traumatic as Preshy had feared. Maître Deschamps merely said that Precious was to have met her cousin from Shanghai, and the police captain said there didn't seem to be much mystery about a tourist falling into the canal and drowning, and that she'd probably had too much to drink. He thanked them for their help, promising the results of the autopsy the following day.

SAM's flight had a stopover in Paris, and it was half-empty. He drank down a vodka as they flew over the Alps, deliberately emptying his mind of the last few days' events.

Looking round, he noticed an Asian woman, an exceptionally attractive woman with a short black bob and almond-shaped eyes the color of warm amber. He wondered what *she* had been doing in Venice. Of course it was ridiculous to think she might have known Lily simply because they were both Asian, but he noted the coincidence.

He'd left Rafferty for two reasons. He could not afford to get involved, and there was nothing more he could do. It was over. Or was it? The question haunted him the entire flight.

He thought of her dealing with the police, taking charge of Lily's belongings, coping with shipping the body back to be buried. He had another drink, but even full of liquor, he could hear her voice saying, "You're coming with me, aren't you?" He could see her aquamarine eyes.

The plane made a bumpy landing in a still storm-tossed Paris, and he strode through the terminal to check in for New York. Halfway there, he changed course and went to Cathay Pacific, where he managed to get a seat on a flight departing for Hong Kong, and from there, a Dragonair connecting flight to Shanghai.

PRESHY's dreams were filled with the image of a woman's body floating just below the surface of the canal. The water lapped over her face, but the arms were outstretched, as though asking for help.

She shot upright, sweating. She glanced at the clock and groaned. Four-thirty. There were hours to be gotten through before the police would know if the body was really Lily's. Hours before she might be asked to identify a woman she had never met. She pictured the cold morgue, imagined the smell of formaldehyde, the covered female shape, the attendant lifting the sheet from the dead face. . . . *She couldn't do it.* But she must. There was no one else.

It was a long sleepless wait for morning. She was in the aunts' suite, having breakfast, when Maître Deschamps called.

"You can relax," he told her. "They were able to identify the body from her passport and from fingerprints. It is Lily Song, I'm afraid. Apparently, the damp cobblestones were slick; she slipped, hit her head and rolled unconscious into the canal. Death was from drowning. It was an accident. And my advice is to simply take her home and bury her and forget what she said on the phone."

"Well," Preshy said to the aunts, putting down the phone, "they are releasing the body. Now all I have to do is arrange for Lily to be shipped home to Shanghai for burial."

"But *who* will bury her?"

"Her friends . . . Surely there must be someone."

Preshy went with her aunts to Lily's room. Lily had not unpacked, and all her things were still in her suitcase. Looking at the small pile of underwear, the black suede pumps, the sweater, Preshy thought how pathetic they were; the leftover belongings of a dead woman. Tears pricked at her eyelids.

"I have at least to go to her funeral." she said.

"Then I'll go with you," Aunt G said quickly.

But Preshy knew that no matter how much her aunt denied being "old," the journey would be too arduous. "No need," she said. "I'll represent us. I'll take care of everything."

Grizelda found Lily's small black leather address book on the nightstand. "It's from Smythson, on Bond Street in London," she said approvingly. "Cousin Lily had good taste."

"Expensive taste, you mean," Preshy said, examining it. A few business cards were tucked into the flap behind the front cover. Lily's own, and others all in Chinese, except for one with the name Mary-Lou Chen, which had the same address as Lily's but with a different phone number.

Figuring Mary-Lou must work for Lily, she called the number. There was no answer. She couldn't just leave a message saying Lily was dead, so she hung up. She would try again later.

Ten

Shanghai

SAM guessed that Aunt Grizelda was not going to allow her "daughter" to stay in any old fleabag, and when he arrived at Pudong Airport, he called the five-star hotels. He'd guessed right. At the Four Seasons he was told Miss Rafferty was expected tomorrow. And yes, there was a room available. He took a taxi there right away.

Once installed, he ordered flowers to be delivered to her room. "Something exotic," he told the florist. "Orchids and peonies, that sort of thing." He wrote a card saying, "Welcome to Rafferty"; then he went to the steam room to clear his head. After that, he had the concierge look up the address and phone number of Song Antiquities, whose name he remembered from the parcel Lily had sent to Paris. Then he took a taxi there.

The area of the French Concession was an odd mixture of old-fashioned charm, high-level noise, speed and urban blight. But the broad leafy avenues had retained some of their glamour, and the narrow lanes were crowded with small businesses and tile-roofed houses hidden behind arched stone gateways. He rang Lily's bell and waited. No one came, but then he had expected that.

He told the cabdriver to take him to the market.

It was evening, and the streets were jammed with noisy people. The scent of temple incense mingled with the aromas from roadside stands, where all kinds of snacks were barbecued or boiled or fried. Sam pushed his way through the throng, dazzled by the flashing neon signs and the harsh rattle of the language; by the gongs and drums; by the children carrying balloons, yelling and darting; and by the crowds streaming in and out of the ornate red-columned temple, where fortunes were told in separate little booths.

He walked over to where the wise men of fortune-telling plied their trade and read the PR written in English for tourists like himself and the faded newspaper clippings tacked on the walls that proclaimed their excellent ability to foretell a man's future. On an impulse, he pulled aside a bead curtain and stepped inside.

The fortune-teller was a small, middle-aged man with narrowed eyes and smooth skin. He was sitting behind an empty table, and he waved Sam to a chair opposite.

Sam expected him to take out a pack of cards or at least a crystal ball, but instead the fortune-teller studied his face intently. Sam offered his palm to be read, but the man said, "Not yet. I am reading your cranium." Uncomfortable, Sam looked away.

"I see that when you were a child, you suffered a life-threatening sickness," the fortune-teller said finally. "Your mind is quick, facile. You are a creator. Success comes easily to you." The man's eyes narrowed to mere slits. "But tragedy stalks you. Images of violence and death have kept you in their thrall. And there is more even now, far from your home."

Startled, Sam said nothing; watching; waiting. He had indeed been very sick when he was only five years old.

The fortune-teller took Sam's palm. "The life line is long, but there are breaks in it. Here, when you were very young, and here again." He looked up at him, eyes narrowed. "Now," he said.

Sam didn't like the sound of that. "I'm searching for two people. I want to know if I'll find them."

The man's eyes met his. "The first person you seek is a woman, and the answer lies in your own soul," he said quietly. "For the second, the answer lies with another woman."

ALMOST TWENTY-FOUR HOURS later, Preshy emerged groggily from the elevator that took her up to the Four Seasons hotel, where she checked in.

"Madame, a gentleman is waiting at the bar for you," the desk clerk told her. "He wished me to tell you as soon as you arrived."

Her brain still reeling from seemingly endless hours of travel, Preshy wondered uneasily who it could be. She headed into the bar, and her heart did a double flip. It was Sam.

"What are you doing here?" she demanded.

"Waiting for you, Rafferty, of course," he said.

She squeezed onto the leather stool next to him. "Why?" she asked, looking into his eyes. They were red-rimmed behind the glasses.

"Because I can't let you go through this alone."

"Hah! The last time we spoke you didn't want to be involved. Anyhow, you look like crap."

"It's merely a reflection of the way I feel. By the way, what would you like to drink?"

She glanced disparagingly at the double vodka in front of him. "Perrier. With lime."

He said, "I had the opportunity to rethink my position on the flight to Paris. Let's just say I changed my mind."

The waiter delivered the water, and she looked into her fizzing glass, her shoulders sagging with weariness. "It was Lily in the canal, of course," she said. "They've shipped her body back. I came to bury her."

"I knew you would. I came here to help you."

She glanced at him. She still didn't know whether to trust him. After all, a man didn't fly halfway round the world to help her bury a cousin unless he had a motive.

"Thanks. But you don't have to." She slid from the stool. "I can take care of myself."

"Good. I'll see you around then."

"Maybe."

She glanced back at him as she trailed from the crowded bar, wanting to believe him.

And then there were the beautiful flowers waiting in her room, and her heart melted. Just a bit.

IN HER room, Preshy saw there were three messages waiting. Casting off her clothes, she showered, put on a robe, then flung herself on the bed, picked up the phone and listened.

The first was Aunt Grizelda, saying she must call and let her know she had arrived safely and tell her what was going on. The second was Daria. "What the hell are you doing in Shanghai? Why can't you leave well enough alone? If Super-Kid didn't have the chicken pox, I'd be on the next flight. Presh, I'm so worried. Please, please, *please,* tell me you're okay."

The last was Sylvie. "Aunt Grizelda told me all about it," she said sternly. "I can't tell you how reckless your behavior is. Why do you feel you have to be involved with this woman? Now you might be in danger." *Oh my God, Sylvie was crying!* "I'm getting a flight tonight. I hope you are still alive, Preshy. I love you."

Clicking off the lamp, Preshy lay back against the pillows, trying to adjust her aching travel-weary back to the soft comfort of the bed. She was so sleepy. . . .

IT WAS still dark when she awoke. She pulled back the curtains and stared out at the blinking neon of the foreign city, wondering what the day would bring. She thought of Sam, hunched over the bar, glass in hand, and wondered how he was feeling. He was probably out to the world. Still, he had come all this way to help her. She picked up the phone and ordered a full breakfast for two, right away. Then she called Sam's room.

It rang and rang, then at last, *"Wha . . . ?"*

She smiled wickedly. *"Bonjour,"* she said.

"What?"

"I said good morning. Perhaps you didn't recognize it in French." She heard him groan, fall back against the pillows. "Rafferty, do you know what time it is? *Five a.m.* Isn't that a *teeny* bit early for a telephone conversation in a foreign language?"

"You said to call as soon as I was ready, so . . . I've ordered breakfast for us. Should be here in ten minutes. I thought we'd discuss procedure."

"Last night I thought you never wanted to see me again."

"Like you, I changed my mind. See you in ten."

He was there in fifteen, arriving with the breakfast. His eyes behind the gold-rimmed glasses looked sunken.

"Try the orange juice." She handed him a tall chilled glass. "I hear it's good for hangovers."

He drank it down, then gave her a level look. "We each have our own way of dealing with our demons," he said. "Mine is drink. Yours, I assume, is cats."

Preshy laughed, suddenly missing Maow. "You're right."

They sat across from each other at the table. She poured coffee, and Sam helped himself to a croissant from the basket.

She handed him the little black leather address book. "You'll find all Lily's contacts in here. I thought about going through it, calling them one by one. But then I came across this card."

He read it. "Mary-Lou Chen. And the same address as Lily."

She stared at him astonished. "How do you know that?"

"The concierge got it from the telephone directory. I went over yesterday to check it out." He patted her hand. "Rafferty, after what happened to Lily, I think we'd better tread carefully."

"You sound like a writer," she said impatiently.

"Probably because I used to be one."

"Used to be?"

He shrugged. "Somehow I've lost the knack."

Looking at his haggard face, she felt pity for him. "I'm sorry for what I said the other day. About Leilani." She swirled the coffee dregs in her cup. "Thank you for coming here to help me."

"That's okay." He got to his feet. "I'll meet you here at nine-thirty to call Ms. Chen." He grinned at her from the door. "Better take a shower. You look like crap this morning."

MARY-LOU DID NOT LOOK TOO good either. She rummaged through her closet trying to decide what to wear. By rights she should wear white, the color of mourning, but she couldn't do that until Lily was found. If she ever was. Weren't there tidal currents in Venice that swept things away? Debris, possessions, bodies . . . She prayed it was so.

She finally put on a pair of khaki pants and a white shirt, tying it in a knot at the waist. She added a coral necklace and gold hoop earrings. She brushed her short black hair and applied her usual scarlet lipstick. She was not satisfied with the result. Murder, she thought, did not add luster to a girl's looks.

Throwing on a red leather jacket, she took the elevator down to the garage, got in the little car she hated and drove to the French Concession. Life must go on. She must act as though nothing was wrong.

She let herself into the courtyard, parked next to Lily's SUV, walked onto the verandah and unlocked the door.

The old house seemed eerily quiet. Not even the ticking of the clock disturbed the silence. The clock had been Lily's mother's, brought over from France, stolen along with the necklace, and it had always been there. Now it had stopped.

Superstitious, Mary-Lou shivered. She opened up the case and gave the hands a little push. The clock still didn't tick. She searched in the drawer underneath, found the key and wound it. There was a whirring; then the clock fell silent. She flung the key back and slammed the drawer shut.

She was heading down the rickety wooden cellar steps to the big safe when her phone rang.

"Yes?" she said impatiently.

"Am I speaking to Miss Chen? Mary-Lou Chen?"

It was a woman's voice, but no one she knew. "Yes," she said in a tone that indicated she was busy.

"Miss Chen, this is Precious Rafferty speaking. Lily's cousin from Paris."

"Ohh." Shock hit her first, then fear.

"Miss Chen, I'm here in Shanghai—"

"You are in *Shanghai?*"

"I need to see you. I have some important news."

"What kind of news?"

"I prefer to speak to you in person, Miss Chen. I can be there in half an hour, if that's okay with you."

Mary-Lou hesitated. If she refused, it might look suspicious. "I'm happy to meet any relative of Lily's. I'm sorry she's not here to greet you personally, but by coincidence she's in Europe."

"I know," Precious Rafferty said, sending new chills down her spine. "In half an hour then, Miss Chen."

Despite the surprise phone call, Mary-Lou had just enough time to pack all Lily's illegal profits in the basement safe into a suitcase and into the trunk of her car. And speaking of cars, Lily's was much better than hers. The keys were probably still in it. She would take possession of that later.

SAM said it would be better if Preshy met Ms. Chen alone, so leaving him in a nearby teahouse, she walked down the lane to Lily's gate, rang the bell and waited. Mary-Lou answered on the intercom and buzzed her in.

The big old house with its fragrant lotus pond, goldfish and trickling fountain made her feel as though she were entering another, more tranquil world. Mary-Lou was standing on the verandah steps waiting for her.

"Won't you please come in," she said. "Lily will be so sad to have missed your visit, but I hope I can make up for it with some small hospitality."

She waved Preshy into the living room, indicating a chair, then excused herself to get the tea. Curious, Preshy looked around, noting the spare furnishings, the shiny bamboo floor, the altar table with the golden Buddha. It was simple and quite beautiful, and for the first time she wished she had known her cousin.

Mary-Lou was back in an instant, and Preshy thought admiringly how lovely she was, with her shiny black hair and wonderful amber eyes and that full scarlet mouth in a shade of lipstick Preshy would never have dared to wear.

Mary-Lou poured the tea into small handleless blue-glazed cups. "It's really a great pity. Lily would have liked to have met you. You are her only relative?" She offered Preshy a cup.

"I'm her only European relative. I don't know about her father's family."

"Lily hated her father," Mary-Lou said bluntly. "She and her mother had no contact with the Song family after he died. Lily is very much on her own. I've tried often—oh so often—to get her to attend parties and functions, but Lily is a loner. She's dedicated to her work," she added, smiling candidly. "Lily has exquisite taste in antiques, but of course most of her business is with the tourist trade copies."

"Fakes," Preshy said.

"If you wish to put it that way, though they are never sold as authentic." She lifted a delicate shoulder in a shrug that made Preshy wonder if she was even capable of making an ungraceful move. "They make us our living."

Preshy looked at her. "I have some bad news, Miss Chen."

"Bad news?" She frowned, looking concerned.

"Lily was in Venice. There was an accident. I'm sorry to tell you, but Lily drowned."

Mary-Lou shrank back in her chair. Her eyes glittered with tears, and she wrapped her arms across her chest. "But why was Lily in Venice? I thought she'd gone to Paris. She even mentioned she hoped to see you. . . ."

Preshy wondered why Mary-Lou hadn't told her that earlier, but she thought perhaps it was just the Chinese way not to discuss personal business with a stranger.

"I'm so sorry," she said gently. "But the fact is I've brought Lily home to be buried." She put the piece of paper with the address and number of the Chinese funeral home on the low table between them. "I was hoping you could help. I don't know the customs and traditions. I don't even know who her friends are."

Mary-Lou said of course she'd take care of it. That there were no friends, only her, and if Miss Rafferty would excuse her, she was a little upset and needed to be alone.

Promising to call later, Mary-Lou saw her out. At the gate, Preshy turned to say good-bye, but the door was already shut. Poor thing, she thought. It's been a terrible shock.

Sam was waiting at the teahouse, sipping a brew he said was called *longjing* tea that he was becoming quite fond of.

"Beats vodka," Preshy said, tasting it.

"What are you, Rafferty? Some kind of reformer?"

"Sorry, sorry . . . Well, anyway, Mary-Lou Chen is a beauty and a sweetheart. Oh, Sam, when I gave her the bad news, that lovely young woman just looked like a frightened child."

"Why frightened? I would have expected shock."

She stared at him. Of course he was right. "I don't really know."

LATER that evening, Sylvie arrived, jet-lagged and furious. "You don't deserve me," she said as Preshy embraced her in the Four Seasons lobby. "I'm a martyr to your emotions."

"Good," Preshy said, "I could use a martyr. It'll make a change from a boozer."

"What boozer?"

"Sam Knight. He's taken to drink."

"I'm not surprised, being around you." Sylvie stopped and gave her a sharp look. "I thought he'd gone back to the States."

"He changed his mind." Preshy laughed. "Either he's got something to do with it or he's succumbed to my fatal charm."

"Seeing as women keep disappearing when Sam Knight is around, has it occurred to you to wonder whether you might be next?"

They rode the elevator in silence, then walked in silence to Preshy's room, which Sylvie was going to share.

Preshy said, "Sylvie, I'm in Shanghai for two reasons. One was to bring home poor Cousin Lily. The other is because Lily said this whole thing had to do with Bennett."

"So?"

"I want to find him, but I've never had an address. Now I have Lily's address book, but I've gone through it page by page and found no Bennett James."

Sylvie sighed as she sank wearily into a chair and looked through the address book. "It might not be under Bennett's name," she said. "For instance, here's a Ben Jackson. And then there's a Yuan Bennett. They might be worth a try."

While Sylvie showered away the travel blues, Preshy called the two numbers. The first was an antiques dealer whom Mary-Lou Chen had told about the funeral. The second number no longer existed. "But there's an address," Preshy said, as Sylvie emerged wrapped in a robe, with her hair in a towel. "Maybe I should go there and find out."

Sylvie threw her a warning look. "Oh no," she said. "Not without me you don't, and I'm going to sleep." She yawned. "Just don't do anything foolish until I wake up, okay?"

But when Sylvie was snoring, in about two minutes flat Preshy put on her coat and went downstairs to the bar.

"Not you again," Sam said, swinging round as she tapped him on the shoulder. "Can't a man drink in peace?"

"Not when he's with me, he can't. My friend Sylvie just arrived from Paris. I showed her Lily's address book. I might be on Bennett's trail." She told him about Yuan Bennett, hoping he would say, "Okay, let's go," but he did not, and he didn't ask her to stay and keep him company either. Finally she stalked off and went outside.

Shanghai glowed like a new planet under halogen arc lights, with illuminated skyscrapers shimmering like stars in the heavens. Signaling a taxi, Preshy climbed in and gave the driver Yuan Bennett's address.

It was a tall expensive condo building, built of shiny pink granite with a pair of rugged bronze lions placed at odd *feng shui* angles outside, to protect the good *chi.* A uniformed doorman opened the taxi door for her.

"I'm looking for a Mr. Yuan Bennett," she told him hopefully.

"So sorry, but Mr. Yuan no longer here."

So it was Bennett *Yuan,* not Yuan Bennett. "Could you tell me where I can find him?"

"So sorry, miss, but Mr. Yuan left after his wife died."

"His wife?"

"Yes, miss. Ana Yuan was in Suzhou, a pretty place with many canals, like the Venice of China, people say."

"Venice?" Preshy repeated, stunned.

"Yes, miss. Unfortunately, Mrs. Yuan tripped. She banged her head and slipped into the canal. She was drowned, miss. They said Mr. Bennett did not inherit his wife's money and could no longer afford this magnificent apartment."

Preshy thanked the doorman. Back at the hotel, she found Sam still in the bar. She slid onto the stool next to him.

"Sam, you're not going to believe this," she said. And then she told him the Bennett Yuan story and how his wife had drowned in the Suzhou canal.

"I still can't believe it's my Bennett though," she said.

"Hah! What do you need, Rafferty? A signed confession? Of course it's him." Sam turned back to his drink. "And why did you go there alone? Anything might have happened."

"Oh no, Bennett would never harm me. It's just a trail of circumstantial evidence. We don't even know it's the same man."

Groaning, Sam drained his glass. "Rafferty," he said, "you need your head examined."

"Maybe I do." She slid off the stool. "And I should have known better than to expect sympathy from you."

"You don't need *sympathy,*" he said. "You need a brain!"

Back in the room, turning the TV on low, Preshy watched Chinese programs, her mind full of Bennett Yuan. Could the two drownings really be just a coincidence?

THERE were only a half dozen mourners at Lily's funeral, and three of them were Preshy, Sylvie and Sam. The others were Mary-Lou Chen; Ben, the business friend Preshy had spoken to on the phone and a frail old man with a stiff goatee beard and flowing hair in worn gray robes.

At the temple they lit bundles of fragrant incense and thin bamboo sticks, watching the smoke spiral upward. They were told this would assist Lily's spirit on her journey to heaven. A small group of paid mourners walked behind the coffin on the way to the burial ground, banging on drums and cymbals and wailing a song for the dead. It was, Preshy thought sadly, the most lonely funeral anyone could ever have.

Tears streamed down Mary-Lou's beautiful face, and she bowed her head sorrowfully. After the burial, the businessman left quickly. The old man went over to Preshy and the others, bowing as he shook each of their hands.

"I came across Lily again only a short time ago," he said. His beard wagged as he spoke, and his rheumy old eyes were soft with sorrow. "Her mother, before she died, entrusted me with something for Lily, to be given to her on her fortieth birthday. And so, a few months ago, I gave her the necklace in its red leather box."

They stared at him, surprised. "A necklace?"

He nodded. "With a history almost as valuable as the jewels themselves. I am sure you will find your grandmother's necklace amongst her possessions, and then it will become yours." He bowed and walked away down the path to the gate.

"What can he mean 'grandmother's necklace'?" Preshy said. "Does he mean the one in the photograph?"

"The photograph that went missing," Sam said.

"Ohh . . . ," she said, remembering that Bennett was the only other person who had been in her apartment.

"Here comes Mary-Lou," Sam muttered. "Just act natural."

Natural! Preshy hardly knew what "natural" was anymore.

Mary-Lou smiled sadly as Preshy introduced the others. Dabbing at her eyes, in a quiet voice she thanked them for coming. "We were childhood friends, Lily and I," she said, "two little half-Chinese outcasts who bonded immediately. Now I would be pleased if you would do me the honor of returning to her house to take some tea."

They had rented a car and driver, and now they followed Mary-Lou back to Lily's home. Looking calm and beautiful in her white Chinese dress, Mary-Lou served tea with special round buns filled with a sweet lotus paste.

"I was sad to see so few mourners," Preshy said. "I'd hoped Lily would have had more friends to say good-bye to her."

Mary-Lou shrugged. "I told you she lived for her work."

"I'm surprised that manufacturing and selling replicas could mean that much to anyone," Sam said, sipping his tea. He was beginning to like Chinese tea very much.

Mary-Lou seemed suddenly flustered. "It does seem odd. But Lily and I grew up poor. Making money was her obsession."

"And yours also?" His eyes lingered on the five-carat diamond on her finger. "Lily must have left quite a legacy."

A flicker of irritation crossed her face. "I have not gone through Lily's things, Mr. Knight. But her world was very small. What you see here is all she had. As far as I know."

"But she must have a lawyer who took care of her affairs."

"Like all Chinese, Lily kept her personal business close to her own heart. I never heard of her using a lawyer. However, I do know there is a safe in her bedroom. And I do know where she hid the key," she added with a half smile. "She kept forgetting where it was, so she always told me." Getting to her feet, she said, "Why don't we go and see?"

They followed her into the bedroom. Mary-Lou fished the key from under the sweaters in the closet and pushed aside the hanging clothes to reveal the small gray door.

There was very little inside. Some gold jewelry, jade bangles and a bundle of papers. Mary-Lou read them.

"These are the title deeds to this house," she said. "Of course now it's quite valuable."

"What about bank accounts, safe-deposit boxes?" Sam looked hard at her, but Mary-Lou did not flinch.

"There is, of course, a business account. Her property will go to her nearest living relative. Miss Rafferty, I suppose."

Preshy looked at her, surprised. "Oh, but I don't think ... I mean, you were her best friend; it should go to you."

"Let's talk about it later," Sam interrupted curtly. "Meanwhile, if you can find the time, perhaps you can go through the house and see if there's anything else."

"Of course." Mary-Lou walked them to the door. "And thank you again for all you did for Lily. It was so tragic, drowning like that, in Venice of all places. I still don't know what she was doing there."

When they got in the car, Sam said, "Of course she knew."

"Knew what?" Preshy and Sylvie stared at him.

"Knew what Lily was doing in Venice. Mary-Lou knew because she was also there. She was on my flight from Venice to Paris."

"Oh ... my ... God," Preshy whispered. "Do you think she had something to do with Lily's death?"

"Why else would she have been there? And my bet is it has something to do with your grandmother's fabulous necklace."

Eleven

Paris

SAM checked into the Hôtel d'Angleterre, just down the street from Preshy's store, and then they went back to her apartment. She had called Aunt G, who had shipped Maow back by special courier so the concierge could let the cat in and feed her, and now she came running with a welcoming yowl. Preshy kissed and hugged her and gave her some of her special cat treats. Then she fixed coffee and went and sat on the sofa opposite Sam, staring gloomily at the empty fire grate.

"We have no proof Mary-Lou was in Venice," she said.

"No, but the police could check the airlines. We also have no proof Bennett James, or Bennett Yuan, or whoever he is, killed his wife, but I'd still bet my shirt on it. And one of them killed Lily."

"How can you say that?" She glared at him. "There's no proof of any of this. The autopsy showed Lily's death was an accident."

"And so was Ana Yuan's. You have to go after Mary-Lou. Somebody killed Lily for your grandmother's necklace. And I *know* she was in Venice."

"But I *can't*," Preshy said, feeling the tears coming.

Sam groaned. "Why not? Are you afraid to know the truth?"

Her temper flared. "What do you mean?"

"Aw come on, Rafferty, admit it: you don't want to know if perfect Bennett—or sweet, beautiful and oh-so-sad Mary-Lou—had anything to do with Lily's death."

"Oh, stop it!" She turned away. "Just leave me alone, why don't you?"

Sam got to his feet. "The trouble with you, Rafferty, is that you always think the best of everybody."

"And the trouble with you, Sam Knight, is that you never think the best of anybody. And anyway, you were not exactly helpful to the police in finding out what happened to your wife."

They stared at each other across a chasm of animosity.

Sam nodded. "You're right," he said. "But you know the old saying, 'Two rights don't make a wrong.' Well, this time those old soothsayers were correct."

Preshy watched as he collected his coat from the back of a chair.

At the door, he turned to look at her, remembering the fortune-teller telling him, "The answer to your second question lies with another woman." That woman was Rafferty. Only she could unravel this mystery.

"Call me—if you change your mind," he said, closing the door behind him.

Tears stung Preshy's eyes. She was exhausted from the long plane journey, battered by the events of the past few days. Sam had no right to treat her like that. She didn't even like him anymore. She would never call him. And if he called her, she would not even speak to him. Ever again.

SHE WAS IN THE SHOWER WHEN the phone rang the next morning. Ignoring it, she let the hot water soothe her bones, wondering why the message center wasn't picking up. It had been acting up for the past few weeks though.

But the ringing went on and on, and suddenly every bad thing that might have happened jumped into her head. Something must be wrong. Why else would anyone keep on ringing like this? Frantic, she grabbed a towel, ran into the bedroom and reached for the phone, just as it stopped. She waited a few minutes, but when it didn't ring again, she went back to the bathroom.

Looking in the mirror, she began smoothing on the face cream that was guaranteed to prevent the ravages of time. Maybe time, but what about stress?

She jumped as the phone's shrill beep split the silence again. She just knew it was Sam and was she going to let him have it for letting the phone ring and ring like that. She ran to answer it. "If it's you, Sam Knight," she said frostily, "I don't want to speak to you ever again."

There was a long silence; then a familiar voice said, "Preshy, it's Bennett."

She stood for a minute, rigid with shock. The blood seemed to drain from her brain, and she thought she would faint. Her knees gave way, and she sank onto her bed.

"Preshy? Please speak to me," he was saying. "I need to talk to you. I need to explain. . . ." His soft tone brought back a thousand intimate moments spent right in this bed.

"I don't want to talk to you ever again," she said, surprised to find that she even had a voice.

"I understand. Believe me, all I'm asking is that you see me, just for the length of time I need to tell my side of the story. Preshy, I can't go through life with this burden of guilt on my shoulders."

She lay against the pillows, eyes tightly shut. Tears trickled across her cheeks. She hadn't expected to feel like this. She'd thought she was over him. No more Pity Days. . . . Move forward. . . . A new life ahead. . . . And within minutes she'd been reduced to a trembling wreck.

"I always loved you, Preshy," Bennett was saying urgently. "But I hadn't told you the truth; that's why I couldn't go through with it. And it was too late. The truth is I had no money, Preshy. I was a poor guy faking it because I was in love. I couldn't marry you and live the lie I'd constructed around me. And I couldn't tell you the truth. It all became too much. I didn't mean to hurt you."

She said nothing.

"Preshy, are you still there?" There was a long silence as he waited for an answer. "Speak to me, sweetheart," he said with a catch in his voice, as though, like her, he was crying.

"I don't know why you're calling me, Bennett," she said at last, sitting up and drying her tears. She wasn't going to be caught out again by his honeyed words and declarations of love.

"I must see you," he was saying. "You have to forgive me, Preshy, because only then can we go on. I'm in Venice. Meet me in Venice, my darling. I'm begging you to at least meet me here and let me explain. You have to *trust* me."

She closed her eyes again, silent.

"There's something else," he said, in a suddenly quiet voice. "I know who killed Lily. And it wasn't me. Believe me. I'll tell you everything when you get here. But you are in danger, too, Preshy."

Oh my God. What was he saying? She had to see him. To find out the truth. Or it would haunt her all her life.

"I'll meet you, Bennett. I'll be there tonight."

His voice seemed to lift with joy and relief as he said, "Oh, sweetheart, it'll be so wonderful to see you again. You're gonna love it here. It's Carnevale time, the pagan festival when everyone wears masks and dresses up. I'll get tickets for a ball. Why don't you bring a costume? We'll pretend we don't know each other, start all over from the beginning, like two new people."

Preshy tried to imagine that but couldn't. "Give me your number" was all she said. "I'll call when I get there."

"I love you, Preshy" were his last words before she rang off.

And despite herself, despite all the progress she'd made, despite Lily, despite all the questions in her head, Preshy still wondered if it were true.

She needed to put closure to Lily's murder and this whole disastrous episode. And she also needed to know the truth about him and who he really was.

QUICKLY, before she could change her mind, she called and got a noon flight to Venice. Then she began to pack. Maybe the carnival disguise was a good idea. She could watch him, and he wouldn't know it was her.

Her wedding outfit still hung in the very back of her closet where she had buried it in its plastic shroud. Now she took out the fur-trimmed cape. It would be the perfect disguise; the wedding cape the groom had never seen. She rolled it mercilessly into a bundle and stuffed it in her carry-on. She rang the Bauer, but they were full, they said. So a small *pensione* near the Rialto would have to do.

She called the concierge to come in and feed the cat, then considered who else to call. She had at least to let Aunt G know where she was going. And why.

She was relieved, though, when she got no reply, because she knew what the aunts' response would be. Jeanne never answered when the aunts were out because the messages were often in foreign languages, so the message center picked up.

"Hi, it's me. I just want to tell you I'm going to Venice to meet Bennett. He wants to see me, to explain. He said he knows who Lily's killer is. I have at least to give him that opportunity to prove himself, don't I?" she said, sounding less sure than she'd meant to. "Anyhow, I'll be at the Pensione Mara, near the Rialto." She left the number, then said, "Love you . . ."

GRIZELDA'S scream brought everybody running. It came from her room, and Mimi, Jeanne, Maurice and the dogs all arrived at the same moments. Unable to speak, Grizelda was on the bed, wafting her face with a hand to stop herself from fainting. She pointed to the phone and mouthed the word "message." Mimi pressed the button. *"I'm going to Venice to meet Bennett. He wants to see me, to explain. . . . he knows who Lily's killer is. . . ."*

"Oh . . . mon . . . dieu." Mimi sank onto the bed next to Grizelda, while Jeanne rushed to get glasses of ice water and Maurice opened the windows for some air. "The silly little fool," Mimi exclaimed. "We have to stop her."

Grizelda nodded. "Call Sam," she said, gulping down the water. "Send a plane for him. Tell him we'll meet him in Venice."

Mimi did as she was told. Sam answered on the first ring. "If it's you, Rafferty," he said, "remember we are not speaking."

"Well, soon you will be, I hope," Mimi said briskly. And then she told him the story. "Drive to the airport at Orly," she said. "A plane will be waiting for you. We'll meet you at Marco Polo."

She didn't have to tell him twice. He was in a taxi in less than five minutes and an hour later was in a private four-seater Cessna on his way to Venice.

So were Mimi and Grizelda, though they were in a Gulfstream. For once they were tense and silent. Every now and then Grizelda would moan, "How could she be so stupid?" And Mimi would answer, "Because she still hasn't learned about men, that's why. The poor fool still believes she's in love."

At Marco Polo, Sam came racing toward them, lanky and lean in his black leather jacket and jeans. They all took a water taxi to the Rialto and walked to the *pensione*. They were told that the *signorina* had checked in, but she was not there right now.

Sam tried Preshy's cell phone, but it was switched off, so Grizelda called the Cipriani and, using her influence, got them rooms. At the hotel, while the two aunts went to freshen up, Sam found a bar and sat brooding over a triple espresso. He was on the wagon—he'd need all his wits to get Preshy out of this one. He was very afraid for her.

Venice

AS DARKNESS fell, Venice came to life. Gondolas full of bizarrely masked and costumed revelers poled down the canals, and crowded motor launches sped back and forth in a surge of spray. Music pounded, and the narrow streets teemed with masked partygoers. Laughter and song echoed across the lagoon, and fireworks split the sky into a million stars. It was Carnevale in Venice.

Sam dialed her number again. *Nothing.* He called her at the *pensione.* Nothing. Grizelda and Mimi had rejoined him and were sitting silently, their faces drawn with worry. "I don't know where she is," he said, "but I'm going over there."

They jumped up. "We're coming with you."

"No. No, you can't." He didn't want to scare them by saying it might be dangerous. "Please," he said. "Let me take care of this. I'll call as soon as I know anything."

"Promise?" they said together, and he nodded.

But the aunts didn't take him at his word. Instead they took the launch right behind him to the Piazza San Marco.

PRESHY was sitting in Quadri's, but she wasn't thinking about Bennett; she was thinking about Sam. She was even sitting at the same table by the window where they had sat together, bickering, over their drinks. She almost wished he were here with her now. But she needed to prove to herself that she could do this alone.

She was wearing the brocade wedding cape with the fur-edged hood thrown back and a feathered eye mask. With her new short hair, she doubted Bennett would even recognize her. Of course *she* would know *him.* How could she not when every aspect of his face and body were permanently engraved on her mind?

Nervous, she took another sip of the hot grappa coffee. It was dark outside, and the winter mist was starting to roll in over the lagoon in great curls of gray vapor. She took her phone from her bag and called Bennett's number. He answered immediately.

"Preshy," he said, in a husky voice filled with emotion. "I'm so happy. I can't wait to see you."

She did not respond to that. "Where shall we meet?" she asked.

"You'll never guess where the ball is. At the Palazzo Rendino. A perfect place for our reunion. Why don't we meet there? I hope you brought your costume."

She nodded. "I did."

"I'm a Plague Doctor," he said with a laugh in his voice. "Like a thousand guys tonight. Black cloak, black britches, tricorne hat, white face mask. Think you'll recognize me?"

"How could I not?" she said.

"And what's *your* disguise?"

"You'll have to wait and see," she said, and rang off.

Her phone rang again immediately. She didn't answer. After a few minutes though, curiosity got the better of her, and she listened to the message.

"Rafferty, where the hell are you?" Sam yelled. "Your aunts told me what happened. Are you out of your mind? I've tried and tried to call you, and now I'm on my way to the Piazza San Marco. I *know* you're there. Call me. And don't do anything dumber than what you already have."

He was in Venice. "Don't do anything dumber!" he'd said. Like meet you, she thought.

Sam had the knack of rubbing her the wrong way. It would almost be soothing to be back in Bennett's company. At least he'd always been nice to her. Before he dumped her, that is.

BENNETT paced the alley that ran down the side of the Palazzo Rendino, linking the small cobbled square with the canal. Music blared from the open windows, and lanterns glimmered in the fog that hovered inches above the water. Every now and again party boats and gondolas filled with drunken young people burst through the mist in a shout of noise and laughter. Everyone was masked; everyone was anonymous. It could not have been more perfect.

His costume was based on the outfits worn by doctors in the great plague that swept Venice in the Middle Ages, and he also carried the "plague stick" they had used in examining their patients in order to avoid catching the disease. Except Bennett's stick was heavier, though playfully disguised with ribbons. It was not so different from the one he'd used when he killed his wife, Ana, and then Lily.

THE Piazza San Marco was erupting with a surging mass of dancing people. A stage had been erected for the band, and the sound of trumpets blared from massive speakers, echoing off the old walls. The entire city was partying in the grand piazzas and at the palaces and on their boats.

But the narrow side streets leading off were empty. The shops and restaurants were closed, and the fog swirled like cotton wool, pressing so close to Preshy's face she could hardly see a foot in front of her. Her gorgeous wedding cape billowed behind as she hurried on, the low heels of her slouchy black boots ringing on the cobbles. She didn't recall coming this way before, but tonight everything looked different, as though Venice itself was wearing a disguise. There were no partygoers here, and, nervous, she looked around. Surely she would come to a landmark soon.

As she crossed a tiny stone bridge, she heard footsteps behind her. Suddenly a Plague Doctor burst from the fog, followed by half a dozen other masked men and women. He brandished his stick, and terrified, she cried out, but their laughter only mocked her as they ran off again.

Now she wished she had asked Sam to come with her. Taking her phone from her jeans pocket, she dialed his number. He answered immediately.

"Please tell me where you are," he said. "I'm begging you, Rafferty; just tell me."

"I'm on my way to the Palazzo Rendino to meet Bennett. There's a Carnevale ball. He's wearing a Plague Doctor costume with a white mask. I thought it would be all right, but now I'm scared."

Suddenly, at the end of an alley, she spotted the familiar square.

"I'm here," she said, in relief.

"Stay right there!" Sam ordered. "Wait for me. And Rafferty, whatever you do, do *not* go near him. Okay?"

"Okay," she said in a small voice as Sam rang off.

His phone rang at once. "Where are you?" Grizelda demanded.

"On my way to the Palazzo Rendino. She's meeting Bennett there."

"Not without me, she's not," Grizelda snapped, and rang off.

Preshy hesitated in a corner of the little piazza. She was wondering what her next move should be when she felt a pair of arms snake round her and breathed the familiar smell of Bennett's cologne. "There you are, my lovely Preshy," he whispered in her ear. "At last."

She swung round in his arms—and looked into the terrifying white mask of the Plague Doctor. But it was Bennett's fierce blue eyes blazing at her from behind it, Bennett's voice saying how happy he was to see her, Bennett telling her she was so good to come . . . and that he could explain everything and protect her from Lily's killer.

Hypnotized, she stared back at him.

"You look so beautiful," he said. "Even though you're masked, I recognized you by your walk." Her hood fell back, and he put up his hand and touched her golden cap of hair. "But you cut off your hair," he said, sounding sorrowful.

She stared at him, like a small animal caught in the headlights of his eyes. Palazzo music buzzed in her ears. It was as though she were not really there, that this was some other woman falling under Bennett's spell all over again.

In the back of her mind she heard Daria's voice. *"Move forward. . . . A new life ahead. . . ."* And she heard Sam. *"You're definitely a Rafferty."* She was strong; she was a new woman. She was herself, and she was no longer Bennett's puppet.

She jerked out of his arms. "Tell me what you brought me here for. And make it good, Bennett, because I don't trust you. I want to know exactly why you left me at the altar. And who killed Lily."

"I told you I was ashamed. And I'll tell you about Lily. But first, tell me where the necklace is," he said in an oh-so-quiet voice that sent chills down Preshy's spine.

Frightened, she took a step back. Of course! That was why he wanted her to come to Venice. *Oh God,* and fool that she was, she had fallen for it! Glancing round the deserted piazza, she wondered desperately where Sam was. The Palazzo and its partygoers might have been a million miles away for all the good they were now.

"I don't have the necklace," she said, stalling for time.

"Yes, you do. I *know* Lily gave it to you." He put his arms round her again. "It's for us, Preshy. I have a buyer for it. We'll be rich, and I can marry you without shaming you. All I'm asking you to do is tell me where it is."

"It's in my room at the *pensione,*" she lied. Then immediately wished she hadn't because if they went to the *pensione,* Sam would never find her. *Where, oh where was he?*

Bennett grabbed her hand. "We'll take a boat there," he said, and dragging her with him, he walked to the steps leading to the canal. Spotting an approaching empty gondola, he let go of her hand for a second to flag it down. In that instant she flew from him, her cape billowing behind her like wings as she raced up the alley.

She kept on running. The fog pressed against her eyes. She could barely see. Out of breath, she had to stop. And then she heard footsteps.

She turned, running alongside the canal now, retracing her path. She *had* to meet Sam at the Palazzo. It was her only chance. But now she was lost again. And were Bennett's footsteps in front of her? Or behind?

The lights of the Palazzo glimmered suddenly from the fog, and with a thankful cry she ran toward it.

Bennett darted from the alley. He got her in an armlock, pressing against her throat. She was choking, gasping for breath. He was talking again, evil words finally telling the truth.

"I felt *nothing* for you, Precious," he said. "*Nothing at all.* Of course I wanted your money, but I planned to kill Grizelda first to make sure you got it. Then I would have killed you. Grizelda managed to escape, but anyway when I found that she wasn't leaving you her money, I walked. You are meaningless, Preshy," he said in low, smooth silken tones. "You offer nothing in life, just another scrap of DNA swept away in a canal. Your only value is that necklace. Tell me where you've hidden it, or I'll kill you right now."

Bennett's words fell on her like blows. He had never loved her. He had killed Lily. And now he was going to kill her.

Anger hit her in a shot of adrenaline. But she wasn't strong enough to fight him off. She struggled to get free, but his arm tightened so she couldn't even scream. She heard footsteps approaching, the feminine clack of high heels along the alley in back of them.

Bennett heard it, too. He turned his head for a split second . . . and found himself looking at a gun.

Aunt G stood there, wrapped in her second-best mink, the dark blue sheared one, holding what looked like a pearl-handled revolver. Mimi was next to her, all in white and silver, looking like an avenging Valkyrie. The pair were like something out of a sixties James Bond movie.

Grizelda said, "Let go of my niece at once, or I'll shoot."

"Go ahead." Bennett positioned Preshy in front of him. "Though if she tells me where the necklace is, she's yours."

Peering into the shadows beyond him, Mimi stalled for time. "What necklace?" she demanded.

But he saw where her gaze went. Just as Sam launched himself, Bennett let go of Preshy, and she hit the ground with Bennett on top of her and Sam on top of Bennett. Grizelda ran to them, still waving the gun, and Mimi shrieked for help.

Preshy wasn't sure what happened next. Flattened, with her face in the cobblestones and all the breath knocked out of her, she heard the sound of running feet. And then a shot.

Oh My God. Aunt Grizelda had killed him.

She got to her feet and saw Grizelda staring at the smoking gun, and Mimi screaming, and Sam running after Bennett.

He'd reached the canal, but Sam was right behind him. An empty party boat waited, moored to the blue-striped pole at the Palazzo's embarcadero. Bennett jumped for it, caught his foot on the edge and slipped and fell, cracking his head on the pole. He staggered to his feet, swayed, then, with a splash, fell backward into the water.

The cold black water rippled gently. The gray fog pressed down on it like a shroud. There was no sign of Bennett.

It was the perfect accident.

"I SHOT him," Aunt Grizelda said in a trembly voice.

"You didn't shoot Bennett, Grizelda. You shot me." Sam took off his jacket and pointed to the blood slowly oozing from his arm.

She clapped a shocked hand to her mouth. "Oh, I'm *so* sorry."

Sam looked at Preshy, staring into the water. "Come on, Rafferty. Bennett's gone, and none of us should be regretting him. The man would have killed anybody that got in his way."

"I know," Preshy said bitterly, and she shook her head, trying to remember the evil hidden behind those blue eyes and behind that soft voice that knew how to say such sweet things. "I'm sorry I got you all into this," she said wearily. "It was my fault." She took her phone from her pocket. "I'll call the police."

Sam grabbed her arm. "Oh no, I'll take care of the police."

Preshy recalled him saying he couldn't afford to be connected to another murder mystery, but now he was going to take full responsibility for dealing with the police. "I can't let you do that."

"You've no choice, Rafferty. For once you'll do as you're told."

"But what about your arm?" Grizelda asked, worried.

"I've seen more blood from a nosebleed. Now, go. All of you. I'll see you in a little while. And remember, this was an accident. You know nothing. You were never here. Just stay cool."

The three women drifted slowly back to Piazza San Marco, where they caught the Cipriani launch. Up in Grizelda's suite they ordered coffee and a selection of little sweet cakes because, Mimi said, they needed a sugar fix after what they'd been through. Then Preshy told them exactly what had happened with Bennett.

"I felt so . . . worthless," she said tearfully. "I was just another scrap of useless DNA was what he said. Which, if he'd killed me, was all I would have ended up as."

"It's men like Bennett who are worthless," Mimi said fiercely. "He's never cared for anyone in his life, except himself."

"And just look where it got him." Grizelda put her arms around Preshy. "*Chérie,* you cannot possibly believe what that dreadful man said. Every word was to hurt you so he could manipulate you. I'm glad he's dead, and you know what? I wouldn't even have cared if I *had* shot him. A *crime passionné,* Maître Deschamps would have called it, and I'm sure he would have gotten me a couple of years in one of the prettier jails. I would willingly have taken the rap for you, my little girl."

"But now Sam's doing it instead," Mimi said.

IT WAS dawn when Sam finally left the *polizia* after making his report. He'd told them he'd seen a man fall into the canal near the Palazzo Rendino. He believed his name was Bennett Yuan or Bennett James. The police questioned him, inspected his passport, asked his occupation and what he was doing there and where he was staying.

"I was on my way to the ball at the Palazzo when I saw this," he said. "Of course I ran to see if I could help, but it was too late. There was no sign of him."

It was all true. Bennett had died in an accident of his own making, Sam thought wearily as he made his way back in a launch over the canal that had claimed Bennett James Yuan's life in a final justice that his wife's Chinese family might find fitting. The evil Dragon River Gods had claimed him and made him their own.

Back at the hotel the three women were sitting in a row on the sofa, eyes wide and alert, waiting, when Sam walked in the door.

"Well?" Grizelda spoke for them all.

"It's okay. Everything's worked out. The cop said his wouldn't be the only body fished from the canal this morning. People get drunk; they fight; it happens at Carnevale."

Sam felt empty inside, drained. Rafferty could have been killed, and it would have been his fault for leaving her all alone. Just the way he had with Leilani. Suddenly near rock bottom, he slumped into a chair and told them everything that had been said at the *polizia,* and that they were free to leave.

Preshy felt the weight lift from her heart. "Let's go back to Paris," she said, meeting Sam's eyes and giving him a smile. His answering smile was filled with tenderness.

And then his cell phone rang. And the moment was lost.

Sam answered it. He said very little. When he put down the receiver, his eyes met Preshy's again.

"That was my agent, from New York," he said in a dead calm voice. "He told me a red jacket was found in the rocks near the beach house. The police believe it was my wife's. They want me back there voluntarily or they will take me in for questioning."

Preshy heard gasps from the aunts. "What will you do?" she asked, shocked.

"I'll go of course. I know the jacket, but it was heavy, and why she'd wear it on a warm summer night, I don't know."

Preshy didn't hesitate. "I'll go with you." She heard the aunts gasp again.

"No, you won't. I don't want you involved. Besides, you've been through enough."

"I *am* involved," she said fiercely. "I'm involved with you, Sam Knight. You just saved my life. Do you really expect me to walk away when you're in trouble? I'm coming, and that's that."

"Quite right," Aunt G chimed in.

"We would come, too, for support," Mimi added, "but you're probably happy with just Preshy."

Sam shook his head, smiling. "I'll be fine," he said. "Alone," he added, looking at Preshy.

"She's coming with you," Aunt G said briskly. "Go now, right away. Get it over with. I'll have a plane waiting for you at Marco Polo. And Sam, our hearts go with you."

Shanghai

MARY-LOU heard the news about Bennett when she bumped into the girl from the health club.

"Tragic," the girl said, eyes brimming, "and him so handsome, so charming. Why do bad things always seem to happen to the good people?" she asked sorrowfully.

"Why indeed," Mary-Lou said calmly, though inside she was trembling.

Of course Bennett Yuan's death was reported in the media, but unlike his wife's, it was played down. Mary-Lou felt nothing. Only relief. She wondered what had happened to the necklace but, remembering it was the cause of all her troubles, decided she didn't want to know.

She had her own life now, running Lily's antiques business. No one else had come forward to claim it, so she had simply taken over, and since Lily's death she had lived alone in the pretty little house where once she had plotted her friend's downfall.

If Mary-Lou had a conscience, she would have considered it clear. She had stolen a few dollars here and there—so what? She had not killed anyone, had she?

Twelve

Outer Banks

SAM was very quiet on the plane flying back to his home. His eyes were closed, and Preshy hoped he was sleeping. He looked exhausted. Drained, in fact, like a man who had reached the end of his rope. He was no longer drinking. Those days of Dutch courage were over.

They touched down at the small local airport. From there Sam went straight to the police station, while Preshy checked into a motel and watched the clock tick the minutes past, thinking about Sam and how their lives now seemed to be so inextricably entangled.

The phone rang. "I'm coming to get you," Sam said, sounding

weary. "We'll pick up some food, go to the beach house. If that's okay with you?"

Preshy said it was and went outside to wait for him. When the black Mustang rental pulled up, she hopped in and took a quick look at his grim face. "How was it?" she asked.

"Okay." He shrugged. They drove a couple of blocks in silence; then he pulled up at a convenience store, and they went in and bought bread, butter, milk, coffee and a couple of cans of gumbo.

The drive along the coast road was wild and windy, with the foaming ocean advancing and retreating in the beginning of a winter storm. They turned off down a sandy lane that led between tamarisk trees to a simple gray-shingled house with a wraparound porch and wide-open view across dunes to the sea.

Sam's shoulders sagged. Different emotions played over his face: pleasure, relief, despair. He looked at her.

"Welcome to my home," he said quietly. And then he took her hand and they walked up the wooden stairway into his house.

Inside was simply one big room with a massive stone fireplace in the center, and walls lined with large somber paintings, done, Preshy guessed, by Leilani. When Sam opened the electric, steel storm shutters, the house was instantly filled with a magical clear gray light that felt, she thought, the way the first dawn must have. So translucent and pearly, so clean and clear; it was like being on the prow of a great ship in the middle of the ocean.

"No wonder you love it," she said.

"Come outside and really breathe," he said. And they went and stood on the deck, inhaling the cold salty air, hearing the wind tear through the trees and the surge of the great ocean.

"Yet just down the beach there's the river and the calm backwaters and marshes," Sam told her. "There's the reeds where the ducks nest, and the mangroves with their gnarled roots are dug deep in the mud. And in summer it's a different world, sun-filled, with white-sailed boats skidding across the gold and blue horizon."

"I'll bet it's humid," Preshy said, thinking of her hair and making him laugh. That was better, she thought. At least he could laugh even though he'd just spent hours with the cops. She still didn't ask him what had happened. If he wanted, he would tell her.

While Sam built a fire, she heated up the gumbo and sawed uneven chunks off the loaf of bread. He brought out a bottle of wine and two glasses.

"The Carolina red?" she asked, tasting it suspiciously.

"So?" he replied, one brow raised in a question.

"Well, it's no Bordeaux," she said, and then she laughed. "But it's pretty darn good, especially on a cold windy afternoon after a long and grueling journey."

"And a grueling questioning," he said wearily, sitting next to her at the white-tiled kitchen counter.

She took a sip of the wine and waited for him to go on.

"They found Leilani's jacket," he said, "not too far from here. A padded red winter jacket. The detective said to me, 'Why would your wife have been wearing such a jacket?' I said it was a puzzle. 'Perhaps the padding holds water better, makes it easier to drown someone,' the cop said."

Preshy drew in a sharp nervous breath.

Sam took off his glasses and rubbed his eyes. "I said, 'I'll remember that for my next book.' And then they showed me what they had found, zippered in the pocket." He held out his left hand to show her. "Leilani's wedding ring. Exactly like mine."

He was a man being destroyed before her very eyes. "She must have taken it off before . . ." She stopped, not wanting to say it.

Sam got up. "I'm going out for a walk." He rummaged in the closet for a jacket. "I'll be back later," he said as he closed the door behind him.

SAM strode along the hard-packed sand at the very edge of the sea where the waves foamed over his boots and the sandpipers scattered in front of him. He was alone with the roar of the wind and the wheeling cry of the birds, with the boom of the surf on the sandbanks. It was the wild power of the ocean.

Turning up the collar of his jacket, he strode on. Leilani was gone. He would never see her again, and his heart would bear the scar forever. He would have to leave this place he loved. It could never be the same without her.

The Shanghai fortune-teller's face came into his mind, clear as a photograph. His words rang in Sam's ears. "The first person you seek is a woman, and the answer lies in your own soul." Sam had been asking about Leilani, and now he searched his soul, asking where he had gone wrong, how he had let her down.

Thrusting his hands deep into the jacket pockets, he emptied his head of all thoughts until he seemed at one with the elements, adrift on the wind and with only the roar of the ocean for company. His left hand closed around something deep down in the crease of the pocket. A piece of paper.

Some old receipt, he thought, but taking it out, he saw it was a folded piece of green paper, the kind Leilani used. "Dearest Sam," she had written at the top.

I'm looking at our beloved dog lying here next to me as I sit trying not to look at the ocean where I know you are tonight. Your dog is old now, Sam. He has not much longer for this world, and you cannot know how I envy him.

I can never "love" the way you do, so direct, so uncomplicated. I wait for my heart to show me how, but it is frozen inside my chest. I wait for simple happiness to happen to me, the way you were this evening, whistling as you prepped your little boat. Why, I asked myself, can't I be like that?

All my life I have tried, and all my life I have failed. Sometimes I was able to lose myself in my painting, and that was the closest I could come to "happiness." But mostly, I was just lost. And now I know I will never find myself.

I can't bear it any longer. All I want, dear Sam, is to be "nothing." And tonight, in a few minutes, I'll take a walk to the small inlet and the sandbank that's uncovered only at low tide. I'll sit and watch the sea come for me. Only you know how afraid I am of the ocean. They say it's a coward's way out, but this is a brave thing I'm doing, Sam, isn't it?

And then, my dearest, we will both be free.

I think about our honeymoon in Paris. That was happiness, wasn't it? I used to remember, but it's lost under darkness.

Do not grieve for me. You must go on, Sam. Believe me, if I knew how to love, it would have been you.

She had signed the note "Leilani Knight." Sam put it back in his pocket, where she must have left it, expecting him to find it right away because he always wore that jacket when he took the dog for walks along the beach. She would have wanted to make sure only he found it and read it. Her message was meant only for him.

He strode along the beach where the wind dried his tears. When he came to the place Leilani had mentioned, where the sandbank was uncovered at low tide, as it was now, he stopped to look.

The tide was turning, and he watched the first wave power over, then retreat, leaving the sandbank clean and empty.

Tears stung his eyes. "I loved you, Leilani," he shouted into the wind. "I will never forget you."

PRESHY saw from Sam's face when he walked in the door that something had happened. She watched anxiously as he threw his jacket onto a chair, took the green paper from the pocket and stood with it in his hand looking at her.

"This was meant only for me," he said quietly. "But I think you are owed some explanation."

She took the letter. All the life seemed to have drained out of his eyes. "It's from Leilani, isn't it?" she said.

He nodded. "She left it in my jacket pocket, thinking I would find it right away. It was crushed into a fold, and somehow the cops missed it."

Preshy walked to the window and began to read. When she had finished, she stood for a long moment, struggling with her emotions. "But why?" she said fiercely at last. "She had everything to live for."

Sam threw himself into a chair. "Manic depression is a serious illness. Leilani told me she was taking her medication, but . . ." He shrugged. "It seems she was not."

Preshy went and knelt at his feet, looking anxiously at him. "You have your answer now, though. The police won't ask any more questions once you show them her letter."

"No! I won't have them reading Leilani's last words. They were meant only for me."

"It's the only way, Sam," she said gently. "You have to do this."

"I didn't expose her illness before, and I won't do it now."

"But you must," she said stubbornly. "It's serious, Sam. You saw *how* serious this afternoon. If you don't show them the letter, they'll arrest you for her murder. And that's not what Leilani meant to happen. You *know* it isn't."

Their eyes linked for a long moment; then he sighed and said of course she was right.

She walked to the kitchen and filled two wineglasses with the Carolina red, then went back to him.

"We're going to drink a toast," she said as he took the glass.

He said it for her. "To my beloved wife, Leilani," he said. "A graceful presence in my life."

And they raised their glasses to her and drank.

Sam called the police. He showed them Leilani's letter, and they checked it against other samples of her handwriting. They gave him back the red jacket and the wedding ring, said they were sorry for his loss and that the case was now closed. It was over so quickly, it was almost as though it never happened.

Preshy stayed on at the beach house with Sam. They were comfortable together, friends, bickering gently as always, but easy now, no longer sparring partners. They took long windy walks, cooked simple meals, drank wine by the fire and talked endlessly into the night. It was as though they had known each other forever.

Time passed, a few days, a week. Then late one afternoon, Sam grabbed her hand and said, "Let's take a walk, catch the sunset."

For once the wind had dropped, and all was calm. Even the sea murmured instead of roaring. Terns swooped over the waves, and the air carried a hint of brine and of sea pines. Sam's hand still clasped hers as they climbed the sand dunes until they came to a sheltered hollow. He let go of her then and flung himself down, lying, hands behind his head, looking up at her.

"Come join me," he said, smiling.

And so she did, lying next to him, matching her length against his as they lay together, staring up into the golden evening sky, tinged with coral from the setting sun.

"Rafferty?"

She turned her face to his. "Yes?"

"You're a good friend, but . . . I'm afraid to say this—in case I spoil our friendship."

She sat up now, staring at him. "Say what?"

"I think I'm in love with you, Rafferty."

"Ohhhh . . ." Her face lit in a smile. "And I think I'm in love with you, too."

"Could it be the real thing, do you think?"

She shrugged. "I don't know." Then she grinned. "But I don't care."

He grinned back at her. "I know I love you. You're unique, one of a kind, a girl in a million. Don't leave me, Rafferty. I'd never find another like you."

"Ohhh," she murmured again, but by now her lips were only inches away from his. And then his arms were around her, and he was kissing her, and she was kissing him back. The cold sand trickled down the neck of her sweater, but she didn't even mind because his warm hands pulled her close and this was what it was all about. The tentative beginnings of "love." It was, Preshy thought, a fine beginning.

Later that night, they sat out on the enclosed porch, glasses of wine in their hands, watching the great gray waves rolling endlessly in, while a softer wind rustled through the tamarisks.

"What will you do now?" she asked.

He thought about it. "I'll sell this place. I'll move on, maybe try my hand at writing again."

"Sounds good to me," she said.

He turned his head to look at her. Their eyes linked. He reached out his hand, took hers. "Don't leave me, Rafferty," he said, quietly. "I am in love with you."

"Funny way of showing it," she said with a sparkle in her eyes. "Why not come over and kiss me?"

And he did. And one thing led to another, and all in all it was another week before they finally headed "home" to Paris and a new life. Together.

Paris

PRESHY had been gone a long time, and Maow was alone and bored. She sat in the exact center of Preshy's bed, a stern look on her narrow face, as though she were plotting something. After a while she got up and stretched one long svelte chocolate leg all the way out in front of her; then she did the same with the other. After that, she went in search of action.

Her first stop was the kitchen, where she sniffed the food the concierge had left that morning and decided against it. She hopped onto the counter and prowled its length, negotiating the stove top. Then tail up—Siamese tails are always up—she stalked into the dining room. The nice big antique glass bowl in the center of the table was just the right size to curl up in. She put tentative front paws on its edge, then aimed her jump. The bowl tipped, crashed under her weight and smashed into a dozen pieces. Maow looked at it, puzzled, then went to see what was doing in the living room.

She stood on the window seat, looking out at the traffic and the people. Bored, she scratched a tentative paw at the glass, looking for an escape route. Impossible.

Filled with a sudden ferocious energy, she spun into a crouching position. Then she took off across the sofa, up the back of the chair, into the bedroom, flying over the bed in one giant leap, spinning the coverlet into a heap, hurling herself back again, over the bed, over the sofa, up onto the shelves, scattering photos and artifacts.

She sat on the shelf, paws together, looking very pleased with herself. She rested her head on the terra-cotta Xi'an warrior, rubbed her ear against it, leaned harder. The warrior tottered for a moment and toppled. Maow stalked to the edge of the shelf looking down at it, smashed into a hundred pieces on the floor.

Back at the window seat, she curled round a few times, then settled down to wait for Preshy to come home.

"There's nothing quite like coming home," Sam said as Preshy unlocked the door. Outside was sleeting and cold, but in Preshy's home the radiators were hissing with warmth, and there was a delighted cry from the cat, who launched herself out of the darkness at them.

"Maowsie, Maowsie." Preshy clasped the cat in her arms, laughing while at the same time joggling her elbow at the light switch. The lamps sprang to life, and the two of them stared, stunned, at the scene of destruction.

"Looks like the demolition derby was here," Sam said, awed.

"Oh, Maow, what *have* you done?" Preshy stared horrified at her antique glass bowl now in shards on the dining room table, at the trampled coverlet in the bedroom. When she surveyed the destruction in the living room, she said urgently, "Sam, come here."

The necklace gleamed up at her from the piece of scarlet silk it had been wrapped in. "It's Grandmother's necklace," she said, awed. "Lily must have hidden it inside the statue and sent it to me for safekeeping. Look, Sam, it's magnificent."

Picking it up, she ran a tentative finger over the giant pearl. It felt cold, and remembering where it had come from, she put the necklace down on the table. They stood, looking at it.

"This is what Bennett killed Lily for," Sam said. "It's probably worth a fortune. And when he didn't get it, the trail led, via Mary-Lou Chen, back to you."

"And now what?" Preshy looked at the sinister corpse pearl, gleaming like moonlight on the black glass table. She shivered. "It doesn't belong to me. It was stolen from a dead empress. It's part of history. It should go back where it belongs, back to China. I'll donate it to them. Maybe they'll put it in a museum."

He nodded. "I'm sure they'll be thrilled with your gift."

She picked up the cat. "If it were not for naughty you, Maowsie, we would never have found it," she said, kissing the cat's smooth chocolate ears.

Maow hooked her paws onto Preshy's shoulders and peeked triumphantly at Sam. He could have sworn the cat was laughing at him. A smile lit his lean narrow face. "Put down that cat and get over here, Rafferty," he said, holding out his arms.

Maow watched from her place on the window seat as Preshy walked right up to him. And then their faces blended in a kiss.

Life was going to be a little different here, in future.

Behind the Scenes with
Elizabeth Adler

BRITISH-BORN Elizabeth Adler and her American husband Richard have lived in Brazil and England and Canada and Ireland, but a few years ago they fell in love with La Quinta, California, a town that calls itself "The Gem of the Desert" and that Adler refers to as "paradise." They share their home with their two cats, Sweet Pea and Sunny.

One reason for Adler's love of her desert home is that "it is so peaceful for writing," she says. But there has to be more to her success as a writer than a peaceful setting, and one has to ask Adler how she does it. Her answer? "I don't know. It's certainly not any magic formula. It's simply something there, inside my head. Maybe it's due to that childhood shyness that cut me off from people and forced me into a world of my own imagination. I

Vital Stats

RESIDENCE: La Quinta, CA
FAMILY: Husband, Richard; one daughter, Annabelle
NUMBER OF NOVELS WRITTEN: 21
FAVORITE COLORS: Blue and yellow
KITCHEN ACCOMPLISHMENT: "I'm a whiz at Yorkshire puddings."
FAVORITE MEAL: An English Sunday lunch in winter
WEBSITE: www.ElizabethAdler.com

was an observer rather than a participant, an eavesdropper on conversations, a gleaner of information. A writer must be all these things."

Adler claims that the inspiration behind her books is the main character. "As I write her, I get to know her, to understand how she thinks, reacts, who she is. Once I have the idea for that character, that person, then the other characters emerge and the story begins to form around her." A character like *Meet Me in Venice*'s Precious Rafferty can practically take Adler over. "When I'm writing these women, I almost become them: I think for them, feel for them . . . It's very personal."

Despite her success, writing is a love/hate occupation for Adler. "I love it when I start a new book," she says, "I can't sleep for the long months I'm writing it, and I love it when it's finished and out of my head, at last." She also finds writing to be a never-ending business. "I write all the time: on my Mac, on the little notepads I keep in my purse and scattered around the house, in the middle of the night when an idea comes to me. It's such a pain, because I have to get out of bed and write everything down immediately. If I don't, I know I'll have forgotten it

by morning. The fact is, there is no rest for a writer."

Adler does have one way of coping with her obsession with writing. "One personal quirk is that I must always have music in the background when I'm writing. And each piece of music in some way relates to the story." When writing about Venice, Vivaldi and "The Four Seasons" was a natural choice. For a story set in Ireland, there was her favorite Van Morrison album, "Avalon Sunset," and the group known as the Pogues. And writing about Paris? For that she needs jazz. Combine the great pianist Bill Evans with some "soft, smooth, sexy" Dexter Gordon, and you begin to get a feel for the all-encompassing nature of the way this author works.

What else does Adler say contributes to her successful writing career? "My biggest passion in life—after my family and my cats and writing—is travel." And this travel does not go to waste, as she works it all into her stories (including, for instance, her exploration of Shanghai in preparation for writing *Meet Me in Venice*). "In my novels, location always plays an important part," she says. "Almost any place my characters go is real—the cafés and restaurants, the streets, the local shops. I've walked

Travel by the Book

Paris. Venice. Shanghai. The French Riviera. We visit these places in *Meet Me in Venice,* and it reminds us that one of the great joys of reading is when a good book takes us to places we've never been, to see sights we've never seen, without our having to leave the comfort of our favorite easy chairs. Among Elizabeth Adler's work there are titles like *Sailing to Capri, The House in Amalfi,* and *Invitation to Provence,* which immediately tell us that we are going to be packing our mental suitcases for an experience abroad.

The history of literature is filled with voyages to new and exotic places, from Homer's cruise with Ulysses to *Gulliver's Travels* to Adler's continent-hopping novels. But many of our favorite armchair adventures are *true* stories, tales told by others of what really happened. Below we offer a selective list of some of the best real-life adventures.

- *In the Heart of the Sea: The Tragedy of the Whaleship Essex* by Nathaniel Philbrick re-creates the whaling expedition that inspired Melville's *Moby-Dick.*
- *The Great Railway Bazaar: By Train Through Asia* by Paul Theroux narrates a rail journey from Victoria Station in London to Tokyo Central.
- *Under the Tuscan Sun: A Home in Italy* by Frances Mayes is a gentle tale of finding a new life in rural Italy.
- *Kon-Tiki: Across the Pacific in a Raft* by Thor Heyerdahl is the classic journey of 4,300 nautical miles from Peru to the Polynesian islands.
- *A Walk in the Woods: Rediscovering America on the Appalachian Trail* by Bill Bryson takes us closer to home, on one of the best hikes in the world.

down those streets, breathed the air, felt how it was to be there."

In the end, Adler describes herself as a writer of romantic thrillers with a sense of place and ambience. The thrills come from her imagination; the sense of place comes from her personal travel. And the romance? Well, she points out that she has been married for over thirty years. "So tell me," she says, "do you think I'm qualified to write about romance?" ∎

JAMES PATTERSON
STEP ON A
CRACK

& MICHAEL LEDWIDGE

PROLOGUE
THE LAST SUPPER

THE back of the table captain's cream-colored evening jacket had just turned away when Stephen Hopkins leaned across the secluded corner booth and kissed his wife. Caroline closed her eyes, tasting the cold champagne he'd just sipped, then felt a tug as Stephen's hand caught one of the silk spaghetti straps of her Chanel gown.

Having this much fun with your husband, Caroline thought, had to be illegal. "You're past *fifty,*" she said. "Not fifteen." That their annual

"Christmas in New York" date got better every year was beyond her, but there you had it. Dinner here at L'Arène, probably the most elegant, seductive French restaurant in New York City, and then back to the Pierre hotel's presidential suite. It had been their Christmas gift to themselves for the past four years. And every year it turned out to be more romantic than the last.

As if on cue, snow began falling outside the windows of the restaurant, big silver flakes that hung in glittering cones from Madison Avenue's black-iron lampposts.

"If you could have anything this Christmas, what would it be?" Caroline asked suddenly.

Stephen raised his glass of Laurent-Perrier Grand Siècle Brut. "I wish . . ." He stared into his flute. "I wish this were hot chocolate."

Many years ago, Caroline and Stephen had been homesick scholarship freshmen at Harvard without enough money to make it home for Christmas. One morning they'd been the only two breakfast diners in cavernous Annenberg Hall, and Stephen had sat down at her table. "Just for a little warmth," he'd said.

They learned they were both planning to be poli-sci majors, and they hit it off. In the Yard outside, Caroline impulsively dropped to the ground and made a snow angel. Their faces almost touched when Stephen helped her up. Then she took a quick sip of the hot chocolate she'd smuggled out of the dining hall—so as not to kiss this boy she'd just met and somehow already cared about.

Caroline could still see Stephen as he had been, smiling in the bright, nickeled winter light in Harvard Yard, clueless to the fact that he would marry her. Give her a beautiful daughter. Go on to become the president of the United States.

The question he'd asked as she'd lowered her cocoa mug thirty years before reverberated poignantly now in her ears: "Does yours taste like champagne, too?"

Hot chocolate to champagne, Caroline thought, lifting her flute. *Now champagne to hot chocolate. Two and a half decades of marriage come full circle. What a life they'd had,* she thought, savoring the moment. *Lucky and worthwhile and—*

"Excuse me, Mr. President," a voice whispered.

A pasty-looking blond man in a metallic-gray suit stood in front of their booth. He was waving a menu and a pen. Henri, the maître d', arrived immediately. He assisted Steve Beplar, the Hopkinses' Secret Service agent, in trying to escort the intruder out of sight.

"I just thought the president could sign my menu," the man said.

"It's okay, Steve," Stephen Hopkins said with a quick wave. He shrugged at his wife in apology.

"I have to say, you guys look terrific tonight," the pale man said over the agent's shoulder. "Especially you, Mrs. Hopkins."

"Merry Christmas, sir," Stephen Hopkins said, smiling back as graciously as he could manage.

"Hope it was no bother," the man said, the sheen of his suit flashing as he backed away, bowing.

"Bother?" Stephen said to his wife after the man had departed. "How could he think that demolishing the most romantic moment of our lives was a bother?"

They were still laughing when a beaming waiter put down their plates and vanished. Caroline smiled at the avant-garde architecture of her terrine of foie gras.

It's almost too beautiful to eat, she thought, lifting her fork.

The first bite was so ethereal that it took a few seconds for Caroline to place the taste. By then it was too late.

What felt like high-pressure superheated air instantly inflated Caroline's lungs, throat, and face. Her silver fork fell from her lips and clattered against china.

"Oh my God, Caroline," she heard Stephen say as he looked at her in horror. "Steve! Help! Something's wrong with Caroline! She can't breathe."

Stephen Hopkins staggered to his feet as Steve Beplar snatched the edge of the dining table and flung it out of the way.

Crystal and china exploded against the hardwood floor. Agent Susan Wu, the next closest of their four-person security detail, pulled Mrs. Hopkins from the booth seat. The female agent got behind Caroline, a fist already under her rib cage as she began the Heimlich maneuver.

Stephen watched helplessly as his wife's face turned from red to almost blackish purple. "Wait!" he said. "She's not choking. It's her allergy! She's allergic to peanuts. Her emergency adrenaline! The little pen thing she carries. Where's her bag?" Stephen found it on the booth seat and upended it, sending makeup and perfume flying. "It's not here!" he said.

Steve Beplar barked into his sleeve mike; then he scooped up the former First Lady in his arms. "Time to get to a hospital, sir," he said, moving toward the exit.

Moments later, in the rear of a speeding Crown Victoria, Stephen Hopkins cradled his wife's head in his lap. Breath whistled weakly from her throat as if it were coming through a cocktail straw. He ached for his wife, watching her eyes tighten in severe pain.

A doctor and a gurney were waiting when the sedan came to a stop out in front of the St. Vincent's Midtown Hospital emergency room entrance on Fifty-second Street.

"You think it's an allergic reaction?" the doctor asked, taking Caroline's pulse as two attendants rushed her through the sliding glass doors on a stretcher.

"She's highly allergic to peanuts," Stephen said, jogging at Caroline's other side. "We told the kitchen at L'Arène. There must have been some mix-up."

"She's in shock, sir," the doctor said. He blocked the former president as Caroline was pushed through a HOSPITAL PERSONNEL ONLY side door. "We'll do everything—"

Stephen Hopkins suddenly shoved the stunned doctor out of the way. "I'm not leaving her side," he said.

They were already attaching an IV drip to Caroline's arm and an oxygen mask to her face when he entered the trauma room. They sliced her beautiful gown to the navel so they could attach the leads of the heart monitor. The machine bleated out an awful, continuous beep when they flicked it on. Then a flat black line appeared on the scrolling red graph readout. A nurse started CPR.

"Clear," the doctor yelled, and put the electrified paddles to Caroline's chest.

Stephen watched Caroline's chest surge upward with a pulse, and then a new, gentle bloop-bloop started on the monitor. A sharp, glorious scratch spiked upward on the spooling readout. Then another.

Tears of gratitude had formed in Stephen's eyes—when the awful *beeeeeeeeeeep* returned.

The doctor tried several more times with the defibrillator, but the screeching monitor wouldn't change its grating one-note tune. The last thing the former president witnessed was another act of mercy by his loyal Secret Service.

Teary-eyed, Steve Beplar reached over and yanked the plug out of the yellow tile wall, halting the machine's evil shriek.

"I'm so sorry, sir. She's gone."

THE pale autograph seeker from L'Arène told the cabdriver to pull over on Ninth Avenue a block north of St. Vincent's Hospital. He stuffed a ten into the grimy divider slot and elbowed open the greasy door latch to avoid touching it. There were reasons he was known as the Neat Man.

When he made it to the corner, he saw uniformed NYPD holding back a throng of reporters and cameramen at the entrance to the hospital's emergency room. He was crossing Fifty-second Street when he spotted a distraught-looking female EMT slumping out of the crowd.

"Miss?" he said, stepping up to her. "Could you tell me? Is this where they've brought First Lady Caroline?"

The Hispanic woman nodded her head, and then she moaned. Tears began to stream down her cheeks. "She just *died,*" she said. "Caroline Hopkins just died."

The Neat Man felt dizzy for a second. He blinked rapidly as he shook his head, stunned and elated.

"She was a saint," the overwrought paramedic said. "All the work she did for poor people and AIDS. Her Service America campaign was one of the reasons I became a paramedic. How could she be dead?"

"Lord knows. But she's in His hands now, isn't she?" the Neat Man said soothingly, brushing past her into the street. He had his cell phone in his hand by the time he made it to the east side of Ninth Avenue. He could hear clattering plates and chefs yelling in French when his call was picked up at L'Arène.

"It's done, Julio," he said. "She's dead. Now get the hell out of there. You killed Caroline Hopkins. Congratulations."

The Neat Man was about to shake his head in wonder at his good luck, but then he stopped himself. Luck had nothing to do with it. Three years to plan, he thought wistfully. Now they had just three days to pull off the rest of this job.

Minutes later, he was in the back of another taxi, heading north up Eighth Avenue. He took a couple of alcohol wipes out of his wallet and scoured his hands and face as he sped through the bright lights, escaping the unclean city.

CHAPTER 1

I'LL tell you this—even on the mean streets of New York, where the only thing harder to get than a taxi in the rain is attention, we were managing to turn heads that gray December afternoon.

If anything could tug at the coiled-steel heartstrings of the Big Apple's residents, I guess the sight of my mobilized Bennett clan—Chrissy, three; Shawna, four; Trent, five; twins Fiona and Bridget, seven; Eddie, eight; Ricky, nine; Jane, ten; Brian, eleven; and Juliana, twelve—all dressed in their Sunday best and walking in size order behind me, could do the trick.

But at the time, the gentle nods and warm smiles we received from every construction worker and hot dog vendor from the subway exit next to Bloomingdale's all the way to First Avenue were completely lost on me.

I had a lot on my mind.

The only New Yorker who *didn't* seem like he wanted to go on a cheek-pinching bender was the old man in the hospital gown who cupped his cigarette and wheeled his IV cart out of the way to let us into our destination—the main entrance of the terminal wing of the New York Hospital Cancer Center.

I guess he had a lot on his mind, too.

"Oh look, Tom," a middle-aged woman said to her husband at the elevator. "A teacher brought some students in to sing Christmas carols. Isn't that so nice?"

We get that a lot. I'm of Irish American extraction, but my kids—all adopted—run the gamut. Trent and Shawna are African American; Ricky and Julia, Hispanic; and Jane is Korean. At six foot two and two hundred pounds, I certainly don't look like what I am—a senior detective with the NYPD Homicide Division. I'm a troubleshooter, negotiator, whatever's needed by whoever needs it.

"Do you know 'It Came Upon a Midnight Clear'?" the woman who had latched on to us persisted. I was about to sharply point out her ignorance when Brian, my oldest son, glanced at the smoke coming out of my ears and piped up.

"I'm sorry, ma'am. We don't. But we know 'Jingle Bells.' "

All the way up to the dreaded fifth floor, my ten kids sang "Jingle Bells" with gusto, and as we piled out of the elevator, I could see a happy tear in the woman's eye. She wasn't here on vacation, either, I realized, and my son had salvaged the situation better than a United Nations diplomat. I wanted to kiss his forehead, but eleven-year-old boys have killed over less, so I just gave him a manly pat on the back as we turned down a silent, white corridor.

Chrissy, with her arm around Shawna, was into the second verse of "Rudolph the Red-Nosed Reindeer" as we passed the nurses' station. The little ones could have been life-size Precious Moments figurines in their dresses and pigtailed hair, thanks to the extreme makeover work of their older sisters, Juliana and Jane.

My kids are great. Amazing, really. They had gone so far above and beyond that it was hard to believe sometimes. I guess it just pissed me off that they had to.

At the end of the hallway, a woman wearing a flowered dress over her ninety-pound frame and a Yankees cap over her hairless head was sitting in a wheelchair at the open door of 513.

"MOM!" the kids yelled, and the thunder of twenty feet suddenly shattered the relative silence of the hospital hall.

THERE was hardly enough of my wife left to get twenty arms around, but the kids managed it somehow. My wife was on morphine, codeine, and Percocet, but the only time I saw her completely pain-free was when we arrived, when she had all her ducklings pressed around her.

"Michael," Maeve whispered to me. "Thank you. *Thank you.* They look so wonderful."

"So do you," I whispered back.

Every day when we came to see her, she was dressed for company, a smile on her face.

"If you didn't want glamour, Mr. Bennett," my wife said, fighting the weariness in her glazed eyes, "I guess you should have married someone else."

It was the morning of the previous New Year's Day when Maeve had complained about some stomach pain. We'd thought it was just some holiday indigestion, but when it hadn't gone away in two weeks, her doctor wanted to do a laparoscopy. They found growths on both ovaries, and the biopsy came back malignant. A second biopsy of the lymph nodes reported even worse news. The cancer had spread, and it wasn't going to stop.

"Let me help you up, Maeve," I whispered as she started to push herself up out of the chair.

"You *want* to get seriously hurt?" she said, glaring at me. "Mr. Tough Guy Detective!"

Maeve fought for her life and dignity like a banshee. She was a nurse herself and used every contact and every ounce of wisdom and experience she'd gained. She underwent so many chemo and radiation treatments, it put a strain on her heart. But even after everything there was to be done had been done, the CAT scan revealed growing tumors in both lungs, her liver, and her pancreas.

I watched Maeve stand on her wobbling toothpick legs to prop herself up behind her wheelchair. Then she sat down on the bed and lifted a white chart from beside her. "Since it looks like I'm going to be stuck here for a while longer, I decided to come up with a list of chores for you," she said.

Some of the older kids groaned. "Mom!"

"I know, I know. Chores. Who needs them?" Maeve said. "But here's my thinking. If you all work together, you can keep the apartment running for me until I get back. Okay, team? Then here we go. Julia, you're on lifeguard duty for baths for the youngins, and you're also responsible for getting them dressed in the morning. Brian, you're my cruise director. Board games, video games. Duck, Duck, Goose. Anything you can think of that's not the TV.

"Jane, you're on homework patrol. Get the house genius, Eddie, to help you. Ricky, I dub you the lunch chef. Peanut butter and jelly for everyone except Eddie and Shawna—they get baloney.

"Let's see. Fiona and Bridget. Table setting and clearing."

"What about me?" Trent squeaked. "What's my job?"

"You're on shoe patrol, Trent Bennett," Maeve said. "All I ever hear from these complainers is 'Where's my shoes? Where's my shoes?' Your job is to gather up all ten pairs and get them next to everybody's bed. Don't forget your own."

"I won't." Trent nodded with five-year-old intensity.

"Shawna and Chrissy, I have a job for you girls, too."

"Yay," Chrissy said, and did a little ballerina twirl. She'd gotten the *Barbie of Swan Lake* DVD for her birthday a month before, and every emotion now came with an impromptu interpretive dance.

"You know Socky's dish in the kitchen?" Maeve said.

Socky was a cat that Maeve had pulled out of the garbage alongside our West End Avenue apartment house. My wife has a thing for the unfortunate and strays. The fact that she married me proved that a long time ago.

Shawna nodded solemnly. At four, she was the quietest and most obedient and easygoing of all my kids.

"Well, it's your job to make sure Socky always has water to drink in her dish. Oh, and listen up, gang," Maeve said. "I want to go over a couple of other things before I forget. In this family, we always celebrate each other's birthdays. I don't care if you're four or fourteen or forty and scattered around the world. We gotta stick by each other, okay? And meals—as long as you live under the same roof, you have at least one meal a day together. I don't care if it's a dreaded hot dog in front of the dastardly TV as long as you're all there. You got me? Trent, are you listening?"

"Hot dogs in front of the TV," Trent said, grinning. "I love hot dogs and TV."

We all laughed.

"And I love you," Maeve said. I could see her eyelids beginning to droop. "You've made me so proud. You, too, Michael, my brave detective."

Maeve was facing the grave with a dignity I was unaware human beings were capable of, and *she* was proud of *us*? Of me? I wanted to start wailing, to put my fist through something. Instead, I took off my wife's cap and kissed her gently on the forehead.

"Okay, guys. Mom needs her rest," I said, fiercely struggling to keep the crack that was in my heart out of my voice. "Time to go. Let's move it, troop."

IT WAS three forty-five when the Neat Man stepped off Fifth Avenue, climbed a set of stone stairs, and walked into St. Patrick's Cathedral.

He took the first seat in the pew beside the nearest confessional along the cathedral's south wall. A fortyish priest with salon-trimmed hair showed up a minute later. Father Patrick Mackey did a double take when he spotted the Neat Man's icy smile. The Neat Man got out of the pew and slid in through the confessional door.

"Yes, my son," said the priest behind the screen.

"Northeast corner of Fifty-first and Madison," the Neat Man said. "Twenty minutes. Be there, or there will be consequences."

It was more like thirty minutes later when Father Mackey opened the passenger door of the Neat Man's idling van. He was wearing a blue ski jacket and jeans. He pulled a cardboard tube from beneath the jacket's puffy folds.

"You got it!" the Neat Man said. "Well done."

The priest nodded as he craned his neck back toward the church. "We should drive," he said.

Ten minutes later, they parked in an empty lot beside an abandoned heliport next to the East River. The Neat Man popped the lid off the cylinder the priest had brought.

The prints inside were old and cracked. The Neat Man stopped his tracing finger at the center of the second print.

There it was! It wasn't just a rumor. It was real.

And he had it. The final detail for his masterpiece.

"No one knows you have these?" the Neat Man said.

"No one," the priest said.

The Neat Man was unable to take his eyes off the architectural drawing. But finally, he lifted a silenced Colt Woodsman from underneath his seat. The double tap of the .22 was subtle to the ear, but it was as if a grenade had gone off inside Father Mackey's head.

Then the Neat Man rolled up the prints and put them back into their cylinder.

A masterpiece, he thought, *in the making*.

THE kids were a blur of activity once we got back home that evening. From every room, instead of television and electronic gunfire, came the satisfying sound of busy Bennetts.

Water splashed as Julia prepped Shawna and Chrissy's bath. Brian sat at the dining room table with a deck of cards, teaching Trent and Eddie how to play Twenty-One.

"Bam," I could hear Ricky, like a miniature Emeril, say from the kitchen as he squeezed jelly onto each slice of bread. *"Bam, bam."*

Jane had the flash cards out on the floor of her room and was preparing Fiona and Bridget for the 2014 SAT.

I didn't hear a complaint, a whine, out of anyone.

Add "brilliant" to the list of my wife's attributes. She must have known how much the kids were hurting, how useless they felt, so she had given them something to do to fill that void. I only wished I could come up with something to make myself feel the same way.

As most parents will tell you, bedtime is the roughest time of day. Everyone, not excluding parents, is tired and cranky, and restlessness can degrade quickly to frustration, yelling, threats, and punishments. I didn't know how Maeve did it every night. It was one of the things that I was most worried about taking on.

But by eight that night, when I went into the girls' room, I saw Chrissy, Shawna, Fiona, and Bridget with their sheets tucked to their chins and Julia closing an Olivia book.

"Good night, Chrissy," I said, kissing her on her forehead. "Much love from your dad."

I continued on my rounds. The boys were all in bed as well. "Good night, Trent," I said, giving him a kiss on his brow. "You did one great job today." As I stepped toward the door, I said, "I couldn't do this without you guys."

"We know, Dad," Brian called from the top bunk. "Don't worry about it. We got your back."

I PULLED the door closed and stood for a moment outside the boys' room. On a normal night, in about a half hour, when I'd come home from my precinct, the living room would be emitting a warm, steady yellow light as Maeve read a book, waiting for me to arrive.

As I stared at the blackened living room, I realized I was experiencing for the first time what darkness truly was.

I went into the living room and flicked on the lamp beside the couch. Then I sat in the silence, passing my eyes slowly across all the memories. The wallpaper we'd painstakingly put up. All the family photographs Maeve had shot and framed.

After we'd adopted Julia, Maeve quit the hospital in order to spend more time with her, and she took a job taking care of an elderly man on West End Avenue. Mr. Kessler was ninety-five, and he was bitter and angry at the modern world and everything in it. But Maeve wore him down with small kindnesses and compassion. She would regularly wheel him out to sit in the sun at Riverside Park, make him remember he was alive, even if he didn't want to.

By the end, he had become a different person, let go of his bitterness, even made amends with his estranged daughter.

After he died, the old man bequeathed to Maeve his apartment, the one our family lives in now. And instead of the antiques a lot of our neighbors seem to be into, Maeve filled our house with children. Four months after we got the apartment, we adopted Brian. Six months after that came Jane. And on . . . and on . . .

"Saint" is a pretty trite term, I know, but as I sat there alone, gazing at all my wife's accomplishments, that was the word that kept popping into my mind.

My heart literally skipped when the doorbell rang. I figured that it was an errant guest of the Underhills, our frequent-cocktail-party-throwing neighbors across the hall. I stood, annoyed, and yanked back the doorknob.

But judging from the wrinkled jeans and dusty navy peacoat of the young blond woman on the other side of my door, I decided she probably wasn't headed to a cocktail party. She clutched a duffel bag in her gloveless hands.

"Mr. Bennett?" she said, dropping her bag. "It's me, Mary Catherine," she said. "I made it."

From her warm Irish accent, I suspected she must be some relative of my wife's. "Made it?" I repeated warily.

"I'm the au pair," Mary Catherine said. "Nona said she spoke with you."

Au pair? Nona? I thought. Then I remembered that Nona was Maeve's mother's name. "I'm sorry, um, Mary, is it?" I said. "I don't know exactly what you're talking about."

Mary Catherine's mouth opened as if she was about to say something. Then it closed. "Sorry I wasted your time, sir," she said quickly and a tad sadly as she picked up her bag. "There must have been some mistake."

Her bag slipped out of her hand as she approached the elevator. I stepped out of the doorway to give her a hand, then noticed my mail on the floor. It had been piling up a little, and the Underhills had dumped it beneath the alcove's table we share in order to make way for their antique wooden nutcracker collection.

I noticed an odd-looking letter sticking out from the pile's center. "Wait, Mary Catherine," I said. "Just a sec."

I tore open the letter. It was handwritten in a tiny script, but I was able to make out the *Dear Michael,* a couple of *Mary Catherine's,* and the *God Bless You in Your Time of Need, Love, Nona.*

I still didn't know what it all meant. One thing I was sure of, though, was that I was too tired to try to figure it all out right now.

"Oh," I said to the girl as the elevator door rumbled open. "You're Mary Catherine, the au pair."

Naked hope twinkled in her bright blue eyes. But where the heck was I going to put her? Our inn was filled to capacity. Then I remembered the maid's room on the top floor; it was currently being used for storage.

"C'mon," I said, grabbing her bag. "I'll show you where you're staying."

It took me a good twenty minutes to get the crib, baby toys, and some old car seats out of the small room.

By the time I came back with some sheets, Mary Catherine was putting her stuff neatly into the drawers of the dresser we'd used for a changing table.

I studied her for a moment. She was in her late twenties, and there seemed to be an energetic heartiness to her, which was good, considering the job she was applying for. "Nona didn't happen to mention how big my family is, did she?"

" 'Quite a brood,' I believe was the phrase she used."

"How many is 'quite a brood'? Where you come from?"

Mary Catherine's eyebrows raised. "Five?"

I shook my head and jerked my thumb upward.

"Seven?"

I watched a ripple of panic cross Mary Catherine's face when I motioned for her to shoot higher.

"Not ten?" she said.

I nodded. "They're all toilet trained. And they're great kids. But if you want to walk away now, I won't blame you."

"Ten?" Mary Catherine said again.

"A one and a zero," I said with a smile. "Oh, and if you're going to work for us, you have to call me Mike. Or idiot, if you want. But please don't call me Mr. Bennett."

"Okay, Mike," Mary Catherine said.

As I left, I noticed the panic that seemed stuck in her face.

"Ten," I repeated under my breath. *The perfect ten.*

DOWNSTAIRS, I couldn't sleep a wink after I slid in between the sheets of my bed. I remembered that tomorrow was Caroline Hopkins's funeral, and that was another sad fact to consider tonight.

For about an hour, I lay in the dark and refused to feel sorry for myself. I wasn't the one whose body had mutinied. I wasn't the one who had devoted my life to helping others for thirty-eight years—and for that trouble wouldn't be seeing thirty-nine.

Then I started to cry. My steely composure was shattered into a thousand pieces, and I was lost.

Originally, I had just gone along with my wife's idea to adopt. After we found out we couldn't have kids, I would have done whatever Maeve wanted. I loved her so much and just wanted to make her happy in any way I could.

But after we got Jane, I was a little reluctant to go on. Three kids in New York? It wasn't like I was Mr. Moneybags.

Maeve showed me that we had room in our home, and in our hearts, for one more. After Fiona and Bridget, I'd roll my eyes whenever Maeve would mention another needy child she'd heard about and say, "What's another pound on an elephant?"

But how can an elephant live without a heart? I thought as I lay there with tears streaming down my cheeks.

There was no way I was going to be able to do this. The older kids were becoming teenagers, and the younger ones . . . How could I be in charge of their lives and their future all by myself?

Then I heard my door crack open.

"Peep-peep," someone small said.

It was Chrissy. Every morning, she'd come into our room with her empty cereal bowl pretending to be a different baby animal in need of feeding.

She padded up to the edge of the bed.

"Peep-peep can't sleep," she said.

I wiped my tears on the pillow. "Big Peep can't either," I said.

She hadn't slept in our bed since she was two, and I was about to get up to tuck her back in her own bed, but then I pulled open the covers. "Get in the nest, Peep, quick!"

As Chrissy dove in beside me, I realized my kids weren't a burden. They were the only thing holding me together.

Chrissy was asleep in about two minutes. After she dug the tiny icicles of her feet snugly into my kidneys, I realized sleepily that maybe you couldn't call this happy. But it was the first time in weeks I'd seen the ballpark.

CHAPTER 2

THE silver chimes of St. Patrick's morning bells were still hanging in the chilled air over Fifth Avenue when the Neat Man arrived outside the cathedral's massive entrance doors. He shook his head at the crowd of loonies who already lined the sidewalk four-deep behind the police barricades.

Caroline Hopkins's funeral wouldn't start for another forty minutes, and already the turnout was as thick as the mounds of donated flowers that buried the base of the block-long church. She had been a popular First Lady, but more important to many, she'd been born and raised in New York City. She was one of their own. Yeah, right. Like the mayor of New York was one of the people.

Up on the front steps of St. Paddy's, the Neat Man watched a marine drill sergeant inspect the army, navy, air force, and marine honor guard just inside the open three-story bronze doors. Then the limousines started arriving.

Mayor Andrew Thurman got there first. He claimed to be a close friend of the Hopkinses.

On his heels came real estate mogul Xavier Brown and his wife, a Chanel-clad fashion diva named Celeste. The power couple was also close friends of the First Lady.

The next to de-limo was New York Giants quarterback Todd Snow. His Super Bowl ring glittered as he put his arm around his attractive model wife. The athlete had done charity work with Caroline Hopkins.

The Neat Man gazed with satisfaction at the freight train of limousines forming to the north up Fifth Avenue. *Hail, hail, the gang's all here. Well, almost.*

Finally, he looked up at the gigantic rose window and majestic three-hundred-foot stone towers at the front of the cathedral. With the ego-per-square-inch ratio this thing was developing, he thought, it would be surprising if there'd still be room for the casket.

JOHN Rooney made a face like the Grinch as his limousine stopped in front of the churning crowds at St. Patrick's. As Hollywood's current lead box-office-grossing actor, he'd come to appreciate the loyal fans who turned out for events of any kind. But now as he looked out at the rapacious faces, he was a little wary. Standing room only at a funeral was a little too close to creepy.

Fortunately for him, the church side of Fifth Avenue was VIP only. Rooney exited onto the street and saw a line of press stacked along both sides of the cathedral's stairs and entrance.

With effort, he managed not to turn when someone from the crowd across Fifth yelled, "WUZ UP, DORK?", the catchphrase from his latest comedy hit. Then he entered the church and showed his invitation to the red-coated security guard.

He heard cameras pop and click behind him like an angry swarm of metal crickets. Mercedes Freer, the twenty-year-old bubblegum pop diva, had arrived wearing a micromini black-widow outfit and veil. Then 1970s rock legend Charlie Conlan climbed out of his stretch and walked up the church's stairs. The tall, hopelessly cool icon had to be close to sixty now, but he still looked real good. He shook Rooney's hand in the vestibule.

Charlie had written and performed three magical songs for a children's movie Rooney had starred in the year before. They'd gone on a brief promotional tour together. The whole time, Conlan had never stopped smiling and had signed autographs for any and all.

"It's a circus, huh?" Charlie said in his patented gravelly voice. "You one of the clowns, Johnny?"

"If I am, then you're the ringmaster," said Rooney, laughing as the cameras went off again.

Another cheer rose from the crowd. Out on the street, Eugena Humphrey was exiting her pink Lincoln Town Car. "Now, now, people," the charismatic talk-show host chided the crowd. "This is a funeral, not the Emmys. Let's have a little respect, please."

Amazingly, the crowd quieted right down.

"Eugena rules," someone said, and that seemed to be the God's honest truth.

NEW York Times reporter Cathy Calvin turned as the First Lady's hearse appeared over the rise of an emptied Fifth Avenue. It was led by a nine-strong V formation of NYPD parade-speed Harleys.

It was as if a contingent of the cathedral's statues had come to life when the honor guard broke rank in the vestibule and marched slowly out onto the sidewalk. The guard arrived at the curb the moment the hearse did. They ceremoniously slid out the American flag–draped casket from the long black car.

Two Secret Service men in dark suits appeared from the crowd and completed the line of pallbearers as the former First Lady's body was effortlessly raised to shoulder height. The soldiers and agents stopped at the top of the stairs, just behind the former president and his daughter, as a low rumbling began to the south.

A moment later, a group of five F-15s appeared low in the sky. As they swooped over Forty-second Street, the westernmost aircraft suddenly broke rank and arced upward while the remaining planes roared over the cathedral in the "missing man" formation.

The pallbearers waited until the last echo of the jet engines' thunder had dissipated from Fifth Avenue's stone-and-steel canyon and then began to enter the church carrying Caroline Hopkins.

A lone bagpiper didn't start playing "Amazing Grace" until the former president passed over the church's threshold.

Cathy Calvin looked out over the crowd. People were taking off their hats, had their hands over their hearts, and were singing with the hymn. Everywhere, jaded New Yorkers were weeping openly.

But that wasn't the biggest shock to her. No, the big surprise was when Cathy Calvin, seen-it-all reporter, put her hand up to her own cheek and realized she was crying, too.

A SEND-OFF like that almost brought tears to your eyes, the Neat Man thought as he stared through binoculars from his swivel chair in the back of his black van. It was parked near Fifty-first and Fifth Avenue, kitty-corner to the cathedral, and for the last hour, through the one-way tinted window at the van's rear, he'd been watching the parade of arriving celebs and dignitaries.

As the church's entrance doors closed behind former President Hopkins and his entourage, the Neat Man lowered the binocs to rip a baby wipe from the top of the plastic canister at his feet. His red hands stung wonderfully when he started scouring them. He dropped the used wipe at his feet and raised the binoculars again.

He scanned the perimeter of the church, lingering at each security post. There was a line of Manhattan beat cops scattered about the front of the church with the press and an NYPD Emergency Service Unit truck blocking the side streets at each corner.

The ESU commandos had submachine guns strapped across their chests, but there were coffee cups and cigarettes in their hands. Instead of being vigilant, they were standing around telling lies about what they would do with all the overtime they were raking in.

Were they that stupid? the Neat Man thought. *Yes, they were.*

His cell phone went off when the bagpiper started winding

down. The Neat Man lowered the binoculars and raised the phone to his ear. "All clear, Jack," the Neat Man said. "It's a go."

IN THE nave of the cathedral, "Jack" bit the antenna of his just-closed cell phone nervously as he gazed out at the dozens of Secret Service agents and cops stationed around the church. *Would this scheme actually work?* he thought for the hundred thousandth time. Well, no time like the present to find out. He holstered the phone and headed for the Fifty-first Street exit.

Seconds later, he unhooked the latch that was holding open the two-foot-thick wooden door. A female uniformed NYPD cop smoking a cigarette in the threshold glanced at him.

"In or out?" Jack said with a smile. "Service is starting. We got to close 'em up."

In the predawn security meeting, law enforcement personnel had been told to give the church security force deference in all matters concerning the ceremony.

"Out, I guess," the cop said.

Good choice, flatfoot, Jack thought, pulling the heavy doors shut and snapping the key off in the lock. *Choose life.*

He hurried up the stairs and around the ambulatory along the back of the altar. It was packed—standing room only—with white-frocked priests. The organ started, and the casket appeared from under the choir loft just as he arrived at the south transept.

Jack jogged down the stairs to the Fiftieth Street side entrance and closed and locked the thick door there, too. He refrained from breaking the key in the lock because they'd need this exit in about a minute. Half of Hollywood, Wall Street, and Washington was now boxed inside the cathedral.

Quickly, he went back along the ambulatory. There was a leather rope blocking off a small, narrow marble stairwell at the rear of the altar. He stepped over the rope and descended. At the bottom of the stairs was an ornate green copper door. The sign above it read CRYPT OF THE ARCHBISHOPS OF NEW YORK.

Jack stepped in and yanked the door closed. In the dimness, he could make out the stone sarcophagi of the interred archbishops arrayed in a semicircle around the stone walls of the chamber. "It's me, idiots," he said in a low voice. "Hit the light."

There was a click, and the wall sconces came on. Behind the caskets were a dozen men. Most were wearing T-shirts and sweatpants. They were big, muscular, and not very friendly-looking.

The men strapped on bulletproof Kevlar vests. Smith & Wesson nine-millimeter handguns in underarm holsters went on next. The black fingerless gloves they put on had cushioned lead shot over the knuckles. Then the mysterious cadre pulled brown-hooded monk robes over the Kevlar vests. Into the pockets were placed what looked like remote controls but were actually the latest in electric-shock weaponry.

They slipped big-bored riot guns up the billowing sleeves of their robes. Half of the guns were loaded with rubber bullets, the other half with canisters of tear gas.

Last, the men pulled black ski masks over their faces. It was as if they were made of shadow when they flipped up the hoods.

Jack smiled approvingly as he threw on his own vest, robe, and black ski mask. As he slowly pulled back the heavy door of the crypt, he said, "It's time to put the *fun* back into funeral."

MOVIE star and comedian John Rooney felt the breath rush out of him as the honor guard finally arrived at the front of the church with the flag-draped coffin.

After the pallbearers laid it down with the organ thundering from above, Rooney turned to his right and saw a line of cowled, brown-robed monks appear. They walked with the same solemnity of the honor guard as they approached the altar. He could see another line of them walking down the aisle to his left. The organ was reaching a crescendo when the monks spaced themselves out and stopped suddenly in the side aisles.

Rooney jumped when he heard a series of muffled blasts under the rumble of the organ. Then smoke, white and enveloping, came billowing from all sides. What had been the austere VIP section looked like a mosh pit as the people in there panicked, clawing at one another to get out of the pews.

Rooney thought he saw one of the monks setting off a shotgun into the crowd. *No,* he thought, blinking hard in disbelief. *That couldn't be right.* He opened his eyes as a uniformed cop stumbled up the center aisle with blood pouring out of his nose and ears.

Then the organ died.

Fear slapped through Rooney. With the music gone, he could hear the screaming of thousands soaring off the high stone vaults.

Someone had just taken over St. Patrick's!

I WAS still groggy when I took a head count and pulled our van away from my building. It was eight forty-one, and I had four minutes to get us to Holy Name on Amsterdam. Or there would be at least one kid from every grade in detention.

From the top of my building, you could probably "roof" my kids' school on Ninety-seventh with a Spalding, but anyone who's familiar with rush hour in Manhattan will tell you that if you planned on going two blocks in four minutes, you were taking your chances.

I knew I could have let them walk. But I wanted to spend as much time as possible with them right now, wanted them to know they weren't on their own. In fact, the only thing that had stopped me from writing out ten bogus sick notes to share my day off with them was Holy Name's principal, Sister Sheilah. My butt already had enough memories of the principal's bench to last a lifetime.

I got them to the school with seconds to spare. I hopped out and threw open the door of our family vehicle, a twelve-passenger Ford Super Duty van I had bought at a police auction.

"Run!" I yelled as I pulled out children with both hands and deposited them on the sidewalk.

Shawna just made it in as Sister Sheilah was taking the hook off the oak door to shut and lock it. I could see the withered old nun scanning the street for me, her stern look cocked and ready to fire. My tires barked as I dropped the Super D's tranny into drive, punched the gas, and fled the scene.

When I got back to the apartment, I couldn't believe my nose: It smelled like coffee. Strong coffee. And that other smell. I didn't want to jinx it, but I had a deep hunch that something was baking.

Mary Catherine was pulling out a tray of muffins when I entered the kitchen. *Blueberry muffins.* And the kitchen. It was sparkling. Every surface gleaming, every cereal bowl put away.

"Mr. Bennett," Mary Catherine said, putting the muffins on the stove. "Where is everyone?"

"At school," I said.

Mary Catherine gave me a questioning look. "What time do they leave?" she asked.

"Around eight," I said, unable to take my eyes off the muffins.

"Then I start at seven, Mr. Bennett. Not nine."

"I apologize. And the name is Mike, remember? Are those . . ."

"For after breakfast. How do you like your eggs . . . Mike?"

After breakfast? I'd assumed they were breakfast. Maybe this au pair thing would work out. "Over easy?" I said.

"Bacon or sausage?" she said.

No maybe about it, I thought. I was contemplating that win-win decision when I felt my cell phone vibrate. I looked at the caller ID. My boss. An express delivery of ill tidings was about to land in my lap. I brought the phone to my ear. "Bennett," I said.

"Thank God," my boss, Harry Grissom, said. Harry is the lieutenant detective in charge of my unit, the Manhattan North Homicide Squad. "You heard what just happened?"

"Where? What?" I said. There must have been a distinct note of urgency in my voice because Mary Catherine turned from the sink.

"All I was told was, about ten minutes ago, at St. Patrick's Cathedral, shots were fired," Harry said. "First Lady Caroline's funeral was going on at the time, so it doesn't sound too good."

What felt like a door breach hit me full in the stomach. "Terrorists?" I said.

"I don't think we know yet," my boss said. "I do know that Manhattan South borough commander Will Matthews is on the scene, and he wants you down there ASAP."

In what capacity? I wondered. I had been on the NYPD's Hostage Negotiation Team before making the switch to Homicide. And wasn't I too fried with my family crisis to take on a much larger one?

"Does he need me for negotiating?" I asked. "Or was there a homicide at the cathedral? Help me out here, Harry."

"I was too busy getting screamed at to ask," my boss said. "Just get down there and find out everything you can."

"On my way," I said, and hung up.

I went into my bedroom and threw on jeans, a sweatshirt, and my NYPD Windbreaker. I retrieved my Glock from the closet safe.

Mary Catherine was waiting in the hall with my travel mug and a bag of muffins. I was struggling to come up with appropriate words of thanks when she opened the front door and said, "Go, Mike."

I PULLED my department-issued blue Impala up to the barricade at Fifth Avenue and Fifty-second Street. I hadn't seen so many cops in front of the landmark church since the St. Patrick's Day Parade. Only instead of goofy tam-o'-shanters, shamrocks, and smiles, they were wearing helmets, automatic weapons, and serious frowns.

I showed my shield to a sergeant by one of the blue-and-white sawhorses. She directed me to the mobile command center, a long white bus parked across the street from the cathedral.

As I got out of my car, a jackhammer throbbing sounded, and I looked up as a police helicopter swung out from behind Rockefeller Center across the street and hovered low over the cathedral. A sniper in the helicopter's open door scanned the stained glass and stone spires over the barrel of a rifle.

I stopped and stared in disbelief. How could this be happening at Caroline Hopkins's funeral?

Will Matthews was standing on the sidewalk in front of the command center bus. Though only five seven, with his broken nose and violently frank way of looking at everybody, he was as pugnacious-looking an Irish cop as you could find on the force.

"Glad you could join us, Bennett," he said.

"Yeah, well," I said, "I hadn't had a chance to see the Rockefeller Center Christmas tree yet."

Instead of chuckling, Matthews looked like he wanted to hit me with a billy club. "I'm in no mood for stand-up," he said. "The mayor; the former president; several movie, music, and sports stars; and about three thousand other VIPs are being held hostage inside by a dozen or more heavily armed masked men."

It was hard to register what Will Matthews had just said to me. The mayor and the former president alone would have been mind-boggling, but all the rest?

"We don't know if the gunmen are terrorists. They took out thirty-one cops and about two dozen federal agents with nonlethal weapons. Tear gas and rubber bullets and Tasers. Twenty minutes ago, they opened the Fiftieth Street entrance doors and bum-rushed all the cops and security personnel. There were a lot of broken noses and black eyes, but they could have gunned them down just as easy as let them go. I guess we can be grateful for small mercies."

I struggled to keep the shock and confusion off my face. "How can I help?" I asked.

"Ned Mason, our top negotiator, is on his way. I know you're not in Hostage Negotiation anymore, but I needed our best option in case these guys call before he gets here. Also, as I recall, you've got a lot of media airtime under your belt. I might need you to run interference with the press. Steve Reno's got the tactical lead. You can consult with him when he comes down off that bird, okay? Sit tight. Think about what to say to the press."

I was following orders, "sitting tight," staring across at the huge, stately church, trying to figure out what kind of person or persons would pull this, when the FBI arrived about ten minutes later. Four black-on-black Chevy Suburbans were let through the barricade, and a fully armed tactical team poured out of the vehicles.

A middle-aged man in a charcoal suit came up and shook my hand. "Mike Bennett?" he said amicably. "Paul Martelli. Crisis Negotiation Unit. The special agent in charge sent us up from Twenty-six Fed to give you guys a hand if we can."

The FBI's CNU was at the cutting edge in hostage negotiation. Martelli, its head, was famous in negotiation circles. A book he'd written was pretty much the bible on the subject.

I usually bristle at the presence of Feds, but I had to admit, I was relieved that Martelli was here. I'd done some standoffs in my three years in Hostage Negotiation, but nothing like this. I'd take all the help I could get.

"I see you guys got the communication and press angles taken care of," Martelli said, looking around casually at the command center and the barricades. "Mike, who's the primary negotiator?"

Even talking about trivial stuff, Martelli exuded tranquil confidence. I could see why he was at the top of the game.

"Me for now," I said, "until our top guy gets here. Then I switch to secondary. ESU lieutenant Steve Reno has the tactical lead. Commander Will Matthews has the final word."

All crisis incidents require a chain of command. The negotiator has to ask higher authorities before acting on a hostage-taker's demands. This buys time and engenders a bond between the hostage-taker and the negotiator. Also, someone has to make the final decision—to keep negotiating or to go tactical.

"Most important thing now," Martelli said, "is to show patience. We have to burn some time. Time for SWAT to gather tactical intelligence. And time for whoever's inside to cool off."

The two of us turned as a cop in a flapping NYPD Windbreaker roared in through the cordon on a dusty black Suzuki.

"Any contact?" Ned Mason barked at me as he got off his bike.

I'd worked with Mason before I had left the negotiation team. A lot of people dismissed the intense sandy-haired cop as arrogant, but I knew him to be a quirky loner who succeeds more by meticulousness and the solitary power of his strong will than teamwork.

"Not yet," I said.

I started to brief Mason, but an NYPD Communications Division sergeant popped his head out the door of the bus holding a cell phone above his head. "It's them!" he said.

Will Matthews joined us as we all rushed inside the bus.

"Call came in to nine-one-one. We routed it to here," a communications tech cop said, offering the phone. "Who gets this?"

Mason snatched the phone out of his hand as Matthews and Martelli and myself pulled on headsets so we could listen in.

"Whoever you are," Mason said into the phone, "listen closely." His voice was powerful, his tone very serious. "This is the United States Army. What you have done has gone beyond the bounds of governmental negotiation. The president of the United States has signed an executive order, and all normal channels are now closed. In five minutes' time, you will either release the hostages or you will be killed. The only guarantee I will give you is this: If you lay down your weapons and let everyone out, you walk away with your lives. Tell me now. Are these the last five minutes of your life?"

Mason was making a bold move, using a controversial strategy designed to end a standoff by basically scaring the hell out of the hostage-taker. He'd just gone "all in" on the very first poker hand.

"If this guy," a voice replied with equal starkness after a short pause, "isn't off the line in five seconds, the former president joins his wife in the afterlife. Five . . ."

I almost felt sorry for Mason when I saw the frown cross his face. It had been a risky bluff, one that had completely blown up on him.

"Four," the voice said.

Commander Will Matthews stepped forward. "Mason!" he said. "Three."

Mason was clutching the phone; he didn't seem to be breathing. "Two."

I had been a good negotiator, but I hadn't done it in three years. But Ned Mason had just crashed and burned, and like it or not, rusty or not, as secondary negotiator, it was my job to step in.

"One."

I pulled the phone out of Mason's hand.

"Hi," I said calmly. "My name's Mike. Sorry, the person who spoke to you wasn't authorized. Disregard everything he said. I'm the negotiator. We will not attack the cathedral. In fact, we don't want anyone to get hurt. Who am I speaking with, please?"

"On account of the fact that I just jacked this cathedral and everyone in it," the voice said, "why don't you call me Jack?"

"Okay, Jack," I said. "Thanks for talking to me."

"No problemo," Jack said. "Do me a favor, Mike. Tell that soldier-of-fortune jerk who was just on that we have every window, door, and wall in this place rigged up to a lotta C-four on a motion-detector laser trigger. He better not breach or everybody on this block is going to be blown to kingdom come. In fact, I'd seriously consider moving that NYPD helicopter off the roof if I were you."

I found Will Matthews with my eyes and made a cutting motion toward the roof of the bus. He spoke to one of his cop entourage, a radio crackled, and the rotor thump of the helicopter fell away.

"Okay, Jack. I got my boss to move the helicopter back. Now, is everybody okay in there? Has anybody been shot?"

"Not yet," Jack said.

I ignored the provocative response for the time being. Once I bonded a little more, I would try to curtail the threats, get him to speak more reasonably. "You guys need food or water?" I asked.

"We're good for now," Jack said. "At this point, I just want to lay two things on you that you need to start wrapping your mind around. You're going to give us what we want, and we're going to get away with this. Say it, Mike."

"We're going to give you what you want, and you're going to get away with this," I said without hesitation. Until we had more of an advantage, I needed him to accept me as quickly as possible.

"Good boy. I know it's a little hard to compute, sitting where you're sitting, Mike. So I just wanted to plant the seed there. Because it's gonna happen. *We're going to get away with this*. Smell you later," the hijacker said—and the line went dead on me.

CHAPTER 3

"WHAT'S your take on these guys, Mike?" Mason suddenly found his voice again.

"Wait a second," I said. Being the closest to the command center window, I was the first to see the movement at the front of the cathedral. "The front door is opening. Something's going down."

A man in a torn blue dress shirt appeared in the doorway, blinking in the pale sunlight as he stepped onto the flagstone plaza.

"I have him," I heard a sniper call over the police band.

"Hold fire!" Will Matthews called back.

A woman in a broken-heeled shoe hobbled out behind the man in the blue shirt.

"What the . . ." Will Matthews said as a thin stream, then a flood, of people started pouring out onto the cathedral's front steps and onto Fifth Avenue. Were the hijackers letting everyone go? The other cops around me seemed as confused as I was.

We watched the unfathomable mob scene. Uniformed cops waded in immediately and guided the people past the barricade.

"Get every detective down here. Robbery, Special Victims, everyone! I want those released hostages identified and interviewed," Commander Will Matthews barked at one of the assistant chiefs.

Then the doors of the cathedral began to close again.

Martelli patted me on the back. "Nice work, Mike," he said. "Textbook negotiating. You just saved thousands of lives."

I appreciated the compliment, but I didn't think what had just happened had much to do with me.

"Is it over?" Will Matthews asked. "Is that possible?"

There was a communal flinch around the room when the phone I was holding suddenly rang.

"My guess," I said, "would be no."

"MIKE," JACK SAID. "HOW'S IT hanging out there, buddy? People make it to safety okay? Nobody trampled to death, I hope."

"No, Jack," I said. "Everybody seems to be okay. Thanks for being reasonable."

"I'm trying, Mike. Giving it my all. I thought I better clear up any misperceptions, though. Now that we've tossed back the *small* fish, I'd like to talk about the *whales* we're still holding on to."

I glanced out the window. My God! He was right. Where was former President Hopkins? The mayor of New York? The A-list people were still inside. *How many of them?*

"To make it easier on everybody, we're holding thirty-four hostages," Jack said as if reading my mind. "Celebrities, of course, some tycoons, couple of politicians. So far, no one's been hurt. But if you guys try to sneak in here and take us out, there's gonna be a bloodbath like this country's never seen. Give us what we want, Mike, and this ugly scene will go away."

"We want to resolve this thing as much as you do, Jack," I said.

"That's good to hear, Mike," Jack said. "Because I'm giving you and these fat cats the opportunity to get out of trouble the good old-fashioned way. I'm going to let you buy your way out."

AFTER Jack disconnected, Paul Martelli took off his headphones and crossed the room. He sat down next to me. "You're doing good, Mike. Cool heads prevail."

"What's your take on this guy, Paul?" I asked him.

"Well, he's obviously not mentally disturbed," Martelli said. "And he sounds confident. I get the feeling that he knows something we haven't figured out yet."

I nodded. I had that same feeling; I just hadn't put it into words.

"The thing he said about explosives on the windows and doors. You think it's legit?"

"Looking at the way he's handled himself so far, I'd say yeah, we have to consider that it's a real threat."

I looked around for Ned Mason. He'd found a seat in the farthest corner of the room. With his failure still hanging heavy in the air, he looked like he was trying to make himself invisible.

"Ned. Tell me," I said, "why do you think they let all those people go when they could have held on to them?"

Mason looked up, surprised that anyone was still talking to him. "Well, let's see," he said. "Logistics, for one thing. Those extra hostages could get sick or hurt. Or worse, they could resist. Controlling a crowd over a long period of time would be tricky."

Martelli nodded. "Also, maybe they thought letting out most of the people would look good for the cameras. You know, let the real people go. Only hold on to the rich. Like a Robin Hood thing."

"Bastards have the angles covered," Mason said. "They must have been planning this for months. Maybe years."

Our coffee cups jumped as my fist hit the counter. *That was it.* What had been bothering me. I couldn't believe it.

"This whole takedown was choreographed, right? No detail was overlooked. But how can you plan to take over a state funeral without a body? Somehow, they killed Caroline Hopkins."

STEPHEN Hopkins sat by himself in a pew in a small chapel behind the main altar. His head was buried in his hands. He was almost glad Caroline wasn't around to see what had happened. She was such a good soul; it would have hurt her deeply.

There were maybe thirty hostages scattered in the pews around him, well-known folks for the most part, whom Caroline had gotten to do charity work. He looked at the three masked gunmen standing at the front of the chapel. He'd been around a lot of soldiers, and that's what they reminded him of. Was that what they were? Former military? Did that make the motivation political?

A short, muscular hijacker stepped into the center aisle and cleared his throat. "Hi, everybody. I'm Jack. You can call my big, bad buddy over there Little John. Our sincerest apologies for detaining you like this. Anyone who needs to use a bathroom, just raise your hand, and you'll be escorted. There's food and water. Again, just raise your hand. Feel free to lie down in the pews or on the floor there in the back. If you cooperate, things will go smoothly. If you don't, the consequences will be very unpleasant."

Who was this twerp to lecture them like they were schoolchildren in detention? Stephen Hopkins stood up. "What do you want with us?" he said angrily. "Why do you dishonor my wife?"

"Mr. President," the hijacker said, smiling as he walked down the aisle. "That tone of voice will not do. I'm going out of my way to be polite. I sincerely urge you to do the same."

Hopkins wasn't used to being spoken to like this. "Oh, I'm sorry. You want decorum. Then would the gentleman in the ski mask deign to let the assembly know why he's holding them hostage?"

A few hostages in the pews laughed nervously.

The lead hijacker laughed, too. Then he leaned in and grabbed the former president by his full head of white hair. "Why, why, why?" he said into his ear. "That was always your weakest side, Stevie-boy. You always had to intellectualize everything."

"You son of a bitch," Hopkins yelled.

"Now you're calling my mother a bitch?" Jack said. "Disrespect me again, and I'll kick your guts out and make you eat 'em." He yanked the former president out into the aisle. Finally, he let go of his hair, and Hopkins sank to the floor.

The hijacker let out a deep breath and smiled at the other hostages. "There goes my temper," Jack said. "Now you've seen my one weakness." After a long, thoughtful moment, he made a thumbing motion at Hopkins. "Mr. President, you know what? You've been through enough today," he said. "Why don't you go home? You're dismissed! Get him out of my church."

Two of the hijackers grabbed the former president roughly by his elbows and started shoving him quickly into the main part of the church, toward the front doors.

JOHN Rooney, *LA Times*–proclaimed "film comic of the decade," was praying. Lapsed or not, he was baptized a Christian, and he was sitting in his pew, silently saying the Lord's Prayer.

He stopped in midprayer when something struck him in the side of the neck. When he looked down, he saw that there was a paper ball, made from a page ripped out of a hymnal, on the pew beside him. Someone had written OPEN ME right over the musical notes.

Rooney palmed the note as he looked up at the hijackers guarding them. The biggest one—Little John, was it?—sat on the altar as if it were the hood of a car and yawned.

Rooney opened the note.

> ROONEY—I'M IN THE ROW BEHIND YOU. SLOWLY SCOOTCH OVER INTO THE CENTER OF YOUR PEW SO WE CAN TALK. DON'T LET THE SCUM IN FRONT SEE YOU!—CHARLIE CONLAN

Rooney shoved the note into his pocket. Over the course of the next few minutes, he slid over the polished wood of the pew.

When he was about halfway, a gravelly voice behind him whispered, "You saw what they did to Hopkins?"

Rooney nodded grimly. "What do you think they want with the rest of us?" he said.

"Nothing good," Conlan said. "I guarantee you."

"What can we do about it, though?" Rooney said.

"Fight back," Conlan said. "Todd Snow's a row behind me. He's talking to the tycoon, Xavier Brown, behind him. With you, it's four."

"To do what?" Rooney asked. "You saw what they did to Hopkins when he just opened his mouth."

"We wait for now. Be patient. Pick our spot. Three of us can take one or two of these guys. We go from there."

THE elation that *New York Times* reporter Cathy Calvin had felt at being released from the cathedral was quickly being burned away by her annoyance at having to wait in line with everybody else to be interviewed by the police. The NYPD had all the detainees corralled outside of Saks Fifth Avenue, and they weren't letting anyone go until they'd been debriefed by one of four detectives.

Calvin noticed the news-van microwave towers beyond the blue-and-white sawhorses, rising above the crowd like the masts of some invading armada. Wait, what was she complaining about? *She was where everyone else was trying to get. Inside the ropes!*

Calvin quickly calculated the strategic advantage of her position. She'd been in the cathedral during the takeover. She was an eyewitness to the siege, which would make it her exclusive.

Just then a hush rolled through the crowd. Calvin peered with the rest of the craning heads toward the cathedral. She could see one of the cathedral's main doors coming open again. *Now what?* She ran forward to get close to the hot breaking news.

And then, for the second or third time this morning, the reporter couldn't believe what she was seeing. "My God," she whispered.

I WAS still in the command center bus, discussing negotiation strategy with Martelli and Mason, when the cathedral doors flew open for the second time. A stunned-looking Stephen Hopkins came stumbling onto the flagstone plaza, and then the doors quickly closed behind him. They'd released Hopkins? But why?

Another unexpected move from the hijackers, I thought with a queasy feeling. It was great that they had released the former president, but the way in which they were doing things was all over the place, impossible to predict. Was that the idea? I doubted it.

A spontaneous, thunderous cheer ripped from both the police and the crowd of civilians beyond the barricades.

"Move in," I heard Commander Will Matthews say. "Pick the president up. Get him out of there. Now!"

Half a dozen ESU cops nearly gang-tackled the former president and rushed him around the sanitation truck barricade.

I stood staring at the cathedral's spooky gothic arches through the bus window. How was I supposed to solve this thing? I thought of Maeve and my kids. I'm not usually one to make excuses, but didn't I have enough on my plate? I needed another crisis?

Paul Martelli's hand found my shoulder. "You're doing the best with a horrible situation, Mike," he said as if reading my mind. "It's the losers inside who are responsible. Not us. Don't forget that."

EUGENA Humphrey sat motionless and numb, staring at the flickering candles in front of the altar.

The Los Angeles–based talk-show host knew that in order to get through any horrifying ordeal, the first thing you needed to do was to calm your emotions. The row of votive candles along the south wall of the chapel had caught her attention immediately. There was something reassuring in the way the tiny white flames burned behind the gold-and-red glass.

I can get through this, she thought to herself. An enormous number of rescuers had to be outside the church right now. And the press. Something this high-profile would be resolved for the simple reason that it had to be. Eugena swallowed hard. Things would be resolved.

When she'd first entered the cathedral, its stone and marble walls seemed too cold, too stark. But after looking upon the votives and feeling the deep silence of this place, she realized it expressed the same spiritual warmness she remembered from the Baptist church her mother took her to every Sunday back in West Virginia.

"My God," a woman whispered next to her. "How will this horror end?"

It was Laura Winston, the New York fashion magazine institution. Poor Laura was trembling. Her gray-blue eyes bulged as if they were about to pop free of her surgically tightened face. Poor woman, Eugena thought with compassion. Her soft black hand found the fashionista's bony white one, and she squeezed gently until Laura looked into her eyes. Eugena put her arm around the distraught woman as she started to hyperventilate.

"Now, now. We're in a church and in His hands," Eugena said soothingly. "Everything's going to be all right. This too shall pass."

"Yes. But will any of us still be alive?"

LAURA Winston had stopped crying and was thanking Eugena for her kindness when there was a commotion up toward the altar.

Somebody was standing up!

From the tangle of blond hair and the black mini, Laura could tell it was the haute-trash pop singer Mercedes Freer. Marble rang as she clicked in her six-inch stilettos toward the rear of the chapel.

"Sit the hell down!" one of the hijackers yelled at her.

"Could I talk to someone, please? I need to talk to your boss, if you don't mind," the diva said.

The lead hijacker arrived on the scene a moment later. "What is it?" Jack said. "Talk to me. How can I help?"

Mercedes plucked her diamond earrings off and offered them to Jack. "These are Cartier. I paid a quarter million dollars for them. Now, I'm supposed to be on *Leno* tonight, and I'm running late. You know what I'm saying? Please take 'em. They're not enough, I'll get my manager on the phone. Let's make a deal, sugar."

Eugena winced at the white girl's attempted inner-city speak. After booking her on the show a year ago, Eugena remembered reading in her bio that she'd been born in white-bread New Canaan, Connecticut. Eugena thought about all the elocution books she'd gotten out of the library to get the sound of poor *out* of her voice. What a sorry state this upside-down world had come to.

The hijacker held up the earrings as if appraising them. Then he flicked them one after the other right into the girl's face. "How about instead," he said slowly, "you sit your slutty ass down."

Mercedes's face darkened. "Slutty what?" she said angrily. "Who you think you're talkin' to, shorty?"

The hijacker pulled out a spray canister from his pocket. He grabbed the singer by her hair and emptied it into her face. Mercedes's face looked like it was blistering as she screamed through the pepper spray. As she fell to her knees, Jack calmly dragged her by her hair to the door of a confessional on the north wall. He opened it, threw the girl in, then slammed it shut.

"Anybody else want to discuss their travel plans?" he said to the wide-eyed hostages.

Jack tapped his foot in the silence. "Guess not," he finally said. "Well, listen up. We need to start an individual interview process, so I'm going to ask everyone to line up in front of the first door to the right at the back of the chapel. *Now!*"

Eugena stood and turned meekly around along with the rest of the hostages. As she came out into the aisle, she could hear Mercedes whimpering inside the confessional.

She almost felt sorry for the girl, but what good was it to antagonize these men? What did she think would happen? She probably thought he would let her go, Eugena decided. When was the last time a human being had said no to the spoiled-brat star?

CHARLIE Conlan waited in line for his "interview" in front of one of the confessionals along the south walkway.

Sounded a little melodramatic if you asked him, more cheesy scare tactics like the masks and robes. It seemed like the hijackers were trying to play off the gothic mood of the place, get people afraid, keep 'em off balance. Fairly intelligent tactics, actually.

Conlan knew most over-the-hill rock legends like him were pretty soft. But few had his background. What growing up poor in downtown Detroit had failed to teach him, an extended stay at the Hanoi Hilton for most of '69 had filled in pretty well.

Conlan steeled himself as the door finally opened and a young actress, Marilyn Rubenstein, emerged shaken from her "interview." She caught Conlan gaping at her as the guards led her past. "Do what they say," she advised in a whisper.

"Next," the hijacker at the door called in a bored voice.

Conlan hesitated; then he stepped into the room.

It wasn't a confessional, Conlan realized. It was a little security room. Sitting at a metal table was the lead hijacker, Jack. He motioned to the empty metal chair on the opposite side of the table.

"Please, Mr. Conlan, have a seat. I'm a big fan, by the way."

Conlan sat. "Thank you."

On the table between them were a pair of handcuffs in a clear plastic bag and a roll of duct tape. Conlan eyed the items, trying to keep the fear in his belly from rising.

Jack lifted a clipboard from his lap. His pen clicked. "Okay, Mr. Charlie Conlan," he said. "I'm going to ask you for the names and numbers of your financial people. Any kind of PIN or access codes that are needed to get to your funds would be most helpful."

Conlan forced himself to smile as he made eye contact with Jack. "So all this is about money?" he said.

The hijacker frowned. "I don't have time for idle chitchat, Mr. Conlan. Are you going to cooperate or not? Last chance."

Conlan decided to push the envelope some. See exactly what they were dealing with here. "Let me think about that for a second," he said, rubbing his chin with his fingertips. "Ummmm, no?"

Jack took the cuffs out of the bag, and then he stood. He walked behind Conlan and expertly cuffed his wrists behind his back.

Conlan clenched his jaw as he waited for the first blow to come.

But the first blow didn't come. Instead there was a quick rustle—and the plastic bag was plopped over Conlan's head.

Tape shrieked, and then a nooselike pressure encased Conlan's neck, closing the bag with an airtight seal. The plastic clung to his skin, rattled in his mouth and nostrils as he took a panicked breath.

"Little hot in there, isn't it?" Jack said near Conlan's ear.

Conlan gagged. His throat was burning. *God, no. Not like this.*

Jack sat down, yawned, and crossed his legs as Conlan convulsed. After an eternity, Jack checked his watch. "You want to sign up for my cash-for-oxygen program?" he asked. "Up to you."

Plastic crackled in Conlan's ears as he nodded vigorously.

Jack reached across the table, and air, sweet air, rushed in around his gloved finger as he poked a small hole in the bag.

Conlan gasped and wheezed with his head down against the table. The clipboard and a pen were slid beside his chin. Two thoughts pounded through Conlan's brain with the returning oxygen. The first was a prayer. The second a curse. *My God. We're completely screwed.*

CHAPTER 4

I HAD just gotten off the phone with Maeve when Steve Reno sauntered into the command bus.

I remembered Steve from several standoffs. The tall, long-haired, muscular tactical NYPD officer was an anomaly. No one was more patient and compassionate on the outside of a barricaded door—and no one was quicker when it had to be kicked in.

Behind him were two FBI commandos in black SWAT fatigues. The shorter of the two could have been a plumber, or a shop teacher, except for the bright green eyes that scanned the trailer and me with the efficient sweep of a copying machine light bar.

"Mike, this is Dave Oakley," Steve told me. "The greatest tactical team supervisor alive."

"Let's just keep it that way, huh, Steve? No mess-ups today," the commando said with a humorless laugh as I shook his hand. "What's the story with our new best friends inside?"

I filled him in as best I could. He nodded when I was done.

"We got our work cut out for us today," Reno finally said. "We spoke to Secret Service. Former President Hopkins told them the remaining hostages are being held in the Lady Chapel at the rear of the church. He said that the kidnappers aren't taking an iota of crap from any of the captives. They seem well disciplined. They're not terrorists. They're American, apparently. New one to me."

"New one to all of us," I said as the door opened again, and another ESU cop came in with an elderly man in a tweed cap. The old man was carrying a large cardboard cylinder.

"I'm Mike Nardy, the cathedral's caretaker," the man said, opening the cylinder's lid. "The rectory told me to bring these here."

I helped him unroll the blueprints. The paper was old, yellowed at the edges, but the detailing of the cathedral was extensive. Reno, Oakley, and Commander Will Matthews also leaned over to look.

The overhead view of St. Patrick's Cathedral looked like a cross. The main Fifth Avenue entrance was at the bottom of the long piece, and the Fiftieth and Fifty-first Street entryways at the sides of the shorter one. The Lady Chapel, like a small extension at the top of the long part of the cross, had no way in or out.

"I got snipers in Saks on Forty-ninth and in 620 Fifth behind us," said Oakley. "I'll have to get one on Madison at the rear to watch the Lady Chapel. Too bad these stained-glass windows are about as clear as a brick wall. Mr. Nardy, is there a clear line of sight from the rose window in the front to the Lady Chapel in the rear?"

"In part," the serious old man said. "Though there are columns along the back of the altar and a fifty-seven-foot baldachin—that's a bronze gazebo-type structure—over the altar."

"The cathedral's a block long. What's that, five hundred feet?" Oakley said to his second-in-command. "We point our fiber-optic camera through one of those windows. Get heat signatures of the weapons to pick out the bad guys. We rappel down the front, blow the rose window and the chapel windows simultaneously."

"I know I must be going a little deaf," the caretaker, Nardy, said. "Because for a second there, I thought you said you were going to destroy the great rose window of St. Patrick's Cathedral."

"You don't have to concern yourself with police business, Mr. Nardy," Oakley said. "Lives are on the line."

"That rose window is a hundred and fifty years old, sir," the caretaker said. "It's irreplaceable, as are the windows of the Lady Chapel. You wouldn't be so quick to blow a hole in the side of the Statue of Liberty, would you? Well, this church is this city's Statue of Faith. You'll destroy it over my dead body."

"Remove Mr. Nardy, somebody, please," Oakley said, annoyed.

"You better listen to me!" Nardy said forcefully as the ESU cop escorted him back outside. "I'll go right to the press."

That's all we needed, I thought. This thing wasn't hard enough without having our hands tied behind our backs.

Oakley turned his black baseball hat around on his head and exhaled loudly. "Would you look at this?" he said. "The granite walls are two feet thick. The doors are foot-thick bronze. Even the windows have stone tracery. There's no adjoining buildings we can try to tunnel our way in from. This place is a fortress. And we have to infiltrate it without leaving a scratch. Would somebody please remind me why I took this job?"

"The fat sneaker contracts and the book deals," I said.

It was a lame joke, but under the circumstances, I needed to provide an outlet for the mounting stress. Everyone, including the stoic Oakley, got a pretty good laugh.

It was either that or cry.

TEN minutes later, we were outside in the frosty air, staring up at the magnificent church. As we stepped around the side of one of the dump trucks, Oakley ordered his snipers to get an angle on the irreplaceable windows of the Lady Chapel.

The gray light cast shadows into the church's second-story windows and its arched entryway. The front of the cathedral resembled a large face, I thought: wide, dark eyes and a very large mouth, gaping open as if in outrage and shock.

I stopped dead still and almost went for my Glock when the bells started sounding. I thought it was another move by the hijackers—until I glanced at my watch and saw that it was twelve. The bells, set on some timer no doubt, were sounding out the Angelus. Each long peal rang out loudly and forebodingly off the surrounding skyscrapers' stone and aluminum and glass.

I scanned the crowd as an idea occurred to me.

I spotted the caretaker, Nardy, talking to a young woman.

"Mr. Nardy, where are the bells located?" I said as I jogged up to him, interrupting his conversation.

"In the north spire," he said.

I looked at the ornate thirty-story cone of stone. About a hundred feet up, I noticed slats that seemed like faded copper shutters.

"Is there access to the bells from inside?" I asked Nardy.

The caretaker nodded. "There's an old winding set of wooden maintenance stairs from a time when the bells were rung by hand."

It seemed risky, but if we could get up there—maybe we could quietly pry loose some of the copper slats and get in.

"Can the inside of the north spire be seen from down in the church?" I asked.

"Why?" asked the woman Nardy had been talking to. "Do you plan to blow it up, too? Detective . . . ?"

I noticed the *New York Times* press pass on the lapel of her cloth coat for the first time. So much for my keen detectively powers of observation. "Bennett," I said.

"You're Manhattan North, right? How's Will Matthews doing?"

Like most cops, I couldn't quite buy the whole "the people have a right to know" argument the press likes to toss around. I might, if all that journalistic nobility didn't have a price tag attached to it. They *sold* newspapers last time I checked.

I gave the young newsie my best pissed-off cop face. "Why don't you ask him yourself?" I said.

"I would. But he has caller ID. So, what's the story? Does nobody know nuttin'?" Her cultured voice dropped into passable New Yorkese. "Or is nobody tawkin'?"

"Why don't you choose the answer you like the most," I advised.

"I wonder if my editor will like BIGGEST SECURITY BLUNDER IN WORLD HISTORY for the headline? Or maybe NYPD DROPS BALL THEN STONEWALLS?" the reporter said. "That's kinda catchy."

I winced. Will Matthews wouldn't like it if I were to single-handedly bring more bad press for the NYPD. "Listen, Ms. Calvin," I said. "Let's not get off on the wrong foot here. I'll talk to you, of course, but strictly off the record. Agreed?"

The reporter nodded quickly.

"You basically know as much as we do at this point. We're in contact with the kidnappers, but they have yet to give us their demands. As soon as we know, and I get permission, I'll give you all the information I can. But we are in crisis mode right now. If the psychos inside have a radio or a TV and get tipped off about what we're going to do, then people will die."

When I turned, I saw Ned Mason waving frantically at me from the door of the bus.

"We all have to come together on this," I yelled over my shoulder as I began to run.

MASON handed me the ringing cell phone just as I made it to the doorway.

"Mike here," I said.

"Mike. Hey, buddy," Jack said. "What's up with letting the phone keep ringing like that? If I didn't know what a sweet guy you were, I might get the impression you were plotting against me."

"Thanks for releasing the president," I said sincerely.

"Ah, don't mention it," Jack said. "Listen, the reason I'm calling is, I've got those demands together, and I was thinking of e-mailing them to you. I'm usually a snail-mail kind of guy, but you know how much of a zoo the post office is around the holidays."

The pseudocasual way Jack was speaking to me was starting to grate on my nerves. I checked my anger by visualizing cuffing him, dragging him past the people he was terrorizing. It was going to happen, I knew. Just a matter of time, I thought as I was handed an e-mail address by a tech cop.

"All right, Jack," I said. "Here's our address."

After I gave him the specifics on the NYPD website, Jack said, "We'll send the stuff over in a minute. I'll give you a little while to absorb things and then call you back. How does that sound?"

"Sounds good," I said.

"I'm really appreciating all the cooperation. We all do. Things keep running this smooth, it's going to turn out to be a real holly, jolly Christmas," Jack said, and hung up.

"THE demands are coming in," called one of the youngish cops in front of a laptop at the back of the bus.

I raced to the rear and looked at the screen. I was expecting a number, but what appeared looked like a long, fairly sophisticated spreadsheet. Down the left margin were the names of the thirty-three hostages. Next to each name was a ransom between two and four million dollars followed by the names of the hostages' lawyers, agents, business managers, and spouses, and their respective phone numbers. At the bottom of the sheet was a bank routing number and instructions on how to wire the money via the Internet into the account.

I absolutely couldn't believe this. The hijackers, instead of negotiating with us directly, were going straight to the source—namely the wealthy hostages themselves. They were acting the way a kidnapper in a concealed location would—not like a dozen guys surrounded by a battalion of heavily armed law enforcement.

"Let's get some people in here to start calling those numbers," Commander Will Matthews said. "And give that account number to the Bureau. See if maybe they can get a lead for us."

JOHN Rooney lifted his chin off his hands when something hard poked into his ribs. He glanced over and saw Little John holding out his billy club.

"Hey, prima donna," he said. "I'm getting bored. Time for you to get up and give us some entertainment. Whattaya say, guy?"

"I'm really not in the mood," Rooney said.

Rooney's teeth clicked together loudly when Little John gave him a love tap on the chin with the end of the club.

"Here's your motivation," Little John said. "Get up on that altar and make me laugh like a hyena. Or I'll shatter your Oscar-nominated skull open."

My God, Rooney thought as he arrived up on the altar and stared out at the other hostages. Just about every face was filled with wide-eyed terror. Talk about a hard crowd to work. What could be funny about any of this? But what choice did he have?

"Hey, everybody," Rooney tried. "Thanks for coming this morning. Heeere's Johnny!"

He heard somebody, a woman, give a real laugh. Who was that? It was Eugena Humphrey. Good for her!

Then Rooney felt something in him flick like a circuit breaker. "Eugena, hey, how YOU doin', honey chile," he said, mimicking the opening tagline from her morning show. She really started cracking up now, along with a few more people.

Rooney faked checking his watch. "Talk about a long Mass," he said. There were more laughs.

"You know what I really hate?" Rooney said. "Don't you just hate it when you go to a friend's funeral and you get *kidnapped?*" Rooney chuckled along with the cackles, maximizing the pause for effect. "I mean, there you are, all dressed up, a little sad about the person gone—but a little happy that it's not you—then *wham!* The monks at the altar whip out sawed-off shotguns and grenades."

Almost everybody was laughing now. Even the hijackers in the back were cracking up. At least his routine was relaxing everyone a little. He spotted Little John doubled over, holding his sides.

Keep laughing, Rooney thought. *I got a million of 'em. Wait'll you hear the one about the kidnapper getting the electric chair.*

FROM the back of the chapel, former rock and roller Charlie Conlan pretended to laugh at John Rooney's shtick as he studied the hijackers one by one.

There were six of the jackals along the rear rail of the chapel. The big one, Little John, was there, but the leader, Jack, along with five or six others, seemed to be somewhere else in the church.

Conlan did his best to recall his army training. He counted the grenades on the kidnappers' chests, eyed the guns they carried, the bulge in their robes where bulletproof vests seemed to end.

He slid a couple feet to the left in his pew. "Todd," he whispered.

"What's up?" the New York Giants football star murmured.

"Is Brown with us?" The real estate tycoon was a big man, in his fifties, who looked to be in pretty good shape.

"He's psyched," the athlete said. "He's going to try to get the mayor on board."

Conlan was glad the quarterback was with them. Out of all of them, the six-four, two-hundred-thirty-pound athlete had the best shot at physically overpowering one of the hijackers.

"That's progress," Conlan said to Snow out of the corner of his mouth. "The more of us, the better our chances."

"What's our move?" the quarterback asked.

"This is between me and you for now. You know how they frisked us? Took away our cell phones and wallets? They missed the twenty-two in my boot," Conlan whispered.

There, he'd said it, he thought. He didn't have a gun, but survival meant keeping up people's spirits, keeping them hopeful.

"We've got a shot," the quarterback said. "Say the word. We go."

THE NEAT MAN PROBED A gloved hand behind the pay phone in the kiosk on the northwest corner of Fifty-first and Madison. *Where was the device?*

His fingers finally found the plastic-coated wire behind the steel box. He clipped a phone company dial set across the pair of hidden colored wires. Three weeks before, his boys had actually snaked a pair of phone lines through a street duct in the rectory basement, into the corner phone company manhole, and, from the manhole, up the pay phone duct here to the street. Anticipating that all cell phone and landline transmissions in and out of the church would be monitored, they had created their own undocumented line.

The Neat Man checked his watch as he lifted the dial set to his ear. At exactly 6:00 p.m., there was a crackle as one of the hijackers inside St. Patrick's attached a simple nine-volt battery to the opposite end of the line, powering it.

"You there, Jack?" the Neat Man said.

"Where else would I be? How's it looking from your end?"

"When you sent out that first wave," the Neat Man said, "they didn't know what to do. Ditto with Hopkins. They're still shaking their heads in disbelief."

"That's what I like to hear," Jack said.

"How'd the interviews go with all our rich friends?"

"Real informative," Jack said. "Question now is will law enforcement stay stunned and stumped for the amount of time we need to get this done?"

"From what I've seen so far," the Neat Man said with a laugh, "they'll be scratching their heads 'til next Christmas."

THE next time I glanced up from the notes I was making on the negotiation with Jack, the command center's window to the outside had become dark. The time had flown. Paul Martelli was talking on the phone beside me. A dozen other cops were working laptops.

The demands had been sent to the FBI's White Collar Crime Squad, and they were crunching the numbers. The grand total of the ransom was nearly eighty million dollars.

It was a massive sum for one person to pay, but if you broke it down to the two and a half million or so for each hostage, it wasn't that outrageous. In fact, it was incredible how willing to pay these people seemed to be. Celebrity spouses and family members were giving me the numbers of their financial people almost before I had a chance to explain who I was.

It irked me, but I had to agree with what Jack had said. The fat cats were more than willing to buy their way out of trouble.

As I stepped outside the bus for some much-needed air, the first thing that hit me was the buzz-saw chattering of diesel generators. A half dozen portable crime scene light carts had been set up, and they illuminated the cathedral as if this were Times Square.

On the northwest corner of the Saks Fifth Avenue roof, I spotted a motionless FBI sniper. The whole thing was totally insane. There should have been families strolling hand in hand down this block around now. Rosy-cheeked visitors from across the country and the world, sipping hot cocoa and smiling.

What was even crazier was that these maniacs thought they were going to get away with it. *How?* Every inch of the cathedral was being scoped out by snipers. There was no basement, no way to get out from underground. It was looking more and more like the hijackers knew something about their exodus that we didn't.

I was rubbing my hands for warmth when my cell phone rang. I rolled my eyes when I saw that the number on my caller ID was my grandfather Seamus. As if I didn't have enough on my mind.

"Seamus, I'm busy. What is it?" I greeted my grandfather. Not the warmest of salutations, but I wasn't filled with Christmas cheer at that moment. Besides, conversation with my seventy-four-year-old grandfather is a form of combat. If you don't put yourself on the offensive immediately, he will eat you alive.

"A fine good evening to you as well, young Micheál," Seamus said. I knew I was in for it when my Hibernian forebear reverted to the Gaelic form of my name. My grandfather didn't just kiss the Blarney Stone, family legend had it. He bit off a chunk and swallowed it.

"And an especially fine way of conversing with the man currently taking care of your flock of goslings," he finished.

I rolled my eyes. My grandfather was the biggest, most blustery stage Irishman alive. He'd come to this country in the 1940s at the age of twelve, but if you didn't know him better, you'd think he'd just put up the donkey after cutting turf from the bog. He was constantly coming in to check on his great-grandkids, though. Underneath the mile-thick crust of blarney lay a heart of pure gold.

"Where's Mary Catherine?" I said.

"Is that her name, now? We weren't formally introduced. Why didn't you tell me you were adopting another child?"

"That's a good one," I said. "You must have been saving that up all afternoon. Mary Catherine happens to be the au pair."

"*Au pair.* Is that whatcher callin'm these days?" my grandfather said. "Be careful, young Micheál. Eileen, your grandmother, caught me talking to an au pair once on a street corner one Sunday in Dublin. She broke three of me ribs with a hurling stick."

"Dublin?" I said. "I thought Grandma Eileen was from Queens."

As he began to stammer out an explanation, I explained to him the letter from Maeve's mother and Mary Catherine's mysterious arrival the night before.

"I don't like it," he said. "This young girl could be after something. Keep track of the silverware."

"Gee, thanks for the heads-up, you suspicious old coot. And speaking of the goslings, I don't know when I'll get a chance to get out of here, but you tell them to get their homework out of the way and to start their jobs. They'll know what you're talking about."

"Does it have to do with that chart on the icebox in the kitchen?" my grandfather asked.

"Yes," I said. "It does indeed."

"Was that your's or Maeve's idea?" Seamus said suspiciously.

"Maeve's," I said. "She thought it would be good to give them something positive to do. Get their minds off everything else."

"It's not a good idea," he said brightly. "It's a great one. No wonder Maeve came up with it." He loved her as much as any of us.

"Any last insults before I hang up?" I said.

"A few," my grandfather said. "But I'll be seeing you later. I might as well save them up."

THE portable generators for the lights were still roaring in the cold when I walked back to the bus. I found Commander Will Matthews inside. All the hostage advocates had been contacted, he informed me. "Now for the excruciating part," Will Matthews said. "It's time to wait this thing out."

"Hey, Mike," Martelli said. "Nothing personal, but you seem beat. Why don't you get out of here for a little while? These jokers say they won't call back for hours, and when they do, we're going to need you calm and collected."

"He's right. Grab a bite. We need you on ice," said Commander Will Matthews. "That's an order, Mike."

The New York Hospital Cancer Center was only twenty blocks uptown, I realized. It wouldn't take very long to swing by there.

I left my cell number with Martelli before I stepped out from the checkpoints. Countless reporters, producers, and technicians were camped out around both sides of blocked-off Fifth Avenue. I had to wake up a burly cameraman who was sleeping in a folding chair in front of my blue Impala. I jumped inside the car and hit the road.

I made two stops. The first was at a place called Burger Joint in the Parker Méridien hotel on Fifty-seventh. Minutes later, I left with a greasy brown paper bag under my arm. The second stop was at Amy's Bread on Ninth Avenue, where I left with another bag.

I put on my light and siren as I made a left onto Park Avenue. Poinsettias and white lights fringed the center median as far as the eye could see to the north. Massive wreaths were hung above the revolving doors of the glass office towers, as well as from the brass doors of the luxury apartment houses I passed farther uptown.

The holiday beauty I saw everywhere made my chest ache with guilt. I'd been so shot to pieces lately, I hadn't even gotten a tree.

No wonder so many people killed themselves around the holidays, I thought. Christmas was geared to make you explode with contentment, to burn with the passing year's tremendous love and good fortune. To be depressed at this time of year, to be actually sick with sadness, felt like an unforgivable sin.

MY SWEET Maeve had her eyes closed as I stepped through her open hospital room door. But her nose was definitely still in working order because she smiled when I put the packages on her tray.

"No," she said in her cracked voice. "You didn't." Her eyes teared with pain as she sat up. So did mine.

"I smell cheeseburgers," she said. "If this is a dream and you wake me up, I won't be responsible, Mike."

"You're not dreaming, angel," I said as I climbed in carefully beside her. "Do you want the double onion or the double onion?"

Though Maeve ate only half of the burger and only about a quarter of the blondie, her cheeks flushed with healthy color as she pushed back the wax paper.

"Remember our midnight junk-a-thons?" she said.

I smiled. When we started going out, we both worked four-to-twelves. At first, we used to hit a bar, but that tired quickly, and soon we found ourselves visiting the local video store and an all-night supermarket, heading for the frozen-food aisle. The rule was anything you wanted, as long as you could cook it in a microwave and eat it in front of an old movie. They were great times. Sometimes we'd stay up after we ate, just talking, not wanting it to end, until birds started tweeting outside the bedroom window.

"Remember all the work I used to bring you?" I said.

Maeve had been in the trauma ward at Jacobi Medical Center in the Bronx around the corner from the Four-Nine, my rookie precinct. I would practically kidnap people off the streets and bring them into the emergency room just to get a chance to see her.

"Remember when that huge, homeless, toothless man you brought in hugged you?" Maeve said with a hard laugh. "What did he say? 'You ain't like those other jive turkeys, man. You care.'"

Her eyes closed, and then she stopped laughing. She must have taken something before I came, and now she was fading into sleep.

I squeezed Maeve's hand gently. Then I quietly rose from the bed, and I knelt beside her. For more than ten minutes, I watched my wife's chest rise and fall. For the first time, I didn't feel angry at the world or at God. I just loved her and always would. I wiped my tears on my sleeves before I leaned in beside her.

"Remember when you changed me forever," I whispered.

I CHECKED in with Paul Martelli on my cell as I pulled out from the hospital.

"Still nothing," he told me. "Take your time. The hijackers are sitting tight. We have you covered, Mike."

I followed Martelli's advice. I made a U-turn and then a left onto Sixty-sixth Street, heading west to check on my kids.

It had started snowing lightly when I was in the hospital, and the dusting on the brownstone walls and tunnels of the Central Park transverse looked like soft shakes of confectioners' sugar on gingerbread. This city, I thought, was determined to break my heart into a million pieces with its incessant Currier & Ives quaintness.

I could hear my kids through my closed apartment door when I stepped off the elevator into the vestibule. Never a good sign, I thought as I turned the knob.

In the foyer, Juliana was sitting on the floor with her back to me, giggling into the phone. I patted her on the head lovingly before I disconnected the cord from the hall jack. "Bed," I said.

My second stop was the girls' room, where a Mercedes Freer song was blasting. With her back to me, Jane was leading Chrissy and Shawna in an inspired dance routine. Though I could have scooped them up in a bear hug they were so cute, I remembered Maeve's dictum on the inappropriateness of Mercedes Freer.

Three crystal-shattering shrieks sounded when I flicked off the radio, followed by an explosion of giggles and blushing when the girls realized I had been watching them dance.

"Well, well. I didn't know Mercedes Freer was having a concert here at our house. I take it you forgot to get your chores done?"

Jane dropped her head. "Sorry, Dad," she said.

"Now that was the right answer, Jane," I said. "No wonder you get such good grades."

Next stop was the living room, where Ricky, Eddie, and Trent were in front of the blaring TV watching CNN's nonstop news coverage of the church takeover. Again, I distinctly remembered that the channels allowed were ESPN, Food Network, occasionally Cartoon Network, and public television.

The three of them almost hit the ceiling when I hopped over the sectional and landed in their midst. "Gathering research for a current events project, are we?" I said.

"We saw you!" Trent screamed after taking his hands away from his face. "On the TV! It's on every station."

"You're still busted," I yelled back at him.

Brian, my eldest son, was so into the game on his computer in his room, he didn't hear me enter. I flicked off the power on his PC.

"Hey!" he said angrily as he looked up. "Dad? Dad!"

"Brian?" I said back. "Brian!"

"I was . . . uh . . . I'll start my chores," he said, *"forthwith."*

I almost knocked down Mary Catherine when I stepped back into the hall.

"Mr. Bennett. Mike. I'm so sorry," she said frantically. "I was trying to get them into bed when Bridget told me she needed help."

"Let me guess," I said. "She told you she had an arts-and-crafts project due for school."

"How'd you know?"

"I forgot to tell you," I said. "Bridget is addicted to arts and crafts. We've been trying to wean her off glue, sparkles, and beads for years now. Arts and crafts are restricted to weekends."

"I didn't know," Mary Catherine said sadly. "I should have done a better job."

"Good Lord," I said. "You're still alive and still here? You should try out for the Navy SEALs."

After I relieved Mary Catherine of command and ordered her upstairs to bed, I found a priest in my kitchen.

The white-haired man in black was holding a steaming iron ready as seven-year-old Bridget put the finishing touches on a pink-and-white beaded pony that covered the entire top of our kitchen island.

"Well, if it isn't Father Shame-less—I mean Seamus," I said.

Nope, it wasn't Halloween. My grandfather Seamus was a priest. After his wife died, he decided to sell the gin mill he'd owned for thirty years and become a man of the cloth. Lucky for him, vocations to the priesthood were at an all-time low, so he was accepted.

He now lived in the Holy Name rectory around the block, and if he wasn't attending to parish business, he was sticking his nose into mine. Seamus wasn't content to merely spoil my children. He felt he was slacking off if he wasn't encouraging mischief.

Even Bridget's freckles seemed to drain of their color when she saw me standing there. *"Goodnightdadgoingtobediloveyou,"* she somehow managed to get out before sliding off the stool she was kneeling on and disappearing. Fiona shot out from the other side of the island and exited a step behind her twin.

"Having a senior moment, Monsignor? Forget how to read a clock? Or did you forget it's a school night?"

"Did you not take a look at this fine steed here?" Seamus said, passing the iron back and forth to melt the collection of beads together. It was nearly the size of a real horse. "That girl is pure artist. And like they say, it takes more than books to inspire creativity."

"Thanks for that nugget of wisdom, Seamus, but if these kids don't get their sleep and stick to their schedules, we're all doomed."

Seamus unplugged the iron and propped it on the butcher block. "If that's the case, why bring someone new into the house now?" he said. "I don't like the looks of Mary Catherine or the situation. Young, single woman in a house with a married man."

That was it. I snapped. I snatched up the plastic pony. Seamus ducked as I Frisbeed it across the kitchen.

"Where do you want me to file your concern, Gramps?" I yelled. "To my wife on her deathbed, or maybe to the thirty-three celebrities in St. Paddy's with guns to their heads?"

Seamus came around the kitchen island and put his hand on my shoulder. "I just thought I was the one who was going to help you," he said in one of the most tired voices I had ever heard him use.

I understood now. Why he was being such a pain about Mary Catherine. He thought he was being replaced. "Seamus," I said, "if I had a staff of twenty, I would still need your help. I need you to help us by helping Mary Catherine. You think you could do that?"

Seamus's mouth pursed as he thought about it. "I'll try," he said with a melodramatic, agonized exhalation.

I stepped across the kitchen and picked up the chore chart. When I lifted the plastic pony, I noticed that it was missing its tail.

"Plug that iron back in, Seamus, would you?" I said, bringing it quickly back over to the kitchen island. "If we don't get this thing fixed, Bridget will kill both of us."

CHAPTER 5

WHEN I arrived back at St. Patrick's, I checked in with my boss, Commander Will Matthews. Still no word from the gunmen inside.

So I poured myself what could have been my twentieth cup of coffee that day and sat.

I hated this part, the waiting, the feeling of powerlessness. It was one reason why I'd transferred out of the Hostage Negotiation Team. In Homicide, there was never a second when there weren't a hundred things to do, never a lack of angles to work a case.

I sat up suddenly in my swivel chair. There actually was one thing I could do to get me away from the oppressive face of the clock, and it could possibly help us.

I found Will Matthews in the rear of the bus. "Hey, boss," I said. "Remember my hunch about Caroline Hopkins's so-called accident? L'Arène, the restaurant where it happened, is three blocks away. I was thinking of swinging by to talk to the kitchen staff."

Will Matthews rubbed his eyes and nodded. "Okay," he said. "Take twenty minutes to see what you can dig up."

The recent tragedy there, and the siege up the street, must have spoiled the appetites of New York's rich and famous because L'Arène looked empty when I jogged in off Madison Avenue. The marble stairs I climbed in the vestibule were draped with a red, white, and blue carpet that seemed more French than American.

Maybe on some other night, the elegant setting might not have been so off-putting. And if I hadn't been grinding so hard in the last few hours, the arrogance that pulsed from the tall, tuxedoed maître d' wouldn't have filled me with such anger.

The dark, curly-haired Frenchman looked like he'd just eaten a bad snail when he spotted me in front of his library dictionary–size reservation book. "The kitchen is closed," he spat, and returned to writing notes in his book.

I closed the tome for him and put my badge on top of it. I savored the shock on his face. "No," I said. "Actually it's not."

When I told him I was there to investigate the First Lady's accident, the maître d' handed me a business card. "Gilbert, DeWitt, and Raby represent us in all legal matters."

I immediately dealt the card back past the sharp tip of the maître d's long nose. "I'm not from the insurance company; I'm from the Homicide squad. Now I can either talk to you and your kitchen staff here, informally, or we can go the formal route. If we go by the book, everyone will have to be brought down to the station house, and of course, you'll make sure each staff member has all his proper immigration papers available for identification purposes."

The maître d's expression underwent an almost instantaneous transformation. It was amazing how warm a smile he'd been able to hide behind his Gallic scowl. "I am Henri," he said with a bow. "How can I assist you, Detective?"

After I told him I needed to interview the kitchen staff, *mon ami* Henri promptly led me through a set of swinging blue doors and translated my question for the chef.

The chef seemed affronted by the questions. He'd personally fixed the First Lady's meal, and there was no way, he said angrily, that he had put any peanuts in her foie gras.

The only explanation he could fathom was that a foolish prep cook had spilled peanut oil on the dish during the controlled chaos of a busy night, but even that seemed absurd to him. The chef then said something in heated French before storming off.

So much for repairing French and American relations tonight, I thought. "Has there been any turnover in the staff since the night she was here?" I said.

Henri tapped a long finger against his lips. "Yes," the maître d' said. "Now that I think of it. One of the prep cooks, Julio, stopped showing up for work a day or so after the terrible accident."

"Any last name on Julio? An address? Off his employment application perhaps?"

A pained expression crossed Henri's features. "It was like you were saying before about formal and informal. Julio was an informal hire. We have no application per se. His leaving was not even a real concern. Our turnover rate for prep staff is quite high."

"I'll bet," I said.

"Wait," Henri said. "I believe he left some things in his locker. Would you like to take a look?"

I did, and in Julio's old locker, I discovered two items. A pair of dirty sneakers and a crumpled Metro North train schedule.

Yet another dead end. I stuffed the things into an empty bag I found under the locker. Maybe we could ID Julio from prints. If he wasn't already back in Central America.

IN HER dream, Laura Winston, the *Vogue* magazine–dubbed "Fashion Queen of the New Millennium," was out on the lake at Ralph Lauren's estate in Westchester. She was lying alone in a canoe dressed in a sheet of white muslin, and she was floating beneath an endless blue sky. When she tried to sit up, she realized that the muslin was wrapped tightly around her arms. She was dead and in her funeral boat, she realized—and she began to scream.

Laura Winston woke with a start and banged her head hard on the wooden arm of the church pew she'd propped it against.

There was a heavy clop-clop of booted feet, and two ski-masked men with grenades strapped across the front of their brown robes passed slowly up the center aisle of the chapel.

What an idiot, she thought. If she had begged off the funeral, she'd be thirty thousand feet above the South Caribbean in a Gulf Four, banking toward her French Renaissance palace in St. Bart's to put the finishing touches on her New Year's Eve celebration. Instead, she had ignored that little voice that had piped up the night before: *Hel-lo! High-profile NYC event, terrorist target. Stay away!*

And then, of course, there was that other little secret voice that was just starting to warm up its dry, agonizing pipes.

She was out of her pills.

The OxyContin had originally been prescribed for a lower-back tennis injury. A month later, after learning that her doctor was more than willing to keep prescribing, she continued to take them. The ultimate energy boost, the ultimate stress eraser.

Laura didn't want to admit it, but for about the last hour or so, she'd been jonesing. It had happened once before on a shoot that had gone a day over in Morocco. The withdrawal had started out like a tiny itch in her blood. Soon she had started throwing up and couldn't stop shaking. She'd managed to survive that episode with half a bottle of Valium mercifully given to her by the photographer.

But now, here, she had nothing. Maybe some of the others had something, she thought. These Hollywood types were known for their Dr. Feelgood prescriptions. She could politely inquire.

No! she thought, shuddering. No one could know about her "hillbilly heroin" addiction. She had to think. What did the hijackers want? Money? Her being alive was important to them, wasn't it?

What if she staged some kind of illness? A heart attack? No, all they'd have to do is take her pulse to see that she was faking. What other kinds of medical emergencies did people suddenly suffer from? Diabetic fits, panic attacks?

That was it! A panic attack! Wouldn't have to fake too hard there, either. She was already sweating; her heartbeat was elevated.

Withdrawal hidden in a panic attack. A brilliant plan. Worst case, she'd be separated from the rest of the celebs to vomit in peace.

EUGENA HUMPHREY WAS SO deeply zoned into her yoga breathing that at first she didn't even notice when Laura stood up. Eugena's breath escaped from her lungs in a gush when the fashion guru started moaning.

A second ago, the fashion diva had been sleeping blissfully. Now, with her pasty face and her hair in a rat's nest, she looked like she might have been sleepwalking. Except that her eyes were open.

"Sit down, Laura," Eugena said. "You saw what happened to Mercedes. These men aren't playin'." Eugena tugged the hem of the fashionista's butter-soft black suede Chanel skirt.

"Get your hands OFF ME!" Laura screamed.

"Laura, what's wrong?" Eugena said as calmly as she could. "Just talk to me. It's okay. I can help you."

"I can't TAKE IT!" Laura yelled, jogging out into the aisle. "HELP ME, PLEASE! Pleeeeeaaaaase! SOMEBODY!"

The short, stocky lead hijacker appeared by the rail as Laura dropped, wailing, to her knees. "We can't have her bugging out like this," he called to Little John. "Take care of her."

The extra-large hijacker lifted Laura up from the marble floor by her lapels. "Ma'am? You'll have to get back in your seat," he said.

"PLEASE HELP ME!" she yelled after a loud, rattling sob. "I can't breathe. I need to go to a hospital."

"To Bellevue maybe," the hijacker said with a chuckle. "Ma'am, you're hysterical. The only way I know how to deal with hysterical people is to slap them. You don't want to get slapped, do you?"

The hijacker grabbed the middle-aged woman by her wrist when she tried to bolt past him. He turned her bony arm around behind her, then took her by the back of her haute-couture top and led her out beyond the rail.

"If that's the way you want to play it," Little John said.

He opened a confessional door. He pushed the screaming Laura Winston inside. When she tried to rush out, he put a combat boot to her chest, sent her flying, and slammed the door shut.

"Jeez," Little John said, shaking his head at the other hostages. "Some people, huh?"

As LITTLE John strutted down the center aisle like a conquering hero, comedian John Rooney lost it. Watching the gunman abuse Laura Winston had set some deep chord within Rooney humming. He forgot about his safety, about the resistance plan. He just sprang up from his seat and jumped the hijacker.

Little John stumbled and dropped when Rooney slammed into the back of his knees. Rooney then managed to wrap an arm around his neck and squeeze with every ounce of his pent-up fear and rage.

Rooney was still on top of Little John when the other gunmen started kicking him. Instead of letting go, he closed his eyes and concentrated on the pressure of his arm on the hijacker's windpipe.

The kicking stopped suddenly. Then Rooney felt something cold and hard press against his temple. He opened his eyes and saw Jack, the lead hijacker, smiling at him from the opposite end of an M16.

"I'm only going to ask you once," Jack said. "Let him go."

"Shoot me!" Rooney found himself saying. Adrenaline burned like acid in his blood. "I'm not going to sit and watch you animals beat up on old people and women!"

Jack squinted at him between the holes in his mask. Finally, he lowered the M16. "Okay, Mr. Rooney. Point taken. I'll take measures to tone down the aggressive crowd control. Now, please release my colleague. If he dies, it'll start quite a bad precedent."

Rooney released the big man and stood up, breathing loudly. His cheek was bleeding from where a boot lace had scratched it, and his right arm felt like it had been in an industrial accident, but his blood sang. He'd actually done something about this outrage.

Jack checked Little John in the chest with the rifle when he leaped up off the floor. "Go get some rest," he told him. "Mr. Rooney, please retake your seat. I'd like to address everyone."

Rooney sat as Jack went to the podium and cleared his throat. Then he smiled, and with his cheerful demeanor, he could have been an airline spokesman updating passengers about a delay.

"Hi, everybody," he said. "We've started the negotiation process, and things seem to be working quite smoothly. If things continue to go this well, there's a shot of getting you back home to your families by Christmas morning."

Rooney thought he detected a collective sigh.

"Now, unfortunately, the bad news," Jack went on. "If things deteriorate, we'll likely be forced to kill a number of you."

A low moan rose from the back of the chapel.

One of the female hostages began sobbing.

"People," Jack chided amiably. "People, please. You act like we're going to torture you. You have my word. All executions will consist of a quick, humane shot to the back of the head."

Jack stepped down from the pulpit and stopped beside Rooney. "Oh, and one more thing," he said, stabbing Rooney in the throat with a stun gun. Rooney's eyes shut of their own accord as every muscle in his body clenched at once. A scream was lost in his throat as he bounced numbly off the floor and rolled under the seat.

"I thought you had to have brains to be successful in this country," Rooney, semiconscious, heard Jack say. "Which part of 'step out of line and we'll kill you' are you morons not getting?"

IT WAS ten to seven in the morning when eleven-year-old Brian Bennett tapped on his sister's door.

"Julia?" he whispered. "You up?"

Julia came out, combing her wet hair. Already showered, Brian thought with disappointment. He'd wanted to be the first one up. He was the oldest boy, after all. When had Julia woken up? Six?

"I was about to get you," Julia said. "Dad still sleeping?"

"Like a dead . . . I mean, like a rock," Brian said quickly. "Who knows when he came in last night. You want me to start getting the cereal out and you wake the monsters?"

"Okay, but if you get finished before I get the girls up, go in and get Trent and Eddie and Ricky," Julia said. "It's going to take me a while to get the girls dressed."

"Okay," Brian said. He began to turn in the dim hall but then stopped. "Hey, Julia, I feel bad about when Dad came in last night and busted us. I really think this will make it up to him. Great idea to get up early and get everyone ready."

"Why, thanks, Bri," Julia said. "That's really nice of you to say."

Man! Brian thought, wincing. She was right. What was he doing being all fuzzy and nice to his sister? "Last one to get their team ready is a retarded loser," Brian called over his shoulder as he left.

He threw open the door to the boys' room after he had quickly set the kitchen table. He was shaking Ricky's foot at the bottom bunk when Trent swung out from the top and hung upside down.

"Did Santa come?" Trent asked urgently.

"No, it's not Christmas yet, you little maniac," Brian said. "Wake up Ricky and go brush your teeth. Now."

Brian smiled when they exited the bedroom five minutes later. The girls were also just coming out of their room. He'd thought Ms. Perfect in Every Way Julia would have the little ladies doing calisthenics or something by this time. But no. It was a tie.

Brian laughed when he flicked on the kitchen light. Even though it was corny, he had to admit, seeing everyone with their costumes on was also hilarious.

It was dress rehearsal today at Holy Name for the Christmas pageant. Chrissy, Shawna, Bridget, and Fiona were garland-haloed angels. Trent and Eddie were shepherds. Ricky had scored the part of Joseph and was sporting a fake beard. Even Jane and Julia, who were in the choir, were wearing long silver robes. Of course, he himself had the coolest costume, being one of the three wise men.

"Look at them," Brian said to Julia. "They're almost, like, cute."

Julia took a camera out of her robe and snapped a picture. What was up with girls? Brian thought. How did they always know the right things to do?

WHEN the muted giggles and bangs and cries of my family getting ready woke me that morning, I sensed the absence on my wife's side of the bed and was grateful. The workday-morning deal between Maeve and me was that she would get them dressed and I would take them to school.

I was reaching for the warmth of her pillow when I felt the cold sheets beside me, and I remembered. As I lay there, taking my first morning sip of personal horror, a chilling question occurred to me. *If Maeve wasn't getting the kids ready, who was?*

I swung my bare feet onto the cold hardwood and grabbed my tattered and holey robe off the bedpost. When I stepped into the kitchen and saw my children fully dressed for their Christmas pageant, I was convinced I was dreaming.

How could they have gotten themselves ready? I thought. What a bad father I was. I hadn't even remembered about the play.

My kids really were angels. Their being able to take care of themselves felt like Maeve had done her job. Like she had tied up all the loose ends and was now ready to go.

I nodded at Julia and Brian. Had anyone, let alone a couple of kids, risen to a horrible occasion with such selflessness?

"I know it's not Sunday," I yelled with enthusiasm, "but who needs a Sunday breakfast as much as me?"

The cries of "We do" and "Me" rang off the walls as I slapped two cast-iron frying pans up on the stove.

Mary Catherine arrived in the kitchen, a quizzical look on her face, as I was dispensing my bacon, egg, potato, and green onion hash to my guys. I handed her a plate.

"I warned you we were nuts," I said, smiling.

THE Bennetts stopped traffic again when we did our morning dash for the front doors of Holy Name. A brunette model crawling out of a taxi in a sequined black dress, no doubt worn the night before, stopped at the curb, put her hand to her décolletage, and actually said, *"Ohhhh!"* at the cuteness of my family pageant.

And far better than that reaction was the one I got from none other than Sister Sheilah. "God bless you, Mr. Bennett," she called with a smile, an actual smile, as she unhooked the door.

I was feeling pretty warm despite the cold when I got back into my van. I decided to sit for a minute. I lifted the *Times* I'd picked up from my doorstep to look at it for the first time.

The spark of holiday joy fizzled instantly in my chest when I looked at a picture of myself under the FIRST LADY CAROLINE HOPKINS'S FUNERAL HIJACKED headline. "We Don't Know Anything" was the cheerful caption under my picture. I looked at the byline of the hatchet job. Cathy Calvin.

I shook my head. She'd hamstrung me but good. Even the picture was bad. There was a pensive, searching expression to my face that could easily be misinterpreted as utter confusion.

Thanks for my fifteen minutes of fame, Calvin, I thought. *You really shouldn't have.* And on that note, I violently hurled the paper over the seat and downshifted into drive.

FUNNYMAN John Rooney didn't know what time it was when he decided to stop trying to fake sleep, but by the wan light glowing behind the stained glass above, he guessed it was near nine. He sat up against the altar rail, rubbing his fists into his eyes.

With the thin pews proving impossible to get comfortable in, the hijackers had allowed them to take the seat and kneeler cushions and sleep on the floor in front of the chapel's altar. The cushions were small, though, and the body-heat-sucking marble floor made a city sidewalk seem like a Tempur-Pedic mattress in comparison.

At the back of the chapel, three masked hijackers sat in folding chairs, drinking coffee from paper cups. Rooney couldn't see Little John or Jack anywhere. With the masks and robes, it was hard to tell how many hijackers there actually were. Eight, maybe a dozen. They seemed to work in shifts, everything very organized.

A hand fell on his shoulder as Charlie Conlan sat up next to him. "Mornin', kid," Conlan said quietly without looking at him. "That was brave of you to fight back like that last night."

"You mean stupid." Rooney fingered the scab on his face.

"No," Conlan said. "Thing now is to do it again, only at the right time."

"You still want to fight them?" Rooney said.

Conlan nodded calmly.

"Yo," whispered a voice behind them. Mercedes Freer, who'd been released from the confessional the night before, sat up from where she'd been sleeping. "You bad boys gonna try something?"

Rooney debated letting her in on it, then finally nodded. "Just being prepared."

"Amen to that," the singer said. "Check it. One of those g's is into me. He was talking to me through the confessional door last night. Skinny one with the shotgun. Yo, we could use that. I could play like I want him or something."

Just then, Little John arrived with a cooler and a cardboard tray of coffees. "Rise and shine, campers," he yelled. "It's chow time."

A sudden booming, sustained sound started from Reverend Solstice three rows behind Rooney. At first, he thought the black minister was having a heart attack. But the sound turned into a note and soared, and Rooney realized that the man was singing.

"Ahhhhhhhhhhmayzing grace, how sweeeeet the sound."

Rooney rolled his eyes. How absurd was this?

But after a while, other people began to join in, and when Rooney saw Little John shake his head in disapproval, he began singing along, too.

The explosive, crisp snap of a gunshot replaced the hostage's last note. Everyone turned back in the pews toward the larger church—where the shot had come from.

After the chilling reverberation of the shot, Rooney felt his resolve go out like a hard-blown candle.

God help us, he thought. *The killing has started.*

HOW could this have happened? With his back flat against one of the cathedral's marble columns, Jack gripped his nine millimeter and listened closely.

He'd been walking the perimeter when a figure in black had bolted out from the gift shop entrance. Thinking that the FBI's Hostage Rescue Team had somehow breached the church's interior, he'd drawn his pistol and fired.

They'd gotten in, Jack thought. There had to be some angle he and the Neat Man had missed.

"What happened?" Little John said, arriving down the center aisle with two men at a run.

"Man in black just popped out of the gift shop. Think I hit him."

"Feds?" Little John whispered. "How?"

"I don't know," Jack said, peeking around the column. "There's a body down by the baptismal font. I'll take that one. You guys check the gift shop. Shoot first."

The men split up and rushed toward the front of the church. Jack swung out into the aisle, his pistol trained on the figure on the floor. It didn't move. He tapped the warm barrel of his gun hard against his forehead when he saw who he'd shot. *What have I done?*

Jack looked down at an elderly priest. Candlelight flickered in the dark pool of blood beneath his head.

Little John almost ran into him. "No one in the gift shop," he said. He looked down at the slain cleric and cursed. "What are we going to do now?" he asked.

At least the boys had his back, Jack thought, looking at the innocent he'd just murdered. He had told them killing might be a possibility, and still they'd agreed. At least he'd have company in hell.

"We use it," he said.

"Use it?" Little John said. "How?"

"Grab the good father's arms and legs," Jack said. "I'm tired of waiting anyway. Time to speed up the clock with a little pressure."

IT WAS just past nine when I arrived at the barricade of the command center. I cut the Chevy's engine and opened the door.

I shook my head at the ongoing life-and-death siege as I threaded my way through the growing media encampment, then was waved through each of three checkpoints.

Reflected in the graphlike black glass of the modern office building neighboring it to the north, the spire of the cathedral looked like a stock that had spiked and was now plummeting. A couple of reporters were doing stand-ups for feeds into their stations. When there was news, the print reporters typed into their laptops, the TV folks did stand-ups, and the radio people filed over their phones.

I had just turned away from the media folks when I caught the movement of the cathedral doors across Fifth. The doors were opening again!

At first it seemed as if the figure that flew from the arched shadow was another person who had been released. But when I saw the black-suited body go facedown on the stone stairs without any attempt at breaking its fall, I knew something was very wrong.

I ran across the avenue, went up the steps, and knelt beside the fallen figure. I couldn't get a pulse out of him. A needle of ice spiked my heart when I turned the body over to perform CPR.

My eyes went from the priest's white collar to the hole in his temple to his open, lifeless eyes. I closed my own eyes for a second. Then I turned and glared at the already closed bronze doors.

They'd murdered a priest!

ESU lieutenant Reno was at my side. "Mother of God," he said quietly, his face faltering. "Now they're murderers."

"Let's get him out of here, Steve," I said.

Reno got the man's legs, and I got his hands. He hardly weighed anything. His scapular, hanging down from his lolling head, scraped the asphalt as we ran with the corpse to the police lines.

CHAPTER 6

I HEARD a phone ring from the open door of the command bus as I laid the murdered priest down on an EMS stretcher. I didn't need caller ID to figure out who it was. Instead of sprinting to grab the phone, though, I let it ring on as I closed the priest's eyelids.

"Bennett!" I heard Commander Will Matthews bellow.

I zombie-stumbled past him without acknowledgment and made my way into the bus. For the first time, I didn't have any butterflies as I accepted the phone, any fear that I would screw something up. Quite the opposite. I was dying to talk to the son of a bitch.

FBI negotiator Martelli must have sensed my fury. He grabbed my wrist. "Mike, no matter what happened, stay calm," he said. "Unemotional. You go ballistic, we lose the rapport you've established. Thirty-three people are still in jeopardy."

Unemotional! I thought. The worst part about it was that Martelli was right. My job was to be Mister Super Calm. It was like getting your nose broken and having to apologize for getting blood on your attacker's fist. I was starting to hate my current role.

I nodded to the com sergeant at the desk. "Bennett," I said.

"Mike," Jack said merrily in my ear. "There you are. Listen, before you guys get all upset, I can explain. Father Stowaway must have been hitting the house wine pretty hard yesterday morning because we told everybody to leave. He jumped out at the wrong time and tried to run for it. With that black suit of his, we thought he was one of you SWAT guys trying to crash the party."

"So you're saying it was just an accident? Not really your fault?"

"Exactly. One of those wrong place–wrong time deals."

"You son of a bitch," I said. "You killed a priest."

"Do my ears deceive me?" Jack yelled happily. "Or did I actually just hear a little real emotion? I was starting to think I was speaking with a computer there, Mikey. All that calming negotiating strategy crap you've been spouting almost made me want to eat my gun. Finally! Let's put it all out on the table, laddie." He laughed. "Either kill us, or get us our money. Just stop wasting my time!"

A CONNECTION-CUTTING dial tone howled in my ear—just as Mike Nardy, the cathedral's caretaker, entered the trailer.

"I'm afraid I have a confession to make," he blurted, looking out over the assembly of cops and agents. "There is another way into the cathedral."

The FBI commander, Oakley, stepped forward. "Tell us about it, Mr. Nardy," he said.

"The reason I didn't say anything before was—it's kind of a secret. The only reason I'm even here is that Father Miller, the priest who was just shot, was a friend of mine, and— Well, I have your word that it won't get out? The passageway?"

"Of course," Oakley said. "Where's the way in, Mr. Nardy?"

"From the Rockefeller Center concourse," the caretaker said. "There's a passage that cuts under Fifth into a, um, bomb shelter. Back in the sixties, after the Bay of Pigs incident, Cardinal Spellman was convinced New York was going to get nuked. So he allocated some funds for an undisclosed construction project. A bomb shelter was built off the archbishops' crypt. With the Rockefellers' permission, an alternate escape passage was dug to the lower concourse of Rockefeller Center, where they now have shops."

"Why didn't you tell us this before?" I butted in angrily. "You knew we were looking for a way to get in."

"I thought things could be resolved peacefully," Nardy said. "Now I know otherwise. Poor Father Miller. He was a good soul."

I was about to tear into the old man for obstructing justice when Oakley cut me off. "Do you think you could show us the way in, Mr. Nardy?" he said calmly.

"Absolutely," the caretaker said.

Oakley called into his radio and ordered half of his commando team to the command center. Finally, some action. I was sick of talking, just like Jack.

"Going somewhere?" Oakley said, eyeing me with surprise.

"With you," I said with a tight smile. "You never know when you might need to negotiate."

AFTER twenty minutes of weapon loading and intense strategy briefing, I joined a dozen joint task force FBI and NYPD commandos. We followed Nardy into 630 Fifth Avenue.

I was all but swimming under a borrowed night-goggle headset, heavy vest, and tactical shotgun. We moved quickly through the Art Deco lobby and down the stairs. Will Matthews had cleared the street concourse below at the beginning of the siege, and it was a little creepy as we trooped through the deserted mall-like corridor.

There were Christmas decorations and lights blinking through the plate glass of upscale clothing stores, toy shops, and a food court, but the aisles and the tables were empty.

Nardy stopped at an unmarked steel door beside a gourmet food store. He removed a ring of keys from his pocket, selected a large, strange-looking key from his ring, and handed it to Oakley.

"That's it," he said, crossing himself. "God bless you."

"Okay, everyone," Oakley whispered. "Radios off and my team in front. Have your night goggles ready for going in lights-out. Single file, space yourselves out."

There were metal flicks of weapon safeties being released, and then Oakley turned the lock. The door made a loud creaking groan as it swung in. We stared over the barrels of our weapons into an unlit concrete-lined corridor. Oakley flipped down his night goggles and stepped into darkness behind his MP5.

When I put on my goggles, the lightless tunnel went to an eerie lime green. Twenty feet in, we had to duck under a bank of rusting iron cable ducts. Another thirty feet after that, we passed along a teakettle-hot steam pipe that was as big as the side of a gasoline truck. The grade of the tunnel pitched downward, and we arrived at a set of spiraling iron stairs also heading down.

At the bottom of the two-story staircase was a metal door with what looked like a steering wheel in its center. If I didn't know better, I would have said we had arrived at the engine room of a ship.

The door moved inward when Oakley put his hand to it. Suddenly, we were in a small concrete room with concrete pews and a cement altar. The only thing not made of concrete was a dull gray metal crucifix. To the right of the crucifix was an iron ladder heading up into a kind of chimney in the ceiling.

Oakley motioned for silence as we moved toward the ladder. The vertical passage was about two stories high. I don't know if they trained in ladder racing at the FBI, but if there was an Olympic event, the Hostage Rescue guys would have gotten the gold.

From the bottom of the ladder, I could make out another steering wheel at the roof of the chimney above the commandos' heads.

Then I saw it spin with a screech.

A few seconds later, I couldn't see anything because a circle of light burned down from above, and I was blinded—blind and then deaf as the world around me shattered with the crackle of gunfire.

Jack was on to us.

I REARED back from the chimney. I tore off my night-vision goggles. Bullets pocked holes in the concrete floor as gunfire rained down into the cramped slot.

It was a miracle I wasn't hit as I pulled the jumping and falling members of the retreating tactical team away from the ladder. The blue-white flashes from the continuing gunfire pulsed like strobe lights as team members performed CPR on their fallen brothers.

I flicked my MP5 to auto and jogged back to the chimney. Then I shoved the machine gun up into the hole beside the ladder, one-handed, and pulled the trigger. The MP5 jumped like a jackhammer in my hand. I didn't know if I'd hit anything, but it seemed to momentarily stop the attack.

A second later, there was a loud, whistling clang, and a smoking canister landed at the base of the ladder. I pulled my Windbreaker up around my face as smoke burned my eyes and lungs.

"Tear gas!" I shouted. "Fall back!"

I almost tripped on a fallen cop behind me. "Hit," he said in a whisper. I lifted him up into a fireman's carry and headed back for the door we'd come in through. I banged my shin on a stair of the spiral staircase and felt blood seep down into my boot.

Back out in the corridor of the mall, I laid the man I had carried out onto the polished marble floor of the concourse. Then I gasped as I stared into his lifeless blue eyes. He was a burly, black-haired NYPD ESU cop, no more than twenty-five. Now he was dead, gone while I'd tried to carry him to safety.

Oakley was putting a helmet over the face of a fallen FBI commando to my left.

What had happened? Two good men, good cops. Down.

Stunned, I bit my lip as I looked back at the black hellhole we'd just climbed out of. *How do they know so much about St. Patrick's? I thought. How do they know so much about us?*

THE Neat Man folded his cell phone closed as an ambulance hopped the curb of 630 Fifth right in front of him. He had to take a step back and prop his back against the cold, filthy side of the crisis bus in order to let out the female EMT from the front cab.

He watched her rush across the plaza, pushing a wheeled stretcher. The tactical team emerged from the revolving door just as she got to the entrance.

The Neat Man counted heads. Thirteen had gone in. Now nine were standing. His boys inside had taken care of business! Thank God he'd been able to tip Jack off.

He winced when he saw that hotshot detective Mike Bennett was still among the living. The EMT was pulling up his pant leg and wiping at a cut on his shin. *What happened, Mikey? Got a boo-boo?*

He watched as Bennett shrugged her off and hobbled, shell-shocked, toward the trailer. Cops and FBI agents patted him on the shoulder as he passed.

"Not your fault," the Neat Man called from the crowd at Bennett's back. "It's those bastards inside. This is all on them."

THIS was a tragedy, thought Jack as he looked down on a fallen pal. The bleeding hijacker resting against the false stone casket moaned as Jack slammed the concrete lid to the bomb shelter shut.

Learning of the existence of the secret escape tunnel from the cathedral's crypt was one of the factors that had swayed him and the Neat Man to go through with the hijacking. It was how most of them had snuck in and the way they were thinking of getting out.

Jack closed his eyes as panic bulged in his chest. Thank heavens he had come up with a plan B. He opened his eyes as his dying comrade, Fontaine, moaned again.

"Calm down now," Jack said as he unseamed the man's brown robe with a Ka-Bar knife, then freed the Velcro straps of his bullet-proof vest with a loud rip. "You're going to make it," he lied.

A return-fire round shot up from the bomb shelter had ricocheted off the lead-lined lid of the hatch. Fontaine had caught the bullet in the back just above his vest collar, to the left of his spine. He was rapidly bleeding to death from where the round had left his body. When Jack peeled the vest off Fontaine's chest, he spotted the blood-gushing exit wound above his friend's right nipple.

"Don't lie to me," Fontaine said. "I'm all sliced up inside. I can feel it. Just do me a favor, will you, when you get out."

"Anything," Jack said.

"Give my share to my girl, Emily. Hell, not even a full share. Just something." The hijacker sobbed suddenly.

Jack sat in the man's blood as he got behind him, cradling him. "You have my word, dog," Jack said in his ear. "She gets a full share. She'll go to college. Just like you always wanted. Ivy, right?"

"For sure," Fontaine said with a soft nod. "She got fifteen hundred on her boards. I ever tell you that?"

"Only about a thousand times," Jack said, chuckling.

Fontaine seemed peaceful now, as if he were drifting off to sleep. Jack saw a final tension jolt through the dying man, followed by a palpable slackening. Fontaine was gone.

Jack was dry-eyed as he stood and handed his Ka-Bar to one of the hijackers who had watched it all. "Cut his hands and his head, and bag 'em," he said. "We take them with us. We can't take the chance they'll identify him."

"BUT *I* want to be the car!" five-year-old Trent Bennett whined across the Monopoly board. Nine-year-old Ricky, sensing trouble, snatched the piece off the GO square. Trent started to cry.

Brian Bennett rolled his eyes. Here he was, doing his job, keeping the squirts busy. He'd busted out an actual board game, and would they cooperate? No way, Jose.

Mary Catherine, their new nanny, had told him she needed to run out and get something from the store. Grandfather was at church. So that left Brian pretty much in charge.

He got up from the dining room table when he heard the front door open. He could see a massive Christmas tree being pushed in through the door. Mary Catherine took off her hat and wiped her hand across her red, sweating, though kind of pretty face.

Brian gaped at her. She'd gone out and gotten them a tree for Christmas. That was, like, *nice*.

"Brian, there you are," she said in her funny Irish accent. "Do you know where your mom and dad keep the decorations?"

Twenty minutes later, all the kids were in the living room, assembly-lining ornaments up to Mary Catherine on the shaky painting ladder. It wasn't the same as their mom, Brian thought. Mom did a tree nicer than the ones in the window at Macy's. But he had to admit, Mary Catherine's was a lot better than nothing at all.

IT WASN'T just the biting cold of the day that made me feel numb as I stopped before the checkpoint media podium. Usually, making a routine statement before the local news outlets filled me with butterflies. But when Will Matthews said that the commissioner had ordered an immediate press conference, I actually volunteered.

I knew those murdering bastards inside were watching—and I wanted them to see me, to hear what I had to say.

I looked out over the clutter of national network and worldwide press cameras and gazed into the lens of the camera in front of me.

"Within the past hour," I said, "a rescue attempt was made to free the hostages. Gunfire was exchanged, and an FBI agent and an NYPD ESU officer were slain. Two other officers were wounded. Names will not be released until the families are notified."

"Why was such a rash move authorized?" a male network reporter called out from the front ranks.

"The decisions of the on-scene command cannot be commented on in light of the ongoing situation," I told him.

"In what part of the cathedral did the rescue attempt take place?" asked a middle-aged female reporter behind him. She had a microphone in one hand and an open cell phone in the other.

"Again, tactics can't be divulged at this juncture," I said. It was scary, even to me, how calm I sounded. "I know everyone wants to know what's going on," I continued, "but now's not the time for full disclosure. We want to extract the thirty-three hostages safely."

"And the hostage-takers as well?" someone called from the back.

I looked steadily into the camera again. "Of course," I said. "We want this to be resolved peacefully."

I ignored the barrage of shouted questions, and as I stepped from behind the podium, I almost knocked down a tall brunette reporter.

"C'mon, Mike," Cathy Calvin said. "Who are these guys? You have to tell us what they want. What's their angle?"

"Why are you asking me?" I said. "Don't you read your own paper, Ms. Calvin? I don't know nuttin', remember?"

I HAD already arrived back in the command center bus and was sitting calmly with the phone in my hand when it rang. I was still boiling, but I knew how useless that emotion was now. What I had to do was to repair things, keep Jack talking instead of shooting.

"Mike here," I said.

"You lying son of a bitch!" Jack screamed.

"Now, now, Jack," I said. "There was a communication flub. I wasn't told about the raid until after it happened." I was acting like I was just a cog in a large wheel that I couldn't control. "And please, Jack, what did you expect? Blowing away a priest wasn't going to have consequences?"

"That was an accident! I told you!" Jack said. "One of you killed my friend. He died in my arms."

"And one of you guys killed two cops," I said. "This is a dead-end game we're playing, Jack. I thought you wanted money. Killing people isn't going to get it for you. Let's put what's happened behind us and get this thing back on track."

"Only part of the track I'm putting this on is the third rail," Jack spat in my ear. "You screwed up, Mike, and now I'm going to punish you for it. Come to the front door and pick up the trash."

I HAD cleared the entrance of the bus and was running flat out across the street when the immense cathedral door began inching open again. I knew another victim was about to be ejected. Part of me wanted to believe I could save a life if I acted fast enough, but I knew better.

I was crossing the wide sidewalk when a human form suddenly flew out the black space of the open door. I couldn't tell whether it was a man or a woman.

The body skidded across the flagstone paving and landed face-down. Male, I registered. Dark suit. I fell to my knees in front of the victim. I didn't even bother looking for a pulse when I saw the torso. The lower back was horribly torn and bloody.

The victim was a middle-aged man. His shirt had been removed, and dozens of stab wounds covered his back. What looked like cigarette burns went up and down his forearms.

The first thing I saw when ESU lieutenant Steve Reno helped me flip the victim was that the poor man's throat had been slit. My heart seized in my chest as I looked at the victim's beaten face.

"This is so wrong," Reno said. His voice was small and wounded, as if he was speaking to himself. "As wrong as it gets."

I nodded as I stared down, unable to take my eyes away.

Andrew Thurman, the mayor of New York City, peered up lifelessly into the leaden sky.

Steve Reno pulled off his Windbreaker and wrapped it around Mayor Thurman like a blanket. "Grab his legs, Mike," Reno said. "Let's get him out of here. Don't let the press get any shots."

As we laid the slain mayor on an EMS stretcher, there was an instant hush in the crowd of law enforcement. They either gaped, goggle-eyed, or stiffened in ramrod postures of respect.

Why the mayor? I thought. Was Jack so overwrought by the death of one of his hijackers that he'd chosen the mayor as the victim who would make us the angriest? Or was it another ploy to push our buttons, to get us to react in a certain way? Was this murder a clue for us? Our first?

BOROUGH Commander Will Matthews had moved the command center to an office in 630 Fifth, the Rockefeller Center building directly across from the cathedral. When I reported there, I spotted my fellow NYPD negotiator, Ned Mason, placing a sheet of computer paper up on a corkboard filled with them. The FBI negotiator, Paul Martelli, was on the phone at a desk beside him.

"So it's true? Thurman is dead?" Mason asked.

I nodded solemnly. "He was dead when they threw him out on the street."

"How could this be happening here?" Martelli said. He looked shocked, too. "Russia. Baghdad, maybe. But midtown Manhattan? Hasn't this city been through enough?"

"Apparently not," I said. "How's the money-gathering going?"

"We're getting there." Mason gestured toward the papers on the board. Each one indicated a hostage, his or her representative, and the amount of the ransom. "I just got off the horn with Eugena Humphrey's people. In addition to Eugena's ransom, they're going to put up the money for the two reverends inside as well."

"That's generous," I said. "How much have we collected so far?"

"Sixty-six million in escrow," Mason said after punching buttons on a desk calculator. "Another ten makes seventy-six, and we'll be ready to wire it."

"Did you subtract the mayor's ransom?" I said.

Mason's eyes widened. "You're right. Okay. Take away his three million, the total goes from seventy-six to seventy-three. Only seven million dollars to go."

CHAPTER 7

JACK sat on the steps of the high altar with his cell phone antenna clenched between his teeth. He'd known the operation would be stressful. He'd even predicted the attempted breach. But dealing with it was a whole nother ball of wax. *Maybe I pushed it too far,* he thought. He'd wanted to make a statement with the mayor, but he wondered if he hadn't gone a little over the top on that one, too.

The whimper Andrew Thurman had made when Jack slid the Ka-Bar into his back still echoed in his ears. The saints on the windows seemed to stare down at him with a malevolent disapproval.

No, no, no, Jack thought with a violent sneer. No way could he even think about going soft now. Killing the mayor had been nothing. Part of a formula that would end with his getting very rich. Besides, the mayor deserved it, he reminded himself. There was a time when Jack had badly needed the mayor's help and had been left twisting in the wind. *Hizzoner had it coming,* Jack thought.

"Jack?" came a voice from his radio. "Come back to the chapel right now! One of the fish has fallen and claims he can't get up."

Jack keyed the Motorola. "On my way," he said.

Not again, Jack thought when he arrived at the rear chapel rail. Another big shot was slabbed out on the marble floor. Real estate tycoon Xavier Brown's eyes were rolled way back in his head. The talk-show woman, Eugena, was sitting almost on top of him, compressing his chest with her hands, saying, "Hold on, Xavier."

"What did you do to him?" Jack said to Little John.

"Nothing," Little John answered. "That's just it. Fatty got up, complained his arm was hurting, and then *boom,* down he goes."

Jack knelt next to the talk-show lady. "How's he looking?"

"Very bad," Eugena said, continuing CPR. "His pulse is very weak. If he doesn't get to a hospital, he'll die."

"Damn," Jack said. Another snag.

He snatched up his phone and hit redial.

"Mike here," came the detective's voice. Jack had to admit the cop was good. He sounded like a concierge at a four-star hotel. *You know it, pal. The hijacker is always right.*

"You got a problem," Jack said. "Xavier Brown's stock has just taken a sudden nosedive. I think his ticker's having trouble keeping up with all the fun and excitement. I'll let him out of here before his aorta explodes, but you have to pay his ransom first."

"We don't have it all together yet, Jack," the detective said. "You have to give us more time."

More time, is it? Jack thought. *Wonder why. To figure out another way in and take us out, perhaps?*

"Go ahead and send his money first, then," Jack said. "Or then again, don't. But tell his people they better decide quick. X. Brown is looking like the next time he makes it into the *Wall Street Journal,* it's going to be on the Obit page. I'll be watching the account. I see my money, I open the front door."

"I'll let them know," the negotiator said.

It took five of Jack's men to drag the heavy financier up the aisle toward the main entrance of the cathedral. Eugena Humphrey tagged along the whole way, even dropping down to give the tycoon CPR in the vestibule.

One of Jack's men called to him from a little security room off the main altar. A laptop sat on a beat-up desk before the man.

"They did it!" the gunman said excitedly. "The money is there."

Jack came over and looked at the screen. A three followed by six zeros was in the column next to their Costa Rican bank account number. By way of a half dozen Cayman Island and Swiss banks, untwisting the pretzel of dummy accounts would be impossible.

Three million. He was a millionaire. Before he was forty.

He was almost giddy when he lifted his radio.

"Release the Fat Man," he said.

HOW could it be Christmas Eve? I thought.

I stood on the corner of Fiftieth Street and watched as snow began to fall, but not the soft, feathery-flake variety. Gritty bits of frozen rain scoured at my face like sand tossed in a wind tunnel.

Over at the command center, I'd heard about a new problem for us to contend with. Along the barricades, tourist crowds had gathered and were resisting being dispersed. Having been denied a peek at the Rockefeller Center tree that had been cordoned off, they were content to stand around and gape at the unfolding spectacle.

I shook my head and wandered over toward Lieutenant Reno and Chief Oakley, who were in front of the black FBI tactical bus. Oakley had a folded blueprint in his hand.

"Mike," Oakley said, "we're going over that first idea you had about the north spire again. Figuring out some way to go in the cathedral up there."

I looked at the commando chief. His face was drawn and weary, but even in the cold murk, there was no mistaking the determination in his eyes. Oakley had lost one of his men, and it didn't look like he would be slowing down until something was done about it.

"It's probably the next best tactical option," I said. "But after what happened in the concourse, I'm worried about getting ambushed again. And it might be a lot harder to fall back from three hundred feet in the air."

"We've spoken to Will Matthews and the FBI special agent in charge," Reno said. "The next decision to go tactical will be a full-force breach from every side. Next time they send us in, we won't stop until every hijacker is taken out, Mike."

I was standing there, trying to shrug off the implications of what Reno had just said, when the crisis cell rang on my belt.

What now? I thought. *What's your pleasure, Jack?*

"Mike here," I said.

"How's it hanging, Mickey?" Jack said.

I thought of the various strategies I could use. I could go passive or aggressive. Ask some questions to feel out his present mood. I was tired of strategies, though. Jack was the one toying with us, and I was sick of pretending it was the other way around.

"Killing the mayor was a mistake," I said. "You wanted us to believe you're a psychopath not to be trifled with? Well, you did a good job. Only that just makes storming in there a foregone conclusion. Which, according to you, blows up the cathedral. Which will kill you. Which makes spending all that money kind of hard."

"So glum, Mick," Jack said. "It's like you're giving up, and it's only the third quarter. Check it out. You've finally started paying. That was good. Now, all you have to do is come through with the rest of the dough-re-mi. Then it will get real interesting. Oh, and before I forget, there'll be another celebrity body at midnight."

"Jack, don't do it," I said. "We can work something—"

"Shut up!" Jack yelled. "I'm tired of the delays. You guys took your best shot and missed, and now it's time for you to pay. I repeat, there will be another body at midnight. No more easy ones like the mayor, either. I've already made my selection. You'll like this one."

WITH another block of excruciating downtime in front of us, I grabbed the opportunity to hand over the crisis phone to Ned Mason. Then I headed uptown to see Maeve.

I noticed a change when I came into her room. The sheets were different, new and crisp, and she was wearing a new bathrobe.

Maeve was awake, watching CNN's coverage of the siege. I found the remote and clicked off the set before I took her hand.

"Hey, you," I said.

"I saw you on the tube," Maeve said, smiling. "You always look so handsome in that suit. Whose christening did you wear it to?"

"Chrissy's," I said.

"Chrissy," my wife said with a sigh. "How is my little Peep?"

"She came into the nest the other night," I said. "I forgot to tell you. I forgot to tell you a lot of things, Maeve. I—"

My wife raised her hand and put her finger to my lips.

"I know," she said.

"I shouldn't have been so concerned with my job. I wish . . ."

She stopped me with a hurt look. "Please don't wish," she said quietly. "It hurts more than cancer. I knew how dedicated you were to your job when we met. It was one of the reasons I married you. I was so proud, seeing you speak to the press. You were inspiring."

"Who do you think inspires me?" I said, tearing up.

"No, not on these nice new sheets. Wait. I have your present."

We always exchanged gifts on Christmas Eve, usually around 3:00 a.m., after putting together a bike or train set.

"Me first," I said, taking a wrapped box out of the bag I had stashed in the trunk of my car. "Allow me."

I tore off the paper and showed Maeve the portable DVD player and the stack of DVDs I'd gotten her. The movies were old black-and-white noirs, Maeve's favorites.

"Look, *Double Indemnity*," I said. "I'll sneak us up some Atomic Wings. It'll be just like old times."

"How awesomely devilish of you," Maeve said. "Now mine."

She produced a black velvet jewelry box from under her pillow and handed it to me. I opened the box. It was a single gold hoop earring. I used to wear one in the late eighties when we first met.

I started to laugh. Then both of us were laughing hard.

"Put it in," Maeve cried.

I maneuvered the earring into the latent hole of my left ear. Miraculously, it slipped right in. "How do I look?"

"Like a well-dressed pirate," my wife said, wiping a rare happy tear from her eye.

"Arrrrrrr, matey," I said, burying my face in her neck.

I backed away when I felt her stiffen. Then I shuddered at the distant look in her eyes. Her breathing became irregular. I blasted the nurse's button half a dozen times.

"I've spilled the water from the spring, Mother," I heard my wife say in the Irish accent she'd fought so hard to erase. "The lambs are all in the ditch, every last one."

What was happening? Oh God no, Maeve! Not today, not now!

Sally Hitchens, the head nurse, came rushing in. She shined a light into Maeve's eye. "Doctor upped her meds this morning," Sally said as Maeve closed her eyes. "We have to watch her closely until she adjusts. Can I speak to you a second, Mike?"

I kissed Maeve's head and followed Sally out into the hall.

The nurse looked directly into my eyes. Bad sign. "We're getting very close to the end now, Mike," she said. "I'm sorry. I'm so sorry."

"How long?" I said.

"A week," the nurse said gently. "Probably less."

"A week?" I said. Even I knew I sounded like a spoiled child.

"Impossible as it is, you have to prepare yourself," Sally said. "Maeve needs you to be strong now."

I closed my eyes and felt my face flush as I heard the nurse walk off. There was something unending about the pain I felt pass through me then. It seemed as if it would burst out of my chest like a bomb blast, stop the world, stop all life everywhere.

It passed after a moment when I heard someone in one of the other rooms click on a TV. *Apparently not,* I thought as I opened my burning eyes and headed for the elevators.

I CALLED home on my cell phone as I left the hospital.

Julia picked up. "How's Mom?" she said.

In homicide interrogations, sometimes it takes lying very convincingly in order to extract a confession. At that moment, I was glad I'd had some practice. "She looks great, Julia," I said. "She's so proud of the way you've been taking care of your sisters. So am I."

"How are *you,* Dad?" Julia said. Was that extremely mature concern in my baby's voice? I remembered that she'd be heading to high school next year. How had she grown up without me noticing?

"You know me, Julia," I said. "If I'm not actually freaking out, I guess I'm doing pretty good. How are things in the barracks?"

"There's quite a line behind me, waiting to tell you," she said.

As I drove through the cold city streets, I spoke briefly to each of my kids, telling them how much their mother and I loved them. I apologized for not being there for their pageant or Christmas Eve. As usual, the kids were taking things in stride. Chrissy was sniffling when she got on the line.

"What is it, honey cub?" I said.

"Daddy," Chrissy said, sobbing, "Hillary Martin said Santa can't come to our apartment because we don't have a fireplace."

I smiled with relief. Maeve and I had heard this lament at least twice before and had devised a solution.

"Oh, Chrissy," I said into the phone. "When Santa comes to New York City, because people in a lot of apartments don't have fireplaces, he lands his sleigh on the roof of the building and comes down the fire escape. Now, Chrissy, do me a big favor? Tell Mary Catherine to make sure the window in the kitchen is unlocked."

"I'll tell her," Chrissy said breathlessly. "Bye, Daddy."

"Mr. Bennett?" came Mary Catherine's voice from the receiver a few seconds later.

"Hi, Mary," I said. "Where's Seamus? He should have relieved you by now."

"He did. He's holding court in the living room with *'Twas the Night Before Christmas.*"

Reading that story had always been my job, but I felt more gratitude than sadness. My grandfather was a wonderful storyteller and would make sure the kids were getting the best Christmas they could under the circumstances.

"Please, Mary, feel free to get out of there," I said. "And thank you so much for picking up all the slack. When this craziness at the cathedral is over, we'll figure out a sane schedule."

"I'm glad I could help. You have a wonderful family," Mary Catherine said. "Merry Christmas, Mike."

I was speeding south past the wreath-and-holly-decked Plaza Hotel when she said it, and for a second, I wanted to believe that it could be. Then in the distance, I spotted the harsh glow of the siege tinting the black sky. "Talk to you later," I said, and snapped my phone shut.

IN THE dark confessional, Laura Winston lay curled on the cramped floor, sweating and shivering.

In the twenty hours she'd been confined, she'd drifted in and out of consciousness. But ever since the dim light had retreated from the stained-glass skylight above her, six or seven hours ago, she'd been completely awake with the fever and pain of withdrawal.

It was around noon when she had noticed her reflection in the polished brass kick plate of the door. Makeup eroded by tears and sweat, honey-blond razor cut flecked with vomit. It had taken a kidnapping, a violent ordeal of historic proportions, but now, finally, she realized the truth. *She was old.*

And she'd actually hurt people, hadn't she? Laura thought. Women especially. Month after month in her magazine, she'd perpetuated the myth of eternal chicness and supposedly attainable beauty. Draped expensive clothes on fourteen-year-old genetic freaks and called it normal, then implied to her readers that if they didn't look like them, they were not living up to their potential.

When she got out of this—if she did—she was going to change, she decided. Go to a rehab facility. Downsize. Instead of building an empire, she would establish a charitable foundation. Insane as it was, this awful experience had changed her for the better.

Give me one last chance, Lord, the fashionista prayed. *At least give me the chance to change.*

It felt like something tore inside her ear when the gun went off just outside the confessional door. When the ringing subsided, she could hear people screaming. Her breath jammed in her throat as she heard a body being dragged past her door.

God have mercy. They'd shot somebody else! Laura felt her heart wallop against her chest. Who could it have been? Why?

The hijacking wasn't really about money, Laura concluded with horror. One by one, they'd be made to pay for their decadent sins.

I'm next, Laura thought with a dry heave.

As I came through the checkpoint, I could see Oakley and a couple more cops running like madmen toward the cathedral steps. That could only mean one thing, I thought.

I checked my watch. Jack had said midnight. It was only ten thirty. Who had they killed now? Why do it before the deadline?

I was already at the ambulances in Rock Center when Oakley and the other cops arrived with a suit-clad body. I couldn't see the face as the medics scrambled over the victim on the stretcher.

After a moment, the paramedics stopped. One of them turned away with tears in her eyes. She sat down in the gutter, and the flashes from news photographers outside the cordon and in the windows of buildings overlooking the cathedral invaded her grief.

I felt my heart flash-freeze when I finally saw who it was. John Rooney, the movie-star comic, lay sprawled on the stretcher.

What felt like a slow electric current crept along my spine. Rooney had millions of fans, many of them children. Being such a star, he'd become part of the country and the world's consciousness, and those bastards had just erased him and all the warm feelings he'd miraculously been able to generate.

For the first time, I wanted to pack it in. I ached to just take the phone off my belt and walk away.

"My God!" Oakley cried in outrage. "How are we going to deliver this bombshell? First we drop the ball with the mayor. Now we let John Rooney get killed?"

Then it dawned on me. I suddenly understood why the hijackers were wiping out celebrities, one grueling murder at a time.

They wanted things to go slow. That way, the pressure was on us. As the bodies piled up, we looked worse and worse. If we screwed up, people wouldn't blame the hijackers; they'd blame us.

I let the crisis phone ring four times before I answered it.

"Hi. It's Jack," he said, and actually sounded gleeful. "Hi-Jack. Get it? Sure, it's not as funny as Rooney, but I'm thinking his stand-up days are over. Time's up, Mike. No more delays. If all the money isn't in my account by nine o'clock tomorrow morning, there'll be so many dead rich and famous people under the tree this Christmas, Santa'll have to leave all the presents in the fireplace."

IT WAS coming on two in the morning when I slowly, painfully, lifted my head off the laptop keyboard I'd been using for a pillow. For the first time in hours, the activity in the command center had died down to a murmur. Our work was almost done. It had taken every ounce of finagling and begging, but we'd somehow gotten all but four of the seventy-three million dollars together.

"Why don't you take a breather, Mike?" Paul Martelli told me with a yawn. He'd just come back from catching some sleep. "Nothing going on here for a little while."

"I don't want to be missing if I'm needed," I said.

Martelli patted me on the shoulder. "Listen, Mike," he said, "we all know about your wife. I can't even imagine the stress you're under. We'll call you the second something develops. Now get out of here. Go be with your family. Mason and I have you covered."

Martelli didn't have to tell me twice. Anyway, I felt the negotiations were over—they'd won. We still had to negotiate the hostages' release and whatever kind of transportation the hijackers thought they would need to get them to safety. But that could wait.

When I got home, I went into the kids' rooms and checked on them. There were probably visions of PlayStation and Xbox dancing in their heads instead of sugarplums, but at least they were snug in their beds. Seamus was snoring to beat the band on top of the chaise in my bedroom, cookie crumbs on his cheeks. My eleventh kid. I tossed a throw on him and turned out the light.

My biggest shock came when I stepped into the living room. Not only was there a grand tree, but it had been decorated to the nines. The kids' gifts had been pulled from the back of my closet, wrapped, and stacked under it. There was a note on the DVD remote. HIT PLAY, it said. MERRY CHRISTMAS! MARY CATHERINE.

I did as instructed. A video shot of Chrissy, dressed as an angel and proceeding up the aisle in Holy Name's gym, filled the screen.

I teared up. What an awesome job Mary Catherine and my grandfather had done. What could be more beautiful than this?

I wiped my eyes to watch as my boys, now shepherds, came wandering from afar toward the stage. *God save the Bennetts.*

CHAPTER 8

I DON'T know what I appreciated more when I woke up early on Christmas morning—the unmatchably wonderful smell of coffee and bacon wafting through my open door or the barely stifled giggling coming from the other side of my bed.

"Oh no," I said, sitting up after a particularly loud titter. "All my children are sound asleep . . . and there's Irish ghosts in my room!"

There was an explosion of laughter as Shawna, Chrissy, and Trent tackled me back onto my pillow.

"It's not ghosts," Trent said. "It's Christmas!"

Tugging one hand apiece, Chrissy and Shawna got me to my feet and pulled me out into the sweetly pine-scented living room.

I got my Christmas present right then when I looked down at my two little ones. Norman Rockwell couldn't have painted it any better. Christmas-tree lights softly illuminating the breathless, saucer-eyed wonder of two little girls on this special day of days.

"You were right, Daddy!" Chrissy said. "I left the kitchen window open, and Santa made it!"

I saw Trent shaking a box.

"How about you little guys wake up the big ones first," I said. "Then we'll open presents together, okay?"

Three little comets rocketed out of the room simultaneously. I headed for the kitchen, following that wonderful smell. Mary Catherine smiled at me as she poured pancake batter into a skillet.

"Merry Christmas, Mike," she said.

"I don't know how I'm ever going to thank you for all you've done for my family," I said. "The tree, taping the pageant, wrapping the gifts. Heck, I'm starting to think maybe Santa is real."

"Please," Mary said with a wink. "Father Seamus did most of it. Wait, I hear the children. Take that tray out. I poured the hot chocolate, and your coffee is there on the island."

I did as I was told. Back in the living room, I thought everyone would be tearing into the gifts, but they were just standing there.

"You didn't have to wait for me, guys," I said. "Merry Christmas. Let the wrapping paper fly!"

"Well, Dad," Brian started. "We had a kids' meeting and . . ."

"What Brian is trying to say," Julia said, "is that we decided that we don't want to open our gifts until we see Mom. We know you have to go back to work, but we're willing to wait until you get home so we can all go over and see Mom together."

I wrapped as many of my kids into my arms as I could. "Game over," I said, closing my eyes tight in the center of the scrum. "You guys are the best kids who ever lived."

After I ate my pancakes, I reluctantly hopped in the shower and got changed. The last thing I saw after I hugged my way to the front door was Mary Catherine charging the video camera battery. How I was ever going to repay this girl, I couldn't begin to fathom.

I almost knocked down Seamus, who'd gone home early to shower and change, as he stepped out of the elevator. He was dressed all in black, with his Roman collar tight at the neck.

"Merry Christmas," he said. "Off to work, are we? That's a fine, fine job you have for yourself. Real conducive to family life, it is."

"Oh, 'tis, 'tis," I said in my grandfather's brogue.

Right. As if I wanted to go to work. It wouldn't have been a holiday without my grandfather busting my chops about something.

"Hey, thanks for what you did for the kids, you nasty old bat," I said with a smile. I stopped the door as it started to slide closed. "Oh, and bah humbug to you, too."

INSIDE the semidarkened cathedral, Eugena Humphrey woke on a hard wooden pew. She sat up and let out a breath of disappointment as she turned toward the votive candles that had given her a sense of peace and hope over the last forty-eight hours. The rows of golden light were gone. Every flame completely snuffed out.

She'd had some pretty bad Christmases before, she thought. But this was worse than getting regifted.

Something hard speared into the back of Eugena's neck.

"Hey, Eugena, Santa got you a cheeseburger this year," Little John said as he dropped a greasy paper-wrapped bundle in her lap.

Maybe the other hijackers were doing this for money, but that son of a bitch, Eugena thought, got off on inflicting pain. He was the one who had walked up and killed John Rooney in cold blood.

An overwhelming sense of despair threatened to overtake her. How could she take another hour of this? Another minute?

She moved her "Christmas breakfast" to the bench beside her. Enough tolerance. It was time to get pissed off. Even if she was a celebrity, she was a person, too! One who wasn't going to take it anymore.

She sat up, clenching her fists. She finally decided that if she got the opportunity, she was going to fight for her life.

ACROSS THE AISLE FROM Eugena, Charlie Conlan checked his watch, then checked it again. He looked up as the skinny hijacker who liked Mercedes Freer came strolling past, doing his rounds.

Conlan turned and saw a lone hijacker sitting on the rear rail. The punk put his shotgun in his lap and took a cell phone he'd grabbed from one of the celebrities out of the pocket of his robe. Was he making a call? No, Conlan realized as the hijacker started pressing buttons with his thumbs. He was playing a video game.

Conlan coughed twice. His signal. Todd Snow at the front pew shot him a look. Conlan nodded as Mercedes, sitting at the end of one of the middle pews, tugged the passing hijacker's robe.

Let's roll.

When the hijacker turned, Snow bolted over the front pew and disappeared under the skirt of the altar.

Conlan swiveled his head to see if the hijacker at the rear had noticed. Nope, still into his game.

Conlan could hear Mercedes chatting up the other punk. "I'm going a little crazy," Mercedes hissed. "C'mon, you and me. I'm serious. Give me a kiss at least."

The hijacker glanced back at his partner, then leaned down and started kissing the pop singer through his mask.

"Not in front of everybody. Behind the altar," she whispered.

"Behind the altar?" he said. "You're even dirtier than your videos. All right, let's go."

Conlan exhaled as Mercedes rose in her pew. This was it.

Two things would happen now. Snow would stomp the hijacker behind the altar, and Conlan would rush the gunman at the back rail. Then they would have two guns and a chance to get out alive.

Conlan wiped the sweat from his palms. He knew how risky this was. But it was either fight or wait to be shot like Rooney. He glanced at Mercedes and the hijacker hurrying up the altar steps.

Now. Conlan stood. Suddenly there was an explosion. What felt like a steel fist slammed into his chin. Without knowing how it had happened, he was down on his back, numb and bleeding.

He heard Todd Snow yell out. Snow had been rushing toward

the gangly hijacker when three others suddenly appeared. They fired on him—rubber bullets!

Conlan watched, horrified, as the quarterback dropped. Then Little John walked out from the larger church. He stepped up to Snow. "You thought you could take us?" Little John put his boot on Snow's chest. Slowly, ceremoniously, he took a rubber-bullet gun from one of his colleagues. He placed the muzzle on the star's right hand, his throwing hand. He stepped on the wrist to hold it still.

The pop of the gun firing was swallowed by Snow's scream.

Conlan looked on as Mercedes walked up to Little John. He watched as she was handed a cell phone. Then a cigarette. He realized what had happened as Little John chivalrously lit it for her.

"You sold us out," Conlan croaked. "You little bitch."

Mercedes rolled her eyes at Conlan.

"Merry Christmas, Momma," Conlan heard her say into the cell phone. "Stop cryin'. It's okay. These boys aren't so bad. They'll let me go, don't you worry about it. One thing you taught Mercedes is how to take care of herself."

WITH the absence of traffic on Christmas morning, I got back to St. Patrick's in near record time. The media crowd had thinned out considerably, but I had a feeling that after they finished opening their presents, they'd be back for their fill of blood sport.

Paul Martelli almost tackled me as I got off the elevator at the command center. "We did it, Mike," he said. "Five minutes ago, we got the last of it. All the money. It's ready to go."

"Any chance we'll be able to trace it?" I asked.

Martelli shrugged. "We know it's set to go to an account in the Caymans. They will wire it somewhere else immediately, then somewhere else. Eventually, we could probably put enough political pressure on the bank down there to tell us where it was sent, but by then it will probably have been shot to another numbered account in Switzerland or who knows where. The white-collar-crime guys are working on it."

I turned as Commander Will Matthews came out of the boardroom. I winced at his stubbled cheeks, the red-rimmed eyes. All he'd gotten this Christmas was an ulcer. "We ready to go?" he said to Ned Mason.

Mason stood up, cupping a phone receiver, and said, "Bank's just waiting on you to give the final word."

Will Matthews took off his cap and clawed a hand through his flattop before he took the receiver. "This is Borough Commander Will Matthews. I hate like hell to say this. Wire the money."

I followed my boss back into the boardroom and stood with him as he silently gazed at the cathedral. Finally, he turned to me. "You get those bastards on the phone one more time, Mike. Tell them they got their blood money. Now let these poor people go."

"How do you think they're going to try to get away, Commander?" I finally said.

"Let's just see, Bennett," Will Matthews said, gazing malevolently across Fifth Avenue. "The suspense is killing me."

I WENT back out to the communications desk in the outer office. The sergeant, who had been the lead tech guy since this thing began, nodded at me with anticipation. "What's up, Mike?"

"Can you ring me into the cathedral?" I said.

The sergeant flipped open a laptop. "Give me a minute."

"Yello," Jack said as the sergeant handed me a phone.

"It's Mike," I said. "The money's been wired."

"Let me see about that," Jack said skeptically.

I could hear some key clicks in the background. They were checking up on the account from inside the cathedral.

"Mikey, what a wonderful gift," Jack finally said after a minute. "I'm about to explode with Christmas joy."

"We fulfilled our part of the bargain," I said. "Now you have to do your part. It's time to let the hostages go."

"All in due time, Mike," Jack said calmly. "The hostages will be released, but on our terms. What would be the point of getting shot like dogs after all this work? Here's what we're going to need. In twenty minutes, I want eleven identical black sedans with dark tinted windows, gassed and ready, parked out front at the Fifth Avenue entrance. The doors will be left open and the engines left running. Fifth Avenue will be cleared all the way to One thirty-eighth, and Fifty-seventh will be cleared river to river. Any effort to detain us will result in a vast amount of death. If all our demands are met, the remaining hostages will be released unharmed."

"Anything else?" I said.

"Nope, that's it," Jack said. "*Arrivederci,* Mikey."

I almost couldn't believe it when I heard a dial tone in my ear. That was it? All they wanted was eleven cars? Where did they think they were going to drive? Mexico?

Behind me, I heard the borough commander radioing the task force to clear Fifth and Fifty-seventh and to block the side streets. He got on another radio and told the rooftop snipers to get ready.

"When they come out, we'll take them down," he said. "Anyone who has a clear line of sight has a green light."

"Roger that," came back one of the snipers.

"Bennett," Will Matthews told me, "get up on the roof and into a helicopter, in case we have to pursue."

Not exactly overjoyed about heights, I can't say I was psyched about that task, but I nodded okay and stepped into the elevator headed to the roof.

I DON'T know how gung ho I would have been to climb into a helicopter on the ground, never mind fifty-one stories up. When I glanced at the pilot beside me, I noticed that it was a woman beneath the aviator sunglasses and helmet. I knew I was in for it the second I saw her cocky smirk. She must have had a healthy sadistic streak, because the second I was strapped in, the aircraft dropped off the side of the building, express elevator down, leaving my stomach back on the fifty-first floor.

After we slowed and stopped to hover four hundred feet over the intersection of Fiftieth and Fifth, I took in the whole of the cathedral for the first time. It really was a beautiful structure, its spires and ornamentation as intricate as a wedding cake's, which was mind-boggling, considering the whole thing was made out of stone.

As I looked down, eleven black Chevy sedans rolled slowly in from the north. They stopped in front of the cathedral, and the uniformed cops driving them jumped out, leaving the doors open.

Squad cars were parked at every intersection to the horizon, their cherry tops flashing as they blocked the side streets on both sides.

Down below, the tall front doors of the church slowly opened. A figure in a brown hooded robe and ski mask stepped out.

There was a frenzied spattering of police radio chatter from my headset as another subject, dressed in the same brown robe and ski mask, stepped out a moment later. Was it the hijackers?

A second later, my jaw dropped harder than the helicopter had off the roof. Spilling out of the cathedral, walking in two straight lines toward the waiting sedans, was a group of twenty-odd people.

All dressed in brown robes. *All* wearing ski masks.

There was no way to tell the hostages from the bad guys.

"Does anybody have a shot?" Will Matthews said over the radio.

There were maybe thirty figures in brown robes moving slowly down the steps toward the waiting sedans.

"*Hold!*" called a voice. "We're scanning with radar for concealed weapons."

On the roof of Saks, a sniper set down his rifle and raised what looked like an extra-long pair of binoculars. He lowered the binoculars finally and called into his sleeve. "Stand down," he said. "Heat signatures indicate that they all seem to have weapons on them. We have no safe shot. We can't tell who is who."

I shook my head. Jack and his hijackers had done it again. They'd anticipated how dangerous it was for them to get from the church to the cars and had somehow disguised everyone.

The brown-robed mass of people was climbing into the cars, three and four per car. The doors started to close one by one. That was that. Another opportunity lost. The bad guys could be the drivers in each car—or they could be in the backseat, holding a gun on a hostage in the driver's seat. There was no way to know.

I stared at the idling cars. The question remained: How did the hijackers think they were getting off the island of Manhattan? With the strange way that things were winding down, I was beginning to believe that nothing short of a bloodbath would resolve this.

We hovered low over the convoy of black sedans. The whirling edges of the rotor couldn't have been more than twenty feet from the building facades on either side of the avenue. I swallowed hard.

When the cars finally pulled away from the cathedral, we tilted forward and inched along in the air behind them as they passed tony Fifth Avenue shops—Cartier, Gucci, Trump Tower. But when they arrived at Tiffany's at the corner of Fifty-seventh, they stopped!

Maybe Jack planned to rob the famous jewelry store as a parting gesture. Anything was possible at this point. The helicopter's rotors thumped in time with my pulse as I waited and watched.

After a pause of a full minute, the lead car made a left—heading west on Fifty-seventh Street. As the next four cars followed, I thought maybe the whole strange procession was going to take a slow tour of the West Side. But the sixth car surprised me by turning east on Fifty-seventh. The remaining cars followed east as well.

I reported the bizarre new twist over the radio. Was one group the celebrities and the other the hijackers?

"Is there any way for you to distinguish who's who?" Will Matthews asked in an anguished voice.

I stared at the two lines of cars. If there was any clue at all, I couldn't see it. "There's no difference I can make out," I finally called into the radio.

"Which way?" the pilot asked, annoyed, as we just sat there over the intersection.

"West," I decided. "Hang a left."

At least if I was wrong, and I got fired, it would be a shorter subway ride back to my apartment.

STRAIGHTENING the wheel of the lead sedan heading east on Fifty-seventh Street, Eugena Humphrey sucked in a deep breath.

The heat of the car was making her sweat, and the stench of the ski mask the hijackers had made her wear was another distraction.

She glanced at two uniformed cops, just standing there on the sidewalk, gaping at the passing sedans.

Nobody was doing anything! How could they?

Frightened as she was, she knew she couldn't break down now. When was the last time she'd actually driven herself around? she thought. Ten years ago? She remembered a red Mustang she'd bought after her transfer out of the Wheeling, West Virginia, affiliate to L.A. What a wild ride she'd been on since then.

And this was how it would end? After all she'd done, pulling herself up out of nothing. She not only had risen above what the world tried to enforce as the limits of her race and class, but had become a force for good in the world, a strong force. But at least she'd lived a full life. Done just about everything there was to do.

Eugena gasped as the gunman in the front seat jabbed her violently with the pipe of a sawed-off shotgun.

"Speed it up," he yelled at her.

Eugena felt her despair pop and her adrenaline surge. She hit the gas, and buildings began to blur past. Outside the windshield, it was as if New York City was coming at her at warp speed.

THE lineup of sedans was still doing a slow crawl west on Fifty-seventh Street. I watched as the convoy passed through the Sixth Avenue intersection at parade speed.

Why wouldn't they do something, make their move?

It was as if the hijacker convoy was reading my mind as it came parallel to the Hard Rock Cafe a minute later. There was a scream of engines, and the five cars suddenly peeled out.

The cops blocking the intersection at Broadway looked like stunned spectators as the vehicles rocketed past them.

The sedans seemed to be drag racing as they shot across Eighth Avenue. By the time they hit Ninth Avenue, they looked like they were taking a shot at the land-speed record.

I thought this sudden need to be somewhere in a hurry a tad peculiar, since they were speeding toward a dead end. There were maybe two blocks of Manhattan left. *Then what?*

I could feel the blood leave my face as I watched the sedans scream down the final slope of street heading toward the Hudson River. Would they try to ram one of the barricades? It appeared that a deadly crash was coming in seconds. And there was nothing I could do except watch from a front-row balcony seat.

HOG-TIED in the front passenger seat of the lead car heading west, rocker Charlie Conlan felt the cut on his chin reopen as the speeding vehicle bounded off a world-class pothole.

Conlan knew that the car was going way too fast. As the sedan's engine roared, he was struck with anger at the animal sitting beside him. Conlan was still breathing, which meant he could still fight. But his arms and legs were taped together. So what could he do?

He glanced at the hijacker behind the wheel to his left. His mask was still on, but the hood was down.

Conlan nodded to himself as he figured it out. *Maybe I'll die, but it won't be on my knees to these bastards.*

The car had just lifted off from a steep crest along Tenth Avenue when Conlan leaned over and bit down into the driver's ear. The scream the hijacker made almost drowned out the engine.

What this worthless vermin had put them through, Conlan thought. He'd killed his friend Rooney, then dragged him outside like a bag of garbage. Conlan wished he could inflict a world of pain on him. But then the front tires shredded as the car touched down off-kilter, turned sideways—and began to flip.

Seconds later, the sedan crashed through the plate-glass window of the BMW showroom on the corner of Eleventh Avenue.

A horrible crunching sound blasted out Conlan's eardrums, and the world went black. Then fluorescent white.

Conlan came out of the fog of shock, blinking up into a bright ice-cube-tray light fixture. He was in an operating room, right? The pile of glass in his lap made a tinkling sound as he turned around.

He was inside a car showroom. They had somehow landed right-side up. He gaped at the twisted metal inches from his throat. The sedan was now a convertible, since the roof had been ripped away.

When he looked out the shattered windshield, his first thought was that the hijacker driver, who was hunched over one of the showroom motorcycles, was trying to escape. Then he noticed that one of the handlebars was sticking out the middle of the hijacker's back. "One down," said Conlan. "That's for John Rooney."

He turned toward the backseat next. The rest of the passengers looked to be all right. Todd Snow undid his seat belt, crawled across broken glass, and ripped at the tape on Conlan's wrists. They stared as the third passenger in the backseat took off a ski mask.

"Great job, fellas," Mercedes Freer said. "You saved us!" She grinned—just before Todd punched out the two-faced diva's front teeth.

BLINKING Christmas lights strung on the fire escape of a brownstone tenement streaked past the copter's window as we hurtled toward the car dealership that the lead sedan had just plowed into. I gawked from above at shattered glass and ripped metal, spinning police lights, running cops.

I turned to my left, away from the milling chaos at the dealership, just as the four remaining cars hit the emptied intersection of the West Side Highway near the Hudson. They hadn't slowed! I thought that they were going to try to turn at the last second and smash their way through the roadblock. But I was wrong.

The world seemed to gray out as I watched helplessly. The black sedans didn't swerve left or right. It was like they were on rails as they rocketed straight for the fence bordering the Hudson River.

The front tires of the cars exploded like pipe bombs as they struck the high concrete curb. Then the sedans bounced high and hit the fence. Chain links parted like wet tissue paper, and suddenly the cars were in the air above the icy river. They hit the water simultaneously, upside down.

I don't know what I had been expecting before that.

But it wasn't mass suicide.

"They're in the water!" I heard on the radio then. "All six cars are in the East River! It's totally insane. This can't be happening."

I thought the report was from a cop watching on the ground beneath me—until I realized they were talking about the other cars. The ones that had headed east.

The hijackers had crashed *all* the remaining cars into two rivers!

The helicopter was swinging down toward the water. We got there just in time to see brake lights disappear under the surface.

"As low as you can go," I yelled to the pilot as I popped my harness and the latch of the helicopter door. I leaned out above choppy, gray water. "And radio the Harbor Unit," I said.

Then I was free-falling.

THE water wasn't so bad. If you were one of those Coney Island polar bear people, maybe.

The temperature, or lack thereof, went through me all at once like an electric shock. Then I bobbed in the ice water until my feet found a bumper. I turned down into the polluted water, reaching forward with my hands.

I don't know how I found the door handle in the opaque water, but I did. I pulled hard, and the door swung open, and a form brushed by me, then another. I was out of breath, and heat, by the time a third and fourth shadow bobbed past me toward the surface, so I kicked up off the sunken car's roof.

As I dog-paddled, I counted twelve people floating in the water. They'd taken their masks off, and I recognized most of them as the VIP hostages. Were they all safe now?

"Is there anybody else stuck in the cars?" I yelled to one hostage flailing in the water.

He stared at me as if I were speaking Chinese. He was in shock. I decided I could do no more, except try to get everyone on the surface out of the water.

That's where the helicopter pilot came in. She was amazing, the best. Using the skid as a gaff, she managed to lift our gasping, hypothermic butts out of the drink and pop us on a nearby dock.

An army of sanitation workers had arrived from their truck depot beside the river, and they dragged us inside a warm building. A blanket was thrown over my back. A hulking sanitation worker gave mouth-to-mouth to a pale middle-aged woman for a moment before she stiff-armed him in his hairy chest.

I realized it was the fashion magazine editor, Laura Winston.

It was maybe half an hour later when I received a call from Will Matthews. All the celebrities who'd gone into the East River had been plucked out of the water and were accounted for. They were bruised and wet, but it seemed as if everyone would survive.

The hijackers, though, were glaringly unaccounted for. Whether they were drowned in the cars or still back at the cathedral had yet to be determined. Before I hung up, Will Matthews ordered me to go to the car dealership up the block to see what was going on.

At least everyone had made it, I thought, heading back outside to the edge of the dock. Except for the people who'd been murdered at the church, of course.

Jack's promise from the beginning of the ordeal galled me as I gazed out at the helicopters searching the frigid water.

He said he'd get away with this, and he had.

CHAPTER 9

AT AN abandoned dock just north of the new Hell's Kitchen Sports Pier, twenty blocks south of where half the cars had driven into the water, a black shape bobbed up from among the rotting piles. With his eyes just above the surface of the water, Jack carefully scanned the choppy gray Hudson behind him for the NYPD Harbor Unit, but there was nothing.

From inside his lightweight Scubapro wet suit, he took out a Ziploc bag. He removed the cell phone inside it and hit redial as he took out his air-tank mouthpiece. "Where?" he said.

"They're still concentrating on the crash sites, still looking to save hostages," the Neat Man said. "They haven't started looking for you yet. Window's open. Move now!"

Jack didn't have to be told twice. He put the phone back into its bag, slipped under the water, and tugged on the tow rope.

Five minutes later, Jack and the four hijackers with him were on a concrete ledge beneath a walkway on the south side of the sports complex, peeling off the wet suits they'd worn under their robes, dumping the air tanks they'd hidden underwater at the crash site.

The most hazardous part, he thought, had been the crash into the river. But the rest—their extraction from the cars and finding the tanks—had gone like clockwork. Not only was it the greatest hijack of all time, but now they were about to pull off the greatest escape!

This was no time to celebrate, though. They had to go to Queens to get the rest of the gang, who'd dumped into the East River. He hoped they had fared as well.

Jack looked back as the last member of his crew shed his wet suit, revealing a track outfit beneath. Now they looked just like everybody else coming off of the sports pier.

"Okay, ladies," Jack said to his men. "Let's move out."

Thirty-five minutes later, they were in a van picking up the rest of the hijackers by the dock of an abandoned bottling plant in Long Island City. Little John grinned as he and the other five men threw themselves in through the sliding door to back slaps and high fives.

"What took you so long?" the big man said, accepting an ice-cold Heineken that Jack handed him from a cooler. "Where's Jose?"

"He lost it as we were coming across Eleventh Avenue," Jack said. "Jose's gone."

Little John looked down at the van floor, ruminating. "What about his prints?" he said after a moment.

Jack smiled. "Remember we told him about the need to not leave any evidence? Well, the crazy mother spent the last month and a half burning off his fingertips with a Zippo."

"To Jose!" Little John said, lifting his beer bottle, happy again. "That *gato* had some nerve."

"And to Fontaine," Jack said, remembering his friend who'd been downed in the firefight in the crypt.

"What do we do now?" Little John said.

"We stick with the plan. Two, three months of waiting to make things look good, and then it's a one-way trip to Costa Rica."

So they'd really done it, Jack thought. It was hard to believe. They'd held the world off. The next part was incredibly easy. They just had to sit back and wait, and not spend their millions.

I HAD to borrow some clothes, so I was decked out in a spiffy green sanitation worker's uniform when I arrived back at the car dealership on Eleventh Avenue.

Two medical examiners in white Tyvek suits were attempting to remove a dead brown-robed hijacker from the handlebars of a motorcycle. Over by a pulverized soda machine, one of my favorite rock singers of all time, Charlie Conlan, and Giants quarterback Todd Snow were being interviewed by detectives from the Major Crimes Unit. From the look of the shredded car, I was surprised the only injury I saw was a fat lip on the pissed-off-looking pop star Mercedes, who stormed by with not a word of thanks to anybody.

I knelt beside the hijacker as the MEs laid him onto the showroom carpet. I borrowed a pair of rubber gloves and pulled off his mask. Then I uncovered a second black rubber mask beneath it.

A skin-diving mask. That's how they did it! They'd used scuba-diving equipment to escape under the water.

I borrowed a phone and told Will Matthews about my discovery. After some choice expletives, he called in more harbor units from Jersey and the Coast Guard.

After I hung up, I pulled off the hijacker's rubber mask. The deceased was a Hispanic man in his late thirties, early forties. Nothing in his pockets. A nine-millimeter Beretta pistol was in an underarm holster, but the serial number had been filed away. I groaned when I looked at his hands and saw his fingerprints were gone, too. I'd seen similar prints on the hands of crackheads, the ridges melted down to a nub from holding too many hot pipes.

I found Lonnie Jacob, a crime scene investigator, and showed him the jacker's hands. "Think you can get anything?" I said.

"Maybe a partial," Lonnie said skeptically. "I'll have to work on him back at the morgue."

"What's up, Mike?" Commander Will Matthews said moments later as he came across the broken glass toward me. "You transferring to Sanitation on me?"

"Thought I'd put out some feelers after this home run," I said.

"We did all we could, Mike," Will Matthews said, staring at the carnage around us. "That's the truth, and it's the story I'm sticking to. I advise you to repeat after me during the impending storm."

"Will do," I said. "Happens to be the truth."

"Now get out of here and see your family. My driver's outside waiting for you," Will Matthews said.

A cold wind was whipping down Fifty-seventh when I stepped outside. This Christmas had turned out to be one of those stainless steel–colored December days when you have the feeling winter will never end. As I got into the back of the cruiser and my thoughts shifted toward my wife, I decided I didn't want it to.

If Maeve wasn't going to see spring, why should anybody else?

SOME say nothing compares to Christmas in New York, but I'd never seen the city look grimmer. After I got home and changed, I drove my brood to the hospital. I couldn't see the wreaths and lights anymore, only the endless gray corridors of blank windows, the grimy concrete, the steam rising from the broken streets.

I stopped our van in front of the hospital and had to hold myself up against the door frame in order not to fall over from exhaustion. Mary Catherine fed my kids out in their good clothes, clutching their brightly wrapped presents. Even the stern nurses seemed teary-eyed as our sad procession passed through the lobby.

"Wait a second," I said, patting my pockets as we approached Maeve's corridor. "The pageant tape. I forgot to—"

"It's right here, Mike," Mary Catherine said, handing me the small plastic case.

I was about to thank her yet again for being such a lifesaver, when the amazing young woman said quietly, "Give my love to Maeve. I'll be in the lounge if you need me. Go."

I could see Seamus kneeling beside Maeve in her wheelchair when we turned into her corridor. A lump formed in my throat when I saw the open Bible in his hand. He made the sign of the cross on her forehead. *Last rites?* I thought.

How was I going to get through this? Today of all days?

Somehow Maeve was smiling when I knocked on the door frame.

Seamus closed his Bible and hugged me hard. "God give you the strength, Michael," he said in my ear. "Your girl is a saint. You are, too." Seamus paused. "I'll be back; I need to get some air."

I guess my heart wasn't already broken because I felt something snap like a guitar string in my chest when Maeve scooped Chrissy and Shawna into her withered lap.

It wasn't fair. Maeve had always exercised regularly, ate right, didn't smoke. I bit my lip as a searing pressure built in my chest. I wanted to, needed to, scream my guts out.

But something strange happened when my son Brian helped her back onto her bed and put the pageant on the TV. Maeve started laughing. Not polite little giggles, either, but gasping-for-breath belly laughs. I moved next to her, and her hand found mine.

For the next ten minutes, the hospital room disappeared, and we could have been on our beat-up couch at home, watching the Yanks or one of our favorite old movies.

"What a great job you did!" Maeve said, throwing high fives all around after the tape had ended. "Bennetts bringing the house down. I'm so proud of all you guys."

"Would you listen to the shameful amount of ruckus coming from this room?" Seamus said to giggles as he came back.

Maeve beamed as he gently took her hand and kissed it. "Merry Christmas," he said, smuggling a gold box of Godiva chocolates behind her back with a wink.

Julia and Brian stepped forward with a black velvet box. Maeve's smile, when she opened it, seemed powerful enough to banish the illness from her body forever. It was a thin gold necklace. The attached pendant said #1 MOM.

"We all chipped in," Brian said. "Even the little ones."

She kissed him on the cheek as he did the clasp for her.

"I want you to keep chipping in, guys," Maeve said, struggling to keep her eyes open. "Many hands lighten the load, and if it's one thing we have a lot of, it's hands. Little hands and big hearts. You couldn't have made me prouder. Dad will show you what I got for you later, kids. Merry Christmas. Never forget, I love you all."

I STAYED behind after Seamus took Mary Catherine and the kids back home. I closed the door to the room and sat behind Maeve in the cold bed, hugging her. I held her hand, staring at where our wedding rings touched.

When I closed my eyes, I pictured Maeve from my first days of courting her in the hospital emergency room. She had always been holding someone's hand then, too, I remembered. I thought about all the human hearts she'd lifted in her life. Mine most of all.

As I stood up to stretch around midnight, Maeve opened her eyes wide and crushed my hand in hers.

"I love you, Mike," she said urgently.

Oh God! I thought. *Not now. Please, not now!*

My hand went for the nurse's button, but Maeve batted it away. A tear rolled down her taut face as she shook her head. Then she smiled and looked into my eyes. It was as if she could see some distant place within them that she was about to travel to.

"Be happy," she said. Then she let go of my hand.

As her fingertips left my palm, I felt as though somewhere deep inside me something shattered and a hole opened.

I caught Maeve as she tipped back. She was so light. Her chest was already still. My hand lowered the back of her head toward the pillow as gently as it did on our honeymoon night.

The room spun as I stood there gasping. It felt as if the wind had been knocked out of me. Everything I had ever felt happy about, every laugh, every sunset, every hope, every good thing there was or ever would be shook loose and plummeted out of my heart.

I shut off the light and lay down beside my wife. *How can I still be alive?* I thought, feeling my heart beat on and on in my chest.

When I found Maeve's hand, I felt the cold of her wedding ring. I remembered the happy tears in her eyes, in the small church we were married in, as I slid it on her finger.

As I closed my eyes, I could no longer hear anything. The sounds of the hospital faded in the dark, and all that was left in the universe was my wife's cold hand in mine and a nothingness that hummed through me like high voltage.

THE head nurse, Sally Hitchens, came in at 4:30 a.m. She smiled as she helped me to stand up. She'd take care of my Maeve now, she promised as I stood disoriented and crazy-eyed over my wife.

I walked the thirty blocks home from the hospital, the cold burning my skin in the predawn dark.

All the kids were up in the living room as I stumbled in.

As I sat down, I thought I had purged away some of the pain from hours before, but my heart got heavier and heavier as my eyes slowly passed over each of my kids' faces. "Mom's gone to heaven," I finally said, gathering them in my arms.

After rising from their sobbing ranks, I stumbled into the kitchen and broke the news to Seamus and Mary Catherine.

Then I went into my room, closed the door, and sat on my bed.

When Seamus came in, maybe ten hours later, I was still sitting there in the same clothes and hadn't slept.

That's when he sat down next to me. "When I lost your grandmother," he said quietly, "I was ready to murder. The doctors who'd told me she was gone. All the people who came to her wake. Because of how lucky they were. They didn't have to go home to an empty apartment. I even thought about picking up the bottle Eileen had pulled me out of. But I didn't. Do you know why?"

I shook my head. I had no idea.

"Because of how insulting it would have been to Eileen. That's when I realized she hadn't really left for good. She'd just gone on ahead a little.

"One thing Eileen taught me is that you get up, put your clothes on, and do what you can do until the day you don't get up. I guess what I'm trying to say is that Maeve isn't really gone. She's just ahead, waiting for you. That's why you can't shut down. We Irish don't always succeed, but we're pretty decent at grinding it out."

"Grind it out until you're dead," I said after a moment. "Words of inspiration from Seamus Bennett."

"Ah, sweet, undiluted sarcasm," Seamus said, rising. "That's the lad. Maeve'd be proud of ya. Music to her Irish ears."

So after I took a shower, we made arrangements. Or, I should say, Seamus and Mary Catherine did. They called the church and then the funeral home, and I just nodded or shook my drooping head. *Grind it out until you're dead.*

IT WAS stone wall to stone wall with friends and relatives inside Holy Name Church two days later for Maeve's funeral. At the wake the night before, and now here at the church, my wife had drawn a crowd that rivaled the one at St. Patrick's for the First Lady.

In the sea of sad faces, I made out her former coworkers, past patients, even most of our snooty neighbors. Not only did most of my Homicide squad show, but most of the NYPD, it seemed, was there, giving their support for a brother in blue.

At the wake, so many people had shared vignettes I'd never heard before about Maeve—about how she had comforted their kid or wife or parent as they were wheeled into surgery or giving birth or dying. The compassion she showed at the hardest of moments. The strength she'd provided when people were most alone.

There are times when New York can be the loneliest place on earth, but as I watched Seamus in his robes come down from the altar and encircle Maeve's casket with incense and heard the sincere weeping of the people behind me, I could feel a sense of community that I would put up against the smallest of small towns.

After the Gospel, Seamus did the eulogy.

"One of my favorite memories of Maeve comes from, of all places, Ground Zero," he said from the pulpit.

"We were both volunteering on the *Spirit of New York,* moored off Battery Park City, helping to give out hot meals to the rescue people. It was during the fourth game of the 2001 World Series, and I was on deck when we heard this earsplitting howl from below. We thought someone had been shot, but when we arrived in the dining room, all we could see was Maeve, wearing headphones, jumping up and down so hard she was nearly rocking the boat.

" 'Tino Martinez tied it up,' she was screaming. 'He tied it up!'

"Now, when I think of Maeve, I will always see her in the middle of those tired men with her fist pumped in the air, her energy and hope and life transforming that black place and time into something unique—something, I think, on the verge of holy."

Seamus's cheeks clenched then. "I won't lie to you. I can't say why God would take her now. But if the fact that she was sent here among us doesn't point toward a loving God, then I can't help you. If we bring away anything from today, it should be the lesson that Maeve herself showed with every full, spent day of her life. Hold back nothing. Leave nothing in the tank."

All through the church, everyone, including myself, was crying shamelessly. Chrissy, beside me, brushed my overcoat out of the way and wiped her tears on my knee.

The sun came out for the burial at Gates of Heaven Cemetery up in Westchester. The kids filed past Maeve's casket with roses. I almost lost it when Shawna kissed her flower before she put it down. And again when the high, bittersweet skirls of an NYPD piper's "Danny Boy" blew off the headstones and frozen ground.

But I didn't.

I asked myself what Maeve would do, and I swallowed my tears and hugged my kids and promised myself and my wife that I would somehow get us through.

I'D OFFERED to stay home from work with the kids, who were on Christmas break, but Seamus wouldn't hear of it.

"Sorry, fella," he told me. "These kids need to be spoiled like no one has ever been spoiled before, and with the mood you're in, you're going to have to leave that job to me and Mary C. Besides, you need to get outside of yourself, Mick. Stop sitting around and go and collar those mopes who jacked the cathedral."

" 'Collar the mopes'?" I said with a faint grin. " 'Jacked'?"

"I watch *NYPD Blue* now and then," Seamus said. "Is it a sin?"

So the Monday morning after the funeral, I arrived back at my desk inside Manhattan North Homicide in East Harlem. I put in a call to Paul Martelli. And I learned that nothing really new had been discovered. Every square inch of the church had been searched and dusted for latent prints, but there had been nothing.

There had been some excitement when a hijacker's body was found in the archbishops' crypt, Martelli told me, but it ended when it was discovered that the man's hands and head, along with any chance at identifying him, had been removed by his partners.

Around noon, I called Lonnie Jacob, the NYPD CSU investigator working the car dealership where the sedan had crashed.

"Mike," Lonnie said after he answered. "I was just about to call you. It wasn't easy, but by sodium hydroxiding our John Doe's hands, I was able to dry them out and peel off the top layer of his charred skin. The second dermal layer is harder to ID, but at least we have something. I already spoke to my contact down in Latent Prints at the FBI. Should I fire it down to D.C. to cross-reference?"

I told him yes, and he told me he'd call me back with the results.

I FELT cooped up in the squad room, so I went for a ride one morning. Four days had passed since I had returned to work. I smiled at the hustle and bustle of loud vehicles and even louder pedestrians around St. Patrick's when I pulled up in front of it. Our city had survived riots, blackouts, 9/11, and now this, I thought as I headed up the cathedral steps.

The church was closed to the public for repairs. The uniformed Midtown North cops stationed at the door stepped aside when I showed them my tin.

I walked up the center aisle and sat in the front pew, looking out on the austere, empty church. You'd think I'd be sick of churches by this point, but for some reason, I felt comforted just being there in the candle-scented darkness. I felt oddly consoled.

My high school graduation had taken place here. I smirked, remembering how wretched at Greek and Latin I'd been. One thing I'd picked up from the Jesuit priests who taught us, though, was the importance of reason. Time and again, they preached the necessity of using our God-given rationality in order to cut through to the essence of things. I guess it was the reason I chose philosophy as my major when I went on to college. And the ultimate reason I had become a detective. The need to get at the truth.

I stared up at the main altar, thinking about the case.

We knew the when, where, what, why, and how. The only thing left was the who. Who was capable of the brilliance, and the brutality? Men with a lot of will, for one thing, I decided, and men not afraid to use extreme violence as a means to a selfish end.

They had killed five people during the siege. An ESU officer and FBI agent had been shot in the tunnel firefight. A priest had been shot in the side of the head "by accident," according to Jack. John Rooney had been executed at point-blank range.

Finally, I thought about the mayor. Why had they stabbed Andrew Thurman to death? The cigarette burns over his arms meant that he'd also been tortured. Why change their killing method for the mayor? Why get personal with the mayor?

There was a reason. I just didn't know what it was. Yet.

I stopped by the row of votive candles at the Lady Chapel before I left. I lit one for each of the souls that had perished here and one for my wife. I hunched onto the velvet kneeler, closed my eyes against my clenched fists, and stifled a tear.

Dear Maeve, I prayed. *I love you. I miss you terribly.*

I was still waiting to hear from Lonnie about the prints, and when I returned to my desk, he still hadn't called. I poured myself a coffee and stared out my window at East Harlem as I waited.

There was still a lot of investigating left to do. We knew the makes of the guns left behind by the kidnappers, and maybe that would turn into something. We'd found shells and spent cartridges. And half a dozen guns that shot rubber bullets. That was an interesting twist. They'd thought to bring crowd-control weapons.

I was hip-deep in hostage interview reports when the phone on my desk rang two hours later.

"Sorry, Mike," Lonnie told me. "No hits on the prints. The dead guy doesn't have a criminal record."

As I laid the phone back into its cradle, I thought I caught Jack's cocky laugh.

CHAPTER 10

THE phone was ringing on my desk when I came in the next morning. I heard a familiar voice when I picked up.

"This is Cathy Calvin from the *Times*. May I speak to Detective Bennett?"

I debated between telling the hatchet-wielding scribe, *No hablo inglés,* or just hanging up. "This is Bennett. I'm really tired of playing games with you, Calvin," I finally answered gruffly.

"Mike," the reporter said brightly. "Please let me apologize for that piece I did. You know how crazy it was. My editor was breathing fire down my neck and . . . What am I saying? No excuses. I screwed up, and I'm sorry. I owe you one. I heard about the loss of your wife. My sincerest condolences to you and your children."

I paused. The reporter certainly sounded sincere, but I was wary. She'd made me and the department look like fools. But then again, having a *Times* reporter owe me a favor could come in handy.

"Accept my apology, Mike," she tried again. "I feel like a jerk."

"Well, at least you're self-aware," I said.

"I knew we were going to be friends eventually," Calvin said quickly. "The reason I called was I'm doing interviews with the celebrity victims. I spoke to the civil rights activist, Reverend Solstice, and do you know what he told me?"

The race-baiting Solstice was famous for basically one thing. Hating cops. "I'm holding my breath," I said.

"He said he thinks the hijackers were cops," Calvin went on. "I just wanted to call and let you hear. Also to tell you that I refuse to print such bull. Okay? See, I'm not all bad."

"Okay," I said. "I appreciate the call."

After I hung up, I leaned back in my chair, thinking about Solstice's accusations. What did he know? Was it anything important? I called back Calvin and got the reverend's number.

Solstice answered on the first ring.

"Hello, Reverend. This is Detective Michael Bennett of the NYPD. I'm investigating the cathedral hijacking. I hear you have an insight into the case. I'd like to hear it."

"Ha!" Solstice said forcefully. "I know what you're doing. What you're trying to pull. The cover-up. Sweeping the truth under the rug. Listen, man, *I know*. I been inside. I know cops. Only pros like you could handle us the way you did. You cops pulled this off, and now you're covering it up."

Could that be true? I sure doubted it.

But Solstice had raised two serious questions: How did the hijackers know so much about siege tactics? And how did they always seem to know what we were going to try next?

THERE are actually ten prisons on Rikers Island in the Bronx, housing as many as seventeen thousand inmates. Rikers is almost a small town, with its schools, clinics, athletic fields, chapels and mosques, grocers, barbershops, a bus depot, even a car wash.

As I arrived there early the next morning, I was hopeful again. I'd had an idea during the night, and now I had the opportunity to execute it.

At a little past eight, I proceeded inside and was escorted to a small meeting room. For the next four hours, I sat in the room and met dozens of inmates. I played them a tape of Jack's voice from the negotiations. Maybe somebody would recognize him from a previous stay at Rikers or another prison around New York.

But not any of the seventy-nine inmates who came to see me in the cramped room had anything for me. How depressing was that?

Until my eightieth visitor, Tremaine, a skinny "older" guy, maybe forty. He said he thought maybe he'd heard Jack's voice before. "Don't know for sure, but *maybe.*"

On the way back from Rikers, I called One Police Plaza and told Lonnie to run the prints from the dead hijacker through the city, state, and national law enforcement employee records.

It was an hour later when the fax rang back at my office. It seemed like a month before the sheet hummed out of the machine. I lifted it up slowly, careful not to smudge the ink.

It wasn't the smiling ID picture of the dead hijacker that I couldn't tear my eyes away from so much as the captioned information underneath it.

Surprise mixed with a sick, guilty feeling that washed through my stomach like battery acid. *Unbelievable,* I thought.

I took out my cell and dialed Will Matthews's office. "This is Bennett," I said when I had him on the line. "I think we got 'em."

IT STARTED to snow as we crossed the city line, racing north on the Saw Mill River Parkway. An eight-vehicle convoy of FBI sedans and NYPD ESU trucks was now speeding through the Westchester woods, but it wasn't to Grandma's house we were going.

We took the exit for Pleasantville and rolled west toward the Hudson. Alongside the wind-scoured river, we stopped before high, harsh concrete walls decorated with razor wire. A barely legible sign was bolted to the rock: SING SING CORRECTIONAL FACILITY.

Nope, not Grandma's house, I thought. *The Big House.*

There was a distinct chill in the air as I got out and stood next to the prison walls. I felt it get even chillier when an armed guard, in what looked like a miniature airport control tower above the wire, swung his sunglasses in my direction. The barrel of the M16 he carried across his chest seemed the only gleaming object for miles.

All this time we were running around trying to send the hijackers to the slammer, I thought, staring at the maximum-security facility. And wouldn't you know it, they were already here.

The print of the deceased hijacker in the car dealership had belonged to Jose Alvarez, a corrections officer who'd worked at Sing Sing prison until six months ago.

A call to the warden revealed that a dozen men on the prison's three-to-eleven tour had staged a sick-out the week of the hijacking.

Suddenly, so many things made sense. The tear gas and rubber bullets, the street lingo mixed with quasimilitary terminology. The answer was right in front of us, but it had taken Reverend Solstice's suspicions and the memory of a prisoner named Tremaine Jefferson, who had previously served time at Sing Sing, to set it free.

Prison guards, as well as cops, were capable of handling crowds and containing people, and capable of being efficiently violent.

"Ready, Mike?" Steve Reno asked.

Our suspects were *inside* the prison, on duty. To arrest them, we were going to have to enter the belly of the beast.

Despite the fact that the wind cutting off the choppy water was like a Mach 3, I was actually smiling. "Let's go meet Jack," I said.

THOUGH none of us was too happy about it, because firearms are under no circumstances permitted in maximum-security facilities, the dozen of us cops and Bureau agents had to check our weapons at the window of the arsenal before being buzzed inside.

"The men who staged the sick-out have already been summoned into the lineup room," Warden Clark said as we arrived in the drab hallway outside his office.

An urgent-sounding squall ripped from Warden Clark's radio as we were on our way. He listened closely.

"What is it?" I said.

"A-Block," the warden said. "Something's happening. A lot of screaming and yelling anyway. Probably nothing."

"Are you sure all the men from the shift are there?" I said as we arrived at the mesh-windowed door of the lineup room.

The warden looked intently through the wired glass. "I think so. Wait. No," he said. "Sergeant Rhodes and Sergeant Williams. The two shift foremen. They're not here yet. *Where the hell are they?*"

The shift foremen, I thought. Sounded like ringleaders to me. "Let me guess," I said. "The foremen are stationed to A-Block?"

Clark nodded. "Our largest maximum-security building."

"We have to go in there," I told him. "Now."

TRAILING behind the warden and a half dozen of his most trusted officers, I climbed countless concrete stairs and went through several paint-chipped corridors before we came to a steel door leading to a barred gate. It buzzed open harshly. Then it swung wide.

I could feel the sound of the prison knock against my chest as we passed through the enormous chamber of the multitiered cell block—radios, inmates yelling, the constant hard and booming echo of steel on steel. The prisoners in the closest cells rose, screaming obscenities from behind double-thick bars as we passed.

"Let's check the gym before we go upstairs to the different galleries," the warden yelled above the racket.

We were buzzed through another locked door at the block's opposite end. There was no one at any of the weight-room benches or pull-up stations. No one on the basketball court. Where were they? Had Jack and Little John gotten away again?

I was leading our group back out onto the bottom level of A-Block when I was shoved from behind. The weight room's steel door boomed to a close as I skidded my palms and knees against the concrete floor.

I turned to see two of the warden's most trusted corrections officers smiling above me as the warden and Steve Reno and the other cops, sealed in the gym behind, began pounding on the steel door. I noticed that one CO was gargantuan, the other short and stocky. Way to go, Professor Bennett. They fit the description of Jack and Little John. That's because they were Jack and Little John.

Jack had a black riot baton in his hand. He spun it easily between his fingers. He had close-cropped curly brown hair and a permanent sneer. "Hey, Mikey," he said. "Long time no talk. So how come you never call anymore? I thought we were buddies."

"Hey, Jack," I said, feigning courage I wasn't really feeling. "Funny, you didn't sound like a midget on the phone."

Jack chuckled at that one. "You made *another* mistake, Mike. Only this one's kind of fatal. Coming into a man's house uninvited. You think that bastard Clark is in charge here? This is my turf."

"It's over, Jack," I said.

"I don't think so, Mike," he said. "We got out of one fortress. We can get out of another. Especially now that we have hostages. Maybe I'll even let you negotiate your own release. How does that sound?"

"Sounds great," I said, taking a half step back. My heel struck the flat, hard steel of the door. There was nowhere to run.

The heavy radio I'd been given by the warden was the only thing remotely resembling a weapon. I hefted it as Little John pulled his baton out with a sickening smile.

"Why don't we just talk about this for a second?" I said as I hurled the radio. Little John's nose and the radio exploded simultaneously. He screamed; then he and Jack lit into me, and I was lifted right off the floor before they both threw me down on my face.

I thought the prisoners had been loud before, but it turned out they were only warming up. As I wrestled on the cement with Jack and Little John, the communal screams off the concrete shell of the cell block sounded like a jumbo jet taking off inside a hangar.

When Jack got in a lick with the riot baton on the back of my head, I went down on one knee. My consciousness was coming in and out like bad radio reception as Little John rolled onto my chest.

I screamed and pushed off the floor with all my might. I was almost on my knees when Little John rolled off me and started booting me in the ribs. I dropped back down, my breath gone. I wondered if Jack, pulling back the baton above me, might be the last sight I'd ever see.

That's when something completely unexpected happened—an arm snaked through the bars behind Jack.

It was so huge, it barely squeezed through. A massive hand

wrapped itself around the back of Jack's collar. It sounded like a gong when Jack's head was slammed into the bars again and again.

"How you like it, CO?" the convict inquired.

When Little John got off me to help out Jack, I managed, wheezing, to gain my feet. The riot baton Jack had dropped was on the concrete. I stooped, lifted it.

It had been a while since I'd had a nightstick in my hand, walking my first beat in the South Bronx. But I guess it was like riding a bike, because Little John's left knee shattered like balsa wood with my first two-handed swing. I had to backpedal immediately as the big man howled and hopped around surprisingly fast on one foot and came toward me. There was rage in his wide, bulging eyes.

I swung from my toes at his jaw. He ducked, but too little, too late. I broke the baton across his temple. He hit the concrete a half second before the splintered wood.

The inmates were cheering something wicked as I stumbled around the big guard's unconscious hulk. I stepped toward the inmate who was choking Jack with both monstrous hands. Jack's face was turning blue. I picked up the other dropped baton.

"Kill, kill, kill, kill!" the inmates screamed in unison.

I have to admit, the suggestion was tempting. I swung the baton hard. But I didn't hit Jack.

I hit the hand that was very close to throttling the life out of him. The inmate yowled, and he let go of Jack, who slumped unconscious to the floor.

"Hey, like, you're welcome, bro," said the muscular convict behind the bars in a hurt voice. He was nursing his injured hand.

"Sorry, Charlie," I said as I started dragging Jack toward the sealed gym door. "I can't arrest him if he's dead."

But I can give him one good kick in the teeth. Because we're such buddies. And that's what I did, and the inmates went wild.

OF COURSE, it couldn't be quite that easy.

They found the two actual shift foremen, Rhodes and Williams, handcuffed in one of the cells on A-Block.

It turned out that Jack and Little John, whose real names were Rocco Milton and Kenny Robard, being close to the warden as shift supervisors, had heard we were coming. They'd convinced the warden that they'd had nothing to do with the siege of St. Pat's, even though they'd taken part in the sick-out. Then they'd ambushed the two innocent foremen—who'd been in on the sick-out but not the hijacking—and hidden them inside the cell block to get us to go into the population so they could make a play.

I Mirandized Rocco "Jack" Milton in the parking lot of Sing Sing before opening the rear door of my cruiser and shoving him in. Steve Reno left in a paddy wagon filled with the rest of the suspected hijackers. Kenny "Little John" Robard was on the way to the hospital with a fractured skull.

I retrieved something in the trunk of my cruiser before I climbed behind the wheel to drive Jack to New York City. Funny as it sounds, a lot of suspects are dying to tell you what they've done. And the more full of themselves, the more they want to give you the dirty details. I had a feeling Jack was pretty fond of himself.

I stayed silent for the first part of our trip back to Manhattan and let his annoyance build.

"Did you know," Jack finally said, "that in the summer of ninety-five, four guards were taken hostage out on Rikers?"

I glanced at him through the mesh behind me. "Is that right?"

"Only two of us made it out."

"You and Little John?" I said.

"On the money as usual, Mike," Jack said. "Suffice it to say that nobody gave a crap about a few corrections officers, especially the mayor."

"So that's why you killed him? Burned him with cigarettes?"

Jack scratched his chin ponderously. "Between you and me?"

"I wouldn't have it any other way," I said, smiling back at him.

"You better believe it," he said. "The animals who'd gotten their hands on us blinded one of my buddies with a butter knife and put out cigarettes on *our* arms. Wouldn't you know it, Hizzoner decided he was above negotiating with the inmates. I didn't see the mayor by my dead buddy's widow at the funeral, either. Guess you have to be a flatfoot like you to get that kind of special treatment."

I nodded neutrally. I wanted Jack to keep talking.

"When my posttraumatic stress disability claim was denied by the city for the third time, I decided to pull off something large, or die trying. The St. Pat's idea came to me when I moonlighted as security at the state funeral for the previous cardinal. I thought it was going to be so impenetrable, with the legendary Secret Service and all, but I found out those guys were soft, all show."

"What about the other jackers? Your coworkers?" I said. "How'd you convince them to go along?"

"Convince them?" Jack said. "I don't know about New York's Finest, but being a guard chews you up. We're inside the belly of the beast, and we didn't do nothing to get there. Put terrible pay on top of that, divorce and suicide rates in the stratosphere, and hassle from the bosses, you got a gourmet recipe for disaster."

"Sounds heartbreaking," I said. "But executing the First Lady, the mayor, a priest, and John Rooney because you were stressed out? That might be a hard sell to a judge."

Jack didn't seem to have heard me. He was staring off at the side of the road. "We did it for each other," he said quietly. "Go ahead and put us back in jail. Won't matter. Guards do life just like prisoners, only we do it in eight-hour shifts."

"If doing life is what you're worried about, then I got good news," I told the cop killer as I clicked off the tape recorder I had running in the pocket of my Windbreaker. "I'll do everything in my power to see you get the death penalty, Jack."

IT WAS eight o'clock and dark when I pulled to the curb down the block from a small house on Delafield Avenue in the Riverdale section of the Bronx. Steve Reno and his guys were already set up. We had the house surrounded and wired for video and sound.

It was time to pick up the final and most putrid bag of garbage. The inside man. The one Jack called "the Neat Man."

According to one of our snipers perched on the backyard wall, our suspect was inside on the ground floor right now, finishing up dinner with his family.

"Car coming from the south," I said into the radio as a blue Lincoln passed my position. I saw the airport taxi placard in its side window as it slowed before our target's house. "Looks like our boy's ride is here," I said. "Where is he now in the house?"

"Just went upstairs," said the sniper. "He's washing his hands. Okay. He's finished. Coming downstairs."

"Heads up, Steve," I said into my Motorola. "I'm going in." I climbed out of my car.

"Get another fare," I told the taxi hack with a flash of my badge as I stopped in front of the house. "His flight just got canceled."

I rang the doorbell and crouched to the side behind a hedge. There was a small window beside the door, and down the hall I could see a woman and three kids cleaning up the dining room table. I guess they hadn't been invited to Costa Rica with Dad.

A form passed the window, and I drew my Glock. Then the door opened. Struggling with a bulky carry-on and a black suitcase, Paul Martelli looked puzzled as he watched the airport limo pull away without him. That's when I stepped out from beside the hedge.

"Paul, how are ya?" I said. "I was just talking to a friend of yours. Jack. He sends his regards."

I watched a terrible flicker in the FBI negotiator's eyes. A tremor suddenly affected his right hand holding the suitcase, the one nearest to a holstered nine millimeter.

I showed him the Glock I was holding beside my leg—as three sniper laser dots danced on his chest like a squadron of angry bees.

"That would be very poor decision making there, Paul," I told him, "going for that nine. But I'd like to see you try, Neat Man."

"I WA-WA-WANT a lawyer," Paul Martelli said when he was handcuffed to the leg of my squad room desk about half an hour later.

The man's hands were shaking, and circles of sweat had formed beneath the sleeves of his shirt. There was an army of Feds out in the hall, waiting to get their crack at him, but not until I was done.

Jack had already told me most of it. How he and Martelli had become fast friends after the Rikers Island hostage situation. How they found that they shared an undying contempt for the system; how they felt their pathetic pay was beneath them.

Martelli had been the inside man during the siege. He was the mastermind working behind the scenes. Literally having written the book on the subject, he knew what our reactions would be. Plus, he could influence what we did.

"I don't have to explain how the game works, do I? Cooperation is the only thing that can save any of you losers," I said.

Martelli sat there blinking and sweating. "I'll tell you whatever you need to know on one condition," he said.

"What's that?" I said.

"This place is filthy," Martelli said. "I need a moist towelette."

"How was the First Lady killed?" I said after I tossed him one from under the takeout menus inside my desk drawer. Martelli didn't speak again until he was finished meticulously scrubbing his face and hands. He seemed to have calmed down considerably.

"Alvarez did her," he said.

"Jose Alvarez?" I said. "The hijacker who was killed at the dealership during the escape?"

"Actually, his cousin Julio," said Martelli. "We had a pretty tall order. To get a state funeral going, we needed to kill somebody high-profile and make it look like an accident. For months, I pored over potential targets. When I read about the First Lady's allergy and her and the former president's annual holiday meal at L'Arène, I figured we had it solved. Julio quit his guard job and got a prepcook job at L'Arène. When the president and First Lady came in, he put peanut oil in her foie gras in the kitchen."

"So it was all over money?" I asked the FBI agent.

"We can't all be Boy Scouts like you, Mr. Mom," the negotiator said, looking me in the eyes for the first time. "Of course it was about money. Money's what makes this world go round, Mike."

I looked away from Martelli in disgust. An FBI agent with a wife and two kids had been killed during the standoff, and it was obvious Martelli couldn't care less. But I could see panic start in his eyes as I motioned at the door and the Feds walked in for him.

"You wouldn't happen to have another Wet-Nap for the road there, Mike?" he said quickly.

I opened the desk drawer, then slammed it shut.

"Wouldn't you know it," I said. "I'm fresh out."

EPILOGUE
SAINTS

THOUGH it was freezing cold and windy, the sun was shining as we Bennetts made our way to Riverside Park on Saturday morning a week later. Beyond the bare trees, the Hudson River—*our river,* as Maeve used to call it—looked like an endless field of molten silver.

It didn't take very long for me to find the orange-taped stake. My darling wife and I had carefully placed it at the edge of a meadow overlooking the water just three months before.

I put down the oak sapling I was carrying on one shoulder and lifted the stake. I glanced at my oldest son. Brian nodded and stabbed the spade he was holding into the earth.

We all took turns. I had to help with Shawna and Chrissy, but Trent insisted on taking his turn by himself. I finally placed the sapling into the hole we'd made. Then I got down on my knees and started pushing the dirt back in with my hands. Pretty soon, I had help. All of us were on the ground, hands buried in the fresh dirt.

I stood up finally, staring at the baby tree silently. I remembered watching the sun go down on a late picnic we'd had in summer two years before. Before the cancer. The kids catching fireflies as I rested my chin on Maeve's shoulder, the sky turning aqua and gold. I could feel her now as I stood there without her, the way an amputee feels a lost limb, a phantom pain in the heart.

"Mommy's present to us," Chrissy said finally, patting the slender tree trunk gently. "Right, Daddy?"

"That's right, Chrissy." I scooped her up and put her on my shoulders. "Ever since you were little, this was Mommy's favorite place to take you guys. She told me that anytime you wanted to think about her or talk to her, she wanted you to be able to come here, or just look out your window at this spot and think of her."

I gathered our family in a circle around the small tree. I was aware of the single earring I still wore in my left lobe and would always wear, whatever the fashion, whatever my age.

"Mom brought us all together," I said. "So as long as we stay together, she'll always be with us."

I felt more than heard Chrissy start to cry as we were leaving the grassy meadow. I lifted my daughter down from my shoulders and cradled her in my arms as she cried. "What is it, honey?" I said.

"Baby Peep misses Mommy Peep," she said inconsolably. "So much. So much."

"I know," I said, trying and failing to dry her tears and mine at the same time. The wind picked up, drew lines across the still river, painted icicles on our wet cheeks.

"Daddy Peep does, too," I said.

Sharing the Spotlight with
James Patterson

WRITERS are often portrayed as solitary creatures, toiling alone in their garrets. James Patterson, however, obviously loves to collaborate. Since 1996, he has worked with five coauthors (Peter de Jonge, Andrew Gross, Howard Roughan, Maxine Paetro, and Michael Ledwidge), all but one of whom (de Jonge) are published authors in their own right. In addition to the twenty-five novels that carry only Patterson's name (not counting his five children's books), there are sixteen additional books that give credit to a collaborator. Why does he use a cowriter so often? Admits Patterson, "I'm not a fast writer. I struggle through the writing. I can get it done. But I know it's not my strength."

Says Patterson's long-time editor, Michael Pietsch, "A lot of great popular entertainment,

Vital Stats

BORN: March 22, 1947
FAMILY: Wife, Susan; son, Jack, eight years old
FAVORITE GENRE TO WRITE: Young-adult books
LEAST FAVORITE GENRE TO WRITE: Love stories
NEWEST GENRE TO WRITE: Horror (*You've Been Warned,* a novel)
WEBSITE: www.JamesPatterson.com

even serious art, comes out of collaboration." Indeed, other famous writers, such as Joseph Conrad and Stephen King, have successfully worked with co-authors (Conrad with literary novelist Ford Madox Ford and King with thriller writer Peter Straub, among others). But James Patterson takes the notion of

New York's "Statue of Faith"

Manhattan's Saint Patrick's Cathedral, site of most of the action in *Step on a Crack*, is a priceless spiritual symbol to millions of New Yorkers. As Mike Nardy, the fictional caretaker, says in the book, it carries the same emotional weight for many citizens as does the Statue of Liberty.

The cornerstone for Saint Patrick's was laid in 1858, but its doors didn't open to the public until 1879, because construction was interrupted during the Civil War. Built of white marble quarried in New York and Massachusetts, it remains the largest decorated Gothic-style cathedral in the United States, with spires that rise 330 feet into the air. The building attracts more than five and a half million visitors per year and seats 2,200 people. Its pietà is three times larger than Michelangelo's *Pietà* in Vatican City. It has two altars—one of which was designed by Tiffany and Company—and three organs. The cathedral's architect, James Renwick, also designed the Smithsonian Institution in Washington, D.C.

As we learn in *Step on a Crack*, Saint Patrick's has a spectacular rose window, a common feature of Gothic architecture. These windows are characterized by their circular shape, ornate tracery, and rose-like appearance. Like many cathedrals, Saint Patrick's also has a lady chapel, a sanctuary dedicated to the Virgin Mary that traditionally sits east of the high altar.

The eight deceased archbishops of New York—six of whom were cardinals—are all buried in a crypt underneath Saint Patrick's. Several well-known Americans have had their funerals there, including Babe Ruth, Vince Lombardi, and Robert F. Kennedy. Special memorial Masses were held there following the deaths of Andy Warhol and Joe DiMaggio. In addition to *Step on a Crack*, the church also figures prominently in Nelson DeMille's 1981 novel, *Cathedral*.

collaboration to a new level. Pietsch believes that Patterson, who maintains homes in Palm Beach County, Florida, and northern Westchester County, New York, is developing nothing less than a Hollywood-style studio system for writers.

The process, Patterson says, is simple. He'll write a detailed outline (the one for *Step on a Crack* ran to thirty pages), and then his coauthor will pen the first draft. Patterson will write the subsequent drafts—often it takes as many as seven to get the story right. For *Step on a Crack,* coauthor Michael Ledwidge sent his work to Patterson several chapters at a time. Revisions came back, mostly having to do with the pace, but through it all the two writers maintained a friendly, cooperative relationship.

Ledwidge says he agreed to become Patterson's coauthor "at about the speed of light." The thirty-six-year-old Bronx-born writer, who lives in Avon, Connecticut, solicited the older writer's advice while working as a doorman in Manhattan and writing his first novel in his spare time. After it was published, Ledwidge came out with two more novels, all with lukewarm sales, and had to take a job as a telephone repair-

man to make ends meet. But now his future as a writer looks rosy. "It's like a dream," Ledwidge says, "to have one job, not two. Everyone is always talking about how to market yourself . . . now I don't have to worry about that."

> Patterson has a folder filled with ideas. . . . "I'd love to write all of them, but obviously I can't."

Patterson's prodigious imagination and his talent for developing storylines are legendary. He has a three-inch-thick folder filled with ideas. "Stories are what light Jim's lamp," says Steve Bowen, the president of James Patterson Entertainment, a firm with five full-time employees devoted to driving sales of Patterson's books and developing his stories in other formats, such as films and video games. Five to ten times a week, Patterson will ask Bowen what he thinks of a new plotline. Says the prolific idea man and author, "I'd love to write all of them, but obviously I can't." ∎

AN

IRISH

COUNTRY

DOCTOR

A Novel

Patrick Taylor

"A grand read from a grand man."
—Malachy McCourt, New York Times bestselling author of A Monk Swimming

1

You Can't Get There from Here

BARRY Laverty—*Doctor* Barry Laverty—his medical internship just finished, ink barely dry on his degree, pulled his beat-up Volkswagen Beetle to the side of the road and peered at a map lying on the passenger seat. Six Road Ends was clearly marked. He stared through the car1's insect-splattered windscreen. Judging by the maze of narrow country roads that ran one into the other just up ahead, somewhere at the end of one of those blackthorn-hedged byways lay the village of Ballybucklebo. But which road should he take? And, he reminded himself, there was more to that question than simple geography.

Most of his graduating classmates from the medical school of the Queen's University of Belfast had clear plans for their careers. But he hadn't a clue. General practice? Specialize? And if so, which specialty? Barry shrugged. He was twenty-four, single, no responsibilities. He knew he had all the time in the world to think about his medical future, but his immediate prospects might not be bright if he were late for his five-o'clock appointment. And though finding a direction for his life might be important, his most pressing need was to earn enough to pay off the loan on the car.

He scowled at the map and retraced the road he had traveled from Belfast. The Six Road Ends lay near the margin of the paper. No Ballybucklebo in sight. What to do? He looked up, and as he did, he glimpsed himself in the rearview mirror. Blue eyes looked back at him from a clean-shaven oval face. His tie was askew. No matter how carefully he tied the thing, the knot always managed to wander off under one collar tip. He understood the importance of first impressions and did not want to look scruffy. He tugged the tie back into place, then tried to smooth down the cowlick on the crown of his fair hair, but up it popped. He shrugged. It would just have to stay that way. At least his hair was cut short, not like the style affected by that new musical group, the Beatles.

Perhaps, he thought, there would be a signpost at the junction. He got out of the vehicle, and the springs creaked. Brunhilde, as he called his car, was protesting about the weight of his worldly goods: two suitcases—one with his meager wardrobe, the other crammed with medical texts; a doctor's medical bag tucked under the VW's hood; and a fly rod, creel, and hip waders lying in the backseat. He leaned against the car door, conscious that his five-foot-eight slightly built frame gave him barely enough height to peer over Brunhilde's domed roof. Even standing on tiptoe he could see no evidence of a signpost. Perhaps it was hidden behind the hedges.

He walked to the junction and looked around to find a grave deficiency of signposts. Maybe Ballybucklebo is like Brigadoon, he thought, and only appears for one day every hundred years. He walked back to the car in the warmth of the Ulster afternoon, breathing in the gorse's perfume from the fields at either side of the road. He heard the liquid notes of a blackbird hiding in the fuchsia that grew wild in the hedgerow, the flowers drooping purple and scarlet in the summer air. Somewhere a cow lowed in basso counterpoint to the blackbird's treble.

Barry savored the moment. He might be unclear about what his future held, but one thing was certain. Nothing could ever persuade him that there was anywhere he would choose to live other than here in Northern Ireland.

As he approached the car, he thought, I'll just have to pick a road and . . . He was pleasantly surprised to see a figure mounted on a bicycle crest the low hill and pedal sedately along the road.

"Excuse me." Barry stepped into the path of the oncoming cyclist. The cyclist wobbled, braked, and stood, one foot on the ground and the other on a pedal. "Good afternoon," Barry said. He was addressing a gangly youth, innocent face half hidden under a soft-crowned tweed hat but not hidden well enough to disguise a set of buckteeth that would be the envy of every hare in the Six Counties. "I wonder if you could help me?"

"Aye?" The cyclist lifted his hat and scratched his ginger hair. "Maybe."

"I'm looking for Ballybucklebo."

"Ballybucklebo?" His brow knitted.

"Can you tell me how to get there?"

"Ballybucklebo?" He pursed his lips. "Boys-a-boys, thon's a grand wee place, so it is."

Barry tried not to let his growing exasperation show. "I'm sure it is, but I have to get there by five."

"Five? Today, like?" The youth fumbled in the fob pocket of his waistcoat and produced a pocket watch. "Five? You've no much time left."

"I know that. If you could just—"

"Och, aye." He pointed straight ahead. "Take that road. Follow your nose till you come to Willy John McCoubrey's red barn."

"Red barn. Right."

"Now you *don't* turn there."

"Oh."

"Not at all. Keep right on. You'll see a black-and-white cow in a field—unless Willy John has her in the red barn for milking. Now go past her and take the road to your right." As he spoke, the youth pointed to the left.

Barry felt confused. "First right past the black-and-white cow?"

"That's her," he said, continuing to point left. "From there it's only a wee doddle. Mind you"—he started to remount his bike—"if I'd been you, I wouldn't have tried to get to Ballybucklebo from here in the first place."

"Thank you," said Barry, stifling his desire to laugh. "Oh, and by the way, you wouldn't happen to know the doctor there?"

The youth's eyebrows shot up. His eyes widened, and he let go a long, low whistle before he said, "Himself? Dr. O'Reilly? I do, sir. In soul, I do." With that, he mounted and pedaled furiously away.

Barry climbed back into Brunhilde and wondered why his adviser had suddenly taken flight at the mere mention of Dr. O'Reilly. Well, he thought, if Willy John's cow was in the right field, he'd soon find out. His appointment at five was with none other than Dr. Fingal Flahertie O'Reilly.

BARRY read the lines on a brass plate screwed to the wall beside the green-painted front door of a three-story house:

DR. F. F. O'REILLY, M.B., B.CH., B.A.O.
PHYSICIAN AND SURGEON
HOURS: MONDAY TO FRIDAY, 9 A.M. TO NOON.

By the grace of Willy John McCoubrey's black-and-white cow, he had arrived with five minutes to spare. He tightened his grip on his brand-new black leather bag, stepped back, and looked around. On either side of the doorway, bow windows arced from gray pebbledashed walls. To his right, through the glass, the furniture of a dining room was clearly visible. So, Barry thought, like many country general practitioners, Dr. O'Reilly must run his practice from home. And if the man's voice, raised and hectoring, that Barry could hear coming from behind the drawn curtains of the left-hand window was anything to go by, the doctor was in.

"You're an eejit, Seamus Galvin. A born-again, blathering, buck eejit."

Barry could not hear the reply. Somewhere inside, a door banged against a wall. He took a step back and glanced over his shoulder at a gravel walkway leading from the front gate, rosebushes flanking the path. He sensed movement and swung back to face a large man—huge, in fact—standing, legs astraddle, in the open doorway. The ogre's bent nose was alabaster, the rest of his face puce, presumably, Barry thought, because the big man must be tiring of carrying a smaller man by the collar of his jacket and the seat of his moleskin trousers. As the small man wriggled and made high-pitched squeaks, he waved his left foot, which Barry noticed was quite bare.

The large man swung the smaller one to and fro, then released his grip. Barry gaped as the victim's upward flight and keening were cut short by a rapid descent into the nearest rosebush. "Buck eejit," the giant roared, and hurled a shoe and a sock after the ejectee.

Barry flinched. He held his black bag in front of himself.

"The next time, Seamus Galvin, you come here after hours on my half day and want me to look at your sore ankle, wash your bloody feet!"

Barry turned away, ready to beat a retreat, but the path was blocked by the departing Galvin, clutching his footwear, hobbling toward the gate and muttering, "Yes, Dr. O'Reilly, sir. I will, Dr. O'Reilly, sir."

Barry thought of the cyclist who had fled at the mere mention of Dr. O'Reilly. Good Lord, if what Barry had witnessed was an example of the man's bedside manner . . .

"And what the hell do you want?"

Barry swung to face his interrogator. "Dr. O'Reilly?"

"No. The archangel Gabriel. Can you not read the plate?"

"I'm Laverty."

"Laverty? Well, push off. I'm not buying any."

"I'm *Dr.* Laverty. I answered your advertisement in the *British Medical Journal*. I was to have an interview about the assistant's position." I will not let this bully intimidate me, he thought.

"*That* Laverty. Well, man, why on earth didn't you say so?" O'Reilly offered a hand the size of a soup plate.

Barry felt his knuckles grind together, but he refused to flinch as he met Dr. O'Reilly's gaze. He was staring into a pair of deep-set brown eyes under bushy eyebrows. He noted deep laughter lines around the eyes and saw that the pallor had left O'Reilly's nose, a large bent proboscis with a definite list to port. It had now assumed the plum color of its surrounding cheeks.

"Come in, Laverty." O'Reilly stepped aside and waited for Barry to precede him into a thinly carpeted hall. "Door on your left."

Barry went into the room with the drawn curtains. An open roll-top desk stood against one green wall. Piles of prescription pads, papers, and patients' records lay in disarray on the desktop. Above, O'Reilly's framed diploma dangled from a nail. Barry stole a peep: TRINITY COLLEGE, DUBLIN, 1936. In front of the desk were a swivel chair and a plain wooden chair.

"Have a pew." O'Reilly lowered his bulk into the swivel seat and pushed a pair of half-moon spectacles onto his nose. "So you want to be my assistant?"

Barry had thought he did, but after the ejection of Seamus Galvin, he wasn't so sure. He sat, settling his bag on his lap. "Well, I—"

"Course you do," said O'Reilly, pulling a briar pipe from his jacket pocket. He held a lighted match over the bowl. "Golden opportunity."

Barry noticed that he kept sliding forward on his seat. He had to brace his feet firmly on the carpet and keep shoving his backside upward.

O'Reilly wagged his index finger. "You'll love it. Might even be a partnership in it for you. Course, you'll have to do as I tell you for a while until you get to know the ropes."

Barry hitched himself back up his seat. "Does that mean I'll have to hurl patients into the rosebushes?"

"What?" A hint of pallor returned to the big man's nose. Was that a sign of temper? Barry wondered.

"I said, Does that mean—"

"I heard you the first time, boy. Now listen, have you any experience with country patients?"

"Not ex—"

"Thought not," said O'Reilly, emitting a puff of tobacco smoke like the blast from the funnels of R.M.S. *Queen Mary* when she blew her boilers. "You'll have a lot to learn."

Barry felt a cramp in his left calf. He shoved himself back up his seat again.

"Lesson number one," said O'Reilly. "Never, never, never"—with each "never," he poked at Barry with the stem of his pipe—"*never* let the customers get the upper hand. If you do, they'll run you ragged."

"Don't you think dumping a man bodily into your garden is a little—"

"I used to . . . until I met Seamus Galvin. If you take the job and get to know that skiver as well as I do . . ." O'Reilly shook his head.

Barry stood and massaged the back of his leg.

O'Reilly began to laugh in great throaty rumbles. "Leg stiff?"

"Yes. Something's wrong with this chair."

O'Reilly's chuckles grew deeper. "No, there's not. I fixed it."

"Fixed it?"

"Oh, aye. Some of the weary, walking wounded in Ballybucklebo seem to think when they get in here to see me, it's my job to listen to their lamentations till the cows come home. A single-handed country GP doesn't have that sort of time." He pushed his spectacles farther up his nose. "That's why I advertised for an assistant. There's too much work in this place." O'Reilly had stopped laughing. His brown-eyed gaze was fixed on Barry's eyes as he said softly, "Take the job, boy. I need the help."

Barry hesitated. Did he really want to work for this big, coarse man? He saw O'Reilly's florid cheeks, the cauliflower ears that must have been acquired in the boxing ring, and a shock of black hair, like a badly stooked hayrick, and decided to play for time. "What have you done to this chair?"

O'Reilly's grin could be described only as demonic. "I sawed an inch off the front legs. Not very comfortable, is it?"

"No," said Barry, pushing himself back up the seat.

"Don't want to stay long, do you?"

"No," said Barry, thinking, I'm not sure I want to stay here at all.

"Neither do the customers. They come in and go out like a fiddler's elbow."

How could a responsible physician ever take a proper history if his practice ran like a human conveyor belt? Barry asked himself.

He rose. "I'm not sure I do want to work here . . ."

O'Reilly's laugh boomed through the room. "Don't take yourself so seriously, son."

Barry felt the flush begin under his collar. "Dr. O'Reilly, I—"

"Laverty, there are some *really* sick people here who *do* need us, you know." O'Reilly was no longer laughing.

Barry heard the "us" and was surprised to find that it pleased him. "I need help."

"Well, I—"

"Great," said O'Reilly, putting another match to his pipe, rising and marching to the door. "Come on, you've seen the surgery. Why our American cousins insist on calling it the office is beyond me. I'll show you the rest of the shop."

"But I—"

"Leave your bag there. You'll need it tomorrow." With that, O'Reilly vanished into the hall, leaving Barry little choice but to park his medical bag and follow. Immediately opposite he could see into the dining room, but O'Reilly charged along the hall, past a staircase with an ornate mahogany balustrade. Then he stopped and flung a door wide open. Barry hurried to catch up.

"Waiting room."

Barry saw a large room, wallpapered with roses. Wooden chairs were arranged around the walls. O'Reilly pointed to a door in the far wall. "Patients let themselves in here; we come down from the surgery, take whoever's next back with us, deal with them, and show them out the front door."

"On their feet, I hope."

The big man chuckled. "You're no dozer, are you, Laverty?"

Barry kept his counsel as O'Reilly continued. "It's a good system; stops the customers swapping symptoms or demanding the same medicine as the last customer. Right . . ." He headed for the staircase. "Come on."

Barry followed up a flight of stairs to a broad landing. Framed photographs of a warship hung on the walls.

"Sitting room's in there." O'Reilly indicated a pair of paneled doors.

Barry nodded but looked more closely at the pictures of the battleship. "Excuse me, Dr. O'Reilly, is that H.M.S. *Warspite?*"

O'Reilly's foot paused on the first step of the next flight. "How'd you know that?"

"My dad served in her."

"Holy thunder. Are you Tom Laverty's boy?"

"Yes."

"I'll be damned."

So, thought Barry, will I. His father had talked about a certain Surgeon Commander O'Reilly who had been welterweight boxing champion of the Mediterranean Fleet—that would account for O'Reilly's ears and nose. In his dad's opinion, O'Reilly had been the finest medical officer afloat.

"I'll be . . . Laverty's boy." O'Reilly held out his hand. His handshake was firm. "You're the man for the job. Thirty-five pounds a week, every other Saturday off, room and board all in."

"Thirty-five pounds?"

"I'll show you your room."

"WHAT'LL IT BE?" O'REILLY stood at a sideboard that bore cut-glass decanters and ranks of glasses.

"Small sherry, please."

Barry sat in a big armchair. O'Reilly's upstairs sitting room was comfortably furnished. Three watercolors of game birds adorned the wall over a wide fireplace. Two walls were hidden by floor-to-ceiling bookcases. From Barry's quick appraisal of the titles—from Plato's *Republic,* Caesar's *De Bello Gallica,* and A. A. Milne's *Winnie-the-Pooh* to the collected works of W. Somerset Maugham, Graham Greene, and John Steinbeck—O'Reilly's reading tastes were wide-ranging. His record collection, stacked haphazardly beside a gramophone, was equally eclectic. Beethoven's symphonies were jumbled in with old 78s by Bix Beiderbecke and Jelly Roll Morton, along with the Beatles's most recent LP.

"Here you are." O'Reilly handed Barry a glass, sat heavily in another armchair, and propped his stoutly booted feet on a coffee table. Then he lifted his own glass, which Barry thought could have done service as a fire bucket if it hadn't been filled to the brim with Irish whiskey.

My God, Barry thought, looking more closely at O'Reilly's ruddy cheeks. Don't tell me he's a raging drunk.

O'Reilly, clearly oblivious to Barry's scrutiny, nodded toward the picture window. "Would you look at that?"

Barry looked past the moss-grown, lopsided steeple of a church across the road from O'Reilly's house, down over the rooftops of the terrace cottages of Ballybucklebo's main street, and out over the sand dunes of the foreshore to where Belfast Lough, the white-capped body of cobalt-blue water that separated County Down from the distant Antrim Hills, stretched out beneath a sky as blue as cornflowers.

"It's lovely, Dr. O'Reilly."

"Fingal, my boy. For Oscar." O'Reilly's smile was avuncular.

"Oscar, er, Fingal?"

"No. Not Oscar Fingal. Wilde."

"Oscar Fingal Wilde, Fingal?" Barry knew he was getting lost.

"Oscar Fingal O'Flahertie Wills Wilde. I was named for him. For Oscar Wilde. My father was a classical scholar." O'Reilly took a deep drink. "Us country GPs aren't all utterly unlettered."

Barry felt a blush start. His first impressions of the big man might not have been entirely accurate. He sipped his sherry.

"So, Laverty," O'Reilly said, clearly ignoring Barry's discomfort. "What's it to be? Do you want the job?"

Before Barry could answer, a bell jangled from somewhere below. "Damn," said O'Reilly, "another customer. Come on."

He rose. Barry followed.

O'Reilly opened the front door.

Seamus Galvin stood on the doorstep. In each hand, he carried a live lobster. "Good evening, Doctor sir," he said, thrusting the beasts at O'Reilly. "I've washed me foot, so I have."

"Have you?" said O'Reilly sternly, passing the squirming creatures to Barry. "Come in and I'll take a look at your hind leg."

"Thank you, Doctor sir, thank you very much." Galvin hesitated. "And who's this young gentleman?" he asked.

Barry was so busy avoiding the crustaceans' clattering claws, he nearly missed O'Reilly's reply. "This is Dr. Laverty. He's my new assistant. I'll be showing him the ropes tomorrow."

2
Morning Has Broken

BARRY woke to the jangling of his alarm clock. His attic room had just enough space for a bed, a bedside table, and a wardrobe. Last night he'd unpacked, put his few clothes away, and propped his fishing rod in a corner near the dormer window.

He rose, drew the curtains, then headed for the bathroom. As he shaved, he thought about last night. O'Reilly had strapped Seamus Galvin's ankle, put the lobsters in the kitchen sink, taken Barry back up to the sitting room, and poured more drinks. He'd explained that for the first month, they'd work together so Barry could get to know the patients, the running of the practice, and the geography of Ballybucklebo and the surrounding countryside.

Somehow the evening had slipped by. Despite a steady intake of Old Bushmills Irish whiskey, O'Reilly had given no sign of ill effects. After two sherries, Barry had been grateful to be shown to his quarters in the attic and wished a very good night.

He rinsed his razor and looked in the mirror. Just a tad of red in the whites of his eyes. Had the sherry affected his judgment so much? Certainly he had no recollection of actually agreeing to take the job, but it seemed that once O'Reilly made up his mind, lesser mortals had no choice but to go along. Well, in for a penny . . . He dried his face, went back to his garret, and dressed. Best trousers, best shoes, clean shirt.

"Move yourself, Laverty. We haven't got all day," O'Reilly roared up the stairwell.

Barry knotted his Queen's University tie, slipped on a sports jacket, and headed for the stairs.

"EAT up however little much is in it, Dr. Laverty dear."

Barry looked up from his plate of Ulster mixed grill—bacon, sausage, fried eggs, tomatoes, lamb chop, and slices of fried soda bread—into the happy face of Mrs. Kincaid. He saw silver hair done up in a chignon, black eyes like polished jets set between roseate cheeks, a smiling mouth above three chins.

"I'll do my best."

"Good lad. You'll be having this for breakfast a lot," she said, setting a plate in front of O'Reilly. "Himself here is a grand man for the pan, so."

Barry heard the soft Cork lilt of her voice, with the habit Cork folk had of adding "so" at the end of a sentence.

Mrs. Kincaid left. O'Reilly muttered something through a mouthful of sausage.

"I beg your pardon?"

O'Reilly swallowed. "I forgot to warn you about Kinky. She's a powerful woman. Been with me for years. Housekeeper, cook, and Cerberus."

"She guards the gates of Hades?"

"Like the three-headed dog himself. The customers have to get up early in the morning to put one past Kinky. You'll see. Now, get stuck into your grub. We've to be in the surgery in fifteen minutes."

Mrs. Kincaid reappeared. "Tea, Doctor?" She poured his tea and gave him a sheet of paper. "That's your afternoon calls for today," she said. "Maggie wanted you to drop round, but I told her to come into the surgery."

"Maggie MacCorkle?" O'Reilly sighed and dabbed at an egg stain on his tie. "All right. Thanks, Kinky."

"Better she comes here than you drive ten miles to her cottage." Mrs. Kincaid cocked her head and studied the mess on O'Reilly's tie. "And take off the grubby thing and I'll wash it for you, so."

To Barry's surprise, O'Reilly meekly undid the knot and handed the tie to Mrs. Kincaid, who sniffed, turned, and left, remarking, "And don't forget to put on a clean one."

"WOULD you take a look?" whispered O'Reilly. "You'd need five loaves and two small fishes to feed that bloody multitude."

Barry stared through the gap where O'Reilly held ajar the door to the waiting room. It was standing room only. How on earth was O'Reilly going to see so many patients before noon?

O'Reilly opened the door wide. "Morning."

A chorus of "Morning, Dr. O'Reilly" echoed from the waiting room.

"I want you all to meet Dr. Laverty," he said. "My new assistant. Dr. Laverty has come down from the Queen's University to give me a hand."

A voice muttered, "He looks awful young, so he does."

"He is, James Guiggan. The youngest doctor ever to take the first prize for learning at the university."

Barry tried to protest that he was no such thing, but he felt

O'Reilly's hand grip his forearm and heard him whisper, "Remember lesson number one." *Never let the customers get the upper hand* echoed in Barry's head as O'Reilly said, "Right. How many's here for tonics?"

Several people rose.

O'Reilly counted. ". . . five, six. I'll take you lot first. Hang on a minute." He turned and headed for the surgery.

Barry followed. He watched as O'Reilly produced six hypo-dermics, filled them with a pink fluid from a rubber-topped bottle, and laid them in a row on a towel on top of a small trolley.

"What's that, Dr. O'Reilly?"

O'Reilly grinned. "Vitamin B-12."

"B-12? But that's not—"

"I know it's not a tonic. There's no such thing. *You* know it's not a tonic, but"—his grin widened—"*they* don't know it's not a tonic. Now, go get 'em."

"All of them?"

"Every last one."

Barry headed for the waiting room. Heavens, this was hardly the kind of medicine he'd been taught. "Would all those for tonics please follow me?"

The six victims trooped into the surgery, where O'Reilly waited by the trolley.

"Along the couch."

Three men and three women dutifully faced the examination couch.

"Bend over."

Three trousered and three calico-dressed backsides were pre-sented. Barry watched, mouth agape, as O'Reilly moved his trolley to the start of the line. He stopped and grabbed a syringe in one hand, a methylated spirits-reeking cotton-wool ball in the other, and dabbed the calico over the first derriere. "Listerian antisepsis," he intoned as he jabbed the needle home.

"Ouch," yelped a skinny woman. The process was repeated down the line—dab, jab, "Ouch"; dab, jab, "Ouch."

"Right," said O'Reilly. "Off you go. You'll all be running around like spring chickens when that stuff starts to work."

"Thank you, Doctor sir," said six voices in unison. The patients filed out and left by the front door.

O'Reilly turned to Barry and said, "Don't look so disapproving, boy. It'll do them no harm, and half of them will feel better. I know it's only a placebo, but we're here to make folks feel better."

BARRY spent the morning acting as a runner between the waiting room and the surgery and sitting on the examining couch watching as O'Reilly dealt with a procession of men with sore backs, women and their runny-nosed children, coughs, sniffles, and earaches. Occasionally, O'Reilly would seek Barry's opinion, always treating the advice with great solemnity.

Barry noticed that O'Reilly knew every patient by name and had an encyclopedic knowledge of their medical history.

At last the waiting room was empty.

O'Reilly sprawled in his chair, and Barry returned to what now was his familiar place on the couch.

"So," asked O'Reilly, "what do you think?"

"Not much about you injecting people through their clothes, and I won no prizes at university."

O'Reilly produced his briar and lit it. "Country folk are a pretty conservative lot. You're a young lad. Why should they trust you?"

Barry stiffened. "Because I'm a doctor."

O'Reilly guffawed. "It's not what you call yourself, *Dr. Laverty*; it's what you do that counts here. All I did was give you a head start."

Someone knocked on the door. O'Reilly looked over his half-moons at Barry. "See who that is, will you?"

Barry walked stiffly to the door. Head start, he thought. As if he wasn't fully qualified. He opened the door to a woman in her sixties. Her face was weathered; her upper lip sported a fine brown mustache. Her nose curved down; her chin curved up like that of Punch in the *Punch and Judy* show. She wore a straw hat with two wilted geraniums stuck in the band. Her torso was hidden under layers of different-colored woolen cardigans, and under the hem of her rusty ankle-length skirt peeped the toes of a pair of Wellington boots. When she smiled, he could see that she was as toothless as an oyster. Her ebony eyes twinkled. "Is himself in?"

Barry felt a presence at his shoulder.

"Maggie," he heard O'Reilly say. "Maggie MacCorkle. Come in." O'Reilly ushered her to the patients' chair and went and sat on the examining couch. "This is my assistant, Dr. Laverty. I'd like him to see to you today, Maggie. Nothing like a second opinion."

Barry stared at O'Reilly, nodded, and strode to the swivel chair. "Good morning, Mrs. MacCorkle."

She sniffed. "It's *Miss* MacCorkle, so it is." Barry glanced to where O'Reilly sat, arms folded, expressionless.

"Sorry. *Miss* MacCorkle. And what seems to be the trouble?"

"The headaches."

"I see. When did they start?"

"They've always been acute, but last night they got something chronic, so they did. They were desperate." She leaned forward and said with great solemnity, "I near took the rickets."

He stifled a smile. "I see. And where exactly are they?"

She whispered conspiratorially, "There." She held one hand above the crown of her flowery hat.

Barry jerked back in his chair. He wondered where O'Reilly kept the necessary forms for certifying that someone was insane.

"Above your head?"

"Oh, aye. A good two inches."

"I see." He steepled his fingers. "And have you been hearing voices?"

She stiffened. "What do you mean?"

"Well, I . . ." He looked helplessly at O'Reilly, who slipped down off the couch.

"What Dr. Laverty means is, do you have any ringing in your ears?"

"Ding-dong or brrring?" Maggie asked, turning to O'Reilly.

"You tell me," he said.

"Ding-dong, Doctor dear. Ding-dong it is. Dingy-dingy-dong."

"Mmm," said O'Reilly. "Are the pains in the middle or off to one side?"

"Over to the left, so they are."

"That's what we call 'eccentric,' Maggie."

That's what I'd call the pair of you, thought Barry.

"Eccentric? Is that bad, Doctor?"

"Not at all," said O'Reilly. "Fix you up in no time."

Her shoulders relaxed. She smiled up at O'Reilly, but when she turned to Barry, her stare was as icy as the wind that sweeps the lough in winter.

O'Reilly grabbed a small bottle of vitamin pills from the desk. "These'll do the trick."

Maggie rose and accepted the bottle.

O'Reilly gently propelled her toward the door. "These are special. You have to take them exactly as I tell you." His next words were delivered with weighted solemnity: "Exactly half an hour before the pain starts."

"Oh, thank you, Doctor dear." Her smile was radiant. She made a little curtsey, turned, and faced Barry, but she spoke to O'Reilly. "Mind you," she said, "this young Laverty fellow . . . he's a lot to learn."

BARRY sat back in his dining-room chair and pushed his lunch plate away. Certainly, he thought, O'Reilly's clinical methods might leave something to be desired, but—he burped gently—he was willing to forgive the man's eccentricities as long as Mrs. Kincaid's cooking stayed at its current level.

"Home visits," said O'Reilly from across the table. He consulted a piece of paper. "Anyone who's too sick to come to the surgery phones Kinky in the morning, and she gives me my list."

"The one she gave you at breakfast?"

"Aye, and she tells me to add any who call during the morning. We're lucky today—just one. At the Kennedys'." He rose. "Let's get moving. There's a rugby game tonight on the telly. I want to get back in time for the kickoff."

Barry followed him down the hall and into the kitchen, where Mrs. Kincaid greeted them with a smile. "Would you like them lobsters for supper, Doctor dear?"

"That would be grand, Kinky." O'Reilly's forward progress stopped. "Kinky, is tonight your Women's Union night?"

"Aye, so."

"We'll have the lobsters cold. Leave them with a bit of salad and get you away early." He charged on, ignoring Mrs. Kincaid's thanks, opened the back door, and ushered Barry through.

He found himself in a spacious garden. Vegetables grew in a plot by the left-hand hedge. Some apple trees were bowed over a well-kept lawn. A chestnut tree at the far end drooped branches over a fence and shaded a dog kennel.

"Arthur!" yelled O'Reilly. "Arthur Guinness!"

A vast black Labrador hurled himself from the kennel, charged over the grass, and leaped at O'Reilly.

"Who's a good boy, then?" O'Reilly said, thumping the dog's flank. "I call him Arthur Guinness because he's Irish, black, and has a great head on him, just like the stout. Arthur Guinness, meet Dr. Laverty."

"Arf," said Arthur, immediately transferring his affections to Barry, who fought desperately to push the animal away. "Ararf."

"Arthur Guinness is the best bloody gundog in Ulster."

"You shoot, Dr. O'Reilly?"

"Fingal, my boy, Fingal. Yes. Arthur and I enjoy a day at the ducks, don't we, Arthur?"

"Yarf," said Arthur, and wandered off in the general direction of his kennel.

"He likes you," said O'Reilly as he walked on and then opened the back gate. "Garage is out here." He crossed a lane to a dilapidated shed and swung an overhead door upward. Barry peered inside and saw a black long-hood Rover, one of a line of cars that had not been produced for at least fifteen years.

O'Reilly climbed in and started the engine. It grumbled, spluttered, and backfired. Barry hopped into the passenger seat. O'Reilly put the car in gear and nosed out onto the lane. The car stank of damp dog and tobacco smoke. Barry wound down a window.

O'Reilly turned left onto the street and drove past his house, past the church with the lopsided steeple, and on along Ballybucklebo's main thoroughfare. Terraces of whitewashed, single-story cottages, some thatched and some with slate roofs, lined the route. They came to a crossroads and halted at a red traffic light. A maypole, paint peeling, leaning to the left, stood on the far corner.

"It's fun here on Beltane—that's the old Celtic May Day," said O'Reilly, pointing to the pole. "Bonfires, dancing, the pursuit of young virgins . . . The locals aren't far removed from their pagan ancestors when there's the chance of a good party." He revved the engine and gestured at the road to the right. "Go down there and you'll end up at the seashore; left takes you up into the Ballybucklebo Hills."

Barry nodded. The light changed. O'Reilly slipped the clutch and roared ahead. He gestured vaguely around. "The throbbing heart of Ballybucklebo."

Two-story buildings now. Greengrocer, butcher, convenience store, and a larger building, upon which hung a sign: THE BLACK SWAN. Barry noticed a familiar figure, left ankle bandaged, limping toward the front door.

"Galvin," said O'Reilly. "That one'd drain the lough if it was Guinness stout." He changed up with a grinding of gears. "Now, you can take this road we're on to Belfast, or if you look to starboard . . . See? You can take the train."

Barry glanced to his right to see a diesel train moving slowly along a raised embankment. Interesting, he thought. He might just do that on his day off. He'd like to visit one of his friends from medical school.

Suddenly he was hurled forward as O'Reilly braked. "Bloody cow!"

Barry saw a black-and-white bovine, eyes soft, reflecting the utter vacuity behind them, ambling along the center of the road, chewing its cud with delicate deliberation.

O'Reilly wound down his window. "Hoosh on, cow. Hoosh."

The animal lowered its head, emitted a single doleful moo, and budged not one inch.

"Right," said O'Reilly. He dismounted, slammed the door, and walked to face the cow. He took a horn in one hand and pulled.

"Move yourself," O'Reilly roared.

The cow flicked her ears, lowered her head, and skittered to the side of the road. O'Reilly climbed back into the car, slammed it into gear, and took off with a screeching of rubber on tarmac.

"Animals," he said. "They're one of the delights of country practice. You just have to get used to dealing with them."

"Fine," said Barry, unaware of how soon Dr. O'Reilly's words would be shown to be true.

O'REILLY grunted and then ground the gears. Barry listened to the grumbling of the engine as the rear tires whined and spun . . . and spun.

"Damn," said O'Reilly. "We'll have to walk." He reached over to the backseat and grabbed his black bag and a pair of Wellingtons, which he now began to change into. "Out."

Barry stepped out—and sank to his ankles in a ditch. He hauled each foot loose from the mud and squelched to the lane's grassy verge. Blast! His shoes and best trousers were filthy. He turned and stared at a farmhouse at the end of the rutted lane. "Is that where we're going, Fingal?"

"Aye, that's the Kennedys' place."

"Is there some other way to get there? My shoes . . ."

"Heaven almighty! You should always bring wellies. All right, we'll cut through the fields." Barry noticed just a hint of pallor on the tip of O'Reilly's nose. "Get a move on. I don't want to miss that rugby match." The big man hefted his bag, pushed open a rusting five-bar gate in the blackthorn hedge, and strode off.

Barry stared at the ruin of his shoes—his only pair of good shoes. He heard O'Reilly yelling, "Is it today you were coming?"

Barry walked to where O'Reilly stood. The grass in the pasture was knee-deep. And damp, very damp. Barry walked purposefully ahead. Oh, well, he thought, at least the dew would wash off some of the mud.

"What kept you?"

"Dr. O'Reilly," Barry began refusing to be intimidated, "I came as fast as I could. My shoes and my trousers are ruined. I—"

"What," asked O'Reilly, "do you know about pigs?"

"I fail to see what pigs have to do with my clothes."

"Suit yourself, but there's one coming." O'Reilly started to walk rapidly.

Barry hesitated. Coming toward them was a pink something with the dimensions of a small hippopotamus. Its eyes were red and distinctly malevolent.

Barry set off at a canter in pursuit of O'Reilly and caught up with him halfway between the gate and the end of the field. "It is a pig."

"Brilliant," said O'Reilly, lengthening his stride. "I've read somewhere that domesticated boars can turn ugly. Bloody big teeth." His gait moved up to a fully developed trot and opened a fair gap between Barry and himself.

Barry risked a backward glance. The beast was gaining. He began to sprint. Ten yards from the far hedge, Barry passed a flagging O'Reilly. The extra helping of Mrs. Kincaid's steak-and-kidney pudding must be slowing O'Reilly down, Barry thought as he cleared a low gate. He almost collided with a small grinning man in a flat cap, who stood in the farmyard. Before Barry could begin to explain, the quiet of the afternoon was shattered by sounds of crashing and rending, and he saw O'Reilly break through the blackthorn hedge like a tank.

O'Reilly came to a halt, examined the rents in his tweed suit, and tried to control his labored breathing. Then he marched over to the cloth-capped stranger, who, Barry noticed, had a ferocious squint but was laughing heartily.

Although O'Reilly's cheeks were scarlet, despite his recent exertions, his nose tip was alabaster.

"Dermot Kennedy," he bellowed, "what's so bloody funny?"

Mr. Kennedy was doubled over, laughing heartily. "Thon's no boar, Doctor dear. Thon's Gertrude," he gasped. "Jeannie's pet sow. She only just wanted her snout scratched."

"Oh," said O'Reilly.

"Right," said Barry. "Animals are, I believe—and please correct me if I'm misquoting you, Dr. O'Reilly—'one of the delights of country practice. You just have to get used to dealing with them.' "

"You can do that if you like, Doctor sir," said Mr. Kennedy, his laughter gone, "but it's really the farmer's job. Doctors keep an eye to the sick, and"—he hesitated and glanced down—"I'm powerful sorry for dragging you out here, so I am, but I'm sore worried about our Jeannie. Would you come and take a look at her, sir?"

BARRY followed Mr. Kennedy and Dr. O'Reilly to the farmhouse, a single-story building, whitewashed and thatched with straw. Smoke drifted upward from a chimney. Black shutters flanked every window.

Barry heard Mr. Kennedy say, "Go on in, Doctors."

He cleaned as much muck off his muddy shoes as he could on a boot scraper and went in. He found himself in a bright kitchen. A black-enameled cast-iron range hunkered against the far wall. A wisp of steam from a kettle drifted up to the varnished ceiling beams. The floor was tiled.

A woman stood, pouring tea into a cup patterned with daffodils. Barry took her to be in her early fifties. "Thanks for coming, Dr. O'Reilly."

O'Reilly parked himself at a solid-looking pine table. "It's no trouble. This is my new assistant, Dr. Laverty."

Mrs. Kennedy nodded. She wore an apron. Her gray-flecked dark hair was untidy, and although she smiled at him, her smile was only on her lips. Her eyes, dark circles beneath, gave away her forced humor. "Sit down," she said. "I'll fetch another cup."

Barry pulled out a chair and sat beside O'Reilly. He thanked the woman when she gave him a cup of tea, dark and stewed.

"And you say Jeannie's been off-color since yesterday?" O'Reilly's tone, for the first time in Barry's short acquaintance with the man, had none of its usual brusqueness.

"Aye. She'll no' eat nothing. Says her wee tummy hurts."

"Has she boked?"

Barry smiled at O'Reilly's use of the country vernacular for "vomited."

"Just the once. And she's burning up, so she is," Mrs. Kennedy said softly.

"Did you not tell all this to Mrs. Kincaid when you phoned, Bridget?" O'Reilly said. "I'd have come sooner."

"Och, we know how busy you are." Mrs. Kennedy's hands twisted her apron. "Sure, it's only a wee tummy upset, isn't it?"

"Mmm," said O'Reilly. "Maybe we'd better take a look at her."

"This way, Doctor," Mrs. Kennedy said, walking to a door.

Barry walked after her into a hall and through the door of a small bedroom. Bright chintz curtains framed the window. A beam of sunlight fell on the counterpane of a child's bed, where a little girl, teddy bear clutched to her flushed cheek, lay listlessly against two pillows. She stared at him with overbright brown eyes.

"This is Dr. Laverty, Jeannie," Mrs. Kennedy explained.

Barry moved to the corner of the room and watched as O'Reilly grinned and sat on the edge of the child's bed. "So, Jeannie," he said, "not so good?"

She shook her head. "My tummy's sore."

O'Reilly laid the back of his right hand on the child's forehead. "Hot," he remarked. "May I take your pulse, Jeannie?"

She gave him her right arm.

"Hundred and ten," said O'Reilly after a while.

Barry mentally added that fact to the rest. With the twenty-four-hour history of abdominal pain, the child not wanting to eat, vomiting, a fever, and a rapid pulse rate, he was already quite sure she had appendicitis.

"Can I see your teddy, Jeannie?" O'Reilly asked.

She handed him the stuffed bear.

"Now, Teddy," said O'Reilly, laying the toy on the counterpane, "put out your tongue and say Ah." He bent and peered at the bear's face. "Good. Now let's have a look at your tummy." He nodded wisely. "Too many sweeties."

Jeannie smiled.

"Your turn," said O'Reilly softly, returning the bear. "Put out your tongue."

The child obeyed. He bent forward and sniffed.

"Have a look at this, Dr. Laverty."

Barry stepped forward. The tongue was furred, the child's breath fetid.

"Can we pull the bedclothes down, Mummy?" O'Reilly asked.

Mrs. Kennedy turned back the covers.

"Jeannie, can you point to where the pain started?"

Her finger hovered over her epigastrium, where her lower ribs flared out.

"And is it there yet?"

She solemnly shook her head and pointed to her lower right side. Barry flinched. The next part of the examination would cause intense pain. Worse, the textbooks called for the doctor to examine the patient rectally.

"Right," said O'Reilly. To Barry's surprise, he gently pulled the bedclothes up over the small body, covering the Peter Rabbit nightgown. "Jeannie, would you like to go for a ride to Belfast?"

The little girl looked at her mother, who nodded. Jeannie stared into O'Reilly's craggy face. "All right," she said. "Can Teddy come?"

"Oh, aye," said O'Reilly. "Now you just lie there like a good girl. I need to have a wee word with your mummy." He smoothed the child's dark hair from her forehead, then rose and headed for the door. "Are you coming, Dr. Laverty?"

Barry hesitated. This wasn't right. O'Reilly had barely examined the patient. The man was in such a hurry to get back to watch his rugby game that he was cutting corners. He'd have this out with O'Reilly later.

"Bye-bye, Jeannie," he said as he left and returned to the kitchen.

Mr. Kennedy stood with one arm around his wife's shoulder.

O'Reilly had the phone clapped to one ear. He'd be arranging for an ambulance. That's it, Barry thought. Send the child to hospital; they'll take over, and you can get back to your rugby match.

O'Reilly's voice echoed from the roof beams: "What the hell do you mean, you've no beds? I've a kiddie with appendicitis here. She'll be at Sick Children's in half an hour. . . . Young man, you get hold of Sir Donald Cromie. . . . I don't give a damn if it is his day off. You tell him that Dr. Fingal Flahertie O'Reilly called from Bally-bucklebo." He slammed the receiver into the cradle.

"You've called the ambulance already?" Barry asked.

"Don't be ridiculous," growled O'Reilly. "We'll take her up to Belfast in my car."

"I thought you wanted to get home to see—"

"Don't be daft. Jeannie needs her appendix out. And quick. We haven't time to wait for an ambulance."

ONCE the Kennedys had been delivered to the Royal Belfast Hospital for Sick Children and O'Reilly was satisfied that Sir Donald Cromie agreed with the diagnosis and would operate immediately, he grabbed Barry by the arm and hustled him to the car.

"Come on. If we get a move on, we'll still be able to watch the second half."

As O'Reilly drove from the hospital grounds onto Falls Road, Barry said, "Dr. O'Reilly, I think you were very lucky to make the right diagnosis."

"Oh?" said O'Reilly mildly. "And why would you think that?"

"You didn't examine the child properly, because you were in a hurry."

O'Reilly stopped at a red light and turned to Barry. "Son, the diagnosis was as clear as the nose on your face from the minute we walked into the room. You could smell her halitosis. Did you want me to prod her belly and stick a finger up her backside just because that's what the book says?"

"Well, I—"

"Well, nothing," said O'Reilly, driving on. "There was no need to hurt her."

"I suppose . . ." Barry could see O'Reilly's logic. He also knew that there had been no real need for O'Reilly to take the family to Belfast.

"You just suppose away," said O'Reilly, "and stick with me, son. You'll learn a thing or two the books don't teach you."

Barry sat quietly in the passenger seat as the car moved past the redbrick wall of Campbell College, his old boarding school. He had made one good friend there, Jack Mills, who was now training to be a surgeon at the Royal Victoria Hospital. They had shared a study at university in their senior year, stuck together as medical students, been interns together. Barry decided he'd give Jack a call to see if they could get together when he had his first Saturday off. He'd be interested to hear his friend's opinion of O'Reilly.

The car left the city traffic. O'Reilly slammed his foot on the accelerator and hurled the Rover at the twisting Craigantlet Hill Road. Barry tensed as the car lurched when a wheel bounced off the curb. "Aren't we going a bit fast, Dr. O'Reilly?"

"Nonsense, my boy." O'Reilly threw the car into a turn. "We're coming to the Straight. We'll be home in no time."

Or upside down in the ditch, Barry thought.

As SOON as they arrived at O'Reilly's house, Barry changed out of his muddy trousers and shoes, then joined O'Reilly to watch the match on television. He finished the last of Mrs. Kincaid's lobster salad and put the plate on a coffee table beside his armchair. The Ireland under-twenty-three rugby squad had beaten the Scots.

O'Reilly belched contentedly, stared through the bay window, and said, "She's a dab hand in the kitchen, is Kinky."

"Agreed." The cold meal had been delicious.

"Don't know what I'd do without her." O'Reilly wandered over to the sideboard. "Sherry?"

"Please."

O'Reilly poured a sherry for Barry and a whiskey for himself. "I'd not have the practice if it hadn't been for Kinky."

"Oh?"

"I came here in 1938, assistant to Dr. Flanagan. Crusty old beggar. I was just out of school, reckoned I was no goat's toe, and he was pretty out of date, and I'll tell you, some of the things he did were very unorthodox, even for back then. You've no idea how cantankerous some old country GPs could be."

"I'm surprised you stayed."

"I didn't. I volunteered for the navy as soon as war broke out."

"What brought you back?"

"When the war was over I'd had enough of the navy, so I wrote to Dr. Flanagan. I got a letter back from his housekeeper, Mrs. Kincaid, to say that he'd died and that the practice was up for sale. I had my gratuity as an ex-serviceman. That, and a bank loan, bought me the house and the goodwill of the practice, and Mrs. Kincaid agreed to stay on. We've been here since 1946, but I damn nearly lost the practice in the first year."

"What happened?"

"Country folk," he said. "You've got to get used to them. My mistake was to try to change things too quickly. The customers stopped coming." He took a long drink. "The mortgage payments didn't."

"You must have been worried."

"Worried sick. I told you I'd have gone under if Kinky hadn't saved my bacon. She's a Presbyterian, you know. She made me go to church with her. Let the locals see that I was a good Christian man."

"That's important here?"

"Back then they liked to think that their doctor was a churchgoer. Didn't much matter if he went to church or chapel as long as he went."

"That's a relief. I spent enough time sorting out the casualties of the Protestant–Catholic street battles when the Divis Street riots hit Belfast."

"You'll not see any of that here," said O'Reilly. "Father O'Toole and the Reverend Robinson play golf together every Monday." He hauled out his pipe. He struck a match. "Anyway," he said, "I was telling you about Kinky."

"Right."

"Off to church the pair of us trotted. Turned a few heads when we took our pew. I'd no doubt who they were muttering about. I heard someone say that I was the young doctor who didn't know his rear end from his elbow. Some of them kept turning round to stare at me. Very uncomfortable."

"I can imagine."

"Do you believe in Divine Providence?"

Barry looked at O'Reilly to see if he was joking.

"Well, I didn't. Not until that particular Sunday. In the middle of the last hymn, a big fellow in the front row let a wail out of him like a banshee, grabbed at his chest, and fell over with a hell of a clatter. The singing stopped, and the minister said, 'I believe there's a doctor here.' Kinky gave me a ferocious nudge."

"What did you do?"

"I grabbed my stethoscope out of my bag—back then you never went anywhere without it—and rushed down the aisle. The man was blue. No pulse, no heartbeat. He'd popped his clogs."

"Was CPR invented back then?"

"Not at all. But I reckoned it was my one chance to make my reputation. 'Someone get my bag,' says I, unbuttoning the man's shirt. Kinky gave me the bag. I grabbed whatever injection was handy, filled a syringe, and stuck the victim in the chest. I clapped my stethoscope on. 'He's back,' says I. You could have heard the gasps of the congregation all the way to Donaghadee. I waited for a couple of minutes. 'He's gone.' I stuck him again. More gasps. 'He's back.'"

"Was he?"

"Not at all. He was stiff as a stunned mullet, but I gave him one more injection."

"I don't see how losing a patient in church in front of half the village saved your practice."

"Kinky did that for me. I heard someone sniff that the demise of the recently departed just went to show what a useless doctor I was. 'Just a small, little minute,' says Kinky. She stared at the minister. 'You have to agree, Your Reverence, that Our Savior brought Lazarus back from the dead.' The minister agreed. Then Kinky said, 'And Jesus only did it once, so. Our doctor, our Dr. O'Reilly, himself here, did it twice.' " O'Reilly finished his drink. "I've been run off my feet since."

"You wily old—"

The doorbell clanged in the hall.

"See what I mean? Be a good lad and see who that is."

Barry opened the front door. He was confronted by a man standing on the step. He was short and sufficiently rotund to warrant being described as spherical. He wore a black three-piece suit, a bowler hat, and a scowl.

"Where the hell's O'Reilly?" The visitor forced his way into the hall. "O'Reilly, come 'ere. I want ye. Now!" he bellowed.

"Perhaps I can—"

"I've heard about you, Laverty." The newcomer turned to face Barry, who was thinking, I'm only a day in the place. News travels fast. "I want himself."

Barry stiffened. "It's *Dr.* Laverty, and if you have something wrong—"

"*Dr.*, is it? Huh!" The little man's eyes flashed. "Do you know who I am? I'm Councilor Bishop, Worshipful Master of the Bally-bucklebo Orange Lodge, so I am."

"Good evening, Councilor," said O'Reilly from behind the man.

Councilor Bishop spun to face O'Reilly, who towered over him. O'Reilly was smiling, but Barry recognized the telltale paleness in his bent nose.

"My finger's beelin', O'Reilly." He thrust his right index finger under O'Reilly's nose. Barry could see the skin, red and shiny round the nail bed, the yellow pus beneath.

"Tut," said O'Reilly, donning his half-moon spectacles.

"Well, what are you going to do about it?"

"Come into the surgery." He led the councilor and Barry inside, then put instruments into a steel sterilizer and switched it on.

"Get on with it. I'm a busy man." Councilor Bishop planted his ample behind in the swivel chair.

"Won't be a minute. And how's Mrs. Bishop?" O'Reilly inquired.

"Look, would you get a move on?"

"Certainly." O'Reilly pushed the trolley toward the councilor. The sterilizer bubbled, wisps of steam jetting from under its lid. He then went to a cabinet, brought out a cloth-wrapped pack, and placed it on the trolley. "Open that, please, Dr. Laverty."

Barry peeled off the outer layer. Inside lay sterile towels and swabs, sponge forceps, a kidney basin, and a pair of surgical gloves. He heard water running as O'Reilly washed his hands, then *snap snap* as O'Reilly donned gloves.

"Dettol and Xylocaine are on the bottom of the trolley."

Barry retrieved the disinfectant and the local anesthetic, relieved that O'Reilly was not going to incise the abscess without deadening the pain.

"Thank you." O'Reilly stuffed a couple of swabs between the jaws of the sponge forceps. "Now, Councilor, if you'd hold your finger over this basin."

The ringing of the sterilizer's bell to indicate that the instruments were now ready almost muffled Councilor Bishop's *"Yeeeowee!"*

Yes, indeed, Barry thought, Dettol does bite. He retrieved the now sterile forceps, scalpel, and hypodermic and carried them over and set them on O'Reilly's trolley. "Local?"

"Of course," said O'Reilly, lifting the hypodermic.

Councilor Bishop stared wide-eyed at the needle.

"I'm going to freeze your finger," said O'Reilly. He filled the syringe's barrel. "This'll sting," he said, pushing the needle into the skin of the web between the index and middle finger.

"Wheee, arr, wowee," howled the councilor, writhing in his chair. "I know you're in a rush, but we'll have to wait for that to work."

"All right," whimpered Councilor Bishop. "Take your time."

"How long has the finger been bothering you?" O'Reilly asked.

"Two, three days."

"Pity you didn't come in sooner. Surgery's always open in the mornings."

"I will next time, Doctor. Honest to God, I will."

There was the merest upward tilt of O'Reilly's mouth as he said, "Do." He picked up the scalpel. "Right. You won't feel a thing."

He sliced into the flesh. Barry watched blood and yellow pus ooze out.

"Oh, dear," O'Reilly remarked, "the councilor seems to have fainted."

Barry looked at the little round man, who lay crumpled in the chair.

"Nasty man," said O'Reilly as he swabbed the mess away. Then he used two clean gauze squares to dress the wound. "Thinks he's the bee's knees because he owns half the property in the village." He pointed to his rolltop desk. "There's a bottle of smelling salts in there. Get them, will you?"

Barry went to the desk, aware that he had seen Dr. O'Reilly perform minor surgery with all the skill of one of the senior surgeons at the Royal. And somehow he had let Councilor Bishop know that while patients might have certain expectations of their physician, courtesy was a two-way street.

3

By the Dawn's Early Light

A TELEPHONE rang. Barry fumbled for the receiver. The night nurse must want him up on one of the wards. His hand smacked into an unfamiliar bedside table. "Ow." The pain brought him to wakefulness, and he remembered he wasn't in his room in the hospital staff quarters. He was in O'Reilly's attic.

The door opened, and a beam of light spilled into his room. A large figure stood in the doorway. "Up," said O'Reilly, "and be quiet. Don't disturb Kinky."

"Right." Barry got out of bed, dressed, and crept downstairs to find O'Reilly, black bag in hand, waiting in the hall.

"Come on," said O'Reilly.

He headed for the kitchen, then out through the back garden. Arthur Guinness stuck his head out of his doghouse.

"I'm not going shooting," O'Reilly said.

"Umph," said Arthur, and retreated into his kennel, muttering something in Labradorese.

Barry climbed into the Rover. "What time is it?"

"Half one," said O'Reilly, backing out into the lane. "Mrs. Fotheringham called. Says her husband's sick, but I doubt it." He headed for the road. "Major Basil Fotheringham's had every illness known to man. He always takes a turn for the worse after midnight, and as far as I can tell, he's fit as a flea. It's all in his mind." He turned left at the traffic light.

Barry yawned, then said, "So why are we going out into the Bally-bucklebo Hills at this hour?"

"Do you know about the intern and the surgeon?" said O'Reilly. "Surgeon comes in to make rounds in the morning. 'How is everyone?' says he. 'Grand,' says the intern, 'except the one you were certain was neurotic, sir.' 'Oh,' says the great man, 'gone home, has he?' 'Not exactly, sir. He died last night.' Once in a while, even the worst bloody malingerer does actually get sick."

"Point taken."

Barry sat back and watched the headlights probe the blackness ahead. Now that Ballybucklebo lay behind, the dark enveloped them as tightly as a shroud. He peered up and saw the Summer Triangle—Altair, Vega, and Deneb—high in the northwest. Barry's dad and mum would be seeing different stars now, he thought. The Southern Cross would sparkle over their heads. Their last letter from Melbourne, where his dad was on a two-year contract as a consulting engineer, had been full of their enthusiasm for Australia.

The car braked in a driveway, and Barry came back to earth.

"When we get in there, I want you to agree with everything I say, understand?" said O'Reilly.

"But doctors don't always agree. A second opinion—"

"Humor me, son. Just open the gate."

Barry climbed out and opened the gate, waited for O'Reilly to drive through, closed the gate, and crunched along a gravel drive to a two-story house, where O'Reilly stood, dark against the light from an open door, talking to a woman wearing a dressing gown.

"Mrs. Fotheringham, my assistant, Dr. Laverty," he said.

"How do you do?" she said. "So good of you both to come. Poor Basil's not well."

Barry followed as Mrs. Fotheringham led them through a hall, expensively wallpapered and hung with prints, up a deeply carpeted staircase, and into a large bedroom.

"The doctors have come, dear," Mrs. Fotheringham said, stepping up to the four-poster bed and smoothing the brow of the man who lay there.

Major Fotheringham sagged against his pillows. Barry looked for any obvious evidence of fever or distress, but no sweat was visible on the patient's high forehead; there was nothing hectic about his watery blue eyes, nor any drip from his narrow nose that hooked over a clipped military mustache.

"Right," said O'Reilly, "what seems to be the trouble this time?"

"He's very poorly, Doctor," Mrs. Fotheringham said. "Surely you can see that."

"Oh, indeed," said O'Reilly, making space among the ranks of salves and unguents on the glass top of an ornate dressing table and setting his bag among the bottles. "But it would help if Major Fotheringham could describe his symptoms."

"Poor dear," she said, "he can hardly speak, but I think it's his kidneys."

"I'd better take a look, then," said O'Reilly. He stepped to the bed. "Put out your tongue, Basil."

Here we go again, Barry thought. O'Reilly had not made the remotest attempt to elicit any kind of history, and here he was barreling ahead with the physical examination. Agree with everything I say. Well, we'll see.

"Mmm," said O'Reilly, pulling down the patient's lower eyelid and peering at the inside of the lid. "Mmm-mmm." He grasped one wrist and made a great show of consulting his watch. "Mmm."

Mrs. Fotheringham stared intently at every move O'Reilly made.

"Open your pajamas, please." O'Reilly laid his left hand, palm down, on the patient's chest and thumped the back of his hand. "Mmm." He stuffed the earpieces of his stethoscope in his cauliflower ears and clapped the bell to the front of the chest. "Big breaths." The major gasped, in out, in out. "Sit up, please." Major Fotheringham obeyed. More thumpings; more stethoscope applications, this time to the back; more huffing; more Mmms.

Mrs. Fotheringham's little eyes widened. "Is it serious, Doctor?"

"We'll see," said O'Reilly. "Lie down." O'Reilly quickly and expertly completed a full examination of the belly. "Mmm, I see."

"What is it, Doctor?" asked Mrs. Fotheringham.

"You're right," O'Reilly said. "It *could* be his kidneys."

And how in the world had he arrived at that diagnosis? Barry thought. No one had said anything about fever, chills, or difficulties or pain urinating, and nothing O'Reilly had done had come close to examining the organs in question.

"Then again, it might not be," said O'Reilly, grabbing his bag. "I think a test's in order, don't you, Dr. Laverty?"

Barry met O'Reilly's gaze, swallowed, and said, "I don't see—"

"Course you do." O'Reilly's tone hardened. "In a case like this, we can't be too careful. You'd agree, Mrs. Fotheringham?"

"Oh, indeed, Doctor." She smiled at O'Reilly.

"That's settled, then." O'Reilly glared at Barry, then rummaged in his bag and produced a bottle that Barry recognized immediately. It would contain thin cardboard strips used to detect sugar or protein in a urine sample. What the hell was O'Reilly up to?

"I'll need your help, Mrs. Fotheringham." O'Reilly handed her several of the dipsticks.

"Yes, Doctor."

"I want you to . . ." He looked at his watch. "It's two fifteen now, so start the test at three. Make Basil drink one pint of water."

"A pint?" she echoed.

"The whole pint. At four give him another pint, but not until he's passed a specimen of urine. Dip one of those dipsticks in it, and put the stick on the dressing table."

Mrs. Fotheringham looked dubiously at her handful of cardboard, sniffed, and said, "Very well."

"And," O'Reilly continued, "I want you to repeat the test every hour until Dr. Laverty and I come back to read the results."

"Every hour? But—"

"It's a terrible imposition, Mrs. Fotheringham, but"—O'Reilly put one large hand on her shoulder—"I know I can rely on you. Should give us the answer, don't you think, Dr. Laverty?"

Barry nodded, knowing any protest he might make would be rolled over with the force of a juggernaut. He despised himself for his lack of courage.

"Good," said O'Reilly to Barry. He turned to Mrs. Fotheringham. "Don't bother to see us out. You're going to have a busy night."

BARRY sat stiffly in the Rover. He was angry about O'Reilly's hocus-pocus and angrier at his own inability to intervene.

"Go on," said O'Reilly, "spit it out."

"Dr. O'Reilly, I—"

"Think your history-taking stinks, and you're up to no good with all that nonsense about the dipsticks." O'Reilly chuckled. "Son, I've known the Fotheringhams for years. The man's never had a day's real illness in his life."

"Then why didn't you just tell them to wait until the morning?"

O'Reilly shook his head. "It's another little rule of mine. If they're worried enough to call at night, even if I'm damn sure it's nothing, I go."

"Always?"

"Lord, aye."

Nothing in O'Reilly's tone suggested pride to Barry. "I see," he acknowledged, "but what was all that business with the test?"

"Ah," said O'Reilly, turning into the lane at the back of his house. " 'There are more things in heaven and earth, Horatio, than are dreamt of in your philosophy.' "

"You'll not put me off by quoting Hamlet, Dr. O'Reilly."

"No," said O'Reilly as he braked. "I didn't think I would, but you'll have to wait until we go back to the Fotheringhams' if you want to find out the answer. Now, be a good lad. Hop out and open the garage door."

BARRY listened to the rain clattering off the surgery's bow windows. Even at almost noon, the lights were needed in the room. He stretched and ran a hand over the back of his neck. He was feeling the effects of a broken night. He watched O'Reilly usher an old man with arthritis to the door. The morning had been busy, and yet O'Reilly showed no signs of fatigue.

"Trot along and see who's next," he instructed Barry.

Barry went to the waiting room to discover that only one patient remained, a young woman with auburn hair and green eyes. "Good morning," he said. "Will you come through, please, Mrs. er . . ."

"Galvin." She stood with some difficulty, one hand on the small of her back, the other holding her swollen belly. "I'm a bit slow getting about," she said.

"That's all right. Take your time. Doesn't look as though it'll be long now."

"A week more." She went into the surgery. "Morning, Doctor."

"How are you, Maureen?" O'Reilly asked.

"Grand." She rummaged in her handbag, produced a small urine sample bottle, and gave it to O'Reilly.

He handed it to Barry. "Pop a dipstick into that, would you?"

Barry took the specimen over to the sink and tested the urine. He found nothing wrong.

"Can you get up on the couch, Maureen?" O'Reilly said.

She turned her back to the table and sat. "Are you sure there's only the one in here, Dr. O'Reilly? I feel like the side wall of a house."

"It was only a week ago when I examined you," he said, "but if it'll make you happier, we'll get Dr. Laverty to lay on a hand."

She lay down. O'Reilly asked the routine late prenatal questions, took her blood pressure, and palpated her ankles to ensure there was no swelling.

"Right, let's see your bump."

She lifted the skirt of her maternity dress, and Barry stepped back and waited while O'Reilly examined her. Maureen's green eyes never left O'Reilly's face, which betrayed no expression.

"Dr. Laverty?"

Barry moved to the table. He examined the belly, felt a single baby's back on her right side, the hardness of the head just above the pubic symphysis. He grasped the head between the out-stretched thumb and finger of his right hand. It refused to budge when he tried to move it from side to side.

"Here," said O'Reilly, handing Barry a fetal stethoscope.

Tup-tup-tup-tup . . . Barry listened, counted, and looked at his watch. "A hundred and forty." He saw questioning lines appear in Maureen's forehead. "Absolutely normal," he said, pleased to see the furrows disappear.

"So?" said O'Reilly.

Barry trotted out the formula he'd been taught. "A singleton, longitudinal lie, vertex presentation, right occipito-anterior, head's engaged, heart rate—"

"A hundred and forty," said O'Reilly. "The rest's right, too. So are you worried now, Maureen?"

Barry looked at the woman's face. The furrows were back. She glanced from O'Reilly to Barry, then back to O'Reilly. "Not if *you* say so, Doctor."

"Just like Dr. Laverty said, Maureen, there's one baby, just the one. Straight up and down, the back of its head is on the right—that's the most normal way—and the head's dropped. The little devil's halfway out already."

Her forehead became smooth, and she gave a contented sigh.

Barry cleared his throat. He saw how he'd baffled the woman with his jargon. She hadn't understood a word of his "singleton, right occipito-anterior" talk, but O'Reilly had gone right to the heart of the matter in plain English.

O'Reilly helped her off the couch. "Right. Same time next week."

"And if the waters break or the pains start, I've to phone you."

"You'll be fine, Maureen," O'Reilly said. "By the way, how's Seamus?"

"His ankle's on the mend, and he hopes you liked the lobsters. Seamus means well. He's a heart of corn, but sometimes—"

"Don't you worry about Seamus," said O'Reilly. "I'll take care of him." He winked at Barry, who had a vivid mental picture of an airborne supplicant with a dirty foot. That Galvin was this young woman's husband?

"You'll not need to much longer," she said in a whisper. "You'll not tell no one, Doctor, but my brother—"

"The builder in California?"

"Aye. He's got a job out there for Seamus, and we've saved up for the tickets. We're going after the baby's born."

"Wonderful," said O'Reilly.

"I'll be in next week." She left.

"I'll be damned," said O'Reilly. He sat at the desk and wrote the results in Maureen Galvin's record. "Maybe the worthy Seamus'll have to do an honest day's work in America. I wonder where they got the money? He's a carpenter by trade, but to my knowledge, he's hardly done a hand's turn here." He looked up.

Barry hesitated. "I'm sorry I didn't explain things to her better," he said.

O'Reilly fished out his pipe and lit it before he said, "Ah, but you will the next time, won't you? Now tidy up. We've another test to go and read after we've had lunch."

"NICE DAY FOR DUCKS," O'Reilly remarked as he hurled the car around the twists and turns on the road to the Fotheringhams, refusing to make any concession to the downpour.

Barry, to distract himself from O'Reilly's driving, muttered, "Water, water, everywhere, and all the boards did shrink. Water, water, everywhere—"

"Nor any drop to drink," O'Reilly finished. "Coleridge, Samuel Taylor, 1772 to 1834, poet and opium addict. Water," he continued, turning into the Fotheringhams' drive. "I wonder how the Fotheringhams have been getting on with it?"

Barry scuttled after O'Reilly and sheltered in the porch until a bleary-eyed Mrs. Fotheringham, hair in disarray, opened the door. "Thank goodness you've come," she said.

Upstairs, Major Fotheringham sat up against his pillows, black circles under his bloodshot eyes. "It's been a hellish night," he croaked. "Hellish."

"Oh, dear," said O'Reilly. "Well, let's see how the test went."

Neatly arranged on the dressing table lay fourteen soggy dipsticks. Not a single stick had changed color.

"Oh-oh," said O'Reilly. "Oh-oh."

Barry was baffled. No color change meant that nothing untoward had appeared in the patient's urine.

"What's wrong with him, Dr. O'Reilly?" Mrs. Fotheringham begged.

"Can I stop the test now?" the major pleaded.

"Certainly," said O'Reilly, "and you are to be commended, Mrs. Fotheringham, on your meticulous devotion to duty."

She simpered. "Thank you, Doctor. But what's wrong with him?"

"What's wrong with you, my dear Major Fotheringham?" O'Reilly paused. "I'm very much afraid it's nothing. Absolutely nothing."

Barry saw Mrs. Fotheringham's jaw drop. "Nothing?" she said.

"Well," O'Reilly allowed, "he might be a bit waterlogged, but other than that? Not a thing. Now we'd better be running along. We've more calls to make. Of course, if you think you need me— anytime, anytime at all, day or night—please don't hesitate to call."

"I THOUGHT THAT WAS THE only call we had to make," said Barry.

"Just a couple more," said O'Reilly as he reversed out of the driveway. "I don't think," he added with a huge grin, "that the major or his lady will call us out again for a while. Do you?"

"I doubt it." In spite of himself, Barry chuckled. "Mind you, it's not the sort of medicine I was taught, but it seems to work."

"Like a charm, my boy." O'Reilly braked at a traffic light. "Twenty years ago I'd have read the Fotheringhams the riot act for wasting my time."

Barry glanced down. His own thoughts exactly.

"What got you into medicine, anyway?" O'Reilly asked.

Barry hesitated. He was always reticent about giving the real reasons. "When I left school, my dad said I was too dim to read physics or chemistry, would never make a living with an arts degree, wasn't a Catholic—so the priesthood was out—and I didn't look like a soldier. So there was nothing left for me but medicine."

O'Reilly guffawed. "Sounds like the sort of thing Tom Laverty would say." He turned and looked into Barry's eyes. "But there was more to it than that, wasn't there?"

"The light's changed, Dr. O'Reilly."

"Right." The Rover charged across the junction, tires shrieking as O'Reilly hauled it into a right turn. He steadied on course. "You didn't answer me."

"Well, I—"

"Don't like talking about it, but you'd a half notion you'd like to help people. Do something useful—"

"How the hell did you know that?"

"Didn't make many friends at school, so you hoped if you went into medicine, people would like you . . ."

Barry's mind went back to his boarding-school days. He'd had no close friends apart from Jack Mills. Barry had been a good scholar, and as a result, he was shunned by the in crowd of his closed-in little world. His four years had been lonely.

"Thought so," said O'Reilly. "Well, most of the customers aren't going to love you. They'll say thank you if you get it right, and treat you like dirt if you don't—and you *will* make mistakes. Never doubt that."

Barry wondered how the big man could have understood so completely.

"A few will have no consideration for the fact that you're on call twenty-four hours a day, and some, like Councilor Bishop, are bloody rude and totally demanding. You simply don't let the Bishops get to you. And there's a good side, too. When you *do* get a diagnosis right, make a difference in somebody's life, find you *do* fit into the local scheme of things, it is all worth it."

"You really think so?"

"I know so, boy. I bloody well know so."

The Rover ran along the shore of the lough, where a grassy verge dotted with sea pinks was all that separated the road from jagged rocks, black in the driving rain. Obsidian-green combers pounded against the shore.

Moments later the car slowed and O'Reilly parked it. "Come on."

Barry climbed out and saw a cottage with gray walls, a slate roof, mullioned windows, and boxes full of bright pansies on the sills. The cottage sat squarely beside the road. O'Reilly knocked on the front door. Barry joined him and immediately recognized the woman who opened the door.

"Come on in out of thon, Doctor," Maggie MacCorkle said. "It would founder you out there, so it would." She closed the door behind them.

A single oil lamp on a small oak table lit the tiny low-ceilinged room. Barry saw dishes stacked to dry in a plate rack beside an enamel sink. Two easy chairs flanked a fireplace. On one chair a huge ginger cat lay curled in a ball.

"Would you take a cup of tea in your hand, Doctor?"

"No, thanks, Maggie. We just popped in for a minute," O'Reilly said. "How's the headaches?" As he spoke, his gaze darted around the room.

"I couldn't have done better at Lourdes," she said, crossing herself. "It's a miracle, so it is. Them wee pills—"

"Good," said O'Reilly, glancing at Barry.

"Away out of there, General." Maggie pushed the protesting cat out of its chair. "Sit down by the fire, Doctor."

O'Reilly sat. "How is the General, Maggie?" He fondled the big cat's head. It had one ear missing, and its left eye was scarred shut.

Maggie's wrinkled face split into a toothless grin. "That one would sow dissension in a deserted house." She turned to Barry. "Have a seat."

He shook his head but out of curiosity asked, "Why do you call your cat the General, Miss MacCorkle?"

She chuckled. "His full name is General Sir Bernard Law Montgomery. Like the man he's named for, he's an Ulsterman, and he loves a good fight."

The General made a deep growling noise and glowered at Barry. Barry took one step back.

"Don't you worry your head about him," she said. "You're not big enough for him to go after."

O'Reilly rose. "We'll have to be getting on, Maggie." He crossed the room to the door. "Now remember, if you're out of sorts, come and see me."

"I will," she said, "and thanks for popping by."

"No trouble," said O'Reilly. "We were on our way to see Sonny."

Maggie cackled. "Poor old Sonny. He's not too well pleased with me. His spaniel came round here yesterday, but the General saw to that dog, didn't you, General?"

The cat arched his back and spat.

Maggie held the door. "Sonny'll tell you all about it, but pay no heed to him. He's only an old goat, anyway."

"I DIDN'T know that Miss MacCorkle had asked you to call," Barry said as he shut the car door of the Rover.

"She didn't," said O'Reilly, driving off. "On slow days, I try to visit one or two of the ones that I worry about."

"You were looking for something back there. What was it?"

"Little things. Dishes washed, no half-filled saucepans on the stove, clean floors." O'Reilly turned onto a narrow road. "Maggie's a bit different, but she's independent, and I need to know that she's looking after herself."

"So you keep an eye on her. That's very decent of you."

"Not a bit," said O'Reilly tersely. "There's more to this job than runny noses and hypochondriacs who drag you out of your bed."

"I see."

"You will," said O'Reilly, "at our next stop."

"Sonny?"

"Sonny. Now there's a story and a half." O'Reilly braked for a tractor crossing the road, then drove on. "I'll tell you about Sonny after we've been there. But if you think Maggie's a bit odd," he said as he pulled to the side of the road, "what do you make of this?"

"Good heavens."

The opposite roadside was cluttered with old cars, television sets, a rusting combine harvester, and folding plastic chairs. Electrical cables drooped from the branches of a larch tree and led to a television set and a glass-fronted spin dryer. The yellow-covered extension cords ran from a roofless house that stood back from the road. The roof beams were weather-stained and half caved in. What should have been the front garden was crammed with old cars, farm machinery, and a yellow trailer.

A man wearing a brown raincoat tied at the waist with baler twine left one of the rusting cars, strode over to the trailer, and opened the door. Five dogs piled out, each yapping and vying for the man's attention. O'Reilly got out of the car and crossed the road and stood beside the television set. Barry followed.

"How are you, Sonny?" O'Reilly yelled.

"I'm coming." Sonny made his way to a gate and let himself out. "Hush now," he called to the dogs that ran along behind a low hedge, yelping and barking. He then strode to where Barry and O'Reilly stood. The noise died away. "Doctor." He offered a hand, which O'Reilly shook.

"Sonny," said O'Reilly, "this is Dr. Laverty."

"Pleased to meet you, Sonny." Barry stared at the man.

He was almost as tall as O'Reilly, older, yet stood with the bearing of a regimental sergeant major. He wore a yellow sou'wester, from under which locks of iron-gray hair flowed to his shoulders. His eyes were pale, and his ruddy cheeks told of years of Ulster winds. And, Barry wondered, was there the faintest tinge of blue in the skin above the man's cheekbones?

"Have you any new potatoes?" O'Reilly asked.

"I have." Sonny reached behind the spin dryer and produced a small sack. "Five shillings and sixpence." He gave the sack to O'Reilly, who counted coins into a hand bent with arthritis.

"I brought you more of these," said O'Reilly, handing over two small medicine bottles.

"How much do I owe—" Sonny was reaching into his trouser pocket.

"Free samples from the drug company," said O'Reilly.

"You wouldn't be having me on? I can pay, you know."

"Not at all," said O'Reilly. "How are the dogs?"

"All grand except Sandy. Silly bugger got into a fight with Maggie's cat."

"I heard," said O'Reilly.

"And how is the old biddy?" Barry heard tenderness as Sonny spoke.

"Rightly," said O'Reilly.

"I'm glad to hear that." Sonny's pale eyes softened. "Silly old duck."

"Aye," said O'Reilly. "Well, we must be getting along."

"WHAT on earth was that all about?" Barry asked.

"Pride," said O'Reilly as he pointed the Rover homeward. "Sonny is the most stiff-necked man I've ever met, and yet he's one of the most contented. He has a Ph.D., you know. He used to work for some big chemical company in Belfast, but he'd rather stay at home and live in his car."

"In his car? But I saw a trailer."

"For the dogs," said O'Reilly. "Sonny dotes on his dogs."

"But why is he in his car? Can he not get the roof of his house repaired?"

"Yes . . . and no. You remember the worthy Councilor Bishop? He's a building contractor. Twenty years ago, Sonny hired Bishop to replace the roof. He wanted the house all done up before he got married."

Barry remembered how Sonny had asked about Maggie Mac-Corkle. "Not to Maggie?"

"To Maggie. But Bishop—and he's a man who'd wrestle a bear for a ha'penny—tried to cheat Sonny on the price of a load of slates."

"After the old roof had been stripped?"

"Precisely. Sonny refused to pay Bishop for the work he'd done already. Bishop said Sonny could whistle for his new roof. Maggie wouldn't marry a man who quite literally couldn't keep a roof over her head. Sonny quit his job, moved into his car, and supports himself selling vegetables and scrap iron."

"I'll be damned. For twenty years?"

"Aye." O'Reilly turned the Rover into his back lane.

"Sonny's not too well, is he? His cheeks are a bit blue."

"Smart of you to notice."

Barry smiled. "Heart failure?"

"Only mild." O'Reilly stopped the car.

"What did you give him?"

"Digitalis and a diuretic. They keep it pretty well in control."

Barry frowned. "Can you get those for free from the drug reps?"

"Ah," said O'Reilly, "them as ask no questions get told no lies. Now be a good lad and open the garage door."

Mrs. Kincaid greeted them in the kitchen.

"Any calls, Kinky?" O'Reilly asked.

"Not one, but there is a small little matter you should see to. Come and see." She led them into the surgery and indicated a wicker basket on the examining couch. "You'd just gone out when somebody rang the bell. I found this thing, so."

"Good Lord," said O'Reilly. He tapped on the side of the basket.

Barry watched the basket jerk for several inches along the couch, as if moved by some primal force. A low growling, harsh and brittle, filled his ears. O'Reilly opened the lid. Barry took a step backward as a white blur erupted from the container and, with an eldritch shriek, landed on O'Reilly's shoulder.

"Begod, it's a cat," he said, reaching up and hauling it off its perch. "Push-wush. Pushy-wushy." He held the animal in one big hand and stroked its head with the other.

It struggled briefly, then seemingly accepting its lot, butted its head against O'Reilly's palm. Barry heard a low rumbling. The animal was purring.

"Mmm," said O'Reilly. "I doubt if we'll find out who left it, and we can't just put it out."

"Will I find it some milk, Doctor?"

"That would be grand, Kinky," said O'Reilly, handing her the little feline. "And could you manage a cup of tea for us while you're at it? I don't know about you, Barry, but I could use a bit of time with my feet up."

Barry yawned.

"Tired?"

"A bit."

"Well," said O'Reilly, "it's only a couple of days till your day off."

4

I'm Standing in a Railway Station

SATURDAY, Barry's first day off, was what the locals would call "a grand soft day." He turned up the collar of his raincoat against the damp that was neither heavy enough to be rain nor light enough to be mist. Mrs. Kincaid had said the train to Belfast would leave Ballybucklebo at ten fifteen. Half an hour to Belfast; fifteen minutes to walk into the city center, where he intended to invest some of his first week's pay in a pair of Wellington boots; half an hour on the bus up Grosvenor Road and he'd still be in good time to see Jack Mills in O'Kane's Bar, opposite the Royal Victoria Hospital.

He strode along Ballybucklebo's main street, then turned onto the aptly named Station Road. At the train station, he bought his ticket and went to the platform.

Moments later he heard the rattle of an approaching train. The brakes screeched. The train stopped. Barry let himself into a compartment where two upholstered benches faced each other and was pleased to see that it was unoccupied. As he sat down, he wondered how often as a student he had ridden on this train from his home in Bangor, farther down the line to the Queen's Quay terminal in Belfast. How many times had he ridden past Ballybucklebo without even paying attention to its existence?

The train shuddered to a halt at Kinnegar Station. Two young women tumbled aboard and sat at the other end of the compartment. Barry tried to ignore them by staring out the window, but their chatter intruded.

"Away on. Charlie Simpson does *not* fancy Eileen." The speaker's voice was harsh, with the flat accents of Belfast. "That Eileen has a face on her like a sheep."

"He's daft about her."

"That's not what I heard."

Poor Charlie Simpson, whoever he was, daft about some girl, Barry thought. He himself had been daft about a student nurse. He closed his eyes and pictured her green eyes, auburn hair, and slim figure and thought about the gnawing emptiness he'd felt when she had told him that she was going to marry a surgeon. Six months ago. And still it stung.

"Do you know it would serve her right to get stuck with Charlie? He's thick as two short planks, so he is."

Barry wished the young woman would shut up. She had a voice that would cut tin.

The other chuckled. Her laugh was contralto, deep and resonant. Barry glanced at her. She had black hair with a sheen. Her face was strong, with a firm chin, Slavic cheekbones, and full lips. Her dark eyes had an upward tilt. A small dimple showed in her left cheek as she laughed. But for that dimple, she could have been Audrey Hepburn in *My Fair Lady*.

"Anyway, Patricia," her friend rattled on, "I says to Eileen . . ."

Would she never stop prattling? He glanced down and then stole another look. Patricia, that was her name. Patricia turned, caught him staring, and held his gaze.

"Excuse me," he said, knowing that he was blushing. "I'm awfully sorry . . ."

She laughed, warm and throaty. "A cat may look at a king . . . if it doesn't think the king's a mouse."

The train slowed, and the sign for Belfast Station glided past the window. As soon as it stopped, the two women left. Barry sat back against the cushions. Why had he not had the courage to find out more about Patricia? In the movies, she would have left something on the train, something he could use as an excuse to run after her. No such luck. Ships that pass, he thought, and yet . . .

He left the compartment not expecting to see any sign of her and her chatty friend, but there they were up ahead, Patricia leaning on the noisy one's arm and limping slowly. Must have hurt herself playing hockey, he thought. She certainly looked the athletic type. He took a deep breath, smoothed his hair, and lengthened his stride until he drew level.

"Excuse me," he said. "Excuse me."

Patricia stopped and faced him.

Words tumbled out. "Look. My name's Barry Laverty. I want . . . that is . . . I'd like—"

"Away off and chase yourself." The friend tugged at Patricia's sleeve.

"Will you have dinner with me tonight? Please?"

Patricia gave him an appraising look.

"You've a right brass neck, so you have." The friend glared at Barry. "Anyway, we're busy the night."

Patricia smiled. "That's right. We are."

"Oh." Barry's shoulders sagged.

"But I'm taking the ten-o'clock train back to Kinnegar."

He saw the laughter in her dark eyes, and his breath caught in his throat.

BARRY sat in the window alcove of O'Kane's Bar, the nearest watering hole to the Royal Victoria Hospital. At his feet, a pair of Wellington boots lay in a brown paper bag. A shadow fell over the table, and Barry turned to see Jack Mills wearing a long white coat and his usual grin.

"Sorry I'm late." Jack sat. "I'd a hell of a night on call, and this morning was murder." He pulled out a pack of cigarettes. "I'm knackered." Jack lit up and stretched out his legs.

"Pint?" Barry asked, looking forward to the afternoon with his friend.

"Can't. Sorry. The resident in Sick Kids is sick himself, and they need a hand on a surgical case in about an hour. I got the short straw, damn it." Jack's smile belied his words. "I wouldn't mind a quick bite, though."

Barry swallowed his disappointment. It would be a long day before the ten-o'clock train. He imagined dark eyes and hoped the wait would be worth it.

"Grub," said Jack. He turned and called to the barman, "Brendan, could you manage a steak-and-mushroom pie, chips, and an orange squash?"

"Right, Dr. Mills." Brendan put down the glass he was polishing. "What about you, Dr. Laverty?"

"That would be good." Barry never ceased to be amazed by how Brendan, owner and barman, remembered the names of the generations of students and junior doctors who used his establishment.

"So," Jack asked, "how's general practice?"

"It's different. I'm working with a Dr. O'Reilly in Ballybucklebo."

"Not Fingal Flahertie O'Reilly? Man of about fifty, fifty-five?"

"That's right."

"Good Lord. Before the war, he was one of Ireland's best rugby forwards."

"I didn't know that." Barry was impressed.

"You, Brother Laverty, wouldn't know an Irish rugby player from a penny bun." He winked at Barry. "But you saved my bacon in anatomy class, so I'll forgive you."

"Here y'are." Brendan set two plates on the table.

"Dig in," said Jack, picking up his knife and fork. "Come on, I want to hear about what you're up to."

Barry did his best to describe his first week as O'Reilly's assistant and the older doctor's eccentricities.

"But you are enjoying it?"

"I think so. There's an awful lot of routine stuff, but I have seen some interesting cases." He told Jack how O'Reilly had driven the Kennedy girl to Belfast in his own car. Jack nodded when Barry mentioned that O'Reilly's knowledge of every patient seemed encyclopedic.

"Now there's a difference," he said. "I never get to know anybody. We're too damn busy." He looked up at the clock over the bar, stood, reached into his pocket, and tossed a pound note on the table. "My half. Sorry, mate, but I'd better run. Sir Donald Cromie is like the wrath of God if his assistant's late."

"Sir Donald who?" Was he the man O'Reilly had consulted on Tuesday?

"Sir Donald Cromie, pediatric surgeon with nimble fingers and a temper like Mount Etna on a bad day. He did an appendix the other night. Now the patient's blown up a pelvic abscess. Sick as a dog."

"You wouldn't happen to know the patient's name?"

Jack laughed. "No. I don't even know if it's a wee boy or a wee girl. I'm off. Good to see you, mate. I'll give you a bell next time I'm free."

MAYBE she wasn't coming. Why would she? Maybe she'd said she'd be on the ten-o'clock just to get rid of him.

The train would leave in five minutes. Barry took one last long look along the Queen's Quay. It was deserted. Oh, well. He hefted his parcel of boots, turned, and made his way toward the platform.

"Barry? Barry Laverty?"

He turned and saw her limping fast toward him.

"Come on." She grasped his arm. "Get a move on or we'll miss the train."

Barry helped her inside and slammed the compartment door after them.

"Just made it," she said, sitting down.

He sat opposite. "I thought you weren't coming."

She laughed, her dark eyes bright in the compartment's dim light. "So your name's Barry Laverty?"

"That's right. I heard your friend call you Patricia."

"Patricia Spence."

He took the hand she offered, feeling the smoothness of her skin, the firmness of her grasp. He knew he was holding on for a moment too long, but he didn't want to let go. He looked into her face. He never wanted to let go.

"I'll have it back, if you don't mind."

He eased his grip, but she let her hand linger just for a moment. Now what? Damn it, why was he always at a loss for words with women?

"You're quiet," she said. "Cat got your tongue? Don't know what got into you, asking a complete stranger to dinner?"

"That's right."

The train jolted and rattled through the dark night.

"If it makes you feel any better, I don't know what got into me, telling you I'd be on this train." She tossed her dark mane. "I think it's the way your hair sticks up . . . like a little boy's, and you looked so lost."

His hand flew to that damned tuft. He saw her smile at him.

Now or never, he told himself. "I just had to meet you, that's all." He swallowed. "I've never seen anyone so lovely." He knew he was blushing. The train clattered to halt. "Sydenham Station," he said.

"Thank you, sir," she said.

"For telling you the name of the station?"

"For telling me you think I'm lovely."

"You are," he said, grateful that no one had boarded, knowing that Kinnegar was only two more stops down the line, happy that the train was on its way again, anxious that his time with her was running out. He wanted to hold her hand, but he was terrified that she might dart away like a startled bird. "You live in Kinnegar?"

"That's right. Number Nine, the Esplanade. On the seafront. I love the sea."

"I grew up in Bangor. I know what you mean about the sea. It's never the same. . . ." He glanced down, then was jerked forward as the carriage stumbled to a halt. He reached out and touched her hand, and she twined her fingers with his.

"I get off at the next stop," she said. "I'm sorry."

"I know, but . . . Patricia, I want to see you again."

"My phone number's Kinnegar six five seven three three four."

Kinnegar 657334. He repeated the number in his head, over and over, as the train moved on. "Can I phone you tomorrow?"

"I'd like that." She leaned forward and kissed him gently, little more than a fluttering of butterfly wings. "Bangor's not far from Kinnegar," she said.

"I don't live in Bangor now. I'm staying in Ballybucklebo."

"You're what?" She sat back and laughed. "Oh, dear," she said.

The Kinnegar sign appeared in the window. The train slowed, then stopped. She rose.

He stood and opened the door. "What's so funny?"

"The ten-o'clock doesn't stop at Ballybucklebo. You'll have to get off here and walk home."

"What?"

"That's right, and you'd better get a move on if you don't want to go all the way to Bangor."

The train jolted. He hustled her onto the platform and jumped down beside her.

"I'm sorry. I shouldn't have laughed," she said.

"It's all right. At least I can walk you home."

"Come on, then. It's not far," she said as the train's red rear lights vanished.

Damn it. He'd left his new Wellington boots in the compartment. She took his hand, and boots forgotten, he walked beside her, shortening his stride to keep pace with Patricia's uneven steps.

"How'd you hurt your leg? Hockey?"

"I didn't hurt it." He detected a hint of bitterness.

"What happened?"

"Nineteen fifty-one."

He stopped. Turned her to face him. "The polio epidemic?"

She nodded. "My left leg's a bit short." She dropped his hand and took one step back. "I suppose I won't be hearing from you now."

He sensed that she had been hurt before, perhaps badly. He knew that to him, her short leg made no difference, none in the whole wide world. "I don't give a damn about your leg, Patricia," he said, watching her face. "I don't care at all."

She stared at him. "I shouldn't, Barry Laverty. I know I shouldn't, but I think I believe you."

He saw something silver beneath her left eye, and he wanted to taste the salt of it, but something told him he mustn't rush her. "Come on," he said, "let's get you home."

5

Deliver Us from Evil

"YOU look like the Hesperus . . . a total wreck," O'Reilly said, leaning forward in one of the upstairs armchairs and peering over the top of the *Sunday Times*.

Barry yawned. "Late night."

"I know. I heard Arthur. What kept you?"

Barry parked himself in the other armchair. "Fate," he said. "Kismet."

"Whatever it was, it's put a grin on your face."

Barry debated whether to tell O'Reilly about Patricia but decided that now was not the time. She was his to relish in private. His musing was interrupted by a rhythmic rending noise.

"Stop that," O'Reilly yelled, tossing the *Times* color supplement in Barry's direction.

Barry ducked. "Stop what?"

"Not you. Her. Lady Macbeth."

The white cat that had been left on the doorstep had been so named by O'Reilly after she'd bloodied Arthur Guinness's nose and chased him back to his doghouse—twice. She was standing on her hind paws, her front claws ripping at the fabric of Barry's chair.

"Stop it, madam." O'Reilly stood over the animal, who clawed away and condescended to give him a feline look. "Stop it." O'Reilly picked the cat up and tickled her under the chin.

Barry watched as she fixed the big man with her green eyes, laid back her ears, and made a throaty sound. She held her tail straight out from her body. "I don't think she's very happy, Fingal."

"Nonsense. Animals dote on me. Don't you?" He went on tickling her until she struck, fangs sinking into the web of O'Reilly's hand. "You bitch," he roared as Lady Macbeth sprang from his arms. He glared at his punctured hand.

"We'd better get that cleaned up," said Barry. "There's a thing called cat scratch disease, you know."

"And tetanus," O'Reilly remarked. "And you can disabuse yourself of any notion, Dr. Laverty, that you're going to stick a needle in my backside. I've already been inoculated."

"Thought never entered my head," Barry lied, thinking of the Dettol that would have to be poured onto the raw punctures. "Not for a minute."

O'REILLY was once again ensconced in his living room. He nodded to where Lady Macbeth lay curled up in a patch of sunlight. "Now, before Her Ladyship remembered she was descended from a long line of albino saber-toothed tigers, I was trying to find out what kept you out so late last night."

"I got on the wrong train. The ten-o'clock doesn't stop at Bally-bucklebo. I had to walk from Kinnegar. That's all."

O'Reilly chuckled. "The exercise'll do you good." He looked at Barry. "I'd hardly call getting on the wrong train 'destiny.' "

"Destiny?"

" 'Kismet,' you said. It's from the Turkish *kisma,* meaning destiny." O'Reilly leaned forward. "What's her name?"

"What?"

"You've had a dreamy look all morning. You were muttering about fate. Two and two usually make four." O'Reilly rose and walked to the window. Without looking at Barry, he said, "You're far too young to be getting involved with a woman. Take my advice. Medicine's a selfish enough mistress for any man."

"I think, Dr. O'Reilly, I can be the best judge of that."

"You'll see." A note of bitterness had crept into the older man's voice.

Mrs. Kincaid bustled in, carrying a tray. "Tea," she said, "and a bit of toasted, buttered barmbrack, so." She set the tray on the sideboard. "And how's my wee princess?" She bent over Lady Macbeth and stroked the cat's head. "You're just a wee dote. Y'are, so."

"With sharp teeth," muttered O'Reilly, showing his bandage.

"Huh," said Mrs. Kincaid, "if you annoy cats, you must take the consequences, so."

"Me?" said O'Reilly. "Have you seen what the beast's been doing to the furniture?"

"You'll just have to train her not to claw it."

"And how do you suggest we do that?"

"Don't look at me," said Mrs. Kincaid, turning to leave, "but Maggie MacCorkle knows as much about cats as you do about the doctoring."

"Now there's an idea," said O'Reilly as he poured himself a cup of tea. He then carried his tea to his place and sat easily in his chair.

Barry was only half paying attention. He'd been disturbed by O'Reilly's attitude toward women. If that was how he felt, Barry's chances of having more time to see Patricia were probably slim, but if he didn't ask . . .

"Fingal?" Barry swallowed. "I'd like to have more time off."

"So it *is* a girl." O'Reilly sipped his tea. "What's her name?"

"Patricia. Patricia Spence."

"And I suppose, to quote Ecclesiastes, if memory serves, she's 'a woman to make men run out of their minds'?"

"All I'm asking for is a bit more free time."

O'Reilly stared over his teacup. "How much?"

"An hour or two the odd evening, maybe every other Sunday."

O'Reilly put his cup on the saucer. "I thought you wanted to be a GP. It's not holiday camp here."

Barry's shoulders sagged. He looked down. He was startled to hear O'Reilly say, "All right. Once I can trust you not to kill too many customers, I wouldn't mind a bit of time off myself. I thought we'd take alternate weekends and have a couple of weeknights each off duty."

Barry looked up. "Do you mean that?"

"Difficult as it is for you to believe, I wasn't always fifty-six. I suppose you'd like to take this afternoon off. Go. I'll hold the fort."

Barry could have hugged the big man. "I'd really appreciate that, Fingal."

"Go on. Phone your Patricia—that's her name, isn't it?"

"It is." Barry sped to the door and took the stairs two at a time. He was just about to lift the receiver when the double ring of the phone's bell startled him. He lifted the phone.

"Hello. Dr. O'Reilly's surgery." No voice came over the line, just a whimper, then deep breathing. "Hello? Are you there?"

"Is that Dr. Laverty?"

"Yes. Who's speaking?"

"It's Maureen Galvin. My waters burst three hours ago, and the pain is every five minutes. I've sent for the midwife. Can you come now?"

"Of course. Dr. O'Reilly will be round right away."

"Thank you." The line went dead.

Barry raced back upstairs. "That was Maureen Galvin. Her membranes have ruptured, and she's contracting every five minutes."

"I'd better get round there." O'Reilly stood, put his cup back on the tray, and faced Barry. "She doesn't live far from here."

Patricia, Barry thought; then he said, "I'll get my bag."

"Good lad. I might need a bit of help."

O'Reilly rapidly organized his equipment, and together they carried the gear to the car. O'Reilly called Arthur Guinness and told the dog to get into the backseat. "We'll give him a run on the beach when the smoke and dust have died down."

The short drive would have been pleasanter if Arthur hadn't insisted on draping his front paws over Barry's shoulders and licking the back of his neck. He was so distracted that he couldn't pay attention to where they were going, and when the car stopped, he found himself in a strange part of Ballybucklebo. By the look of the narrow-fronted terraced houses that lined the street, he could have been in one of the slums of Belfast.

"Where are we, Fingal?"

"Council estate. Cheap housing for the less fortunate. Council voted the budget and chose the building contractor. Bishop sold them the land and finagled the contract. He cut so many corners it's a bloody miracle that these houses aren't circular."

O'Reilly slammed the car door, and Barry grabbed the equipment.

"Come on. Let's get at it." The big man crossed the footpath and pounded on the front door. Barry joined him.

A slim woman wearing the blue uniform of a district midwife answered the front door. "Dr. O'Reilly."

"Miss Hagerty, this is Dr. Laverty. How's Maureen?"

"Grand, Doctor. Three-minute contractions, and the fetal heart rate's fine."

"Right." O'Reilly charged down a narrow hall and up a steep staircase.

There was barely space for Barry in the small bedroom. Maureen Galvin lay in bed. The midwife had spread a rubber sheet under the laboring woman. O'Reilly and Miss Hagerty stood on opposite sides of the bed. The doctor finished tying the belt of a chest-high rubber apron; then he bent over and put his ear to a fetal stethoscope pressed to Maureen's belly.

"Uuunnnhhh," she groaned. Barry watched her face contort.

O'Reilly straightened and took her hand. "Squeeze," he said. "You're doing fine."

"Uuunnnhhh."

"Pant, Maureen. Pant. Like this." Miss Hagerty began to puff. Short breaths through barely open lips.

"Good lass," O'Reilly said. "You're not quite ready to push yet." The contraction passed. Maureen lay back on her pillow.

"Could you open the big pack, Dr. Laverty?" O'Reilly asked.

Barry set to work preparing the sterile towels, scissors, clamps, bowls, and a suturing kit.

"Now, Maureen, Miss Hagerty and I are going down to the kitchen to wash our hands. Dr. Laverty'll keep an eye to you." Together they left.

Barry moved closer and hoped that O'Reilly would get a move on. He'd never been left alone with a woman in labor before.

Maureen grabbed his hand. "Oh, Lord. It's coming, Doctor."

Barry tore off his jacket, flung it aside, and rolled up his sleeves. "Can you bend your knees up, Maureen?"

She parted her legs and bent her knees. "Hail, Maaaary . . . ummmh." Maureen was pushing with all her might, and a circle of damp baby's hair appeared.

Barry's hands went to work unbidden as he remembered what he had been taught and controlled the rate of descent of the baby's head. The contraction passed.

"Are you all right, Barry?" He looked up to see O'Reilly standing at the foot of the bed, Miss Hagerty behind.

"I think so."

Miss Hagerty moved to the top of the bed.

"I'll get the gear ready," said O'Reilly. "You carry on."

Maureen sat up now, supported by Miss Hagerty. "Come on, big puuush."

Under Barry's fingers, the baby's head advanced. He let it come farther, farther, a little farther. As it rotated, a wrinkled forehead appeared. A squashed nose came next, and in a rush, a puckered rosebud of a mouth and a tiny chin. Even before the shoulders were born, the baby gave its first wail.

Barry used both hands to guide the slippery infant out of its mother and onto the rubber sheet, conscious of the warmth of the body, the beating of the heart under his right palm.

He heard Maureen ask, "Is it a boy or a girl?"

"It's a boy," he said. "He's fine."

"Here," said O'Reilly, reaching out with gloved hands to swathe the little one in a green sterile towel, "we'll just pop him on Mum's tummy."

"Thanks, Dr. Laverty," Maureen said when the umbilical cord was cut and the placenta expelled. "You've a quare soft hand under a duck, so you have."

He laughed at the country description of gentleness. "You did very well, Maureen. What are you going to call the wee lad?"

"Well, if it's all right with the pair of you, I'd like him to go by Barry Fingal Galvin."

"That's a mouthful for such a little lad," Barry said, grinning.

"What'll Seamus think of that?" Miss Hagerty asked.

"Seamus? He'll be happy enough. He's down at the Black Swan with his mates, wetting the bairn's head."

BARRY hardly noticed the time pass as Miss Hagerty busied herself tidying up the mess of the delivery and then went to make the new mother a cup of tea. O'Reilly expertly examined the newborn as Barry repacked the instruments.

"Right," said O'Reilly, "young Barry Fingal's fit as a flea." He gave the baby back to Maureen.

"Thanks again, Doctor," said Maureen. "He'll make a grand wee American, won't he?" Barry remembered that the Galvins intended to emigrate.

"Indeed," said O'Reilly. "Now we'd better be going. Dr. Laverty could use a bath and a change of shirt. He's off somewhere tonight."

Barry nearly dropped the bag he was carrying. In the excitement of the delivery, he had completely forgotten about Patricia.

"You run on, Dr. Laverty," said Maureen. "You did grand, so you did."

As soon as they were back in the car, Barry remembered something that had been bothering him. "Fingal, is Jeannie Kennedy home yet?"

"No. She's still in the hospital. She blew up an abscess. They opened her again yesterday, but she's on the mend now."

So Jack *had* been going to assist in Jeannie's reoperation.

"I always phone the hospital to see how any of my lot are getting on. Sir Donald spoke to me this morning, so I was able to let the Kennedys know they mustn't be too worried."

"Decent of you."

"Rubbish."

When the car pulled up to the garage, O'Reilly said, "I'll take Arthur for his walk. You go get cleaned up, make your phone call, and tell your lassie you'll not be able to see her until after supper."

"But—"

"No buts. You still have to go and tell the proud father."

"Could you not do that?"

"I didn't deliver the wean, you did. And son, you did it well. Now go get organized and walk down and meet me in the Black Swan."

BARRY bathed, changed, and gratefully gave his splattered clothes to Mrs. Kincaid to be washed. Then he phoned Patricia. He mouthed a silent "Oh, yes" when she said she'd be happy to be picked up at seven.

He walked with light steps past the church and the row of thatched cottages. What a day. The sun shone; he'd delivered Barry Fingal Galvin *and* to Dr. Fingal Flahertie O'Reilly's satisfaction. Now he'd drop into the pub to congratulate the father, go home for a quick supper, and then . . .

He paused at the maypole. He could see the Black Swan ahead. He didn't want to stay at the pub too long. It wouldn't do to show up at Patricia's the worse for drink.

He crossed the road and went in. The bar, loud with competing voices and hoarse laughter, was a single timber-beamed, low-ceilinged room. The place was packed. Seamus Galvin, left ankle strapped, stood swaying in the center of the crowd. Barry peered through the throng but saw no sign of O'Reilly.

Councilor Bishop, seated at a table, beckoned with a crooked bandaged finger. "Laverty, tell O'Reilly it's time he had a look at my finger."

"It's *Dr.* O'Reilly, Bishop," Barry said smoothly, "and you know when the surgery's open."

"It's *Councilor* Bishop to you, you young puppy."

Barry turned away as the door opened and O'Reilly appeared, followed by a panting, tongue-lolling, sand-covered Arthur. Barry glanced anxiously at his corduroys, his last clean pair of trousers.

"Good afternoon to this house," O'Reilly bellowed.

Conversation died. Every eye turned toward the door. The men who sat at the table nearest the door rose and joined those standing at the bar. Without a word of thanks, O'Reilly took one of the chairs. "Under and lie down," he called.

Arthur obeyed, much to Barry's relief.

"Take the weight off your feet, Barry."

Barry sat, carefully tucking his legs out of the way of the drooling dog.

"The usual, Doctor?" he heard the barman ask.

"Aye, and a pint for Dr. Laverty."

Two pints of Guinness were delivered to the table, and moments later the barman reappeared, carrying a bowl. He bent and shoved it under the table.

"Arthur likes his pint," O'Reilly remarked.

Barry heard lapping noises under the table.

"Lovely," said O'Reilly, swallowing half the contents of his glass. "Come on, boy. Don't let yours go flat."

Barry sipped the bitter stout, then sensed someone standing at his shoulder. He turned to see Seamus Galvin, a lopsided grin pasted to his narrow face.

"So's a boy, Doctors? S'a wee boy?"

O'Reilly nodded.

" 'Nother round here, Willy," Galvin shouted to the barman. "On me."

"Easy, Seamus," O'Reilly said quietly. "You'll need your money now."

"Ah, sure, I'm like Paddy Maginty; I'm going to fall into a fortune." He favored O'Reilly with a drooping wink.

"Oh?" said O'Reilly. "And where would that come from?"

"Least said, soonest mended."

As two more pints arrived, he climbed onto a chair, where he stood swaying like a willow in a high wind. He whistled. Silence.

"Just wanna say . . . best two doctors in Ulster—in all of Ireland."

Councilor Bishop yelled: "That bloody O'Reilly couldn't cure a sick cat."

Barry looked at O'Reilly, who lifted his glass to Bishop and smiled.

"Are you not going to say something, Fingal?"

O'Reilly shook his head. "Revenge," he said, "is a dish best eaten cold. I'll say no more today."

"They got me a wee boy, so they did," Seamus Galvin roared. "Everybody have a drink to Farry . . . Bingal . . . Gavlin." He finished his pint to the cheers of the crowd.

Barry felt duty-bound to join in the toast. He regarded his empty glass with surprise. That stout had vanished quickly.

"A wee boy." Galvin continued to the renewed cheers of the patrons, waved both arms over his head, hands clasped like a boxer who had just KO'd his opponent. Then, with great solemnity, he fell off the chair.

"Drink," said O'Reilly. "It's the curse of the land." He turned to Barry. "Drink up."

Barry took a goodly swallow from his second pint, surprised by how much better than the first it tasted.

I<small>T HAD BEEN A</small> W<small>ONDERFUL</small> afternoon, Barry thought as he accompanied O'Reilly and Arthur on the short walk back to O'Reilly's house. Wonderful. But when he stumbled and grabbed O'Reilly's arm, it dawned on him that he was not entirely sober. He'd better pull himself together. Nothing was going to spoil his evening.

"I wonder," said O'Reilly as he opened the back gate. "I wonder how Galvin's going to 'fall into his fortune.' I'd not like to think it'll be the cash Maureen's been saving for their emigration."

Barry might have been concerned, too, if Arthur Guinness had not cocked one leg and, with the unerring accuracy of a marksman, peed all over his trousers.

B<small>ARRY</small> left the parked Brunhilde, smoothed the tuft of hair on his crown, and looked down. He was a sight. Bloody dog. With one pair of trousers still wet from the wash and his only others reeking of dog pee, he'd had to accept O'Reilly's offer of the loan of a pair. Wearing brightly checked trousers cut for a man of six foot two, even with the cuffs rolled up and the waistband cinched with a belt, he knew he looked like an escapee from a touring circus. Nor was he convinced that a short nap, Mrs. Kincaid's liberal doses of black coffee, and the greasy fry-up she'd made him eat had restored him to complete sobriety. If they had, he probably wouldn't be standing here outside Number 9, the Esplanade, Kinnegar, giving a fair impression of a clown. He looked at the row of bell pushes, each accompanied by a hand-lettered card. "Patricia Spence. Flat 4." He rang the bell and waited.

The door opened, and Patricia came out. "Hello, Barry Laverty." She turned to close the door behind her, and her high ponytail danced impertinently as she turned back to him, her dark eyes wide, her dimple deep as she smiled. She was wearing a white silk blouse and a mid-calf green skirt.

His breath caught in his throat.

"What in the world?" She stared at his trousers.

"It's a long story." He felt the heat in his cheeks. "I'll tell you in the car."

He held the car door and waited until she was seated. He rushed to the driver's side, climbed in, started the engine, and drove off.

"Now," she said, "tell me about those trousers, Mr. Laverty."

Mr. Laverty. He hadn't told her last night he was a doctor. "I only own two pairs. I got both of them dirty today, so I had to borrow these from a friend."

"A stilt-walker?"

Barry laughed. "No, but he's big."

"So's the Atlantic Ocean, and you're drowning in those. But don't worry about it. Where are we going?"

"I thought we'd go to Strickland's Glen. Walk down to the shore."

"You'd ask a girl with a game leg to go for a walk?"

Was she teasing him? Was she being caustic? He couldn't tell. "Patricia," he said, "if you'd rather not go for a walk, say so."

She leaned over and kissed his cheek. "I like you, Barry Laverty."

For the rest of the drive, they chatted about the weather and about tennis and pop music. She said she liked the Beatles.

"Here we are," he said when they arrived at the glen. "Hop out."

He led her onto a path strewn with needles from the evergreens above, the air redolent with their piney scent. Rays of sun filtered through the trees. Other walkers were taking advantage of the sun-soaked evening. But Barry was barely aware of them.

"Listen," she said. "Song thrush. You can tell his song a mile away. I love birds. My dad's an ornithologist. He taught my sister and me about them when I was little, growing up in Newry."

"Mine taught me astronomy."

"Bit of a stargazer, are you?"

"Yes," he said softly, and careless of passersby, he bent and kissed her.

"Mmm," she said, "nice, but we should move along if we're going to get to the shore."

A boy of five or six ran past, stopped, pointed, and yelled, "Mommy, look at the man in clown's trousers."

Barry heard Patricia's laughter, warm as butter on fresh toast.

"Come on, then, Pagliaccio." She tugged at Barry's hand.

"Pally who?"

"A clown. In an opera. The Beatles aren't the only ones I listen to."

"I'm not much up on opera."

"I'll teach you. I've tons of records back in the flat. I'm going to Queen's. Taking extra courses this summer. I want to graduate as soon as I can. It's too far from Newry to Belfast to travel up to town, and the rent's cheaper in the Kinnegar."

"I see. So you're a student and you like opera. Do you like to read?"

She frowned for a moment. "I've tried Hemingway, but he's too curt. I prefer John Steinbeck."

He took her hand. "Come on. Just over this bridge," he said, and they walked onto a small wooden arch over a stream. "Might be trout in there."

"Or a hobbit under the bridge. I've just finished *The Lord of the Rings*."

She knew Steinbeck, Tolkien. "So you're taking an arts degree?"

"No." She stopped walking. "Why would you say that?"

"I dunno. You certainly seem to know the kinds of authors that I'd expect an art student to know."

"And women should take arts or nursing? Is that it? And there's plenty of work for good secretaries? I'm twenty-one, and I'm the youngest student in my class—my civil engineering class—and there are only six of us."

"Six what? Engineers?"

"No. There are eighty-two in the class. Only six are women."

"I still don't understand. We'd ten women in our lot at university."

"What exactly don't you understand?" Her eyes were narrow, lips tight.

"What are you making such a fuss about? Why shouldn't a woman be an engineer or a doctor? If you want to be an engineer, you ought to have the chance." Barry did not like the way this discussion was going.

She pursed her lips and spoke, as if to herself. "Bloody right I should. But a lot of people wouldn't agree. It's a damn sight tougher if you're a woman. Women have to fight for their rights."

Barry moved closer. "Fair enough. But you don't have to fight with me."

"You're right."

"Right as rain," he said. Then he grinned at her.

Like a summer squall, her anger passed. "I shouldn't have yelled at you, but . . . damn it . . ." She grabbed him and kissed him hard. "Am I forgiven?"

He would have forgiven her for not one but all of the seven deadly sins.

"To the beach, woman," he said with mock sternness.

"Yes, sir." She took his hand, and they walked to the shore, where they stood and looked out across Belfast Lough.

"So tell me about Barry Laverty," she said.

"Well, apart from my unshakeable belief that women should never be admitted to faculties of engineering—"

"Just cut that out." She was smiling. "I'm sorry I got shirty with you."

"I'm twenty-four, no brothers or sisters. I like to read, to fish. I used to sail, but I'm a bit busy now." He paused before looking her right in the eye and saying, "My dad's a mining engineer."

"And what does the son of a mining engineer do?"

"I'm a GP. I'm an assistant to Dr. O'Reilly in Ballybucklebo."

She pointed at his ridiculous, oversized baggy trousers and giggled. "Well, Doctor, I hope none of your patients have seen you this evening." She snuggled against his chest as the sun slipped behind the Antrim Hills, leaving one last molten streak across the darkening lough.

BARRY peeped through the double doors of the upstairs sitting room. He saw O'Reilly sprawled in his chair, his head drooped to the left. Lady Macbeth lay tucked into the angle between his neck and his right shoulder.

O'Reilly opened one eye. "You're home."

"Sorry, Fingal. I didn't mean to disturb you."

"Had a good evening?"

Barry savored his memories of the slow walk back through the moth-fluttering gloaming. The drive to Patricia's flat, her invitation in, and his polite refusal. He'd known from the minute he'd seen her that she was different—special—and sensed that if he were too hasty, he would be rebuffed. Better to let things percolate.

"I presume by your dewy-eyed silence that the answer is yes." The cat slid down O'Reilly's waistcoat and curled up in his lap.

"It was wonderful."

"Huh. Women."

Barry glanced at the big man, expecting from his tone to see distaste written on his face, but instead he saw sadness. "You don't mean that, Fingal."

"Don't I, by God?" O'Reilly rose, and Lady Macbeth slipped to the carpet. The doctor paced to the window and stood, staring out. "Women? Nothing but grief." He turned, and for a second, Barry thought he could see moisture in his brown eyes.

"Good Lord, would you stop it?" O'Reilly swore at Lady Macbeth, who had happily returned to reducing the furniture to tatters. "Give over."

Barry was relieved that the animal had distracted them. Whatever was troubling O'Reilly was none of his business. "Maybe Kinky's right. We should ask Maggie what to do about Her Ladyship."

"It's not Maggie we need. It's a bloody exorcist. I think she's possessed." O'Reilly yawned. "I'm off to bed. We'll be busy for the next few days."

"How come?"

"Thursday's the Twelfth of July, of 'glorious and immortal memory,'" he said, referring to the annual celebration of the victory of Protestant King William III over Catholic James II at the Battle of the Boyne. "Unless someone's at death's door, they'll not want to miss the parade, so anyone with blepharitis, a blister, a bunion, or bursitis will be bellyaching in the waiting room first thing tomorrow, Tuesday, and Wednesday. You'll have to wait for a few days to go back and see the light of your life."

"Well, I—"

"Don't worry," said O'Reilly as he left, "you can have Friday night off."

"Thanks, Fingal," Barry said to the departing back. He sat down. It was too soon to go to bed. He'd too much to think about: Patricia. He'd phone her tomorrow and hope she was free on Friday.

"Excuse me, Dr. Laverty, but I've a pair of trousers dry and pressed for you, so." He hadn't heard Mrs. Kincaid coming in. "You can get out of himself's bags now. You don't seem to fill them too well."

"I know." And, Barry thought, I don't think I'm ready to fill the big fellow's shoes, either. He hesitated. "Mrs. Kincaid, would you mind if I asked a question? It's about Dr. O'Reilly. I'm a bit worried about him."

"How so?"

"He gets very upset when I mention a young woman I've started seeing. And earlier—now please don't laugh—I thought he was going to weep."

"Did you?" Her eyes softened. "Sometimes I wish to God he would." She stuffed her bulk into an armchair, glanced at the closed door, lowered her voice, and said, "You'll keep what I'm going to tell you to yourself?"

"Of course."

"He doesn't know I know. He's a very private man, so. Old Dr. Flanagan told me. In 1941, April, Easter Tuesday, them Germans dropped bombs on Belfast, aye, and Bangor." She clenched her fists. "A young nurse was killed. They'd been married six months. He worshipped that girl, so."

"My God."

"Himself was away on that big ship. He didn't get told until June that she was dead." She looked up into his face. "It hurt him sore, Dr. Laverty."

"It still does," Barry whispered.

"Aye, so." She rose and stood before him. "I think he worries that you'll get hurt like him. He's taken quite a shine to you, Doctor. I can tell."

"Mrs. Kincaid, I thank you for telling me this."

"Not a word now, but"—she smiled at Barry—"there's only you and me to look after the big buck eejit."

"I understand."

Mrs. Kincaid stood like a guardsman, her three chins thrust out, eyes hot. "I hope you do, for I'll not see him let down again." She crossed the room and turned. "It's not my place to say it, Dr. Laverty, but I'd take it kindly if you'd think of staying on here. He's a good man, and he needs you."

6

For Marriage Is an Honorable Estate

ALTHOUGH Monday morning's surgery started slowly, with three men waiting for tonic injections, their departure opened the floodgates. It seemed to Barry that every case in Ballybucklebo of back strain, sniffles, cough, hay fever, and hangovers following the welcoming of Barry Fingal Galvin poured through the place. Several of the hangover sufferers had also needed attention for blackened eyes and skinned knuckles.

As the last of them left, O'Reilly said with a grin, "I just hope we don't get a rematch on the Twelfth." He stretched. "Are there many more today?"

"Two children and a young woman. I think that's it."

"Get them, would you?"

Barry brought the children from the waiting room. He had assumed, incorrectly, that the woman was the mother of the two children. The boy, who Barry guessed was five or six, wore short tweed trousers and a gray shirt. The blond girl wore a pale blue pinafore dress that matched her solemn eyes. She was probably a year older than her companion.

"Good morning, Colin Brown. Good morning, Susan MacAfee, and what can I do for the pair of you?" O'Reilly peered over his half-moons.

"Mr. Brown and I want to get married."

"Indeed," said O'Reilly without a flicker of expression. "Married? And how do you feel about it, Mr. Brown?"

The little boy looked down and tugged at the front of his trousers.

"I see," said O'Reilly. "Well, marriage is an honorable estate not to be entered into lightly."

"Yes, Dr. O'Reilly," said the little girl. "We know that."

"Uh-huh," said Mr. Brown. He shifted from foot to foot.

"We've saved up," said the little girl. "A whole shilling."

"You know," said O'Reilly, "maybe you're a bit young."

Mr. Brown nodded, yanked the girl's hand, and whispered into her ear.

"You'll just have to wait," she said.

"Before you see the minister?" O'Reilly asked.

Mr. Brown hauled so hard on her hand that she had to take a step toward him. "I said you'll have to wait. What . . . ?" She bent to him. "Oh," she said. "Dr. O'Reilly, we'll have to be running along."

"Fine," said O'Reilly. "So you *are* going to wait?"

"No," she said, putting a hand on her hip and pouting at the little boy. "Mr. Brown here's just wet himself."

"Oh, well," said O'Reilly, "perhaps Mrs. Kincaid can help. Come on." He rose and took the girl's hand. "I think she's in the kitchen." O'Reilly turned to Barry. "Get the last one in, will you? Start taking her history."

"Right." Barry waited until O'Reilly and his charges had left before he surrendered to laughter. He was still chuckling when he reached the waiting room. "Will you come with me, please?" he asked a young woman who sat all alone staring at the floor. She wore a white raincoat and black high-heeled shoes. She clasped a patent-leather handbag with both hands. Her corn-silk hair was held in place by an Alice band, and when she looked up, her eyes were dull and red-rimmed, and by the look of the shadows beneath, she must have been short of sleep.

She stood. "Dr. O'Reilly?"

No one from Ballybucklebo would have mistaken him for Fingal. "No," he said, "Laverty. But Dr. O'Reilly'll be along in a minute."

She said nothing, even when she was seated in the patients' chair.

"Now," said Barry, spinning the swivel chair and reaching into one of the desk drawers to pull out a blank patient-record card. "I'll just get a few details. You're not from round here, are you?"

She shook her head. "Rasharkin."

"County Antrim? You're a long way from home." He glanced at her left hand. No ring. "Miss . . ."

"MacAteer. Julie MacAteer."

He entered the name. "How old are you?"

"Twenty." There was a catch in her voice. "Next week."

"And what brings you to see us?"

A single tear fell from her left eye. She opened her handbag and brought out a handkerchief. "I'm late," she whispered. "Three whole weeks. And I'm always on time."

Barry swallowed. "Do you think you could be—"

"I know I am." Her eyes flashed. "I've thrown up every morning for the last week, and I'm main sore here." She put her hand to her breast.

Barry heard O'Reilly enter. He looked over to see the big man put a finger to his lips. "Have you told anyone?" Barry asked her.

"Who could I tell? Da would kill me, so he would."

"Julie, you could be wrong. Hormones are funny things. It's not unusual for young women to miss a period if they're worried about something."

"I'm not wrong. I know I'm . . . pregnant, and I don't know what to do."

"I think we should find out for sure. Did you bring a urine sample?"

She pulled a small glass bottle from her bag. "Here."

Barry took the bottle. "I'll have to send it to Belfast for a test." He saw O'Reilly hold up a thumb. "We'll know for sure on . . . ?"

"Friday," said O'Reilly.

She swung round and stared at him.

"This is Julie MacAteer," Barry said.

"It's all right, Julie. I'm Dr. O'Reilly."

She turned back to Barry. "I'll just have to wait, then."

"Will you be going back to Rasharkin today?" Barry asked.

"No. I'm stopping here."

"Where?" Barry realized he had forgotten to take her address.

She tugged at the handkerchief. "I'm not telling."

"But—"

"It's not important." O'Reilly put a hand on her shoulder. "Dr. Laverty only needs it for the records. Barry, just put 'local' on the card."

"Dr. O'Reilly?" She straightened her shoulders and stared up into his face. "If I am . . . you know . . . I can't keep it."

"You'll not have to," said O'Reilly. "I promise."

Barry sat bolt upright. He could understand why a single woman wouldn't want to consult a physician in her own community, and he'd assumed that was why she'd traveled to Ballybucklebo. But was O'Reilly an abortionist?

"Do you mean it?" she asked.

"I do," said O'Reilly. "I promise."

Good God. Barry could not believe what he was hearing. Abortions were illegal. "Dr. O'Reilly, I won't—"

"Hold your horses, Barry. It's not what you think."

Barry, unable to trust himself not to say something he might regret, left the surgery. How could O'Reilly tell her that everything would be rosy when the odds were that she was pregnant and there wasn't a damn thing they could do about it?

He almost bumped into Mrs. Kincaid as she let the two children out through the front door. "Sorry," he snapped.

The surgery door opened, and O'Reilly, holding Julie's arm, took her to the front door. Barry saw Mrs. Kincaid peer at the young woman's face and a look of puzzlement cross her own. Then he heard O'Reilly say, "Come back on Friday. Try not to worry. We'll take care of it, I promise." The front door shut. "Kinky. Lunch," O'Reilly said. "We've a lot of calls this afternoon."

Barry went into the dining room. O'Reilly came in and sat at the table.

"You promise, do you, Fingal?" Barry could barely stop his hands from trembling. "How can you promise her? Do you do abortions here? Is that why she's come all the way from Rasharkin?"

O'Reilly folded his arms and looked levelly at Barry, who rushed on. "Are you one of the charlatans who take money from well-to-do ladies and make sure they can get rid of their little inconveniences?"

"At least," said O'Reilly mildly, "those fellows use a sterile technique."

"And you think that sterility's justification for what they do?"

"It's better than the backstreets."

Barry stood straight. "I won't be party to it."

"You won't have to be."

Barry swallowed. He saw clearly that although he was now enjoying working in Ballybucklebo, he wouldn't, couldn't, stay here. He half turned, fully intending to leave, when he heard O'Reilly say clearly and distinctly, "I don't do abortions."

Barry spun back. "What?"

"I said, I don't do abortions."

Barry frowned. "But if you don't . . . how could you promise Julie she'd not have to keep it?"

"I didn't say she wouldn't have to have the baby."

"Come on, Fingal. How could she go on living in a place like Rasharkin or here in Ballybucklebo? The shame would kill her."

"Why don't you take a deep breath, count to ten, and sit down?" An edge of command laced O'Reilly's words, and Barry sat slowly. "If she's pregnant, I'll arrange for her to go to Liverpool. There's a charity there. A home for the Piffys."

"Piffys?"

"PFI's. Pregnant from Ireland. Piffys. The people there will look after her until the baby's born and then arrange an adoption. The folks in Rasharkin can suspect, but they can't be sure that she's had a wee bastard."

"Oh." Barry could not meet O'Reilly's gaze. "Look. I'm sorry, Fingal. I shouldn't have jumped to conclusions."

"No, you shouldn't. But I'll say one thing. I admire a man who has the courage to speak his mind."

Barry looked up and saw a soft smile on O'Reilly's face.

"So we'll say no more. Mind you, it would make life a lot easier all round if the baby's daddy would make an honest woman of her."

"I wonder why she's here. In Ballybucklebo."

"Haven't a clue." O'Reilly looked over Barry's head to where Mrs. Kincaid stood holding two plates of steaming food. "What do you think, Kinky?"

"About what?"

"About why a pregnant young woman would come here from Rasharkin to see me?"

"So, the wee girl's in trouble?" She set two plates on the table.

" 'Fraid so." O'Reilly grabbed his knife and fork and set to.

"I'll need to ask about," said Mrs. Kincaid. "I've seen that girl before."

"You do that, Kinky. I want to know by Friday."

"I will." Mrs. Kincaid handed over a piece of paper. "And here's your afternoon list."

"WHO'VE we to visit today, Fingal?" Barry asked as they climbed into the car.

O'Reilly consulted his list. "Archie Campbell's arthritis is playing up; Katy Corrigan's bronchitis is getting worse; Mrs. Mallon thinks her Jimmy's broken his ankle. I doubt it, but that's very handy."

"What is?"

"The Mallons live near Maggie's place. We'll make our last call with her and see if she has any suggestions for what to do with Lady Macbeth."

The actual consultations didn't take long. Most of the time was consumed driving from place to place, and Barry soon understood why it was important to know the geography of the area.

At last, O'Reilly pulled up outside Maggie MacCorkle's cottage.

"Hello, Doctors dear," said Maggie as she turned from a window box, trowel in one hand. Barry noticed that the geraniums in her hatband had been replaced with marigolds. "Grand day."

It was. Out past her cottage, far out on the whitecapped lough, Barry could see a fleet of yachts running down the wind. In the sunlight, their multihued spinnakers billowed like fairies' parachutes. I'd like to be out there with them, he thought.

"How are you, Maggie?" O'Reilly asked.

"Grand, so I am. I'm glad you dropped by. I need a wee favor."

"All in good time, Maggie. We've come to ask advice."

"Oh? What about?"

"Cats," said O'Reilly. "I've just got a new one."

"Good. It'll be better company for you than that great lummox of an Arthur Guinness." Maggie looked gently at the big man.

"I'm having trouble training her."

Maggie cackled. "Sure, you can't train cats."

"Oh," said O'Reilly, looking crestfallen. "So I'll just have to wave good-bye to my living-room suite? She's clawing like a tiger with fits."

Maggie frowned. "You could try doing what I did for the General. Come inside and I'll show you." She led the way, leaving the front door open.

The General lay on a chair beside the unlit fire. Maggie went into another room and came back carrying a T-shaped piece of equipment. The base was a bit of flat plywood. A post, two by two by thirty-six and covered in old carpet, rose vertically from the base.

"One of these might do the trick," she said. "It's a scratching post, so it is."

The General opened his eye, stared at the scratching post, and made a moaning sound. Then he scuttled, belly to the floor, under the table. "The General used to rip my bits and pieces, didn't you?"

She waved the post at the cat, who put a paw over his eye and retreated out of sight.

"I see," O'Reilly said, "and every time he tried to scratch the furniture, you showed him the post, and he learned to use it instead. Brilliant."

"Not at all," said Maggie. "When he tried it, I took the post . . . and I fetched him a right good belt on the head, didn't I, General?"

Barry was aware of an orange streak that rushed past him and out through the open door.

"Maybe," said O'Reilly, when he finally stopped laughing. "Maybe a piece of rolled-up newspaper would work."

"Maybe," Maggie said. "It's the best I can think of."

"Thanks, Maggie." O'Reilly walked to the door, stopped, and said, "I nearly forgot. What was the wee favor you wanted?"

Maggie fidgeted, cocked her head to one side. "I sometimes take a walk up past Sonny's place. I don't go that way often, you understand."

"Of course," said O'Reilly.

"But I was there this morning, and I don't think the old goat's right. He usually hides in his car if he sees me coming. He just sat in his chair. "Morning, Maggie," says he, and he coughed. A great big long hack. He looked terrible blue in the face, so he did. Would you maybe take a gander at him?"

"Of course. We'll head up there right now."

THERE was no sign of Sonny. Nor did he appear when O'Reilly bellowed the man's name. Four of his five dogs ran barking through the scrap yard to the gate in the hedge. The spaniel stood outside a derelict car, front paws on the sill of an open rear door.

"He must be in there," O'Reilly said, opening the gate. He brushed aside the dogs and made his way, Barry in tow, along a path through weeds and rusting metal. He bent at the open car door.

"Are you there, Sonny?"

Barry heard a hacking cough and a feeble "Go away."

"It's Dr. O'Reilly." The doctor clambered through the open door.

Barry peered through the dirty windows to make out a figure curled up on the backseat.

"Ah, Doctor, let me be." More coughing.

O'Reilly backed out of the car, dragging Sonny. "It would be a hell of a sight easier if you'd cooperate," O'Reilly panted. "You're sick as a dog."

He straightened up. He held Sonny in his arms, the man's legs dangling to one side, his head pillowed on O'Reilly's chest. Barry could see that Sonny's cheeks were slate gray. His nostrils flared like a scared horse's, and his neck muscles stood out like cords every time he tried to inhale. There was no need of a stethoscope to hear the damp rattling of each labored breath.

"Come on," O'Reilly said, "we'll have to get him to the surgery."

O'REILLY laid Sonny on the examination couch. Barry helped him remove Sonny's raincoat, a heavy sweater, and a collarless shirt. It took several minutes to peel away the layers of old newspaper that lay under his shirt. With each rasping inhalation, the muscles between Sonny's ribs were sucked inward and he whimpered.

"Hurts to breathe?" O'Reilly asked as he took Sonny's pulse.

"Yuh-huh." Sonny put a hand to his ribs.

"When did it start?"

"Just after . . . *hack* . . . the storm . . . *hack* . . . got soaked."

"Help me sit him up."

Barry put an arm round Sonny's shoulders. He could see that the jugular veins were distended right up to the angle of Sonny's jaw, a sign that blood was backing up behind a heart that lacked the strength to pump it farther.

O'Reilly percussed Sonny's back. Barry heard sullen thumps where a resonant sound should have been. Either the lungs or the pleural cavities were filling with fluid. O'Reilly stuffed his stethoscope in his ears and listened.

"You daft old beggar. Why the hell didn't you send for me?" Sonny hacked.

"Right," said O'Reilly, pulling his stethoscope from his ears. "Hang on." He rummaged under the examining table and swung the upper end to an angle of forty-five degrees. "Let him lie back now."

Barry eased the old man's head back onto the pillow. "Heart failure?" he asked.

"And pneumonia and pleurisy. Both sides." O'Reilly shook his head. "It's the hospital for you, Sonny."

Terror filled Sonny's eyes. "Who'll look after . . . *hack* . . . my dogs?"

"Your dogs'll do a damn sight better if you're around to take care of them," O'Reilly said, "and you won't be if we don't get you to the Royal. And quick." He turned to Barry. "Go and call the ambulance. The number's by the phone. We need oxygen down here as quick as we can get it."

"SHERRY?"

"Please." Barry sat in his by-now usual chair in the upstairs lounge.

O'Reilly gave Barry a glass, set his whiskey on the coffee table, shoved Lady Macbeth out of his chair, and sat. The cat leaped into his lap, and he fondled the animal's head. "Lord," he said, "it never rains but it pours. What a day. Surgery packed to the gills, a pregnant lass from Rasharkin. I'll need to give the folks in Liverpool a call about her tomorrow . . . and that's not the half of it." O'Reilly frowned. "I'm worried as hell about Sonny and his place."

"Do you not think he'll make it?"

"Touch and go. Pneumonia, pleurisy, and a dicky ticker? Still, he's a tough old bird, and they'll do the best they can for him in the Royal. That's not what I'm concerned about."

Barry looked at Lady Macbeth. O'Reilly had a soft spot for animals. "You're not going to see to Sonny's dogs?" he asked.

O'Reilly shook his head. "No. Maggie'll look after them if we ask her. It's more than his dogs that's got Sonny scared."

"Oh?"

"Bishop." O'Reilly spat the word. "Sonny told me when you were phoning for the ambulance. There's some council bylaw that if a property's derelict and the owner moves away, the council can have it repossessed. Then they sell it to the highest bidder. And who do you think that is likely to be?"

"Ah, no."

"Ah, yes. Bloody Bishop's been trying to get his hands on Sonny's place for years." O'Reilly ground his teeth. "I'm damned if I can see a way out, but Bishop may not hear for a day or two, and the council offices will be closed for the Twelfth week. Maybe we can come up with something."

"I hope so, and I hope Sonny recovers."

"That," said O'Reilly, "goes without saying." He took a deep breath. "I said you could have Friday off. Should you give that lass of yours a call?"

"I'd like to."

"Go on, then."

Barry ran downstairs, dialed, and waited.

"Hello, Kinnegar six five seven three three four."

"Patricia? It's Barry. Look, I'm off on Friday. Would you like to go out for a bite?"

"I'd love to, but I've got an evening seminar."

"It's my only night off."

"I suppose I could ask someone to let me borrow their notes."

"Do it. We could go to my boat club in Bangor." The grub's cheaper there for members, he thought.

"Super. I look forward to it. Got to run now."

TUESDAY and Wednesday sped by. O'Reilly's phone calls to the Royal brought the news that Sonny was holding his own. He wasn't out of the woods, but his condition had not deteriorated. Maggie had agreed to take care of his dogs. Somewhere in the village, Julie MacAteer tried not to worry about the results of her pregnancy test. Councilor Bishop's finger needed attention. And despite the long hours, Barry began to feel truly at home in his choice of career in general and in the village in particular.

Seamus Galvin had come into the surgery on Tuesday morning. He sat in the patients' chair and pulled off his cloth cap.

"Morning, Seamus. How's young Barry Fingal?" Barry asked.

"Grand. Mind you, it's a good thing men can't feed wee ones. He has Maureen up half the night, so he has."

"Huh," said O'Reilly. "I don't suppose you'd think of giving the child a bottle once in a while?"

"Not at all. That's Maureen's job, so it is."

O'Reilly looked at Barry and shook his head.

"Ah, sir. It's time for you to take a wee look at my ankle."

"And I suppose you want a line?" said O'Reilly.

"Oh, indeed, sir, I do that. I'll have to go on the burroo."

Barry understood. Seamus wanted a medical certificate so he could draw disability insurance from the Bureau of Unemployment—the "burroo."

"We'll see," said O'Reilly. "Show me your ankle."

The ankle in question looked perfectly normal. No swelling.

"Can you bend it?" O'Reilly asked.

Galvin made a show of trying to extend his foot. "Ah. Ooh."

"Hmm. Right. Let's see you walk on it."

Galvin stood and teetered across the room, hauling his allegedly wounded ankle behind him and moaning, "Ooh, ah."

"You're one for the textbooks, Seamus," said O'Reilly. "You've managed to hurt the side that was fine when you showed that hoof to me first."

Galvin hung his head and hobbled back across the room.

"You want me to give you a line?" asked O'Reilly.

Galvin brightened. "Yes, please, sir. For two weeks, if that's all right."

"I might," said O'Reilly, "but I'd need to know about the fortune you said you'd be falling into."

Galvin sat back in the forward-tilting chair. "Ach, you don't, sir. Ach, no."

"Ach, yes, Seamus, I do. Or it's no line."

Galvin took a deep breath. "Maureen gave me the money."

O'Reilly's nose tip blanched. "She what? The money for California?"

Galvin hung his head.

"You skiver. Give it back to her, do you hear?"

"I can't, sir. It's spent. On ducks. Rocking ducks."

O'Reilly's shaggy eyebrows rose. "What are you talking about?"

"I'm going to make rocking ducks. Just like rocking horses. There'll not be a kiddie in Ballybucklebo won't go daft to have one. The lumber and paint's all bought. I can sell them for twice what they'll cost to make. That's why I want two weeks off, so I can finish making them and get them sold."

"How many will you make?"

"About a hundred, sir."

"And how many kiddies that would want a rocking duck do you think live in Ballybucklebo?"

"I don't know, sir."

"Forty, maybe fifty. Do you reckon they'll buy them in pairs?"

"I never thought of that, sir. But it will all work out. You'll see. So you'll give me the line, Doctor sir?"

Barry was surprised when O'Reilly said, "A promise is a promise," and returned to the desk to scribble on a government form.

"Here," said O'Reilly, handing Galvin the form. "Two weeks. But you build those damn ducks. I might know a business in Belfast that'll take the lot. And Seamus," O'Reilly added, "get out of your bloody bed and give that wife of yours a hand. Do you hear me?"

"I do, sir. I will." Galvin left.

"MIGHT be a bit difficult to park the car on Main Street. They'll be getting it ready for Thursday," said O'Reilly, finishing his lunch. "We've to nip round to Declan Finnegan's. He lives over the grocer's. It's not a bad day. Let's walk."

"Fine." Barry would be glad of the exercise. He thought wistfully of his fly rod, propped up, unused in his attic.

"Is it nice in there?" O'Reilly asked.

"Where?"

"Wherever the hell you've gone off to in your head. I suppose your young man's fancy is lightly turning to thoughts of love?"

"If it's any of your business, I was thinking about fishing."

"Were you? I noticed you've a rod. You like to fish?"

"Very much."

"I'll have a word with His Lordship. The Marquis of Bally-bucklebo. Nice old fellow. He owns a beat on the Bucklebo River. He'd probably let you on his water if I asked him."

"Would you? I'd love a day on a good trout stream."

"I'll see to it." O'Reilly rose. "Come on."

The town was busy. Shoppers and children on their summer holiday filled the narrow footpaths. A gang of men were painting the curbstones in bands of glistening red, white, and blue. The maypole had been touched up in the same Loyalist colors, and from its peak hung a large flag: the Red Hand of Ulster, centered on the red cross of St. George, set against a white background. Union Jacks dangled from upstairs windows.

Other men struggled to erect an arch across the road. In its center was a picture of a man mounted on a rearing white horse. One hand held the reins; the other waved a saber over the rider's head.

"Pity," said O'Reilly, "that William of Orange's charger has a squint."

Barry looked more closely. O'Reilly was right.

"Derry, Aughrim, Enniskillen, and the Boyne." O'Reilly read the names of battles that were lettered on painted scrolls on either side of the mounted man. "In 1690 or thereabouts. Old battles that should be forgotten."

"You said it was all sweetness and light between the Protestants and the Catholics in Ballybucklebo."

"There's nothing overt. Not like the taunting and ranting that go on in Belfast. But I don't like it," said O'Reilly. "I was a boy during the Troubles back in the 1920s. I'd hate to see the Troubles come back, and when you keep on rubbing folks' noses in it with flags and parades . . ."

"I'm sure there'll never be anything like the Troubles again. Not here."

"I hope you're right," said O'Reilly, "but long memories are the curse of Ireland. The Twelfth's just a holiday to most folks, but there's a bunch of bigots keeping the old hatred alive . . . like our worthy councilor. If he can spare the time from trying to drive a decent old man off his property, he'd be happy to string up the odd Fenian from a lamppost." The doctor sighed. "I don't know about you, but I'm no closer to sorting out how we can help Sonny, and now I have to find a way to get Maureen Galvin's money back for her."

"I thought you knew a company in Belfast that would buy the ducks."

"I can phone a fellow I played rugby with, but would you want to try to sell the things?" O'Reilly started to cross the road. "Something will turn up," he said, stepping back onto the footpath. "Just what the dickens do you think this is all about?"

Barry saw the ginger-haired Donal Donnelly waving at them as he forced his way across the street. It was Donal who had directed Barry to Ballybucklebo his first day. Donal was accompanied by a gray dog. "Dr. O'Reilly, sir. Could I have a wee word?" Donal's buckteeth trembled against his long lower lip.

"Of course."

"This here's Bluebird." He tugged on a thin piece of rope. The dog raised its narrow muzzle. "After your man Donald Campbell's speedboat."

"Races, does she?" O'Reilly asked, examining the dog's flanks.

"She does, sir, but she hasn't won yet."

"So if she's slow, why do you call her Bluebird?"

"Because, sir"—Donal's left upper eyelid drooped in a slow wink—"she runs on water. But on Friday at Dunmore Park, she'll be running dry."

"Will she, by heaven?" O'Reilly's eyes widened.

Barry was baffled. What were they talking about?

"Thought you'd like to know." Donal peered around. "Not a word now."

"Thanks, Donal. I might just take a trip up to Dunmore. Dr. Laverty could look after the practice."

Barry flinched. Oh, no. Friday was to be his night off.

"We'll be running on," said Donal, tugging at the rope. "Got to get you fit, girl."

"Fingal," said Barry. "You said I could have Friday night off."

"Don't worry. We'll both get away. You just hold the fort till it's time for you to go. I don't do it very often, but if no one's baby's due and the shop seems reasonably quiet, Kinky takes the calls. Either she asks the customer to wait until the morning or, if she thinks it is urgent, she arranges for an ambulance to take the patient up to the Royal. So you can see the light of your life, and I can have a bit of fun myself." O'Reilly chuckled.

"You've utterly lost me."

"I do that sometimes," said O'Reilly, "and I've no time to explain now. We're running behind. Come on and we'll get Declan Finnegan looked at."

IN LOCAL parlance, O'Reilly went through Tuesday's afternoon calls—and most of the patients who had come to the surgery on Wednesday morning—like grease through a duckling. Barry could barely keep pace. He was glad of the respite when Mrs. Kincaid set his lunch plate on the table.

"Your list, Doctor. It's not too bad." She handed O'Reilly the sheet.

"Thanks, Kinky." O'Reilly consulted it quickly. "Not bad at all. Any luck with finding out about Julie MacAteer?"

"I'm not getting very far. The wee girl is living somewhere here, but nobody knows where. I—" Her reply was interrupted by the jangling of the front doorbell. "I'll see who it is, so." She left, and when she returned, her color was high. "It's his exalted excellence, Councilor Bishop. Wants to be seen now. Will I tell him to wait?"

"No," said O'Reilly, pushing his plate aside. "Pop these in the oven, Kinky. Come on, Barry."

"Right."

Councilor Bishop stood in the hall. "You took your time."

"Ach," said O'Reilly mildly, "we were at our lunch. Could you not have come during surgery hours?"

"And wait forever with the unwashed? Don't be stupid."

Barry saw a spark deep in O'Reilly's brown eyes.

"Come into the surgery," said O'Reilly, crossing the hall and opening the door. When the councilor was seated, he said, "What can I do for you?"

Councilor Bishop thrust his bandaged finger under O'Reilly's nose. "I need this better for tomorrow."

"Right," said O'Reilly as he went to a tray of instruments and picked up a pair of scissors and a set of fine-nosed forceps.

Bishop gave his hand to O'Reilly, who picked up the bottom end of the bandage with the forceps, slid one blade of the scissors beneath the gauze, and began to snip. When the dressing was divided from finger base to fingertip, O'Reilly gave a ferocious yank with the forceps. Bishop let out a deafening *"Yeeeow!"*

"Sorry about that, Councilor," O'Reilly said. "I could have soaked it for fifteen minutes and softened the old blood, but I know you're in a rush. Go and rinse it in the sink."

The councilor obeyed.

"All set for the big day tomorrow?" O'Reilly inquired.

"Don't talk to me about big days. I've bigger fish to fry. Sonny's in hospital, and that parcel of land—"

Barry needed to hear no more. "I think that's the meanest—"

"Nobody asked you to think," O'Reilly snapped. He shook his head.

Barry bit back his words. He felt heat in his cheeks.

Councilor Bishop turned off the tap and glowered at his fingertip. "Doesn't look too bad. Good. I'll be off, then. I've work to do."

"Fine," said O'Reilly as he accompanied the councilor to the surgery door. "And how's Mrs. Bishop today?"

"She's fit to be tied. That new maid of ours. The Antrim girl. She's given her notice, and where in the hell can you find good help these days?"

"I wouldn't know," said O'Reilly, smiling at Mrs. Kincaid, who was busy in the dining room. He opened the front door and let the councilor pass.

Barry stood at O'Reilly's shoulder as the fat man marched down the path. "You were too civil to that man," he muttered. "And I thought we were going to have it out with him about Sonny's place. When I tried to say something, why did you jump all over me?"

"Arguing with men like Bishop's no use. All it does is stiffen their resolve. If we're going to sort him out, we need an argument he can't resist."

"And what could that be?" Barry was not satisfied.

"I'm beginning to wonder, but I'm starting to get an idea. I didn't know his maid came from County Antrim." O'Reilly looked up at the sky as if seeking divine inspiration. "Would you look at that?"

Barry stared at the sky. Ranks of cumulonimbus clouds were marching like dark-cuirassed dragoons toward the little town of Ballybucklebo.

"I think," Barry said, "we're in for a storm."

"Indeed," said O'Reilly, glowering at the distant departing back of Councilor Bishop. "You could be right."

7

Don't Rain on My Parade

O'REILLY opened the upper half of one of the sash windows in the upstairs sitting room and said, "We'll watch from here."

Barry looked across to the church steeple, dark against a leaden morning sky, and on down Main Street where red, white, and blue bunting strung between lampposts drooped listlessly. The street was flanked by the citizenry. Many carried tiny Union Jacks or Ulster flags. Youngsters were hoisted onto their daddy's shoulders. Stray dogs yapped. Borne on the humid air, the rattling of side drums and the distant wailing of bagpipes drifted into the room.

"That'll be the Ballybucklebo Highlanders warming up down at the maypole," O'Reilly remarked. "As brave a bunch of musical heroes as ever blew into a bag. Pipe major Donal Donnelly, bass drummer Seamus Galvin, and the rest." O'Reilly chuckled. "We could be busy when the parade's over and that lot have gone to the field for the speeches and the hymns and a bit of good old neighborly Pope bashing. Bagpiping's a thirsty business."

"I know," Barry said. "I worked in the first-aid tent last year at the Bangor Field. I put in more stitches than a shirt factory."

"And I'll bet some of the worst offenders were members of temperance lodges," said O'Reilly. "But maybe we'll get lucky today and that thunderstorm will break before they get too much of a head of steam up." He looked at his watch. "Eleven o'clock. Should be starting soon."

Tah-rah-rum, tah-rah-rum. The distant side drums broke into the double triple-roll that Barry knew signaled the start of a pipe band's advance.

"Here they come," said O'Reilly. "That'll be the worshipful master Bertie Bishop on the off-white horse at the head of them."

Barry could see a man riding an off-white horse. Behind him tramped the members of an Orange Lodge following its banner. Next came a drum major marching in front of a kilted pipe band.

"Ballybucklebo's finest," said O'Reilly. "The Highlanders."

Now Barry recognized Councilor Bishop at the head of the procession. He could see that, even for a Clydesdale, the animal was making heavy weather of carrying the councilor's weight.

"You should see—" O'Reilly was cut off by a series of shrill whinnies.

At the head of the procession, Councilor Bishop's mount was rearing. The animal bucked, unseated its rider, and galloped off down the road.

O'Reilly doubled over, hands clasped to his ample belly. "Better," he said, laughing hard. "Better than a bloody pantomime."

Barry watched the Ballybucklebo Lodge members clustering around their fallen worshipful master. "I hope he's not hurt."

"So do I. He's the last one I'd want to have to minister unto today. I think he'll be all right. He's getting up."

"Lord, Fingal. Look."

The councilor's mishap had brought the marchers to an untidy halt, blocking the progress of the pipers. The drum major dropped his mace. He fell to his hands and knees trying to retrieve it. The front rank of pipers shambled to a halt.

"That's Donal Donnelly there at the left of the front rank," Barry said.

"Pipe major. How do you like his uniform?" O'Reilly snorted.

Donal's saffron kilt hung from his skinny hips. It ought to have ended at knee level but instead drooped to half-calf.

"Look out, Donal!" O'Reilly bellowed uselessly.

Barry watched open-mouthed as the red-faced piper in the rank behind, his eyes closed, fingers running up and down the chanter, marched smack into Donal's skinny back. Accompanied by the tuneless yodeling from the rapidly deflating pipes of the man behind him, Donal's kilt slipped off. He dropped his pipes, bent, and hastily hoisted his garment.

Collapsing pipes wailed as rank tangled with file.

As if in celestial solidarity with the ructions below, the heavens joined in. The storm broke, rain lashing the participants and the spectators. Bandsmen scurried for shelter. Lightweight raincoats appeared as if from nowhere, and family groups shared the dubious protection of the plastic held over their heads.

"I'd call this a humdinger," said O'Reilly, closing the sash window. "No point getting this room soaked."

O'Reilly strolled to the sideboard. "How about a sherry?" he asked as he filled his glass with Bushmills. "I don't think there'll be much business for today."

By Friday the thirteenth, the thunderstorm had passed and bright sunlight streamed in through one dining-room window.

"Big day for the pair of us," said O'Reilly, finishing his breakfast.

"I know," said Barry, trying not to think too hard of his evening to come with Patricia. "You're going to the dogs."

"I'd hardly put it that way, but yes, I want to see how Donal's Bluebird runs. And I'm meeting an old friend."

"Not by any chance the one that might buy Seamus Galvin's ducks?"

"The very fella," said O'Reilly. He rose. "But the dirt has to come before the brush. How'd you like to run the surgery this morning?"

"Me? Seriously?"

"I've been watching you, son. Time for you to fly solo. Well, dual control, for a start. I'll keep you company, but you do the work. I'll not interfere."

Barry straightened his tie, smoothed his tuft of hair, rose, and said, "If you really think so, we'd better get at it." He started toward the waiting room.

O'Reilly stopped him. "I'll fetch the customers. Explain to them who's in charge today. And you"—O'Reilly grabbed Lady Macbeth, who was trying to get into the surgery—"can get lost. Dr. Laverty will not be in need of your advice today. Into the kitchen. We'll have a word with Kinky. She was going to find out about Julie MacAteer. Julie should be in today to get her results." He headed for the kitchen, stuffing a protesting Lady Macbeth under his arm like a rugby football. "I'll bring the first customer back with me."

With each case that morning, Barry's confidence grew. True to his word, O'Reilly offered no advice unless asked, and sat quietly on the examining couch.

Just before lunchtime, O'Reilly brought in Maureen Galvin, carrying baby Barry Fingal wrapped in a blue shawl.

"Good morning, Maureen," Barry said as Maureen laid the little lad on the table.

"How's Seamus?" O'Reilly asked as Barry examined the healthy newborn.

"He's very busy. Him and his rocking ducks." Her green eyes sparkled. "He says you've fixed it up for him to sell the whole lot of them to a firm in Belfast. That we're going to make a mint."

"I hope so," said O'Reilly.

When she left, Barry heard Maureen singing, " 'California, here we come.' "

O'Reilly closed the surgery door. "I hope she's right. I'll just have to put the screws on my friend or think of something else. And we're going to have to sort out Julie MacAteer. She's next."

"What did the test say?"

O'Reilly grunted. "Bloody typical." He pulled an envelope, newly arrived with the morning's post, from his jacket pocket. "Look at that."

Barry read the results of an Aschheim-Zondek pregnancy test, which were inconclusive. "Oh, great."

"Right, and Mrs. Kincaid's no further on finding out about the mystery woman of Ballybucklebo." He blew out his cheeks. "I'll go and get her."

He returned moments later and offered Julie MacAteer a seat.

She sat, knees together, hands folded in the lap of her tartan skirt. "Am I?" she asked, her voice steady.

"We don't know. The test didn't work. I'm really very sorry," Barry said.

"My period's not come."

Barry swallowed. "Julie, we can do another test. It'll only take a few days."

"I know I'm pregnant," she said flatly.

"You may be right," Barry said, "but let's make sure."

"I suppose so. Mind you, if I just wait another few months, I'll know for certain, won't I?" She sniffed and used the heel of one hand to dry her eyes.

O'Reilly spoke quietly. "That's true."

She spun in the chair to face him. "What'll I do?"

"Dr. Laverty's right. "We'll repeat the test. But in the meantime, we've made arrangements for you to go to Liverpool. Just in case."

"Liverpool?" Julie sat back in the chair. "In England?"

"They'll take good care of you there. No one here need know."

"I'd have to have the baby. Give it up?" Her tears flowed.

"Yes. It'll be hard on you," O'Reilly said. "I know that."

She took two deep breaths. "I've no choice, have I?"

"I'm sorry," O'Reilly said gently. "Unless you can tell us who the father is . . ."

Julie shook her head, tossing her corn-silk hair. "No." She stiffened her shoulders. "Can I bring in a specimen this afternoon?"

"Yes," said O'Reilly. "Give it to Mrs. Kincaid when you come back."

"All right." Julie sniffed. "Liverpool. Oh, God. I just knew I'd have to go away. I've already given my notice."

"Oh?" said O'Reilly. "And who's your boss?"

"I'm not telling." She stood. "I'd better be going."

"I'll tell Mrs. Kincaid to expect you," O'Reilly said as he opened the door.

"FOUR o'clock. Time I was going," said O'Reilly, leaning against the mantel in the lounge, his briar belching. "I've to pick up Donal and Bluebird and drive them up to Dunmore Park; then I'll go over to the Royal. See how Sonny's getting on."

"He should be on the mend by now."

"I hope so, but what we're going to do with him when he gets out of hospital is beyond me. He can't go on living in his car. Anyway, you just keep an eye on the shop until it's time for you to go out yourself."

"I'll do my best."

"I know that," said O'Reilly, looking Barry in the eye. "I told you I've been watching you, son. You've the makings of a damn good GP. And you have fun tonight. You've earned it."

"Thanks, Fingal." Barry knew he was grinning, but why not? Praise from O'Reilly was praise indeed.

Barry sat back in his chair. O'Reilly had been right. There was a great deal of satisfaction to be gained from the routine of a busy general practice. Still, being left alone was a little unnerving. He stood up and strolled over to the window just in time to see Julie MacAteer walk down the front path. She must have brought her urine specimen. Poor lass. Why wouldn't she tell her physicians who she worked for? Something worried away at the back of Barry's consciousness. Something that somebody had said about a maid giving her notice. An Antrim girl.

He hadn't heard Mrs. Kincaid come in, and he jumped when she said, "Would you like some tea, Dr. Laverty?" She set a tray on the sideboard. "I made it for that nice MacAteer girl, the wee lamb."

"How is she, Mrs. Kincaid?"

"She puts up a brave front, so. Very private. Himself asked me to try to find out about her." She handed him a cup. "Milk's in it, the way you like it."

"Thanks." Barry took the cup. "And what have you discovered?"

"Not much. No one in the village seems to know her. But she works somewhere here or out in the country a ways. Her hands are soft, so she'll not be working on a farm. Maybe she's in service."

And then Barry remembered that it was Councilor Bishop who'd said his wife was fit to be tied because their maid had given her notice. "Mrs. Kincaid?"

"Dr. Laverty, I'd be very pleased if you'd call me Kinky, like himself."

Barry felt flattered. "All right . . . Kinky. Could Julie MacAteer be working for the Bishops?"

Kinky's small black eyes narrowed. "Aye, so. On Monday I'll be going to the Women's Union. Mrs. Bishop's a member. I will ask her, so."

"Good," said Barry before drinking his tea. He then heard the front doorbell. It might just be my first patient, he thought. "I'll go," he said.

A large familiar-looking woman stood on the step. She wore a floral-patterned dress with the dimensions of a small tent.

"Dr. Laverty? Could I have a wee word?"

"Certainly, Mrs. . . ."

"Sloan. Cissie Sloan. I'm one of the tonics."

"Come into the surgery." Barry stood aside to let her squeeze by. She was one of the patients O'Reilly injected with vitamin B-12.

"What can I do for you?" He closed the door and went to the swivel chair.

She perched her bulk on the patients' chair. "Cold in here," she said.

Barry was surprised that she felt cold since the room was overly warm.

"I feel the cold something chronic."

"Do you? Is that why you came?"

She shook her head. "I've been under Dr. O'Reilly for six months, and he's doing me no good. I come for a second opinion. He's away, isn't he?"

"Yes." News traveled fast in Ballybucklebo, Barry thought.

"Donal Donnelly's my nephew. Him and his dog and Dr. O'Reilly's away to Belfast. So I want you to tell me what's wrong with me."

"I'll try. Can you give me a few clues?"

Barry, with great patience and with growing concern that the consultation would make him late for Patricia, managed to mine a few nuggets of clinically relevant information from the slag heap of Cissie's detailed reminiscences.

"I first took poorly on a Thursday. No, no. I'm wrong. It was the Wednesday that Donal's other dog died. The one with the wee short tail. . . . So I said to Aggie—that's Aggie Arbuckle that was. Now she's Mehaffey. Married to Hughie, him that's Maggie MacCorkle's second cousin. . . . Anyway, Dr. O'Reilly says to me—you'd think he was Jehovah giving out the Commandments to Moses—he says to me, 'You're run down, Cissie. You need a tonic.' And here's me taking the tonic every six weeks for six months and I'm no better—"

"Right, Mrs. Sloan." Barry finally managed to stem the tide. "Let's see if I've got this right. You've been tired for six months, and it's getting worse?"

"Aye."

"Muscle cramps?"

"Desperate. In my legs. And you'll not believe this, Doctor. I've been putting on weight."

"Never," said Barry, inwardly congratulating himself for being able to keep a straight face. "Has any of your hair fallen out?"

"How did you know that?"

Barry ignored her question but asked, "Are you constipated?"

"Constipated? I've been like an egg-bound hen for months."

Barry peered at her face. Her complexion was pasty yellow, and there were puffy bags beneath both eyes. "Let me have a look at your neck." He stood and moved behind her chair. "I'm not going to strangle you," he reassured her as he placed his fingers over the front of her throat. Underneath the fat, he could feel a solid rubbery mass. Barry stepped back. She was right. She wasn't simply tired. She had all the classic manifestations of an underactive thyroid gland.

"What do you think, Doctor?"

Barry coughed. He was unsure how to answer her honestly and at the same time preserve O'Reilly's professional reputation.

"I'm not sure. We'll need to arrange a test at the hospital."

"Have I cancer?"

It was possible, but her thyroid gland was smooth, not hard and craggy. "I don't think so. I think your thyroid is a bit underactive."

"Why'd O'Reilly not do the test?"

"Um . . ." The truth was, he'd probably been in a hurry and had missed the diagnosis. "It's new. I only heard about it this year. But if the test shows what I think it will, we'll need Dr. O'Reilly to prescribe your treatment. He's much more experienced than I am. Now I'll just go and make a phone call."

The laboratory was still open when Barry phoned. Yes, they'd arrange for her to have a radioactive iodine uptake test.

"Here," he said, handing her a requisition form. "Monday morning, ten o'clock at the Royal. Go to the information desk. They'll show you to the lab."

"Thank you, Dr. Laverty sir." She rose and left.

"My pleasure," he said, and he meant it. He had been worried about being left all on his own, but unless something dramatic happened between now and half past six, when he would leave to pick up Patricia, he would be quite happy to feel just a little smug.

BARRY took one last look in the mirror. He brushed his hair, knowing that it was a futile gesture. Before long the tuft would be sticking up again like the crown of a broken hat. He glanced down.

His shoes were newly polished and his corduroys pressed. He silently thanked Mrs. Kin . . . no, Kinky.

He ran downstairs. The telephone began ringing as he cleared the last stair. He hesitated. O'Reilly had said to let Kinky take care of any calls. He lifted the receiver. "Hello?"

"I want to speak to Dr. O'Reilly."

"I'm sorry. He's in Belfast. It's Dr. Laverty. Who's speaking?"

"This is Mrs. Fotheringham. It's very urgent. I want you to come at once. The major's been taken ill. Very ill."

"What seems to be the trouble?" He glanced at his watch. Six fifteen.

"It's his neck. He's got a terrible pain in his neck."

He is a terrible pain in the neck, Barry thought. "Could it wait until morning?"

"I want him seen now."

Barry knew he couldn't justify sending for an ambulance for a man with a stiff neck. "Very well," he said. "I'll be right over."

"Don't be long." The line went dead.

Barry raised his eyes to the heavens, then saw Kinky, who had appeared from her kitchen. "Major Fotheringham has a stiff neck. I'll nip round there."

"I'll telephone your wee girl. Tell her you'll be late. What's her number?"

"Kinnegar six five seven three three four."

"You run on, Doctor. I'll take care of things here."

MRS. Fotheringham opened the door. "Come in, Laverty. The major's in the drawing room." Her tone was haughty.

Barry followed her, amused by her changed attitude. On the last visit, she had fawned over O'Reilly; now she was treating Barry like an underling.

"Major Fotheringham," Barry said to his patient, who lay on a long sofa between two armchairs. "How are you?"

The major put a limp hand to the left side of his neck. "It's my neck," he said. "It's awfully stiff. It started this morning."

"Were you doing anything when the stiffness started?" he asked.

"He was carrying stepladders," Mrs. Fotheringham said.

"You've probably just strained it." Barry laid the back of his right hand on the major's forehead. Meningitis was one serious cause of neck stiffness, but then there'd be a fever, and the major's skin was cool and dry. The pulse rate was normal. "Look into my eyes," he said to the major. Both pupils were the same size. No early clues of increased pressure inside the head there.

Barry put a hand on the side of the major's neck. He could feel the tension in the sternocleidomastoid, the strap of muscle that runs from the clavicle to the base of the skull. It was probably torticollis, spasm of the muscle, which was frequently a manifestation of hysteria. He could see the clock. Twenty to seven. "You've got a wry neck, Major Fotheringham."

He saw Mrs. Fotheringham's shoulders tense, her lips purse.

"Its correct name is torticollis," he said, and he watched her relax. "We'll soon put it right." He opened his bag and pulled out an aerosol canister of ethyl chloride. "This is pretty cold." He depressed the red button, and a cloud of vapor hissed out onto the skin.

"*Wheee.*" The major flinched as a thin rime of frost formed.

"Sorry, but it makes the muscles relax." Barry stuffed the can back into his bag. "If it's no better in the morning or if it gets worse, give us a call."

The fact that Mrs. Fotheringham called him Dr. Laverty when she said good-bye was not lost on Barry.

BARRY drummed his fingers on the steering wheel. It was nearly seven. He could only hope that Patricia would understand that not only was a doctor's time not always his own but also that people did get stuck behind tractors on country roads. As the car crept along, he thought about the recent consultation. The only thing that bothered him was a niggling worry that perhaps his examination had been a bit hurried. He hadn't made a full neurological evaluation, testing skin sensation and reflexes, but that would have taken at least half an hour and almost certainly would have shown absolutely nothing. Stiff necks could have sinister causes, but most were rare as hen's teeth.

And that bloody tractor up ahead was going at the speed of a snail. Blast. He saw the tractor's driver stick out his right arm. Barry braked. The tractor swerved right, then, as if having second thoughts, turned a good one hundred and twenty degrees and went into a field on the left-hand side of the road. At least the road ahead was clear.

Barry trod on the accelerator. Brunhilde's engine spluttered, wheezed . . . and died. Damnation. He knew he could have written his entire knowledge of the working of the internal combustion engine on a postage stamp. He turned the key, to be rewarded by a grinding of the starter motor—a grinding that became fainter as the battery began to expire.

Lips pursed, he climbed out. The tractor was nosing back out onto the road.

"Hello," Barry yelled, gratified to see the Massey-Harris halt and to recognize the driver, who'd come in last week for some liniment for sore knees. "Sorry to bother you, Mr. O'Hara, but do you know anything about engines?"

"Aye."

"Could you take a look at mine?"

"Aye." He moved to the driver's door and peered inside the car. "Excuse me, Doctor, but take a look at thon gauge. Engines go better if there's a wee taste of petrol in the tank."

"Oh, no! And I'm late."

"I could give you a lift to Paddy Farrelly's garage."

"Would you?"

"Aye." He set off, and Barry followed. His watch said ten past seven. Now he was going to be much later. Would Patricia understand?

EIGHT thirty. Barry's trousers were stained from the tractor's muddy seat, and his hands stank of gasoline. The door opened. "I'm sorry I'm late."

She laughed. "It's all right. Your Mrs. Kincaid phoned." She kissed him on the cheek, a short, chaste kiss, like brother to sister. "So did you save a life?"

"A life? One life? I eradicated bubonic plague from the hinterland of Ballybucklebo, brought a moribund malingerer back from the brink, gave three pints of my own blood—"

"Stop it." She laughed. "You are very late. It must have been important."

"Not exactly. Some hypochondriac with a stiff neck. It didn't take long to sort him out. Then my car ran out of petrol. I had to get a lift on a tractor. That's why . . ." He gestured at his dirty trousers. "Look, we'd better get moving. The kitchen at the club closes at nine."

"No need. I phoned them and canceled. I've made us a bite. Why don't you go and have a wash." She took his hand and pulled him into the hall and showed him to the bathroom.

What a girl, he thought to himself as he scrubbed his hands. Beautiful, self-possessed, and able to accept and adapt to changing circumstances.

When he returned, Patricia brought him into a small room. "You really don't mind?" he asked.

"I like cooking. It's hardly your fault you had to do your job. And it's the first time I've heard of a fellow running out of petrol on his way to a date."

"I know. I usually arrange that for the drive home."

"Well, you'll not be able to try that one on tonight."

"Me? Try it on? Never." He looked around the room. Books were neatly stacked on shelves improvised from planks laid on piles of bricks. Many were engineering texts, but he also saw works of Steinbeck, Tolkien, and—what a strange title—*The Feminine Mystique* by a Betty Friedan. A table was set for two, close to a window overlooking Belfast Lough.

"Nice place you have here," he said.

"Thank you." She put on a record.

Barry listened as a soprano sang in Italian. The notes swelled, rose, and fell in cadences that touched something deep in him.

"What's that? It's beautiful." And so was she, standing there, backlit by the light reflected from the lough's calm waters.

"Mozart," she said. *The Marriage of Figaro.*

"It's amazing."

"I hope you like lasagna," she said. "Italian music, Italian food, and Italian wine." She handed him a corkscrew. "Open it, would you?" She indicated a bottle of Chianti.

"All we need now are a couple of strolling mandolin players to make this a *Bella Notte.*"

"You speak Italian?"

"Not at all, but I've seen *Lady and the Tramp.*"

"Eejit." Her laughter filled the little room. "I read once that women should beware of men who make them laugh. I'll have to keep an eye on you, Barry Laverty."

And I'll keep mine on you, Patricia, he thought, seeing the curve of her breast and the slimness of her waist and not noticing her limp at all as she went through a doorway that led to her kitchen.

"THAT," he said, laying his knife and fork on a tomato-smeared plate, "was great." He sipped the dark red wine, tasting Tuscan sunshine. "Great."

"Glad you liked it." She lifted their plates. "I'll just be a minute. Sit where you are. These can soak in the sink."

Barry, replete, stretched his legs in front of him.

Patricia reappeared and bent over the gramophone. "This is my very favorite," she said. "Listen."

It was a duet. Two sopranos with voices like liquid silver and molten gold flowed together in harmony.

"It's 'The Flower Duet' from Delibes's *Lakme.*"

He stood and put his hands on her waist, and she leaned against him. He lifted the hair from the nape of her neck and kissed her there. He heard her breathing quicken as he turned her to face him, holding her close, feeling the softness of her. He kissed her slowly, deeply, and his hand found her breast, firm through the silk. She whimpered. He felt her hand on his wrist as she moved away.

"Not yet, Barry. Please. Don't spoil it." Her voice was low.

Barry swallowed. "All right." Had he scared her? Had he been too fast?

"I'm sorry, Barry. I want to, but . . . not yet. Not tonight."

He stroked her hair. "I understand. It's all right."

"Thank you." She led him to a small sofa. "Barry." She hesitated. "Barry, I think I could fall in love with you, but I'm not sure I'm ready."

"Why not?"

"I want to be an engineer."

"I know that."

"I haven't time to fall in love."

"I have." He knew that he was already in love, in love to the depths of his soul.

"You don't understand," she said. "It's not about sex. It's about me. I want to do a man's job in a man's world, so I have to work twice as hard. You know what it took for you to get through medical school."

"But I still had time for a bit of fun. I had time for a girlfriend."

"I don't . . . for a boyfriend, I mean. Not a serious one. I daren't fall behind." She stood up, her arms folded. He could tell by the set of her jaw that arguments would be futile.

"I'd better go." His words were more clipped than he had intended.

"Please . . . Please don't be angry. I like you a lot, but I don't want you or anybody else to—"

"I understand." He stood.

"I'm sorry," she said.

He waited for her to say something else, anything, but she had half turned to stare into the dark night.

"All right." He walked to the door. "Thank you for a lovely dinner." His words were politely cold.

"Barry, I'd still like to see you again." She moved closer to him.

To tell me that your career is more important? he thought. To hold out a hope and dash it again? "I'll not be free again for a couple of weeks."

"Will you phone me?"

He hesitated.

"Please?" She moved closer still, but he simply held out his hand. She ignored it and kissed him, and he held her.

"I'll phone," he said, and swallowed, telling himself he was being stupid. But there could never be another Patricia. Not for him.

"Thank you," she said softly. "Please try to understand."

"Good night," Barry said, and closed the door behind him.

8

I Fall to Pieces

"YOU'VE a face on you like a Lurgan spade," O'Reilly said, referring to the extra-long turf-cutting implement peculiar to that town in County Armagh. "Bad night?"

"Not really." Barry sipped his tea and stared out through the dining-room window. Yes, it had been a bad night. Things had not gone at all the way he had been hoping with Patricia, and as a result, he had slept badly, but he saw no reason to confide in O'Reilly.

"Kinky said that you were busy."

"I saw Cissie Sloan." Barry hesitated. "And I think you're wrong about her." He studied O'Reilly's face.

"Is that a fact?"

"I'm sure she has hypothyroidism." Barry quickly listed her symptoms.

"You might just be right." O'Reilly went to the sideboard and helped himself to a kipper. "Good lad."

Emboldened, Barry said, "I'm sending her for a radioactive iodine uptake on Monday."

"Better and better." O'Reilly tucked into the butter-dripping smoked herring. "If you are right, it'll do wonders for your reputation."

"What about yours?"

O'Reilly grunted. "I'm big enough and ugly enough to look after myself. Kinky said you went to see Major Fotheringham."

"Another false alarm. Torticollis. I gave him a squirt of ethyl chloride and told him to call us if there was no improvement."

"Lord," said O'Reilly. "One day that man *will* have something wrong and we'll miss it. He'll not have just cried wolf. Since I've known him, he's roared on as if he were being attacked by a whole bloody pack." He chuckled. "I always liked the wolves. *Canis lupus,* to give them their Latin name."

"I know. You've one of their descendants, *Canis familiaris,* in your backyard."

"Good old Arthur," O'Reilly said fondly. "And by heaven, I'd a lot of fun with another canine last night."

"Donal's Bluebird?"

"The darling dog excelled herself. She won in the third race at twenty to one."

Barry's fork stopped. "And I suppose you backed her."

"Wouldn't you have if you'd had inside information?"

Barry savored a morsel of kipper, swallowed, and said, "All that business about running on water, then running dry? Fingal, would you explain?"

"Look. At the races, a bunch of dogs rush round an oval track chasing an electrical hare. After a few races, the bookies figure out the likelihood of any given dog winning and, on that basis, offer odds. When there's money involved, people will always try to fiddle the system. It's not been above some of the doggy fraternity to help their contender along a bit."

"How?"

"Stimulant drugs. That's why all dogs that place are immediately tested. But they don't test the losing animals. What do you think the odds will be after a dog has come last in half a dozen races?"

"Relatively good."

"See, you're beginning to understand."

"The hell I am."

"Water," said O'Reilly conspiratorially. "When Donal told me the dog had been running on water, he meant that he'd kept her thirsty until immediately before each one of her previous outings. Just before the race, he let her have all she wanted to drink. No dog can run when it's waterlogged."

"So the odds go down?"

"Right," said O'Reilly. "You're not as green as you look."

"And when Donal said the dog would run dry last night . . ."

"Exactly. No water. No handicap. Great odds and not a thing to show up on a drug test."

"But isn't that dishonest?"

"Totally. But it keeps the bookies humble."

"How much did you bet?"

"Twenty quid."

Barry whistled. "But that means you won four hundred pounds."

"Indeed," said O'Reilly, "but it's going to a good cause."

The Fingal Flahertie O'Reilly Benevolent Fund, Barry thought. "And I suppose to top it off, Sonny's better and your friend is going to buy Seamus Galvin's rocking ducks. You said you were going to see Sonny."

"And so I did. He's off oxygen. Temperature's normal. Unfortunately, my business friend doesn't want Galvin's ducks. He's probably still laughing about them. Can't say I blame him, really. But I'm sure something will turn up for Seamus." He winked at Barry. "I did have one other bit of good luck, and so did His Lordship, and that should please you."

"Why me?"

"The old boy likes a night at the dogs. I gave him the nod about Bluebird, and when he'd collected his winnings, I asked him if you could have a day or two's fishing on his water. 'Anytime,' he said."

"Thank you, Fingal."

"I presume you'll be spending a bit of time there soon."

"Why do you say that?"

O'Reilly pushed his plate away. "Young fellows who've been out on dates with beautiful young women generally beam a bit the following morning. You are decidedly deficient in the beaming department. I'd guess you and Patricia didn't hit it off."

"You could say that," he said quietly.

"I just did. You'll get over it. But it'll take time. I know."

I know you do, Barry thought. As he wondered how to reply, he heard the telephone ringing in the hall.

"If it's one of the customers, I'll go, Barry."

"Thanks, Fingal, I—"

Mrs. Kincaid burst in. "It's Mrs. Fotheringham. She says to come at once. Her husband's unconscious."

O'REILLY hurled the Rover along the narrow road. Barry tried to answer O'Reilly's questions and keep an eye on the road.

"Tell me again. Exactly what did you find when you examined him?" O'Reilly's fists grasped the steering wheel. He stared ahead.

"Not much. Bit of spasm in the left neck muscles. His pupils were equal in size, not dilated or constricted."

"What about his reflexes?"

"I didn't test them. I thought Fotheringham was up to his usual tricks."

"I'd probably have done the same."

"Would you?"

"Probably." O'Reilly stamped on the brakes, and Barry was thrown forward. "Out. Open the gate."

Barry obeyed, and waited for the car to pass. He then ran up the gravel drive and into the Fotheringhams' house. He caught a glimpse of O'Reilly disappearing into the upstairs bedroom and raced up the stairs. He was short of breath when he arrived.

Mrs. Fotheringham stood at the foot of the bed. O'Reilly sat on the side of the four-poster taking the pulse of a clearly unconscious Major Fotheringham and barking questions at his wife.

"Dr. Laverty sprayed his neck and the pain got better?"

"That's right. Basil said the spray was working, but his head had started to feel funny, so he thought he'd go to bed. He was still asleep when I got up. I was going to bring his breakfast up to him, but I heard him calling for me."

"When did he vomit?"

Barry was aware of the acrid smell. Stiff neck, headache, vomiting, coma. It couldn't be.

"I came back up, and he said he thought someone had hit him on the head. I told him not to be silly . . . then he boked."

Barry could see the lines in the textbook, word for word, the ones he'd memorized before his finals: ". . . and headache may be so abrupt in onset as to make the patient think he has been struck."

O'Reilly produced a penlight and bent to examine the major's eyes. Barry knew, he just knew, that one pupil would be widely dilated and would not respond by constricting when O'Reilly directed the thin beam under the eyelid. Barry held his breath.

"Right pupil's fixed," said O'Reilly.

Barry exhaled. Major Fotheringham had suffered an intracranial hemorrhage. And his stiff neck last night had been the earliest sign.

"I'm afraid your husband's had a kind of stroke."

Mrs. Fotheringham crossed her arms and rocked back and forth, all the while making little keening noises.

And if I'd not been in a rush . . . Barry's thoughts were interrupted when O'Reilly said, "I'm sorry Dr. Laverty didn't make the diagnosis last night." Barry stiffened. "But I doubt if anyone could have."

"I know. He was very nice." She forced a tiny smile.

Barry blessed the older man for his support. What O'Reilly had said would have been true if last night's examination had been thorough, if he had tested the reflexes and found them to be normal. But that hadn't happened.

"Right," said O'Reilly. "We'll have to get him to the Royal."

"Is he going to die?" Mrs. Fotheringham asked.

O'Reilly nodded. "I'll not lie to you. He could."

Mrs. Fotheringham yelped and stuffed a fist into her mouth.

"He could live but be paralyzed. But until the specialists have done a test called a lumbar puncture and maybe take special X-rays, we'll not know what's caused it." Maybe it's just a bleeding aneurysm, Barry thought, and heard O'Reilly echo the idea. "If it's just a leak from a thin-walled blood vessel, they can usually operate. Some patients make a complete recovery."

"Really?" There was hope in her eyes.

"Yes. But I won't make any promises. Dr. Laverty, would you phone for the ambulance?"

"I WONDER where Lady Macbeth is," O'Reilly remarked, walking directly to the sideboard in the upstairs sitting room.

Barry neither knew nor cared.

O'Reilly handed him a tumbler of whiskey. "Get that into you."

"I'd rather have a sherry." Or perhaps some hemlock, Barry thought.

It had been more than an hour since Major Fotheringham and his wife had been dispatched to the Royal. O'Reilly had driven back home. They had exchanged few words.

"That's a medicinal whiskey. Sit down, drink up, and shut up."

Barry sat. The whiskey was peat-flavored, sharp on his tongue.

O'Reilly fired up his briar pipe and lowered himself into the other armchair. He looked Barry in the eye and said, "I'm disappointed."

Barry flinched. "There's no point making excuses, so I won't."

"Excuses? What for?"

"I was in a hurry. I didn't do a complete examination."

"And if you had, what do you think it would have shown?"

"Enough so that I could have got him to a hospital before the bleeding into his head got any worse."

"Maybe, but what did his wife say?" O'Reilly took a sip from his glass.

"What do you mean?"

"Everything blew up this morning. Hours after you were there. If he'd had a decent bleed last night, don't you think it would have been as plain as the nose on your face? But he hadn't bled, and it wasn't plain."

"I was wrong last night."

"And that's why I'm disappointed."

"Because I didn't do my job right?"

O'Reilly stood and loomed over Barry. "No, you buck eejit. You knew your patient's history of malingering. You went to see him, and you didn't have to. You put him before yourself, and there was no need to. I know how much you wanted to see that wee girl. I told you Kinky could have handled things. Fotheringham would have been no worse off if you hadn't been conscientious enough to go last night and we'd not gone out there till this morning."

"It's still no excuse."

"Good Lord, man. Who do you think you are? Hippocrates? Listen, what makes you think you're the only physician to make mistakes? Do you think missing Cissie Sloan's thyroid is the only mistake I've ever made?"

"Well, I—"

"Of course not. And not living up to your own personal standards last night may seem like the end of the world to you. It's not. You'll make mistakes. You're beating the hell out of yourself because you think you should be infallible. That's why I'm disappointed. You should know better than that. Go easy on yourself."

Barry looked up at the big man. The hint of a smile was at the corner of his lips as he said, "How long have you been here?"

"Two weeks."

"That's long enough for me. I've told you, you've the makings of a damn good GP. But you'll never last if you insist on taking everything to heart."

"I still think I could've done a better job."

"Yes," said O'Reilly levelly, "but you recognize it, and that's to your credit. What happened can't be helped. Learn from it and put it behind you."

A huge grin erupted on O'Reilly's face, and Barry had to smile back. "Good man, Barry." O'Reilly finished his whiskey and looked at his watch. "It's only two o'clock. Why don't you grab your rod and head down to His Lordship's? Nothing like a few hours in the open air, away from whatever you do for a living, to give you a chance to get your mind straightened out."

"I'd like that, Fingal."

"So off you go. Kinky'll make you some sandwiches. Forget about Fotheringham. Forget about your broken heart. I'll look after the shop, and Barry, would you do me a favor?"

"Of course."

"Take Arthur Guinness with you. He loves an afternoon by the river."

"How did you make out?" O'Reilly asked when Barry walked into the kitchen that evening.

Barry grinned, parked his rod, opened the creel, produced two shining brown trout, and dumped them into the kitchen sink.

"Not bad," said O'Reilly. He opened a drawer, took out a knife, and handed it to Barry. "You caught 'em. You gut 'em."

"Fair enough." Barry turned on the cold tap, took the first fish, and expertly slit it open and cleaned it.

"That was slick," said O'Reilly. "Ever consider a career in surgery?"

Barry shook his head. "No, but I did think over what you said." Barry laid the cleaned fish aside and reached for the other. "I didn't do all I could have for Fotheringham, but you're right. I will try to put it behind me."

"Good lad. 'To err is human.' "

" 'To forgive, divine.' " Barry sliced into the second fish. "Alexander Pope."

"And you'll be pleased to hear that the Divinity must have been keeping an eye on you. Fotheringham had a small aneurysm. The surgeon reckons he got it tied off and that the major should make a reasonable recovery."

He turned and saw that O'Reilly was smiling. "Honestly?"

"Honestly." O'Reilly slapped a hand on the counter. "Now," he said, "tomorrow's Sunday. No surgery. I'd like to nip up to Belfast for the day. Think you could manage on your own?"

Barry hesitated.

"Best thing you could do. Just like falling off a horse. Most riders think it's a good idea to get back into the saddle as soon as possible." He turned. "I'm off upstairs. Come and have a jar when you've cleaned yourself up."

THE next morning, Barry stood in the recess of the bay window. The rain was lashing down, blackening the tiles of the steeple opposite and drenching the members of the congregation, most of whom were hurrying away on foot. He saw Kinky cross the road and felt the door slam as she let herself in.

He heard the phone jangle below. The ringing stopped. Kinky must have taken the call. If someone needed him, he hoped it would be a simple case. O'Reilly had left an hour ago.

"Dr. Laverty?"

He walked to the door.

"There's some foreign gentleman says he has to speak with you."

"Right." Downstairs. He took the receiver. "Dr. Laverty."

"Crikey. How is it being the great, healing sahib?" The man's muffled voice had the singsong cadence of what was known as Bombay Welsh. "I am very much wishing to consult the man of medicine, Dr. Lavatory."

Barry laughed. "Stop mucking about, Mills. You're not Peter Sellers."

"But I am thinking it is a pretty damn good impression of his Mr. Banerjee, isn't it? How are you, mate? What are you up to today?"

"I'm on call."

"I'm not . . . for once. I thought I'd take a trip down to see you."

"That'd be great. Hang on." He turned. "Kinky, could you manage lunch for two?"

"Aye, so."

"Come and have lunch." Barry gave directions.

"Great. I'll see you in about an hour." The phone went dead.

Barry said to Kinky, "Jack Mills is an old friend. He'll be here in about an hour. Look after him, will you, if I have to go out?"

"I will, so." She bustled off to her kitchen, pausing only to ask, "Would you like them fishes for your lunch?"

"Yes, please." Barry went back upstairs. He lifted the *Sunday Telegraph* from the coffee table, found the cryptic crossword puzzle, and settled into the chair, welcoming Lady Macbeth when she jumped into his lap.

"THAT there trout," said Jack in the accents of Belfast's dockland, "was cracker, so it was. Dead-on. Bloody wheeker."

"I take it you approve?" Barry smiled. Jack Mills hadn't changed, not since they'd met eleven years before. Solid. Dependable. Never serious for long.

"Isn't that what I just said?"

"I caught them yesterday."

"So you do get a bit of time off?"

"A bit."

"Have you seen that bird you were telling me about?"

Barry's smile faded. "Patricia? I don't think she'd be too happy to hear you call her a bird. She's an engineering student."

"Good Lord. What is the world coming to? The next thing you know, women'll be playing rugby."

"I doubt it. Mind you, she's pretty single-minded about her engineering. She told me on Friday night that she didn't want to get serious. Her career was too important." He glanced over at Jack.

"And you did? Want to get serious?"

Barry nodded.

"Is it getting to you, mate?"

"A bit."

"So what are you going to do about it?"

"I'm not sure. She asked me to phone. I thought I might tonight."

"I wouldn't. Remember when you tried to teach me about fly-fishing? You said that trout would be scared off if we rushed up to the riverbank, that we'd have to move up quietly, take our time?"

"So I should take my time with Patricia?"

"Definitely. If she's serious and doesn't want to see you again, you'll not hear from her. If she does want to see you, she'll call."

9

All Professions Are Conspiracies Against the Laity

ON TUESDAY, Barry was disappointed that he'd not had a chance to speak to Kinky the previous night after her return from the Women's Union. After a packed Monday-morning surgery, he and O'Reilly had been called out to attend another confinement. He wasn't going to complain. It worked wonders for the morale to see a baby safely delivered by a grateful, healthy woman. It might not be as challenging as brain surgery, but it felt right. He headed for the dining room.

"Morning, Fingal."

"You look like the cat that got the cream." O'Reilly glanced up from a plate of lamb kidneys. "Feeling pleased with yourself?"

"Well, I . . ."

"So you should. You've a knack for midwifery."

Barry helped himself to a small portion from the sideboard.

"I know," said O'Reilly. "You came down here to give general practice a try. I'd not want to force you to stay." His gaze was level. "You might do better if you specialized in obstetrics and gynecology."

Barry wasn't sure what to say. He had wondered last night about that very possibility.

"You have to do what's right for yourself, son. Now eat and shut up. I've a lot I want to think about." He hunched over his plate, shoveled in another mouthful, and chewed fiercely.

Barry sat just as Kinky strode in.

"Kinky?" Barry asked. "Did you get a word with Mrs. Bishop last night?"

Kinky beamed. "Aye, and you were right. The wee Rasharkin lassie is a housemaid at the Bishops'."

"How long has she worked there?" O'Reilly asked.

"Three months."

O'Reilly nodded. "Interesting. And how does she get on with the Bishops?"

"Mrs. Bishop's heartbroken that Julie's given her notice. The wee girl wouldn't give a reason for a while. Now says she has a sick sister living in Liverpool. Mrs. Bishop thinks that there's no such thing."

"What does she think?"

"That Bertie Bishop's always had an eye for the ladies. Mrs. Bishop thinks her husband maybe pinched the wee lass's bottom once too often."

O'Reilly's eyes were wide. "Now there's a thing."

Barry was not quite sure what O'Reilly might be hinting at. "Do you happen to know, Kinky, if Julie has a boyfriend?"

Kinky frowned. "I did ask. Mrs. Bishop didn't know, but once or twice a fellow with ginger hair had come round to the servants quarters at night. She only caught a glimpse of him."

"Damn."

"Don't let that bother you, Barry." O'Reilly was rubbing his hands with, Barry thought, the enthusiasm of Ebenezer Scrooge surveying a heap of gold sovereigns. "Thanks a million, Kinky. You're a better spy than James Bond. And *he* can't cook."

"And you're full of blarney for a man with work to do."

"How much work?"

"Not too much. Half a dozen of the regulars. Julie MacAteer'll be in later." Kinky's brow furrowed. "And Cissie Sloan's here, and it's not her tonic day."

Kinky was right. The waiting room was half empty.

By mid-morning, two reports had arrived in a buff envelope: Cissie's and Julie MacAteer's. Barry's pleasure when he saw that the radioactive iodine uptake test had confirmed his diagnosis was dulled by one word on the second piece of paper: "Positive."

He tried to smile at Julie, who sat in the waiting room. "Just be a minute, Julie. Will you come in, Mrs. Sloan?"

Cissie followed him to the surgery like a battleship in the wake of a tugboat.

"Morning, Cissie. So, Dr. Laverty?" O'Reilly held out his hand. Barry handed him the pink laboratory form. O'Reilly peered at it, then gave it to Barry. "You'll have to tell me what this newfangled stuff means."

Was O'Reilly serious? Barry spoke to Cissie but kept his eyes on O'Reilly's face. "Mrs. Sloan, in a nutshell, a gland in your neck isn't making enough of a little thingy it releases into your bloodstream. The little thingy—called thyroxine—is supposed to help you feel full of get-up-and-go, so it's no wonder you've been feeling frazzled."

Barry looked at O'Reilly, who said, "Do you think some thyroid extract might do the trick, Dr. Laverty?"

"Indeed. Will you write the prescription?"

"I will," said O'Reilly, scribbling away.

"I told you," said Barry, "Dr. O'Reilly's the expert on the treatment."

"And amn't I the lucky one having the pair of you to look after me? This'll put that there Aggie in her box. She said you near killed that snooty Major Fotheringham."

Barry flinched.

"Says I to her, 'Nobody's perfect, Aggie.'" She looked directly at O'Reilly as she delivered those oblique words of forgiveness.

O'Reilly inclined his head, then gave Cissie instructions for using the medication and accompanied her to the door.

"Well done," said O'Reilly when she'd left. "That was a smart diagnosis, and you're getting the hang of explaining things. And thanks for that bit of professional courtesy, letting on that I know more about the treatment."

"There's honor among thieves," Barry said, smiling.

"Sure, 'All professions are conspiracies against the laity.'"

Barry frowned. "Who said that?"

"Fooled you that time. George Bernard Shaw in *The Doctor's Dilemma*."

"One to you, Fingal. And speaking of dilemmas"—Barry handed Julie MacAteer's results to O'Reilly—"she's next."

"I'M SORRY, Julie . . ." O'Reilly began.

"It's positive, isn't it?" She looked up.

He nodded. "I'm afraid so."

She squared her shoulders. "I knew it." She took a deep breath. "So that's me for Liverpool?"

"Not for a while, but yes. Before you start to show. . . . Unless—"

"Unless what?"

"The father?"

"He can't."

O'Reilly scratched his chin. "Do you mind me asking why?"

"I don't mind you asking, Doctor, but I'm not going to tell you."

"Fair enough. I had to ask," O'Reilly said. "Now, we should start your prenatal blood work. I'll go get the laboratory forms." He left.

"So, Dr. Laverty," she said.

Barry decided to take the bull by the horns. "Julie, do you enjoy working for the Bishops?"

She jerked back in her chair. "How did you know where I work?"

"It's a small village. Is Councilor Bishop the father?"

"What? That lecher?" Her brow furrowed, and her cheeks reddened. She rose and stood. "I've better taste than that."

O'Reilly came back, pink lab forms held in one hand. Barry plowed on. "If he is, we could at least make him pay for—"

"Not him." Her lip curled.

"Who's him?" O'Reilly inquired.

"Councilor Bishop. I asked Julie if he could be the father."

"And I told Dr. Laverty . . ." A single sob interrupted her words. "He tried to have a go at me. I'd not let him anywhere near me."

"It's all right, Julie," O'Reilly said gently. "Dr. Laverty was only trying to help."

"I know that." She dashed the tears away with the back of one hand. "But just thinking of that man gives me the creeps." Her green eyes flashed.

"We'll say no more about it." O'Reilly waited.

She held out her hand. "Give me them forms. Where've I to go to for the tests? Can I get them done here?"

O'Reilly gave her the requisitions. "If you want to keep this to yourself, maybe you'd be better to nip down to Bangor to the health clinic there."

"I'll do that," she said. "Would tomorrow be all right?"

"Of course. We'll have the results by Friday."

"I can't get any more time off this week. Could I come in on Monday?"

"Of course, and we'll have all the information about Liverpool."

She forced a smile, stuffed the forms into her handbag, then held out her hand to O'Reilly.

O'Reilly smiled and shook her hand. "You'll be all right, Julie."

"She took it well, Fingal," Barry said after she'd left. "I hope I didn't upset her too much, asking about Bishop, but I thought—"

"I know exactly what you thought, Barry," O'Reilly said. "And it's given me an idea. I'll need your help, and we'll have to bend a few rules, but . . ."

Barry's eyes widened as O'Reilly unfolded his plan.

As SOON as the morning surgery was finished, O'Reilly began to make telephone calls. "Hello? Royal Victoria? Put me through to Ward Six. . . . Hello? Nurse Gordon? Fingal O'Reilly here. . . . I'm grand. How's your bad knee? . . . Good. I'm delighted it's on the mend. How's Sonny? . . . My customer with the pneumonia and heart failure . . . I see. . . . Right. . . . Right. . . . Another week? Fine. Now you look after yourself." He hung up.

"Sonny's on the mend. They'll discharge him on Saturday. The almoner's been to see him—nice word, 'almoner'; some bloody bureaucrat wants to change it to 'medical social worker'—and she won't let him go back to his car. She's got a bed for him in the convalescent home in Bangor, and he'll be all right there until we get things sorted out. And to do that . . ."

He consulted the telephone directory, then dialed again. "Dr. O'Reilly here. I want to speak to Councilor Bishop." He winked at Barry and waited.

"Councilor. Sorry to bother you." O'Reilly's voice oozed solicitousness. "I won't keep you a minute. It's about Sonny's property. I know you want to acquire it. Perhaps I can help." He held up one hand, finger and thumb forming a circle. "Not on the phone. Could you drop in about six? . . . Splendid." O'Reilly replaced the receiver. " 'I gloat!' " he roared. " 'Hear me gloat!' "

"*Stalky and Co.*, Rudyard Kipling," Barry said. "So he's taken the bait?"

"He's risen like a trout to a mayfly."

THE front doorbell rang. Barry looked at O'Reilly, who said, "Kinky knows to bring him up here. Just follow my lead. Agree with everything I say."

Barry heard footsteps on the stairs. Kinky showed Councilor Bishop into the upstairs sitting room. "It's the councilor, so." She had a look on her face as though she had found something unpleasant on the sole of her shoe.

"Come in, Councilor," said O'Reilly, rising. "Have a seat. Would you like a wee . . ." He inclined his head toward the decanters on the sideboard.

"I've no time for that. I'm here on business, so I am."

Bishop lowered himself into O'Reilly's recently vacated chair. Barry sat opposite. O'Reilly leaned against the mantelpiece.

"So," said the councilor, "is the old devil going to die?"

O'Reilly shook his head. "Sonny? He's very much on the mend."

"Pity." Bishop crossed his short legs. "Ballybucklebo would be a damn sight better off if we could see the back of him and them scruffy dogs."

"You're probably right," said O'Reilly, "but I think old Sonny'll be around for a day or two yet."

"All right. How much for Sonny's place?"

"I'm only a country GP. I've no idea."

Bishop steepled his fingers. "I'm a fair man."

"Oh, indeed," said O'Reilly, "everyone knows that."

"Two thousand pounds."

Barry's knowledge of land values was limited, but the figure seemed low.

O'Reilly put a match to his briar. "I'm sure that would be very fair," he said, "but we're not actually talking about selling Sonny's land."

"You said you could help me get the property."

"Not exactly," said O'Reilly. "I said I knew you wanted to acquire the property and that perhaps I could help. I meant I thought I could help prevent you from getting within a beagle's gowl of the place."

Councilor Bishop's face turned scarlet. "Listen, you stupid country quack, there's not a damn thing you can do to stop me. I'll have Sonny's place, lock, stock, and barrel, by the end of next week, so I will. Two thousand pounds. Take it or leave it."

"I think we'll leave it." O'Reilly blew a cloud of smoke toward the ceiling.

"Right." Bishop stood. "I'm for home."

"I hope Mrs. Bishop will be pleased to see you."

"What are you on about?"

"And little Julie MacAteer. She's up the pipe, you know."

Barry clenched his teeth. This bending of the rules, this breach of a patient's confidentiality, bothered him a lot.

"What's that wee guttersnipe being pregnant got to do with me?"

O'Reilly said softly, "She says you're the daddy."

Councilor Bishop rocked back on his heels. "She what? The wee bitch. I'll kill her. I'll kill her dead, so I will."

"I don't think so," said O'Reilly. "I don't think so at all."

Councilor Bishop's face went from scarlet to puce. He took a deep breath, clearly pulling himself together. "If she's a bun in the oven, it's no concern of mine. Mind you, I wouldn't have minded giving her a wee poke."

"You did, Bertie."

"Lying slut. She'll have no reference from me. She'll never get another job—"

"Our tests don't lie." O'Reilly moved closer to the councilor.

"What tests?" Bishop's narrow forehead wrinkled. "What tests?"

"You tell him, Dr. Laverty."

Barry stood. "I think you'd better sit down, Councilor."

Bishop looked from O'Reilly to Barry and back to O'Reilly. Then he slowly sat.

"It's a new test," said Barry. "You left some pus on a couple of swabs from the night Dr. O'Reilly lanced your finger. If you take a blood sample from a pregnant woman and mix it with pus from the putative father, there can be an anaphylactoid progression of the polylobed acido philic granulocytes." Barry knew he was spouting gibberish, but it was what O'Reilly wanted.

"A what?"

"Pay attention," said O'Reilly.

"An anaphylactoid progression of the acidophilic granulocytes. It's absolutely . . . pathognomonic." Barry stumbled over the last word. It came hard to lie to a patient.

"Pathognomonic means that it's money in the bank," O'Reilly said. "You're the daddy, all right. I wouldn't have thought a wizened-up miserable scoundrel like you would have had it in him."

"There's got to be some mistake. I never laid a finger on her." Bishop fiddled with the knot of his tie. "Your stupid test's wrong. I can prove it."

"How?" asked O'Reilly.

"It's her word against mine."

"Not exactly," said Barry. "It's your word against hers . . . and two qualified medical men, and some highly sophisticated science."

"But you doctors—and I know this for a fact, so I do—you doctors can't discuss a patient in public."

"Normally you'd be right, Bertie," said O'Reilly, "but in your case, we'd be prepared to make an exception. Old Hippocrates would understand."

"Oh, God." The councilor buried his face in his hands.

"Of course, Bertie, there's an outside chance that the test *could* be wrong," O'Reilly said.

"Could it?" Councilor Bishop's bluster had gone completely.

O'Reilly fiddled about, relighting his pipe. "I suppose so, but we wouldn't know for at least two weeks. By then, I imagine your loyal brethren down at the Orange Lodge would have had something to say. I hear they can get a bit right-wing about Orangemen who indulge in extramarital hanky-panky. Tend to ask for resignations. The town council could be a tad upset."

Bishop made one last attempt to bluster. "You're bluffing."

"And then," said O'Reilly sweetly, "there's Mrs. Bishop. She told Kinky she'd seen you having a go at Julie MacAteer."

"Honest to God, I only ever tried to feel Julie's breasts. Just the once."

"Dirty old man," said O'Reilly. His voice hardened. "I might just believe you, Bertie Bishop, but I'll take a lot of convincing."

Bishop looked up at O'Reilly. "How?"

"Not much. A wee favor, that's all. You'll fix Sonny's roof and the rest of his place . . . free of charge."

"What?" Bishop whimpered.

"You'll settle five hundred pounds on Julie MacAteer. You'll write her a letter of reference that would get her through the Pearly Gates . . . and if you breathe a word that she's pregnant—"

"I won't. I swear I won't."

"Good," said O'Reilly. "Very good . . . and just one other little thing. Seamus Galvin is looking for someone to buy a clatter of rocking ducks. About four hundred quid would see him right."

Barry chuckled inwardly. He'd completely forgotten about the Galvins.

"I'll be ruined," Bishop muttered.

"Indeed you will be, Bertie, if you don't do as I've told you."

Bishop hung his head. "Can I go?" he asked.

"If you must," said O'Reilly. "And I'm sure that when the laboratory retests the sample, it'll all turn out to have been a horrible mistake. Oh, and while you're here, Bertie"—hardened steel was in O'Reilly's voice—"if you ever call me a quack again, if you ever forget that Dr. Laverty and I worked hard for our degrees, I'll gut you like a herring."

WEDNESDAY-MORNING surgery and lunch were over. O'Reilly consulted his list. "Great," he announced, "not one sick one."

"So we can put our feet up?" Barry rose from the table. "I'm off to have a go at today's crossword."

"The hell you are," said O'Reilly, shaking his head. "We need to drop in on a few folks that we've been neglecting."

Barry sighed. "All right. Who do you want to go and see?"

"The Galvins. I want to hear if Bishop's kept his word. The Kennedys. See how Jeannie's doing; then we'll have a word with Maggie. Let her know about Sonny."

"That shouldn't take long."

O'Reilly's expression clouded. "They're the easy ones. We'll have to make a stop with Mrs. Fotheringham. I'll bet she won't have a clue what's going on. The specialists at the Royal are too busy to talk to relatives. I'll phone the ward. Check up on Fotheringham's progress."

Barry steeled himself before saying, "Could I do that? It should be me who tries to explain things to Mrs. Fotheringham."

O'Reilly cocked his head on one side. "You know, I hoped you'd say that." Barry heard the satisfaction in his senior colleague's voice as O'Reilly continued, "You'll need to get put through to Ward Twenty-one. I'll see you at the car."

Barry spoke to one of the medical staff on the ward and was gratified to hear that Major Fotheringham's recovery was progressing as anticipated. He'd be left with some impairment, but he should be able to live a fairly normal life. He'd have his stitches taken out on Friday and be discharged for outpatient follow-up and physiotherapy the following week.

"ISN'T it grand, Dr. O'Reilly?" Maureen Galvin, eyes bright, showed O'Reilly a pile of twenty-pound notes. "Some fellow came round first thing this morning. 'I hear your husband's got a load of rocking ducks for sale.' 'Right,' says I. 'I'll take the lot,' says he. And would you look at that? Four hundred quid.'

"I'm delighted," said O'Reilly.

"You never saw such things in your life," said Maureen. "Not one of them looked like any duck I'd ever seen. Anyway, we got our money back and a bit of a profit." She hesitated. "Would you do me a wee favor?" She handed him the notes. "Would you take care of these? I'd be happier if Seamus—"

"They'll be safe as houses," said O'Reilly, stuffing the money into his pocket.

She smiled at him, cocked her head to one side, and asked, "Would you be free on Saturday, Doctors?"

Barry had hoped for some time off. He wanted to see Patricia if she did phone, or perhaps he'd meet Jack if she didn't. He looked questioningly at O'Reilly.

"We might," said O'Reilly.

"We're having a wee going-away party. We'd like for you both to come."

"What do you think, Dr. Laverty?"

"We'd have it here. In the afternoon," said Maureen.

Barry could tell by the way she looked up into O'Reilly's face that the presence of her medical advisers was important. "I don't see why not," he said.

"Grand," said Maureen.

"I tell you what," said O'Reilly. "Could you or Seamus get your hands on the marquee the Ballybucklebo Highlanders use? Just in case it rains. There'd be a lot more room in my back garden."

Maureen beamed. "You wouldn't mind, sir?"

"Not at all. You never know how many'll show up at a Bally-bucklebo party."

"Seamus'll get the big tent. We'll put it up on Saturday morning."

"Right," said O'Reilly. "Now we'll need some grub. Mrs. Kin-caid'll take care of that. I'll get a couple of barrels of stout over from the pub."

"But that'll cost a fortune."

"No," said O'Reilly. "Willy the barman'll have to charge the guests. I'm not made of money."

"We'll not have time to get a permit," Barry said. In Ulster, if anyone wanted to sell alcohol anywhere but in a registered public house, they had to apply for a special permit.

"We'll not need one. We'll not sell drink; we'll sell glasses of water," said O'Reilly with a grin. "Grand stuff, water. You don't need a permit to sell it, and there's nothing to stop you giving away a free drink with every glass sold. To be on the safe side, we'll invite Constable Mulligan. If there is a law being broken and him at the hooley, he'd have to arrest himself."

Barry laughed, and his laughter woke young Barry Fingal.

"I'd better see to the wean," said Maureen. "Saturday it is, Doctors."

TO BARRY'S great relief since he still lacked a pair of Wellington boots, the lane to the Kennedys' farmhouse was dry. Jeannie was playing in the farmyard, throwing a stick for her Border collie.

"Hello, Dr. O'Reilly." She took the stick from the dog. "Stay, Tessie."

"How are you, Jeannie?" O'Reilly walked over from the car.

"Much better now, thank you."

Barry followed. He could see that this was a different little girl from the one he'd met three weeks ago. She had color in her cheeks, and her eyes were bright.

"She's really on the mend." Mrs. Kennedy appeared in the doorway of the farmhouse, her hair neatly tied up in a bun. "We were main worried about her for a while, but them doctors at Sick Children's were smashing, so they were. There was a young one, a Dr. Mills. He said if you and Dr. Laverty hadn't been so quick off the mark . . ." She swallowed.

"All's well that ends well," said O'Reilly. "Lots of fresh air, plenty to eat, and she'll be fit as a flea in no time. Ready for school in September."

"WOULD YOU LIKE SOME TEA and scones?" Mrs. Fotheringham asked when O'Reilly and Barry were seated in the antimacassar-draped armchairs.

"No, thank you," said O'Reilly. "We can stay for only a minute. Dr. Laverty has something to tell you."

Barry swallowed. "I've had a word with the hospital about the major. He's fully conscious. Weak on his left side. His speech is a bit slurred. He's never going to be quite right, I'm afraid, but the speech therapists and physiotherapists can work wonders . . . with time."

"I see." Her face was expressionless. "Perhaps if he'd gone to the hospital sooner?" she asked through thin lips.

Barry inhaled. "Yes. He might be doing better if I'd recognized what was wrong when I saw him on Friday. I didn't think it was more than a muscle spasm in his neck."

"But you were wrong, weren't you?"

"Yes, Mrs. Fotheringham, I was."

"I'm glad you admit it, young man."

"Ahem," O'Reilly grumbled. "You know, Mrs. Fotheringham, I don't think I would have done any better. There wasn't a lot to go on on Friday."

She sniffed haughtily. "Of course you medical men always stick together. I've had time to think this over," she said, rising, "and I have decided that my husband and I will be seeking our medical advice elsewhere."

"That is, of course, your choice, Mrs. Fotheringham. I hear Dr. Bowman in Kinnegar is very good." O'Reilly's tone was measured.

"In that case"—she crossed the room and held the door open—"perhaps you would be good enough to transfer our records?"

"With pleasure."

Barry, his head held low, walked slowly to the hall. "I'm sorry."

"Sorry won't give me back a healthy husband."

Barry looked at O'Reilly, then stepped outside.

"Good afternoon, Mrs. Fotheringham," O'Reilly said from the front step. "I hope the major makes the best recovery possible."

"Huh," she said, and closed the door.

A short time later O'Reilly pulled the Rover to the side of the road by Maggie MacCorkle's cottage. "Come on. Let's tell Maggie about Sonny."

Sonny's dogs spilled out of the front door and clustered around the car. Maggie thrust her way past them, and Barry noticed the fresh pansies in her hatband.

"You're just in time, Doctors dear. The kettle's boiled."

"Great," said O'Reilly, "a cup of tea would hit the spot."

"Away with you, General Montgomery." Maggie shooed the cat off one of her chairs. "Have a seat, Dr. O'Reilly. Light your pipe."

She bustled around her stove, warming the teapot.

"I'm glad you came," she said. "I've run out of them wee pills, and I'd another of those eggycentwhat-do-you-muhcallum headaches the other night, so I had. Would you have any more tablets with you?"

O'Reilly shook his head. " 'Fraid not, Maggie. Eccentric headaches can be funny things. Could you pop in tomorrow? I'd like to take another wee look at you before I give you any more pills. Just to be on the safe side."

Barry smiled. He wasn't the only doctor in Ballybucklebo who would be taking a complaint of headaches more seriously.

"I'll be round," she said, pouring tea into three mugs. "Milk and sugar?"

"Just milk," Barry said as O'Reilly nodded.

"We just popped in to let you know about Sonny," O'Reilly said. "He's getting out on Saturday."

"Told you," said Maggie. "They'll have to shoot that one." She sipped her tea. "That means he can have his dogs back."

"Not exactly," said O'Reilly. "He'll have to go to Bangor to convalesce until his roof's fixed."

Maggie sat bolt upright. "Until what?" Her eyes widened.

"His roof's fixed. Councilor Bishop told me he's had a change of heart."

"Bertie Bishop?" Maggie grunted. "I'll believe it when I see it."

"It's true, Maggie," Barry said. "Honestly."

"Aye," said O'Reilly. "I'm going up to the Royal on Saturday. I'll run him down to Bangor, but first we're having a bit of a party at my place. To send the Galvins off to America. Sonny'll be fit enough to drop in for a wee while. How'd you like to pop by and tell him about the roof?"

Barry watched as, from somewhere deep under Maggie's leathery cheeks, a glow rose and spread. "Away off and chase yourself," she said. "Him and me barely give each other the time of day."

"I know," said O'Reilly, "but the last time I saw him, Sonny said he wanted to have a wee word . . . to thank you for taking care of his dogs."

"That would be civil of him, right enough."

"So you'll come?"

"I'll mull it over," she said. "If I do, I'll bring one of my plum cakes."

10

Now Is the Time for All Good Men to Come to the Aid of the Party

O'REILLY had left for Belfast to collect Sonny. Barry yawned and toyed with a slice of toast. He looked through the dining-room window. The weather forecast had been right. Sunshine and a few low clouds. Perhaps the tent that was being erected in O'Reilly's back garden might not be needed.

He rolled his shoulders. Thursday and Friday had been hectic. Droves of patients, and last night there had been a traffic accident. Two men had needed to be given morphine, splinted, and sutured before being sent to the Royal. It had been four in the morning when he and O'Reilly got into their beds.

A bit of a sleep-in wouldn't have gone amiss, but he had been woken by the sounds of Seamus Galvin and his team putting up the big tent. Barry sighed, picked up his breakfast plates and cutlery, and carried them through to the kitchen. Perhaps his tiredness somehow made his disappointment more real. It seemed that Jack's advice to wait for Patricia to phone had been wrong. Not a peep from her, and it was eight days now.

Kinky straightened up from the oven. "Pop the dishes in the sink. I'll see to them, so," she said. "Grand day for the hooley."

"Suppose so." Barry put the plates down. "I'm not in much of a party mood."

Kinky squinted at his face. "It's none of my business, Dr. Laverty, but . . . is it that wee girl that has you sore tried?"

Barry wondered how she had seen through him so easily. "A bit," he admitted. "She told me she didn't want to get too involved."

Kinky tutted. "Silly girl. If you don't give, you'll not get back. I know that for a fact, so."

Barry had wondered what had happened to Mr. Kincaid. "You were married, Kinky, weren't you?"

She nodded slowly. "I was, and it was grand, so. But I lost himself. I was only eighteen. He was a Cork fisherman. He was lost at sea, and I was lost on land. It was like half of myself gone." She moved to the counter. "But life has to go on." She grabbed a rolling pin and with steady, strong strokes began to flatten a mound of pastry dough. "I thought I'd see the world." She chuckled. "It was a brave step from Cork to County Down before the war, so I took a job with old Dr. Flanagan here . . . just till I found my way again."

"And you never left?"

"I never met another lad like my Paudeen." She sprinkled flour onto the now flat pastry. "After a year or two of feeling sorry for myself, I looked hard for another lad, but I never did find one."

Barry thought he felt the same way about Patricia, but at least Kinky had made an effort after she had been widowed.

"Are you content here, Kinky?"

"I am. I've had a good life, so. I'll not complain, but it pains me to see a young man moping."

"It's daft, isn't it?"

She smiled. "Sure, there are times the heart rules the head." She sprinkled flour on the sheet of pastry. "The newspaper's in the hall. Go up to the sitting room. It'll be quieter there. I'll call you if there are any patients. And who knows? Maybe things will turn out for you after all."

He collected the paper and went upstairs.

BARRY wrinkled his nose. Something was tickling his nostrils. He was dimly aware of a gentle whiffling and a persistent rumbling. A weight was on his chest. He blinked, opened his eyes, and shook his head. He'd nodded off. Still not fully awake, he made out a dim white blur. Lady Macbeth was crouched on his chest.

He wriggled in the chair, fondled the cat's head, and asked, "What time is it?" He looked at his watch. Good Lord. One forty-five. He yawned and stretched, and Lady Macbeth sprang to the floor, disturbed by his movements.

Pursued by the cat, Barry trotted downstairs and into the kitchen, where Kinky was busy loading plates of sandwiches onto a tray.

"Is Dr. O'Reilly back yet?" he asked.

She shook her head, then batted Barry's hand away as he tried to steal a sandwich. "Leave you them be. They're for the guests. I've left a plate on the shelf for you, so." She pointed to a platter of sandwiches and sausage rolls.

"Thanks, Kinky." Barry helped himself.

She lifted the tray. "I'd better be getting these outside."

He held the back door open. Kinky, burdened by the tray, moved sideways into the garden. Tail high, Lady Macbeth slipped past them both.

Barry was curious to see what arrangements had been made, so he followed Kinky and her tray out into the bright sunlight. The tent stood on the left side of the back garden, close to the house. Willy the barman was ready for action behind a trestle table that occupied the greater part of the rear wall. Pint and half-pint glasses, glasses for whiskey, and glasses for wine stood there in ranks. A skirmish line of lemonade and orange squash for the children was flung out on both sides of the main array.

The side walls of the big tent were lined with more tables, covered with plates of sandwiches, sausage rolls, cheeses, barmbracks, a ham, and a cold leg of lamb. Kinky finished depositing her burden.

She turned to Barry. "I think there should be enough, so."

"Enough? You could feed five thousand. You've done a wonderful job."

Kinky smiled. "It'll be like a flock of locusts in here in the next couple of hours, and I have to be sure no one goes hungry."

As she bustled away, Barry wandered out of the tent. Rows of folding chairs were lined up from the side of the tent to the back fence. An open space lay between the house, tent, and chairs. He noticed something at the far end of the garden, near Arthur's kennel under the chestnut tree. An irregular shape covered in a tarpaulin. "Any idea what that is, Willy?"

The barman stopped polishing a glass. "No idea, and don't you go near it, Doc. Seamus Galvin brought it over. It's to be a surprise for Dr. O'Reilly."

"Oh," said Barry, almost tripping over one of the ropes. As he struggled to regain his balance, he was jolted from behind.

"Aaarf," said Arthur happily.

"Arthur. Sit, you great lummox."

The black Lab subsided onto the grass, tongue lolling.

"That's better," Barry said. "Now, behave yourself."

He turned and started to walk back to the house. From behind, he heard a hissing like a pit full of vipers followed by a sudden yelp. Barry spun on his heel. Lady Macbeth, back arched, tail fluffed, made what must have been her second attack on Arthur Guinness's nose. Her paw, claws unsheathed, flashed forward in a rapier thrust that drew a howl from Arthur, who put his tail between his legs and slunk off toward his kennel.

"It's a tough old life, Arthur," Barry said at the same time as he heard the back gate creak. He looked up to see the guests of honor, Seamus, Maureen, and Barry Fingal Galvin. Seamus wore his best suit. Maureen wore a yellow pleated skirt, pale green blouse, floppy hat, and white gloves. She pushed a perambulator, a massive contraption, the sort of vehicle that had been popular with the nannies of the Victorian upper classes.

"Good afternoon, sir." Seamus touched the peak of his cloth cap.

"Seamus. Maureen." Barry moved to the pram. "And how's Barry Fingal?"

"Grand, so he is," said Maureen, her green eyes smiling fondly into the massive vehicle. "Growing like a weed."

"Would you look at that?" said Seamus, taking in the contents of the tent. "Feast fit for a king."

"Can I get you something, Maureen?" Barry asked.

"I'll see to it," Seamus said.

Maureen sat down on the nearest deck chair, steadying her hat with one hand, holding the pram's handle with the other as Barry Fingal gurgled happily. "It's a great day for the party," she said. "Where's himself?"

As if her question had worked to summon Dr. Fingal Flahertie O'Reilly, the big Rover pulled into the back lane and juddered to a halt. O'Reilly opened the passenger door and helped Sonny out.

Barry opened the gate. "How are you, Sonny?" he asked as O'Reilly guided the old man into the garden. Sonny's gray hair was neatly combed, and his weathered cheeks had lost their ominous blue tinge.

"I am very well, thank you, sir," Sonny said.

"You'll be even better when you take the weight off your feet," O'Reilly said, helping him to a chair beside Maureen. "Do you know Mrs. Galvin?"

"I've not had the pleasure," Sonny said, starting to rise again.

O'Reilly put a hand on Sonny's shoulder. "Sit down. You've not all your strength back yet."

Barry smiled at the man's old-world gallantry.

"Afternoon, Doctor sir." Seamus Galvin appeared, balancing a glass of lemonade on a plate piled high with sandwiches in one hand and clutching an already half-empty pint of Guinness in the other. "Here you are, love." He gave the plate to Maureen. "I never thanked you proper, Dr. O'Reilly, for getting them Belfast folks to take the rocking ducks. Can I buy you a jar?"

"No," said O'Reilly with a huge grin. "I've a thirst like the Sahara Desert. You can buy me two." He headed for the tent with Seamus, paused, and said to Barry, "Would you look after Sonny?"

Barry nodded. "Can I get you something, Sonny?"

"A bit of that ham would be much appreciated, and do you think I'd be allowed a small glass of stout?"

"Of course," Barry said. "I'll get them."

By the time he'd brought Sonny his plate and glass, the garden was filling up. Groups of women arrived, all dressed in their Sunday best, and Barry had to jostle past knots of men, some of whom he recognized as members of the Ballybucklebo Highlanders.

As he listened to the ever swelling drone of voices and laughter, someone tapped him on the shoulder. He turned to see the open face of Jack Mills.

"How's about you, Barry?" Jack said.

"What the blazes are you doing here?"

"Your boss was up in the Royal today. He was having a chat with Sir Donald Cromie. I was there and got introduced. Seems O'Reilly saw me play rugby for Ulster. He asked me if I was your Jack Mills and said I should come on down to the party."

"I'm delighted," Barry said. "Come on, then. Let's get a drink."

Jack lowered one shoulder and started to clear a way toward the tent. He stopped. "Good Lord, who is that?"

Barry had to look twice before he recognized Maggie Mac-Corkle. Her skirt was ankle length, but instead of being its usual black, it was scarlet. She wore layers of cardigans, each one buttoned only at the neck. All were of different colors and resembled the icing on a layered sponge cake. The ensemble was crowned by a hat of such dizzying proportions that it could have been left over from the Ascot scene in *My Fair Lady*. And as ever, there were fresh flowers in the hatband, this time orange lilies. She carried a bundle in one hand and Lady Macbeth under an arm.

"There you are, Dr. Laverty," she said. "Here." She thrust the squirming cat into his arms. "Get that wee scared moggie inside. She doesn't like the crowds. This is a Ballybucklebo ta-ta-ta-ra, and it's not hardly even got started yet. So"—she waved her bundle— "I'll just go and put this plum cake on the food table." She scanned the crowd. "Someone said that oul' goat Sonny was here. Have you noticed him about the place?"

"He's sitting under that apple tree," Barry said, pointing.

"Right," said Maggie.

O'REILLY, pint glass in hand, beamed down to where Jeannie Kennedy was playing on the grass with young Colin Brown and his bride-to-be, Susan MacAfee. "See how your appendix abscess made out, Dr. Mills?"

"I hardly recognized her," said Jack.

"Come on," O'Reilly said to Barry. "I want to hear what's happening with Maggie and Sonny." He winked and sidled across the lawn.

Barry and Jack Mills followed. They stood behind the apple tree, unashamedly eavesdropping on Sonny and Maggie.

"I have to thank you for looking after my dogs, Miss MacCorkle."

"It was no bother. I'll keep them till you get home, so I will."

From where he stood, Barry noticed that neither Maggie nor Sonny would look each other in the eye.

"That would be most generous." Sonny cleared his throat.

"Are you sure you're all right?" The concern in Maggie's voice was plain.

"Just a little tickle. A frog in my throat."

"I hope so. No wonder you near caught your death, living in that old car."

Sonny sat stiffly. "It suits me, and I'll not pay that despicable man, Bishop."

Maggie's toothless grin was as radiant as the sunlight. "You'll not need to—pay him, that is."

Sonny frowned. "Why not?"

"Because, and don't ask me how it happened, Councilor Bishop started fixing the roof yesterday."

Sonny's eyes widened. "I'll not pay. Not a penny."

O'Reilly stepped forward. "You'll not have to, Sonny. The worm has turned. Bertie Bishop came to see me a few days ago. Said he'd had a change of heart, he was sorry you were so sick and he'd fix your roof for free."

"I don't know what to say." Sonny looked from O'Reilly to Maggie.

"I do," said Maggie, leaning over and planting a great wet kiss on Sonny's forehead. "And if you'd ask me as nicely as you did all those years ago . . . I'll say 'I do' properly when the Reverend asks the question, so I will."

Sonny took Maggie's hand in his arthritic grip and raised it to his lips.

O'Reilly turned to Barry. "Come on." He lowered his voice. "I think that pair of turtledoves would like to be left alone."

"Right," said Barry, nodding to Jack.

"What was that all about?" Jack asked as the trio made its way back toward the tent.

Barry smiled. "The Lord and Doctor Fingal O'Reilly both move in mysterious ways their wonders to perform. It's a long story."

Barry's explanation was interrupted by a ferocious wailing. He swung around to see Seamus Galvin, bag under his arm, drones over his shoulder, cheeks puffed, foot tapping in time to the lively notes of "The Rakes of Mallow." Arthur Guinness sat at Seamus's feet. The dog had his head thrown back at an impossible angle. His ululations quavered and rose and fell. In the space at the house end of the lawn, men now coatless and women with their Sunday hats cast aside had formed a set and were dancing a reel.

O'Reilly grinned. "Who needs another pint?"

"Me," said Jack. Barry shook his head.

"Come on, then, Mills," said O'Reilly. He glanced at the yodeling dog. "Arthur'll be thirsty with all that singing. I'll see if Willy the barman has a can of Smithwick's."

Barry stood and watched the dancers.

"Doctor, sir."

Barry turned to see the bucktoothed, ginger-topped Donal Donnelly grinning like a mooncalf. "Could I have a wee word, Doctor sir?" He had to shout to be heard over the row of the pipes, the bellowing of the dog.

"Certainly." Barry's mouth fell open. Donal was holding tightly to Julie MacAteer's hand.

"Julie and me wanted to say thank you to you and Dr. O'Reilly."

"Don't tell me . . ." Barry started.

Donal blushed to the roots of his ginger hair. "We couldn't afford to get wed," he said, scuffing his boots on the grass, "and Julie wouldn't tell nobody I was the daddy."

"So what happened to change things?"

Donal swallowed. "I won some money on Bluebird. It wasn't enough, but then Julie got a parcel of cash for severance from Councilor Bishop."

"I'm sure," she said with a wry smile as she looked into Barry's eyes, "I'm sure the doctors don't know anything about that."

"Not a thing," Barry said. He glanced away.

"Anyway," said Donal, "I've a new job now. I'm laboring on Sonny's house for the councilor."

"So you're getting married," Barry said. "I'm delighted. And Dr. O'Reilly will be delighted, too. There he is. Go and tell him."

Sometimes, he thought, the ends *do* justify the means. Sonny and Maggie. Julie and—hard to believe as it was—the bucktoothed Donal Donnelly. Neither pair would be together if O'Reilly, with Barry's complicity, hadn't broken the rules of confidentiality. Indeed, there wouldn't be a reason for this party at all if O'Reilly hadn't forced Councilor Bishop to buy Galvin's rocking ducks.

Barry watched Donal and Julie, still hand in hand, walk over to O'Reilly, who clapped Donal on the shoulder and whose cheerful "Bloody marvelous!" boomed over the end of the music.

Barry wandered back to the bar, acknowledging the greetings of partygoers. It was a pleasant feeling to know he was becoming accepted in the village. A fiddle started to play. Someone had a penny whistle. A large man rattled out the percussion on a bodhran, the Irish drum of parchment stretched over a circular frame. Barry recognized the tune and started to hum.

"Another sherry, Doctor?" Willy asked.

"No. I'll have a pint."

"Good man," said Willy, pouring the Guinness. "One and six for your water please, sir," he said with a wink.

Barry paid and made his way back into the sunlight. He was just about to put his pint to his lips when Kinky, whom he hadn't noticed approaching, whispered, "Would you come into the house, Doctor Laverty? There's someone wants to see you, so."

"Could they not wait?"

"Ah, no. I can tell that this one is an urgent case. And they particularly asked for yourself."

"Very well." He handed his glass to Jack Mills. "Look after that for me. I've a case to see." Barry then followed Kinky to the house.

"In the surgery, sir."

Barry grunted, walked down the hall, opened the surgery door—and stopped dead.

"Hello, Barry," Patricia said. "I thought you were going to phone me."

Barry's mouth hung wide open.

"You said you'd call." Her voice was deep, just as he remembered.

"I know," he said, trying to collect himself. "I thought you were being polite . . . letting me down gently."

She shook her head, almond eyes laughing. "No. I meant exactly what I said. I wasn't sure that I was ready to get deeply involved."

"Oh."

"And before you start getting any notions, I'm still not sure."

"Then why are you here?" Barry felt his fists clench. Dear God, but she was lovely.

"Because"—she limped close to him and looked into his eyes—"there's something about you, Barry Laverty, that I think I'd like to get to know better. And it just seemed that if you wouldn't phone me, then I should come and see you."

He took her hand. "I'm so glad you did." Jack had been right, he thought. "And you picked the best day. There's a bit of a party going on."

"I'd never have guessed," she said with a smile as the sounds of the pipes and a burst of applause came from the back of the house. "Can I come?"

"In a minute." He pulled her to him and kissed her in O'Reilly's surgery, beside the rolltop desk, the swivel chair, the patients' seat with the uneven legs, the old examining table. He was kissing her in a room that in three weeks had become as familiar to him as his old bedroom back in his folks' house in Bangor. And he might as well have been kissing her on the far side of the moon, so lost was he in her kiss.

Their lips parted. She moved back. "Now," she said, pulling away, a little breathless. "What about the party?"

"Come with me," he said. Taking her hand again, he led her through to the kitchen, where Kinky was lifting yet another tray of pastries from the oven.

"Mrs. Kincaid, I'd like you to meet Patricia Spence."

"We met at the front door, so." Kinky put the tray on the counter and shook off her oven mitts. "Nice to meet you, Miss Spence. Now, I've work to do, so run along with the pair of you."

"Right," said Barry, heading for the back door. He tugged on Patricia's hand. "What can I get you from the bar?" he said, holding the back door open. He barely noticed Lady Macbeth slip past him out into the sunlit back garden.

"Beer, please."

"If we ever get to the front of the queue," Barry said, watching two men who were in a heated argument up ahead of them.

O'Reilly appeared and grabbed each of the belligerent parties by a shoulder. He roared. "You, you daft scoundrels, quit your argy-bargy and get the hell out of the way before all these other folks die of thirst."

"That's Dr. O'Reilly," Barry said to Patricia.

"Is he really such an ogre?"

Barry shook his head as O'Reilly roared, "Pint, Barry, and what's your friend having?"

"A beer," Barry yelled.

O'Reilly juggled three pint glasses between his hands and drove a way through to Barry and Patricia. "Here you are." He gave them a glass each.

"Fingal, this is Patricia Spence."

O'Reilly smiled at her and extended his hand. "How do you do, Miss Spence? And what do you think of the party?"

"Very nice," she said.

"I'll tell you," said O'Reilly, lowering half of his pint in one swallow, "parties are like those rockets the Americans and Russians fire into space. Once they leave the launching pad, they either wobble and blow up or roar off and head for the stars."

"I think that's called escape velocity," Barry offered.

"It is," said Patricia. "A rocket has to achieve a critical rate of speed to overcome the gravitational pull of the earth."

"Patricia's an engineer," Barry explained.

"Good for you," O'Reilly remarked. "Escape velocity? Well, the last time I saw Seamus Galvin, he was definitely flying."

Seamus swayed gently in time with the music. He and a couple of Ballybucklebo Highlanders were piping for sets of dancers. Half a dozen men, arms around each other's shoulders, were well on their way into the later verses of "The Rocky Road to Dublin."

"Now, Barry," O'Reilly said, "before Seamus drinks himself beyond redemption, I think it's time we got any formalities over and done with. It's the Galvins' going-to-America party. Someone should say a few words."

"Right," said Barry. "What do you want me to do?"

"Get hold of that friend of yours, Mills. Take one of the smaller tables from the tent and cart it up to the house end of the garden."

Barry found Jack, and they lugged one of the smaller tables to the end of the garden to make an improvised dais in front of the rows of chairs. O'Reilly appeared, holding Kinky by the arm. She and Patricia had deck-chairs-of-honor beside Maureen in a chair and Barry Fingal in his pram. Jeannie Kennedy and the want-to-be-weds, Susan MacAfee and Colin Brown, found spots on the grass.

"Would the Ballybucklebo Men's Choral Society care to join us?" O'Reilly roared. The fiddling and whistling stopped, and the singers drifted across the lawn. "Nip over and bring Seamus, will you, Barry?"

Barry skirted the apparently tireless dancers. "Seamus." He tugged at Seamus's sleeve.

Seamus stopped his pipes and raised a questioning eyebrow.

"Dr. O'Reilly would like everybody to gather round up there."

"Right, sir. I'll see to that."

From the corner of his eye, Barry caught a glimpse of Lady Macbeth sidling into the now empty tent. He then made his way to where everyone stood, rank upon rank, waiting expectantly. Now that the piping had stopped, all that could be heard was a gentle murmur of conversation.

O'Reilly hoisted his bulk onto the unsteady table. "Ladies and gentlemen," he said. "We are here today to bid farewell to three of Ballybucklebo's more illustrious citizens. Seamus and Maureen and wee Barry Fingal are off to start a new life in the New World."

"Will Seamus be working?" a voice inquired from the crowd.

"I will, so I will," Seamus yelled back.

"Mother of God," said the voice, "miracles still do happen."

"Now," said O'Reilly, "you all know I'm a man of few words—"

"And the Pope's a Presbyterian," a man called.

"Watch it, Colin McCartney," O'Reilly said. "I have my eye on you." The crowd laughed, and O'Reilly continued: "All right, all I want to do is wish the Galvins a safe journey and a grand new life." He held his glass aloft. "To the Galvins."

"The Galvins," echoed the crowd.

"Come on, Seamus. Speech!" Donal Donnelly shouted.

O'Reilly beckoned to Seamus. "Up here." The doctor leaped from the table.

"Right." Seamus had to be helped to climb up. He swayed, then said, "I've said it before . . . an' I'll say it again. Best couple of doctors in Ireland. Best village in Ireland. Best country in the whole world." Seamus's voice cracked. "And I don't want to go to America," he said, tears dripping.

"We're going. The week after next," Maureen stated. "Dr. O'Reilly's holding the cash, and the tickets are ordered. Me and Barry Fingal's going anyhow."

"And I'm coming with you, love," Seamus announced, blowing her a kiss.

"You've a job to do right now, Seamus Galvin," Maureen said, handing her husband a parcel.

"Right. Nearly forgot." Seamus held the package over his head. "This here's for Dr. Laverty." The crowd applauded. "You'se folks is very lucky he came to work with Dr. O'Reilly."

"Hear, hear!" yelled Cissie Sloan.

Barry knew he was grinning fit to bust as, glass in hand, he walked to the table.

"Here you are, Doc." Seamus bent forward and handed Barry the gift. "Open it."

Barry ripped off the paper. Inside was a burnished aluminum box. When he opened the lid, he could see it was full of beautiful hand-tied flies. A lump was in his throat, and he took a deep breath before facing the crowd and saying, "Thank you, Seamus and Maureen. Thank you all."

He struggled to find something more appropriate to say, but his thoughts were interrupted by a sharp, deep bark and a screech. Lady Macbeth tore past in a white blur. Hot on her heels galloped Arthur Guinness, bashing into Barry's legs and knocking him over. He felt the dampness of his spilled drink soaking into his trousers.

He then felt O'Reilly pulling on one arm. "Up with you, m'son." Barry struggled to his feet.

"One more thing," Seamus continued. "This here's a token of

our undying esteem for Dr. O'Reilly." He jumped from the table and stood by the canvas-covered object. "I'd like for himself to open it."

As O'Reilly strode across the grass, Barry returned to stand by Patricia.

She was laughing as she stared at his sodden trousers. "I think that's what I find most interesting about you, Barry. Your trousers. I've only seen you once in a clean pair." She stood and kissed him. "Could you by any chance get away tonight? I'll cook you dinner."

He looked into her smile and saw the promise there. "Come hell or high water," he said. "And I'll wear a clean pair of trousers."

He turned when he heard Seamus say, "It's like one of those unveiling jobs that the queen does. You've to pull this rope here."

"This one?" O'Reilly tugged.

The tarpaulin slithered to the ground and there, in all its splendor—three feet tall by three feet long, green head and yellow beak bright in the afternoon sunlight, brown saddle painted on its beige back—was a rocking duck.

"Good Lord," said O'Reilly as gasps of pure amazement rose all around. "It's a thing of beauty, Seamus." He crossed the grass, lifted up Jeannie Kennedy, and sat her in the saddle. She started to rock back and forth, laughing and fending off a line of children who were noisily demanding their turns.

"See," said Seamus, "I told you they'd go down a treat with the kiddies."

"You might just be right," said a thoughtful O'Reilly.

"Whoever bought them'll make a fortune," Seamus added.

Barry wondered if his timing might be poor, but he left Patricia and walked up to O'Reilly. "Fingal? I don't suppose I—"

"Could have the night off?" O'Reilly stared hard at Patricia. "Buy me a pint and I'll say yes."

"You're on." Barry started to head for the tent before the queue grew too long. He felt O'Reilly's hand on his arm and turned back.

"Take tomorrow off, too. I can manage without you. Although I'd like you to stay here for the long haul . . . as an assistant . . . partner in a year."

Barry looked back into the big man's brown eyes and said, "I'd need to think about it, Fingal. But you know, I might just do that."

"You think about it," said O'Reilly, "but get me a pint like a good lad . . . and a Smithwick's for Arthur."

Barry made his way to the makeshift bar and waited his turn in the queue, glancing over to where Patricia was deep in conversation with O'Reilly. Sunlight dappled her hair. She waved to him and smiled. He waved back. Right, he told himself, he'd get the drinks for O'Reilly and his daft dog; then he'd make his excuses and leave. With Patricia.

"Ahem?"

Barry turned.

Donal Donnelly stood there. "Doc, I know you must have been thinking of something important, but the queue's moved a bit."

Barry shuffled ahead. Something important? Nothing was more important to him at the moment than Patricia.

"So, sir," remarked Donal, "I was just thinking about that day you asked me for directions to Ballybucklebo. Do you remember?"

"Yes, I do." Indeed, he remembered—the yellow gorse, the drooping fuchsia, the blackbird's song, instructions not to turn at the black-and-white cow, how anxious he'd been about his interview with Dr. O'Reilly, and how Donal had fled at the mere mention of the man's name. He'd not understood why Donal had pedaled away back then, but by heaven, he did now.

Donal nodded his head to indicate that the queue had moved on again. Barry took several paces forward.

Donal tilted his head to one side and said, "Can I ask you a wee question, sir?"

"Fire away."

"You've been here a fair while now, sir. How do you like Ballybucklebo . . . and working for himself?"

"I like it fine," Barry said without a moment's hesitation. He thought about the little quiet village with its maypole, pub, and thatched cottages on the shores of Belfast Lough, and of course its inhabitants: Kinky, Donal, Julie MacAteer, Jeannie Kennedy, the Galvins, Maggie, and Sonny.

Barry was distracted by O'Reilly's laughter roaring through the softness of the Ulster summer evening. Dr. Fingal Flahertie O'Reilly, odd as two left feet, but Barry knew that if he himself were ever ill, there was no one he'd rather have to look after him.

He smiled at O'Reilly and Patricia and murmured to himself, "I don't think 'like' is the right word. I love it here." And Dr. Barry Laverty knew it was the truth.

A Conversation with
Patrick Taylor

Vital Stats

BORN: 1941, Bangor, County
Down, Northern Ireland
RESIDENCE: Bowen Island, British
Columbia, Canada
MEDICAL TRAINING: Queens
University, Belfast
NEXT BOOK: *An Irish Country
Village*
FAVORITE SPORT: Sailing
TRAVEL: Visits Ireland twice yearly
WEBSITE: www.PatrickTaylor.ca

PATRICK Taylor, MD, was born
and raised in Northern Ireland.
An Irish Country Doctor is based
on journals he kept of his early
days as a doctor in rural Ireland.
In 1970, he and his family left Ireland for Canada, where he still re-
sides, though he is contemplating
a return to his native County
Down. Now retired, Dr. Taylor
devotes his time to writing, sailing, and enjoying Irish cuisine.

We recently interviewed Dr.
Taylor about his life and career.

SELECT EDITIONS: How did
your career as a doctor begin?

PATRICK TAYLOR: I graduated
in Belfast in 1964 and, after a year
as a houseman [intern], studied
anatomy while working weekends, evenings, and holidays as a
supply doctor in rural practices to
make ends meet. I loved general
practice and applied for a job
in England. Unfortunately, they

were looking for someone with experience in midwifery, so I went to Glasgow to get the experience, fell in love with obstetrics, and went back to Ireland to train in obstetrics and gynecology. I continued to make ends meet by "moonlighting" as a rural GP—and those were the years that inspired *An Irish Country Doctor.*

SE: Do you miss Ireland?

PT: I miss the Ireland I knew, that's why I try to re-create it. It was a simpler, quieter place than it is now.

SE: Tell us about Ballybucklebo, the setting of your novel.

PT: The setting is a fictional village, the name of which came from my high-school French teacher who, enraged by my inability to conjugate irregular verbs, yelled, "Taylor, you're stupid enough to come from Ballybucklebo." *Bally* (Irish, *baile*) is a townland, *Buachaill* means "boy," and *bo* is a cow. In *Bailebuchaillbo,* or Ballybucklebo—the townland of the boy's cow—time and place are as skewed as they are in Brigadoon.

SE: What do you do to relax?

PT: There's a pub on the island where I live that's small and cozy. When I finish work each day at about 3 p.m., I walk the mile and a half downhill to the pub to meet

Ancestral Isle

Northern Ireland, which for centuries has been the venue of civil conflict and religious strife, is unquestionably one of the most beautiful locales of the British Isles. Lovingly evoked by Patrick Taylor in *An Irish Country Doctor,* Northern Ireland, or Ulster, as it is sometimes called, is rich in lakes, rivers, and captivating countryside. Since the early eighteenth century, it has also been the point of origin for many North American immigrants—Patrick Taylor included.

An ambitious lot, once across the ocean these Scotch-Irish (so named for their shared Scots ancestry) excelled as frontiersmen, lawyers, soldiers, entertainers, and politicians. Notable Ulster-Americans include pioneer Davy Crockett, Presidents Andrew Jackson and Woodrow Wilson, actor Jimmy Stewart, and music icon Dolly Parton.

the same coterie of people, so there's always good conversation to be had. Then I walk the mile and a half uphill back home. The exercise just about negates the beer calories and stops me getting too tall around! ∎

ACKNOWLEDGMENTS

Page 158: Wendy Werris. Pages 5, 159, 305, and 575:
Clipart.com. Page 303: Raz/Jobee Photography, Los
Angeles. Page 429: Sue Solie Patterson. Pages 5 and
430: iStockphoto.com. Page 574: Sarah Taylor.

The original editions of the books in this volume are published and copyrighted as follows:

THE OVERLOOK, published at $21.99 by Little, Brown and Company,
a division of Hachette Book Group USA, Inc.
© 2006, 2007 by Hieronymus, Inc.

MEET ME IN VENICE, published at $24.95 by St. Martin's Press, LLC
© 2007 by Elizabeth Adler

STEP ON A CRACK, published at $27.99 by Little, Brown and Company,
a division of Hachette Book Group USA, Inc.
© 2007 by James Patterson

AN IRISH COUNTRY DOCTOR, published at $24.95 by Forge Books,
an imprint of Tom Doherty Associates, LLC
© 2004, 2007 by Patrick Taylor

The condensations in this volume have been created by The Reader's Digest Association, Inc.,
by special arrangement with the publishers, authors, or holders of copyrights.

FIRST EDITION: Volume 295

The volumes in this series are issued every two to three months.
The typical volume contains four outstanding books in condensed form.
None of the selections in any volume has appeared in Reader's Digest itself.
Any reader may receive this service by writing
The Reader's Digest Association, Inc., Pleasantville, NY 10570
or by calling 1-800-481-1454.
In Canada write to:
The Reader's Digest Association (Canada) Ltd.,
1125 Stanley Street, Montreal, Quebec H3B 5H5
or call 1-800-465-0780.

Some of the titles in this volume are also available in a large-print format.
For information about Select Editions Large Type call 1-800-877-5293.

Visit us on the Web at:
selecteditions.blogspot.com
rd.com
readersdigest.ca (in Canada)